THE WOLVES OF ETERNITY

THE WOLVES OF ETERNITY

KARL OVE KNAUSGAARD

Translated from the Norwegian by Martin Aitken

Harvill *Secker*

LONDON

1 3 5 7 9 10 8 6 4 2

Harvill Secker, an imprint of Vintage, is part of the Penguin Random House group
of companies whose addresses can be found at global.penguinrandomhouse.com

First published by Harvill Secker in 2023
First published with the title *Ulvene fra evighetens skog*
in Norway by Forlaget Oktober, Oslo in 2021

The epigraph is from Revelation 21:4 in the King James Version

Excerpts from Status Quo's 'Rockin' All Over the World', written by John Fogerty;
Metallica's 'Welcome Home', written by Lars Ulrich, James Hetfield and Kirk Hammett;
and Rainbow's 'Tarot Woman', written by Ritchie Blackmore and Ronnie James Dio

This translation has been published with the financial support of NORLA

A CIP catalogue record for this book is available from the British Library

penguin.co.uk/vintage

HB ISBN 9781787303355
TPB ISBN 9781787303362

Typeset in 10/15 pt Swift LT Std by Jouve (UK), Milton Keynes
Printed and bound in Great Britain by Clays Ltd, Elcograf S.p.A.

The authorised representative in the EEA is Penguin Random House Ireland,
Morrison Chambers, 32 Nassau Street, Dublin D02 YH68

To Michal

And God shall wipe away all tears from their eyes;
and there shall be no more death,
neither sorrow, nor crying, neither shall there be any more pain:
for the former things are passed away.

HELGE

I've just been listening to the Status Quo album *Rockin' All Over the World*. I'm still shaking. I played it non-stop when it first came out. That was in 1977, and I was eleven years old. I hadn't listened to it since. Not until now, when, sitting bored in the office, I began wandering along some pathways back into the past, a band that reminded me of another band, and then another, on the screen in front of me. The cover alone sent a tingle down my spine. The image of the world, shining in the darkest firmament, the band name in electric lettering and the album title underneath in computer script — wow! But it didn't really knock me out until I pressed play and started listening. I remembered all the songs, it was as if the melodies and riffs hidden in my subconscious came welling up to reconnect with their origins, their parents, those old Status Quo songs to which they belonged. But it wasn't only that. With them came shoals of memories, a teeming swathe of tastes, smells, visions, occurrences, moods, atmospheres, whatever. My emotions couldn't handle so much information all at once, the only thing I could do was sit there trembling for three-quarters of an hour as the album played.

I had it on cassette — no one I knew owned a record player back then, apart from my sister, who only ever listened to classical and jazz anyway — and I played it all the time on the black cassette player I'd got for Christmas the year before. It ran on batteries and I used to take it outside with me nearly everywhere I went. Invariably, I sang along too. How brilliant to hear the album again now!

Status Quo, Slade, Mud, Gary Glitter, they were the bands we listened to. Those a bit older than us added in Rory Gallagher, Thin Lizzy, Queen and Rainbow. Then everything upended, at least it did for me, and all of a sudden it was Sham 69, the Clash, the Police, the Specials, nothing else would do. But they're bands I've kept listening to, on and off. That's never been the case with Status Quo. That's why it hit me the way it did, like an explosion. And it's why suddenly I cried when I heard the chorus of the title song.

It wasn't as if there was much good happening that year, 1977, certainly not in my own life, it was more the feeling that *something* was happening, and not least that something *existed*.

That I existed. And that I was *there*.

In my room, for example.

Yes, the smell of the electric heater.

The music on the cassette player.

Not too loud, because Dad was home, but loud enough for the feelings to pervade me.

The snow outside. The smell of it when it was wet, as much rain as snow.

An ai laik it ai laik it ai laik ai laik it ai la la la la laik it la la la laik it.

Hilde, opening the door.

'There's a girl hanging around outside. Do you know her?'

I stepped over to the living-room window. Sure enough, a girl was traipsing up and down the road out there, on the other side of the fence. She stopped and looked up at the house. She couldn't see me, but still. And then she started again, disappearing from view behind the bushes, reappearing, back and forth, following the line of the fence.

'Do you know her, then, or what?' said Hilde.

'Yes,' I said. 'It's Trude. She's in the same year as me at school.'

'So what's she doing here?'

I shrugged.

'Following me around, maybe.'

'Ha!' said Hilde. 'You're only eleven, you know.'

'I've had loads of girlfriends,' I said.

'Kissed them on the cheek, have you?'

'I've snogged a few.'

'Go out to her, then.'

I shook my head.

'Why not? Are you seeing someone else?'

'She's a bit special.'

'Not right in the head?'

'No, not like that. Just different.'

'Sounds all right to me.'

'That's because you're special yourself,' I said, and looked at her; she lit up when I said it.

'Not right in the head, I mean,' I added.

Then the doorbell rang.

'It's Trude,' Hilde said. 'Aren't you going to go?'

'Can you do me a favour and say I'm not in?'

'What's it worth?'

'Something.'

'Half your sweets on Saturday.'

'OK.'

I stood behind the stairs and heard Hilde say I wasn't in and that she didn't know where I was. I could see Trude trudge off home through the snow.

I don't know if that was exactly how it was. I remember seeing her, and I remember having to give Hilde a load of my sweets for lying for me. But the thing I remember best is the snow, the feeling of snow, the atmosphere of it. It was foggy too. Soft white snow, grey fog. And *Rockin' All Over the World*.

Is there ever a memory that *isn't* affirmative?

Of course not, a person consists of memories that can only ever be affirmative, they're what that person *is*.

But one of my memories stands apart in a way. One that isn't connected with anything else. It was something I saw. And it was that winter, a few weeks before Christmas, 1977. But I can remember it without the help of any music. It's a memory that shimmers, ungraspable inside me.

Across the road from our house, woods sloped away towards a narrow inlet of the sea, on this side was our housing estate. If you followed the road down to the junction and took a right there, you came to a low bridge that spanned the inlet. There were some pontoons below the bridge and a bit further away was the strait.

That night, I went down the road on my own. It was dark and still foggy, the snow had partly melted during the day, the road was covered in slush. I don't know where I was going, or where I'd been, all that's been erased from my mind. Maybe I was going down to the pontoons to see if there was anyone there, it was a place where we often used to hang out. Whatever: dark, foggy, the slushy road. Anorak gleaming in the road lighting. Across the bridge. The water black and cold.

But what was that?

Something shining down there.

Deep down in the black water, something was shining.

A few seconds passed before I realised what it was.

It was a car.

I saw then that a kerbstone was gone, there were wheel marks that went to the edge.

It must have just happened, if the headlights were still working.

I turned round and ran back up the road. I had to get to a phone and call an ambulance. But when I got to the houses I wasn't sure any more. It didn't have to be a car. It could have been something else. I might have been about to set a massive rescue operation in motion for nothing. What was Dad going to say then?

I came to our house and went in, took off my coat and my boots. Dad poked his head out of his office as soon as he heard me.

'Where have you been?'

'Up to the new shop,' I said.

'Tea's on the table,' he said. 'And straight to bed afterwards.'

'OK,' I said.

I did what I was told. Ate the sandwiches he'd made, then went to bed. Lay for a long while in the dark, thinking about the headlights in the water, the car in the water, its headlights shining as I lay there.

The next day there was an ambulance, a police car and a crane truck down there. The day after that it was on the front page of the newspaper. Everyone was talking about it. Except me. Now, thirty-five years on, I still haven't told anyone what I saw that night, or what I did. I know, you see, that I could have saved him if only I'd done the right thing. But I didn't do the right thing, and he died. No one needs to know. It's my memory, and mine alone, and unless something unforeseen happens, I'll take it with me to the grave.

SYVERT

The airport shuttle was waiting outside the little arrivals hall in the drizzling rain with the engine running and its headlights on. I jogged towards it, put my rucksack in the open luggage compartment and got on, then sat down on one of the seats at the back. I recognised the driver who was standing smoking under the canopy wearing the bus company's shapeless grey uniform; it was Eva's father, Eva, a girl I used to go to school with. He gazed emptily across the car park, the car roofs, while shielding his cigarette in his cupped hand.

I wondered what he might be thinking. Sunday roast, with sprouts? The fact that no one liked sprouts, but ate them anyway because they went with the roast? Or did appearances deceive? Was his mind on kinky sex when he drove his bus?

He was so heavy the vehicle swayed slightly as he stepped inside. I counted the passengers absently, there weren't many, ten including myself. They sat apart in silence. One, a guy my own age, but with much longer hair, had a pair of headphones on. The sound that leaked from them was like buzzing bees or something.

With his money bag at his hip the driver started coming down the aisle for the fares. When he got to me all I had was a thousand-krone note.

'Haven't you got anything smaller?' he said.

'I'm afraid not,' I said.

He looked at me a second, diverted his gaze when I looked up at him, and began picking through the notes in his bag. The peak of his cap was wet and glistened in the light of the ceiling lamp just above his head.

'I can't give you change for that,' he said.

'What do we do, then?'

'I'll have to let you off, won't I?'

'Thanks,' I said.

Shortly after, he threw the big engine into gear and pulled away from the forecourt. I got my headphones out of the pocket of my anorak and put them on, turned the cassette over in the Walkman and pressed play. It was Van Halen, their first album, and with that in my ears, the asphalt, the road lighting, the airport fencing and the faint thrum of the bus engine were as if foregrounded, while the landscape of trees, small outcrops of rock, river water and sand-covered shores seemed to draw back as if they belonged to some second-order reality.

It had been four months since I'd last been home. It had been Christmas then, I'd been on leave, the town was full of people I knew, and I'd been out every night. Now it was April, everyone else was back in Oslo or Bergen or Trondheim, and I'd done my stint. I thought it'd be a good idea to take a couple of months off and work out what I was going to do with my life, but as the bus went up the hill after the bridge, and the flatland outside the town emerged in front of us, I had the feeling I was only going to be bored. What was I going to do in the daytime?

I could forget about lying in bed all morning, unless I wanted Mum going on at me. She'd allow it for a week, maybe, as a kind of well-deserved holiday, but then she'd start nagging. I could hear her voice in my inner ear, the way she could shout my name as if pronouncing sentence.

We stopped at some lights. I lifted my knees and wedged them against the back of the seat in front, slid down into my own. On the other side of the window a cyclist stood with one foot on the ground, the other poised on the pedal. His lightweight rain jacket billowed like a carrier bag in the wind.

Either drawn-out and torturous — *Syy-yvert!* — or else a short, stinging lash — *Syvert!* — that was the sound of my name when it was she who uttered it. The fact that it had also been my father's name was in there somewhere too. At least I imagined it was. At any rate, she was still angry at him for dying and leaving her saddled with everything.

Some teenagers were hanging around in a little group outside the Narvesen when we pulled into the bus station, but apart from that the place was as good as empty when I crossed the concourse to change buses. I tried the same trick with the new driver, only for him to thumb out nine hundreds and a fifty without a word, before pressing the rest of the change out of his coin machine and issuing me the familiar small, square, pale yellow ticket.

Just before the bus was due to leave, Gjert came running towards it. I could tell it was him straight away. We'd played for years on the same teams together, handball as well as football, so I could hardly fail to recognise his short, rather stocky, angular frame.

He stopped in front of the driver after he got on, produced a bus card from his wallet and started walking up the aisle towards the back, undoing the cord of his hood with one hand, pulling the hood back with the other.

'Getting the bus now, are we?' I said. 'Lost your licence?'

He halted abruptly and his face lit up in a smile.

'Syvert,' he said. 'Have they given you leave again?'

'No, I'm discharged, as of today.'

'Well done,' he said, and sat down on the seat in front of me, leaning back against the window and putting one leg up on the seat beside him.

'Not sure about it, to be honest,' I said. 'I wouldn't have minded staying on a few months, if I'd had the chance.'

'You were a cook, weren't you?'

'Yes.'

'Sounds like a decent turn.'

'It was all right.'

The door closed, the bus pulled out from the empty departure area towards the traffic lights next to the railway station.

'*Have* you lost your licence?' I said.

'No, course not. Only I bashed my car.'

'Wouldn't they give you a courtesy car?'

'It'll cost me more to get it fixed than I paid for it. I'm looking for a new one.'

'I see,' I said.

'Can't be helped,' he said. 'What are you thinking of doing now, then?'

I shrugged.

'You're going to be home for a while, though?'

'I reckon so.'

'See you at practice, then?'

'Seriously?'

'Tomorrow night.'

'Why not,' I said.

'But give Terje a ring first, make sure it's all right. I'll have to warn you, though. We've got a new trainer now. Mads. A Dane. A lot of talk in him.'

'How do you mean?'

'Theory.'

'Theory?'

'Tactics. He's even got a board with him when we train.'

We sat and chatted for half an hour, the time it took to get home. Gjert lived a couple of kilometres from ours, on an estate from the seventies, while we lived in a house from the thirties, built by my grandfather on my dad's side, on land where his parents still had a farm at the time. We lived as if in the remnants of a bygone age, I'd often thought. Most of the others I'd known at school were newcomers, though not from far away, whereas maybe ten or twenty per cent were like me, with parents who looked like they belonged to a different generation from the parents of the kids on the estate, as if there was something in the times we hadn't quite cottoned on to. Gjert was somewhere in between, and we were actually related, albeit distantly, even though he'd grown up on the estate. The ties he felt were transparent now; while the others who'd lived there had moved away, at least into town, he'd stayed put.

His hair was that reddish colour the English call *ginger*, he had blue eyes that gazed rather coldly, and a wide, narrow mouth. He laughed a lot, but wasn't the sort to tell jokes, he wasn't verbal or inventive like that, but he'd always been respected, even if he hardly ever drew attention to himself. He was a bastard to play against, a real hard case, never afraid to use his body, throwing himself into tackles and one-on-ones like he had nothing to lose. I was a big lad too, bigger-boned and a good deal taller, but I was more the easy-going type. He'd go mad if we let a goal in, he'd mouth off at the ref then, telling him he didn't know what he was doing, that he wasn't up to it, sometimes he'd snap completely and would lunge in and take the legs away from whoever it was he wanted to get back at.

'Anyway, nice to see you in a good mood for a change,' I said as we came to where he'd be getting off. 'Found yourself a girlfriend, have you, or what?'

'Well, now you mention it,' he said, and looked up abruptly to see where we were.

'You're joking?' I said.

'No,' he said.

'Who is she? Anyone I might know?'

He shook his head.

'Met her at a New Year's Eve party on the other side of town.'

'Is that where she's from?'

He nodded.

'How old is she?'

'Sixteen.'

'Get in there,' I said. 'First-year gymnas?'

'Vocational school.'

'Has she got a name?'

'Bente.'

It had stopped raining by the time I got off the bus and walked towards the house. It was set back at the edge of the woods a few hundred metres from the stop, at the end of a narrow gravel track soggy with puddles whose surface the wind would rip up as it came sweeping across the flatland from the sea which, although hidden from view, could always be felt.

A vague sense of unrest went through me when I saw the lights in the windows. I knew Joar was excited about me coming home and had probably been looking forward to it for days.

It was important not to disappoint him.

I had no idea if Mum felt the same. I didn't doubt that she appreciated me coming home, it was her reasons I was unsure about, whether she was just glad of a helping hand, more than it being my hand in particular.

It didn't matter. I wasn't going to be staying long.

Joar was standing in the hall waiting when I opened the door.

'I saw you get off the bus,' he said with a smile.

'Are you allowed to be up this late?'

His smile vanished and he gave me that intense look of his.

'I am twelve, you know,' he said.

'Oh, I'd forgotten!' I said. 'Only joking.'

I ruffled his hair before dumping my rucksack. The house was full of cooking smells. I went through and saw Mum standing at the cooker with a spatula in her hand.

'Hello, Syvert,' she said. 'Journey all right?'

'Yes, fine,' I said. 'Everything all right here?'

'Yes, fine. I've fried us some beefburgers.'

'Just the job,' I said.

'I set the table,' said Joar.

'It's all ready now,' Mum said. 'Put one of those down to put this on, will you?'

She lifted the frying pan off the hob. I took a table mat from the sideboard and put it in the middle of the table. She'd fried eggs and potatoes as well.

'It might not be good enough for a cook like you,' she said.

'You know what they say about food and the armed forces,' I said.

After Joar had gone to bed I sat with Mum in the living room watching telly. It wasn't that late, but she fell asleep anyway, mouth open, head tipped back. Now and again, a low, rumbling snore came out.

'Don't you want to see the news?' I said after a while.

'Hm?' she said, and sat up straight.

She looked first at me, then at the telly. Wiped her mouth with her hand.

'I must have nodded off,' she said.

'Willoch's still negotiating by the looks of things,' I said, and gave a smile to annoy her; the last thing she looked like she wanted was to talk politics. 'Do you think he'll have to go as PM?'

'Think and hope,' she said. 'I reckon your friend Hagen might give him a push in that same direction.'

'He'll be choosing between plague and cholera,' I said.

She exhaled, leaning forward to roll a cigarette.

'I was hoping you'd see sense in the forces,' she said.

'Hagen's reasonable.'

'Humph. He's a slippery customer. I don't like him one bit.'

'I never said I *liked* him. You've got to distinguish between the issue and the person. It's politics that interests me. Not politicians.'

'So you say. You'll come round in the end.'

'To thinking the same as you, you mean? To thinking you're right?'

'Not at all,' she said. 'It's good you've got your own opinions.'

'Only you'd prefer them to be different?'

She looked at me and smiled.

'You always were an awkward one, Syvert.'

'And where would I have got that from, I wonder?'

'Awkward and bloody-minded,' she said. 'Ever since you were little.'

'What, because I don't just agree with you on everything?'

She said nothing, her gaze went from me to the telly, it was the weather forecast now.

'That's exactly what's wrong with politics in this country,' I said. 'People vote Labour because they always have done. It's the safe bet. But why does there have to be one way of doing things, one way of thinking? There's four million people in this country! Only nobody thinks they can *change* things any more. It doesn't *have* to be like that. Why do we have to have only one TV channel, for example? We could have hundreds! Why should that lot at Marienlyst decide what we can watch? And why does the *state* have to own and run everything? Why do the shops have to close early? Why can't they stay open all night if they want to? Why do *others* have to dictate *our* lives?'

'We're well off in this country,' she said. 'You can't deny that. Not with all the misery in other parts of the world.'

'But we've got no freedom. It is actually possible to be well off *and* free, you know.'

The testcard came on the screen, Mum sighed, took a couple more drags, stubbed her cigarette out, picked up the ashtray and got to her feet.

'Time for bed, I think, don't you?' she said. 'You must have had a long day.'

'No, I'm all right. You go on, though. Goodnight.'

'Goodnight.'

She took the ashtray with her into the kitchen and pottered about there for a few minutes before I heard her shuffle up the stairs. I switched the telly off, stood at the window and looked out. The light from the lamps on the outside of the house and the barn pooled out into the yard the way it had always done, reaching across the field at the front, dissolving eventually into a sea of darkness.

I was a bit annoyed with Mum, I couldn't let go of it. She never took me seriously, it was like she never really thought I meant what I said.

I went and picked up my rucksack in the hall, took it upstairs to my room and unpacked before getting into bed. The last thing I did before I went to sleep was have a wank while thinking about Bente, Gjert's girlfriend, who I'd never seen.

A noise woke me up in the middle of the night. Before I managed to work out what it was, it was gone. It had sounded a bit like a whinging cat. I decided that was the most likely explanation, and closed my eyes.

But it came back, and I could hear then that it was coming from inside the house, not outside.

Was it Joar?

Was he *crying*?

I got up and went out quietly onto the landing, stopping at his door.

Yes, he was.

I opened the door and looked in on him.

'Are you all right?' I said softly.

He was lying facing the wall and didn't answer.

I stepped inside.

'Joar?' I said. 'Are you all right?'

He'd gone quiet.

I went over to his bed and sat down on the edge, put my hand on his shoulder.

'Did you have a nightmare?' I said. 'A bad dream?'

He turned towards me.

'I dreamt about Mum.'

'What did you dream?'

'She came out to the front of the house and looked up at the sky. And then she opened her mouth and a bird flew out.'

'A bird?' I said, and had to bite my lip so as not to smile.

'A sparrow,' he said.

'That sounds like a nice dream,' I said. 'Strange, but nice.'

'Don't you understand anything?' he said. 'She's going to die.'

A sob escaped him after he'd said it. I ruffled his hair, he twisted away.

'But, Joar — it was a *dream*.'

'She's going to die,' he said into his pillow.

I didn't know what to say, and ruffled his hair again.

'Don't touch me,' he said.

I took my hand away.

'I won't touch you,' I said. 'But you have to realise, there's a difference between dreams and reality.'

He said nothing.

Was he even listening?

'You might be *scared* Mum's going to die,' I said. 'Especially because Dad died. But being scared of it happening can be enough to make you dream just that. Do you follow me? The dream doesn't mean Mum's going to die, it means you're scared she will.'

He looked up at me with his dark eyes.

'You're so stupid, Syvert.'

I stood up.

'You're the one crying because of something you dreamt, not me,' I said. 'I was only trying to be nice to you.'

'Why are you angry?'

'I'm not angry,' I said. 'But you can't just say what you like to people.'

'But it's true. You *are* stupid. Why can't I say so when it's the truth?'

'You were crying like a baby. Because you thought your mum was going to die. How stupid do you think that is?'

I regretted it as soon as I closed the door behind me, and stood for a moment on the landing, wondering whether to go back in.

If he started crying again, I would.

But all was quiet, so I returned to my room and got back into bed.

I woke up again only a few hours later, this time at the sound of Mum starting the car outside. I went back to sleep and didn't wake up again until she came home around nine. I got up, wound a towel around my waist and went out onto the landing, opened the door of Joar's room and then remembered it was Friday, not Saturday as I'd thought, and that Joar would be at school.

He was used to going to school on his own when Mum was at work, so it didn't matter that I'd been asleep, I supposed, and went to the bathroom.

Mum had two cleaning jobs, one doing some offices in town, where she'd been now, the other at the school near where we lived, that was in the afternoons. Quite often she'd do shifts at the old people's home too, at weekends. With no education to speak of, she had to make do with what she could get. I wish I could say she never complained, but she did.

I let the towel drop onto the floor and looked at myself in the mirror. My best asset was my upper body, the thing to do was to get them to notice it once they'd got past the first impression and my face.

I twisted round. My back was broad and full of pockmarks from zits. Neck short and powerful.

Like an ox.

'Syvert, are you in the bathroom?' Mum shouted from downstairs.

I didn't answer, turned the water on in the shower and stood underneath. For some reason I thought of Keith, the vainest man I ever knew. The way he always stood preening in front of the mirror after practice, combing his hair, slick as you like, black pointed shoes, pale, delicately coloured jackets with the sleeves pushed up, always in a new pair of jeans. No one ever held it against him, he was too cool for that, and anyway, there was something moody and dangerous about his eyes. It wouldn't have surprised me if one day he'd pulled a knife and not a comb out of his back pocket. On the other hand, all that went out the window as soon as he got on the pitch. It wasn't that the kit made him look ordinary, because he could look sharp in that too, with the collar turned up, shirt tucked into his shorts, expensive shiny boots on his feet, it was the way he played: as soon as we got started he turned into this awkward, overly eager, technically-not-very-good left wingback.

His face could have been a girl's. Maybe that was what they liked? Whenever we walked into a place, all the women looked at him, it never failed. His name was an advantage too. Everyone asked about it. Keith? Then he could say his dad was English, and how exotic was that? It gave him a head start.

He was welcome. With him on the team at least there'd be girls hanging around.

I squirted some soap into my hand, washed and rinsed myself properly, rubbed myself dry, put deodorant on, wrapped the towel around my waist again, and went back to my room to get dressed.

When I came down into the kitchen, Mum had fried eggs and bacon and put it all on a dish in the middle of the table. She'd sliced some bread and put the butter and cheese out too, and the pot was full of coffee. I sat down and got started. The saturated fields outside the windows stood out yellow against the still, grey sky. I noticed the car had made deep ruts in the soft gravel and thought maybe we should order a new load and make some repairs before the summer came round.

'Did Joar get off to school all right?' Mum said, appearing from the laundry room.

'I don't know,' I said. 'I was asleep. I think so, though. He wasn't here when I woke up at any rate.'

Reaching up to get a mug from the cupboard, she stopped suddenly in mid-movement and clutched her back, leaning forward with a wince.

'You've not put your back out, have you?' I said.

She shook her head and straightened up slowly, filled the mug to the brim, sat down at the other end of the table, blew on her coffee and took a sip.

'What is it then?' I said.

'Just a shooting pain in my back, it happens sometimes.'

'Have you been to the doctor's about it?'

She snorted.

'Not much he can do. It's the work, isn't it?'

'A physiotherapist would sort you out in no time,' I said.

said.

ou, then?'

I am, thank you very much,' she said. 'I'll make you a list
at need doing.'

' I said with a smile.

'Perhaps you could start by changing the tyres on the car? It'll save
me paying the garage.'

'I didn't know you used the garage for that. I thought Uncle Einar
did it for you when I wasn't here?'

'Well, you're here now, aren't you?'

'I'll do it, of course I will,' I said. 'Only it won't be today.'

'What have you got on for today that's so important?'

'Thought I'd go into town, that's all,' I said.

She looked at me.

'You can take the car, if you want. As long as you're back by two.'

'Not a problem.'

'Perhaps you could do some shopping for me while you're at it?'

'I thought there had to be a catch somewhere,' I said, and laughed.

'We've got to have food in the house,' she said. 'At least we do when
you're here.'

'All right,' I said, as I cut the yolk out of an egg, then shovelled it onto
my fork and lifted it into my mouth, where it broke open and ran out,
no longer warm, onto my tongue. 'Just write me a list.'

Mum didn't have a cassette player in the car, only the radio, so I put my
headphones on before turning the key in the ignition. I had AC/DC on
and sang along to 'Hells Bells' as I drove up to the main road. I put my
foot down as soon as I turned onto the smooth asphalt, there was hardly
another car out and I tore through the woods, past the school and the
sports hall, where kids in brightly coloured jackets and hats, all reds
and blues, highlighted the dismal greys, past the local shop and the
new salon there. *Hells bells, Hells bells*, I screeched, my hand tapping out
the beat on the steering wheel. Up on the E18 I got stuck behind an
articulated lorry and every time there was a bend I drifted out towards
the other side of the road like a dinghy being towed, but there was
always some idiot coming the other way, so it wasn't until we got to the

long, slow rise where there was a crawler lane the lorry decided to use that I was able to get past and pick up speed again.

I shouldn't have lost my temper with Joar like that. Only he'd caught me unawares; he'd been crying and frightened.

There was nothing wrong with him. Quite the opposite, he was genuinely quick-witted and a lovely lad. He just couldn't tell a lie. Couldn't say a word that wasn't true.

Which should only ever be a good thing.

I looked over at the enormous factory. It loomed out of the landscape, especially with the surrounding vegetation having been cleared.

Was I really stupid?

Of course not. He'd been referring to what I'd *said*, about dreams.

But that wasn't stupid either. It was fact. He was scared Mum was going to die and so he dreamt about it.

He barely remembered our dad, he was only four when he died.

Daddy, Daddy, he kept saying when all of a sudden he wasn't there any more. Daddy, Daddy.

But Daddy never came back, and eventually he forgot about him.

At least that's what I'd thought.

A year afterwards he was sitting on the back seat as we were on our way into town, and out of nowhere he said Daddy was sitting in heaven doing the driving.

I turned and looked at him and asked what he meant.

'Mummy's driving the car, and Daddy's driving Mummy. And me and you.'

At the time, I just smiled at him and turned to face the front again. Mum pretended not to have heard.

Now I wondered how a thought like that could have occurred to him.

Where did he get it from?

Ahead of me the town lay as if on a dish at the mouth of the river valley, the sea behind it and the low, wooded hills on either side. The sea was quiet and grey, the surface a kind of metallic sheen that made the contrast with the low-hanging, likewise grey sky more distinct that you'd have expected.

I left the car in the multi-storey on Festningsgaten and walked down to the jobcentre, where I had to sit for nearly an hour and wait my turn. I'd thought I'd just have to fill in a form, only it turned out signing on wasn't that easy. Besides the form I'd have to have an interview with a needs assessor, but I'd have to come back the following week for that, and then I had to sign up for a jobseekers' course, the weary-looking employment officer said. Only after that, and several weeks to assess my claim, would I get to know if I was eligible for unemployment benefit.

'What does a person do if they haven't got any money?' I said. 'If they're in urgent need, I mean?'

'Then you'd have to go to the social security department,' she said.

I thanked her, took the little pile of forms and brochures she'd given me and went towards the door. Two of those sat waiting were people I recognised. They'd both been a year below me at gymnas. One was called Håvard, I seemed to remember, his hair was in a crew cut on top with a long plait hanging down his back, he was always dressed in black and had his own programme on one of the new local radio stations. It wasn't surprising at all to run into him there, but it still got my back up, he was against everything in society, it was his big thing, it was what he was all about, and yet there he was waiting his turn for a handout from that same society.

I felt sick to my stomach as I went along Dronningens gate. Signing on meant I'd lost face, it was the opposite of everything I stood for politically. I'd thought of my national service as a duty, I hadn't asked to do it, then when I got discharged in March, mid-term, when you can't start a course of education, I reckoned it had to be their duty to tide me over. But surely that was bollocks, a poor excuse? It didn't matter how many people were sat in there cap in hand, I knew there were plenty of jobs to go round for those who wanted them.

I bought two newspapers at the newsagent's on the pedestrian street and sat down in the cafe at the library. First thing I did was look up my shares in the business paper. They hadn't budged, even though it was a fortnight since I'd last checked. It meant I was still down by just over half my investment. Believing I'd get my losses back any time soon felt a bit like believing in Father Christmas. Instead of putting my money into Statoil or another of the big players, I'd gone with two small offshore companies. I'd given them what my dad had left me, nearly the whole lot, money I'd received when I reached eighteen. Mum didn't know, but it wasn't like I'd done anything illegal with it or squandered it all gambling. I'd been meaning to tell her once the investment got going and started earning me some good money, enough to put paid to her objections.

There was still time, stock investments were always a long-term thing.

I folded the paper and shoved it out of the way, then picked up the local rag. Labour still had their knickers in a twist and were only going to accept petrol surcharges if top-bracket tax rates went up at the same time. In other words, they agreed with Willoch but were tabling a demand they knew he couldn't meet, meaning he'd have to step down and they could resume power. Talk about double standards. They supported the bill, but would vote against. And Hagen's hands were tied, he *couldn't* vote for surcharges. His party's whole platform was anti-taxation. It was their bedrock.

But then of course that Håvard guy had to come in. He sat down at the table next to mine with a couple of his mates. He gave me a nod, probably because he'd seen me at the jobcentre and to his mind it meant we were allies. I nodded back, got up and went out. Through the window I saw he'd taken my paper and had started reading it.

I walked along to the square and went into the reception area in the corner building where the local paper had their offices. An elderly man in a navy-blue coat, with white hair that was so thin it looked like dust, stood chatting with the receptionist, something to do with his paper not having arrived, so I gathered. The receptionist kept nodding politely. She had long blonde hair and a tanned face, long dark eyelashes. It wasn't the first time it had gone missing, he said, and she nodded, it was clearly a serious matter. She must have been on her holidays somewhere sunny over Easter, I reasoned, she didn't look like the sort who spent time in the fells. She apologised for what had happened and said he could take today's paper with him when he went, only he wouldn't, it was the principle that was important. When he left, his umbrella under his arm, she turned to me and smiled.

I smiled back.

'Dag, is he in? Or is he at the main office today?'

'No, he's in. I don't know if he's in right at the minute, though. Let me just find out for you. Sorry, who should I say wants to see him?' she said, the receiver already poised at her ear, clamped into place by her raised shoulder.

'Syvert,' I said.

She wasn't bad at all. A bit old for me maybe — she looked like she was at least twenty-five — but I still felt the stirrings of a hard-on.

'Visitor for you,' she said into the phone. 'Syvert.'

I'd known Dag all my life. We were cousins, he was the son of my dad's brother, we'd grown up together and were in the same class at school for nine years, and although we'd chosen different gymnasium schools after that — he'd gone to the Cathedral School in town, the posher choice — we'd still seen a lot of each other. We'd take the same bus in the mornings, the same one back in the afternoons, and even if we went out with our new friends at the weekends, we'd still often end up at the same table. He'd started writing for the paper when he was sixteen, they had a weekly page dedicated to local youth, and he did well too, well enough for them to offer him a short-term position after he finished gymnas, now he was into his second year.

He was sitting hunched over his typewriter when I came into his office.

'All right,' he said without looking up.

'All right,' I said, and sat down on the chair on the other side of the desk.

'Just need to get this done,' he said. 'Won't be a minute.'

'Don't mind me,' I said, unzipping my jacket as I looked down at the square below the window, the little park beyond, the way everything so impassively let the rain drizzle down on it.

Dag had a pigmentation disorder, what they called partial albinism, which meant his hair was white and his skin was white, but his eyes were brown. He'd been proud of it when he was little, it made him stand out, but once he got into puberty it tormented him.

'When did you get back — yesterday?' he said after a bit, leaning back in his chair and draping an arm over the backrest.

I nodded.

'Cup of coffee? I forgot to ask,' he said, and was on his feet before I even answered, disappearing into the corridor and returning a few moments later with a cup in each hand.

'Cheers,' I said as he handed me mine.

'So, dickhead, you did your stint!' he said, sitting back down again.

'Yes,' I said.

'*Yes*?' he said. 'Is that all you can say? Aren't you happy?'

'I wouldn't have minded staying on.'

'Then join the pros.'

'What, as a cook? No, thanks.'

'It's a career opportunity, that is. They'll be calling you Captain Cook by the time you're finished.'

'Captain Cuckoo, more like,' I said.

We laughed.

'What's that girl's name in reception, anyway?'

'Marianne?'

'The one who's down there now.'

'That's her, yes. Fancy a go, do you?'

'I wouldn't say no,' I said. 'How about you?'

He shook his head.

'People from work are out of bounds. It's a principle of mine.'

'You're only saying that because you've got no chance with anyone here,' I said.

'Are you going out tonight, then?' he said. 'Celebrate and all that?'

I gave a shrug.

'I wasn't planning on it. I'll have to see. What about you?'

'Don't know yet. Managed to get down the off-licence, though, just in case,' he said, nodding in the direction of a carrier bag that was dumped against the wall underneath the coat peg where his jacket was hanging.

'What did you get?'

'Rum.'

'Bacardi?'

'No. *Dark* rum. Can't remember what the brand's called. Have you tried it? It's not half bad. Takes the back of your throat off.'

'Can't say I have, no. Do you mix it with something?'

He shook his head.

'I suppose you can. I don't know. I just like it neat.'

'I've been on the margaritas recently,' I said. 'Have you tried that?'

'Course I have. With the salt on the rim of the glass?'

'Mm.'

'That's really nice too, that is,' he said.

'Then there's tequila slammers, of course,' I said. 'Have you tried them?'

'Once or twice, yes.'

'No, you haven't,' I said, and laughed.

'How the fuck do you know?'

'Because you said *once or twice*. You'd only say that to make it sound plausible. Am I right or am I right?'

'OK, so I've *seen* people who were on them and made a note to try one myself sometime. Will that do you?'

'Ha ha!'

He took a packet of cigarettes out of his shirt pocket and lit up, shoved his chair back and put his feet up on the desk.

'What were you thinking of doing now, then?' he said.

'Got to get off home. Get some shopping in for my mum on the way back.'

'With your life, stupid.'

'Oh, that,' I said. 'I don't know. I've just been down the jobcentre, thought I'd sign on to begin with.'

'Straight up?'

'Not much choice really.'

He put his feet down again, pulled his chair back up to the desk, reached his arm out and tapped his cigarette above the ashtray.

'Do you fancy being interviewed about it?' he said then.

'About what?'

'About being unemployed. There's a story in there, you know. Young man does his national service, only to go straight onto the dole queue. Where's the idea in that? Whose responsibility is it? And what's to be done?'

He looked at me.

'How about it, then? I can't interview you myself, the two of us being family and all, but I can give it to someone else who can. It's a good story. Important, too. The unemployment figures are ridiculous now.'

'I don't think so,' I said. 'I can get a job, easy. And no way I'm going to make myself out to be a victim.'

'It's not your fault! Go on, Syvert. You're out of work, it's a fact. Writing about it won't do any harm, surely? Anyway, have a think about it.'

'I can think about it all right,' I said, getting up. 'But I won't be doing it. You can forget all about it.'

He shrugged.

'See you in town, maybe.'

'It wouldn't surprise me,' he said.

I put the shopping bags down in the kitchen so Mum could put it all away, then went out again, rolled the summer tyres down from the barn, fetched the jack from out of the garage and set about changing the wheels on the car. I thought about Dad. It wasn't often I did these days, but on special occasions, Christmas, 17 May, or when it was my birthday, or if something out of the ordinary happened, if someone came to see us unexpectedly, for instance, or if I came at something familiar from a new angle, like I'd done now, after I'd first gone into the barn, then the garage, I could find myself thinking about him.

The jack sank a few centimetres into the grit that welled up around its red metallic foot. It had stopped raining, but the air was still moist and the sky heavy; the fog stood grey among the green pines at the edge of the woods.

After I'd changed the wheels on one side and was jacking the car up again on the other, the school bus pulled in down on the road at the bottom of the drive. A few minutes later Joar was standing beside me in his shiny down jacket, a white woolly hat pushed up his forehead.

'You can roll those tyres up to the barn for me, if you like,' I said.

His face lit up, which he then immediately tried to hide.

'I'll just take my bag inside first,' he said, and went up to the house, checking his stride I sensed: he looked like he wanted to run.

He changed the last wheel all on his own, all I did was tighten the nuts, and then we went inside for our tea.

We were having cod, and the whole kitchen smelled of fish.

With her slotted spoon, Mum lifted the chunks out of the pot and put them down on the serving dish as Joar and I sat down at the table. The potatoes had already been put out and lay steaming in their bowl, next to them a dish of boiled carrots and cauliflower.

'What's the first thing you can remember?' Joar said, his eyes glancing up at me, his head lowered.

'From when I was a kid, you mean?'

'What's the first thing you can remember?' he repeated, as if about to throw a strop.

Mum put the fish on the table and went over to the sink to fill the jug with water.

'I'm not sure if it's the very first thing,' I said. 'But I'm standing on a little suspension bridge, and I'm jumping up and down to make it sway. I suppose I must have been three or four, something like that.'

I looked across at Mum.

'Can you remember that? That we went somewhere and there was this little bridge?'

She shook her head and sat down.

'Here we are,' she said. 'Tuck in.'

'Can you describe it?' said Joar.

I put a lump of fish on his plate and one on mine.

'I'm holding on to the rope and jumping up and down, and the water's rushing underneath the planks.'

'What does your face look like?'

'I'm laughing. I feel joy. That's probably why I remember it.'

'So you can see yourself from the outside?'

'Yes,' I said.

'Is it a memory then, do you think?' he said.

'Of course it's a memory,' I said.

'But we don't see ourselves from the outside, do we?' he said, and then shaped a little slot in front of his eyes with his fingers and thumbs. 'We look out.'

'True,' I said, pressing my knife between the white flesh and the tough, grey skin that came away almost by itself.

'So you've altered what actually happened.'

'It would seem so, yes,' I said. 'I still *remember* it though. So it did happen. I just saw it from the outside rather than from the inside, that's all.'

I parted the piece of fish in two and removed the hunk of bone. It looked like a prosthesis, a foreign body in all the softness of the flesh.

'What made you think of that, Joar?' said Mum.

'I saw myself from the outside in a dream,' he said. 'And then I realised that's how I mostly see myself when I'm dreaming, from the outside. I just think it's a bit weird. Don't you think so too?'

'Yes, I suppose,' said Mum.

'Do you see yourself from the outside when you dream?' he said.

'I wouldn't know, I've never thought about it,' said Mum.

'Joar changed the wheels all on his own,' I said.

'Only one of them,' he said.

'Very good,' said Mum, and she smiled for a second or two before her face fell into repose again, as when a smile is only forced.

Shortly after half past five as I was lying on my bed listening to the new album I'd bought in town, *Master of Puppets*, a car came up the drive. Mum never had visitors at this time of day, and none of Joar's friends would come in a car, so it had to be someone for me.

I got up and went to the window. It was an Ascona, it pulled up outside and sounded the horn.

'Syvert!' Mum shouted from downstairs. 'Gjert's here!'

Oh, bloody hell.

I snatched a pair of shorts, a shirt, a training jacket out of the cupboard, a pair of socks, hurried down the stairs, got my football boots from the laundry room and ran out to the car that stood waiting with the engine turning over.

'All right,' said Gjert as I opened the door and got in.

'All right,' I said, pulling the seat belt across my chest as he swung back down the drive. The headlights swept over the ramp of the barn before flooding across the field, making the signs on the main road faintly luminescent before locking onto the gravel in front.

'Had you forgotten?'

'Yes.'

'Not to worry. I had a word with Terje today, he said no problem if you wanted to come.'

'Great,' I said. 'Anyway, I thought you said you hadn't got a car. This looks like a car, if you ask me.'

'Just bought it today.'

'How much did that set you back?'

'Five grand. Stereo and everything,' he said, and leaned forward to switch it on. The panel lit up and music thudded from the speakers. 'Nice sound too.'

'What are we listening to?'

'Don't you recognise it?'

I shook my head.

'Accept. *Balls to the Wall*.'

'I do actually, now you mention it,' I said.

As we walked over towards the pavilions I saw several shadowy figures cross fleetingly between the trees on their way to the floodlit all-weather pitch. Five or six were there already, in hats, mittens and bulging training jackets, kicking some balls about.

'What kind of a person would have football practice on a Friday night?' I said.

Gjert shook his head.

'It is a bit daft. There's not been a single time when everyone's come.'

The rain that fell was invisible apart from in the floodlight beams, where the wind made it look like something someone was throwing onto the pitch.

In the changing rooms, Keith, Vegard, Karsten and Glenn were getting ready.

'H-e-e-y,' they said as soon as they saw me. 'The Elk's back!'

'Whelk, more like,' I said. 'I've not moved a muscle since Christmas.'

I pulled off my shoes and trousers, sat down on the bench, bent over my bag and fished out my shorts, socks and T-shirt.

'Are you home for good now, then?' said Glenn and looked up, he was bent forward while he tied his laces, his dark fringe flopping in front of his eyes.

I nodded.

'He got his discharge yesterday,' Gjert said.

'Straight up?' said Keith. 'Celebrating tonight, then?'

'Not sure really,' I said. 'Are you lot going out?'

'Has a zebra got stripes?' said Glenn.

'Has Karsten got a dick?' said Keith, jumping to his feet. We laughed and he grinned, pleased with himself, and crossed the room, stiff-legged, the peculiar gait that comes of wearing studs. They clacked against the floor.

'You know why they call me the Elk, don't you?' I said. 'And it's nothing to do with long strides either.'

'Arf, arf,' said Karsten, now rubbing his thighs with muscle rub from a little jar. The pungent menthol smell cut through the air. Karsten didn't look that big when he was sitting down, his face seemed like it belonged to someone smaller, or maybe it was the way he was, unforthcoming in a way, always a bit cautious, but then when he drew himself up to his full height, as he did now, his build and features came together and everything fell into place. He was a strapping two metres tall, and ample to go with it. His best mate ever since junior school had been Glenn, who was small and wiry, or at least looked like he was next to Karsten. We sometimes called them Stan and Ollie.

I put my boots on and did up the laces, zipped up my top, then glanced over at Gjert, who was sitting in his shorts, meticulously unfolding his socks. No one took as much time getting changed as he did. And no one wore as many layers in winter as he did.

'I'll get out there, then,' I said. 'I'll be here all night if I have to wait for you.'

He nodded deliberately, as if immersed in some demanding task. I got to my feet and went out, together with Vegard and Glenn and Karsten. The air nipped at my bare thighs. On the other side of the trees, which shimmered in the fog and the light from the windows, we broke into a trot. I didn't know the trainer who'd taken over after Christmas. I jogged up and stopped in front of him.

He was quite young, thirtyish. His features were sharp. Narrow mouth topped by a thin moustache. Pale skin, dark straight hair. He looked more like someone in a synth band than a football trainer.

'Hey,' I said. 'I'm Syvert. I used to play for the juniors here. I was wondering if I could join in tonight?'

He nodded.

'Terje mentioned someone new was coming. What position do you play?'

'Midfield,' I said.

'Right, then,' he said.

We jogged a couple of laps first, then put in some short intervals, rounding off with a series of sprints across the width of the pitch. I was nearly throwing up by the time we'd finished, then when we kicked off with some five-a-side my legs were like jelly and shaking so much I could hardly pass straight. After a while, though, my body seemed to adjust and I managed to get into the game a bit more.

I realised I'd been missing it, the whole thing. The fluorescent bibs, the plastic cones, the floodlights, the grit, the constant alternation between building up your own game and breaking down the opponents', the different kinds of players there were in every team, regardless of what level you were playing at. The rhythm of your breathing, bodies clashing together, the falling rain, the shouts for the ball, the warnings, the body language when someone scores, ironic, triumphant, indifferent.

We played defence v. attack for a while, the trainer kept blowing his whistle to stop us, correcting and explaining. He wanted us to play out from the back, long balls from your own half weren't allowed. Gjert and I were to drop deep so we could pick up the ball, turn it round and feed it out wide.

After a bit, he blew the whistle and gathered everyone round.

'Football's simple,' he said. 'It's all about scoring more goals than you concede. Are you with me?'

No one said anything.

'To make that happen, there's only one thing we need. Space. Empty space. The aim is to create space when we're on the ball, making it *easier* to move it forward and put it in the back of the net. The second aim is to close our opponents down when *they're* on the ball, making it *harder* for them to move it forward and put it in the back of *our* net. Are you with me?'

'If you say so,' said Glenn.

He got a couple of laughs.

'When Gjert and Syvert drop deep, they pull opposing players with them, leaving space in behind. That's where the ball has to go, into that space. As soon as we do that, we're past the first line of pressure, and more pockets of space will open up as a result. But none of that space is going to open up if all we do is welly the long ball from the back. That ball's always going to be easy to defend against. Are you with me?'

'Yes, but we're not Juventus either, are we?' said Keith.

'Speak for yourself!' said Vegard.

We laughed.

'All right,' said Mads. 'We'll do midfield and attack against defence. Gjert, you go with defence, in front of the four.'

Again he kept interrupting the play, sometimes telling everyone to freeze in their positions so we could see what opportunities there were and what the various options would lead to.

It was annoying, I wanted to play football, not chess. But after fifteen minutes of that he let us play out the rest of the session seven v. seven on the full pitch without stopping us. We finished off with some more intervals. Strictly speaking I didn't need to do that bit, I was only there for fun, I just didn't think it was on to go and stand under the showers while the rest of them were killing themselves like that, so I clenched my teeth and ran until I was nearly blacking out.

In the changing room afterwards everyone was quiet. We just sat there, faces flushed and sweating, no one had the energy to take their boots off. Once we got some strength back, our movements gradually found some fluidity, they quickened, our voices rose, the showers were turned on, laughter resounded between the walls. It was Friday night, most of them had been working all week. Many had jobs at the cellulose factory. The older ones, those in their mid and late thirties, were people I didn't know other than by their names and faces, what they'd be doing later on I had no idea. I'd never seen any of them at Sundown, which was where I normally went.

'You'll be knackered now, then?' said Kjetil, the square-jawed striker, naked next to me, rummaging for something in his holdall.

'I'll say,' I said. 'I've been living on a *boat* these last few months.'

'You won't have done much running about there, then,' he said, pulling out a towel and a soap case. It was an old Liverpool bag, looked like it was from the mid seventies, I'd had one the same when I was little.

'Are you coming out with us afterwards?' he said, and stood up.

'Where are you off to?'

'Fun Centre, I imagine. A bit of bowling. A few pints, I shouldn't wonder.'

'Fun Centre,' I said. 'I've not been there yet.'

'Haven't you? It's about time you did, then.'

'Maybe it is,' I said, and pulled off my soaking wet T-shirt.

Gjert sat in the car outside the house while I went in and changed into something more presentable. He switched the engine off, but left the ignition on; I could faintly hear the bass from his music. The beams of his headlights projected like two yellow cylinders into the dark night, the wipers moved gently back and forth across the windscreen. I did the top button of my shirt up, raised the collar, draped a tie around my neck and tied it. I put some aftershave on my fingertips and dabbed my cheeks. On my way out I put my head round the door of the living room, where Mum and Joar were watching telly.

'What are you watching?' I said.

'The video charts,' said Joar.

'Aha,' I said. 'Any good videos on tonight?'

He shrugged.

'Who's that, then?' I said. 'I've heard that song a few times.'

'It's "Peter Gunn" by Art of Noise, but it hasn't come out yet, so you can't have heard it that many times,' he said, the little smart-arse.

'OK,' I said. 'I'll be off out, then. Have a nice time.'

'Where are you going?' Mum said.

'Over to Gjert's,' I said.

'Don't stay out all night,' she said.

'I won't,' I said.

Joar was staring intensely at the screen.

'Joar?' I said.

'What?' he said.

'Do you fancy going to the swimming baths with me tomorrow?'

'What time?'

'Any time,' I said. 'We'll leave that till tomorrow.'

He nodded. I put my jacket on, trotted across the yard and opened the car door. Gjert started the engine without looking at me.

'Do you really think smelling nice is going to help you, as ugly as you are?' he said.

'I always get so horny when I look at you, Gjert,' I said. 'Your face looks just like a cunt.'

'If looking at me makes you horny, it's because you're a bloody puff with gel in your hair,' he said.

'I'll give you gel up your arse, if you don't watch out. You can sit on the gear lever then and enjoy yourself while you're driving.'

He laughed and leaned forward, wiping the windscreen with a cloth he must have had in his hand for the purpose, braking as we got to the road.

Gjert opened the boot and got out two carrier bags of beer, handed me one and closed the boot again. The thud rebounded between the silent houses.

'Are you all right with me buying these off you?' I said as we started walking to the bus stop.

'Course,' he said. 'I wouldn't have said otherwise, would I?'

He put his down on the ground and took a tin of *snus* from his inside pocket before tucking a pouch under his lip.

'You look like an idiot,' I said.

'You don't look too good yourself,' he said. 'And you don't even use it.'

From somewhere nearby, presumably one of the houses behind the treees where we stood, music came drifting. It was so faint I couldn't hear what it was. Apart from that, everything was quiet.

'Is there a party on there, do you think?'

Gjert shook his head.

'It's from over at Susanne's. Probably just warming up before going on somewhere.'

'Don't you fancy going over?' I said, stepping outside the bus shelter and craning towards the house.

'We're not in their league,' he said.

'Only the best's good enough,' I said.

'Dream on,' he said.

A car came tearing along the road. It slammed the brakes on when it saw us. Terje leaned across and rolled the window down on the passenger side.

'Need a lift, lads?' he said.

'We're off up to Karsten's,' said Gjert. 'If you're going that way?'

'You're in luck.'

As we got in, me in the front, Gjert in the back, the bus came round the bend at the far end of the flatland, and the sight of the big vehicle, which when I was a kid I'd always thought of as good-natured, perhaps because of the rumble it made, struck me as immensely sad and lonely. What were its headlights searching for? Like-minded friends. What did they find? Fields, trees, rows of houses.

Terje pulled away and soon we were doing a hundred an hour, the road cutting through the woods. Terje spent so much time in his car it was more like his body. He drove fast, but safely.

'What do you make of Mads then, Syvert?' he said without taking his eyes off the road.

'Seems like a decent enough bloke,' I said. 'But all I want is to play football. Like we've always done.'

'He was coaching a second division team in Denmark,' Terje said. 'So yes, decent bloke, I reckon.'

'How come he's ended up here?'

'He's with Lene. Moved here last summer.'

'Vegard's sister?'

'That's right. They're getting married next summer.'

We turned onto the E18, it led us down towards the sea again, into the housing estate behind the little shopping hub with its petrol station and supermarket, where Terje seamlessly, not unlike a boat putting in at a jetty, sailed into a driveway and pulled up next to Karsten's dad's Granada.

We went in without ringing the bell. They were in the basement watching videos and drinking beer.

*

I woke up the next morning when Joar came into my room. Everything around me swam as I opened my eyes. He was holding a bag in his hand.

'You've got to get up now if we're going,' he said.

'Going where?' I said, and closed my eyes again.

'The swimming baths.'

'Joar,' I said, peering out now. 'We'll go tomorrow instead, OK?'

'But you promised,' he said.

'I know I did. But it'll be better tomorrow. Weren't you doing something else today, anyway?'

'All you think about is yourself,' he said, and left the room, and I must have gone straight back to sleep then, because the next thing I knew Mum was calling up the stairs, lunch was on the table, it was two o'clock. I got up, still reeling from the night before, got dressed and went down. She'd made rice porridge, which was the last thing I felt like, but luckily she'd put some ham slices out too.

'Where's Joar?' I said as I sat down.

'He's over at Rickard's. He'll be having something there, I imagine.'

I poured myself some juice, took a couple of slices of ham, then spooned a couple of dollops of the rice porridge onto the plate, put a knob of butter on top that soon melted and formed a little yellow pool in the middle, and sprinkled it with some cinnamon and sugar.

'I've got to go to work tonight,' she said. 'So you'll have to stay in and look after him.'

'That's all right,' I said.

'Is the porridge still hot?'

'Yes,' I said. 'It's fine.'

'Good.'

'Mum?'

'What?'

'I'd thought I'd go to the shop, only I'm just about skint. I don't suppose you've got any spare cash lying about, have you?'

'In my purse. It's in my bag.'

'And where's your bag?'

'Where it always is.'

'By the phone?'

She nodded.

'How much can I take?'

'Take what you need.'

She had quite a bit as it turned out, just over nine hundred kroner, in fact. Plus I still had a few hundred myself. So maybe I could take three hundred, I told myself, standing with her bag in front of me on the little telephone table, her purse open in my hands. That would do me for a while. And I wouldn't have to pester her for more later on.

I put the three notes in my trouser pocket, put my anorak on, and my boots, and went off in the direction of the shop. I didn't want to chance taking the car yet, and besides, a bit of fresh air would do me good. A fog was hanging over the fields again, the air shimmered slightly, some gulls were standing on the barn roof with their wings tightly folded. I sensed Mum at the window watching me as I started walking, but I didn't turn to look. I was still on a bit of a high from the night before, a lingering excitement at the loud music, the people and the flashing lights, so alien it all seemed in this landscape, with its dark green, towering spruce, its sodden fields beneath a low and unmoving sky.

As so often before, nothing had happened, we'd just been out, drinking and having a laugh, and at the end of the night we'd pooled together for a minibus home around three in the morning. Now, as I walked along the road, it felt like that glittering, throbbing space, whose wide-open faces, as if caught in some terrific thunderstorm, had repeatedly been illuminated and thrown back into darkness, was emptying out into something so much greater, something motionless and still.

At the same time, the feeling got me wondering if I should get a few beers in at the shop, just in case. For all I knew, Joar might want to stay the night at his friend's, wasn't he still at that age, when they did that?

I spent just over a hundred on a football coupon, as Dad had always done, which gave me a sense of contentment, bought some Coke and some crisps, a six-pack of Carlsberg, and a couple of newspapers, *VG* and *Dagbladet*.

It was Signe on the checkout.

'You're back, are you?' she said with a smile.

'Looks like it,' I said. 'And you're working here now?'

'Looks like it,' she said, entering in the price of the six-pack with one hand while shoving it along the shiny metal counter with the other. Her jutting breasts that we'd leered at during the last couple of years of school filled out her green shop jersey.

'Full-time, is it?' I said, pulling a carrier bag out of the cardboard box under the counter.

'You must be joking. It's only weekends, and the odd night in the kiosk. I'm doing my entrance exams.'

'University, wow. You'll be moving away soon then, I expect?'

'I reckon so.'

'Oslo?'

'Maybe.'

I handed her some money, the drawer of the till jumped out and she counted my change.

'Can you give me some extra coins?' I said.

'I'd have thought you'd have grown out of the kiddie ride,' she said.

I laughed.

'Don't be giving me ideas,' I said. 'Is it still here?'

She handed me the change, I bagged the last of my items, said see you and went out. I gave Dag a ring from the phone box to see if he fancied coming over. He said he would.

I put the beers and the Cokes in the fridge, the crisps in the cupboard, then went to the toilet for a shit, only there was someone in there, so I went into the living room and put the telly on in the meantime. The only thing on was the harness racing, so I turned it off again, went and stood at the window and looked out. Three unusually big crows were standing in the field a bit further away. Or were they crows? They were completely black, there wasn't a bit of grey on them. I'd never seen that sort before. Had they got lost? If so, where had they come from?

The phone rang behind me. I turned round and answered it. It was Evert, Mum's brother. We exchanged a few words and then he asked if she was in. I told him to hang on a minute, lowered the receiver and put my hand over the microphone part.

'Mum!' I called out. 'Phone! It's Evert! Can you talk to him now or do you want to ring him back?'

'Just a minute!' she shouted. I put the receiver to my ear again.

'She's just coming now,' I said. 'Anyway, speak to you again soon.'

'Yes, look after yourself, Syvert. Thanks a lot.'

Mum came in at the same moment. I handed her the receiver and went straight to the toilet.

There was blood in the sink. A streak of red blood down the sloping side of the porcelain, and some half-diluted drops that clung to the wet metal strainer over the plughole.

I stared at it for a few seconds, it was as if everything inside me went dead. Then I turned the tap on and rinsed it away. It was almost certainly nothing serious, if it had been she'd never have forgotten about it like that. She must have had a nosebleed or something.

And it had nothing to do with Joar's dream.

How stupid a thought was that?

When I came back in again she was sitting in the chair reading a women's weekly, *Hjemmet*. She looked up at me. Nothing untoward there.

'Dag's coming round,' I said.

'That's nice,' she said.

We'd been watching the English football on telly together for years. There were no more matches on now, but the Norwegian league was starting that weekend, so instead we listened to one of the local radio stations that had live updates on the scores. For a long time it looked like I was going to have ten right on my coupon, only then it all went to pot like it usually did, three teams scored in the last fifteen minutes, meaning I ended up with only seven. Dag got five.

'Not bad going,' I said. 'Getting five right's as hard as getting eleven.'

'No, it isn't,' he said. 'Five right's about the same as seven on a scale of probability. One right's the same as eleven.'

'Can't be,' I said. 'It's got to be a lot harder getting none right than twelve?'

'Why should it be?'

'It feels like it should, that's all. None right's impossible, surely! Do you know anyone who's ever got none right?'

'No,' he said.

'But you know someone who got twelve?'

'Yes. My dad, for one.'

'There you are, then.'

'How do you mean? You can't put your money on getting none right, that'd be negative betting. There must be loads of people who get none right, if you take hedges into account, it's just that no one can be bothered to check.'

'The dead,' I said.

'What?' he said.

'The dead, I imagine they'd be into negative betting.'

'You reckon they watch the footy?'

'Yes. Or the ytoof, as it's called where they come from.'

'Sey! Sey! Laog! Laog!' said Dag.

I laughed and went to the fridge to get another beer. Dag was driving and wasn't having any, so I don't suppose I was being much of a mate starting on my fourth, it occurred to me, opening the cupboard under the sink with one hand and tossing the top into the bin while holding the bottle, slender and cool, in the other.

'I'm turning this off now, is that OK?' said Dag from the living room.

'Of course it is,' I said, and went in to join him, grabbing a handful of crisps as I sat down. 'When I was a kid I used to think the lettering on the ambulances, you know the back-to-front lettering on the bodywork, was for the dead to read.'

'Seriously?' he said.

'Yes, I couldn't understand why else it'd be back to front. I didn't think anyone could read back to front. It wasn't until I passed my driving test and saw an ambulance coming up behind me one day that I realised the point.'

'Straight up?'

'Yes. It's not that weird, is it?'

'Maybe not. But you didn't still think it was for the dead by the time you passed your test?'

'No, of course not. No, no.'

'Anyway, I can talk,' said Dag. 'Nan told me once when I was little that the swallows slept at the bottom of lakes in winter. I believed it for years. At least until the end of junior school.'

I got up and went over to the unit against the wall, rummaged through my cassettes there, put one in the deck and switched it on.

'What are you doing tonight? Anything?' I said.

'Stopping in, I reckon.'

'Same here.'

'You could have fooled me, the way you're going.'

'What, a couple of beers while the football was on?'

'I'd best be going now, anyway,' he said. 'My mum's doing pizza tonight. I promised them I'd be there.'

'OK,' I said.

'Come by the office next time you're in town,' he said, and got to his feet.

'Will do,' I said.

He went out into the hall, and I followed him with the bottle in my hand.

'I'll do that interview, if you want,' I said.

He looked at me as he put an arm through his coat sleeve.

'About being unemployed?'

'That's right.'

'Seriously? That's brilliant!'

'On one condition, mind.'

'Which is?'

'That you don't make me out to be the sort who can't look after himself and people have to feel sorry for.'

'Of course, understood,' he said. 'Do you want to stop by on Monday? We could do it then, if it suits you?'

'OK,' I said.

From the living-room window I watched his car grow smaller as he went down the drive, until he turned onto the main road at the bottom and was gone.

I went into the hall, up the stairs and into my room. The high I was on from the beers I'd drunk felt like a sort of currency, to stop there would be like throwing good money out the window. But sitting at home drunk wasn't much cop. I flicked through my records, stood in front of the window and looked out, decided to ring that friend of Joar's, went downstairs and dialled the number Mum had written on the pad that hung from the wall above the telephone table. It was the mother who answered, I told her who it was and she went and got Joar. Was he coming home after, or was he stopping there the night? No, he was coming home. It might be late, though. Why was I asking? Just wondered, that's all. Because you want to go out? he said, the little clever clogs. I wouldn't mind, I said. You can if you want, he said. I can look after myself. I know you can, I said. Only I promised Mum. Ah, he said. I wouldn't worry about that. You go out, I'll be fine. Are you sure? Sure.

It was pouring when I stepped out. I locked the door, left the key under the mat and started walking to the bus while big raindrops detonated in the puddles and threw up little columns of water. They pattered against the hood I'd tied tight under my chin. I hadn't phoned anyone, and I'd never actually done that before, gone into town on my own without arranging to meet someone. But if I didn't run into anyone I knew, however unlikely that was, I could always go home again, it'd be all right, and Mum would have nothing to complain about then either.

I stood at the deserted stop for ten minutes before the bus came. The back seats were taken up by a group of sixteen-year-olds, I gave them a nod and sat down, got my Walkman out of my pocket, unravelled the cord, put the headphones over my ears and switched it on. Led Zeppelin's *Physical Graffiti* on one side, Van Halen's *Fair Warning* on the other. The bus stopped at nearly all the stops on the way, but no one I knew other than by name and appearance got on. It wasn't surprising, it was only eight o'clock, most of them would still be drinking at home.

I got off at the bus station and walked along the quayside. The murky water was lit up as far as about ten metres out by the light from the many lamp posts, their illumination perforated by raindrops. Further away, the water merged into almost black air. The high I'd been on was wearing off, and for a moment I thought about catching the bus back again; I wondered what I was doing there. But if I went back, nothing would happen, that much I could be sure of. And I wanted so much for something to happen. It hardly mattered what.

In front of me a car went down the ramp that led into the hotel's underground car park. Another had pulled in at the petrol station's pumps, a Mazda from my own neck of the woods by the looks of it, the foxtail dangling from the aerial was a dead giveaway. But the driver who was filling up, a guy in his twenties wearing a denim jacket, jeans and clogs, was someone I'd never seen before. He glanced at me as I went past, totally uninterested. A girl with long blonde hair was sitting in the front passenger seat in a white down jacket, and I'd definitely seen her before, more than once, she was from one of the villages a good way up the valley alongside the river. Her clog bloke wouldn't be able to see, so I sent her a smile. She turned her head away slowly as if she was too good for me.

There were twenty-odd people sitting in the bar area of the cafe, mostly men. I found a stool at the end of the long counter and ordered a rum and Coke.

'Roman Coke? Never tried it myself,' the bloke next to me said, his accent suggested the Østland, he had a suit and tie on and his belly hung down to his thighs.

I couldn't think of anything clever to say, but smiled a brief acknowledgement, pulled a hundred note out of my pocket and put it on the counter as the bartender put my drink down in front of me.

'It's like this, you see,' the fat bloke said. 'I'm from Eleverum myself. The Swedes think I mean a big house.'

I looked at him blankly.

'Eleven rooms, get it?'

He chuckled to himself. His cheeks drooped on either side of his mouth, his eyes were small and narrow, as if squashed together by the fat that surrounded them. But he was enjoying himself.

'From the town here, are you?' he said.

I nodded while I scanned the room to see if there was anyone I knew.

'I'm not really from Eleverum. That was only for the joke. I live in Drammen. I could have said something funny about that too. But that would have been too cheap, even for me. Have you ever been there?'

'Only the station,' I said.

'Like most people. Drammen's a place for passing through.'

There were some chairs free, but no tables that weren't occupied. I wondered if I should go and sit down at one anyway, just to get away from him. The asphalt outside glistened in the street lighting. The cars that came sailing past had their wipers going, swishing across the windscreens. Now and then, someone came walking along the pavement, their umbrellas were like little Japanese roofs. They glanced through the windows as they went past.

He lit a cigarette and held the packet out to me, I shook my head, and the bartender placed an ashtray in front of him.

'What happens on a Saturday night, then, in a town like this?' he said.

'Not much,' I said.

'No?' he said, and looked at me with a raised eyebrow.

'No,' I said.

'No,' he said.

I put my empty glass down, caught the bartender's attention and raised a finger in the air. Was he homo or just looking for someone to talk to? It was hard to tell, but I knew one thing, I didn't want to sit there long enough to find out. So when my drink came I downed it in a couple of mouthfuls, got to my feet and went outside into the rain, the alcohol glowing warmly in my blood. There was a new place a couple of streets away, I remembered, downstairs in a basement. I'd never been there, it was Dag who'd told me about it the last time I'd been home. No one else I knew went there, at least not as far as I was aware, and I'd never thought of going there myself either, not before then, until I was on my way. Some cars from out of town cruised slowly through the streets; they'd do so all night, pausing only for the occasional pit stop at one of the petrol stations or to congregate out at the docklands where they always got together on Friday and Saturday nights.

When I came to where the pedestrian street cut across, and was about to turn right, a car honked its horn and pulled in at the kerb. It was Gjert's Ascona. He rolled his window down.

'All right,' he said, looking up at me, his elbow on the sill, his other hand on the wheel. 'Out for a walk, are we?'

'All right,' I said, and peered at the dimly lit girl in the passenger seat. Long dark hair, she had, and a pale, narrow face. She was looking straight ahead.

'I was thinking of going to that new basement place,' I said. 'Have you been there?'

He shook his head.

'Where are you off to, then?' I said.

'Nowhere, really, just cruising. I'm sure we'll think of something, though. I've heard there's a party on at Jarle's, we might go there. Do you fancy it?'

'No, I was thinking of going on to Sundown at some point. See if there's anything happening. Don't you fancy going there instead? I can't really be arsed sitting around in someone's basement again.'

Gjert looked at me and jerked his head ever so slightly in the direction of the passenger seat. She was only sixteen, I remembered, so she wouldn't be allowed in anywhere.

'You've not met Bente, have you?' he said.

'No,' I said.

She turned her head towards me and gave a faint smile.

'Hello,' she said.

'Hello,' I said, and reached my hand past Gjert. 'I'm an old friend of Gjert's. Syvert.'

Her hand was cold, and the act of shaking hands itself seemed like it was something strange to her, something she wasn't used to doing, her eyes glazing over in shyness, as she looked straight past me.

'Anyway,' said Gjert. 'You doing all right?'

'Yes, fine,' I said. 'You?'

'Can't complain,' he said.

'See you, then,' I said.

'See you, mate,' he said, winding his window up and then throwing the car into gear as I started walking.

As soon as I set foot in the dark room, I realised it wasn't a good move. Round tables with tall bar stools occupied mostly by people dressed in black, like that guy I'd seen at the jobcentre, what was his name again? Håvard, that was it. Candles on the tables, new wave coming out of the speakers. Still, I sat down at the bar and ordered a beer. I'd drunk nearly half of it before I discovered there was actually someone there that I knew. Susanne and three of her mates were sitting at a table over in the corner. I picked up my beer and went over. She looked up.

'Syvert,' she said. 'It's been a long time.'

'It has, yes,' I said. 'Sixteen months, to be exact. I've been away doing my national service. Mind if I join you? I'll be off soon, anyway.'

She was looking really good. Black leather jacket, dark hair, bright red lips. And something dark around her eyes.

'No, not at all,' she said.

I sat down on the empty chair next to her.

'Do you come here often?' I said. 'Decent place. I've never been before.'

'Sometimes,' she said.

'Pretty often, I'd say!' one of her mates said.

'This is our corner,' said one of the others.

Susanne picked up the packet of cigarettes that was on the table and her upper arm brushed against mine. I looked at her, she looked down at the packet and opened it at once, and when she lit her cigarette her eyes were fastened to a point somewhere in the middle of the room. Her upper lip quivered faintly, and then again, before she clamped her mouth around the filter and sucked in smoke.

'Are you moving into town?' she said.

'Not sure yet,' I said. 'Probably. It's as good as anywhere else, I suppose.'

'Not!' she said with a smile. It wasn't a friendly smile, but the sarcasm it signalled wasn't aimed at me, or so I understood.

'You've changed a bit,' I said. 'I can tell, not having seen you for so long.'

'We're not teenagers any more,' she said. 'That's what you can see.'

'I am,' I said with a laugh.

'You are, that's right,' she said.

'Not for long though. My birthday's in October.'

'You don't say.'

This time the sarcasm *was* aimed at me.

'Yes, I do, as a matter of fact,' I said. 'When's yours, anyway?'

'Why would you want to know?'

'Routine question.'

'Syvert was in the year below me at junior school,' she said.

'And secondary school, and gymnas,' I said.

'I'm a Sagittarius,' said Susanne.

'Means nothing to me,' I said, and supped a mouthful of beer.

'Sagittariuses are restless,' one of the others said. 'They want to travel.'

'Do you believe in that rubbish?' I said.

'It's true for me, at least,' said Susanne.

'What are you doing sitting here, then?'

She glanced at me.

'Nosy all of a sudden, aren't we?'

'Oh, come on, we're only talking!' I said. 'Anyway, I'm not stopping. Meeting some people down at Sundown in a bit.'

I stood up, drained my beer, put the glass down on the table, said see you and went out, through the rain-soaked streets to the club. The queue outside wasn't too bad, I was in after ten minutes. I stood at the bar and ordered a gin and tonic while scanning for someone I knew. Wasn't alcohol sometimes known as firewater? I thought it was a good name, because if the high it gave you diminished after a while, it was a bit like when the flame in a stove dies down and the wood lies there glowing, and then when you chuck a new log on, even hours afterwards, the flames immediately start dancing again. That was what it felt like.

No one there I knew, as far as I could see.

I sat down on one of the stools at the bar counter, angling myself away from it so I could keep an eye on who was coming in, and ordered another drink. Discreetly, I counted the money in my wallet, it had gone down in no time. Three hundred and something left.

I saw the blood in the sink so clearly that for a few seconds it was almost as if I was there. There was no need to be worried, she'd been normal as ever afterwards, in a good mood even, I told myself, survey-ing the room again, noticing the floor was carpeted from wall to wall, with the exception of the dance floor, as yet deserted at the far end, illuminated by shifting colours, now and then blitzed by strobe lights that made all movements jerky and disconnected, like in a silent movie or something.

'Love me bartender,' said a voice beside me. 'Love me true.'

I turned. The fat bloke from before smiled and lifted his hand to his forehead in a salute.

'Aren't you too old to be hanging out in a place like this?' I said.

'Now you're doing me an injustice,' he said. 'How old do you think I am?'

'Fifty-five,' I said.

'I'm forty-three,' he said.

'I wasn't far off.'

'My *dad's* fifty-five.'

'He was twelve when he had you, was he?'

'Exactly. Early bloomer.'

At that moment, Keith, Vegard, Karsten, Glenn and Terje all came in. I stayed seated and studied them a moment instead of getting up and going over, which had been my first impulse. Terje big and heavily built, Karsten towering, fleshy, Glenn small and slight, Keith confident and cool, the sleeves of his jacket pushed up his forearms. Vegard unhurried as always in his green army jacket and longish black hair. They didn't look like brothers, that would have been an exaggeration, but they still looked like they belonged together. The way they made a beeline for a table on the other side of the dance floor, all in agreement, no discussion, and sat down there. The air of controlled excitement they had about them, as if quietly confident of success. Their poring over the menu, the way they fingered their hair, their money, a brief exchange as to whose round it was first, decided in seconds, Glenn getting up and making straight to the bar. Yes, they were a squad.

Glenn came up on the other side of the fat bloke and didn't see me.

'Can I get you a drink, my southern friend?' the bloke said, nodding at my now empty glass.

'I've got my own money,' I said. 'Thanks all the same.'

Glenn turned his head, maybe he recognised the voice, and I looked straight at him.

'All right, Syvert,' he said.

'All right,' I said.

'Who are you with?' he said.

'Just on my own,' I said.

'On your own?' he said, and gave me a perplexed look as the bartender came over, then turned to face him and ordered their drinks. Five pints, five Jägermeisters.

'That's right,' I said. 'I was only sitting at home bored.'

'Why didn't you give us a ring? We were at Vegard's.'

'Too short notice,' I said.

The bartender put a tray down on the counter and started pulling two pints at once.

'Oh, I see,' Glenn said. 'Anyway, we're over there.'

'Got you,' I said. 'I'll be over in a minute. Anyone else out tonight?'

He shrugged. The bartender put the first two pints down on the tray.

'What's that you're drinking?' said Glenn.

'Gin and tonic,' I said.

'It's the malaria he's frightened of,' the fat bloke said with a laugh. 'We're that far south.'

Glenn threw me another bewildered look. I gave a shrug.

'You knew that, of course? The gin and tonic was invented by the English to protect themselves against malaria in the tropics. Tonic water contains quinine. As good an excuse as any, I'd say.'

The bartender placed another two pints on the tray. At a table close by, I saw someone I knew. I couldn't quite place her at first. Then I remembered. It was the girl from the reception desk at the newspaper offices. What was her name again? Dag had told me.

Marianne. That was it.

'Nothing like a Jägermeister after a long day with the hunt,' the fat bloke said. 'Dare I ask what you've bagged today?'

'Give it a rest now, eh?' I said. 'It's not funny.'

'I'm not from Drammen for nothing,' he said. 'Bar jokes are my speciality.'

Glenn gripped the tray of drinks and carried it back to where they were sitting. I smiled at Marianne, but she didn't notice, or else she was ignoring me. The lads, however, all looked in my direction, and I could hear Glenn's voice in my inner ear: Syvert's on his own at the bar with some fat homo from Drammen.

Time to make a move.

I got to my feet and went over to the table where Marianne was sitting.

'Hello,' I said. 'You work at the newspaper offices, don't you? I was there yesterday, and I recognised you just now.'

'Yes, I think I remember,' she said.

'You haven't seen Dag here, have you?'

She shook her head.

'Is he supposed to be?'

'No, I don't think so,' I said. 'I just wanted to say hello to you, really.'

'Well, now you have,' she said.

I retreated with a smile, and went and sat down with the others.

'Who the hell was that dope you were with?' said Glenn.

'I don't actually *know* him, if that's what you're thinking,' I said. 'He was sitting there when I got here, that's all.'

When the club closed we stood for a while outside trying to get an after-party together. Glenn's dad had the use of a flat somewhere along the quayside, it was his trade union that owned it, apparently, but he had a key and Glenn had borrowed it. It was the first any of us had heard about it, but it sounded like a good idea, if only we could get some girls to go with us. So when I caught sight of Marianne, who in my mind was now almost like an old acquaintance, crossing the street and walking away, I didn't hesitate, but ran after her, the inside of my head all lit up and fizzy, and put a hand on her shoulder.

'Hey, Marianne,' I said. 'There's a few of us going on to an after-party,' I said. 'Do you fancy coming?'

'No, I don't,' she said.

'Go on! It'll be fun!'

She shook her head and pressed her lips together, then started walking again.

'OK, if you want to be like that about it,' I said, and turned away from her, hearing her footsteps carry on along the pavement in the opposite direction as I trained my attention now on the crowd outside the club, which was already beginning to thin out. Susanne and her three mates were standing with Glenn and Keith, it looked like they were negotiating. A bit further away, outside the cinema, was another girl I knew, I just couldn't place her for the life of me. I went towards her hesitantly.

'All on your own?' I said.

She turned her face to look at me. It was the girl from the petrol station.

'What's it to you?' she said, turning away from me again to study a film poster.

'We've got an after-party on just down the road. Would you like to come?'

She shook her head without looking round.

'Maybe something fantastic will happen,' I said. 'You never know. Maybe something that'll change your life for ever.'

'Like what?' she said. 'You knocking me up, for example? Leaving me an ugly little kid like you to look after?'

'Is that what usually happens when you go to an after-party?' I said.

'No,' she said. 'I just like to get the measure of people. Have you got a smoke, then, or what?'

I didn't smoke myself, but I always had a packet with me in my coat whenever I went out, in case a situation like this ever happened. I patted my pockets, produced a packet of Marlboro and handed it to her. Out of the corner of my eye I saw someone peel away from the crowd and come towards us. When I turned to look, it was the guy in the denim jacket and the clogs.

He came up to us.

'Are you trying to get off with my girl?' he said.

'No,' I said. 'She asked me if I'd got a cigarette.'

'He was inviting me to an after-party,' she said, and lit the cigarette.

'Oh yeah?' the guy said. He stepped closer and was squaring up to me all of a sudden.

'All right,' I said. 'I didn't know she was with someone.'

'He said he was going to do fantastic things with me,' she said, and blew smoke out while staring me in the face, as if to see what sort of effect her words were going to have.

'Oh yeah?' he said.

'No,' I said. 'I didn't say that at all.'

'She's lying then, is that what you're telling me?' he said, and grabbed me by the coat with both hands.

It really pissed me off.

'What the hell's wrong with you people?' I said.

He shoved me hard up against the window.

'And what sort of shoes do you call those, anyway?' I said. 'Haven't you learned to tie your laces yet, is that it? Or do you actually think they look good?'

His girlfriend laughed.

That was when he headbutted me.

I wasn't expecting it, and at first I didn't quite realise what had happened. All of a sudden I was decked, with a strangely warm feeling in my body as if something good had just occurred. As if a painful abscess had finally burst and the abscess was me.

Then everything came unpleasantly into focus. A prickling pain radiated from the root of my nose. I felt with my hand and looked at blood. My other hand was throbbing from a nasty scrape. My trousers were wet with rain from the pavement.

Glenn and Karsten were standing over me now.

'What did he fucking do to you?' said Glenn. 'Did he butt you?'

'I reckon so,' I said, and got to my feet with my hand held over my nose.

'Let's have a look,' said Glenn.

I moved my hand away.

'Ouch,' he said. 'It's bent!'

'Oh no,' I said. 'I had such a good nose.'

'Do you want us to get you to casualty?' said Karsten. 'It's no problem.'

'No, you just go along to the party,' I said. 'I'll be fine.'

'You'll need to tidy yourself up a bit, at least,' said Glenn. 'There's that petrol station over there.'

They went with me to the petrol station round the corner, stood and waited between the shelves while I washed the blood off me, smiled when I appeared again.

'There you go,' said Karsten. 'New man.'

'Are you sure you don't want to let them have a look at you in casualty?' said Glenn. 'It looks a bit broken to me.'

'I don't think it is,' I said. 'It's just a bit sore, that's all.'

'What got into him, anyway?' said Karsten. 'Did you say something to him?'

'I may have done, yes,' I said, and smiled.

'You've always had a bit of a gob on you,' said Glenn. 'Someone was bound to take you up on it eventually.'

'My mum always told me never to speak to strangers. Now I understand why,' I said. 'Anyway, you lot go on. I'll get off home, I think.'

'Are you sure?'

'Yes, I'll be fine. See you around!'

I didn't really have the money for a taxi, but the expense was warranted by the situation, I told myself as I went towards the taxi rank over by the bus station.

I felt strange. It was as if nothing of what had happened concerned me, almost as if it had happened to someone else. My surroundings too, as I looked around me, the huge ferry that was moored at the quayside, the buses lined up in their bays at the bus station, the cars that went by in the rain, none of it seemed to have any connection to me at all.

It was like everything was a film set and the real world hidden behind it.

I nodded to the driver of the first taxi in line, he nodded back from the other side of the window, folded his newspaper and adjusted his seat, while I opened the back door and got in.

'I'm going to Vindsland,' I said. 'Do you know where it is?'

'I do,' he said. 'And you've got enough money? It's weekend and night rates, you know.'

'I know,' I said, and liked the feeling it gave me, to be someone who could afford it, however much it was going to be.

He turned the radio up as we drove out of town. Night-time requests. The music wasn't much to get excited about, 'Forever Young' and then 'I Won't Let the Sun Go Down on Me', but the female DJ had a sexy voice and I found myself wondering what she looked like as I stared out into the darkness and the trees that now and then rose up like a wall out of the heathland, now and then opened towards the sea.

Red hair, white skin, warm eyes, cheeky mouth.

No, that was the woman from that kids' programme on TV, surely?

Another go.

Dark hair, round, slightly chubby face, blue eyes.

That station had their studios up in Trondheim, didn't they?

I could just as well move up there as anywhere else.

Not that I knew what I'd do there.

No, the best thing was to hang around here for a bit and see if anything turned up. I didn't need to start on anything until the autumn, anyway.

The bastard, I thought, and put my hand to the ridge of my nose again, gingerly testing to see if it wobbled. Wouldn't it feel loose if it was broken?

Butting someone for no reason in particular.

As if I was going to run off with his girlfriend.

We drove past the ski slope. The seats of the lift hung motionless from their wires above the hill. You'd have no idea what it was if you saw it for the first time, I thought, and didn't know what snow was. Just a clear-felled area of the forest, I supposed. But what about the lift? Machinery to transport the logs?

The last twenty minutes of the way I just sat and dozed and thought about nothing. Then we crossed over the little bridge and I leaned forward.

'You can just pull in at the bus stop over there,' I said.

'Right you are,' he said, and put the indicator on.

Mum could still be up, and I didn't want her to know I'd got a taxi. Besides, I thought the extra walk in the rain might clear my head a bit.

I paid the fare, thanked him for the ride and started walking while he turned round and set off again.

'Where have you been?' Mum called out from the kitchen the minute I opened the door.

'Out,' I said, and hung up my soaking wet anorak.

'Joar was all on his own when I got back,' she said, appearing in the doorway. 'You promised me you'd look after him.'

'I thought he was staying the night at his friend's?' I said, looking at her to gauge her mood.

She didn't look happy.

'It didn't suit them. You should have checked before you went out.'

'I'm really sorry. He's a big boy now, though.'

'He's scared of the dark. He wouldn't tell you that.'

She sighed.

'You can't just come here and not lift a finger, you know. I've got two jobs so we can make ends meet. If you're going to be staying here, you're going to have to pull your weight.'

'I know, Mum,' I said.

'You've been out two nights running now.'

'But I only got my discharge two days ago. I deserve a breather, surely?'

I smiled and looked at her again.

Her eyes narrowed.

'Have you been fighting?'

'Fighting, me? No, of course not. It's my nose you're looking at, isn't it? I turned round to look at this really fit girl and walked straight into a lamp post.'

'You're not getting yourself into trouble, Syvert, I hope? That's the last thing I need.'

'Relax, Mum. Everything's fine. I'll help you as much as I can. I'll get a job if I can find one. And if I can't, there's enough to be getting on with here. Get yourself to bed!'

But she didn't, I heard her coughing downstairs as I got undressed, and I still hadn't heard her come up the stairs by the time I fell asleep. It wasn't like her, but the sense of unease it gave me had gone the next morning, the way all problems and difficulties do, showing themselves in their true light. They belonged to the night-time; the hours of confusion and turmoil.

The only thing I regretted was telling Dag I'd do that interview. I couldn't understand how I could have agreed to something so stupid. I phoned him after I got up, only he didn't answer, and I didn't manage to get hold of him until late in the evening. He told me I couldn't back out, it was all lined up.

'Don't I have a say in the matter?' I said, twisting the telephone cord around my forefinger and staring distractedly into the kitchen, where Mum was clearing the table after tea.

'I'm responsible for it now,' he said. 'I put the idea forward at an editorial meeting and they were all for it. I can't call it off now, I've got the journalist and the photographer already set up, it's all slated for tomorrow!'

'It wouldn't be the first time something fell through, surely?'

'But it'd reflect badly on me, you can understand that, can't you? All you've got to do is answer a few questions. It's no big deal.'

'The thing is I don't look at myself as unemployed,' I said.

Mum, now filling the sink to wash up the few plates and glasses we'd used, looked at me. I smiled at her and turned away.

'Did you sign on or not?' said Dag.

'I did, yes. But only because they gave me my discharge halfway through the semester. I'm not *unemployed*, as such.'

He sighed.

'So you signed on as unemployed, only you're not unemployed?'

'You understand what I mean.'

'I understand you're letting me down. That's what I understand.'

'OK, OK,' I said. 'I'll do it.'

The next morning I caught the bus into town and met up with Dag and his colleague at the cafe by the park. His colleague, who was from Sunnmøre, was called Ove and was somewhere in his late twenties. He was tall and thin, with a small head and a serious expression, and nodded at everything that was said.

'I'll leave you to it, then,' Dag said after a bit and got to his feet. 'Enjoy yourselves, and I'll catch you later, Syvert.'

'Is it all right if I record this?' said Ove.

'Yes, no problem,' I said.

He placed a tape recorder on the table between us and got out a thick notepad. The first few pages were dense with writing.

'That's a lot of questions,' I said.

He pressed play and glanced at his notes before looking up at me.

'If you could start by just saying your name and a little bit about yourself,' he said.

'OK,' I said. 'My name's Syvert Løyning, I'm nineteen years old and I come from Vindsland.'

He nodded.

'That's about it, really,' I said.

'And you've just completed your national service, is that right?'

'That's right, yes.'

'Can you tell me a little bit about it?'

It went on like that. He probed, I answered as best I could. After a while, the photographer turned up, a woman in her thirties with a husky voice and a Palestinian scarf, and we went outside to take some pictures.

'Can you sit down over there?' she said, pointing to a bench in the little park.

I nodded and went and sat down.

'Do you think you could sit at one end?' she said. 'And keep your legs together?'

'Like this?' I said.

'Excellent, yes! A bit more on the edge, maybe? And if you could look over in that direction? Put your hands in your lap! That's it! Brilliant!'

There was no one in when I got home. Joar was at school and Mum must have gone somewhere after work. I felt restless and impatient, wanting something to happen, but of course nothing did. The interview had gone all right, so it couldn't have been that that made it so hard for me to relax.

I had a shower and lay down on my bed with one of the thrillers that were still on the shelf in my room, *The Key to Rebecca* by Ken Follett, one of my favourites. I'd read it loads of times, but realised quite soon that I could barely remember the storyline.

Although the interview had gone well, I knew I never should have done it. That must have been what was tormenting me.

I went to the cupboard and looked at all my old things. Two boxes of school exercise books, what did I want them for? The pile of board games.

In the corner at the back was my old air rifle. I'd got it as a present off my uncle Einar and my auntie Ida for my twelfth birthday, almost certainly because Dad was fond of shooting and would probably have bought me an air rifle himself if he'd still been alive then.

I hadn't used it for years.

I got it out, put it to my shoulder and took aim at a sparrow that was perched on a twig on the tree outside the window.

Double standards. A lack of principles. Not being honest with myself.

I wondered if there might still be some paper targets in the garage.

Maybe it was something that would amuse Joar?

With the rifle under my arm I went out to have a look. And there was too, a pile of mouldering cardboard targets, tucked away on top of one of the beams under the roof.

I strung one up between the two apple trees that formed a kind of portal between the garden and the field. No one would ever go out there, and even if someone did, I'd be able to see them a mile off.

I fired a few shots from the wall of the barn, first standing, then lying down. It would have been an understatement to say I wasn't very good; half my shots missed completely, the rest were nowhere near the bull's eye. I decided to keep at it at least until I got a bit closer. Then, just as I was changing targets, I heard a car come up from the road and went round to the front of the barn to let Mum know where I was.

Joar was on his way inside with his school bag on his back and a carrier bag in his hand, while Mum had put two bags of shopping down so she could close the car boot.

'You've done the shopping, I see,' I said.

'Are you *shooting*?' Mum said.

'I found my old air rifle in the cupboard. Do you fancy a go, Joar?'

He nodded from the doorway with his face turned towards me.

'He's only twelve,' Mum said.

'I was twelve when I got it for my birthday, or can't you remember?' I said, and laughed. 'It's only an air rifle, anyway.'

I leaned it against the barn and carried her shopping inside. After that, I took Joar round the back of the barn with me, just as Dad had done with me that time.

'You've never tried before, have you?' I said, handing him the rifle.

He shook his head.

'I know how, though.'

He nestled the butt against his shoulder, closed one eye and took aim at the target.

'That's it,' I said. 'But you might want to load it first?'

I took the rifle and showed him how to do it before handing it back.

'Deep breaths, in and out, exhale slowly, and then fire while you hold your breath.'

He did as I said. Loaded, held his breath and fired, then again, and again after that.

He looked up at me and beamed.

'It's fun, isn't it?' I said. 'Let's go and see if you hit the target, shall we?'

He had.

'Eight, seven and four.'

'Is that good?'

'I think it's very good,' I said. 'Beginner's luck, if you ask me!'

'What did you get?'

'We won't talk about that,' I said. 'Do you want another go?'

He nodded. I strung up another target and stood beside him as he loaded and took aim. He was really enjoying himself, a picture of concentration.

'You should join a club,' I said.

He raised the rifle slowly as he breathed out, and I realised suddenly that he was aiming towards the apple tree, where a raven stood watching us.

'No, don't shoot it!' I said, but it was too late, he squeezed the trigger and the next instant the bird collapsed to the ground. As if in slow motion, it fell over onto its side, its wings still folded against its body.

'Wow!' he shouted. 'I got it!'

I grabbed him hard by the arm.

'What the hell are you playing at?'

'Let go,' he said. 'I want to see where I got it.'

'You don't shoot birds just for fun.'

'You're not my dad.'

'But it's my rifle,' I said, and took it from him. 'You're coming in now.'

'I want to see where I got it,' he said.

He tried to twist free. I gripped him tight.

'Let go!' he shouted.

I saw myself dragging him inside as he twisted and writhed, shouting and screaming. What was I going to do once we got in — lock him in his room?

So I let him go.

He ran over to the bird. I went after him, saw him bend down and pick it up.

'I shot it in the head!' he said. 'Look, there's hardly anything left of it!'

'All right, you've seen it now,' I said. 'Put it down and come inside.'

The little head was a mess of bloody goo and splintered bone.

'It's still warm,' he said.

'That's because it was still alive three minutes ago,' I said. 'But now it's not. It'll never be alive *ever again*. Do you understand that?'

'Of course I do,' he said, and threw the bird into the field. 'Is that good enough, or do you want to bury it too?'

I said nothing to Mum about what had happened. I knew what she'd think. It'd be my fault for letting him try.

And in a way she'd be right.

Instead, I went upstairs to his room after tea to have a word with him.

He sat hunched over his desk, drawing.

'What are you drawing?' I said, and sat down on the edge of his bed.

'Just my room,' he said.

'Do you want to show me?'

He held the drawing up for me to see. The room was recognisable down to the smallest detail, the bed, the wardrobe, the bookcase, even the posters on the wall were there. And at the desk, hunched over some drawing paper, he'd drawn himself, seen obliquely from behind.

'It's not finished yet,' he said.

'It's very good,' I said. 'You could draw comics when you grow up.'

He pulled a face.

'Is it *this* drawing you're doing there in the picture?'

'How could it be?' he said, and smiled.

I looked closer and saw that it was; the little drawing he was drawing in his drawing was of his room too.

'Do you want to see some others?' he said.

'Yes, if you want to show me.'

He pulled the drawer open, took out a pile and handed it to me.

The first one was of a crouching ape that seemed to be staring into thin air. The second was a big crab. The third a helicopter.

'You're getting really good,' I said. 'They're very accurate. Where do you find the ideas?'

'I usually draw from pictures. Copying's easy.'

'Not everyone can. I can't, for example.'

'You probably never tried.'

'That's true. But listen, there's something I want to talk to you about.'

'Is it that bird?'

I nodded.

'I realise it's tempting to shoot at something that's alive rather than just a piece of cardboard. I can understand that. But it's against the law, for one thing. And for another it's wrong. That bird could still be alive.'

'Or a cat could have got it,' he said. 'They kill birds all the time. You wouldn't go and tell a cat off.'

'A cat follows its instincts,' I said. 'But you can think.'

'Don't you think cats can think?' he said.

'Don't be argumentative,' I said. 'I'm being serious. If you ever want to borrow my rifle again, you must promise me never to shoot at anything living.'

'What if I hit the tree?'

'Joar, I mean it.'

'The tree's living.'

'You know what I mean,' I said, and stood up. 'Can you promise me?'

'You're *not* my dad,' he said. 'Can't you get it into your head?'

I sighed and went out again without saying any more. It was no use arguing with him, he always had to have the last word. An expert at splitting hairs, he was, even at twelve years old.

The clock on the wall above the worktop in the kitchen said a few minutes to half past seven. I got my football boots and holdall out of the laundry room, and the carrier bag with the things I'd bought from the sports shop, then went and sat down in the living room where Mum was watching the telly.

'Have you got football practice?' she said.

I nodded, unscrewed the lid from the tin and started treating my boots.

'Good idea,' she said.

I had to have a talk with her about Joar. His attitude. It needed to be nipped in the bud, before it went too far. It'd be too late then.

Only not tonight.

'He's looking a bit fraught, our prime minister,' I said instead, a nod at the screen as a bravely smiling Willoch forged a path through a gaggle of reporters in a corridor somewhere.

'He's smiling, though,' Mum said. 'Perhaps he knows something we don't.'

'The angrier and more offended Willoch gets, the more he smiles,' I said. 'It's a fact.'

I rubbed the boots clean with an old sock, pulled the laces out and threaded in the new ones I'd bought, before screwing in the new studs and tucking the boots into my holdall.

'There we are,' I said, and leaned back in the chair.

'He always looks so frightened, that newsreader,' Mum said.

'Bryn? He's still only young, maybe he just hasn't got the experience yet.'

'How old would he be, do you think? Thirty?'

'Something like that,' I said. 'Do you think I'd make a good newsreader?'

'A newsreader? I think you would. You can read, at any rate.'

I laughed.

'*And now to news of a radioactive cloud detected today over Norway, Sweden and Finland,*' Bryn said, looking earnestly into the camera. '*An increase in natural radioactivity levels of sixty per cent was recorded in the Østland, though this is not considered to be hazardous.*'

'What?' I said. 'Were you listening to that?'

'It's been on the news all day,' Mum said. 'It's not hazardous, they say.'

'They've got to say that, haven't they? Of course it's hazardous.'

It turned out a Swedish nuclear power plant had detected the cloud that morning. At first they'd thought it was a leak at their own facility, the readings they were getting were that high, but then they'd realised it was coming from somewhere else.

'*A dense mist hung over Oslo and the Østland area today,*' the reporter said to pictures of a foggy capital. '*Although the mist is unconnected with the high levels of radioactivity, today's levels were significantly above the norm. The National Institute of Radiation Hygiene recorded increases of up to sixty per cent on naturally occurring radiation levels. Does this mean that we have been shrouded in a dangerous radioactive cloud in Scandinavia today?*'

The man they interviewed was standing on a rooftop looking out over Oslo and said he wouldn't call it a dangerous radioactive cloud, but the general public should try to avoid as much extra radiation from non-natural sources as possible, because such things weren't good, as he put it, before adding that it wasn't in the slightest bit dangerous.

'What exactly is it they're saying?' I said. 'They've said so many times now that it's not dangerous, that what they're actually saying is that it *is* dangerous. Am I right?'

'It certainly can't be good with all that radioactivity,' Mum said.

'That's your socialists for you,' I said, and got up.

'They don't know where it's from,' she said.

'Where else would it be from?' I said. 'Anyway, I'd best be off. Get some radioactive air in my lungs.'

The story of me getting butted had of course spread and I had to take a lot of banter when I walked into the changing room. I hung up my coat and sat down, laughed along with them as I got changed, and after a short while the talk moved on, mostly to people who weren't there but who everyone knew. People at work, people in the village, people on other teams. The radioactive cloud wasn't a topic. Nor, for that matter, was the crisis in the government.

'Have you all heard about Arne's lad?' Glenn said, and started laughing just at the thought.

'Arne who?'

'Arne Olsen. The maths teacher. They went to get some building materials in town. Ha ha ha! When they ha ha ha! When they were coming back over the bridge, it was so windy that Arne ha ha ha! told the lad to get out and ha ha ha! hold the planks down on the trailer.'

'No!'

'Ha ha ha! He only blew away himself, the lad, didn't he ha ha ha! broke ha ha ha! . . . broke . . . ha ha! . . . broke his arm . . .'

I smiled and zipped up my top.

'We locked Arne in the sports hall garage once,' I said. 'At first he was spitting feathers. We stood all quiet outside, so he'd think we'd gone home. Then he started shouting for help. Heeeelp! Heeeelp! We were laughing our heads off.'

I bent forward to do up my boots.

'It's a wonder his nerves ever held up, the amount of stick he had to take from us,' said Karsten.

'Actually, they didn't,' said Gjert. 'Or maybe you didn't know? He was away from school nearly two months. In the loony bin.'

'I don't believe that,' I said. 'It was only a rumour.'

Gjert gave a shrug.

'Sounds quite likely, if you ask me.'

'He knew his maths, though,' said Glenn. 'I'll give him that.'

'I learned *nothing* in his lessons,' said Vegard.

'That's not Olsen's fault,' said Glenn. 'It's to do with your restricted intellectual capacity.'

I stood up and went towards the door.

'My what?' said Vegard. 'I don't understand the words you're using . . .'

When I stepped out of the pavilion there were a couple of figures over on the pitch floating long passes to each other while the trainer was putting cones out. The sky was grey, but thin, with no sign of rain.

Full of invisible radioactivity.

Every time I breathed in I was drawing it into my body. And if there was enough I'd be damaged. I could start bleeding uncontrollably.

But what was it exactly?

I broke into a run, onto the pitch towards the two senior players, what were their names again, Kjetil and . . . ? Vennesland. That was it.

Kjetil saw me coming and sent me a long ball. I took it down and slid one back to Vennesland, who curled it on to Kjetil on the half-volley.

I knew nothing better than this. Cushion, centre, run, dribble, shoot.

Soon the pitch was teeming with players and the session got started. Just as the last time, Mads had us doing various drills after the warm-up, kept stopping the play, and just as before he blew his whistle after a while and had us all gather round.

'Football's simple,' he said. 'It's all about scoring more goals than you concede. Are you with me?'

So he was going to say the same thing every time, was that it?

'With you,' said Glenn.

'To score goals you've got to have the ball. Are you with me?'

'With you,' someone at the back said. A few laughed. Mads grinned.

'It's basic, I know. But that means it's important. So, the opponent has the ball. How do we get it off him? By denying him space. Space means time. More space, more time. Less space, less time. And less time will often mean more mistakes. The quicker we are to put them under pressure, the greater our chances of winning the ball. If we stay compact, that gives them no space, and if we press the man on the ball, he can't put it behind our defence either. That means we can stay high. And if we stay high, the way forward will be shorter once we win the ball. Are you with me?'

No one said anything. He produced his board and showed us how we wanted us to position ourselves.

'But aren't we leaving a whole load of space behind us then?' said Gjert.

'Yes!' said Mads. 'But as long as we're pressing the man on the ball, they can't exploit it. Do you understand? If there's no press, then of course the whole back line has to drop back. And the midfield after them.'

I was getting sick of it. It was almost like being back at school again. And everything he said and tried to explain went out the window anyway as soon as we started playing. Especially when, like now, he started shouting at us to raise the intensity, to run more, because all we got then was a tangle of legs and arms between the small goals we were using for practice.

But I did what he said, ran and ran.

'Good, Syvert!' he shouted when at one point I tackled Kjetil and won the ball. 'That's the way!' he shouted, even though I had so much jelly in my legs by then that my next pass went out over the touchline.

Mads jogged after it and kicked it back into play.

He kicked the ball the way someone who's never played football would kick it.

I was gobsmacked.

Maybe he couldn't actually play?

What was he going on about then?

We played on and I continued running and chasing and harrying until I could taste blood in my mouth. That must have been why he came up to me after the session and put a hand on my shoulder.

'You're carrying out your tasks really well,' he said. 'Do you fancy giving it a go, if we make room for you in the squad?'

I was standing bent over with my hands on my knees, gasping for breath.

'Yes,' I said. 'I'll give it a go. I don't know where I'll be after the summer, though.'

'We can look at that if and when,' he said. 'Let's say you're in for now, OK?'

I nodded and straightened up. And I was still OK about it on my way home half an hour later. It made sense, I'd been missing it more than I'd realised. Playing proper matches again, that peculiar mixture of physical exertion and excitement, the joy there was in that, in scoring a goal, delivering a good pass, winning. Even the disappointment when we lost, the way it kept stabbing at you the rest of the day and well into the next, was something I'd missed.

But thinking of football in terms of spaces to be opened and shut down, I'd never thought of it like that before. And I never wanted to either. Football was something to be played, not thought. Of course you closed down your opponents, of course you stopped them passing the ball, of course you put it in behind if there was space. But you didn't have to bloody *think* about it.

That night I dreamt about Dad. I didn't very often, and when I woke up from the dream I was confused; for a few seconds I didn't know if he was alive or not.

He'd been standing in the laundry room when I came into the passage, and had turned towards me. He smelled of machine oil and tobacco.

'Listen, Syvert,' he said.

'What is it?' I said.

'Can you look after your brother for me?'

'Of course. But why, where are you going?'

'Away, that's all.'

'What about Mum?'

When I said that, he took off his glasses, shaped his mouth and blew on the lenses, then dried them with the corner of his shirt while scrutinising me with that exposed, defenceless look he always had when he didn't have his glasses on.

'Son, your mum's been dead for years,' he said.

As he said it, I knew immediately that she *had* been dead for years, and it was as if with a fingersnap the entire past was turned on its head, and all my assumptions in life upended.

He put his glasses on again, wound his scarf around his neck and buttoned up his jacket, the one with the lambskin collar, stepped past me, picked up his briefcase and went out into the snow, turning then momentarily with a wave of his hand and a 'Look after yourself, son'.

I closed the door after him. What had he been doing in the laundry room? I wondered, and just as the question occurred to me I woke up and found I was in bed.

After the first seconds of bewilderment, when I didn't know what was real and what wasn't, it was as if an enormous grief exploded inside me.

I realised that Dad actually *could* have been here.

If he hadn't died.

But he had died.

So he wasn't here.

The room was flooded with light, the sun was coming up outside. The sky was open and blue, and the birds were singing. I knew I wouldn't be able to go back to sleep, even though it was hardly seven o'clock, so I got up and had a shower. When I came down into the kitchen, Mum had left a note on the table. *Syvert, can you empty the washing machine and do another wash?* she'd written. *And perhaps sort out the garage? It's like I don't know what out there. And if you could give the kitchen a quick once-over, and the living room as well, before I get home?*

She's pushing things a bit, I thought, and got the peanut butter out of the cupboard, the bread from the bread bin, the butter from the fridge. Normally I'd have been pissed off about it, only now I was feel-ing rather guilty towards her, because straight after I woke up the thought had occurred to me that maybe it would have been better if things had been like in the dream, if Dad had been alive and Mum dead.

As if I could choose.

I poured myself a glass of milk, turned the radio on and sat down to my breakfast.

Glorious sunshine outside.

It must have been Joar's dream that had triggered mine.

But why the laundry room in the basement? What had Dad been doing there?

I didn't like it.

He'd been so alive. It had been just like he was still living.

Only he wasn't.

The peanut butter stuck to the roof of my mouth and I gulped some milk.

He'd said I had to look after Joar.

Of course, I realised it hadn't been my dad talking at all, that it was something in myself that had been using the figure of my dad to remind me it was what I had to do. Something good in me, telling me to take care of my brother.

That the good in me felt it had to tell me meant presumably that there was something bad in me too. Something that wouldn't take care of Joar, or was going to forget.

The news came on and I pricked up my ears. I hadn't heard any more about the cloud since the television news the evening before. But the first story was about the government crisis that had only got worse since yesterday. Not until that was out of the way did they turn to the radioactivity.

As expected, it had come from the Soviet Union, a nuclear power plant not far from Kiev had exploded. They'd been keeping it secret for three days, despite the radioactivity drifting through Europe in the meantime.

The expert they interviewed repeated that the radiation values they were detecting in this country weren't hazardous, and I looked out of the window. That the landscape outside could be contaminated was hard to imagine, even if what they were saying was true and it was only tiny amounts.

I remembered as a kid reading a series of biographies for children. One was about Marie Curie. She died of a blood disease, almost blind, her fingers burned and scarred as if from the inside. All because of radioactivity, whose dangers at the time were unknown. At school, I'd read in another book about what had happened to the people of Hiroshima and Nagasaki who had survived the explosions of the atom bombs that had dropped on those cities.

It was the fact of it being invisible and that it was everywhere and could eat up the body from inside that had frightened me then. How did the radioactive atoms get inside the body, and how did they manage to destroy it? How did they make it bleed, how did they make it burn? How did they know what to do inside the body to destroy it?

Some of that fear had never gone away, that was the only way I could explain the concern I felt. No one else seemed to care.

When Joar came downstairs an hour later, I'd just finished hoovering. He cast a glance at me, that was all, before getting his breakfast ready.

'So, there you are,' I said, and smiled at him as I stepped on the button that gobbled up the cord. It flew across the floor like a snake. 'Did you sleep all right?'

He nodded without looking at me, pouring milk over his oatmeal and raisins.

'Good,' I said.

I took the Hoover down into the laundry room in the basement and couldn't help looking for signs there, something Dad might have been trying to draw my attention to. The big utility sink, the shelves of detergent and all sorts of articles for one thing and another that had accumulated over the years. The washing machine and the tumble dryer. The boots and winter shoes, the rainwear.

What had I been expecting? The key to a safe deposit box? A letter? A secret diary containing his innermost thoughts about us?

I heard Joar go up the stairs. I could feel I wasn't looking forward to the day, so many hours to kill. Everyone I knew was at work.

I emptied the tumble dryer, it was stuffed full, took the whole lot into the living room and dumped it on the sofa, went back down and transferred the wet clothes from the washing machine into the dryer, which I then switched on, loaded the washing machine with a pile of clothes from the laundry basket, switched that on, then went back up the stairs to the living room to fold the clean, dry clothes I'd left on the sofa.

'Do you want me to drive you to school?' I said when Joar came down again. This time he had his school bag.

'Mum's got the car, hasn't she?' he said, baffled.

I slapped my forehead.

'You're right, she has! How stupid of me!'

'That's OK,' he said, and went out, clearly in a better frame of mind now. 'See you later!'

The door closed after him and I went back to folding the clothes like I was a housewife. I even put them away.

Then there was the garage.

Mum never parked the car in there, and over the years it had filled up with all sorts of junk. I wasn't sure if she wanted me to chuck things out or just tidy up, but when I pushed the big door open and saw the state of the place in clear daylight I decided to sort through everything, burn what was no use and store the rest in the barn.

Surely that would make amends for my two nights out.

I started by getting everything together that needed burning, collecting it all in a pile in the middle of the floor, then carrying it all out behind the barn, where I heaped it up in front of the little bank where we always made our bonfires, sprinkled some petrol on and set light to it. The ground was still wet and there wasn't a breath of wind, so there was no danger of it spreading, but I stood and kept an eye on it anyway.

For as long as I could remember I'd loved to stand there and watch our bonfires. There was something magical about flames. Maybe it was because they came out of nowhere. The cardboard and other materials, the plastic and the paper, came first, piled up on the ground, but then, when I set fire to it, the flames would all of a sudden emerge, as if from inside the very things they were going to consume, as if they lived inside them and were now peeping out. Hesitant at first, as if they didn't really believe they were being set free, but more eagerly then, and soon as if enraged, yes, they became as if possessed, the flames, racing up and down those things. Trembling, in some places almost transparent, in others, often closest to the wood or cardboard, blue, then fat and orange as they took hold.

And then they transformed the things. Completely and comprehensively. From a big and roomy cardboard box to a handful of ash. All as the fields stretched calmly away into the rising heathland.

What was the difference between fire and radioactivity, exactly?

Both were chemical reactions, weren't they?

One was natural, the other was unnatural.

But why was it unnatural?

It was the sort of thing Joar likely knew.

There'd been no reason to get so angry with him. We'd targeted birds with our catapults when I was his age, for no other reason than to kill them. It was what boys did. It certainly didn't mean there was something wrong with him.

I went over to the target between the trees to see if I could find the bird, maybe bury it somewhere, but of course it was gone, taken by some animal or other.

From there, the flames were almost invisible in the daylight. They were getting on with the job, there was no need to stand around until it was done, I told myself, and went back to the garage.

It was still a tip in there. I counted seven bikes in all, none of them used any more: Mum's old one, Dad's old one, my old racer and four kids' bikes, two for little kids, two for bigger ones. I could no longer imagine Mum on a bike. But when I was little we'd often go out for a ride, all three of us. Down to the river, sometimes all the way out to the beaches.

It was nothing to get in a state about, it had all been nice.

Nice memories to have.

My old moped was in there too, filthy dirty, a sorry sight. It had been Dad's when he'd been young, but even after he stopped using it he still made a point of looking after it. It was going to be mine when I reached sixteen. He taught me to ride it when I was ten, round and round in big circles at the front of the house. When I got to sixteen I started using it on my own. It was an old Corvette, I never got it up to more than forty kilometres per hour, which had been a bit embarrassing, I remembered, but all right at the same time, because it got me around for two years before I passed my driving test, and if anyone ever called me an old fart or grandad, I didn't care.

I'd leave that where it was. Same went for my bike, and Joar's and Mum's. The other four I carried up to the barn. After that I began stacking all the firewood. Mum had got a big load delivered that winter, but hadn't stacked it and had just been taking logs in off the pile as she needed them. I hung the tools up on the wall, sorted all the loose screws and nails, bolts and hinges, the fishing tackle that was lying all over the place, spinners and ledgers, hand lines and otter boards, hooks and reels, and all the bike things that had accumulated over the years. When that was done I lugged some bin liners full of old clothes up to the barn, a better place for them, I thought. Besides, it was where she'd put all Dad's things. Maybe ten boxes stacked against the far wall, and I put the bags of clothes down next to them.

That corduroy jacket with the lambskin collar he'd been wearing in the dream, his glasses, his brown, unpolished shoes, the brown leather briefcase, it'd all be here, wouldn't it?

The dream had been so vivid that something in me resisted the thought. Those clothes *couldn't* be here, packed away, not if he was still going around wearing them. It was a law of nature. Things could only be in one place at a time.

Apart from in dreams. Dreams of course didn't abide by the laws of nature.

I bent forward and loosened the duct tape on the side of the box that was nearest, pulled it carefully away and opened the flaps. I hadn't seen his things since he died. Not because I'd been grieving over him and couldn't bring myself to look at them, but because I hadn't been interested in them. In him.

On top was the blue-grey cap that belonged to the uniform that was neatly folded underneath, also blue-grey. Then there were some shirts and sweaters, layers of them, and at the bottom his best pair of shoes.

The next box contained his overalls, rainwear, all just as clean and neatly folded. At the bottom: his work shoes, his clogs, his boots.

Why hadn't she just got rid of it all? He was dead and wouldn't be needing any of it, nor would she, or any of us.

The corduroy jacket was in the third box. A shudder ran down my spine when I saw it. I picked it up, pressed it to my face.

It smelled faintly, of machine oil and tobacco.

In the same box was his leather briefcase. It was squashed flat, and apart from a couple of old receipts, empty.

A taxi receipt from 1976 for twelve kroner, a dry-cleaning receipt for five kroner.

That was it.

As I returned the briefcase to the box, it struck me that it would be radioactive now.

Everything here was radioactive.

Maybe it altered dreams too?

Maybe that was what had happened?

I left the garage door open when I was finished so Mum could see I'd tidied up and she could start parking the car in there again. I checked the bonfire, it had gone out, and I wondered what to do next.

I wasn't used to being on my own so much, and I didn't like it either, it was as if I retreated into myself. And nothing was ever going to happen there, the only things there were old feelings and old thoughts.

I decided to go into town. Not that I'd be talking to anyone there either, but at least there'd be faces to look at.

The next bus was in fifty minutes. I fetched the paper from the mailbox and sat down with it in the living room. I read about the crisis in the government first. Willoch's time was definitely up now, it seemed. It would be Brundtland, then, a socialist government, at least until the next election. Roll out the grey carpet: the state would be running everything now. Higher taxes, zero private initiative and full indoctrination. Annoying that it was Hagen who got the blame, he'd had no choice, he couldn't go against his own party programme, not even if the end result was a Labour government. It was all Willoch's mistake, there'd been no need to go out on a limb like that, he'd had nowhere to turn when it all came to a head.

I moved on then to the reports on the Soviet nuclear disaster. There was a picture of army trucks in convoy, on their way through the forests outside Chernobyl, that was the name of the town where the power plant was, and another of a helicopter flying over the reactor itself. It was still on fire, they were trying to put it out with sand, the reports said. Helicopters emptying load after load onto the place.

A fire that wouldn't go out.

Wasn't that what hell was like?

Outside, a car came up the drive. It was Mum. She parked where she normally did, clunked the door shut behind her and came across the yard. She didn't even notice the garage door was open.

'Up already?' she said sarcastically as she came in.

'Not only that,' I said. 'All jobs done.'

'Good,' she said, and carried on into the kitchen.

I see, I thought. Was that all she had to say?

'Can I borrow the car?'

'Sorry, what?' she said, filling a glass with water from the tap, her back turned.

'Can I borrow the car?'

'If you're back by two.'

'No problem,' I said.

She turned towards me and smiled faintly before popping two tablets in her mouth and swallowing them with a mouthful of water. She emptied the rest of the glass out in the sink.

'What are the tablets for?'

'Nothing,' she said. 'A bit of back pain, that's all.'

'Still?'

'Looks like it. Where are you going, anyway?'

'Just into town.'

She nodded absently.

All of a sudden I saw her for what she was. Not as *Mum*, but as a woman in her mid-forties. Her face, the lines around her mouth and on her brow, the corners of her mouth that had started to droop. Her frame, her slightly stooping posture, her long and narrow fingers still curled around the glass.

'What are you gawping at?'

'Maybe you should see the doctor about that back,' I said.

She snorted.

'It's nothing. I'm not young any more, in case you hadn't noticed.'

'You're not exactly old either.'

'It's nice of you to say so, at least,' she said, and smiled.

I smiled back.

'The car key's on the table in the hall,' she said.

'Is there anything we need?'

She shook her head and so I went and got in the car, shoved the seat back, adjusted the mirror, put the sun flap down, the key in the ignition.

I was feeling a bit out of sorts, it would do me good to get out in the car. Even if the engine was barely bigger than a sewing machine's. Onto the main road, across the flatland, into the woods, along the coast. The sea was the brightest blue, great swathes of light erasing all other colours.

I remembered another spring day when Dag and I had come out here with Dad and Dag's father, my uncle Einar, to do some fishing. I cast the lure, a great glittering arc in the air, only when it landed and I started reeling in there was nothing there, the lure had come off in the cast.

And how I'd hoped Dag would lose that fish when he got a bite. I even prayed to God.

But no, of course he didn't. He reeled it into the shallows, and Dad — why not Einar? — thrust the gaff into it. A fine, big codfish.

Dag beamed from ear to ear at the praise he got, and I knew that I had to smile too, only I couldn't, it was impossible.

Dad had looked at me then. He couldn't say anything with Dag and Einar there, but the look he gave me said all that needed to be said. Learn to be pleased for others.

A lot of Dad today.

It had to be the dream that had him filling my thoughts.

But Mum was the one who was alive. She was the important one.

I put the radio on to give me something else to think about. It was the Soviet nuclear plant again. Hundreds of thousands of people had been evacuated, they were saying. A huge area would be laid waste for ever. But the main thing at the moment was to get the fire under control.

I switched it off.

When I looked at Mum, I saw *Mum*, the same as when I was a kid. It was the way it was.

Was it the same with everyone? When I looked at Dag, was it *Dag* I saw?

I hadn't cared to see her disentangle from *Mum* to become someone else. But why, exactly? Why did it make me feel so terribly despondent?

The big, dark, windowless factory loomed up, then disappeared into the distance behind me, and a few minutes later the town lay out ahead. I didn't really have anything I wanted to do there, but I could always traipse about, browse some records, have a coffee somewhere. If I was lucky, I'd run into someone I knew. I could always look in on Dag, of course, but every time I thought about him I started thinking about that stupid interview he'd roped me into, and if there was one thing I didn't want to think about now, that was it.

I left the car in the car park on Festningsgaten and went first to the second-hand shop a bit further up the street, where they sold LPs, magazines and books, and I flicked through the heavy section, found Dio's debut, *Holy Diver*, at only a tenner, and bought it. I'd got it on cassette, but the tape was worn, and in any case I liked LPs better. The guy behind the counter, fair-haired, in his thirties, with a pigeon chest and a little pot belly, who always wore a shirt with a V-neck pullover on top and corduroy trousers, even though he was a massive metal fan, and was always smiling no matter what was going on around him, asked me as he entered the amount into the till if I'd heard Dio's latest. I told him I had, and handed him the tenner. But it wasn't as good as *Holy Diver*.

'You're right there,' he said, slipping the album into a bag. 'What about the new Judas, have you heard that yet?'

I shook my head.

'Any good?'

'No idea. It only came out in England two weeks ago. I've ordered it, but it hasn't come in yet. From what I've heard, though, or read, they're using synthesisers now. On this one, at least.'

'Aren't they heavy any more?'

He shrugged.

'Doesn't sound like it, no.'

'They sold out ages ago anyway,' I said.

'Couldn't agree more,' he said. 'Didn't you come in and buy some Metallica the other day?'

'That's right,' I said.

'Have you heard Pentagram?'

'Can't say I have, no. Pentagram, are they a new band?

'Old, but re-formed with a different line-up. They put a new album out last year. American, they are. Really ace. Terrible production, but totally raw.'

'Hm,' I said.

'Not that I've got it in,' he said. 'Just thought someone who thinks Judas have sold out and who likes Anthrax might want to check them out.'

'I will,' I said.

'And maybe Dead Bodies Society too, while you're at it,' he said.

I nodded.

'Thanks a lot.'

'You're welcome,' he said, and with a smile went back to whatever he'd been doing behind the counter.

As I went back out into the sunshine, I wondered why he was starting to recommend far-out stuff to me all of a sudden. What made him think we were the same?

I turned onto the street where the library was. The old fogies were all lined up on the benches outside. The ever-greedy pigeons were never far away, strutting about between their feet, looking a bit like distant ancestors, it occurred to me, with their bald heads and rigid, twitching movements.

I hung my jacket over the back of a chair at an empty table, bought myself a coffee and half a bap with a slice of cheese on it, and sat down, took the record out of the carrier bag and looked at the cover for a bit, put it back and looked out onto the square outside.

A fire that wouldn't go out.

It was as if the accident had opened a gateway to the other side and something had got out.

That was it.

That was why I was feeling so unsettled.

An invisible gateway into an invisible place.

And now it was all flooding in to where we were.

I drained my coffee, got up, picked up the carrier bag with the record in it, and my jacket, and went into the library. I didn't want to ask for help, it was no one else's business what I wanted to read, so I started browsing on my own. I spent a long time looking along the shelves where the books on the natural sciences and mathematics were, but found nothing that had radioactivity in the title, and the books on nuclear physics seemed impossible to fathom, so instead I took an encyclopedia volume over to one of the desks and looked up radioactivity.

Radioactivity is a property exhibited by certain types of matter whereby energy is emitted from an atomic nucleus. Such emission is termed nuclear radiation, often erroneously referred to as radioactive radiation (the radiation itself is not radioactive).

So the emission itself wasn't radioactive? But then what was it that was drifting about in the air? Atoms? That'd be it. Damaged atoms floating about on the wind. But how did they get there? The radiation was emitted from them, but what about the atoms themselves? What was it that got them drifting? The explosion?

I read some more.

The radiation associated with radioactivity may be damaging to the health in instances of incorrect use or as a consequence of accident or misadventure. Exploited correctly, radioactivity may safely be put to use for scientific, industrial and medical purposes to the greater benefit of society.

May be damaging to the health in instances of incorrect use? The greater benefit of society? It was pure propaganda! I looked up, my blood boiling with a sudden rage. What's more, it was dishonest. And this was the *Great Norwegian Encyclopedia*!

It was something that really got me going, when biased opinion was sneaked into supposedly objective communication. When our history teacher had suggested there might be a connection between a historic earthquake and the waves parting for Moses, I'd written to the principal about it and got more than half the class to sign the letter. There'd been no more Bible in our history lessons after that.

I felt like writing to whoever published the encyclopedia too.

A bit like I'd done a couple of years back when I'd penned some razor-sharp letters to the local paper about the Progress Party when everyone else was turning their noses up at them and ridiculing them a lot more than they were now. I'd done it under an assumed name, not wanting Mum to be ashamed of me, she didn't like it when people drew attention to themselves, and the last thing she'd have wanted, so I reckoned, being from a family who were Labour through and through, was for her son to come out as a Progress Party supporter.

People had been provoked and bombarded the paper with replies.

Apart from Dag, no one knew it was me.

It had been a laugh, like having a secret life, it meant I could go on about things I knew would get people going.

Bloody-minded, Mum always called me. It didn't exactly come out of nowhere. But the thing was I meant it, and that was what she didn't understand.

A simple relation describes the attenuation of the gamma-radiation in an absorber: $I(x)=I_0. \exp(-mu\ x)$ (Lambert–Beer's) law, where I_0 is the intensity of the radiation incident on the absorber, $I(x)$ is the radiation intensity exiting the absorber, mu is the linear absorption coefficient of the material and is characteristic for each type of material, and x is the absorber thickness.

The entry was clearly written for people who already had some considerable knowledge of physics and chemistry — I certainly didn't understand a word. There was nothing either about how radioactivity affected the body or the environment, what actually happened. Apart from the following short passage that I didn't latch on to until I looked at it a second time:

In addition to the absorbed dose, the biological effect of the radiation, which is quantified by the equivalent dose, also depends on the dose rate (absorbed dose per unit time), that is, it depends on how long a period a given dose is accumulated. There is a larger effect from a high dose rate than from a low dose rate even if the accumulated dose is the same.

The equivalent dose is quantified in the unit sievert (Sv), which equals the absorbed dose measured in gray multiplied by a quality or efficiency factor, which equals 1 for low dose rates of beta- and gamma-radiation, but which equals 20 for alpha-radiation, and increases with increasing dose rates.

But what was it even saying? Something about how the effects of radioactivity on living creatures were measured, but *nothing* about the nature of the effects themselves.

What could be more important than that?

It was a bit funny though that the unit of measurement for radio-active effects was the same as my name! All right, the spelling was slightly different, but if you said it out loud it was almost impossible to tell the difference between Syvert and Sievert.

I closed the book and put it back on the shelf, and went outside again into the street.

I'd hardly spoken to anyone all day. When had that happened last?

It wouldn't harm to pop in on Dag and see if he had a few minutes to spare, I decided, and went across to the offices on the corner.

Marianne had the phone wedged between her shoulder and cheek while she noted something down on a pad in front of her. She glanced up when I came in and gave a little nod in the direction of Dag's office. She didn't smile, but at least she remembered who I was.

'All right,' said Dag, swivelling to face me in his chair.

'All right, Tintin,' I said. 'You busy?'

'Just about done for today.'

'You what?'

'Came in at six this morning.'

'The working man's lot,' I said, sitting down and crossing my legs. 'I can give you a lift home, if you want.'

'Can you? That'd be great. Now, you mean?'

'Now's fine.'

He nodded, grabbed his coat and picked up his bag, and was halfway out the door before I'd even stood up.

'You're in a hurry,' I said when I caught up with him.

'I can stay on, if it suits you better.'

'That's not what I meant. You just seem a bit hyped up. Something got you going?'

He shook his head.

'Pressures of work, that's all. Been trying all day to get hold of someone from Kjeller who can give me something on Chernobyl. Only no
one's called back. Probably got every journalist in the country clamour-
ing after them. I had to make do with someone from the technical
college here instead. And the spokesperson from No to Nuclear
Weapons.'

He looked at me and smiled.

'Better than nothing, I suppose.'

'You could always have tried Jönsson,' I said. 'He'd have stepped up.'

'Ha ha.'

'But I wonder how much he actually knows. We never heard a word
about quantum theory or nuclear physics, did we? It was as if it didn't
exist.'

'I don't think it's on the curriculum until you get to gymnas,' he
said.

'Do you know much about it, then?'

'A bit,' he said. 'The gist of it.'

'Go on, then.'

He looked at me again. His curly white hair took on a slight blush in
the sunshine.

'You are joking?'

We emerged onto Festningsgaten and went left.

I shrugged.

'I just found out I know *nothing*. I don't even know what radioactivity
is. Not *really*.'

'It's not like you to make an admission like that.'

'That there's something I don't know?'

'Mm.'

'But quite like you to make out you know something you don't,' I
said. 'So go on, then. What is radioactivity?'

'OK,' he said. 'Basically, the nucleus of an atom consists of protons
and neutrons. You with me so far?'

He laughed before going on.

'Protons are positive and neutrons are neutral.'

'That'll be why they're called neutrons?' I said.

'Exactly.'

'So how come protons aren't called positons?'

'All right, stop arsing about. When the atomic nucleus is broken apart, energy is released. That's the protons. Or actually, I'm not sure about that. Sounds right, though, doesn't it? Anyway, that's what a radioactive process is.'

'The atoms get broken apart,' I said. 'And energy abandons ship.'

'You could say.'

'But why is radiation dangerous? That's what I don't understand. What does it *do*?'

'It gives you cancer, for a start,' he said.

'I know that,' I said. 'But *how*?'

'Don't ask me,' he said.

We stopped by the car and I unlocked the driver's side, got in, put the carrier bag with my record in it on the back seat, leaned over and opened the door for him on the passenger's side.

'And how come radiation lasts such an incredibly long time? It's like hundreds of years, isn't it? I mean, if radiation is protons that have been slung out, how many protons are there exactly?'

'In a nucleus?'

'Yes,' I said, and started the car, reached my hand over the back of his seat and turned my head so I could see to reverse out.

'Not that many protons. But all the more atoms. We're talking billions, aren't we? Or are we?'

'I haven't a clue. I might have to give Jönsson a ring when I get in.'

I turned onto Festningsgaten and drove up to the lights, waiting there for what seemed like an age, Dag gazing emptily out of the window, while I turned the radio on, only to turn it off again a second later, before the lights went green and we swung up onto the main road.

I'd had no idea he wanted to be a journalist or even had the remotest interest in that sort of thing until he went for an interview to be taken on as the new youth section reporter. He was sixteen at the time. I don't think anyone else knew either. It was typical Dag. I could never keep my mouth shut about anything, never had a secret from anyone, whereas he had quite different limits as to what he'd share with others.

It had always been like that. I was an open book, he was a cagey bastard.

'Jönsson's not there any more, anyway, I suppose you know that?' he said as we flew along the motorway, the car shuddering as we headed west.

'He was forced out, wasn't he?'

'I believe so. He runs a kind of marriage bureau now. Thai women.'

'Oh? I didn't know that. What's that about?'

'He arranges contacts between Norwegian men and Thai women.'

'Any good ones?'

He looked at me and laughed.

'Are you that desperate?'

'Desperate? Now you're being prejudiced. What's wrong with Thai women?'

Jönsson had been our science teacher at secondary school. He'd been wildly unpredictable, sometimes turning up drunk to our lessons, and of course we'd all had a laugh when he set about his experiments or dissections in that state, his clothes dishevelled and his hair all over the place, dull-eyed and a wide smile on his lips. Something blew up in his face once, it was bedlam, he was all black with soot. Another time, this was in junior school, we'd been scrumping apples in his garden when he appeared with an automatic pistol and demanded to know our names while pointing it at us. Dad had known him, they'd gone to school together, and he wasn't angry after the phone call he got; when he spoke to me about it he just said it was best to stay away from Jönsson and that there were many other places where we could be kids in the same way as we'd thought we could in Jönsson's garden.

We passed the steelworks. Two great rusty ships lay moored at the quay. The water on this side was in shadow and completely black, while towards the sea it was bright blue and glittered with tiny shards of light.

'Does Einar ever talk about my dad?' I said.

The question came unexpectedly, I saw the way Dag seemed to stiffen in his seat before looking across at me and then relaxing again.

'Sometimes, yes. Of course he does,' he said. 'Not at any great length, but a bit now and again. Why do you ask?'

'I don't know. I've been thinking about him today, my dad. I don't normally. But I dreamt about him last night, that's probably why. Anyway, I've been thinking I don't actually know very much about him. Which is my own fault, because I've never really asked. And Mum never talks about him.'

'Never?' said Dag, looking straight ahead at the road now.

'No. I think she might be bitter. But she doesn't talk about that either. She doesn't say anything.'

'So you want to talk to my dad about him, is that it?'

I glanced at him immediately.

'No, no, no. That's not why I was asking at all.'

Neither of us spoke for a moment.

'Wasn't there one year when they weren't on speaking terms?' I said then. 'Do you know anything about that?'

'Not that I ever heard about. Dad and Syvert?'

'That's right. I don't know where I got it from. Maybe I just got the wrong end of the stick at the time and was never put right about it.'

'Well, I don't know,' he said. 'Come over for dinner one night. They both ask after you. And you haven't been round ours for ages.'

'I will,' I said.

Dag stared out at the forest we were going through, it was still dark and sopping wet after the winter.

'Are you not doing too good at the moment?' he said after a second.

'How do you mean?'

'You seem a bit down, to be honest.'

'No, not at all! Everything's fine. Just a bit bored, maybe, that's all. I imagine that's what you can see.'

'That'll be it, then,' he said.

We followed the river in silence the last part of the way before I turned onto the estate and drove up the winding road to the top where their house was.

'You can do entrance exams in town here, you know,' he said. 'You don't actually have to do them at the university.'

'What's got into you now?' I said, changing down a gear to make it up the last steep hill. 'Are you giving me advice? Well, I'll give you some in return: shut your gob and mind your own business.'

'All right,' he said. 'Thanks for the lift, and give them all my best at home! Hope I never see you again.'

'I doubt you'll be that lucky. Say hello to Einar and Ida.'

That night I dreamt about Dad again. He was sitting by himself on the living-room sofa when I came in. All the lights were on. He was wearing his checked flannel shirt, staring into space.

'What are you sitting here for?' I said.

I wasn't used to seeing him sit like that, he was always busy doing one thing or another, mending the car or the bikes, soldering something, knocking something together out of some lengths of wood, touching up some paintwork.

'Just a bit tired, that's all,' he said, and smiled at me kindly. 'There's been such a lot on the go of late.'

'Are you feeling a bit down?' I said.

He nodded a couple of times while looking at me, a bit perplexed, as if he hadn't expected it of me.

'I suppose I am. Your mum and I aren't getting on too well, you see.'

He stood up and tousled my hair.

'Are you going now?' I said.

He nodded again.

'Where are you going?'

He didn't answer, just gave me that mild smile of his, bent down and picked up the brown leather briefcase I hadn't noticed until then.

'But before I go, I want to give you something. We'll do it the other way round this time. You get the present when I go, instead of when I come back. OK?'

'OK,' I said. 'What is it?'

He opened the briefcase and took out two stones. They were rough and jagged, grey-white with something red in them, they looked like granite.

'Here you are, son. These are for you. Look after them. I'll see you again when I get home.'

When I took them, one in each hand, they were so much heavier than I'd expected, so my hands were pulled downwards until my brain recalibrated itself and my arms adjusted to employ the strength required to hold them up.

They were a tiny bit warmer than I'd anticipated as well, as if they'd been put on top of the stove for a short time.

The next thing, Dad was crossing the yard outside, leaning slightly into the wind that was making the tree sway and rippling the surfaces of the puddles.

Then I woke up.

It was completely dark outside, raining and windy as it had been in the dream. I got up and went downstairs, anxious to see if the living-room lights were on.

They weren't, thank goodness.

I drank a glass of water and went back upstairs to bed. I'd never had such vivid dreams before. Normally, I never remembered them either, only occasionally, and then only vaguely, and if I tried to think about them, they dissolved like mist in the sun.

This was something else.

Could it have something to do with the radioactivity?

The stones did, definitely. The dream had recast the radioactivity in a simple image: two warm, heavy stones.

But what about the dreams themselves? The radiation wasn't enough to be dangerous, all the experts had been saying so. But it was there nonetheless. All around. Invisible atoms that had been destroyed and were giving off their invisible rays. Penetrating into animals and plants, flesh and bark. And our brains too, surely?

Rubbish.

I'd dreamt about Dad, nothing odd about that. I'd come home and some memories had been triggered.

Only he'd been so vivid.

As if he were still among us.

Rubbish, I told myself again, closed my eyes and lay listening to the sounds of the rain and the wind until I fell asleep. Faintly registered the car as Mum went off to work, Joar shutting the front door behind him. By the time I eventually woke up it was already twelve o'clock and Mum was rummaging about in the kitchen downstairs.

I had a shower and went down for some breakfast.

She was sitting at the table with the radio on, smoking and drinking coffee.

'So there you are,' she said.

'I did clear out the garage yesterday,' I said. 'And did the hoovering in here.'

'Have I said you didn't?'

'You were criticising me getting up late.'

'I wouldn't say that, exactly,' she said, and stubbed her cigarette out in the ashtray. 'You never used to sleep for so long, though, did you?'

I sighed and got the corn flakes out, a bowl, the sugar and the milk.

She lit another cigarette as I began to eat. I'd never cared for it, the smell of smoke while I was eating, it smothered the taste of the food, but I said nothing, she'd got too much on me with my nights out for me to be able to complain.

'Do you ever dream about Dad?' I said.

She turned her head towards me, slowly.

'Of course I do,' she said, meeting my gaze before looking down at her hands, picking the nail of one index finger with that of the other. 'Why do you ask?'

'I dreamt about him last night. And the night before, as it happens. It's strange though, because I don't usually. Or else I just don't remember. I remember these ones, though.'

She looked out of the window again.

Wasn't she going to say anything about it?

I wouldn't either, then.

I crunched a few mouthfuls of corn flakes. The radio played an Øystein Sunde song. The sky looked to be clearing up over the fields, a line of blue visible through a crack in the grey-white blanket of cloud.

'How were things between you and Dad, anyway, when he died?'

I stared at her.

Her eyes darted this way and that a couple of times. But she sat just as calmly as before, and when she looked up at me, her eyes were calm too.

'What makes you ask that?'

'In the dream I had, Dad said you weren't getting on.'

She smiled. It was a smile of relief, I thought.

'So you think you're a seer?'

'It was an odd thing to dream.'

'We got on fine,' she said. 'He was away a lot, but he always was.'

'Where did he go?'

'You know where he went,' she said. 'To various airports at first. Then to shipyards and factories round about.'

'Yes,' I said. 'I remember when he used to come home.'

'You were always so excited, you and Joar,' Mum said, and smiled again.

'How is it you never talk about him?'

'Don't I?'

'No, never. It's like he never existed.'

'I didn't realise,' she said.

There was a silence then. She got up and poured herself another cup of coffee.

'It's just so awful to think about.'

The paper boy hadn't shut the mailbox properly, so the newspaper was soggy when I went to get it. It annoyed me, not so much because it made it harder to read the paper, more because he must have known it'd get ruined in this weather, but still hadn't bothered to make sure he'd put the lid down right before biking off again.

I almost felt like phoning the newspaper offices to complain. But it was probably only an empty-headed twelve-year-old, and a telling-off wasn't exactly going to make the paper dry.

I put it down on the kitchen table and tried to turn the pages to Dag's section without tearing them, but they were so stuck together I couldn't separate them, so instead I went to the shop to buy a new one. Mum wouldn't like it, she hated waste more than anything and could always see the value of things no matter what. But she didn't have to know.

It had clouded over again and the light had faded. The river ran dark under the trees. I probably merged into the surroundings in my dark green anorak, I thought, and so every time a lorry came thundering through the flatland I stepped well back from the road just in case.

There were no customers in the shop when I came in, and the woman

on the till, who'd worked there always, was sitting reading one of the
weekly glossies.

NORWAY'S NEW PRIME MINISTER, *VG*'s headline said, and there
was a picture of Brundtland with her index finger pressed to her
temple — apparently she'd ridiculed Syse in parliament the day before.

I took a copy out of the rack. The checkout woman looked at me.

'All very quiet in here,' I said.

'Always is before lunchtime,' she said.

'Isn't it a bit boring?'

'No, it's all right.'

'I don't think I've ever been in at this time,' I said, and picked a basket from the top of the stack. 'Apart from at weekends, that is.'

'You've not missed much,' she said, and met my gaze. Her eyes were
gigantic behind her glasses. What lenses did she use? She must have
been nearly blind!

'You never know what can happen,' I said. 'All of a sudden, an American film star could walk in through that door and ask for a packet of
chewing gum.'

'I've worked here twenty-five years.'

'And nothing exciting's ever happened?'

She shook her head.

'That minister from the government was here once. Stray. That's the
only time.'

'What did he buy?'

She smiled.

'I can't remember.'

'I met someone in the military whose parents own a hotel in the
Vestland. One day, all of a sudden, Al Pacino was there playing billiards, he told me.'

'It goes to show, I suppose.'

'He's a very good actor, Al Pacino,' I said, and went down the aisle,
picking up a two-litre carton of milk, a loaf of bread and some cheese,
the newspaper under my arm.

'So you're following your father's footsteps?' she said as she entered
the amounts.

'How do you mean?'

'You said you were in the forces.'

'No, just my national service, that's all.'

I took a carrier bag and put my items in it, got my wallet out and paid.

'Did you know him?' I said.

'Oh yes,' she said. 'He went to school with the rest of us.'

'What was he like?'

'Like? I don't know, really. Just normal, I suppose. Like everybody else.'

I nodded.

'Thanks, anyway,' I said and smiled. 'And remember, before you know it, it'll be Sylvester Stallone standing here!'

Mum had gone to work again by the time I got home. She'd switched the coffee maker off, but the coffee was still warm in the pot. I switched it on again so it wouldn't go cold and poured myself a cup before sitting down at the table and opening the paper. Dag had got a whole page, and as far as I could judge his pieces were all good. The bloke from No to Nuclear Weapons said the nucleus of the atom was unchanged by any chemical process, and splitting it, as we were now doing, went against Nature and was in fact a threat to life on earth as we knew it. Are we playing at being God? Dag had asked him. No, we're playing at being the Devil, he'd answered.

I tried to phone him to tell him I thought his work was good, and to ask if he fancied coming round to watch the international match, but he wasn't in. Instead, I went up to my room, lay down on the bed and carried on reading my Follett. When I got to the scene where the main character shaves a woman's cunt in a bathtub at a hotel in Cairo, I got a hard-on, undid my trousers and started wanking as I'd done so many times before when I got to that scene, the only one I could remember in the whole book.

Just when I was about to come, someone opened the front door downstairs.

'Hello?' Joar's voice called out.

I tried to keep going, but my fantasy couldn't contend with reality, it all fell apart and the climax that had been so near was suddenly so very far away.

'Syvert?' Joar called out.

I did my trousers up and got to my feet.

'I'm up here,' I shouted.

'OK,' he shouted back.

OK?

'What is it?'

'Nothing!' he shouted. 'I'm home!'

He was slicing some bread when I came down. His school bag was dumped in the hall, his wet coat on top.

But I wasn't his dad, so I said nothing.

'Can we have some cocoa?' he said.

With his pale face tilted down and his rather pointed or at least thin nose, the whirl of hair at the crown of his head, he looked like a little bird.

'Of course we can,' I said.

'Will you make it, then?'

'You can make it yourself, can't you?'

'Mum says I'm not allowed.'

'You're allowed when I'm here.'

'But I don't know how to make it.'

'You don't know how to make *cocoa*?'

He shook his head.

'Mix two spoonfuls of cocoa and a spoonful of sugar with a bit of water in a mug. Then you heat the milk and pour it on top. Nothing could be easier. Can't you fry an egg either?'

'I've never tried,' he said.

'What's Mum thinking?' I said. 'You're *twelve* years old!'

'Were you allowed to cook when you were twelve?'

'Allowed? I *had to*. There were all sorts of things I had to do. Look after you, for a start.'

I smiled at him. He looked at me, but didn't smile back.

'I'm sorry I killed the bird,' he said.

'I'm sorry too for getting so angry,' I said.

He took a plate from the cupboard, put his bread on it and went over to the fridge to get something to put on the bread.

'I don't know why I did it.'

'You did it because it was exciting. All boys have done it at some point. Think no more about it. Are you going to make that cocoa, then, or shall I?'

'I can do it.'

His voice cracked slightly as he spoke.

'What was that?' I said.

'What?'

'Is your voice breaking now?'

He blushed and turned his face away from me as he took the milk over to the cooker.

'Have you got hair on your . . . ?' I said, not knowing whether to say *willy* or if he was big enough for me to say *dick*.

'It's none of your business,' he said, still looking the other way. 'Where's the cocoa?'

'So you have, then!' I said.

He busied himself without saying anything, poured the milk into the pan, mixed the sugar and cocoa into a paste and whisked it into the milk.

'Do you want some?' he said with his back to me.

'I wouldn't mind,' I said.

'Can you pour it, then? I'll only make a mess.'

'You're a big lad now, you'll have to do it yourself,' I said, and laughed.

He said nothing, but from the look on his face when he put my cocoa down in front of me I could tell he wasn't just embarrassed, but proud of himself too.

'Have you got homework to do?'

He nodded.

'We've got to write a composition for Friday.'

'About what?'

'Either "My Dog Says" or "A Day I'll Never Forget".'

'It'll be a cinch for you,' I said.

'I hate writing.'

'What do you like, then? Maths?'

'A bit. We might be able to take computer studies in ninth. That'd be good.'

'I'm *really* glad I'm finished with school,' I said.

'Aren't you going to university?'

'I'm not sure. Maybe, maybe not.'

He looked at me over the rim of his mug, that probing, penetrating gaze of his. He put the mug down and began buttering a slice of bread.

'Why do we die, exactly?' he said.

'*Why?*'

'Yes, why do we die?'

'Are you thinking about the bird now.'

'Maybe.'

'It died because it got shot to pieces. You can't function any more when a bullet's just gone through your brain, can you?'

'But if that hadn't happened, it would still have died sooner or later.'

'That's just the way it is.'

'But why?'

I shrugged.

'No one knows.'

'There must be a reason,' he said.

'Things get old and wear out. A car will only keep going so many years before it starts breaking down, and eventually there's nothing you can do other than scrap it.'

'But you can take a car to the garage and get it mended.'

'Like hospital,' I said, 'it only helps for a while.'

'That's not right,' he said. 'You can put new parts in a car when the old ones stop working. You can't with people and animals.'

'I wouldn't speak too soon,' I said. 'They'll be putting artificial organs in humans next.'

'Will death disappear then, do you think?'

'Yes, I think it will, don't you? If everything that stops working can be replaced?'

'The first thing about that,' he said, looking down, with his elbow propped on the table, his slice of bread in his hand, 'is that if you had all the parts in your body replaced, then you'd no longer be you, would you?'

'I suppose you're right,' I said.

He smiled, then seemed to retract it again.

'The second thing is that it doesn't answer the question of why death exists, does it?'

'It doesn't, no,' I said. 'You were a bit ahead of me there. Was that the point?'

'Hm?' he said, chewing his bread.

'You were just briefing me, was that it?'

He shook his head while he swallowed.

'I've been thinking about it for a while, that's all. Why a bird dies, but a stone doesn't.'

'That's simple,' I said. 'It's life that dies, and a stone isn't alive.'

'I know *that*,' he said. 'But why does life die?'

'No one knows, and no one ever will,' I said, and got up. 'Thanks for the cocoa, mister. Now go and do your homework!'

'Where are you going?' he said as I went into the hall and put my anorak on.

'Out, that's all. Won't be long.'

It had cleared up again. The light from the white sky made the sodden fields shimmer faintly. I didn't know what I was going to do, or where I was going to go, all I knew was I didn't want to stay in a second longer.

But Mum still had the car and none of my mates lived within walking distance. Besides, I supposed they'd all still be at work.

I walked towards the main road. Luckily, we had practice at six. It had never been the highlight of the week before, but it definitely was now. It was our first match at the weekend, so most likely we'd be given the team sheet tonight. I wasn't expecting much game time to begin with. But it was still something to look forward to, and think about.

And then there was the international after that. It was only a friendly, but it was Argentina we were up against, and Maradona would be playing.

As I walked along the road, the river running grey next to it, a wall of dark green spruce on the other side, it occurred to me to go down to the moorings and have a look at the canoe. It had been under a tarp more than six months, easy to steal for anyone who knew what they wanted. Not that I was afraid of that. It wasn't exactly worth much anyway.

Several boats were in the water already. The canoe was still there, on the ground under a tree at the bottom end.

Maybe I could go out for a paddle, I thought as I lifted the tarp and the green hull became visible.

I'd have to go and get the paddles first.

Could I be bothered?

Yes, I could.

I could ask Joar if he wanted to come.

I ought to.

It'd be good for him to get out.

But was that what I wanted?

I'd been big brother enough for one day, I reckoned.

A little trip down the river, it'd be good.

I went back and found the paddles at the far end of the barn, together with the life jackets and a bailer, almost yellow in the grainy grey light. Next to them were the boxes of Dad's things.

Something in me wanted to see what else was in them. Not to get closer to him, more the opposite, to remove him from me, put him back in his boxes, back with his things.

I crouched down and opened the one that was nearest.

The things from his desk. Passport, driving licence, wallet. A folder full of bills, some loose soldering schematics, circuit boards, small bundles of wires, pens and pencils, typewriter ribbons, his Polaroid camera. And the Chinese figurine of a human with a monkey's head that he'd kept on his desk and which I'd thought was made of gold, only it wasn't. I hadn't seen it since he died, when I was eleven, and all sorts of emotions ran through me as I held it in my hand. There were some ring binders too, with documents in them, mostly with the Royal Norwegian Air Force letterhead. And at the bottom, spines facing up, five books. I'd never seen him read anything other than the newspaper and occasionally my comics, which he sometimes borrowed when he was tired, so I picked one out.

The alphabet it was written in was indecipherable. It had to be Russian. The others were the same.

Why on earth would he have books in *Russian*?

I put everything back in the box again, picked up a paddle in one hand, a life jacket in the other and went outside. Mum's car was parked out front now, and I saw her in the kitchen. I thought maybe I should tell her where I was going, but on the other hand she didn't need to know everything. I was an adult. Even if she didn't necessarily see things the same way.

There was no one around at the moorings. The river flowed by with barely a sound. I put the life jacket on, pulled the tarp away and dragged the canoe over the grass between the trees and the gravel, down to the river. I got in and paddled out midstream. Little galaxy-shaped eddies formed here and there in the water around me. Behind the wall of tall spruce trees that were almost black under the overcast sky, the heathland rose up, and behind it, where again it sloped away, was the sea.

I wondered if I'd have sensed it, if I hadn't known.

It felt that way. You always sensed the sea, if it was close by.

Then I thought of the Russian books.

Maybe they'd been a present from someone. But who would give a person books they couldn't read?

I reckoned he must have bought them himself on one of his trips abroad, as a curiosity. The Chinese monkey man was something he'd bought in a big city somewhere, Berlin, if I remembered right, but it could have been London; wherever it was, I remembered him coming home and showing it to me, telling me about the shop he'd bought it from. An old Chinese man had been sitting stock-still behind the counter, and his shop had been filled to the rafters with all sorts of weird things. He'd bought Mum a silk dressing gown from the same place, though I'd never seen her wear it, and I got a mechanical bird that lifted up its head and sang. It broke after only a few days. I hadn't told them, just left it on the windowsill.

If he'd bought things from a shop like that, he could have bought the books from a similar place, intrigued by them being in Russian and not knowing what was in them.

I'd have to ask Mum about it.

I let the canoe drift downstream on the current, adjusting its course now and again, but otherwise resting the paddle on the gunwale. It was going to be hard work paddling back the other way, so I had to make sure not to drift too far. Under the bridge, where the river narrowed, the boat went slightly faster, slowing again on the other side, where it opened out again, and I had to start paddling. I loved to feel the heaviness of the water when I thrust the paddle down and pulled it back, so hard that it gave a shudder, propelling myself slowly forwards at the same time.

A wall that was also an opening.

Two hours later, Gjert pulled up outside the house in his black Ascona and tooted the horn.

'All right, loser,' he said without looking at me, his hand rummaging for something in the glove compartment as I got in.

'All right, gobshite,' I said, putting my holdall on my lap. 'Anything been happening?'

'Like what?' he said, and pushed a cassette into the stereo, threw the car into gear and set off back towards the road.

'How should I know?' I said.

The first chords of 'War Pigs' came through the speakers.

'When was the last time you had a shower, anyway?' I said.

He gave me a quick look.

'Only it's a bit whiffy in here.'

'Seriously?' he said.

'Have you been wanking in here, or what?' I said.

He stopped at the road, there was a bus coming. I could nearly hear his brain creaking. Did his car smell of spunk?

'Ha ha,' he said, and pulled out as soon as the bus had gone past, speeding up and overtaking it before we got to the bridge.

'Were you there, by the way, when Glenn told us what he used to do when he started wanking?' I said.

'No,' he said. 'How many different ways are there?'

'He used to fill a sock with warm porridge. And then off he'd go! Ha ha ha!'

'Ha ha ha!'

'Only a sick mind could think that up.'

Apart from his brief moment of uncertainty, he was the same as he always was. As spiritless as ever, no sign of any joy in him, no inkling of any triumph. If it had been me with that girlfriend of his, I'd have been dying to go on about it.

But it wasn't me.

'Paranoid' came on.

'It's held up well, that album,' I said. 'Better than Ozzy, at any rate.'

'He's not doing too bad.'

'Didn't you see him on Live Aid? All pudgy and waxen, and covered in sequins. Not much devil and darkness there any more.'

'It's all just image, that,' said Gjert. 'You should just stick to the music. That's what counts. His voice is still as good.'

'What kind of music does Bente like, anyway?' I said.

'So we're going to talk about Bente now, are we?' he said, almost as if he was annoyed.

'She is your girlfriend,' I said. 'It's only natural to talk about her.'

'She's pretty straight,' he said. 'She likes . . .'

'Come on, out with it!' I said.

He went quiet, his eyes on the road as he changed gear before the bend and the hill.

'It can't be that bad, surely,' I said.

'No, of course not,' he said.

'Go on, then!' I said.

'Phil Collins, for one,' he said.

'PHIL COLLINS?' I said, and burst out laughing, more because of his embarrassment than her liking the bald little drummer.

'I know, I know,' he said. 'It gets worse, though. She really likes Sting as well . . .'

'STING?' I spluttered.

'All right, that'll do.'

'I hope for your sake she's got a good pair of tits on her.'

'Well, she has.'

On my way up the stairs after practice I saw Mum sitting in the kitchen with some papers in front of her, pen in hand, her reading glasses on the tip of her nose. I knocked on Joar's door and opened it before he answered.

He looked up at me from his bed where he was lying reading.

'Aren't you going to watch the match?' I said.

'I don't think so,' he said.

'What? It's Argentina. Maradona's playing!'

'But there's nothing at stake,' he said. 'Come and get me when they've qualified for the World Cup.'

'Listen,' I said. 'Football's football. It's exciting whatever kind of match it is. Maradona's the best player in the world. How many times have you seen him play?'

'None.'

'Exactly. Come on!'

He shook his head and went back to his reading.

'All right, I can't force you,' I said. 'Even if I do feel like it.'

He didn't say anything, so I went downstairs again, stopped in the kitchen doorway and looked in on Mum.

'Doing the bills?' I said.

She nodded.

'Are you on top of them?'

'Yes. I can tell you're here, though.'

'Now you're being funny,' I said, and went in. 'Am I an expenditure item now?'

'The food budget's up, I can tell you that much.'

'I've not been here a week yet!'

'But you'll be here the rest of the spring and the summer too, won't you?'

'Where else am I supposed to stay?'

She shook her head.

'You need to be a bit more grown up now, Syvert. You can stay here as long as you want. You know that. But you're going to have to chip in. I haven't got that much money.'

'Me neither,' I said. 'None, to be exact.'

'Can't you get a job up at the factory? Just for a few months?'

'Mum, you can't just *get* a job these days. It's 1986.'

'You could at least try. Didn't you know someone who's a foreman there?'

I didn't answer, went into the living room and switched the telly on, and sat down on the sofa to watch the match. But I was too annoyed to enjoy it. I was nineteen years old, not a kid any more. She had no right to tell me what to do and what not. I'd been here *six* days, and even if I had been eating like a horse, it couldn't possibly have shown up on that idiotic budget of hers.

Giske made a dreadful mistake, Thorstvedt had thrown it out to him, it was an easy ball to control, only it rolled under his foot, straight to Maradona, who touched it forward to an Argentinian who then shot from the edge of the area, Thorstvedt had to go full stretch to fist it out for a corner.

It was only the first minute of the game!

It was going to be a massacre.

Two corners later, Maradona got the ball again outside the area. Norway were running around like headless chickens.

'Syvert?' Mum said from the kitchen.

'What?' I said as forbiddingly as I could.

'There was something else I wanted to talk to you about.'

'I'm watching the football.'

'Can we talk afterwards, then?'

I didn't answer.

The silence that followed was oppressive, but I forced myself not to say anything. Forced myself to focus on the match.

Giske and Hareide cocked it up between them, and again Maradona was there, but they managed to get away with it.

There wasn't going to be much point watching this.

Jørn Andersen was useless up front, I'd seen him play twice at our place, he had no technique, could hardly control a ball, how he'd got to be leading scorer was beyond me, it was sheer luck. But Larsen Økland was good.

Argentinians swarming everywhere. Osvold lost the ball far too easily.

He was good when he played here, I liked him then.

Not now, though.

The Norwegians looked like they were playing on stilts compared to the Argentinians.

No, I couldn't be arsed with this.

I switched it off and went and stood in the kitchen doorway.

'What was it you wanted to talk about?' I said.

She smiled tenderly.

'Will you sit down a minute?'

I'm all right standing here, I said to myself, but at the same time I could see how childish it was, that it wasn't going to lead to anything good. So I went in with a loud sigh, pulled a chair out and sat down opposite her.

'I wasn't telling the truth this morning,' she said. 'When you asked about your dad.'

I looked at her.

She took off her glasses, put them down on the table.

'You asked how your dad and me were getting on before he died.'

'And you said you were getting on fine.'

'Yes,' she said. 'I shouldn't have said that. And I'm sorry. I didn't have time to think.'

'So things weren't good between you?'

She picked up her glasses, held a stem to her lips, as she looked the other way.

'He wanted to get divorced,' she said.

'*What?*' I said.

She glanced at me. Put her glasses down again.

'But why?'

'He'd found someone else.'

'What? Dad had?'

She nodded. I had to look down. Her eyes were moist.

'Are you sure? How do you know?'

'He told me. And said he wanted a divorce.'

'When? When was this?'

She shrugged.

'A few days before he died.'

'But, Mum, that's terrible!'

'Yes, it is.'

'How come you never said anything?'

'You were eleven years old at the time. You wouldn't have understood. And the most important thing was for you to be all right, wasn't it? Besides, it wasn't something you *needed* to know.'

'But I've not been eleven years old all this time.'

'Why would you want to know?'

'Because it's the *truth*,' I said, and stood up. 'And because it changes everything!'

I went upstairs to my room, lay down on the bed, but couldn't just lie there, and so I got up again, gazed around the room, found nothing I could attach myself to, nothing that could be a refuge, and went downstairs again, took the car key from the table in the hall, snatched my coat from the peg.

'Syvert?' Mum said from the kitchen. 'Where are you going?'

I didn't answer, slammed the door behind me, crossed the yard and got in the car. Drove off, turned onto the main road, followed it aimlessly alongside the river. There was practically nothing on the road, so I drove fast.

Too late to go and see anyone. Not that I felt like it. All I wanted was to get away. Take off somewhere, disappear into something else. A town I'd never been to, people I'd never met.

For nearly nine years she'd made out she was still his wife.

But he hadn't wanted to stay with her.

It hadn't been Mum and Dad. It had been Dad and someone else.

How could she bring herself to lie about *that*?

I was never going to forgive her.

At the bridge that crossed over the falls I turned left along the narrow road that followed the river on the side where there were almost no houses, where the forest would soon be taking over completely. It was a hilly road, with lots of sharp bends, climbs and descents. A few kilometres further up, in what seemed like the deepest forest, was a rallycross circuit. Apart from that there were only trees in the headlight beams.

Would he have left Joar and me too?

Was that why he was away such a lot, because he didn't want to be with us?

No, it was Mum he didn't care for, not us.

He'd been kind and caring in the dreams I'd had.

Sitting there with his head in his hands. Despondent.

But that had been me dreaming, me making him out to be like that. So how would I know, that he was unhappy, that things weren't good between them?

I had no recollections of anything like that at all.

There was some frost heave on the road and I slowed down. The headlights picked out an unmade road leading off into the trees, and without thinking I braked and turned off.

The gravel was fresh and the wheel ruts broad and deep. Most likely it was for transporting timber, I thought, and changed down as it grew steeper. At the top, there was a turning area. From there, it got muddy and was more of a track than a road, impossible to negotiate for anything but a tractor, so I pulled in and continued on foot. The ground was covered with the rotting leaves of the deciduous trees that grew on both sides. The rain, which had been like a film while I'd been driving, little drops that spattered the windscreen, swept aside the whole time by the swishing wipers, was suddenly real; cold and wet, it blew into my face as I walked, invisible, but certainly audible: all around me in the darkness it pattered in the trees and bushes, the moss and the heather.

I could just keep on walking, I told myself, on and on, day in, day out, until the forest swallowed me up and I was consumed, vanished. It would mean I'd gone mad, but what difference did that make if there was no one else to know?

There was a bend up ahead, and suddenly there were no more trees. The whole area had been cleared. The hillside was bare stubs. It looked like there'd been a war there, or a fire.

I carried on slowly, upwards through the vandalised landscape, the ground littered now with branches, twigs, bits of bark, sawdust, and stopped at the top. The hill was just as bare on the other side. At the bottom I could see a sheeny surface I realised was a lake.

Once, in year nine, we'd paddled canoes on a lake much further inside the forest, lit a fire when evening came, slept under the canoes in the night. Our teacher had told us the lake was connected with other lakes and rivers, a network spanning hundreds of kilometres, I remembered. Perhaps this was where it began?

Mum hadn't cried at the funeral. I'd thought her grief had been too immense for tears. It was a thought that had put my eleven-year-old mind at rest. I'd never returned to it until now.

Who had she been, the other woman?

I didn't suppose she came to the funeral.

But her grief must have been just as immense.

If they'd really been serious about each other, that is.

They must have been.

Maybe Mum knew who she was.

Not that I was going to do anything about it, I told myself, and turned back, descending through the stumps, the bracken that grew among them.

How could she not have said anything? I was her son, I had a right to know. For nearly nine years I'd been living a lie.

Her bloody lie.

I'd have to move out. Find a place of my own.

That was for certain.

A vague sense of relief welled in me, it was as if joy's little bird were flapping its wings in there, but just a couple of beats, then it died, and the worm of despair started wriggling again. There was something shoddy and senseless about it, him having an affair and wanting to get divorced, then dying like that, her not saying a word about it, not a word, as if it never happened, and that was what I'd grown up in, a lie, a deceit, and it meant our lives too were somehow all wrong. Shoddy and inexcusable.

How could she have done that?

I was nearly at the road again and could see the turning area and the car where I'd left it. I got in and switched on the ignition, the gravel and the bare trees suddenly illuminated, the rain that slanted in the beams.

Mum was sitting in the kitchen when I got home. I took my shoes off, hung my anorak on the peg and went upstairs to my room without saying anything.

It had to be past midnight. It wasn't like her to be up so late during the week. I supposed she wanted to talk to me about it. Apologise, get me to understand. But I'd already made my mind up I wasn't going to discuss it, not a single word. She could burn in her own shame.

I couldn't even be bothered getting undressed, but got into bed still with my clothes on. It felt right too, in a way. I didn't like the thought of making things easy for myself.

Shortly afterwards I heard her come up the stairs, the door of her bedroom closing quietly.

I woke up around ten; the phone was ringing. When it stopped, I got up, went downstairs and decided to fry myself an egg, bacon and a couple of beefburgers for breakfast. The fields outside were yellow and brown with occasional puddles, mirrors reflecting the grey sky.

The phone rang again. I turned the heat down on the hob and went into the hall.

'Hello, the Løyning household,' I said.

'Hello, Løyning,' said Dag. 'How's tricks?'

'Good.'

'Good.'

'But not good enough for me to ask how you're doing.'

'Is it what I said about those entrance exams?'

'Don't be daft! I've not given it a thought.'

'Glad to hear it.'

'What do you want, anyway?'

'Mum and Dad are asking you round for dinner on Friday. Can you come?'

'I reckon so, yes. What time?'

'Not sure, to be honest. Seven, maybe?'

'OK. And go out afterwards?'

'Sounds good to me,' he said. 'By the way, I read your piece yesterday. It's going to be really good.'

A moment went by before I understood what he meant. My interview in the paper.

'Oh Christ,' I said. 'I should never have agreed to it.'

'Don't be so precious,' he said. 'You're doing a lot of people a favour.'

'Spokesman of layabouts, is that it?'

'No, seriously. It's an important debate.'

'Sod it,' I said. 'What's done's done.'

'And what's dunce is dunce,' he said. 'See you Friday, then.'

'See you. Say hi from me!'

I put the receiver down and went back into the kitchen. As I was having my breakfast, Mum's car came up from the road. She still hadn't got it into her head that the garage was empty, and parked out front like she always did.

Why had she got her posh coat on?

The door opened.

'Hi,' she said, and took the coat and her shoes off in the hall.

'Hi,' I said. 'Do you want some coffee?'

'Yes, I think I will.'

She poured it herself and stood by the worktop, the steaming mug in her hand.

'Is there something special on today?' I said.

'I don't think so. Why?'

'You're all done up.'

She looked down at herself.

'I wouldn't go that far,' she said. 'No, it's the holiday, that's all.'

I looked at her, perplexed. What was she on about?

'What holiday?'

'It's the first of May, International Workers' Day. It never was your cup of tea.'

'So it is,' I said. 'I'd forgotten. Is everything closed?'

She nodded, fetched an ashtray and sat down at the table to roll herself a cigarette.

'How's your back, anyway?'

'A bit better at the moment. Thank you for asking.'

I carried on eating. She shoved the rolling machine's little handle forward and picked out the finished cigarette, lit it and sat smoking in silence, without the slightest consideration for me having my breakfast. I hated it.

'I understand you being angry and upset,' she said after a bit.

'I'm not,' I said, and removed some ketchup from my lip with the tip of my forefinger, then glanced around for something I could wipe it off on. I couldn't see anything, so I rubbed my fingers together instead, until there was nothing left of it apart from a bit of moisture on the skin.

'I think you are.'

'You've no idea what I think. And it's going to stay that way too.'

I stood up, took my plate and cutlery over and put them down on the worktop next to the sink, picked up my coffee and went into the living room.

'We must be able to talk about it,' Mum said from the kitchen.

'No, we mustn't,' I said. 'We've been living a lie for nearly nine years. Your lie. There's nothing else to say other than that.'

She went quiet.

I knew I wouldn't be able to sit there in silence without caving in. I was too soft for that.

'Can I borrow the car? I said.

'Yes, you can,' she said. 'As long as you're back by two.'

I drove the same way I'd gone the night before. There was hardly anything on the road. It was raining, people would be staying in, if they weren't taking part in the parade in town. What then had been darkness with small pockets of light here and there was now an array of colour, greys, browns and yellow-whites, the hills green with conifers, an occasional red-painted barn on the other side of the river.

It wasn't just radioactivity I didn't understand. Colours were something I couldn't grasp either, even when I'd had them explained to me. Because if colours didn't exist in themselves, but were actually different wavelengths of light that the brain turned into colours, what was it we saw when we saw colours then? Colours were an illusion, they didn't exist, and yet we *saw* them, so they did exist, not outside, in the world, but inside us.

But how did they get there?

Colours are all in the head, my teacher had told me when I'd asked about it. Colours are a product of our sensory system.

But *where* in the head?

'Now you're being belligerent, Syvert,' he said. 'Light entering through the pupil is detected by the retina and converted into electrical signals that are sent to the visual cortex at the rear of the brain. There are cells in the retina called cones and rods, which react differently to different wavelengths of light, and the electrical signals they send out determine whether we see colours or black and white. But we don't actually see colour until those signals are processed in the visual cortex.'

'But I see colour,' I said. 'Not signals.'

'It all happens in the visual cortex,' he said. 'Now, no more questions about the eye. Everything's perfectly well explained in your textbook.'

But it wasn't.

The world was outside us, it was something we were *in*. But *seeing* it, it became a part of us. So wasn't the world then *inside* us? If it was only on the outside and nothing of it got in, everything would just be dark. The same surely applied to hearing and smell and touch. Our senses took what was *external* and turned it into something *internal*. If the world couldn't get inside us, it wouldn't exist.

That would be like the way a stone existed in the world. Nothing in the world got in, the stone couldn't hear, see, smell, taste or feel anything, so the world as far as it was concerned didn't exist. A stone didn't even know it existed itself.

Was that what life was? Was that what set it apart from what was not living? What was living was living because it internalised the world? And both the world and what was living were thereby felt to exist?

That had to be it.

But how did the visible world get inside us?

That was the bit about light entering through the pupils.

It was from there on it got hard to grasp.

The world came in as two narrow beams of light, and that light contained so much information that the brain could construct for us an identical image of the world on that basis alone.

Where was that image?

It seemed like it was outside us.

The river was down there, not inside me.

And then there was the fact that colours were something *added on*. Like some kind of emotion.

Was everything in the world colourless?

It had to be.

Could there be other things that were added on too? Things that didn't exist, which we constructed and *believed* to exist?

I indicated left and slowed down to allow a VW Beetle to come chugging over the bridge before I turned off onto the narrow road and followed its climb along the river.

If Mum kept on about it, I *would* cave in soon.

I'd nearly felt sorry for her as she sat there in the kitchen on her own with her thoughts, wanting to talk to me about it. No, I *had* felt sorry for her.

He'd left her twice. First when he told her he wanted a divorce, then when he died. That made a difference. If it had just been the divorce, she'd have been able to deal with it in a way, she'd have been able to talk to him about it, and to her family and friends, that way she'd have come to terms with it. But him dying like that meant there was no closure, they never got as far as actually divorcing. In her mind, though, they had divorced, and without her having been able to share it with anyone.

He must have had his reasons for wanting to leave her.

But I'd never know what they were.

I passed the rallycross circuit that lay in a former sand quarry, empty and desolate in the grey drizzle, old tractor tyres stacked up at the bends, a weather-beaten hot-dog stand at the far end. I didn't know why I was there, but it was as good a place to come as any, I thought to myself, slowing almost to a stop and hugging the verge: an enormous lorry laden with timber was on its way through the bend above me.

The hearses of the forest.

Who was it who'd said that?

It rumbled past, a minor inferno of metal and timber, and I pulled away again, shortly afterwards turning off onto the soggy unmade road and driving up to the turning area at the top again. There was a car there now, a red Lada. There was no one in it, and no one around either as far as I could see when I got out, locked the door and set off along the track that went up the side of the hill. My mood was a different one now, of course, the light falling from the sky all around me, the trees standing out so clearly, in places I could see quite far between them.

Had Dad told the other woman about Joar and me?

He must have done.

Maybe she lived in town.

Maybe she was even from the village? An old flame that had been rekindled?

Or else he'd met her on one of his trips abroad.

I remembered hardly anything from the year he died, it was as if from the day of the funeral the memories of the months in both directions dissolved, the ones that had been and the ones that were to come.

The clear-felled tract opened out in front of me. It seemed even more extensive in daylight, even more brutal. But we needed timber, we needed houses and furniture and paper, and forest would always grow again.

As I stood on top of the hill looking down in the direction of the lake, I noticed a figure a couple of hundred metres below. It looked like a woman, she was wearing a red anorak and army trousers, a moss-green rucksack on her back. She was crossing the bare rock that sloped down towards the lake, walking briskly and full of purpose. This was a person out hiking, I thought to myself, my eyes following her until she reached the trees on the eastern side of the lake and disappeared into the forest.

Where was she going? I wondered. It wasn't exactly hiking terrain. Or actually it was, I thought then, forest and hills and lakes stretching away in all directions. Maybe that was why no one ever came here. It was so unspecified. No landmarks of note, no spectacular views or well-known buildings, hardly any history at all. Just bogland and forest, lakes and rock.

I went down to the lake and sat on a mound. I could bring Joar out here with the canoe in the summer. It'd be a nice trip. Good for the both of us. We could camp out, cook some food on the Primus.

At the lakeside, somewhat further away from where she'd vanished from sight, the woman emerged from the trees again. She halted and took off her backpack. It looked heavy. As she straightened up again, she looked out across the water. Then she waved to someone.

Shortly afterwards a canoe came gliding into view from the other side of the spit. The person paddling was a man, his movements were measured, and I took him to be elderly. She looked to be a good bit younger, though I was too far away to be able to see her face. Maybe the man was her father and they were going off on a trip together?

She'd chosen a good spot to meet him, there was a flat slab of rock where he was able to land side-on and she could basically just step into the canoe after handing him the rucksack.

She sat down on the bow seat, picked up a paddle and they set off, seamlessly and in perfect sync, and in a couple of minutes they were out of sight behind the spit.

Maybe they had a cabin somewhere close by.

I'd never come across any in the area, and never heard of anyone who had. But then I'd never been here before, not here exactly.

I got to my feet and trudged back towards the car. At the turning area I stopped in front of the Lada, cupped my hands at the side window and peered into the car through the little tunnel they made. The usual things: chocolate wrappers in the footwell on the passenger side, Krokanrull and Bounty by the looks of it, and an empty bottle of Tab, an umbrella on the back seat, a pile of envelopes and bumf that had slid to one side, a carrier bag that said MEKKA, with what looked like some books in it.

Not exactly revealing.

But then hardly mysterious either. An ordinary car belonging to an ordinary woman who'd met up with an ordinary man in a canoe and paddled off across an ordinary lake.

I got into the car, turned the ignition and saw to my horror that the clock on the dashboard said quarter to two. I'd never get home in fifteen minutes, it didn't matter how fast I went. But I could try.

Mum opened the door and came out as I pulled up at the front of the house. She must have been standing ready with her coat on.

'I'm really sorry,' I said. 'I forgot the time.'

'I'm ten minutes late.'

She closed the car door without saying anything else, started the engine again and drove off.

As if deceiving me for nearly nine years wasn't enough, I thought. Now she was in a nark with me as well.

'Joar?' I shouted as I stepped into the hall.

'What?' he shouted back from upstairs.

'I'm home!'

'OK.'

I thought maybe I should make us some tea, even if it was a bit early, so I went into the kitchen to see what we had. A variety of ready-made soups, vegetable, onion, pea, cauliflower. A tin of Mexican stew and another, much the same, though with pineapple for the exotic touch. Mushy peas and some mashed turnip. In the fridge there was some *lungemos* that Mum liked and which I didn't mind, it was just a bit boring, I thought. There was a packet of potato dumplings as well, and half a kilo of mince. The freezer in the basement was nearly full, mostly stuff that had been there ages, she could never throw anything out.

I took some fillets of saithe and a packet of frozen prawns and left them to thaw on the worktop in the kitchen before sitting down in the living room with a cup of coffee and yesterday's paper. I froze for a second as I unfolded it and saw the masthead: they'd be running that stupid interview on Saturday.

Oh well.

At least we were playing football on Saturday, I was looking forward to that. And besides, there was so much else going on in the world that no one was going to care less about a filler interview with some saddo on the dole.

Outside the window, a small figure on a bike came into view. It was Rickard, Joar's friend. He leaned his bike up against the tree, took the bag that was strapped to the luggage rack and went towards the front door.

'Joar!' I shouted up. 'Someone to see you!'

At the same moment, a car came up from the road. It looked like Terje's, I thought as I opened the door and watched it turn into the yard.

'Is Joar in?' said Rickard.

He came bombing down the stairs behind me.

'Come in!' he said.

'All right,' said Terje, who'd now extricated himself from behind the wheel and was standing with his hand on the top of the open door.

'Tea's in an hour,' I said to Joar. And then to Rickard: 'Do you want your tea here, Rickard?'

'What are you having?' he said, kicking off his shoes, still with his bag in his hand.

'Fish soup,' I said.

'No thanks,' he said, and the two of them went up the stairs.

'All right?' I said to Terje.

'Not seen you for a bit,' he said. 'Anything happening?'

'Not much. You?'

'We're at Tor Egil's. He's got the house to himself. Do you want to come round?'

'Could do. Got to make the tea first, though. Who else is there?'

'Glenn and Karsten. Harald. Tor Egil, of course. Trond and Jensen.'

'No girls?'

He shrugged.

'None that I noticed.'

'OK,' I said. 'Only I haven't got the car. The buses will be a Sunday service today, won't they?'

'I can come and pick you up. What time are you having your tea?'

'In an hour.'

'Around five then?

I nodded. He squeezed his frame back into the seat and drove off.

Tor Egil was the only person I knew whose parents were rich. His dad imported agricultural machinery and sold it across the country. They lived in a big house with an indoor swimming pool at the top of the estate. Tor Egil wasn't the sharpest knife in the drawer, a bit of a daddy's boy who wore V-neck pullovers with a shirt underneath, boat shoes and posh jackets, but there was always some benefit in having him around. As there was now: a fridge filled up with beer, and pizza for anyone who wanted.

They'd rented three films and everyone was a bit comatose after the night before.

'All right, Syvert,' they said when Terje and I came into the living room.

'Happy first of May, workers,' I said.

'Didn't see you last night,' said Glenn. 'Where were you?'

'I didn't realise it was the night before a holiday,' I said. 'I was at home watching the footy.'

'Not a bad choice, that,' he said. 'Who'd have thought that bunch of clodhoppers could beat Argentina?'

'You mean they *won*?' I said.

They all looked up at me.

'You just said you watched it!'

'They were so rubbish I switched it off.'

'Well, they won,' said Glenn. 'One–nil against Argentina with Maradona playing.'

'Bloody hell,' I said, and sat down on a chair by the dining table. 'Who scored?'

'Osvold.'

'The jammy bugger.'

'Great goal, long-range effort. Played a good game too.'

Tor Egil appeared from the kitchen with four bottles of beer in his hands.

'Do you want one of these?' he said as he came up to me.

'I wouldn't say no. Have you got a bottle opener as well?'

He fetched it from the coffee table and handed it to me.

They'd rented *The Deer Hunter*, *Octopussy* and *Rambo*.

I'd seen them all before, but it didn't matter. I could hardly remember what happened in any of them, apart from the Russian roulette in *The Deer Hunter*.

'Do you think it happens in real life? People playing Russian roulette for money?' said Karsten when we watched it.

'No way,' said Glenn.

'I wouldn't mind having a go,' I said. 'I could do with some cash.'

'As if you'd have the guts,' said Karsten, and laughed.

'Why wouldn't I? Surviving and pocketing the money's the most likely outcome.'

I held my index finger to my temple.

'Bang!' said Glenn. 'Sorry, Syvert. Better luck next time. Oh, that's right, there won't be a next time!'

We sat there drinking the whole evening, Tor Egil's beer supply was inexhaustible, or so it seemed. I'd decided I wanted to get back by ten, before Mum got home, but it slipped my mind completely, the alcohol took over, coursing so gorgeously through my veins, and making me feel so breezy and buoyant that it didn't even occur to me until it was gone eleven and Terje said he had to get going.

It didn't matter much. Joar was used to being on his own when Mum worked evenings. And his friend had still been there when I went out,

they were playing a game on the Commodore he'd brought with him
and were in a world of their own.

'Don't you get sick of always driving and never being able to drink?'
I said to Terje when we got in the car.

'Don't you get sick of going for a piss all the time?'

'I've never thought about it like that,' I said.

The headlights lit up the reflective verge markers far ahead of us as
we passed through the woods. Terje pushed a cassette into the stereo. A
quiet synth grew louder, then came what sounded like a peal of thunder, then a deep drone, with tinkling notes wafting above it.

'Great stereo you've got.'

'It's not bad, is it?'

He turned the volume up, a picky guitar came in, followed by some
piano, then all the floaty bits came tightly together as bass and drums
were introduced.

'What sort of crap's this you're playing?'

'Don't you know it? "Telegraph Road". Dire Straits.'

'I see.'

'Perfect road music.'

He hummed along for a bit, tapping his thumbs against the steering
wheel.

'Do you reckon I could get a job at the factory for a few months?' I
said.

He looked at me.

'I doubt it. I can ask, if you want.'

'I wouldn't mind.'

'Aren't you going to uni after the summer?'

'I don't know yet. Probably.'

'It's not always a good idea, you know, starting work in those circumstances. You can soon get used to earning a wage, money in your
pocket every month. Good money, at that.'

'Boring work, though.'

'It's not that bad, if you ask me. I could think of a lot worse.'

'Like what?'

'Teacher, maybe? How much of a laugh is that?'

'You're right.'

'Dentist.'

'Nope. No laughs there either.'

'Dental receptionist.'

'I take your point,' I said. 'There's a lot of boring jobs out there.'

'I'll have a word with them tomorrow,' he said. 'Don't build your hopes up, though.'

'I won't.'

We crossed the bridge, and for some reason I thought about Gjert's girlfriend. It wasn't beyond the realms of possibility that he'd end up with her. He was a determined sort, but he never took on more than one thing at a time. A bit like a badger that wouldn't let go. He looked a bit like a badger too, come to think of it, with that slanting brow and those piercing eyes of his.

'Anyway,' said Terje, 'see you Saturday, then.'

'Thanks for the lift,' I said, unclicked my seat belt and opened the door. The cold air outside streamed into the car. 'And thanks for asking about the job for me.'

'No problem. See you!'

He reversed a bit, swung round and drove off again. I noticed the lights were on in the kitchen and the living room, before I looked up at the sky. It was full of stars.

When I went inside, Mum was standing in the hall.

'Where have you been?'

'At Tor Egil's.'

I bent down and undid my shoes.

'Are you drunk?'

'Drunk? Of course I'm not drunk,' I said, concentrating as best I could on keeping my balance. 'Why would you think that?'

'You reek of it.'

I straightened up and took my coat off, hung it on the peg.

'We were watching videos and had a few beers. But even if I *was* drunk, there's no law against it. I'm over eighteen, in case you'd forgotten. You've got no right to decide over me.'

'Joar was on his own here.'

'What about when you're normally at work in the evenings? He's on his own then, isn't he?'

'Yes, and I only wish he wasn't. But now you're here he doesn't have to be. You can understand that, can't you?'

'I'm not his dad,' I said, and went up the stairs. 'And unlike you, I've got a life to lead.'

I woke up the next morning feeling strange. I was trembling inside, the way you do before a test. It was as if my body knew something I didn't.

I hadn't dreamt anything I could remember. I pulled my trousers and T-shirt on while looking out the window. There was a fog on the fields. The trees over by the barn were like dark, slender figures reaching their arms into dismal sky. The fields beyond were quite invisible in the fog.

Everything I saw was radioactive.

Maybe my body was reacting to it. It was only natural if I was a bit scared.

Or else it was Dad. The way he'd said in my dream that things weren't good between him and Mum.

In a dream.

How could that be?

I went downstairs and had some breakfast while I thought about what I was going to do. One thing was certain, I couldn't just sit there and do nothing. I didn't want to be in either when Mum got back. At the same time, I didn't have the car before then. I didn't feel like cycling. Maybe go somewhere on the bus?

Not into town again, though.

The moped!

I'd be able to get it going, surely?

I put my boots on, grabbed my anorak from the peg and put it on as I went over to the garage. Switched the light on and wheeled the moped out. Wiped away the cobwebs from it, and all the bits and debris that had collected in them. Fetched a bucket of water from the house and then washed it down. Cleaned and lubricated the spark plugs. I'd always enjoyed tinkering about with it, and Mum never chucked anything out, so everything I needed was there: motor oil, oil filter, cable grease and brake fluid. Once I'd changed the oil, I cleaned and lubricated the chain and adjusted the slack, before greasing the cables and eventually putting some petrol in the tank.

It started third go.

Vroom vroom!

I killed the engine and went back to the house, put a thick sweater on and a set of waterproofs, wondered for a moment if I should leave Mum a note, but decided she didn't need to know, took the crash helmet from the nail on the garage wall, kick-started the moped again and wobbled slowly out into the yard.

It was a model from the late sixties, but so simply and solidly built that it was running just as good twenty years on. Or maybe *good* was pushing it a bit; on the steeper gradients it could only just make it over the top.

My helmet was a black full-face job with a tinted visor; I'd thought it made me look hard when I was sixteen, completely unaware of how comical it actually came across, that cool helmet with such a feeble machine. Now of course, as I chugged across the flatland, I didn't think it was funny. The fog clung to the green spruce on the hillside across the river, making the top of the hill invisible. It looked as if the world came to an end there. Ahead of me, it was draped like a curtain at the end of the plain, the cluster of buildings that were the former shop, the garage and the disused petrol station seemed like the final outpost.

But once I'd gone past and up the short, steep climb that followed, a new world opened out, of spruce and heather, moss and upward-reaching deciduous trees, though it too was bounded by fog, and after the bend another, this one comprising a timber merchant's and a plant-hire firm in whose shared car park there stood three cars, gleaming with moisture, and an orange forklift backed up against a corrugated-metal fence.

I didn't know where I was going, I was just riding around. When I got to the bend where the main road entered the woods, I turned off for some reason down the narrow road to the right that led to the flatter bit where the church was.

I hadn't been there for ages. Probably not since my confirmation. But I could see nothing had changed when the church came into view ahead of me with the river grey and heavy behind it.

Dad was buried there. And Gran and Grandad on my dad's side. And Grandad's two brothers and their wives.

I hadn't thought about it when I'd turned off the main road, so that wasn't why I was there. But now that I was, I could just as well go over and pay my respects, I thought, and pulled in by the stone wall, turned off the engine, kicked the stand out, hung my helmet on the handlebars and went into the churchyard.

The oldest graves, from the end of the previous century, were those nearest the church itself, while the most recent were furthest away, Dad's right over by the wall at the far end.

On top of the hill was the old people's home. I couldn't help but smile when I saw it. They looked down on the churchyard. What had they been thinking, whoever's idea that had been? And what was it like for those who lived there to look out on a churchyard every single day, knowing that before long they'd be ending up there themselves?

Eww!

In the ground *right* under my feet lay the dead. In their hundreds.

Hey, there's one just gone over there, mate. Get her in the soil, then.

Hey, there's another. Get him in there as well.

Shovel plenty on top, and we'll say no more about it.

Again and again. Not just over the course of a few years, but hundreds, thousands, tens of thousands, hundreds of thousands of years. Non-stop. Dead, dead, dead. Soil, soil, soil. No prayer ever a help, there was no way out: bang, stop. Dead, soil, dead, soil for all eternity.

And we just accepted it.

Bloody hell. It was terrible once you got thinking about it.

It wasn't at all out of place, that question Joar had asked.

Why do we die?

Well, Dad died because he was driving too fast on a slushy road, the car skidded unfortunately, and unfortunately went over the kerb and ended up in the water.

There's always some explanation.

Every single death has its own explanation.

But not death as a whole. That has no explanation.

I stood in front of the headstone that had his name on it and looked across for a moment at the river that came gliding by, wide and calm after the rapids further upstream. The trees in the background were so still it was almost scary.

Syvert Løyning
1940–1977

A car engine sounded, and as I turned round I saw a red Toyota pull up behind my moped and could just about see the faces of an old man and an old woman through the windscreen.

I tried telling myself that red didn't exist, but it seemed so incomprehensible, seeing the red Toyota standing out so brightly in the grey surroundings.

The grave wasn't untidy, but it wasn't exactly immaculate either, which in a way was all right, I thought, and started to go back to the moped as the two old people with their white hair and moist-looking eyes came towards me.

I had a clear recollection of what Dad looked like, even with my eyes open I could picture him quite clearly. He was stored as a certain combination of electrical signals in my brain. A pattern of a kind, which didn't alter, a bit like the pattern in a rug.

That was basically what was left. A pattern in the brains of those who'd known him.

'Afternoon,' I said.

'Afternoon,' said the man, and his wife gave me a silent nod. He had a little rake and a trowel in his hand, while she carried a plastic bag that I took to contain flowers or a plant.

As I came round the other side of the chapel, I looked at the church itself with its thick white walls of stone, its green spire. I definitely hadn't set foot in there since my confirmation. The centre of false hopes, as I'd called the church in an essay I'd written when I was at gymnas. I should never have been confirmed, but none of the others had been opposed to it, and of course there was the money everyone gave you. What sort of fifteen-year-old could turn that down?

He rose from the dead on the third day, to return and judge the living and the dead — who actually *believed* that?

It was an insult to those left behind. Instilling such unrealistic hope in weakened souls should have been against the law, the same as telling cancer sufferers they'd get well again if only they'd swallow a spoonful of ash-tree essence.

I stopped at the moped, wiping the moisture absently from the saddle with one hand as I put my helmet on with the other.

I'd been fifteen years old, so it was only understandable I'd sold out for the money. And it was because everyone else was getting confirmed too, and because there was a camp afterwards, and everyone said it was the highpoint of eighth.

But I wasn't fifteen any more. I could choose to opt out.

I *ought* to opt out.

I fastened my helmet and got on the moped, started the engine. But then I switched it off again.

I could opt out now, while I was here.

I looked over at the clergy house. The lights were on.

Why not?

I crossed the road and went towards the house. My footsteps crunched in the still air. The house was whitewashed like the church, squat and big, with a garden that ran all the way down to the river, full of leafless old fruit trees and bushes.

I opened the gate, the black wrought iron was freezing cold to the touch, and went up to the side entrance where the pastor had his office. I rang the bell.

He took his time in there, but eventually he came to the door and poked his saggy face out.

'Hello, Syvert, is that you?' he said with a smile.

I was surprised he remembered me, my confirmation was years back, and he'd have instructed lots of candidate groups since then.

'Hello,' I said. 'I hope I'm not interrupting?'

'Not at all. Come in!'

He opened the door wide and stepped back. He had a grey cardigan on over a black shirt, and a pair of grey trousers. His feet were in a pair of thick, grey-white woollen socks that looked like they were home-knitted.

'You can hang your coat up over there,' he said, indicating with a nod the coat stand in the corner.

'I won't stop long,' I said, but took my coat off anyway; it was wet.

'Something to drink, perhaps? Coffee?'

'No thanks.'

'In that case, let's go inside, shall we?' he said, and showed me in room leading off the hall. A pair of sofas were positioned either side of a low table on a thick red patterned rug, and a desk stood in front of the window with a view of the church and whoever might be coming or going along the road. There was a fireplace too, with a fire burning in it.

'This is very homely,' I said. 'You could almost live here in this one room.'

He smiled.

'Thank you,' he said. 'I almost do, the time I spend here. Have a seat!'

'I won't stop long,' I said again, sitting down on the nearest of the two sofas.

'Do you mind if I smoke?' he said.

'No, not at all. Smoke all you like.'

He went over to the desk and came back with a packet of cigarettes and an ashtray.

'You haven't exactly been pounding on the door since your confirmation, Syvert.'

'I'm impressed you could even remember my name,' I said. 'You must have had a hundred kids in through the door since then.'

'But not many as eager as you to discuss everything.'

He lit a cigarette and the smoke curled into the air in front of him. He seemed livelier than I remembered him, more *present*, in a way. At the time of my confirmation there'd been something a bit listless about him, as if it had all been a dull routine. Someone said he was probably still depressed after his wife had died two years before.

That would be her standing beside him in the photo on his desk.

He looked at me without saying anything.

'I was thinking . . .' I said.

He raised his eyebrows slightly.

'The thing is I don't believe in God or Jesus, or any of that stuff. So I was thinking it's a bit hypocritical of me still belonging to the Church of Norway. Don't you agree? That it's hypocritical to stay a member?'

He nodded.

'That's fair enough, certainly,' he said. 'But what is it you don't believe in when you don't believe in God?'

'How do you mean?'

hat is it you don't believe in when you don't

re's anyone behind it all.'

ted itself?'

'Yes.'

He nodded a couple of times without saying anything.

'So, is there a form I need to fill in or something?'

'There is, yes,' he said. 'But is it so very urgent?'

'I wouldn't say it was *urgent* as such,' I said. 'But now that I'm here, I might as well get it done.'

'When you say there's no one behind it all, what do you mean by that exactly?'

'A god.'

'Would that be a person? Or a higher power of some sort, perhaps?'

'It wouldn't be a person, at any rate. But it wouldn't be a higher power either. That's what you worship, isn't it, a higher power? Or is it a father in heaven?'

'If there were no higher power, how then was the world created?'

'Big Bang.'

'You mean the entire universe came out of nothing?'

'Yes.'

'But why? And how?'

I shrugged again.

'A chemical reaction.'

'So the cat over there . . .' he said, nodding towards a cat I hadn't noticed that was lying stretched out on its side on the rug. 'Billions of years ago there was nothing, and out of that nothing the entire universe came into being in an enormous explosion? Which all on its own then led to a creature as advanced as that cat asleep over there, and not least to the two of us sitting here chatting? Out of nothing? An *explosion* out of *nothing*?'

He looked at me with a smile. His saggy cheeks made him look a bit like a dog.

'You're a pastor,' I said. 'It's your job to make people believe in fairy tales.'

'Doesn't Big Bang sound rather like a fairy tale, too?'

'It's science. It's proven. The world consists of atoms. That's what I believe. And I don't think I need to convince you I'm right just to opt out.'

He laughed.

'No, of course not. I'm just curious, that's all.'

'What do you believe in, then?' I said.

'I believe in God.'

'But what do you believe in when you believe in God?'

'I don't know. No one knows what God is.'

'So you believe in something, but have no idea what that something is? Well, that's confidence-inspiring, I must say.'

'We're human beings, Syvert. We see only what human beings can see. We understand only what human beings can understand. We know we're here, and we know it's not something we can take for granted. But we don't know how, or why. Do you agree?'

'No,' I said. 'We do know how. That's evolution. And the reason we don't know *why* is because no particular reason *exists*.'

He stubbed out his cigarette and got up.

'I want to quote you something,' he said.

I got up too.

'I've got to be going, actually,' I said. 'So if I could sign that form now?'

He didn't answer, but went over to the desk, opened one of the drawers and took out a book.

'There's something here to which I hope you'll give some thought.'

Again, he looked at me and smiled.

'Don't worry! It's just a single sentence. It goes like this: "Religion is the connection of humanity and the world with the absolute principle and focus of all that exists." '

He closed the book.

'Did you understand that?'

I shook my head.

'It was written a hundred years ago by a Russian philosopher called Solovyov. I like it because it goes both ways. Everything we see leads into the absolute principle, and from the absolute principle a focus radiates towards all that exists.'

'So the absolute principle is God?'

He looked out of the window at the road, where at the same moment a yellow car came driving along.

'It's not a definition of God, but a definition of religion. What he's saying is that religion is what connects us with the absolute principle. Which is to say, the teachings of Christ.'

He turned to face me again.

'Syvert?' he said. 'How about I send you that form in the post?'

'OK,' I said. 'As long as you send it.'

He laughed.

'Nice talking to you, Syvert.'

'Same here,' I said.

He followed me into the hall and saw me out. The yellow car had parked behind the red one and a woman in a dark blue coat was on her way into the churchyard. The old couple were still there, the woman bent forward over one of the graves, the man standing next to her.

As I put my helmet on and kick-started the moped, I realised I was feeling sad. I didn't know why, only that it wasn't because I'd visited my dad's grave. I assumed it had something to do with going to see the pastor. I put the moped into gear and set off along the wet road in the direction of the hill, it was clad with oak trees on both sides and still possessed a faint reddish tinge from all the leaves that had fallen in the autumn. But why visiting the pastor would have made me feel sad, I had no idea.

Mum stole a march on me and made us our tea that afternoon. She'd boiled some florets of fresh cauliflower in the ready-made cauliflower soup and heated up some frozen supermarket baps in the oven. I was eating at Dag's with his mum and dad later on, but that wasn't until seven, and I was starving, so I sat down with Mum and Joar as soon as the food was ready. Outside, the sun had come out and there wasn't a wisp of fog left. Apart from the temperature, it could almost have been a late afternoon in summer, I thought, with the wide blue sky and the rich light that slanted in through the window.

The feeling I'd had when I'd woken up that morning, of something not being right, had blown away.

Mum put the saucepan of soup on the table, the bread basket with the baps and the margarine next to it. A tractor was moving methodically across the field from one side to the other. The noise of its engine rose and fell as it approached and drew away. Some gulls followed in its wake as if it was a trawler and the fields were the sea it was ploughing.

'While I remember,' said Mum. 'The fluorescent light above the cooker's stopped working. Can you fix that, do you think, Syvert?'

'Of course.'

'Maybe they've got them at the shop.'

'Yes, they've got all sorts there,' I said. 'But if they haven't, I'll go to the supermarket in the morning. I could do that anyway, I'm sure we need to get some shopping in. Do you fancy coming with me, Joar?'

'Could do,' said Joar, his head lowered as he guided a spoonful of soup carefully towards his mouth.

'How did you get on at school today?' I said.

He sucked in air through his teeth and blew it out again in quick succession, presumably he'd got a hot piece of cauliflower in his mouth.

'All right,' he said after a few seconds, and gulped some water from his glass. 'We watched a film in general studies. It was quite good. *The Wave.*'

'Oh yes, *The Wave*!' I said. 'I've seen it a few times. It's brilliant.'

'Have you seen it, Mum?' he said.

'I don't think I have,' she said. 'What's it about?'

'It's about this teacher who performs an experiment with his class where he gets everyone to follow really strict rules so that they can understand what made Nazism possible,' he said, and looked up at me. 'That's right, isn't it?'

'Yes,' I said. 'The teachers love that film. I saw it three times when I was at school. It could be a warning against communism too, of course. Mention that to your teacher and see what he says!'

'She,' he said.

'Hm?'

'You said see what *he* says. But it's a she.'

'Ah,' I said.

'Are there any Nazis in our family, Mum?' he said.

'No, thank goodness,' she said.

'Only communists,' I said.

'There's one communist in our family, and that's Evert,' she said. 'You know perfectly well!'

'What about Dad, then?'

'Dad?'

'Yes. I saw he had some books in Russian. Which is a bit peculiar. Not many people have. Not round here at any rate.'

She looked at me in surprise.

'He studied Russian, so of course he'd have Russian books.'

'*Dad* did?' I said.

'Yes. Didn't you know?'

I shook my head.

'Hasn't anyone ever told you? He learned Russian in the military. He never put it to any use, though.'

'*Dad* went to the armed forces intelligence school and did their Russian course? But that's only for the real brains!'

'Your father wasn't stupid, you know.'

'But how come no one ever told me?'

'You were so young when he died. I never thought about it. I suppose I just assumed you knew.'

'Did you know?' I said, and looked at Joar.

He nodded.

I looked back at Mum.

'Is there anything else you've not told me about him?'

'There's no need to carry on about it, Syvert. You were eleven years old at the time.'

'Joar's twelve,' I said. 'You've obviously told him.'

'It cropped up, that's all. Anyway, what difference does it make if your dad did go there?'

'It makes a difference, because I didn't know! And it's not exactly a little detail. That's an elite course. People who've done it are politicians now or hold down key positions in the business world.'

'But he never put it to use.'

'That's beside the point!' I said, raising my voice. 'It's the principle that matters! He was my dad, for God's sake!'

I sprang to my feet and left the table. Even as I was going up the stairs I regretted it. Joar was there and everything. But I couldn't go back and sit down again and pretend nothing had happened, and I couldn't say I was sorry either, I'd be humiliating myself then, and I definitely didn't want Joar to see that.

I'd just have to stand by what I'd done.

Anyway, I had a right to be angry.

I put the new Metallica album on and lay down on my bed. In between songs I could hear the birds chirping in the trees outside and the rumble of the tractor that was still going backwards and forwards in the field.

I couldn't lie here.

I couldn't just go out either, not without saying where I was going. I hadn't told Mum I was going over to Dag's. Or had I?

No.

The softest of the album tracks kicked in, 'Welcome Home'. I tried to focus on listening to it instead of my thoughts. It was hardly thrash metal to begin with. More like a power ballad. But it built up gradually and got heavier as it went on.

Welcome to where time stands still
No one leaves and no one will

Instead of turning the record over when the needle locked into the final groove, I took it off and went for a shower. Once I'd got changed, I knocked on Joar's door.

'I'm off over to Dag's,' I said.

'OK,' he said.

'If Mum asks, that's where I am.'

'Haven't you got the guts to talk to her?'

I glared at him.

'Why wouldn't I have the guts to talk to her?'

'*I* don't know,' he said, and looked at the floor.

'It's only in case I don't see her before I go. OK?'

'OK, OK.'

Annoyed, I went down the stairs, put my anorak and shoes on and went and got the crash helmet out of the laundry room where I'd left it. Mum came into the hall as I was on my way out.

'We need to talk, Syvert. A proper talk. We can't be having this.'

You've only yourself to thank for it, I thought, but said nothing. She looked so troubled.

'I'm off over to Dag's,' I said. 'I don't know what time I'll be back.'

'Are you taking the car?'

'The moped.'

'Maybe we can talk when you come back, then.'

'Maybe,' I said, and closed the door behind me as I went out.

Dag and his family lived in a housing-estate house like any other from the seventies. The outside was painted black, the window frames were red, and on the parcel of land it had been built on, which like all the others on the estate was exactly one thousand square metres in area, a few tall pine trees grew between the ornamental shrubs and flower beds. At the bottom of the garden, where Einar had established a vegetable patch, there was an outcrop of moss-covered rock that for some reason had never been blasted away when the estate was being developed, and this remnant of the forest had always spoken to me in a way, even if I wasn't sure why. The bracken that grew against the low stone wall did too, and the little boggy area that lay behind it, where a few stunted birch trees poked up, before another garden began on the other side.

I parked at the edge of the drive, next to the bikes that were leaned up against the wall of the house, took my helmet off and rang the bell.

Einar came to the door.

'Syvert!' he said with a wide smile, and put out his hand. 'Long time no see!'

His grip was firm and dry, like himself.

'How's things?' I said as I followed him in.

The smell inside stirred up all kinds of emotions in me, all of them good.

'Oh, everything's fine here,' he said. 'How about yourself?'

'Not bad.'

'Not bad? Is that all?'

He laughed.

'Dag's not home yet. How about a cup of coffee?'

'That'd be good,' I said. 'It's a bit chilly on the moped. The weather's not that cold, though. I'm sorry if I'm a bit early. Dag did say seven o'clock.'

'Not at all, it's good to see you,' he said. 'Ida's gone to the shop. We discovered we had no cream.'

They'd done the place up since the last time I'd been there, I noticed straight away when we went up the stairs. New wallpaper, new furniture, and a completely new open-plan kitchen and living room where they'd knocked down the dividing wall.

'You've been busy here,' I said.

'Well, we had to do something, it was getting to feel like we were living in a museum.'

'It's very nice.'

'Do you think so?' he said, and smiled at me. 'We're pleased with it ourselves. Anyway, sit yourself down, I'll make us some coffee.'

I sat down on the sofa. It was new and blue with white cushions on it. There was a little pile of newspapers on the coffee table, mostly the one Dag wrote for. They'd always been very proud of him.

I wondered whether to ask Einar about Dad, seeing as we were on our own. I wanted to ask him if he knew Dad had been involved with someone else, and maybe if he knew who it had been. But if he didn't know, it was going to come as a shock, it'd ruin the whole evening, and even if we didn't talk about it, he'd still be thinking about it. And all I wanted really was to chat and have a nice evening with them.

My gaze drifted to the photos on the opposite wall. A big colour photo from their wedding, one from Dag's confirmation, one from when he was little, his first day at school maybe, and one from when he was a baby, lying starkers on a woolly rug.

'Do you take milk in your coffee, Syvert?' Einar said from the kitchen area.

'No, black's fine, thanks!'

He came over with a mug in each hand.

'There you are,' he said, putting mine down on the table in front of me. He pinched his trouser legs above the knee and hitched them up slightly before sitting down, he was that sort of bloke. Always properly dressed, shirt and slacks, corduroys perhaps, and the few times I'd seen him wear jeans they looked like they'd been pressed. His belt had to be the same colour as his shoes, and he wore a proper overcoat in winter, a blazer in summer.

He was so unlike Dad that it was hard to believe they could have been brothers. Dad was never exactly shabby in the way he dressed, but somehow there'd always been a hole in his sock, a stain on his pullover or his old trousers. I don't think I ever saw him polish his shoes. Their faces too were very different. Einar's was like a pencil drawing, narrow lips, thin nose, tight cheeks. Dad's features had been heavier, fleshier. Thick lips, a high brow, and his eyes had been darker too, richer in a way. His hair had been more unruly than Einar's was, he'd been going a bit thin on top, and the frames of his glasses were black and chunky, not thin and silvery like Einar's.

Einar was always striving, whereas Dad was content to be the person he was.

It hadn't occurred to me before.

But both enjoyed fiddling around with electronics and machines, anything that whirred or ticked. Dad was an air-force engineer for a good many years before taking on a civilian job only a couple of years before he died, whereas Einar had always worked as a civil engineer for the local authority. He was head of something now, I didn't know what exactly, but it was something to do with developing road infrastructure.

He could get really angry sometimes, I knew as much from Dag, but I'd never seen him like that myself, and Dag was still living at home, so it couldn't have been that bad.

'How's Evelyn?' he said.

'Good, I think,' I said. 'She works a lot, though.'

'We haven't seen her for ages. Give her our best. And Joar?'

'He's good, too. Bit of a clever clogs these days. He's as sharp as a knife.'

'How old is he now?'

'Twelve.'

'We should get together soon, all of us.'

'Good idea.'

'And how was the national service. Any use?'

'Well, it's taught me how to cook.'

'Is that what you're thinking of doing?' he said, gazing out the window.

'Kitchen work? You must be joking!'

'What plans have you got, then?'

He drank a mouthful of coffee and put his mug back down on the table.

I shrugged.

'Dreadful question, I know!' he said. 'You've plenty of time to work something out, though.'

'Yes,' I said.

Neither of us said anything for a moment.

'Dag said you were asking about your dad.'

'Was I?'

'I've maybe not been very communicative with you about him. And I probably should have been there for you a lot more than I have been.'

'What are you talking about?' I said with a laugh. 'I was here nearly every day for at least a few years. If that's not being there for me, I don't know what is.'

'Well, that's true, I suppose,' he said. 'Nice of you to see it that way.'

'And I'm not a kid any more, either.'

'So it's too late now, you mean?'

He smiled.

'Yes. What I haven't made sense of yet, I never will.'

'You're more right than you know,' he said. 'But *that's* something you won't understand until you're my age.'

'Understand what?'

'That we never get older, not really. It just looks that way. Inside, we're still nineteen, all of us.'

I couldn't work out if he was joking or not, and smiled a bit tentatively before having a drink of my coffee. Outside, the trees were swaying in the wind. Three birds came flying through the air; two of them settled in one of the pine trees over by the low stone wall, the third landed on the grass. It was those big black ones I'd noticed for the first time the other day.

Not the *same* ones, surely?

What a stupid thought.

There were some more birds in one of the fruit trees, little grey fluff-balls perched on the bare branches, probably sparrows.

'Do you want some more coffee?' he said.

'Yes, please.'

He took my mug and went into the kitchen area again. I stood up and went over to the window. Two kids in dark blue anoraks went by outside, one with a grey ball under his arm. There was a small football pitch tucked away a couple of hundred metres behind the houses, stamped earth with two goals, the neighbours had got together to put them up when we were little. I supposed that was where they were going.

Einar came back, handed me the mug and stood beside me looking out too.

'You'll remember quite a lot about your dad, I imagine?'

I nodded.

'I remember him well.'

'He was always a bit different from his siblings,' he said, continuing to gaze out of the window. 'When we were growing up, I mean.'

The two kids disappeared between the birch trees where the boggy bit began.

Some clouds scudded across the sky, the way they did in spring and autumn.

'In what way?' I said.

'He used to sit up at night, I remember. And he was extremely restless.'

I couldn't see how that set him apart from anyone, but I let it pass. I hoped he was going to tell me more.

'He was exceptionally bright at school. But of course you know that. Left gymnas with top marks in every subject.'

'I didn't know that,' I said.

'Didn't you?'

He glanced at me, I sensed, but I didn't look back at him.

'Joar's very much like your dad, the way I remember him when we were growing up,' he went on. 'You've got more of your mother in you, I'd say.'

Something sank inside me. Whatever it was that whirled up as it hit the bottom was grim and dismal. But I said nothing. What could I say? He'd made up his mind that was how it was. And why did I want to be like Dad? Dad had been dead half my life. And I'd never see him again.

'He could have become whatever he wanted. He was that capable.'

'But then why . . . ?' I began.

'Why didn't he make more of himself? Is that what you're thinking?'

I didn't answer. He did make something of himself. He'd done well.

I didn't want to hear any more and went back towards the sofa to change the setting, but Einar wasn't letting go.

'The thing about your father, Syvert, was that he suffered from anxiety. It was a hindrance for him.'

'Dad?' I said, and turned. 'How do you mean? What kind of anxiety?'

'Anxiety,' said Einar, still staring out of the window.

'But . . . ?'

'When you were little, he was off sick for a year. He should have been in hospital, but he stayed at home. Spent his days lying on the sofa or in bed. He ground to a complete halt. I was there many times, but there was nothing I could do. He couldn't be helped, or didn't want to be.'

I felt a stab in my chest.

'I didn't know anything about that.'

'No, it's never been an easy subject to broach.'

It occurred to me then that Einar must have been speaking to Mum about it. She'd asked him to tell me. There was no other explanation for it cropping up now, not when I'd just been asking her about him.

I sat down on the sofa. Einar came over and sat down on the one opposite.

'He could never lie down and rest his head on his arm, I remember, because he'd hear his pulse then and the fear of dying would come over him. We were just boys. But it never left him. He could be so afraid of dying that it disabled him completely.'

'But he was just normal when I was little,' I said. I felt almost nauseous, and cold. 'He didn't have anxiety then, or anything else, not as far as I can remember.'

'He went through his good and bad patches. And he was very conscious of making sure everything around you stayed settled.'

There was a silence. At the front of the house a car came up the road and pulled into the drive.

'That sounds like Ida,' he said, and looked at me. 'I hope that didn't come as a shock to you. It doesn't change anything. Your father was a good man in every respect, and being off work because of anxiety is a lot more common than you might expect. It doesn't *change* anything.'

So why are you telling me? I wondered.

'Syvert was *exceptionally* capable, but he was of a very nervous disposition. Meeting your mother was a stroke of luck. Everything fell into place for him then. He got a job like everyone else and made a good life for himself. Especially when you and Joar came along.'

'But he was right,' I said as the front door opened and Ida called a hello up the stairs.

'What do you mean?' said Einar.

'He was right to be afraid of dying. Because that's what happened, isn't it? He died.'

Einar looked at me as if I was stupid.

At the same moment, Ida came up the stairs, and behind her Dag.

'You again, is it?' he said. 'I thought we said seven o'clock?'

I stood up.

'Hi, Syvert,' said Ida, putting down the bag she was carrying to give me a hug. 'Good to see you!'

She stepped back and looked into my face, as if to scrutinise me.

'Good to see you, too,' I said. 'I hear there was a bit of a crisis.'

She gave me a puzzled look.

'Ran out of cream?'

'Oh, that!' she said, and laughed. 'Got the cream.'

'It'll be your famous potatoes *au gratin*, then?'

'Right first time!'

'Are you coming, or what?' said Dag, already on his way to his room.

After a few beers with Dag, followed by a glass of wine with the meal and a stiff cognac over coffee, I wasn't competely sober as I rode back in the dark, but not exactly drunk either.

The air was icy cold and the sky twinkled with stars.

It was as if there'd been two different people inside me when we'd been having dinner. One on his own, immersed in thought, so filled with confusion he couldn't think at all, and another who chatted and laughed.

Or no, that wasn't it.

It was more like my thoughts had been trying to get away from my feelings, which to a certain extent they managed, removing themselves at least far enough to be unconcerned with them, even if they could still sense them. They knew they were there, and that it was important they kept their distance.

There was nothing shocking as such about what Einar had said.

Dad had suffered from anxiety and had been off work for a year because of it.

It was just that it didn't accord with the picture I had of him. It was way off. It wasn't *my dad* at all. To me, he'd been nothing but solid, stable, dependable, calm, unflappable. That he'd been tormented by anxiety was something I'd never have guessed. And I'd never have thought anyone could think he'd never made anything of himself.

So what *was* the truth?

Was the picture I had of him false? Had he *in fact* been a different person altogether?

But what hurt the most was what Einar had said about me not being like Dad, and that it was Joar who was.

I'd always thought of myself as taking after him. I may have been a bit taller, and more powerfully built, but as far as I was concerned we shared the same level-headed temperament, the same sociability. I liked the same sort of things as he used to like. Tinkering about with the bikes and the moped, woodwork, fishing, shooting. And even if he'd never played football himself, he'd always been interested and had taken me to the match in town a few times. We'd watched Norway together on the telly, and FA Cup finals as well.

Had he been riddled with anxiety then? Had he been nervous and afraid then?

And how did the relationship he'd embarked on fit in with that?

Einar had said everything had fallen into place in his life when he'd met Mum. That couldn't be true. Einar wouldn't know anything about their relationship. If he did, he wouldn't have put it like that, surely?

Or maybe he just wasn't aware that I knew.

He was constructing a version of Dad's life for me. Keeping his own version to himself.

Exhausted and confused by all these new thoughts, I tried to put them aside. Dad was dead, it didn't matter what he'd said or done, or who he was.

Look after Joar, that was his message to me.

Joar was *now*.

Bloody hell, it was freezing!

The air was that much more raw by the river and gusted cold as I rode along.

Footy tomorrow.

Maybe I'd get twenty minutes. That'd be good.

Maybe a goal too?

I crossed the bridge and turned up the drive. The lights were on in the windows, darkness all around, tiny glittering stars strewn across the sky.

My hands were red and I was shivering as I got off the moped. It was all I could do to unfasten my helmet.

'Hi, Syvert,' said Mum as I stepped into the hall. I put my helmet away in the laundry room, hung my anorak, so sadly inadequate, on the peg and poked my head into the kitchen. She was doing a cross-word and smoking.

'Hi,' I said. 'I'm going to have a shower then straight to bed.'

'You do that,' she said, and smiled. 'Did you have a nice time?'

'Yes — they all said to say hello.'

'Thanks,' she said.

'Did you ask Einar to have a word with me about Dad?'

'No. What makes you think that?'

She sounded like she was telling the truth. Not that she couldn't lie. She'd done it before.

'Just wondered,' I said. 'Goodnight.'

*

The first thing I did when I got dressed the next morning was go to the mailbox at the end of the drive. Might as well get it over with, I thought as I lifted the lid, took the newspaper and unfolded it.

The photo of me covered half the front page. I realised immediately why the photographer had wanted me to sit at one end of the bench. It made me look lonely. She'd got me to look away as well, and there I was, staring into the distance like I was completely lost.

But the headline was worse. My stomach hurt when I saw what it said.

SYVERT (19): FROM NATIONAL SERVICE TO JOBLESS — 'NO FUTURE FOR ME'

They'd made me out to be a loser.

But I'd told them that was the one thing I didn't want!

The bastard. The absolute fucking bastard.

I hid the paper under my anorak so that Mum wouldn't see it if she happened to look out of the window, and then stuffed it under some rubbish in the bin.

'It hasn't come,' I told her. She was standing at the worktop slicing a loaf, a steaming saucepan on the cooker beside her.

'Hasn't it? That's funny. It's gone eleven o'clock. It won't be coming at all now, then.'

She put the slices of bread in the bread basket and looked at the clock, then took the saucepan off the hob.

'Yes, it will. The paper boy's having a lie-in, that's all.'

'Give them a ring and tell them, would you?' she said, and poured the boiling water carefully into the sink before turning the tap on and letting cold water gush into the saucepan. The eggs clunked against each other.

'The newspaper offices? There's not much point in that. I'll buy one when I go out, if you want.'

'Honestly, Syvert,' she said, glancing at me before putting the eggs in a bowl she then placed on the table. 'We've paid for that paper. I can't afford to buy things twice. Give them a ring, they'll send someone out with it. Or else we'll get two on Monday.'

'OK,' I said.

'Give Joar a shout, will you?'

I nodded, went to the stairs and called his name. When he came and sat down, I saw him in a new light. Dad as a boy.

Had Dad always started such serious conversations?

Brainy, unable to tell a lie.

That journalist had put one over on me.

Taken me for a ride.

I sawed the top off my egg with my knife, sprinkled salt inside its little lid, dug out the white flesh with my spoon and popped it in my mouth before salting the yolk and scooping out nearly half the egg in one go.

That's why he'd kept going on about the future. He knew exactly what he wanted.

'What plans have you got for the future?' he'd asked.

'Nothing in particular,' I'd answered. It was the truth, I'd just done my stint in the armed forces and was planning on taking it easy for a few months before deciding what I was going to do. But that wasn't what he was after.

'But not having a job, that makes things difficult, doesn't it?' he'd gone on.

'Yes, I suppose it does a bit.'

'So if you're looking at the future, what do you see?'

'I don't know, really.'

'Does it look bright, do you think? Or is it less straightforward than that?'

'Probably less straightforward, I imagine. But that's OK.'

'So what do you think about when you think about the future?'

'I don't go round thinking about it that much, to be honest.'

'But if you had to?'

'Then I'd think: what future?' I'd said and laughed.

'So you don't think you've got a future, is that it?'

He'd grinned as if he was just carrying on the joke.

'Something like that, yes,' I'd said.

He'd tricked me deliberately. And there was nothing I could do about it.

Mum got up and came back with the coffee pot.

'Do you want some?'

'Yes, please,' I said, holding out my mug and glancing at Joar. 'Do you want to go to the shop with me afterwards?'

'Walking or taking the car?'

'The car. We'll go to the supermarket.'

'All right.'

After I'd found a space in the shopping centre's enormous car park, which was nearly full, it struck me I might actually be recognised. The whole region read that newspaper.

I took a trolley outside the entrance, found the shopping list Mum had made out and with Joar beside me went into the brand-new hangar of a shopping centre, trying my best to look casual and to think about something else. But it was easier said than done, there were racks of newspapers outside the supermarket kiosk to the right as you went in, as well as at all the checkouts. And the papers themselves were all placed with the headline and the photo of me facing out, visible to any-one who cared to look.

'Will you get some chops?' I said to Joar. 'Some beefburgers and some bacon?'

'How many?'

'You can decide when you get there.'

I dropped two loaves into the trolley and a woman my mum's age who I'd never seen before stared at me. She looked away when I looked back at her.

They could think what they liked.

But not Joar. I didn't want him to see.

I took some fish fingers and some fillets of cod, a packet of beef burgers and some bags of peas and chips from the frozen counters.

Joar stopped in front of the trolley and put his items in it.

'I got six chops,' he said. 'Two for each. Is that all right?'

'That's fine. What kind of pizza do you like best?'

'Grandiosa.'

Of course, it could have been my good looks that had grabbed her attention, I reasoned, and put four pizzas in the trolley.

'What are you smiling at?' said Joar.

'Was I smiling?'

'Yes, like this,' he said, and put on a smug-looking smile.

'I was thinking about something,' I said, and carried on down the aisle.

'About what?'

'Nosy! A joke, that's all.'

'What sort of a joke?'

'All right,' I said, looking obliquely at him as he walked along with his hands in the pockets of his quilted body warmer, his shoulders slightly hunched. 'Did you hear about the man who hated fish so much he kept sausages in his aquarium?'

'That wasn't what you were thinking about, no way. You've told me that one loads of times.'

'It's a good one, though!'

'If you're five years old, it is.'

'All right, clever clogs,' I said. 'Have you got a better one?'

'As a matter of fact, yes,' he said, and looked up at me with a big grin on his face.

'Go on, then.'

'What's the skin around a woman's cunt called?'

'Hey,' I said. 'You're not old enough to be telling jokes like that.'

'Do you give in?'

'That depends,' I said.

'The woman,' he said, and looked at me in anticipation.

I laughed. Not so much at the joke, more because it was him telling it.

'You can tell that one to your friends,' I said. 'And to me. But not to anyone else. Do you hear me?'

'I'm not stupid, you know.'

'Now, we need a bag of flour and a bag of sugar. And some yeast as well. Can you get that for me?'

While he was gone, I got some eggs, milk and yogurt, and thought again about how I was going to keep him away from the newspaper racks.

Something he could fetch from the car?

No, what would that be?

I looked in the direction of the checkout lanes. Behind them was the kiosk. And the betting corner!

He could fill in a pools coupon. That would keep him occupied. He'd be concentrating so much he wouldn't be able to think about anything else.

'Do you want to fill in a pools coupon for me?' I said when he came back.

'The football pools?'

'Yes. You can do one for twenty kroner. As long as you win, mind!'

I told him he could go over and get started and as soon as I was finished I'd come and pay. He went straight there as I put the first of my items on the conveyor.

The girl on the checkout didn't look at me, not even when I handed her the money, and no one else paid me any attention either, despite my picture staring at them from all eight checkouts.

In the car on the way home, Joar went on at length about all the predictions he'd made and why. It sounded like he knew the names of every player on every team, not only in Norway but also in England.

When Mum still used to read to him at bedtime, he'd known all the books by heart. He only needed to listen to them once or twice and he'd be able to tell you everything that was in them. He used to pretend-read on his own, I remembered.

The sun came out between the clouds and he went quiet. It changed the mood of the landscape completely, no longer oppressive, but open.

Streams rushing white down the hillsides, clouds hastening across the sky, driven by the strong wind that made everything flap and flutter.

'When can we go camping again?' said Joar.

I shrugged.

'The weather will need to get a bit better first, I think.'

'I suppose so.'

'But we could go off for the day somewhere, if you like?'

'Yes, I'd like that.'

He looked at me.

'Can we go out in the canoe today?'

'Maybe not today,' I said, indicating left while waiting for two cars to come past so I could turn onto the drive.

'That's what you always say.'

'What?'

'You always say *some other day.*'

'That's because I've got other things to do,' I said, slowing down as we turned onto the gravel and spinning the steering wheel to avoid the potholes.

'Like what? You never do anything.'

I glanced at him.

'You do know I just got home after a year and a half in the armed forces?'

'So what?'

'Listen, you cheeky thing. We can have a short paddle upstream this afternoon. But only because you're pestering me, not because I want to.'

'Hooray. At two o'clock?'

'Why not three minutes to?'

'Deal,' he said, and grinned.

I turned in and pulled up in front of the house. Joar helped me take the shopping bags inside and I started putting the things away while he went upstairs to his room.

'Syvert?' Mum said from the living room.

'What is it?'

'Come here a minute.'

I put the empty carrier bag I had in my hand in the drawer and went in.

She was sitting on the sofa with the paper in her lap.

'It came, then!' I said.

'What's all this about?' she said. 'You're not unemployed! You only got home from doing your service a week ago.'

I shrugged.

'Dag asked me to do it. I was doing him a favour.'

'You humiliate yourself for the whole village to see, and now it's Dag's fault?'

'I'm not humiliating myself at all. It's just a normal interview. And what it says isn't untrue.'

'Have you no pride?'

'Mum,' I said, 'it's nothing to get worked up about. It's only an interview.'

'What do you think your father would have had to say?'

I turned round and went into the hall, snatched my anorak, slammed the door and got in the car, started the engine and drove off.

To hell with her.

Always sticking her oar in. Always knowing best.

She was a bloody cleaning woman.

Never a good word to say about anyone. Always having a go. Miserable as bloody sin.

I had to get away. Not just for now, for ever.

The river gleamed softly beyond the fields, glittered between the trees as the valley narrowed in on it a few kilometres further on. Without actually deciding to, I turned off towards the track in the forest, the lake. The houses and farms became more scattered, and then there was nothing but the forest to see. Not a human being anywhere, not a car. It suited me fine.

Why was everything so difficult all of a sudden?

It hadn't been before.

And it wasn't because anything had *happened*.

Dad hadn't left Mum, they'd still been married when he died. And Einar had probably always been jealous of Dad, if he really had been as capable as he said he was. Dad's illness would have been to Einar's advantage then, so it was possible he'd been exaggerating to big himself up.

It was quite likely, in fact.

To my surprise, the red Lada was still parked in the turning area. I pulled up beside it, got out, locked the door, and peered in through its side window again. Everything was exactly the same as before, it didn't look like it had been anywhere since.

Could she have had an accident? Was she lying out there in the forest somewhere with a broken leg?

If she didn't have a cabin she was staying in. That wasn't inconceivable. New cabins were appearing all over the place these days. Mostly in designated areas, but some people liked a bit of solitude, and there'd just as likely be a plot or two available here once in a while as anywhere else.

Anyway, it was none of my business.

I put the key in my anorak pocket and trudged off up the path.

*

When I got back, the red Lada was gone. It was a bit disappointing for some reason. A little mystery had come to an end.

At least she wasn't lying distressed in a ravine somewhere.

I got in, turned the ignition and pulled away down the hill.

It was just gone two o'clock, so I didn't have that much time, I was playing football at four and needed to be there an hour before kick-off. I'd still make it, though.

No future for me.

Everyone would think it was what I'd said. That it was what I thought and believed.

And with the photo on top of that they'd think I felt sorry for myself.

That was why Mum had felt ashamed of me. *What will other people think?* was always the first thing that came into her mind.

They could think what they bloody well liked, I told myself.

All the ways she had of expressing her disapproval. It didn't matter what I did, there was always going to be something wrong. I was like a fish on her hook. Every now and then she'd cut me some slack and I'd think I was free, but then she'd reel in again and I could put up as much of a fight as I wanted, she was always in control.

There was only one thing to do about it.

I came down the hill by the bridge and turned onto the main road, which was busier now. It was blowing a fair bit. It wouldn't be conducive to a good game of football. But then neither was the bumpy pitch.

It was never much fun when conditions had too much of a say.

As I came past the shop, where the local paper was piled up in the rack, it occurred to me that *everyone* I knew, the neighbours, people I'd gone to school with, relatives and friends, would now be seeing my photo on the front page and reading the headline. What's more, they'd be talking about it too.

You know Syvert, don't you? Things haven't quite turned out for him, have a look at this.

Syvert Løyning? Evelyn's lad? Poor woman, having a layabout like that for a son. Look here.

There's something about Syvert Løyning in today's paper. I knew his father, of course. He was called Syvert as well. Very sharp mind. Highly intelligent he was. Not much of a chip off the old block there, it seems.

The clock on the dashboard said twenty to three when I turned up the drive. Only then did it hit me that Mum might be working. In which case she'd have needed the car an hour ago.

Oh no.

I parked out front and hurried in.

The house was all quiet. The radio and television were switched off and there was no one in the living room or the kitchen.

'Mum?' I called out.

Her voice came back from upstairs, but so faintly I couldn't make out what she said. It was unusual, so I went up the stairs to check.

'Where are you?' I said.

'In here,' she said.

I opened the bathroom door. She was sitting on the floor with the wash bucket next to her.

'I felt such a pain in my back,' she said. 'I can't get up.'

'How long have you been sitting here?'

'Not that long.'

'Let me help you,' I said. I bent down, took her by the armpits and pulled her upright.

She was a lot lighter than I'd expected.

'Help me into the bedroom, will you? I don't think I can manage on my own.'

'Have you pulled a muscle, do you think?' I said, and put my arm around her for support.

'I don't think so. It's further in than that. I think you'll have to carry me. Can you manage?'

I carried her like a child to her room, drew the duvet aside and put her down on the bed.

'What do you think it is?'

'Nothing. It's my back, that's all. All it needs is a bit of rest.'

'OK. But if it's no better tomorrow, I'll take you to the doctor's.'

'There's no need for that. You could get me an aspirin, though.'

I did, and a glass of water. She took two, then closed her eyes. I looked at Dad's side of the bed, his bedside table, then at the aerial photo of the house when it had still been part of a working farm.

'You should have a bell you can ring if you need anything!' I said.

What if she needed the loo? I thought then. Would she need help for that too?

'Does it still hurt?'

'Not really. Just a bit. It'll be better tomorrow.'

'I hope so.'

'Joar's over at Rickard's.'

'OK. How long's he staying there?'

'I don't know.'

'I've got to get going in a minute,' I said. 'I'm playing football. I could take him with me, I suppose. Then when we get back I can make us something to eat.'

'Thanks, Syvert.'

'Are you going to be all right?'

'Yes.'

'OK. I'll be off, then. See you later.'

'Take care,' she said, and lay looking at the ceiling as I closed the door behind me.

Joar's friend Rickard lived on a small farm that was tucked inside a dell on the other side of the river. His father farmed part-time, like so many others in the area, the rest of the time he had a job with the local authority. As I parked the car outside he came out of the woods with a chainsaw in his hand, in blue overalls, high-leg safety boots and a safety helmet.

I lifted my hand in a wave and he waved back. I caught sight of Rickard's sister Helene through the kitchen window. I remembered her from secondary school, she'd been in seventh when I was in ninth, she was decent-looking, even if she had always come across as a bit of a prude. At least to me.

I went to the door and could see she was baking.

I rang the bell. A dog barked inside, followed by a kid's voice telling it to be quiet.

The dog was called Thief, Joar had told me once. It was for a joke, it meant they could shout *Stop, Thief!* when it ran away from them.

They probably didn't think it was funny any more.

Rickard opened the door with one hand, holding the dog back by its collar with the other. Its claws clicked and scraped against the stone floor.

'Hi, Rickard,' I said. 'Is Joar here?'

'I'll go and get him,' he said, and disappeared again.

Behind me, his dad came over.

'Hello there,' he said as I turned round.

'Hi, how's it going?' I said.

'Fine,' he said, halting in front of me. 'I hear you're in a bit of a spot at the moment?'

It took a few seconds before I realised what he meant.

'No, not at all. That journalist's just blown things up out of all proportion.'

His head was big, his face flat and broad, his yellow hair thin, and the skin around his eyes and mouth was creased. A pot belly bulged in his overalls, making them too tight around the waist. He'd always been a jovial sort, but I'd noticed his eyes were different from the rest of him, they were always so serious.

'How long have you been out of work now?' he said.

I couldn't tell him a week, he'd wonder what all the fuss was about.

'A while,' I said instead. 'Not that long.'

Joar appeared in the doorway.

'You said we were going out in the canoe at two o'clock,' he said, as if Rickard's dad wasn't there at all. 'Why didn't you come? You promised! That's three promises in a row you've broken!'

'Something came up,' I said. 'Something important. Anyway, you can come with me now. We're in a bit of a hurry.'

'Why? Where are we going?'

'Up to Solvallen. I'm playing in a football match.'

'I'm not going.'

I glanced at Rickard's dad and smiled.

'You've got to, I'm afraid. I'll explain in the car.'

'No,' he said. 'I'm staying here.'

A sudden rage welled in me.

Behind him, Helene went through to the living room without looking at us.

'Joar,' I said as gently as I could. 'You've got to come with me. It's not up for discussion.'

'No!' he said, and glared at me in defiance.

'He's no bother,' said Rickard's dad. 'You can come and collect him after your football, if it makes things easier.'

I felt like grabbing hold of Joar and dragging him to the car, it didn't matter how much of a fuss he kicked up, shake some reason into him. This was about more than his own little world. Mum was in bed, in pain, and all he could think about was himself.

I steadied my breathing as I turned to Rickard's dad.

'Are you sure?'

'Yes, no bother.'

'All right,' I said, and looked back at Joar.

He smiled at me sarcastically.

'As long as you know you're coming with me when I get back.'

'Yes, master,' he said, and disappeared into the house again.

'Thanks,' I said to Rickard's dad. 'I'll see you later, then.'

By the time I came into the changing room, everyone else was already there. It wasn't good, all focus was on me straight away.

'Here he is, local celebrity!' said Glenn.

'How come you're late? Job interview, was it?' said Karsten.

'You've got no future on this team, that's for sure,' said Svein.

They all laughed.

I tried to think of something witty to say, about the future being in our own hands and wanking, only the wording wouldn't quite come together, so I gave up after a few seconds, laughed with them and sat down on the bench next to Gjert, where I started getting changed. Some of them were all ready in the new kit. Blue shirts and white shorts as always, but this season they'd jazzed the shirts up with a white stripe that ran diagonally across the chest.

Terje tossed me a set and gave me a wink. They'd given me number thirteen.

'Right, now that we're all here,' said the trainer. 'It's windy as hell today, so no long balls out from the back, not if you can avoid it.'

'I didn't think we were supposed to, anyway,' said Vegard.

'That'll do. Now listen. Trond and Karsten, Keith and Glenn, I want you getting past their first press when we play out from the back, *no exceptions*. As soon as you're through, you look for Gjert or Atle. Gjert and Atle, that's when you drop deep. Make yourselves playable. Svein, you do what you want, but *don't* lose the ball when we're going forward. Kjetil, I want shots from outside the box. As soon as they're on the ball, what do we do? We *press* like bloody hell. Now, you've been training well all winter, and what have you been training for? To *win*. And in order to *win* you've got to *run*. If you run, we'll win this. I want you tasting blood after ten minutes. Run, run, run. Press, press, press. Win, win, win. Right?'

'Right,' everyone mumbled back.

'RIGHT?' he shouted.

'RIGHT!'

Everyone got up and filed out, but I was still getting changed. There was nothing in the world as cold as watching football in spring and autumn, and seeing as I didn't think I'd be coming on, I wrapped up warm: shorts, socks, tracksuit bottoms, shirt, hoody and windproof training jacket.

'Do you want to play, Syvert?' the trainer said when I came trotting out to the bench.

'Yes, of course,' I said.

'In that case, you get here on time,' he said as he looked out across the pitch where the eleven who were starting came jogging towards us side by side as they warmed up.

'Yes,' I said. 'I'm really sorry about that.'

'I realise you're going through a hard time at the moment. But if you're going to play for us, you don't come late.'

'I won't, I promise. Sorry about that.'

He turned his back on me and went over to Terje, who was out on the pitch with a stack of cones and a net full of balls.

That bloody interview.

I wasn't going through a hard time at all. I was getting along fine. But the interview made me look like some sorry deadbeat.

Dag wasn't going to hear the last of this.

Terje slung a few balls over to the other subs. I jogged over and we started kicking them about between us, long passes from one side of the pitch to the other.

How could kicking a ball be so much fun?

But it was.

I tried to make every pass perfect and relished every touch.

Playing in an actual game was different, everything was chaotic then, there was never any time, and often I just ran around, hoofed the ball up the pitch if it came my way, half in panic, though most of the time I never even got near it. But sometimes, strangely enough it always seemed to be in the autumn, it was as if a great calm settled in me, everything was so easy then, when I got the ball I'd always have plenty of time, I could drive forward with it, dribble past a couple of opponents, the pitch almost opening out for me, I could see every movement, even at the very edges of my field of vision, and could thread a decisive pass through a defence if the space was there.

It was strange, because my technique, physical condition and reading of the game were no better or worse then than at any other time. I imagined that was what it meant to be good, what really set the good players apart from the mediocre, that there was never a hint of panic in them and that they could do what they did regardless of the circumstances, no matter how hard the press.

One of the lads from my class at gymnas, Tore, was on the books of a first division team now. He'd started college and got in touch with the local club in his new town, played for their academy and then after a couple of months graduated to the senior squad. He hadn't had a game yet, but he'd been on the bench. Which was brilliant in itself. We'd played together for the school and he'd never actually been *that* good, technically he wasn't much better than me. It was his composure that made the difference.

The eleven who were starting went back into the changing room. I jogged about a bit to keep warm, with one eye on Kilsund who were doing a five-a-side drill. They looked like they were good. But then so did every team before the match got started.

Vegard came jogging up alongside me.

'Sorry to read that interview,' he said. 'I didn't know things were that bleak for you.'

I rolled my eyes.

'I'm absolutely fine. The journalist made a meal of it, that's all.'

'I've got an uncle in town,' he said. 'I could ask if he needs anyone? If you're interested?'

'What does he do?'

'He runs an undertaker's business.'

I stopped in my tracks and looked at him.

'Are you having me on?'

He smiled.

'No, seriously.'

'You think I'd want to work in a bloody *undertaker's*? Is there something the matter with you?'

'I'm sure it's not that bad. It's just lugging coffins, isn't it? And you wouldn't have to work there for ever.'

I started jogging again. He followed suit.

'It could tide you over, until you sort yourself out,' he went on.

'Give over,' I said, and kicked him one of the loose balls we passed. He toe-poked it back, I stopped and waited until he was a bit further away before floating him a pass just as our opponents headed back to the changing room and their reserves started doing what we were doing.

'Do you want me to ask, then?' Vegard shouted once he'd collected the ball.

'Over my dead body!' I shouted back.

'Ha ha!'

On the terrace behind me, a few spectators had turned up already. Twenty or so people standing around, a few cigarettes in mouths, a hot dog poised in a hand here and there. A few more came straggling across the road.

It wasn't much of a terrace, barely more than a few slabs of concrete dumped along one side, the rudiments of a proper terrace that had never got any further.

Girlfriends would come, a few dads, the odd brother or sister, and a steadfast core of old-timers who'd played for the club in years gone by. Occasionally there'd be players from the juniors or the old boys, maybe a group of secondary-school girls who were bored and looking for something to do. Never more than fifty in all, rarely fewer than twenty.

Some would watch from their cars on the other side of the pitch.

The eleven starters came trotting out and I went and sat down on the bench. Keith had leggings on under his shorts. Leggings or gloves in a match were a no-go, too girly. Keith was the only one exempted.

They ran a few circles, each on his own, while waiting for the other team to appear. When they came out, in red shirts and green shorts, Mads got off the bench and clapped his hands together.

'Give it all you've got, lads!' he yelled in his tinny voice.

The ref, who was about the same age as me, his cheeks pockmarked with acne scars, and the sort of mouth where the lips never quite closed properly over the teeth, blew his whistle and got the game started.

'They look like a bunch of Christmas trees,' I said to Vegard, who was sitting beside me.

'They do and all,' he said.

'Are they any good, do you know?'

'They played in the division above us last season, so they should be fairly decent, I reckon.'

The ball was played back to their central defender who wellied it up the park. Trond rose up and headed it away, straight to a little Kilsund player who immediately fed it wide, their wing-back bursting past the wrong-footed Keith to receive the ball in full flight and tear down the line. Our defenders raced back, but one of their strikers had read what was happening and was all on his own in the box when the delivery came.

One—nil to them.

'What the hell are you playing at?' Mads screeched.

'We're too high up the pitch,' Vegard said to me in a low voice.

Kjetil kicked off, Vennesland played it back to Gjert, who gave it to Atle. Straight away, two Kilsund players were all over him and all he could do was play it back to Karsten. But Karsten's first touch was too heavy, and their striker nicked it from him, seamlessly touching it on to one of theirs as he spun round and headed towards our goal. The pass that came back to him from the same little player as before was perfectly weighted into his path. Kjell Inge came rushing out of his goal and made himself big and star-shaped, only for the striker to drill it far-post, low into the goal.

Mads put his head in his hands.

'What the hell's going on?' said Vegard.

'They've had nine touches and are two–nil up,' I said. 'That's what's going on.'

'Atle and Karsten!' Mads shouted. 'Pull your fingers out!'

Karsten looked towards the bench and threw his arms in the air.

'We haven't even had the ball yet,' said Vegard.

'Two presents for the Christmas trees,' I said.

'Gjert!' Mads shouted. 'Atle!'

When they looked across, he waved his hand a few times to shift them back into more defensive positions.

Gjert nodded.

'We need to be going the other way, if you ask me,' Vegard said quietly.

'It'll be ten–nil by half-time if we do that,' I said.

'Ten–one,' he said.

We couldn't get our game together, kept giving the ball away after only a couple of passes, but at least we didn't concede further before the break. Basically, we were playing six at the back and all we could do when we got the ball was play it long up the park. Karl and Vennesland would chase like a pair of dogs up there, but always in vain, the ball was gone by the time they got anywhere near. Svein had barely had a touch all first half. Kilsund's playmaker, the little wiry lad with the long hair who looked like he was no more than sixteen, was all over it; every ball went through him, he was bossing the game for them, slipping away from every challenge with a little dummy or a flick, firm, accurate passes forward to their strikers or out wide to their wing-backs, playing the long cross-field pass if it was on, going short whenever it was advantageous. I'd never seen such a good player at this level. Svein was probably just as good technically, one on one, but he didn't bring anything to his team the way this lad did.

'What's happened to you?' said Mads at half-time. He was standing in the middle of the room with a tactics board in his hand. 'Have you forgotten *everything* we've done in training during the winter?'

'No, but they're bloody good,' said Karsten.

'So are you,' said Mads. 'As long as you do as we agreed. You're panicking as soon as you get the ball. Calm down! Play each other. It's not rocket science. Make them run.'

'That's easy for you to say,' said Karsten.

Mads glared at him.

'As easy as putting you on the bench, in fact. Vegard, you're in at centre-back. Syvert, you go in for Atle.'

Karsten shook his head and stared at the floor, but said nothing.

'If we sit as deep in the second half as we have done in the first, we'll lose the game,' said Mads, lifting up his board. 'We need to get up the field. And we need to keep hold of the ball. Kjetil, you stay up top. Svein, you go in behind Kjetil, into this area here.'

He moved the coloured magnet that was Svein further into the middle, the two that were Gjert and me in behind, and then one either side of us.

'We've got to win the midfield, so we're going four-five-one. Syvert, you've seen their seven?'

I nodded.

'Get as close to him as you can, OK?'

'You want me to stick to him?'

'No, you don't need to follow him all the time, but you've got to get in close when he's on the ball. Without him, they're not nearly as impressive. Svein, your job is to hold on to it until reinforcements arrive. Kjetil, shoot at every opportunity. And Trond, for Christ's sake, when they're on the break and there's none of ours around, you've *got* to get in there. That goes for one on ones as well. OK? They scored twice in two minutes. So can we. Now, get out there and show me what you're all about. And stay calm for fuck's sake!'

'So we're meant to run around like madmen *and* stay calm,' Vegard said as we jogged onto the pitch.

'I can't believe he thinks we can *play* our way out,' I said. 'We're a bunch of clodhoppers next to this lot.'

Kjetil got the second half started, rolling it to Svein, who strode forward on his own. He went past the first man, but got stopped by the second, and the ball was kicked high into our half. Trond headed it back, Gjert picked it up in midfield and played it to me, and straight away I hoofed it blindly forwards.

'Take your time, Syvert!' Mads shouted. 'Play your nearest man!'

I ran to pick up their little number seven, who looked at me and smiled. He knew what was happening.

'They always put the ugly ones on me,' he said to one of theirs, making sure I could hear him.

He was already asking for it then.

He jogged towards his own half. Their centre-backs played it between them a couple of times, before one of them put it out to the wing-back, who then touched it on to one of their midfielders who came to receive. I was right on the back of their number seven, knowing the ball was coming to him, but it was no use, as soon as the pass was made and I wound my leg around him to get the first foot on it, he flicked it to his right, turned and left me on my arse. I got up as fast as I could and legged it after him. He'd got the ball again now, his flick of course having found one of his own, and now he threaded it low and hard in between Trond and Vegard to their striker, who fortunately was unable to control it.

He winked at me as I came up beside him again.

Kjell Inge bounced the ball a couple of times in front of him as he prepared to launch it upfield.

'We *play* it out from the back!' Mads yelled.

But Kjell Inge waved us up the pitch, took a couple of steps forward and sent the ball arcing high over the midfield. Kjetil won the header and the ball landed for Svein, who immediately cut into the box, dummied the wing-back and got his shot away even before it seemed possible, so although there wasn't much power in it, the keeper was wrong-footed and had no way of reacting as the ball passed him and went in off the near post.

Svein wheeled away with one arm in the air. The rest of the team ran up to celebrate with him, me bringing up the rear, keeping a bit of distance rather than diving in.

'Well done, lads!' Mads shouted.

His upper body inclined forward as he clapped his encouragement.

For the rest of the match I marked their seven as close as I could. He was a cut above, ghosting away from me constantly, and there was nothing I could do about it. It was as if he could draw the ball towards him, it didn't matter how it arrived or how close I was, it was drawn to his feet. I'd never felt as big and clumsy in my life. The only weapon I had to counter with was my strength, I was a lot stronger than him, of course, his spindly legs were like a pair of pipe cleaners by comparison, his arms the same, and his chest was like a little bird's, but whenever I managed to take his legs from under him while going for a ball that was already gone, or when he danced past me and I grabbed his shoulder and pulled him backwards to the ground, the humiliation I felt was only that much greater.

The goal he scored was a cut above too. He fell deep to pick up the ball, shrugged off two tackles, stepped past me and laid it off to the striker, who'd found space to make himself available and who then held it just long enough to give it back to him as he came into the box. There, he stopped completely, nudged it coolly to his right to get the required angle and then curled it into the top corner.

If I'd been on the terrace, I'd have applauded. But he was my responsibility on the pitch, so his goal was my fault. Added to that, he was a sixteen-year-old squirt who kept calling me things and taunting me. *Come on, arse-face. You can do better than that, surely?* How could I feel admiration for him when he kept on at me like that and was totally outplaying me at the same time?

Still, I can't explain what I did.

Not that it caused him any damage, but it was so unlike me.

Driving home after the match, I could hardly believe it had even happened.

But it had.

We were on the attack, he hadn't tracked back and was strolling in the middle of the park. I stayed with him. No one was looking, they were all watching the ball.

'You're not just ugly,' he said. 'You're a shit player, too. How many times have I done a number on you now?'

I said nothing.

I knew I had to hit him.

It wasn't a rush of blood. It was something I knew I had to do.

I stepped in front of him, turned round and punched him as hard as I could in the stomach.

He crumpled and fell to the ground.

I carried on walking.

'He hit him! He hit Gustav!' one of their players shouted. 'Ref, stop the game! He hit him!'

The referee turned and looked in the direction of the injured number seven, who was curled up on the ground clutching his stomach, then came running and bent over him.

'What happened?' he said.

Seven sat up.

'He punched me,' he said, pointing at me. 'That bastard punched me.'

'Send him off!' one of his teammates screeched.

'It's a red card, ref!' blustered another.

'Number thirteen, over here!' the referee said.

I went over.

'What's up?' I said.

'Did you punch him?' said the ref.

'Of course not,' I said. 'I don't know what he's talking about. He's having you on, ref.'

'He's lying,' said number seven, and got to his feet. 'He punched me in the bloody stomach!'

'It's your word against his,' said the ref. 'I didn't see anything. Are you all right?'

Seven nodded.

'You're going to send him off, though, aren't you?'

'Can't do that,' said the ref. 'Now, calm down, the lot of you. I want no more funny business.'

I held my hands out to my sides, palms upwards, and gave number seven a smile.

'Syvert!' Mads shouted. 'Come here!'

I ran over to the touchline as play resumed at their end of the pitch.

'I saw what happened,' he said. 'What's got into you?'

I didn't say anything, but felt my cheeks turn red.

'Gjert takes care of their seven for the remainder. You stay away from him. If we'd had more subs, you'd have been in the dressing room. Do you understand?'

'I understand,' I said, and ran onto the pitch again. When the ref blew the final whistle a few minutes later and we went in to get changed, my cheeks were still burning. I couldn't joke about it, couldn't lift my gaze to look the others in the eye, I felt like I'd run into a wall. I put my clothes in my holdall, put my training jacket on and went out to the car without showering, without a word to anyone.

I couldn't think straight, not even when I was on my own in the car. I'd never done anything like that before, never even come close. It was as if it had happened by itself, outside of me. As if I hadn't been a part of it. But I had.

'Christ!' I said out loud, and slammed the steering wheel a couple of times with the heel of my hand.

The story would get around, in a day or two everyone would have heard.

Syvert punched one of the other team's players during the match on Saturday.

They'd think I was the sort who went around hitting people.

But I wasn't!

The wind swept up through the river valley, flapping everything that was slack. The clouds that scudded across the sky were flat and all at the same height. There was something harsh about the landscape, not like in summer when everything was soft and deep and even the gusts of wind had something curvy and enveloping about them.

I might have understood if I'd been so incensed that I'd lost control of myself. But actually *deciding* to do it? It had felt like it was something I had to do. An obligation of some kind.

I parked the car in the garage, closed the door behind me and went into the house, finding it empty and quiet.

That's when I remembered that Mum was in bed.

'Hello!' I called up the stairs. 'I'm back!'

I slung my bag into the laundry room and went up to see how she was.

She was lying on her back and looked at me as I opened the door. She'd dropped the pillow onto the floor beside the bed, I noticed. Her face was pale, paler than usual.

'How are you feeling, Mum?'

'I'm fine,' she said. 'Where's Robert?'

'Robert?'

'Joar.'

Hell, I'd forgotten!

'He's still over at Rickard's,' I said. 'I'll go and pick him up in a minute.'

'All right.'

'Is it painful still?'

'No, not at all. Just a bit sore, that's all. It's not much.'

'Do you want another aspirin?'

'Yes, that'd be nice. Bring the packet, would you?'

'OK,' I said, and went to the bathroom. The packet was nearly full, she never did pain relief, not even when she needed it.

'Here you go,' I said. 'How many? Two?'

'Yes, please.'

I put two tablets into her hand, and then the glass from her bedside table, which still had a couple of mouthfuls of water in it.

'It might help if you keep yourself mobile,' I said. Maybe you could come downstairs for dinner? I'll make something.'

'Yes, I was thinking the same thing. Let me rest a few minutes more, I'll come down in a bit.'

'I might as well go and collect Joar, then. I won't be long!'

Why had she called Joar Robert? I asked myself as I went down the stairs. It was weird. Could a couple of aspirins have made her that woozy?

I thought I'd better have a shower and get changed first, I didn't want to turn up in my football gear, but then again he'd been there all day and it probably didn't matter that much anyway, they shuffled about in jogging pants themselves at Rickard's when they weren't wearing overalls that smelled funny.

A few minutes later I was on my way up through the river valley again. Passing the shop, I noticed the sign for the physiotherapy clinic. It had been there for years, I must have seen it a thousand times without thinking about it. But now suddenly it was relevant. It was just what Mum needed.

I turned the car and went back. The shop was closed, but the owner and his wife, who ran the clinic, lived in the house round the back.

I rang the bell, and the wife, whose name was Ellen or Marianne, something like that, a woman I took to be in her mid-fifties, came to the door and smiled when she saw me.

'Hello,' I said. 'Is it possible to book a physio session on the spot, or is there some procedure to go through first? I was driving past and saw the sign just now.'

'Yes, of course,' she said. 'Wait a minute and I'll get my appointments book.'

A smell of fishcakes and onion wafted through the hall. What had happened during the match seemed even stranger as I stood there.

Now my reaction started to torment me too. The way I hadn't looked at anyone or said anything, just retreated inside myself and left without a word.

'Here we are,' the woman said, appearing in front of me again with a book and a pen in her hand. 'When were you thinking would suit?'

'It's for my mother. She's got this terrible pain in her back, it just came on today. She does cleaning work.'

'I see.'

'Monday, maybe? Would that be possible?'

She looked in her book.

'Twelve thirty?'

'That'll be fine, I think.'

'What name should I put?'

'Evelyn.'

'Lovely!' she said, and looked up. 'Monday at half past twelve, then.'

The dog started barking inside the house even as I crossed the yard. This time it was Rickard's dad who came to the door, holding the boisterous hound by the collar.

'Joar!' he shouted. 'Your brother's here!'

He turned to face me again.

'How did your game go?'

'We lost three—one.'

'Oh well. Still, it's a long season. Who were you playing against?'

'Kilsund. They were playing in the division above us last year.'

Joar appeared behind him. He sat down on a chair up against the wall to put his shoes on. It always took him such a long time. First loosening the laces, then sliding his feet into the shoes and wriggling them properly into place before eventually commencing the slow and methodical process of tightening and at last tying them with double bows.

It was no use telling him to hurry up, he couldn't even if he wanted to.

'Someone been baking today?' I said.

'You've a good sense of smell,' he said. 'Helene's baked some buns. Do you want one?'

'No thanks. It's very kind of you, only we've got to be getting back for dinner.'

'Take some with you, then! You can have them later on. Just hang on a second, I'll go and fetch you some.'

He disappeared inside, still bent forward because of the dog, which only reluctantly went with him. Voices came from the kitchen.

'Have you had a nice time?' I said.

'Yep,' said Joar.

'Mum's got a bad back today.'

'She has had for ages.'

'A bit more than usual today, though, I think. She's in bed having a rest.'

Rickard's dad appeared again, without the dog this time, but with a carrier bag full of buns instead.

'Here you go,' he said as he handed it to me.

There were at least ten buns inside.

'You needn't have,' I said. 'But thanks ever so much.'

'Thank Helene,' he said. 'She's the one who baked them.'

Joar was ready at last and stood up from his chair.

'Rickard! Come and say goodbye to Joar!' Rickard's dad shouted.

'We've said goodbye,' said Joar.

Rickard's dad smiled at him in a way that made me shudder. It was a smile so indulgent as to say it didn't matter what Joar said.

As if there was something wrong with him.

Rickard came into the hall.

'Bye, Joar,' he said.

'Bye, Rickard,' said Joar.

And then we left. Rickard's dad shut the door behind us and I turned round to see if I could catch a glimpse of Helene in one of the windows, but there was no one there.

'It might be cancer,' said Joar after we got in the car.

'What?'

'Mum's back pains. It might be cancer.'

'Yes,' I said as I reversed before turning the car round. 'It might just be a bad back as well.'

He didn't say anything.

'Mum does cleaning work, it's very demanding physically. It's hardly surprising if she's put her back out.'

It was impossible to tell what he was thinking.

'Joar?' I said. 'I understand you not wanting to come and see me play. It's quite all right. And I'm sorry about not taking you out in the canoe like I promised. If I said we could do that tomorrow, would you believe me?'

'No.'

'Cross my heart and hope to die?'

'No.'

'But you'd come if we did?'

'No.'

'Fair enough,' I said. 'We'll put it on hold, then.'

We said no more all the way home. I could tell that he was worried about Mum, and was hoping she'd be up by the time we got back.

But she wasn't.

He went straight to his room even though I told him to look in on her and say hello.

She opened her eyes when I came in.

'Joar's in his room,' I said. 'I'll get some dinner on the go. Is there anything you want? Some more water, maybe?'

'Yes, please.'

'I've made an appointment for you on Monday at that physiotherapist's down the road.'

'Thanks,' she said, as if it were the most natural thing in the world.

'Do you want me to bring the radio up?'

'There's no need,' she said. 'I'll be down soon.'

Outside the sun was going down. I liked when the dusk was allowed to come inside too, and left the light off. The rooms became almost a part of the flatland out there. I got an onion and some mushrooms out of the fridge and started preparing them.

Music came from Joar's room, though I couldn't hear what it was he was playing. He couldn't be that worried, then, I thought.

I put the chops on the chopping board, drizzled some olive oil on them and sprinkled them with salt and pepper. The oil lay like a film on the surface of the meat, with its little grains of salt and pepper. If Mum died, I thought as I rinsed my hands under the tap, I'd inherit the house. I'd be able to sell it then and move wherever I wanted.

'No, no, no!' I said out loud.

I couldn't think like that, not *ever*.

Furious with myself, I got the two frying pans out of the cupboard, turned the cooker on and dropped a knob of butter into each, sweeping the onions and mushrooms into one while waiting for the butter to melt and turn brown in the other so I could put the chops on, filling a saucepan with water for the rice and putting it on the hob.

Then the phone rang.

I froze for a moment, not knowing what to do. Should I answer it straight away and tell whoever it was I'd phone them back? Turn the cooker off while I answered it? Or just let it ring?

Joar came bombing down the stairs.

'Hello?' I heard him say in the hall. 'Yes, he is. Just a minute.'

Louder then:

'Syvert, it's for you!'

I turned the cooker off and wiped my hands on the tea towel before going out into the hall, where Joar was standing with the receiver held against his chest.

'Who is it?'

He shrugged and handed me the phone, disappearing up the stairs again as I put it to my ear.

'Hello?' I said.

'Is that Syvert?' a girl's voice said.

'His very self, in person.'

'Hi,' she said. 'This is Lisa speaking. We met last weekend. It was my boyfriend who headbutted you, if you remember.'

'I've got a vague recollection, yes.'

'I just wanted to apologise. He gets really jealous.'

'But he doesn't mean anything by it, is that it?' I said.

She went quiet.

What was I doing?

I was in! A girl had phoned me up!

'Anyway, I just wanted to say sorry,' she said, and sounded like she was about to hang up.

'How did you get my number?' I said.

'It's in the book.'

'But I never told you my name, did I?'

'We read the paper here, too.'

'Ah!'

There was a pause.

I wondered where she was, what sort of surroundings she was in. And how to stop her from hanging up.

'Does he know you're phoning me?' I said.

'No,' she said. 'I've broken up with him, actually.'

'What, because of me?'

She snorted derisively.

'No. Because of him.'

'How does it feel?'

'Pretty shit.'

'You liked him, then?'

'We'd been going out with each other nearly two years,' she said. 'Of course I like him.'

'But, it couldn't go on . . . ?'

Another pause.

'I don't know what I'm talking to you about it for,' she said.

'Because I'm good to talk to, maybe?' I said. 'I've got lots of other good qualities too, as it happens!'

'I doubt it very much,' she said, and something in her voice suggested a tiny smile.

'So we're not going to meet up and talk about it, then?'

'Are you not right in the head, or what? I rang you up to apologise,
not to get chatted up. I'm actually upset about it.'

And then she hung up.

Nevertheless, I was bubbling with joy as I went back into the kitchen. She knew who I was, and I must have made at least some sort of
impression on her? She'd smiled, and confided in me, however little it
had been.

The light had dwindled even more outside, I could only just make
out the outlines of the hills on the other side of the river. I turned the
ceiling light on and the kitchen immediately appeared reflected in the
windows, as if it was what the switch was for.

The onions and mushrooms were soon sizzling gently in their pan,
the chops spitting in theirs, the rice boiling happily away, steaming up
the cold windowpanes. I added a good mesasure of cream to the onions
and mushrooms and allowed it to reduce down before putting the
chops onto three plates and pouring the sauce on top, straining the rice
and spooning it into a little pile at the edge of each plate.

It looked good.

'Dinner's ready!' I shouted.

No one answered, so I went upstairs to fetch them.

Mum opened her eyes when I went in.

'Dinner's on the table,' I said. 'Can you manage the stairs, do you
think? If I give you a hand?'

She shook her head, the smallest movement.

'I think Joar's going to be really worried if you stay in bed much
longer.'

'I know,' she said. 'We'll give it a try, at least. Can you help me up?
Careful, mind.'

I leaned over her and slipped one hand under her back, the other
under her shoulder. Cautiously, I drew her into a sitting position.

'Ow, ow,' she said. 'Argh! Oh! Ohhhh!'

She managed to put her feet to the floor on her own.

Sat there a moment without moving.

'Are you all right?' I said.

'Yes.'

I put my arm around her and helped her up.

'The stairs might be a bit tricky,' I said.

'I'll manage,' she said. 'As long as you help me.'

It felt like five minutes before we got downstairs. As soon as she was seated on her chair, I went up and got Joar.

He said nothing, but took his place with his eyes fixed on the table.

'Did you have a nice time at Rickard's, Joar?' Mum said.

'Yes,' he said.

'They'd been baking,' I said. 'We've got a whole bagful of buns now.'

'That was kind of them,' she said.

We ate for a while without speaking. With the bright light from the ceiling and the darkness outside, it was like we were seated on a stage. But the chances of anyone seeing us were minimal. There were no houses on the kitchen side, and no roads either, only the fields and the hills behind them, the woods and forests stretching away.

Mum picked at her food.

Couldn't she eat just a little bit, for Joar's sake? Couldn't she tell how worried he was?

Joar put his knife and fork down and drank some water. His chop wasn't even half eaten.

'Didn't you like it?' I said. 'It's a recipe I picked up in the forces. It went down a treat there, I can tell you!'

'It was all right,' he said.

'You're just not hungry, is that it?'

'Not really.'

'What do you two normally do on a Saturday night, anyway?' I said. Joar looked at Mum.

'We normally have pizza, don't we?' she said.

'Yes,' he said. 'And sweets or crisps later on.'

'While you're watching telly?'

'Yes.'

'Is there anything on tonight, do you know?'

He shrugged.

'There's a children's programme. It'll be finished now, though.'

'We could rent a video?'

'I suppose so,' he said.

'Come on, daft arse!' I said. '*I suppose so*'s hardly going to get me driving all that way to rent a film, now, is it?'

'All right, I want to.'

'That's the spirit! What do you fancy watching?'

The petrol station lay illuminated like a little palace at the end of the plain, a truck stop on one side, forest on the other. There was a transport cafe with slot machines, and next door to that a low, boxy building called Video Shack. It was because of Video Shack that I'd always somehow connected video games and VHS films with the forest. Even films that took place in New York and other big cities were tinged with it. Not the forest itself, as nature, but things I associated with its general environment. Fenced-in storage buildings, plastic bags of rubbish half hidden under trees, decaying farm buildings and desolate housing estates, groups of youths hanging around their cars, empty paper cups tossed onto the roadside, parties in basement rooms.

I pulled in at one of the pumps.

'Do you want to go in while I fill up?' I said. 'See if there's anything you fancy?'

'OK,' he said, and unbuckled his seat belt.

'Violence is good, but nothing with sex in it, all right?'

He looked at me dumbfounded.

'I'd be too embarrassed,' I said with a wink. 'Only joking. Go on, get going!'

He rolled his eyes and got out of the car.

After I'd got some petrol and paid, I found him at the action movies. He was holding one in his hand.

'Can we get two?' he said. 'So we can watch one tomorrow as well?'

'Of course we can. What's that you've found?'

He showed me the cover. *The Guns of Navarone*.

'Haven't you seen that one?'

'Yes.'

'Wouldn't it be better to get something new, then?'

'But I know this one's good. It means we won't come home with something rubbish.'

'Good thinking. Let's find another, shall we?'

'*Rambo*?'

'I don't think Mum would be too keen.'

'She wouldn't have to know, would she?' he said artlessly.

I didn't care for him wanting to exploit the situation like that. I said nothing, but he must have cottoned on, because he picked up a film straight away and studied it conspicuously for some time.

'What about this one?' I said. '*The Beerhunter*?'

'*The Beerhunter*? What's that?'

'Sorry. *The Deerhunter*. I forgot my glasses. Do you fancy it? It's really good.'

'How do you know? Have you seen it?'

I didn't want to say I'd only just watched it, that would have gone against what I'd just said about *The Guns of Navarone*, so I told him it was well known that it was good.

'Isn't it for grown-ups?' he said.

'It *is* for grown-ups, yes,' I said, and put it back. 'Would you rather see *Granny and the Eight Children Have Fish for Dinner*?'

'How about a James Bond film?'

'Now you're talking. Which one, though? The newest?'

He nodded.

I handed the two films to the guy behind the counter and asked to rent a Moviebox too, and a few minutes later we left the lit-up forecourt and pulled away onto the dark road that ran through the forest.

Joar sat looking out of the window. I glanced at him a couple of times. His face was expressionless.

It struck me that I never wondered what he was feeling or thinking, what it was like to be him. Not really. All I did was check if he was in a good mood or if something looked to be troubling him.

It meant he was a sort of robot to me, didn't it?

What had it been like for him living on his own with Mum?

Was he fond of her?

'Are you thinking about Mum?' I said.

'Maybe.'

'There's no need to worry, you know. She's put her back out, that's all. Not that it doesn't hurt, mind. She's definitely in a bit of pain. But it's not *serious* in the way you're thinking. She works too hard, that's the trouble. It's a strain on her back. So maybe the two of us should try and help her a bit more around the house. And I'll see if I can get a job so she won't need to put as many hours in. How does that sound?'

He nodded.

We crossed the bridge over the river and I glanced down at the falls and the lights from the cellulose factory below.

'You could get a job there,' said Joar.

'Maybe I could, yes,' I said, slowing to give way to a bus that was pulling out from the bus stop up ahead. 'I think it's pretty dreary, though. Not much of a future in it either.'

'I didn't think you had a future anyway?'

I looked at him.

'Have you read that interview?'

He didn't answer.

The bus snailed its way up the hill, but the road was too narrow for me to overtake. A pair of headlights came up behind us, blinding me in the mirror.

'Dag asked me to do that.'

'I'm not bothered.'

As I spoke, the car behind pulled out and squeezed its way past. The driver couldn't possibly see if there was anything coming the other way, the road wasn't only narrow, there was a bend there too. On the other hand, I thought to myself as it was overtaking the bus, there was so little traffic about that the chances of a car appearing right there, at that moment, were probably microscopic.

'About what? The interview or my excuse?'

'Neither.'

'That's all right, then,' I said. 'It's nothing to be bothered about anyway.'

When I woke up the next day it was with the feeling that something good had happened the day before. I just couldn't remember what. As I thought about it, everything else that had happened came back into

my mind. Me punching their number seven. Me coming across like a
saddo in the paper. Mum lying in bed. Rickard's dad looking at Joar as
if there was something wrong with him. And then there was what Einar
had told me about Dad. But at the back of all that was the gleamy glow
of something else. Something good.

But what?

I went and had a shower. I still hadn't bought my own shampoo, so
I had to use Mum's again. I stepped away from the shower head and
started working it into my hair. It lathered up too much, and its honey-
like smell wasn't exactly masculine.

She was employed on a full-time contract, so she'd still get paid even
if she had to go off sick. But I didn't know for how long. Maybe she'd
end up on an invalid pension?

I stepped back under the shower and rinsed the shampoo out. Thick,
soapy rivulets ran down my body.

Lisa!

That was it! The phone call!

And she'd chucked her boyfriend.

I'd sensed a smile.

I turned the water off, took the towel that I'd hung over the top of
the shower cabinet, stepped out onto the floor and dried myself.

The only thing was I didn't have her number.

And I didn't know her surname either.

Lisa Larsen?

Lisa Olsen?

Lisa Løyning! It sounded quite good.

Syvert and Lisa Løyning.

How could I get hold of her number?

I got dressed in a hurry, as if something big was about to happen.
And even if I knew it wasn't, I did nothing to stop the impulse, but
pursued it with a sense of joy.

The hall was full of cigarette smoke.

Was Mum up?

She was.

With a cup of coffee in front of her, she was sitting at the kitchen
table with the radio on, smoking and doing a crossword.

'Wonders never cease!' I said. 'You're up!'

She smiled and put her pen down.

'I was feeling much better when I woke up this morning. Perhaps it was just a pulled muscle.'

'Do you want me to cancel the physio?'

She looked at me like she didn't know what I was talking about.

'I made an appointment for you. I told you.'

'Did you? That was thoughtful of you. When for?'

'Tomorrow. Half twelve, I think it was.'

'I think maybe I'll keep it,' she said.

'Joar's going to be glad at any rate. Is he up yet?'

'Yes, had his breakfast and everything. Could the two of you do something together today, do you think?'

I nodded and poured myself some coffee. The weather outside was the same as the day before, sunshine and windy.

'I'll see if he wants to go out in the canoe.'

'That'd be nice.'

The phone rang. My heart immediately beat faster.

Maybe it was her?

I put my coffee down and went into the hall to answer it.

'All right, you dosser,' said Dag. 'How's it going?'

'Fine, until that paper of yours came out yesterday and the whole world started feeling sorry for me,' I said. 'I told you I'd only do it on one condition, that you didn't make me out to be some kind of pathetic failure. And yet that's exactly what's happened. It's the worst thing I've ever done.'

'What are you on about?' he said. 'The piece is brilliant. I've had loads of positive reactions, and I didn't even write it. People love a good human interest story, don't they?'

'People love to see someone more pathetic than themselves, you mean. Of course they love it. But OK, I won't hold a grudge. What do you want, anyway?'

'I wouldn't say *want*, exactly. Only I was thinking of going to the pictures tonight. Do you fancy it?'

'What's on?'

'Either *Out of Africa*, *A Room with a View* or *9½ Weeks*.'

'The first two are for girls, so I'm hardly going to watch them with you, am I?'

'9½ Weeks, then?'

'All right. Nine o'clock, is it?'

'Yes.'

'Are you going to pick me up?'

'If you like.'

'See you later, then.'

'Great, see you later.'

'Was that Dag?' Mum said when I came back into the kitchen.

'It was, yes. We're going to the flicks tonight.'

'That sounds nice.'

I took a sip of my coffee and studied her for a moment.

'Are you *really* feeling better?'

'Still a slight pain. Nothing to go on about, though.'

Joar was sitting drawing when I opened the door of his room.

'Do you want go out in the canoe with me?'

'When?' he said without turning round.

'How about now?'

'Can do,' he said, and got to his feet straight away, placing his drawing on top of the pile and putting his pencil away in his pencil case.

'Put a windproof jacket on. It's windy today, and nowhere near as warm as it looks.'

He stepped past me without a word.

Rickard's dad saw him as a kid, nothing else, and he was the sort who didn't care much for kids. It was as simple as that, I told myself, and went down the stairs behind him.

'We need to get the paddles and the life jackets from the barn,' I said.

'OK,' he said.

'We're off out, Mum!' I called.

'Have a nice time!' she called back.

Sunlight shone through all the cracks in the roof and walls of the barn. Whenever the wind came gusting, the woodwork creaked and something outside that was obviously loose rattled.

Joar went over to the far corner where the canoeing gear was stored.

'Can I use the yellow paddle?' he said.

'If you want,' I said. 'Did you know those boxes are full of Dad's old stuff, by the way?'

He shook his head. It didn't seem to interest him much.

'What do you remember about him, exactly?' I said.

'I remember him pushing me in the red plastic pedal car, and I remember him burying it in the garden.'

I laughed.

'He buried your pedal car?'

'It broke.'

'He didn't bury it, though, surely? Where did you get that from?'

'He did. I remember.'

'What more do you remember?'

'We went swimming once, and when we got in the car to go home he sat down on the front seat and screamed.'

'Why, what happened?'

He shrugged.

'Perhaps the seat was really hot. It was summer and he only had his swimming trunks on.'

'You might be able to remember some more, if you see his things?'

'I don't need to remember any more.'

I stepped forward and opened the box I'd been looking in last. Curiosity got the better of Joar's indifference, and he came closer.

I took out the passport and opened it at the page where the photograph was.

'Is this how you remember him?'

Joar nodded.

'Can I see?'

'Of course you can,' I said, and handed it to him.

He turned the pages and studied the stamps.

He'd been all over the place.

Italy, Greece, Spain, the UK, Germany.

'What country's this?' said Joar, holding the passport up in front of me. It wasn't just a single stamp, but a whole page that had been glued in with his picture on it and a lot of different stamps.

'It looks like the Russian alphabet,' I said. 'He must have been to the Soviet Union.'

'Was he a spy, do you think?'

I laughed.

'I doubt they'd have given him a visa, if he was!'

'Why did he go there, then?'

'No idea. I was just a kid then, too, remember? We'll have to ask Mum. She'll know. But he did do a Russian-language course with the military. He had some Russian books, as well. Look.'

I picked one up. He took it out of my hand.

'What does it mean?' he said, staring intensely at the strange writing. 'What does it say?'

I laughed again.

'You've got me there.'

He turned the pages, as if to understand.

I lifted the Chinese monkey out of the box.

'Do you remember this?'

He looked up from the book.

Shook his head.

'There's a letter here,' he said, and held out some folded sheets of paper.

'To Dad?' I said. 'Let me have a look!'

He handed them to me. The writing paper was small in size, but the pages were many. The writing was all in Russian.

Maybe it was some notes he'd been taking.

But there was a space between the first line and the next, likewise between the last line and the one above. Dear Syvert, yours whoever?

I slipped the pages back inside the book and returned it to the box.

'Shall we get going, then?'

'What did it say?'

'It's all in Russian,' I said. 'I'm not even sure it *is* a letter.'

I pressed the duct tape to the cardboard, but it wasn't sticking any more, so I picked up one of the other boxes and put it on top to keep the flaps closed, then got my paddle and life jacket and went out again after Joar.

*

The canoe was where I'd left it, under the tarp at the far end of the moorings. We paddled on a gentle current all the way as far as the church, and it wasn't until we were approaching the rapids where the river narrowed that it got more strenuous.

We manoeuvred into the backwater the way we usually did and carried the canoe along the path to the top of the rapids. The water was white where it ran over the edge, streaming down over the smooth rock of the riverbed. It had to be the most fun Joar could imagine, I thought when he turned to look at me, his face beaming as the current seemed to grab hold of the hull and sweep us away.

'WHOO-HOO!' he shrieked as we went over the edge, and for a few seconds it felt like we were free-falling.

It wasn't far off the most fun I could imagine either, I thought, ploughing into the pool at the bottom where we could start paddling once more.

'Let's do it again!' he said.

'Next time,' I said.

'OK,' he said, without seeming the least bit disappointed. He was growing up. Soon he wouldn't be a boy any more.

Joar had a dad, even though his dad was dead. But Dad didn't have Joar, he had no idea who he was. He'd only known the four-year-old.

'What do you want for your birthday?' I said.

'A Commodore,' he said without looking at me.

'Not on the cards, I'm afraid.'

'I know. But you asked what I wanted, not what I thought I'd get.'

Through the bare trees I could see people pottering in their gardens, cars moving along the road, some people gathered outside the church. It felt unreal to be on the river then, as if we belonged in a different age. It was something to do with being so close to the water's surface, I supposed, and also that we were propelling ourselves by our own muscle power.

Returning to the moorings, we put the canoe back in its place and walked the short distance home.

'Are you going to help me wash the car tomorrow?' I said when I saw how filthy it was, parked there in the sunlight.

'Can do,' he said.

*

The streets surrounding the hotel and the cinema were packed with people as always on a Sunday night. Cars were cruising around. The sun was low in the sky, giving it a blush of pink. The air was cold, but the feeling of spring was intense. There was a buzz everywhere, a hum of chat and laughter, young people hanging out, excitement, different altogether from the winter, when the mood was checked and inhibited, or at least more so than now.

Dag was in a good mood too. He was wondering whether to start his journalism degree in the autumn or wait a year and stay on at the paper. If he stayed, he'd rent a flat in town, he said.

He asked me what I thought. I said I didn't know, but both options sounded good.

'You're a bit quiet tonight,' he said as we wandered along Dronningens gate, killing time before the film started. 'What's up, did you shit yourself?'

'Quiet?' I said. 'I didn't realise.'

'I've known stones more talkative.'

'Stones are silent, not quiet.'

'Same difference.'

'Silent as a stone means not letting on about something. Quiet's what mice are.'

'So what are you, then? Quiet or silent?'

'I punched a player from the other team during our match yesterday.'

'Seriously? Did you get sent off?'

I shook my head.

'The ref didn't see it.'

'What made you hit him? It doesn't sound like you at all.'

'That's just it. I've no idea. He was giving me verbals all the time, I got sick of it and punched him in the guts.'

'What did he say to you?'

'Nothing, really. At least, not enough to excuse me hitting him like that.'

'Come on,' said Dag, smiling at me. 'He must have said something to get you going!'

'But that's the thing. It didn't get me going at all. I just felt I had to hit him.'

'What did he say?'

I shrugged.

'The usual stuff you say to any opponent. He called me ugly, that kind of thing.'

'Ah!'

'But it didn't bother me! That wasn't it at all.'

'Obviously.'

'It's true.'

'So how come you hit him, if you weren't bothered?'

'That's what I don't know!'

We'd got to the petrol station and could see the bridge that spanned the river, the new estate on the other side.

A snot-green car was parked slightly away from the pumps. A girl in a white down jacket, blue jeans and black clogs got out of the passenger side.

It was Lisa!

She crossed over the forecourt and went into the shop.

'Let's just go over to the petrol station a second, eh?' I said.

'The film starts in . . . seventeen minutes,' said Dag, checking his watch.

'I just want to get some chewing gum. Anyway, there'll be ten minutes of adverts first.'

'OK,' he said, and went with me over the road.

'You can wait outside, if you want,' I said. 'I won't be a minute.'

'No, I think I'll get something as well.'

'What do you want? I'll get it for you.'

He gave me a funny look.

'I can do these things on my own, you know.'

I shrugged again.

'Just trying to be helpful.'

He shook his head and went in. Lisa was standing in line by the counter holding a bottle of cola and a bag of peanuts, waiting her turn. Dag took a packet of Ms off the shelf and went and stood behind her. I went up beside him, my heart thumping.

Unaware of me standing there, she put her items on the counter when her turn came, asked for twenty Prince Mild, got her money out of her pocket and paid.

'We meet again!' I said.

She spun round to see who it was.

'Small world,' she said, and headed for the door, stuffing her cola in one jacket pocket, her peanuts and fags in the other.

Dag looked at me quizzically, I gave him a smile and went after her.

'How are you doing?' I said. 'All right?'

'I was doing fine until now,' she said, opening the door and going back outside without the slightest indication she was going to pause for a chat.

'Aren't you going to give me your number?'

'Not likely,' she said with a snort.

She went towards the car.

'Go on!' I said. 'Please?'

I folded my hands and gave her my best impression of a begging look.

She opened the car door.

'You're such an idiot,' she said.

'Idiots are people too. Some are even quite nice. Go on! I'm not asking for much. A few digits, that's all!'

She got in the car shaking her head.

'You could at least tell me your surname!'

The guy behind the wheel peered out at me. He had an unlit ciggy in his mouth and long black hair.

'Dønnestad,' she said, and slammed the door.

The guy revved the engine and and tore the few metres to the exit.

Dag came up behind me.

'What was all that about?' he said. 'Who the hell was she?'

'Lisa Dønnestad,' I said. 'Shall we get going? We don't want to be late for the adverts!'

I got myself so worked up thinking about her during the film that I was exhausted by the time it was finished and we walked back to the car. It was Sunday, everywhere was closed, and Dag was working the next day anyway, so there was no point in hanging around town, even if going home was the last thing I wanted.

'Well, that was crap,' said Dag.

'She wasn't bad, though,' I said.

'Not my type.'

'So you'd turn her down?'

'Too cold for my liking.'

'Not bad, but too cold?'

'That's about right.'

'So you'd rather have someone hot who wasn't not bad? Ha ha ha!'

'Ha ha.'

He hadn't asked who Lisa was yet, but I knew it was only a matter of time, he was a nosy bastard who loved a bit of gossip, he just didn't want to come across that way.

We got into the car. Dag pushed a tape into the cassette player and a moment later the car was filled with Dag music. Tinny stuff for the world-weary. The Clash, U2 and Big Country, bands he'd been trying to get me into for ages.

'What's this we're listening to, then?' I said as we pulled out onto the road.

'Imperiet. *Blå himlen blues.*'

'Ah. The world-weary Swedes.'

There was hardly any traffic once we got out of town, the motorway was almost deserted. The odd speeding car on a long journey, a few lorries.

'I heard you had a good talk with my dad the other day,' he said.

'Yes,' I said.

'It can't have been easy, your dad passing away when you were that young. I've never really thought about it that much since. Should I have done?'

He glanced at me.

I laughed.

'It's a bit late to start now,' I said. 'No, not at all. I've never thought about it much myself, to be honest.'

The darkness above us had something of the greyness of summer nights, that was how it seemed, lighter now than only a few weeks before. But maybe I was imagining it.

'I found out something weird,' I said. 'About my dad, I mean. I found his passport, he had a Soviet visa. I think that's what it was, anyway.

There were some Russian books in among his things, too, and a letter in Russian. Have you any idea what that might be about?'

'Didn't he take the Russian course at the intelligence school?'

'You mean you knew too?'

'Yes. Didn't you?'

'Not until a couple of days ago, no.'

'I've always known that.'

'Joar has as well. No one's ever thought of telling me, though. It makes me wonder what else I don't know. What else I *ought* to know. My mum's been holding back information.'

'Hardly holding back, surely? You make it sound like a conspiracy.'

'Not far off, though. I'm going to tell you something now. Can you promise you won't mention it to your mum and dad?'

'Yes, what is it?'

'You promise?'

'I just said, yes! Mention what?'

'Dad was involved with someone else before he died. He wanted a divorce. He told Mum and everything. Only he died before he could do anything about it.'

'Are you having me on?'

'Of course not. Mum told me just before the weekend.'

'That's a shock.'

'Do you think Einar knows?'

'Dad? No, I don't think so. Or rather, I wouldn't know. It's not the sort of thing he'd have told me about, really.'

Neither of us spoke for a moment.

'Who was she?' Dag said after a bit.

'Who? The girl at the petrol station?'

'No, you idiot. The woman your dad was involved with.'

'Oh, her. Ha ha. I haven't got a clue. Mum didn't know. And there's no one else I can ask.'

We went quiet again.

Then Dag laughed all of a sudden. I looked at him.

'The girl at the petrol station!' he said.

'What about her?'

'Why would you think I was asking about her? Because you can't stop thinking about her. Am I right, or am I right?'

The house was still and dark when I stepped into the hall. The sound of Dag's car disappeared into the distance. I cut myself a slice of bread in the kitchen and headed for my bed.

'Syvert?' Mum said from her room.

'Yes?' I said, and opened her door.

'I'm staying off work tomorrow. Can you get up with Joar and see him off to school?'

'Of course I can. Is it your back again? Do you want me to drive you to your physio tomorrow?'

'We'll see.'

'Is there anything you need?'

She shook her head slightly.

'All right, then,' I said. 'Goodnight!'

'Goodnight,' she said.

I wound up my old alarm clock, set it for seven and put it down on the floor over by the wall on the other side of the room so I wouldn't just turn it off and go back to sleep.

When it did go off, it felt like I'd only just got my head down, and my first thought was that I must have set it wrong, but the room was light and the air outside busy with the sound of cheeping birds, so there was nothing else for it than to get up.

Lisa Dønnestad!

At once it was as if all fatigue evaporated.

Tra-la-la-la-la, I sang as I went to get showered, knocking hard on Joar's door when I was finished, finding him with his cheek pressed into his pillow and one arm dangling down from underneath the cover.

'Rise and shine!' I said, pulling his curtains aside. 'It's gone seven o'clock!'

Without lingering to gauge his reaction, I skipped down the stairs and into the kitchen where I got some coffee on the go, fried some eggs and bacon and heated up a couple of Mum's frozen baps from the supermarket.

With the table set and everything ready I went out into the hall and looked Dønnestad up in the phone book. There were more than twenty people with that name, five of them in the area I was sure she was from. It wasn't a problem, I could just phone them one by one and ask for Lisa.

'Breakfast's ready!' I shouted up the stairs.

I could heard Joar thudding about, but nothing from Mum's room.

I went up and knocked on her door, then put my head round.

'How are you feeling?' I said. 'Do you fancy some breakfast?

She looked up at me. There was no sign of a smile, not from her lips, not from her eyes.

'Not good?'

'I think I will go to the doctor's, after all,' she said.

'Now?'

'Sometime today, if I can get an appointment.'

'Of course. But you've got your physio later on. Maybe that'll help. You could go to the doctor's after that, if it doesn't. What do you think?'

'I'd forgotten all about the physio. Perhaps you're right.'

'Do you want some breakfast? Or can't you manage the stairs?'

'I don't think I can.'

'Shall I bring you a tray? Breakfast in bed?'

A faint smile passed across her face.

'That'd be nice.'

I cut a bap in two, put a slice of cheese on one half and a slice of salami on the other, lifted an egg onto the plate and some of the bacon that was nice and crisp — getting it crisp is easy when you know how, just turn the heat up high without any butter or oil or anything — and then poured a mug of coffee, put some milk in and put everything on a tray I then carried up the stairs for her.

'Where do you want it?' I said. 'If you sit up, I can put it on your lap. Wait a minute, I'll get you a cushion.'

I went back down into the living room and picked up a cushion from the sofa. She managed to pull herself upright, I slipped the cushion behind her back and put the tray on her lap.

'Thanks,' she said. 'Go down and see to Joar now, will you?'

'Of course,' I said.

Joar was sullen, the way he often was in the mornings, he wasn't touching his eggs or his bacon.

'All the more for me, then,' I said, and gave him a smile. 'Cheers for that.'

'Isn't Mum coming down?'

'She's not feeling too well. I've taken her breakfast in bed. But listen, little man, you've got to eat, you know.'

'So I can grow up big and strong?'

'Exactly! You're growing every day at your age. But you've still got to eat properly.'

'I'm not hungry.'

'You will be without your breakfast. How about I make you a good packed lunch? Then you can have a glass of milk, at least, and maybe a banana, too?'

'I don't like bananas.'

'An apple, then.'

I went into the living room and took an apple from the fruit bowl, put it down on the table in front of him and poured him a glass of milk.

He drank a couple of mouthfuls and left the apple untouched.

I looked at him. His pale face, the skin under his eyes almost blue, his dark hair with its unruly tuft. Dark, dark eyes.

'I'll eat it on the way,' he said.

'That's the idea,' I said as I piled some bread slices onto my own plate. 'What do you want in your sandwiches?'

'Anything. Salami, maybe.'

'Salami in all of them?'

'Salami in two. Then two more with cheese.'

'Coming up,' I said.

He started playing with his fork, moving it around the table, backwards and forwards, while I buttered his sandwiches. He pushed some of the breakfast things out of the way and ran his fork between them.

'What are you doing that for?' I said after a bit.

'What?'

'With your fork.'

'It's a tractor harrowing the field. That's the hill,' he said, indicating the bread basket. 'This is the rock sticking up. Here's our house. And the road and the river are here.'

'How old did you say you were again?' I said.

'I'm twelve.'

Was he being ironic?

No, the look he gave me was serious.

'I'm only pulling your leg,' I said. 'I know how old you are, of course I do.'

He carried on driving his tractor through his little landscape while I got the greaseproof paper.

'I dreamt about Dad last night,' he said without looking at me.

'Did you?'

'Yes.'

'What happened?'

'He came up the stairs. I was sitting on the floor and he went past me into the bedroom.'

'Was that all?'

'Yes.'

'What did he look like?'

'Like Dad.'

'Did he look happy? Sad? Angry?'

Joar shrugged.

'He looked like he was very busy.'

I tore off a length of the greaseproof paper and tore it into four smaller pieces to wrap his sandwiches in.

'Do you dream about Dad a lot?'

He shook his head.

'I think it's the first time. But I can't remember everything I dream.'

'No, of course not. How did it make you feel?'

'Feel?'

'Yes. Did you feel anything when you saw him?'

'No.'

I wrapped the sandwiches as neatly as I could and put his finished lunch down next to his apple.

'There you are,' I said. 'What time do you normally get going?'

'Quarter past.'

'Are you going to brush your teeth, then?'

'In three minutes,' he said with a look at the clock on the wall.

As soon as he was gone, I went upstairs to check on Mum and collect her breakfast tray. She'd fallen asleep with the big cushion in her back and the tray still on her lap. She was obviously exhausted. I felt sorry for her. It must have been the pain that made her tired. It was often the way, I reasoned, that fatigue followed on from illness, as if it had all been pent up in the body.

I picked up the tray as carefully as I could, and when I turned to look at her as I reached the door she was still asleep.

It was too early to phone Lisa.

I went absently from one downstairs room to another with my coffee. After a while I slipped my feet into my old Adidas sandals and shuffled over to the barn. The sky was bright blue, the air surprisingly mild. All of a sudden it felt like it was closer to summer than winter.

I opened the box with Dad's books in it and took out the letter or whatever it was that we'd found. Joar's dream had made me feel like he was actually with us, in the house, but we could only see him in dreams. It was a stupid thought, obviously, with no base in reality. It wasn't that I believed it to be true, it was more the feeling that he was there, restless and despairing, that made sense somehow.

I looked at the Russian handwriting. It was in blue ink, and there was something about it that made me think it was a woman's. The letters were small and round. It could have been the unfamiliar shapes of the different characters that gave me the impression, but I didn't think so.

What had Dad's handwriting looked like, anyway?

I rummaged through some of the other boxes until I came across some papers I could see were accounts of some sort, which I was almost certain were in his own hand.

The characters were small and pointed, not small and round, and with relatively big spaces between the words. It looked a bit odd, small words and big spaces, it made me think of people spread out in a landscape.

The Russian definitely wasn't the same handwriting. Not his at all. The letter had to be from someone else.

I stared for a long time at the indecipherable symbols, as if suddenly they might become meaningful.

Who did I know who knew Russian?

No one.

Maybe Dag would know someone?

He had all sorts of contacts now. And if he didn't know anyone personally, he'd know someone who did.

I went back to the house and dialled the newspaper offices.

'Is that Marianne?' I said when a female voice answered.

'Yes, who's speaking?'

'Hi, it's Syvert here! Could you put me through to Dag?'

'Just a moment.'

A few seconds later, Dag's voice came through at the other end.

'Løyning here,' he said.

'That's funny,' I said. 'Løyning here, as well. How's things?'

'Good. Thanks for the date!'

'Same to you. But listen, I was thinking.'

'You're going to ask me a favour now, aren't you?'

'I am, yes. Do you know anyone who knows Russian?'

'Russian? No.'

'Can you find me someone who does?'

'What for?'

'That letter I was telling you about. The one I found in Dad's things. I want to get it translated. It's probably nothing, it's just so incredibly frustrating not knowing what it says.'

'There might be someone at the college who speaks Russian,' he said. 'I can ask, anyway.'

'That'd be brilliant, Dag, if you would.'

'You don't have to actually use my name, even if you are grateful, Syvert.'

'I'll bear it in mind, Dag. Speak to you soon!'

Mum slept all through the morning. It was nearly twelve o'clock when I went up the stairs to wake her up. She was sitting on the edge of the bed in her nightie when I opened the door.

'Morning!' I said. 'Are you feeling any better? Ready for your physio?'

She nodded.

'I'll need a shower first, though. Have we got time?'

'Yes, if you're quick about it,' I said. 'It's only a couple of minutes in the car. Do you need any help?'

'No, I'm fine. It's much better now. I don't know what it is. It's the strangest thing. I was in *such* pain yesterday. Now I'm as right as rain again.'

'Maybe you're just a bit fatigued. The physio will do you good. Then perhaps you can take things easy the rest of the week.'

'We'll see,' she said, and stood up, wriggled her feet into her slippers and shuffled past me on her way to the bathroom.

While she was in the shower, I went and got the newspaper and the post. There was a parcel for me. I wasn't sure I'd ever received one before, and I opened it standing next to the mailbox.

A book and a letter.

From the pastor.

Was he trying to win me over now? I wondered, slipping the letter back into the envelope to read in the house and turning my attention to the book. It was a dog-eared paperback entitled *Crime and Punishment*. Written by Fyodor Dostoevsky.

It was quite timely, I thought as I walked back up. A Russian writer, the same day I'd phoned Dag to see if he could find someone to translate Dad's letter.

Maybe the pastor knew Russian?

But why would he?

The clock on the kitchen wall said ten past twelve and I went and sat down in the living room while I waited for Mum to get ready. I took the letter out of the envelope again.

Dear Syvert,

Thanks for coming to see me the other day! It was a most pleasant surprise, even if the reason for your visit might have been a happier one for an old clergyman such as myself. But I believe in the freedom of the individual to think for himself. Which is exactly what you're doing – and that does please me. The form you requested is attached herewith. I've also taken the liberty of sending you this book, which I hope you will read,

preferably before signing the form! I think you'll understand why once
you've read it – if indeed you choose to read it at all!
  Very best wishes from your old confirmation pastor,
  Gerhard Krøgenes

He had a bit of a cheek, didn't he? Trying to get me to change my
mind after I'd clearly said I wanted to opt out.

But he meant well.

And it felt rather good.

I slipped the letter inside the book, which I left on the coffee table,
and threw the envelope in the bin in the kitchen.

'How are you doing up there?' I called up the stairs.

'Ready in a sec,' she answered.

A few moments later, she came down. She looked different, younger
in a way, even if she did take the stairs slowly and with some caution.
She'd put on a blue sweatshirt I'd never seen her in before, and a pair
of jeans she hardly ever wore either, that must have been it.

I didn't care for it, the look was too young for her somehow.

'Good to see you up and about again,' I said. 'Do you want to drive,
or shall I?'

'You drive.'

I pulled up outside the shop. Mum opened her door and swung her legs
out, gripped the handle and tried to heave herself up. I hurried round
from the driver's side and helped her before she had a chance to ask, I
knew how embarrassed she'd feel if she had to ask.

'There we are,' she said once she'd drawn herself upright. 'I can
manage on my own now. If you'll just hand me my bag?'

I did so and closed the door.

'Do you know where it is?'

'Oh yes. I've been doing the shopping here for twenty years, it hasn't
escaped me.'

'I'll go in with you so they can tell me when you'll be finished.'

The clinic was through a door at the rear of the shop, it was open
when we got there and the physiotherapist herself was seated at a desk
reading something with her glasses on the tip of her nose. She got up as

we came in. She couldn't have very many clients, I thought to myself, it was probably more like a hobby she had.

'How long will it take?' I asked.

'Forty-five minutes,' she said.

'I'll pick you up again at quarter past one,' I said to Mum, who stood clutching her bag, looking quite lost all of a sudden.

A lorry thundered past on the road when I came back out, a corner of its tarp flapping wildly. Sand from the winter's gritting whirled up in its wake.

Another week of weather like this and the leaves would come out, I thought as I got in the car. It was hardly worth going home again, but it made even less sense hanging around outside the shop, so I turned the ignition and pulled out to get back on the road. A red Lada was coming towards me and I tried to see what the driver looked like, thinking it could only be the woman I'd seen in the forest. There weren't that many red Ladas about. But the sharp sunlight on the windscreen was a glare that erased every detail. A blurred figure wearing sunglasses was all I could see as she passed.

Then, with a stab of joy, I thought about Lisa Dønnestad.

Only then did it occur to me I must have been feeling down.

Why?

Mum had looked so lost in there. So helpless in her youthful clothes, with her drained-looking face.

I had to do better for her. And for Joar, too.

I could, easily!

I could get the breakfast ready in the mornings. Good breakfasts, with juice, perhaps even pancakes.

I could bake in the evenings, so there'd be nice fresh bread for us.

I could make the dinners.

And get Joar out of his room. Do some shooting practice with him. Take him out in the canoe.

Talk to Mum a lot more.

Forget that business with Dad.

He was dead. She was alive.

Yes, that's what I'd do.

I turned off the road onto the gravel track of our drive and carried on

slowly up to the house, parking in front of the step so the hosepipe
could reach and I wouldn't have to carry the bucket very far when I
started washing the car. But when I got out and saw how dirty it was, I
realised that with only half an hour until I had to go and pick Mum up
again I wouldn't have time, so it was all pretty pointless.

Oh well.

Maybe she'd got her own flat or a bedsit, with a phone of her own?

I hadn't even thought of that.

Her features were still rather vague when I tried to think about her,
but the feeling she gave me was strong and clear.

She may not have been a supermodel, but she was bloody gorgeous
all the same.

A bit trashy perhaps, but who cared?

There was no one by the name of Lisa Dønnestad in the book, so I'd
have to try all five, unless of course I got lucky and found her first go.

But not now, not at one o'clock in the afternoon.

I wondered what she did.

It was hard to tell how old she was. Anything between sixteen and
twenty, I reckoned.

But not sixteen. And not twenty either.

I poured myself some coffee and rang the paper.

'I have got a job to do as well, you know,' said Dag as soon as he
realised it was me again. 'But since you're asking, I phoned the
college.'

'And?' I said, looking out of the living-room window. The spruce on
the hillside across the river seemed to glitter in the sunlight.

'No one there who knows Russian.'

'But?'

'What makes you think there's a but?'

'I could tell by the way you said it.'

'But,' he said. 'The woman I spoke to told us to get in touch with
Terje Krag.'

'Who's he?'

'You don't know?'

'I wouldn't have asked if I did.'

'He's in the paper every other day!'

I didn't say anything, but stepped backwards so I could see the clock in the kitchen. Five to one.

'He's a local cultural figure,' Dag said. 'Writes all sorts of books that people round here give each other for Christmas. *Our Town of Sailing Ships*, for example. You'll have seen that one, surely?'

'Probably,' I said. 'And he knows Russian?'

'Apparently.'

'And lives in town?'

'Lives and breathes the place. Puts himself about as well. Local history society, that sort of thing. Anything for a preservation order.'

'Is he in the phone book?'

'He is, so I suggest you give him a ring. But listen, I've got to get back to work. Let me know how you get on. You've got *me* interested in that letter now.'

'You haven't mentioned what I told you in the car, have you?'

'Course not.'

'Good. Thanks for all your help. Speak to you soon.'

'Yes, catch you later.'

Mum was standing in the sunshine outside the shop with her bag on her arm when I turned into the car park. I pulled up next to her, leaned across and opened the door.

'How did it go?' I said. 'Can you feel any difference?'

She nodded and got in, gave me a faint smile.

'Thanks for booking the appointment.'

'No problem. Was she rough on you?'

She shook her head. I swung round to get back on the road, giving way to three cars that came past in close succession.

'A little bit. But she's good is Johanne.'

'Do you know her?' I said, pulling out and moving quickly through the gears.

'Oh yes,' she said.

'When do you think you'll be able to go back to work, then?'

'Tomorrow.'

'That's good!'

'Yes, I suppose it is,' she said.

I looked at her before turning up the drive, taking care so as not to give her too bumpy a ride.

After I pulled up and she opened the door to get out, I went round to help her as I'd done earlier on, and although her movements were slow and her facial expression pained, I thought it would be best for her to manage on her own as much as she could. It could so easily become a frame of mind.

'What are you going to do the rest of the day, then?' I said. 'Savour your freedom?'

She put her bag down on the table in the hall and hung her short jacket on the peg.

'I'll go for another lie-down, I think,' she said. 'You don't mind, do you?'

'No, of course not. Sounds like a good plan! Do you want me to bring you some coffee?'

'Later, perhaps.'

'OK. Shout down if you need anything.'

She went slowly up the stairs into her bedroom. It didn't look like the physio had helped much. But then again, it was bound to be a bit gruelling to begin with, before the benefits kicked in. I should have asked if she'd made another appointment.

If she hadn't, I could do it for her.

I sat down on the sofa with the phone book in my lap. I looked up Terje Krag first, which was easy enough, he was the only person in town with that name. After that, I wrote down the numbers of all the Dønnestads that looked like they could be a lead on Lisa. My heart beat faster in my chest as I wrote.

'Steady now,' I said to myself with a smile. 'She's just an ordinary girl, that's all.'

I went and got Dad's letter and put it on the telephone table in front of me before dialling Krag's number.

As I did, I heard a car pull up outside. I hung up just as it started ringing and went over to the window. It was Terje. He'd parked, and when I went out he stood slouched over the open car door, the way he'd done the last time he was here.

'All right,' he said.

'All right,' I said. 'How's things?'

'Good. Just on my lunch break. Thought I might as well pop over rather than phone. I had a word with the foreman. No jobs just at the minute, I'm afraid,' he said.

'That's OK,' I said. 'I didn't think there would be. But thanks for asking, all the same.'

'Nothing steady, anyway. There's always some casual work to be had, though. The odd few hours here and there. Mostly at weekends, I think, and when they've got big orders going out. I can get you in, if you're interested? They'd ring you up when they needed you.'

'What sort of work would it be?'

He shrugged.

'Sweeping up, that sort of thing. Tidying up in the stores. Shifting stuff.'

'Haven't they got youngsters doing that after school?'

He nodded.

'You'd be top of the list, though. I mean, they'd ring you first.'

'Thanks, but I think I'll pass,' I said. 'I need something more stable.'

'I can understand that.'

'Do you want a coffee?'

He shook his head.

'Got to get back. Are you coming to practice tonight?'

'Of course.'

'OK, see you later!'

He slipped back into the driver's seat and sat like a kind of mollusc in its shell as he reversed and pulled away down the drive.

I went back in and dialled Krag's number again.

'Hello?' a gravelly voice said after a couple of rings.

'Hello, is that Terje Krag speaking?'

'It is, yes.'

'Hello, my name's Syvert Løyning. I'm calling because I've been told you know Russian. Is that right?'

'That's right, yes.'

'I've got something I'd like to have translated, you see. I'd pay you for your trouble, of course!'

'I see,' he said. 'Is it much?'

'No, no. It's a letter of some sort. Four short pages of handwriting, that's all. I'd like to know what it says, only it's all Greek to me.'

He laughed.

'So someone sent you a letter in Russian?'

'Not exactly. It was sent to my father. He's been dead for some years now. I found the letter among his things.'

'Did *he* know Russian?'

'Yes.'

'What was his name, if I might ask?'

'The same as my own, actually. Syvert Løyning.'

'And he was from here?'

'Yes. At least not far away. The countryside, you'd probably call it.'

'Hm. I thought I knew everyone in the area who knew Russian. Still, I'd be happy to help. Just bring it round. I'm usually in. Apart from the evenings, that is.'

'Excellent!' I said. 'Thanks very much indeed. Would it be convenient if I came later today?'

'Yes, why not?'

I made a couple of sandwiches and poured some milk into a glass for Mum before I got going. She was fast asleep, so it seemed, so I put the tray on the bedside table and crept out again. I scribbled a note for them both telling them I'd gone into town, and left it on the worktop in the kitchen. I could wash the car when I got home, I thought when I saw it there with its filthy windows in the sunshine. Or maybe tomorrow, if I didn't have time before football practice. I had the dinner to make as well.

I could heat up some frozen pizzas. Joar wouldn't mind, at least.

I stopped off at the shop first to get some batteries for my Walkman so I could listen to some music on the way there. I put a cassette in, Whitesnake on one side and Rainbow on the other, turned up the volume and set off. Out by the sea, the sun was so bright I had to get Mum's sunglasses out of the glove compartment as I sang along to 'Tarot Woman'.

I don't want to go
Something tells me no

It was still the dog's bollocks, that old Rainbow album.

I pictured the cover, the enormous hand gripping the rainbow. *Rainbow Rising* in Gothic lettering above. For a long time I'd thought it was mountains in the background, but then one day I realised the hand was emerging from the sea, and the mountains were in fact waves.

Vidar's brother had had the poster on his wall. We'd thought it was totally wicked! Not to mention the music itself. We weren't old enough yet, we knew that, but we'd grow into it.

Steinar, his name was. Long, dark hair. He took his guitar with him on the bus in a guitar case. Lived in the basement of their house, with his own entrance.

One day we'd crept up on him and his mates from outside as they sat with the window open, tiptoed up close so we could hear what they were talking about.

Craft-verk, someone said clearly. *Three-dimensional*. And *synthesiser*.

Vidar shook his head vigorously as I snuck closer before craning to look in. Steinar's two mates were sitting on the floor studying an LP cover, while Steinar himself was bent over the record player.

Robot music streamed suddenly into the room, and as Steinar straightened up he caught sight of me and I scrambled to my feet and legged it with Vidar close on my heels.

Why I remembered it so well, I had no idea. It was just etched into my memory.

Maybe it was the feeling that the three young men in that basement room had stepped into the future. Or at least were in touch with it.

Three-dimensional — for me it was a word of the future. I didn't know what it meant at the time, so it must have been the sound of it that made such an impression on me.

Did Vidar remember?

I doubted it.

Where was he these days, anyway?

It was 'Do You Close Your Eyes' now and I sang again while taking in the sight of the town that had come into view after the bend, its roof-tops and windows shimmering and glittering at the end of the valley.

Did he still have that job at the hunting and outdoor pursuits shop?

It wouldn't have surprised me.

He was the sort who always had a smile on his face, and giggled so much that no one, male or female, ever took him seriously, he was like a nobody in that respect. It didn't seem to make much difference that he was good-looking, got top marks in all subjects and was even a district shooting champion.

There was nothing wrong about him. But nothing right either.

I'd always liked him, and we'd always been friends. But even I had a tendency to forget about him the minute we weren't actually hanging out together. He never left an impression, there was never a trace of him afterwards.

I could stop by the shop on the way and see if he was there. Yes, that's what I'd do.

The car park on Festningsgaten was full, so I carried on down to the quayside and parked there instead, even if the address I was going to was at the other end of town. The sun was shining and the air was still and rather warm, so it didn't matter much. Hopefully, Mum was going to be feeling stronger when she woke up, at least strong enough to be up with Joar.

What was strange wasn't so much the dream he'd had about a bird flying out of her mouth, but that he actually believed it was telling him something was going to happen.

Where did he get that from?

He certainly didn't take after Dad. There was a slight physical resemblance, but that was all.

The outdoor tables at the quayside restaurant were packed with people drinking golden beer with their prawn sandwiches or fish soup, soaking up the sunshine. What kind of jobs did they have, I wondered, since they could afford not only the monetary cost, but also the time in the middle of an ordinary working day?

The pedestrian thoroughfare was busy too, almost like a day in summer. At the entrance to the Arcade, a covered passage tucked between two buildings, a white van stood parked with its rear doors open, and a small man in white overalls was manoeuvring a large red cylindrical object of some sort, by turns dragging and wriggling it from the inside of the van onto the ground. I slowed as I approached, there was something familiar about him. He drew himself upright and put one hand to the small of his back, the unwieldy object now standing on its end in front of him. I didn't realise until then that it was a rolled-up carpet. He looked over his shoulder and at once I recognised him.

It was Mads!

'Hey!' I said

'Hello, Syvert,' he said, seeming a bit uncomfortable.

'What are you up to?'

'Just taking this carpet in there.'

'Do you need a hand?'

'No, no. No, no, no.'

'OK,' I said. 'Is this your job, then?'

He nodded.

I read what it said on the side of the van.

'Kaspersen's Carpets,' I said. 'Your own firm?'

'No, I work for them, that's all.'

His eyes were looking everywhere except at me.

'Well, I won't hold you up. See you tonight!'

He gave a brief nod, I smiled at him and carried on up the street. When I turned round a few moments later he was back to grappling with his carpet again.

So weird seeing him away from the football pitch!

And how different he'd come across.

I stopped to look in the window of the music shop, they sold records as well as instruments, and thought about going in, but I didn't have enough cash on me to buy a record, not even a Nice Price, so I carried on walking.

Two girls of the well-to-do spoilt type who looked like they were still in gymnas were sitting on one of the benches in the middle of the street, each with a cornet of ice cream, each wearing sunglasses and a plump down jacket, each with their legs crossed.

I stopped in front of them.

'Those ice creams look nice,' I said. 'Where did you get them?'

One of them pointed towards a kiosk about twenty metres away. Her forehead and chin were full of zits she'd tried to cover with some sort of make-up. Dark hair, round sunglasses. She stuck her tongue out and licked her ice cream methodically from bottom to top to catch what was melting and beginning to drip.

'Thanks,' I said with a smile. 'What's that you've got sprinkled on?'

'Get lost,' the other one said. She had big, protruding lips that seemed not to belong to the rest of her face, pale skin, broad shoulders, a stubby neck.

'Just wondering. It looks delicious.'

'Caramel crunch,' the first one said.

'Do they still let you have caramel crunch on one side and cocoa powder on the other?'

'How old are you, five or something?' her friend said, before nipping off a mouthful of ice cream with her lips.

'Just a thought. Another thing that's good, of course, is biting the bottom off the cornet and sucking the ice cream out that way. Have you tried it?'

The one with the stubby neck put her index finger to her temple and twisted it in the air a couple of times. But I noticed that the one with the zits smiled as I walked on. They were probably sagging off in the fine weather. Their jackets would have been presents from Daddy, and the only worries they had in life were about how they looked.

The kiosk had the business paper in the rack outside, so I took a copy out, turned to the share pages and looked down the list until finding mine.

I shouldn't have done. They'd dropped again.

'Are you buying that, or what?' the guy at the counter said.

'Just needed to check something,' I said, returning it to the rack and walking off again before he could say anything. To get to Krag's place I had to turn left down the next side street, but wasn't there something else I was going to do first?

What was it?

I walked slowly while racking my brains. Something I'd been thinking about in the car.

What had I thought about in the car?

Three-dimensionality.

Vidar.

That was it!

The shop where he worked was in one of the side streets leading down to the railway station, so I turned and went back. I glanced up at the clock on the church tower. I was in no great hurry. And it'd be good to know what Vidar was up to now. I could have a look at some outdoor gear while I was at it.

A few minutes later I opened the door of the shop and went inside. There was no one behind the counter. At a low bench in the middle of the room, an assistant was bent over a shoebox in front of a male customer in his sixties who was taking off his shoes.

'Does Vidar still work here?' I said.

The assistant glanced up at me. His face was ruddy and his eyes somewhat unfriendly.

'He's in the storeroom.'

'Can I go in? I just stopped by to say hello.'

'That's not allowed, I'm afraid. He'll be back in a minute, though.'

'OK,' I said, and ambled past the shelves and racks towards the rear wall where the fishing tackle was. The tackle we had at home was all from the seventies, most of it Dad had bought. The rods you could get now were much better, but cost a packet.

A door, barely discernible in the wall next to the shelves of footwear, opened and Vidar emerged carrying a stack of shoeboxes. He didn't see me, but headed for the bench in the middle.

I gave him a few seconds before going after him.

'All right, Vidar?' I said.

'Syvert!' he said. 'What are you doing here?'

'Thought I'd see if you still worked here. Which obviously you do.'

Vidar nodded briskly. It was good to see he still had the same enthusiasm.

'And you're in the navy?'

'Got out a week ago.'

'Nice one!' he said.

'Thanks,' I said. 'Have you got time for a coffee?'

He looked at the clock first, then at the sales assistant who had now straightened up to thread some laces into a pair of new fell boots.

'Jørgen?' Vidar said.

No reaction.

'Jørgen? Do you mind if I just pop out for a bit? Ten minutes, at the most!'

Jørgen glanced at him sideways and nodded curtly.

'Ten minutes?' I said when we got outside into the street. 'We'll have to get a move on, then!'

Vidar giggled.

'Is Jørgen your boss?' I said, narrowing my eyes to focus in the bright sunlight.

'No, no. He just works there the same as me. But he's older, so it's only natural he has more of a say. If that's what you mean?'

'Shall we go up to the Bakery?' I said.

'OK,' he said.

A pair of old fogies were sitting inside with their cake; apart from that the place was empty. A fly, imprisoned in the glass display case, wandered across the icing on a sponge cake. I'd read once that they tasted with their feet, so I supposed it was doing all right for the moment.

'Coffee?' I said to Vidar, who'd already sat down at a table by the window.

He nodded.

'Anything else?'

'Are you having something?'

'Maybe a custard and coconut bun?'

'Sounds good.'

I went back to the table with the cakes while the woman at the till entered the amount, then went back to pay, poured the two coffees from the self-service, took them back to the table, and put one down in front of him, the other where I was sitting. Then the door opened and a woman backed in, dragging a pushchair.

'I haven't seen you for ages,' I said. 'How's things?'

'Good,' he said. 'I retook one of my exams in the winter to improve my grade and now I've got in to study medicine. He he he.'

'Brilliant! So you're going to be a doctor?'

'I hope so.'

'Doctor Andersen!'

He laughed a bit sheepishly and shifted in his seat before realising he could sip his coffee and conceal his embarrassment that way instead.

'You were always good at school,' I said.

'Not really.'

'What do you mean, not really? You got As in every subject in ninth, as far as I remember.'

He shook his head.

'I got a B in home economics.'

'But that was with Martinsen. She never liked any of us.'

'He he he.'

The bun was a bit dry on the outside, so I cut it in two so I could go straight to the custard in the middle.

'How about you?' said Vidar. 'What are you going do when autumn comes?'

I shrugged with my mouth full. Swallowed, sipped some coffee.

'Haven't a clue,' I said. 'Any suggestions?'

He shook his head and giggled.

'Maybe Trondheim, the Institute of Technology,' I said. 'I'll have to see. I'll need to do a retake as well, though. I'm not sure, I haven't really looked into it yet. Maybe not. What do you think?'

'Depends what course you want to take.'

'That's just it. I've no idea, really. I've got to do something, though. Only I can't help thinking that the choice I make now means I'll be stuck with it for the rest of my life. Which isn't that appealing, seeing as how I've no idea what I want.'

'Then do a foundation course. It'll give you six months to think about it.'

'Maybe. Signe's doing that now, by the way. I ran into her in the shop a few days ago.'

Vidar nodded slowly a couple of times.

'You had a thing about her, didn't you, now I come to think about it?' I said.

'He he he.'

'Doctor. I can see you as a doctor. It'll be a tough course, though?'

'Yes, I think so. Medicine and law are meant to be the hardest.'

'You'll be off to Oslo, then?'

He shook his head.

'Bergen.'

'Great city, Bergen,' I said, my eyes inadvertently finding the gaze of the little kid in the puschair who was staring at me mesmerised, mouth wide open.

It happened quite a lot, that little kids I didn't know stared at me like that. Sometimes I wondered if it was because I looked funny, other times if they saw something special in me, something only they could see.

'Do you remember that time we crept up on Steinar and his mates when they were sitting in the basement with the window open even though it was winter? We'd have been ten or eleven, something like that.'

He looked at me as he lifted his cup to his lips.

'No, of course you don't, and why would you?' I said. 'We must have done a million things just like it.'

He put his cup down and wiped his mouth with the back of his hand.

'I do remember that.'

'Do you?'

'Yes, of course.'

'How come?'

'Because that's when you found out . . .'

His voice trailed off as he looked at me in surprise.

I said nothing, waiting for him to go on.

'Don't you remember?' he said.

'Remember what?'

'That was when your mum came.'

'My mum? When? Then?'

'Yes. You mean you don't remember?'

Bang.

I remembered.

We'd run as fast as we could around the side of the house. When we got to the front, in stitches from the excitement, Mum's car came up the drive. I remembered standing quite still with my hands at my sides, watching her as she got out. I knew something had happened. She bent forward and held her arms out, standing beside the car looking at me, I was perhaps ten metres away. She was waiting for me to come to her, so that she could hold me.

But I didn't want to.

'Syvert, come here,' she said.

'What for?' I said. 'What is it?'

'Come here.'

I stayed put. She straightened up and came towards us. Stopped in front of me and leaned forward again.

'There's been an accident,' she said. 'It's your dad.'

She put her arms around me. I turned my face to the woods. In the car, Joar was starting to get impatient.

'I remember now,' I said to Vidar, and smiled faintly. 'I'd just forgotten it was the same day.'

'It was terrible,' said Vidar.

'Yes, it was. But it's a long time ago! Nearly nine years, can you believe it?'

He didn't say anything, just shook his head.

'How about going for a drink on Saturday?' I said.

'I'd love to, only I'm in Evje then. There's a shooting tournament on there at the weekend.'

'You've kept up the shooting, then? How's it going?'

'He he he.'

We parted outside the Bakery with a vague agreement to go out somewhere soon. Not that I was desperate to go out drinking with Vidar, but having looked him up like that it felt like I had to follow up in some way.

As I went back down the pedestrian street, I took the letter out of my back pocket and looked at it again. It could have said anything at all.

Why couldn't they use the ordinary alphabet in the Soviet Union like the rest of us? Everything they had was turned in on itself. Even some of their cities were secret, so I'd heard. They weren't on any map, and it was forbidden to go there.

What had Dad been doing in a country like that?

And why hadn't anyone ever told me?

I put the letter back in my pocket and made a right turn, the shops petering out after a couple of hundred metres, superseded by low, white wooden houses. Krag lived a bit further along, next to what looked like a scrapyard. Two ship models in the window. No doorbell, just a little brass knocker.

Thunk, thunk.

A door opened inside. Footsteps came across a floor.

A man with a big halo of white hair, a grey beard and small, round specs came to the door.

'Syvert?' he said.

'That's right,' I said. 'I hope I'm not intruding?'

'Not at all. Come in.'

After the bright sunshine outside, my eyes took a few seconds to adjust to the dim hallway.

'Coffee?' he said, already on his way through a door further inside.

'If it's no trouble,' I said, and bent down to take my shoes off. The walls were painted dark green and a crimson mat ran the length of the varnished floor. Old photographs covered the wall on one side, small paintings on the other. A staircase led up to the first floor, next to it was the door through which Krag had just disappeared. I heard the sound of running water and followed it, entering the kitchen just as he put the coffee pot on the hob and switched it on. He turned towards me.

'So, a letter in Russian. To your father, you say?'

I nodded.

'Actually, I'm not really sure what it is. It *looks like* a letter. I found it among my dad's things. It could be just notes or something, for all I know.'

'We'll soon find out. Let's have a look, shall we?'

I got the letter out of my pocket and handed it to him.

'It would seem to be a letter,' he said. 'Syvert is the name in the salutation. Your father's name too, is that right?'

'Yes.'

'Care for a biscuit with your coffee?'

Without waiting for an answer, he reached up and took a tin from on top of the cupboards.

'They're rather good, which is why I keep them up here. If I didn't, they'd be gone in a jiffy. It gives me time to pause and reconsider, and usually I come to my senses. Usually, not always! Ha ha ha! When you get to sixty, as I will soon, a person can't eat the way they used to, not without it showing. Not that *you* need to worry!'

He took two small white plates with a floral pattern from the cupboard and put them down on the worktop as the coffee pot spluttered. Then two cups and saucers with the same pattern. They were so thin and delicate I had difficulty connecting them with him, his tanned, leathery face, the lines in his brow, the wrinkles around his eyes, his thick, tufty hair, his big hands, etched with scars.

The cupboards were painted blue and had an old-fashioned feel to them. Next to them was a shelf of dinner plates that were displayed upright on their rims. The table by the window was old-fashioned too, its legs blackened with age.

The coffee pot began to spit. Krag swivelled and pressed it down on the hob. It spat even more. He opened the biscuit tin and put some of the biscuits onto a plate.

'They've a honey topping of some sort, you see. I've no idea how they make them. Have you had them before?'

'I don't think so,' I said.

'Do you want me to do this out loud, like a simultaneous translation? Or would you prefer to have it in writing? As if it were a letter in Norwegian?'

'In writing, I think. I'd probably just forget otherwise. It'd be good to have it written down. If that's OK?'

'Yes, of course. It'll take a bit longer, that's all.'

He took the coffee pot off the heat.

'Let's go into the studio,' he said, nodding towards a door.

The room behind it was a kind of library, one wall covered with books from floor to ceiling, a desk strewn with papers up against the other. Another door led off into a glass extension crammed with art materials and unfinished paintings, a pair of tired sofas and a low table at one end where he put the coffee things down.

'Sit thee doon,' he said. 'Coffee before work, always.'

I remained standing a moment, looking at what surrounded me, while he went back to get the coffee. Some of the paintings were completely blue, layer upon layer of blue in different shades. Others were orange, yellow and brown, and seemed to represent the skerries.

Who painted the sun brown and the sea yellow?

'I see you're an artist,' I said when he came back in with the coffee pot.

'Perhaps,' he said. 'Or perhaps just a painter!'

He laughed and sat down.

'There we are,' he said. 'Now, where were we? A letter to your father that you'd like to have translated.'

'Yes,' I said.

'And your father is dead, is that right?'

'Yes.'

'And you found this letter among his things.'

'Yes.'

'What was his surname again?'

'Løyning.'

'Hm. And the reason he spoke Russian was . . . ?'

'He learned it in the armed forces.'

'Aha. One of that lot!'

'And what would be the reason *you* speak Russian?' I said. 'Anything to do with socialism, by any chance?'

He poured a small amount of coffee tentatively into his own cup, then poured it back into the pot without looking at me.

'What makes you think that?' he said, throwing me a glance.

'Nothing, really. It's just the impression I get. And with the Soviet Union being a socialist country, well . . .'

He laughed.

'You couldn't be more wrong, young man. The Soviet Union is most certainly not a socialist country. In fact, it has nothing *whatsoever* to do with socialism.'

'I'm sorry, but I happen to know quite a lot about it. The Revolution in 1917 was a Marxist–Leninist revolution, in other words socialist. Everything to this day is state-run and collectivised.'

'The Soviet Union is a totalitarian autocracy, my friend. Which is anathema to socialism. Socialism is government by the people.'

'Socialism is the tyranny of the state,' I said. 'The state owns everything and decides everything. Ordinary people have no say in a socialist society. That's what your protest generation left us.'

'It sounds like you've been exposed to some capitalist propaganda.'

'Maybe someone who talks about socialist government by the people should keep his voice down about propaganda.'

He picked up the coffee pot, then put it down hard again on the table.

He looked at me with his blue, rather moist eyes.

'You're wrong,' he said. 'I didn't learn Russian because I was a communist. I learned it because I read Dostoevsky as a teenager. I decided then that I would read him in his own language. It took me twelve years. But the rewards have been rich.'

He poured coffee into my cup, and into his own, then offered me a biscuit from the plate. I took one.

'Rather good, don't you think?' he said, popping one into his mouth.

'Very,' I said.

'Have you read Dostoevsky?'

I shook my head.

'But I've got one of his books.'

'Which one?'

'I can't remember the title. Something to do with a crime.'

'*Crime and Punishment.*'

'That's it, yes.'

'You're just the right age for it. I wish it was me who'd yet to read it! Go home and read, young man!'

'Is he a socialist writer?'

'Dostoevsky? Good lord, no. Don't they teach you anything at school these days? Dostoevsky, Dostoevsky is a *Christian* writer. Perhaps the most Christian of all writers. More Christian than Christ himself even, you could say. Does that sound boring?'

'A bit.'

'Well, it isn't! Listen. I'll translate your father's letter for you. Gladly. I won't have money for it, though. I want you to read *Crime and*

Punishment instead. OK? How does that sound? I translate the letter, you read Dostoevsky.'

I wanted to say I'd rather pay, but something told me he'd take offence, so I nodded and told him it was a deal.

'It'll take a short time,' he said. 'Do you want to wait here or come back later?'

'How long do you think it'll take?'

'Half an hour, at least. Perhaps longer.'

'I'll wait,' I said. 'If you're sure it's all right?'

'Of course. Help yourself to biscuits and books!'

He stood up and went into the adjoining room. I remained seated, crunched a biscuit, poured myself another coffee. The books he'd mentioned filled a row of shelves up against the wall. Thick volumes that looked like they were all about art. I didn't look any closer than that, but crept about, looking at the pictures he'd painted. Blue, slightly irregular vases of blue flowers in blue rooms, various versions of the same motif. A girl in a green T-shirt sitting at an angle on a chair in a yellow room, it looked like something a child could have painted, it too in a number of versions.

Maybe he kept some of his own books in here?

I went over and studied the titles.

Yes, there they were. Lined up on the bottom shelf.

Our Town of Sailing Ships. Terje Krag.

Russia's Heart, Russia's Grief. Terje Krag.

The Great Storm and the Little Town. Terje Krag.

The Chronicler of Bestiality. Terje Krag.

Conservation Blues. Terje Krag.

The Wildest Dance. Terje Krag.

The Wildest Dance?

I plucked one of several copies of the book from the shelf and took a closer look.

14 July 1518. A woman takes to dancing in the streets of Strasbourg. She dances day and night, and is joined by increasing numbers. Eventually, more than four hundred people are dancing with her, seemingly unable to stop. For several weeks, they dance. They dance until their feet bleed, dance until they drop, dance until they die. Incidents of the same phenomenon, referred to variously as the Dancing Plague, Dancing Mania or St Vitus' Dance, are recorded as having occurred on numerous occasions in medieval Europe. In The Wildest Dance, *Terje Krag investigates this extraordinary episode in European history, drawing parallels with similar occurrences in our own age.*

I sat down again, poured some more coffee into my cup, and took another biscuit, promising myself it would be the last. After all, he was fond of them, and his stash probably wasn't inexhaustible.

They were really good. The honey topping was chewy and hard at the same time, whereas the biscuit itself was crisp and porous. The combination was irresistible.

If Lisa and I had been been going out with each other, I could have slipped one into my pocket and taken it with me for her to taste. I could have told her about all the paintings and the books, the wildest dance. And our little discussion about the Soviet Union.

'He's a communist, I'm sure he is,' I'd have been able to say.

'What's wrong with that?' she'd have been able to say then.

'Nothing, nothing at all. People can believe in what they want. It's just that they can't in a communist country, can they? Do you get what I'm saying?'

'I'm not thick, you know. But maybe he wants communism *with* free speech. Have you thought about that?'

I smiled to myself as I sat there. Now that I was thinking about her, it wasn't such a long stretch to think about getting her clothes off. She was in a white T-shirt and light blue jeans, and she was sitting on the other sofa across the table. But if I got up and went over to her in my mind, and kissed her and took her T-shirt off, and her bra, and fondled her white breasts, it'd only give me a stiffy that'd be impossible to get rid of, I'd go all red in the face, there'd be no way out.

Too late.

It had already happened.

There was only one thing for it.

I buried my hands in my pockets and went into the adjoining room where Krag sat bent over his desk, writing busily on a sheet of paper, the letter next to it.

'Sorry, do you think I could just use your loo?' I said.

'Of course,' he said. 'Up the stairs and right in front of you. Very interesting letter, by the way! Soon be done.'

The staircase was painted in a thick blue paint that made me think of the deck of a ship, even though I'd never seen a blue ship's deck before. The bathroom was small, with an old-fashioned bathtub on claw feet that took up nearly all the space, a toilet and a small sink with a narrow shelf and a stingy little mirror above it. I put the hook on the door and turned the tap on so no other sound would escape. Lisa was still looking at me with a little smile on her face. It was an ironical sort of smile, she was an ironical sort of girl, I'd realised that, but I couldn't care about it now. I imagined myself getting to my feet and going over to her. I pulled her T-shirt over her head and took it off, undid her bra. Put my hands on her white breasts, fondling.

'I've never done it before,' I whispered, my heart thudding.

'It's all right,' she said. 'It's not exactly difficult. But it's really nice. Oh, you're so good.'

'Oh, yes,' I said. 'You're so gorgeous, Lisa. You're everything I want.'

'You've got me now,' she breathed. 'I'm yours. Do what you want with me.'

The first delivery splashed against the wall before I managed to direct the next into the toilet bowl. When it was over, I stood still for a few seconds to listen in case there was someone there. Then I wiped up the mess, washed myself and went back downstairs to Krag, who looked up at me from his desk as I came in.

'Here we are,' he said. 'We now have a letter in Norwegian. Not a perfect translation, not by any means, but good enough to give you an impression of what the original says! Would you like me to read it to you?'

'I think perhaps I'd like to read it on my own.'

'Well, if you can decipher my scribble,' he said, handing me the letter.

I took it and read the first couple of lines.

My dear, beloved Syvert,
*   You've just left me as I write this. The bed is still warm from your body.*
How unbelievable that I should miss you already! I never would have
thought I could feel such happiness. And such sorrow!

Oh God. Oh dear God.

It was from her. The woman he was going to leave us for.

She was Russian! She lived in the Soviet Union!

Krag studied me as I folded the letter, my heart trembling.

'Can you read the writing?' he said. 'Or would you like me to type it for you?'

'I'm really grateful to you for this. I'd like to pay you for it.'

He shook his head magnanimously.

'Read *Crime and Punishment.* That's my price. Deal?'

'Deal,' I said, my whole body now strangely cold, and I felt nauseous too. 'Thanks very much indeed.'

'Was it something you weren't expecting?' he said, getting to his feet.

'No,' I said. 'Not at all. It's what I thought it was.'

I went into the hall, put my shoes on and bent down to tie the laces. Krag stood in the doorway waiting.

'Is your mother Russian?'

None of your bloody business, I thought, but kept it to myself.

'No,' I said.

'I thought so. She'd have been able to translate it for you herself, if she was. Unless she's . . . no longer with us, that is.'

I said nothing, but straightened up and returned his gaze as I put out my hand.

'Thanks a lot indeed,' I said. 'I owe you a favour.'

'We've already agreed about that,' he said, and shook my hand. 'Nice meeting you.'

'And thanks for the biscuits as well! They really are delicious.'

I opened the door and stepped out into the sunshine, closed it behind me and went down the three steps to the pavement. For a short moment, I didn't know where I was, not even what town I was in, everything was a blank, all I could see was shimmering white wood and an empty street, blue sky and some seagulls on the roof of the house across the road. It was like I was in a dream.

I looked at the letter that was still in my hand.

For crying out loud.

For crying out bloody loud.

I folded the pages once more, slipped them into my inside pocket and started walking. I didn't want to read it there, standing in the street. And not in the car either, I decided. In my room, when I got home? No, not with Mum and Joar in the house.

It felt like the letter was on fire in my chest.

She'd been totally in love with him. And he with her, presumably. Enough for him to want to leave Mum and us.

But he wasn't the sort of man women fell in love with! Not like that, anyway.

Maybe it was a long time ago? Maybe it was when he was a student. Before he met Mum? Was the letter dated? Was it? Was it?

I snatched the pages out of my pocket and looked again.

It wasn't dated.

So it could have been from an old flame.

But *inside* the Soviet Union?

It didn't have to be! She could just as well have written it in Norway!

That had to be it. He knew Russian, she lived in Oslo, worked at the embassy there or something, they met and had a relationship. Before he met Mum.

I looked up and discovered I was already on the pedestrian street again, right by the Bakery. Could I sit down and read it in there? No, not with other people around me. But I had to read it.

He'd made a woman tremendously happy.

Dad? That quiet, timid man? Immersed in all his little interests, never saying much.

But Einar had been jealous of Dad for having been so *capable*, as he'd put it.

Intelligent, in other words.

More than ordinarily intelligent.

That was what he'd meant.

And then there was him suffering from anxiety.

Nothing aligned with what I remembered.

I certainly couldn't see him in bed with another woman.

I never would have thought I could feel such happiness.

Mum hadn't to see the letter, not ever. Even if the woman had been there before her, it would still hurt too much. A woman who'd never felt such happiness. Dad had never made Mum happy like that.

Or had he?

They had two children together.

That had to mean something.

I stopped in front of the car, turned round and scanned the quayside, the outdoor tables of the restaurant where people still sat crammed together like nesting birds on a cliffside. A small bridge led over to the island in the harbour, so close it barely seemed like an island at all. That was where I could go. It'd be quiet there, even at this time of day.

Ten minutes later I was sitting with my back against the wall of a towering silo on the industrial quay where forklift trucks flitted about and cranes slowly swung their catches through the air. The sun obliterated all colour from the sea out at the horizon, where the water became just a gleaming gold, whereas at the quayside it was dark blue, and in the shadow of the spruce on the other side almost black.

I sat with the letter in my lap without yet reading it. There was no reason *not* to read it, what it said had been said now for nine years at least, possibly a lot longer, and nothing would be altered by my reading it.

But still, that was how it felt. That what the letter said was going to change everything. And if I didn't read it, everything would stay the way it was.

For crying out loud. It was only a *letter*, for God's sake.

From someone who'd been very fond of Dad.

How could that be so threatening?

I shaded my eyes with a hand peaked at my brow, and began to read.

My dear, beloved Syvert,

*You've just left me as I write this. The bed is still warm from your body.
How unbelievable that I should miss you already! I never would have
thought I could feel such happiness. And such sorrow! I hope you feel the
same, the happiness at what we have, and the sorrow at our difficult
plight. Please don't misunderstand me, for naturally I wish you no pain!
But during our time together these past two weeks, I have wondered if
what we share means as much to you as it does to me, if we are committed
in the same way, with the same feelings. Nothing you have said or done has
sown this doubt in me. It was there even when you came. Of course it was
there! You live in a faraway country with a family of your own, and
although we had such a joyous time when first we met, it was but a single
occasion, a few days only! And so I looked for signs when you came, signs
that you were here with all your heart. Or whether I was simply someone
with whom you were having fun on one of your trips abroad. When I saw
you and you embraced me and whispered my name, I knew it was not so.
But now that you are gone . . . Oh, how I miss you! Write as quickly as you
can, write, write and tell me how you feel, and what you think.*

Yours, always,

Asya

I sat for a long time looking at the sea without a thought in my head.
Then I read the letter again, as slowly as I could.

They'd met each other in the Soviet Union, it was almost certain,
seeing as she'd written that he lived in a faraway country. And she
wrote too that he had a family of his own. It meant he'd met her while
he was married to Mum, not before. Obviously, she was the woman he
was going to leave us for just before he died. It couldn't have been anyone else.

Did she know he was dead?

All of a sudden his letters would have stopped coming. There could
have been any number of reasons.

I got to my feet and started walking back to the car. I felt such a desperate sadness, for Dad, for the Russian woman, for Mum.

There had to be other letters too. He wouldn't have kept just the one,
surely?

Mum couldn't read them anyway, so he wouldn't have had to hide them exactly.

I had to talk to someone, tell someone.

Dag was the only one who'd understand, who would keep it to himself.

But I didn't trust him completely. I had a feeling he'd tell Einar. They'd been brothers. And his loyalty would be more towards his dad than me.

If only I had Lisa!

I stopped at the car, unlocked the door and got in. My heart seemed to constrict every time I thought about the letter.

What had he been doing in the Soviet Union anyway? A few days to begin with, when he first met her, then two weeks after that. Entering the Soviet Union wasn't exactly straightforward!

The only person I could ask was Mum. But I wasn't going to do that. I had to keep a barrier between the Soviet Union and her.

Einar, perhaps? I mulled it over as I pulled away across the car park, turned onto the road and headed up through town towards the motorway on the outskirts.

It was much the same with Einar as with Mum, I reckoned. He wasn't to know. It would have to be my secret.

Mum was in the kitchen making dinner when I got back, while Joar was seated at the table doing his homework.

'This is all very cosy,' I said, going over to fill the coffee maker with water. 'Are you feeling better?'

She nodded.

'Much,' she said, and smiled. 'The physio helped.'

'I thought it might,' I said. 'That sort of thing often results in a bad back.'

'What sort of thing?'

'Stress. Fatigue. The daily grind, it wears you out.'

'Is that what you've been thinking? That I'm worn out?'

I shrugged.

'It's crossed my mind, yes. You've got two, three different jobs. It wouldn't be that strange.'

She snorted.

'It's just a pinched nerve or some such thing.'

'If you say so,' I said, spooning four measures of coffee into the filter. 'What's for dinner?'

'Barley soup with sausage and vegetables.'

'Lovely,' I said. 'What about you, kiddo? Anything exciting to tell me about?'

Joar shook his head without looking up from his book.

'What's that you're reading?'

'It's about the Greeks and the Romans. We've got to find out what differences they've made to our own age.'

'The most important thing is that the Greeks invented salad,' I said. 'To this day, we eat Greek salad. And the Romans improved on it when Caesar invented the Caesar salad.'

'Ha ha.'

'It's true! You know what kind of salad's used in a Caesar salad? Romano salad. That's because it's Roman.'

'Don't confuse him,' Mum said with a little smile on her face.

It was a smile that made my heart sink. I thought again about the Russian woman writing her letter to Dad just after he'd gone.

But that was a long time ago. It wasn't now, even if now was when I'd read it. It had happened more than nine years ago.

What if I opened up about it?

What if I just showed Mum the letter?

No, no, no! I couldn't ever do that.

The last fond memories she had would be destroyed.

'Set the table, will you, Syvert?' she said.

'Of course. Are we having bread to go with it?'

'If you want.'

I put three soup bowls on the table, and spoons and drinking glasses, filled the jug with water and sliced some bread while Mum put the mat down on the table, then the pot of soup on top of it.

'There we are,' she said.

Joar closed his school book, put it on top of his exercise book and shoved the little pile to one side with his pencil case to crown it.

'Do you want to come out and do some shooting afterwards?' I said.

'Could do,' he said as Mum ladled some soup into his bowl. As if he couldn't manage himself!

'You could join a club, if you wanted,' I said. 'You're good at it, I could see that straight away. My friend Vidar, you know the one with the curly hair? He's been in a shooting club for years. He competes in the national championships and everything. He's taking part in a tournament in Evje this weekend, in fact.'

'Good idea,' said Mum.

'I don't think I want to,' said Joar.

'You don't go to anything,' said Mum. 'A healthy interest would do you good.'

'I've got interests.'

'I know you have,' said Mum. 'I'm thinking about things with other kids.'

Joar gave me a sour look.

I smiled as best I could.

'You know what'd be really good?'

He didn't answer, but gave a slight shake of his head.

'Hunting. With a rifle. In the forest or up on the fells. Don't you think so?'

'I suppose.'

'Don't you need permission for that, a licence?' Mum said. 'You can't just go out shooting any time you like, surely?'

'No idea,' I said. 'I can ask Vegard's dad. He'll know all about it.'

I put a slice of bread down on the table and started buttering it. The butter was hard and the bread got torn by the knife as I drew it across.

'Is it true you hit someone when you were playing football?' said Joar.

'What are you talking about?' I said, making sure not to look up at Mum as I lifted the bread to my mouth and took a bite.

'They said so at school. They said you punched someone from the other team and knocked him to the ground. Is it true or not?'

I chewed my bread and swallowed.

'There was a bit of handbags, that's all. It happens in football.'

'It doesn't sound like handbags to me,' said Joar. 'They said you punched him as hard as you could in the stomach and that you'd have been sent off if the ref had seen it. Is that what happened?'

'Like I said, it was handbags,' I said, and dipped my spoon into the soup.

'And they said you got headbutted when you were on the town last weekend.'

'Is that what they say?'

I sipped my soup cautiously as I looked at him.

'Yes.'

'I see.'

'Is it true, then?'

'Sort of.'

Mum concentrated on her soup as if she wasn't listening.

'You've heard about the feather that becomes five hens?' I said.

'No,' he said.

'It's from a story, by Hans Christian Andersen, I think. Someone mentions a feather to someone, who mentions it to someone else, and so on, and by the time they're finished the feather's become five hens. You mustn't believe everything you're told. People exaggerate all the time. They'd rather tell a good story than tell the truth.'

I looked at him.

'Are you ashamed of me?'

'No.'

There was a silence. I scraped up a big curl of butter with my knife and tried to butter another slice. I wondered what Joar and Mum talked about when they were on their own.

'Those buns you brought home the other day, Syvert. Did you put them in the freezer?'

'Yes.'

'Are there many left?'

'Loads. Ten, at least. Why?'

'Synnøve and Vibeke and Randi are coming round tonight. I've got to give them *something*. And I'm not really up to baking. But if you want to keep them, I can get some biscuits or something at the shop.'

'No, you have them.'

'All right.'

'The soup was good,' I said. 'Especially with the sausage in it.'

'I'm glad.'

I stood up and took my bowl with the spoon in it and my glass over to the sink as Joar disappeared up the stairs with his books under his arm.

'I'll do the dishes,' I said. 'You have a rest.'

'No, you won't,' she said. 'I'm perfectly fine now.'

'Are you sure? I don't mind, you know.'

'No, I'll do them. You see if you can drag Joar out with you.'

'Joar?' I called up the stairs. 'Are you coming out?'

He didn't answer, so I went up to get him.

'Are you coming out?' I said again as I put my head round the door.

'No,' he said. He was lying on his bed with his hands under his head.

'What do you mean, no?'

'I've changed my mind.'

'OK,' I said. I didn't want to do any shooting anyway, so it was only a relief. Instead, I wandered over to the barn and started going through the boxes of Dad's things, meticulously and more methodically this time, now that I knew what I was looking for.

At the bottom of the box with his accounts in it there were some more letters. All without their envelopes. Some running to several pages, others quite as short as the first. Eight in all.

What was I going to do?

I wasn't going to ask Krag again. He knew too much already. He knew Dad's name and that he'd had an affair with a woman in the Soviet Union. He even knew *her* name.

Besides, there was something nosy about him. The way he'd asked if Mum was Russian.

I emptied an A4-size envelope, put the letters inside and took them up to my room with me, slipping the envelope behind the paperbacks on the shelf. After that, I packed my holdall and went and sat downstairs in the living room to wait until it was time to go to football practice. Mum was busy in the kitchen with the radio on. A faint smell of buns came wafting through. Chernobyl was hardly mentioned on the news any more, but I could hear them talking about it now. They were saying the radioactivity had entered the ecosystem, especially in northern Norway, where the reindeer and other animals had got it in them and now they couldn't be eaten. In the Soviet Union they believed huge areas would have to stay uninhabited for hundreds of years, entire towns would be left empty.

What if Dad's woman lived there?

It wasn't impossible.

But not very likely either.

Asya.

What if she didn't know Dad was dead?

How would she know? Their relationship was a secret, no one here knew who she was. Added to that, she lived in a closed country with no possibility of coming here or getting in touch with anyone to find out what had happened.

She probably assumed he'd got cold feet and left her in the most cowardly fashion without a word. It wouldn't have been like him at all, but how was she to know?

But in fact he'd told Mum he wanted a divorce.

What had he been planning to do after that?

He couldn't exactly move to the Soviet Union.

A chilling thought occurred to me.

Perhaps he wasn't dead. Perhaps he'd staged the whole thing so he could live there without anyone knowing.

Ha ha.

My dad, the master spy.

I got up and went into the kitchen. Mum was sitting in the chair by the window with some plates and cups from the good tableware put out on the table in front of her. Briskly, she snapped the cigarette-rolling machine together and took out the finished cigarette, then stifled a cough before lighting up.

'I'm off to practice, then,' I said.

'All right,' she said.

'What time are your ladies coming?'

'They should be here any minute.'

'Can I take one of those buns with me? If you've got enough?'

'Yes, course you can. I'm not sure if they're quite ready yet, mind.'

I opened the oven and took one of them out. It was too hot to hold in my hands, so I tossed it into the air a few times, then put it down on the worktop while I filled a bottle with water from the tap. When I'd done that, I picked up the bun and went out to the car.

                                             *

I was nearly the first to arrive, only Terje had got there before me and was lifting a net of balls out of the boot of his car when I pulled up alongside him.

'All right, thug,' he said. 'How many have you punched today?'

'You'll be the first, if there's any more lip.'

'You can have a go.'

'I could hardly miss, not with that stomach.'

He grinned as he stood there, the bulging net slung over his shoulder like he was Father Christmas. He shut the boot, locked the car, picked up the orange cones that were stacked at his feet with his free hand and tucked them under his arm before we both walked over to the changing rooms. Some small figures were running around out on the pitches, they looked to be under sevens or under nines. As I sat and got changed, they all came charging in. I could tell they were a bit put out by my presence, they weren't used to seniors in their changing rooms, so I made sure I got a move on.

Terje was out in the middle pumping balls. I ran over and nicked a couple, placed them on the edge of the box at an angle to the goal and practised my free kicks. I managed to get a decent bend on them both, but the first sailed over the bar, the second went wide. I ran to get them and repeated the drill. I remembered one summer when Gjert and I snuck inside the ground and spent a whole morning taking free kicks until the groundsman came to water the pitch and chased us back out.

How much easier life had been then. We'd bike out to the tennis courts in the woods early in the morning and play there all day, the whole day would just be that. Or we'd bike to the beach at the mouth of the river, or to the low, smooth rocks at the sea, and spend the day swimming. We'd have our tea, watch telly, sleep, and wake up to another day.

Over by the changing rooms the others were arriving, holdalls dangling from shoulders. I flicked the ball up onto one foot, skied it, cushioned it with my head as it came down, and volleyed it way over the bar.

'Get your body over the ball, man!' Terje shouted.

I collected the balls and jogged back over to him.

'Who are we playing at the weekend?' I said.

'Vågsnes away.'

'How did they get on in their first match?'

'Drew one—all against Stampa. So we should be able to beat them.'

The sun was low in the sky now, the trees that edged the training ground and we ourselves threw long, thin shadows. Soon, the others began to emerge from the changing rooms, and before long the pitch was teeming with players, laughing, shouting, running.

After the warm-up, Mads gathered everyone around for his little talk.

'We lost our first match,' he said. 'And we need to be honest enough to admit that a lot of the time they played us off the park. That said, we got better as the game progressed, and Svein got us a cracker. That's what we take with us. The question is why they outplayed us to the extent they did.'

'They were better than us,' said Vegard. 'Simple as that.'

'I'm doing the talking now, Vegard,' Mads said. 'It was a rhetorical question. If you know what that is?'

'Is that a rhetorical question too, or do you want me to answer?'

A few of us laughed.

'All right, so you do know,' said Mads. 'Well done! But we still need to know why we were outplayed. What went wrong? What did we do wrong? Even if they were better than us, which in my opinion they weren't — they had one good player, he was brilliant, but that was it — we shouldn't have conceded that easily. We're a team, for Christ's sake, eleven players. We have to keep our shape. Defence, midfield, attack. That's three lines they need to penetrate. If we keep our shape tight, and if we press, if we run, if we're aggressive, they're not going to get through us. They won't be able to. But you didn't press, you didn't run and you didn't keep your shape. You left acres of space wide open, and when you do that all it takes is one good player, they're through on goal and it's in the back of the net. So that's what we're going to practise tonight.'

After he'd explained what he wanted us to do, just as we were about to run out onto the pitch, he raised his hand in the air.

'One more thing,' he said. 'We're footballers, not thugs. What happened during the match on Saturday, Syvert, is something I *never* want to see again. Understood?'

'Understood,' I said. 'I'm sorry. I don't know what got into me. It won't happen again. You can count on it.'

'Five laps of the pitch. Ten push-ups after each.'

'You're joking?'

'No, I'm not joking. Go on, get going.'

My first impulse was to just walk away and go home. But if I did that, I'd never be able to come back.

The others were grinning and laughing at me.

I started jogging, angry and in turmoil. There was no need for him to humiliate me.

'Pick up the pace, Syvert! I want you tasting blood!' he shouted.

Danish prick.

He was full of wind and nothing else.

What he knew about football was something he'd read in a book.

But I wanted to play. It was the only thing that kept me going at the moment. So I picked up my pace, did the ten push-ups in front of his nose, got to my feet again and ran on, while the others played football and forgot all about me and my punishment.

As I'd anticipated, Mum and her friends looked like they'd be sitting in the living room all evening, so I couldn't phone Lisa as I'd originally planned. I couldn't watch telly either.

I flicked through my thirty-nine LPs and put Black Sabbath's *Master of Reality* on, their best album, I reckoned, and I hadn't played it for ages. I lay on my bed, staring at the ceiling while I listened to it. After a while, I got up and scanned the paperbacks on the shelf, but found nothing I fancied reading again. I even looked at some of my old magazines — *Fotballrevyen*, which Dad used to buy me, and *Sport i Bilder*.

Only then, after skimming an article about Helge Skuseth, I remembered the book I'd promised Krag I'd read. It wasn't a promise I was bound to keep, of course, but the pastor had wanted me to read it too, and the fact that two people I basically didn't know had recommended I read the same book, and had done so independently of each other in the space of a week, made me curious. What could it be about, since they thought it was so important?

I went downstairs to get it.

Mum had got the cherry liqueur out and what looked like the left-over biscuits from Christmas, as well as the buns.

'You all look like you're having a nice time,' I said.

'Do you want a glass?' said Mum.

'No thanks.'

'A biscuit, then?'

'No thanks,' I said again. 'I just came down to get a book. It was on the table here. Have you seen it?'

'On top of the newspapers over there,' she said.

'You used to have such a sweet tooth,' said Randi. 'I remember how over the moon you'd be whenever I brought you chocolate.'

'I haven't forgotten,' I said. 'How come you stopped?'

'I suppose it didn't seem right any more once you were as tall as me,' she said.

I'd known Randi, Synnøve and Vibeke for as long as I could remember. Randi was round and fair, always cheerful, always with the same short haircut and big hooped earrings. Synnøve had a long and narrow, rather bony face, equine was probably the word. Her gums showed when she smiled, she had dark hair and serious eyes. Vibeke was curvy and a bit fit, and when I first started wanking I used to think about her, even though I knew it was a bit perverse with her being Mum's friend and me only thirteen.

'What book is it you're reading?' she said.

'It's a Russian novel,' I said, and regretted it straight away, but there was nothing about Mum's expression that suggested the word Russian triggered anything in particular.

'Oh,' said Vibeke. 'It's not *Anna Karenina*, is it?'

I glanced at the title.

'*Crime and Punishment*.'

'I love *Anna Karenina*,' said Vibeke. 'Has anyone else read it?'

The others shook their heads.

She started giving a summary as I went towards the door.

'Enjoy yourselves, ladies,' I said, and went upstairs again, lay down on my bed and began to read.

After only a few pages I knew he was going to kill the old woman. He had no reason to in particular, she hadn't done anything, it was nothing but a fanciful turn of his mind. I lay uneasily as I read. He was heading straight for the abyss. For no reason! And all around him was misery and wretchedness. Beggarly derelicts drinking themselves into oblivion. It hurt in the pit of my stomach to think that people could humiliate themselves to such an extent, and when after a short time I put the book down, it was as if its entire mood had seeped into my own reality.

What was it the pastor wanted me to see in such a book?

That to kill was a sin?

Downstairs the phone rang.

'Syvert! It's for you!' Mum shouted up.

'Coming!' I shouted back and went down the stairs into the hall, where the receiver lay on its side on the table. I closed the living-room door and picked it up.

'Hello?' I said.

'Hello,' said Lisa. 'How's your nose?'

'Lisa,' I said, sensing to my horror that my voice was shaking. I cleared my throat. 'It's coming along fine, thanks. The rest of me's all right as well!'

'Good to hear it. I feel guilty about what happened. There'd have been no trouble if it wasn't for me.'

'I'm glad it happened,' I said.

'Glad?'

'If it hadn't, you'd never have called me.'

'You needn't start fancying your chances.'

'No, I wouldn't. I'm the least conceited person you've ever met.'

'You could have fooled me.'

'It's true!'

'Hm,' she said.

There was a silence.

I racked my brains in panic for what to say next.

Nothing came.

She was expecting something of me, she wouldn't have phoned otherwise.

Say something, say something!

Anything!

Go on!

'There's something I should tell you,' I said. 'When I saw you at the petrol station . . .'

'Yes?'

'I realised then that I . . . well, you know?'

'No.'

'I realised . . .'

'Spit it out! Realised what?'

'I realised . . . I'm in love with you.'

She went silent again.

'No, you're not,' she said after a moment, and now there was irritation in her voice. 'You just think you are. You don't even know me! You don't know me in the slightest!'

'I don't need to know you to know the person you are,' I said.

'That's the most brainless thing I've ever heard.'

'I think about you all the time.'

'Pack it in! You're even more stupid than I thought.'

'Can we see each other?'

'No, we absolutely can *not*. I'm glad Kjeld didn't hurt you seriously. But that's all. Have a nice life.'

She hung up.

For a few seconds I must have been completely gone inside, because slowly, almost bit by bit, I became aware that I was standing with the receiver in my hand, the dialling tone sounding angrily in my ear as I stared at my own face in the wall mirror.

I put it back on the hook and went upstairs.

I'd ruined everything.

How could I have said that?

I could have said anything!

She *phoned* me and I'd bollocksed it up!

What was I going to do now?

There was nothing I *could* do.

I'd frightened her off for good.

I sat down at the desk and switched the lamp off so I wouldn't be able to see my reflection. The lights along the road stretched away into the darkness, pooling then at the shop and the little cluster of houses there.

I hadn't lost anything exactly, because I'd never had anything to begin with. Nothing was more pathetic than someone going on about the enormous fish they'd hooked and almost landed, only for it to get away.

So near and yet so far.

But I hadn't even been near.

She'd phoned out of concern, not love.

Love!

I had no right to even think about the word.

I stood up. Maybe I could lie down and carry on reading? But the Russian novel didn't appeal, it was too unpleasant. And the Follett book only made me think about the shaving episode in the bath.

The voices of Mum and her friends drifted up from downstairs. It sounded like they were on their way home.

I waited until everything was quiet before going down.

Mum was clearing the table in the living room.

'Did you have a nice time?' I said.

She nodded.

'I'm tired now, though. And a bit tipsy from that liqueur!'

She laughed.

'I'll tidy up,' I said.

'We'll do it together,' she said. 'There's not much.'

I went into the kitchen and filled the sink. Mum put the things on the side and sat down on the chair by the window.

'Who was that on the phone?'

I was going to say Dag, but remembered it was Mum who'd answered.

'Just a girl I know,' I said.

'And?'

'We're not going out, if that's what you think,' I said. 'She's just a friend.'

'Where did you meet her?'

I turned the tap off and squirted a bit of washing-up liquid into the water.

'Nowhere, she's more a friend of a friend of a friend, really.'

She took a pinch of tobacco from her pouch, teasing out the strands before cramming them into the recess of the rolling machine.

'How are you feeling now?'

'Much better. But I'm staying off work another day to be on the safe side.'

'Good idea.'

I heard the click of the machine behind me as I rinsed the first plate in cold water in the other sink and put it on the rack.

'Mum?' I said.

'Mm?' she said, and I realised she had a cigarette in her mouth and was about to light it.

'I'm sorry for losing my temper the other day.'

'That's all right.'

'But I really am sorry,' I said, turning round to face her. 'It was just that I didn't know that about Dad. That you'd been keeping it from me. But I understand why, I was just a little kid at the time. I'm actually glad you never told me, I wouldn't have understood.'

'Do you understand now?'

'Of course.'

'I'm not sure I do,' she said.

I washed the small glasses, rinsed them and placed them upside down on a tea towel next to the sink. My hands were red from the hot water that prickled my skin fiercely every time I immersed them.

'It's made me realise how little I actually know about Dad,' I said. 'And about you, too.'

'About me?'

'Yes.'

She huffed.

'What don't you know about me?'

'The person you were when you met Dad, for example.'

'The person I was? More or less the same as now, I expect.'

'What sort of person was Dad, then? When you first met. How did you meet? Did you fall in love with him straight away? Or did it take time? What was he like exactly?'

'What a lot of questions,' she said.

'I don't mean you have to answer them all. You know what I mean, though. I don't know anything about all that.'

'Not everything needs to be known. I don't know anything about my parents and their relationship before I was born.'

'Granny and Grandad?'

'That's right. They never told me anything. It wasn't something we ever talked about.'

'Did you ask?'

'No. It never occurred to me.'

'But did you wonder about it?'

'Do you know, I don't think I ever did.'

I dried the teaspoons and put them away in the drawer, lifted the plug out of the sink and folded the tea towel before hanging it over the oven door handle.

'Do you want a drink of something?' I said. 'Tea, or a beer maybe?'

'A cup of tea would be nice.'

'Did you know Grandad told me how he and Granny met?' I said as I filled a saucepan with water, put it on the hob and switched it on.

She shook her head and looked at me.

'I don't think I told you. I think I thought it was a bit embarrassing, to be honest. It was when he was in hospital. He might have been a bit confused. I'm not even sure he knew it was me he was talking to.'

'You never told me, no.'

'Granny and her two sisters were spending some time in the hills that summer and he went up to see them with a friend of his.'

'I knew that.'

'Then the next night he went back on his own. Did you know that bit, too?'

She shook her head slowly.

'*I didn't get her then*, he said. *But the next night I did.*'

'Is that what he said?' said Mum, and looked down at herself as she blew out smoke, her elbow propped on the table.

I wished I hadn't said anything, it was a lot more intimate somehow, me telling her than him telling me.

I turned round and got two tea bags out of the box in the cupboard, dropped one into each cup and went to the fridge for the milk.

'Well, you'll get nothing of the like about your dad and me, I can tell you!' Mum said. She looked at me with a gleam in her eye.

'I wouldn't want to know anyway,' I said, and smiled back at her.

'But you know where we met?'

I nodded.

'In a park in Oslo,' I said.

'That's right. I looked after two children for a family up in Frogner. We used to spend whole days in the park. Your father came along one day and sat down under a tree nearby. He was in uniform and on his own, and I remember I was a bit curious about him. He sat reading the newspaper and smoking. Then he lay down and had a little sleep. The children I looked after, two boys, were playing football.'

'The ball hit him in the head.'

'And we got talking. We met up that same evening and got drunk together.'

'I've never heard that part before!'

'Is it really so strange?'

I laughed and poured the boiling water into the two cups, dipping the tea bags a few times until the water turned cloudy and tan, after which I dropped them in the bin and added a touch of milk to each cup.

'What was it that made you fall for him?' I said, putting her cup down in front of her.

'He was so well balanced, at ease with himself and the way he related to everything. And of course he was handsome, too.'

'Was he?'

'Your dad? Yes, he was.'

She paused for a moment before going on.

'I don't know, really. Some people you just like straight away, do you know what I mean? And some you like a lot. It's hard to explain why. I don't even know myself.'

'So you were a couple from the start, after that first night out together?'

'Yes. We saw each other again the next afternoon as soon as I got off work. And the day after that, too.'

I sat down and took a sip of my tea, then got up again and fetched the sugar from the cupboard, spooned three heaps in and stirred them round with the teaspoon.

'What did you talk about then?'

'The first day?'

'Yes.'

'All sorts, I suppose. He asked me about my job. I made him laugh, I remember, when I told him about the couple I worked for. And of course I asked him about what he did as well.'

'Were you in love with him even then?'

'Yes, I think so. Yes, I was. It was all I could think about when I went home afterwards.'

She looked like she was immersing herself in the memory of it. All of a sudden she looked younger as she sat there, or more full of life, as if illuminated from the inside.

I shouldn't have got her going. There was nothing here that could absorb such feelings.

She fell quiet for a bit. I was quiet, too.

Then she looked up at me.

'You like that girl, don't you?'

I felt my face go warm.

'A bit,' I said, and swallowed some more tea.

'What's her name?'

'Mum, there's nothing in it. She's not interested.'

'We'll see.'

She got up.

'Goodness, look at the time,' she said.

'What makes you say that, exactly?'

'Say what?'

'*We'll see*, you said. As if you knew something I didn't!'

'She phoned you, didn't she?'

I didn't answer.

'Put the lights out when you go up, will you?' she said.

What I'd said to Lisa had ruined everything. That much was incontestable, I told myself as I lay in the dark, waiting for sleep to come. But it had been true. Why did truth have to ruin things? If not telling the truth had worked things in my favour, that would have been deceitful.

Ha! As if she'd ever been interested in me!

She felt guilty because her boyfriend had headbutted me. It was because of her that he'd done it.

I turned over onto my other side, put my head against my arm and heard my pulse beat in my ear. That was what had made Dad so scared, Einar had said.

Ba-dum. Ba-dum.

How could it have made him scared?

Ba-dum. Ba-dum.

It was the sound of life.

Maybe it wasn't true. Maybe it was Einar who'd been scared.

I opened my eyes.

Mads had punished me because I'd seen him in his job.

That was why!

He'd felt humiliated and wanted to exact revenge.

A dogsbody for Kaspersen's Carpets.

A carpet-lugger.

When I woke up the next morning I lay there trying to think of something to look forward to, and came up with nothing. There wasn't even football practice later on. And Lisa had hung up on me.

But I couldn't let it get me down. Normally, I'd never even have thought I had a chance with her, so it was no great loss in that respect. You can't lose what you've never had.

And if things were at a standstill now, I needed to draw up a plan and then stick to it.

I climbed out of bed, yawned and stretched my limbs.

I could apply to start that foundation course this autumn.

But where?

Oslo, Bergen or Trondheim?

There! Three possible futures all of a sudden!

I went to the bathroom, turned the shower on, took my underpants off and tested the water with my hand until it was hot enough to step underneath. I thought about Eilif, who began every day with an ice-cold shower *to get started*, he said. He'd done such a good job of talking it up that I'd actually tried it once. Never again.

What sort of person chose something grim and nasty rather than something good and nice?

I ought to give him a ring and hear how civilian life was treating him up there in Steinkjer.

I reached for the soap in the little recess in the wall. There was only a sliver left.

Maybe there was a new packet in the cupboard under the sink?

I stepped out of the shower, opened the little cupboard door and found a triple pack of Sterilan soap in the corner at the back. The plastic wrapping was almost impossible to remove, I had to bite it to get some purchase and tear it off. The paper around the soap bar itself was easier. With the coarse green soap in one hand and the wrapper in the other, and water still dripping from my hair, I looked around for the waste bin. It wasn't there, so I crumpled the wrapper and tossed it into the corner for the time being, before stepping back into the shower again, shivering a bit already, then lathering myself while I sang 'Slow an' Easy' by Whitesnake.

When I came down into the kitchen, Joar was sitting at the table eating a slice of bread he'd sprinkled with sugar.

'You do know everyone can hear you when you sing in the shower?' he said.

'That's the whole point,' I said. 'To spread a little joy.'

'Suffering, more like.'

I smiled and filled some water in the coffee pot, then poured it into the coffee maker.

'Are you actually allowed to put sugar on your bread?'

He shook his head.

'Not really.'

'Why have you, then?'

'Mum's not here.'

I slotted the filter bag into place and spooned some coffee into it. I didn't want to tell him off. He'd go into a sulk if I did, anyway. But if I didn't, no one else was going to.

'It's for your own good that rule,' I said. 'It's not for Mum's sake.'

'I know.'

'Good.'

He shoved the last bite into his mouth and gulped down the rest of his milk before getting to his feet and going upstairs to his room.

I carried his plate and glass over to the sink, put the butter back in the fridge, the sugar in the cupboard, and the bread in the bread bin.

The branches of the tree in the yard outside had a faintly green lustre about them, I suddenly noticed. They hadn't yesterday.

What had the first ever humans thought when the trees shed their leaves and winter came? They must have been scared, because nothing would have told them the leaves would come back again. And when they did come back, it must have been like a miracle. Maybe it made them think the dead could come back too and start living again?

I emptied some oatmeal into a bowl, poured on some milk and was still eating when Joar came back down.

'What do you think the first ever humans thought when winter came?' I said. 'Do you think they were scared when the leaves fell off the trees?'

He looked at me as if seeing me for the first time.

'Humans emerged in Africa, as everyone knows,' he said. 'Their winters aren't exactly like ours, are they?'

He laughed out loud and went out.

My face burning even though I was on my own, I carried on eating.

The little devil.

What was it like for Mum? I wondered.

I'd never seen him laugh at her.

Didn't she ever say anything stupid to him?

He respected her. He knew she was above him.

Above him?

In what way?

She was no intellectual, exactly. He knew lots of things she didn't. But it was as if everything that Mum was to him blanketed him completely. Enveloped him.

It had never been the case with me.

I ought to make her some breakfast. The coffee was already made.

I could fry her an egg. And some bacon.

No, too substantial, she wouldn't want that. Some bread, perhaps. An apple.

I prepared a tray and took it upstairs.

'Morning!' I said. 'How are we feeling today?'

'Fine, thanks,' she said, and sat up, her face drawn after sleep. 'Sorry I've had such a lie-in. I didn't mean to.'

'Why shouldn't you sleep as long as you want? Is your back all right?'

She nodded. I put the tray down carefully on her lap.

'I thought I'd give the car a wash today.'

'That's nice of you.'

I gave a snort and went towards the door.

'Let me know if you need anything.'

'I'm getting up now anyway.'

'OK,' I said, and went downstairs again to do the dishes. After I'd finished, I took a packet of fish fillets out of the freezer and put them in a dish on the side before filling a bucket with hot water, squirting in some detergent, fetching a sponge from the laundry room and going out to wash the car. The sun glittered from the sheeny surfaces, but the air was surprisingly cold. Was it because the sun was further from the earth than later on in summer?

I hardly felt bold enough to even entertain such questions after what Joar had said. All of a sudden, my ignorance seemed to know no bounds.

I connected the hosepipe to the tap inside the house and rinsed off the soap. The suds ran down the bodywork and trickled away in little rivulets, the bubbles shimmering colourfully in the bright sunlight, almost like petrol. How strange that washing away dirt and muck to reveal shining metal and glass should be so satisfying. But it was. I wiped the hubcaps clean too before fetching the Hoover. The cord just reached without me having to move the car, and once the footwells and the seats were vacuumed, it was all as good as new. Or at least as spick and span as could be.

When I went back in and through the hall, Mum was standing facing the wall, talking on the phone. I went upstairs to my room, took Dad's letters from the envelope I'd put them in, and looked at them again. It was hard to understand that she was contained in them, concealed behind those unfamiliar symbols. But it was a fact. I was dying to read what she'd written to him. Surely it was more important than the reluctance I felt towards Krag? He hadn't done anything wrong. He'd done me a favour.

Would he be able to translate them for me this afternoon?

I went downstairs and found his number in the book. Mum was in the living room, so I closed the door before dialling.

'Hello, Krag speaking,' his gravelly voice said.

'Hello, this is Syvert Løyning again. Thanks for helping me out with that translation!'

'Hello, Syvert,' he said. 'Was it any use?'

'Very much so, yes! But there was something else I forgot to mention.'

'Oh yes?'

'It was just that if you could treat it as a matter of confidence and not mention it to anyone, I'd be really grateful.'

'What do you take me for?' he said. 'I realise perfectly well it's a sensitive business. Not just for you, but for your mother, too. So there's no need to be concerned on that account.'

'Thanks very much indeed. I knew you'd understand, of course, but since I hadn't mentioned it I felt I just needed to make sure we were on the same wavelength.'

'Have you kept your part of the bargain?'

'My part?'

'Yes, *Crime and Punishment*. Have you been reading?'

'I've started.'

'Excellent! What do you make of it?'

'It's . . . good, yes.'

'Yes?'

'I haven't got very far yet. But listen, there was something I was wondering —'

I heard Mum coming and stopped short just as she opened the living-room door and came out.

'Hello?' said Krag.

'Sorry. Just a second.'

She went through into the kitchen. When I reached out to shut the door behind her, the receiver still pressed to my ear, she winked at me.

'Sorry about that,' I said to Krag. 'I'm with you again now. What was I saying? Ah, yes. Feel free to say no, of course. Only I've found some more letters. The same kind, in Russian. I was wondering if you'd have time to translate these ones for me as well? There's no hurry. And I'd pay you properly this time. They're a bit longer than the first one, you see.'

'Yes, of course. No trouble.'

'Really? That's brilliant. Thanks very much indeed!'

This time, I found somewhere to park outside his house. I tapped the little knocker against the door a few times and admired the shiny clean car while I waited. When there was no reponse, I knocked again. I heard a toilet flush, the sound increasing in volume as a door opened, and then his figure appeared behind the frosted glass.

'Ah, Syvert,' he said, looking at me as he buckled his belt under an untucked shirt.

'I've brought those letters for you,' I said, handing him the wad of pages.

'Rather more than last time, I see,' he said, glancing up again. 'It'll take some days. A week, perhaps. If you give me your number, I'll phone you when they're ready.'

'Yes, good idea.'

He went inside to get a pen.

'Cup of coffee?' he said once he'd written the number down.

'Tempting, but I'm afraid I've got an appointment,' I said.

'A shame,' he said. 'I imagine it'd be quite refreshing, discussing Dostoevsky with a member of the Progress Party youth wing.'

'What makes you think I belong to them?'

'I'm right, though, am I not? Your pro-American views would point to either the Young Conservatives or the Progress Party's youth section. But the way you dress would seem to exclude the former.'

He chuckled to himself.

'Anyway, finish the book, at least. Then we'll talk about it when you come to collect your letters.'

'All right, I will,' I said.

I didn't really have much choice. He was doing me a massive favour and the letters were in his hands now, he'd got me where he wanted.

I hadn't expressed a single pro-American view, I thought to myself as I got in the car. That was just his prejudice showing through. Just because I was critical of socialism as an ideology, and opposed to a country like the Soviet Union for oppressing its people, it didn't mean I was an ardent defender of America.

I was, but how the hell was he to know?!

Another prejudgement.

Bloody Socialist Left deadbeat!

I reached for Mum's sunglasses in the glove compartment as I came onto the motorway, the sun hitting me smack in the face. With the glorious weather and the empty road ahead, it would have been natural to put some music on and turn the volume up, but I'd left my Walkman at home, and the radio was just chat.

If it had been Wednesday, I might have been able to talk someone into going out drinking, even if they had to go to work the next day. But it was only Tuesday, so there was basically no chance.

It would all have been so different if Lisa and I were going out with each other. I'd have been able to go over to hers! We could have done whatever we wanted. We could have gone out and got pissed, even if it was only Tuesday. Or we could have stayed in at hers and played Yatzy or whatever else she wanted.

I could have taken her clothes off and held her naked body.

If we were going out with each other, she wouldn't mind. We'd be able to do it all the time, whenever we felt like it.

What would happen if I called her?

The worst that could happen would be that she'd hang up.

She'd already done that. So it wouldn't exactly alter anything.

She'd rung me.

It had to count for *something*.

Mum was in her room when I got back, or at least that's where I assumed she was, because she wasn't downstairs, and she didn't have the car. I decided not to disturb her, it was good for her to rest another day after being so exhausted.

It was the fourth day now. But people with job burnout could be off work for months, and she'd been up and about today and yesterday. She'd even had her friends round and had sat up late with me.

I felt despondent all of a sudden. Her recalling the time they first met had brought her to life. While I was having letters translated from the woman he'd loved.

Why did he have to tell her and then go and die?

He didn't know he was going to die. But he wanted to get away. Presumably to live with her.

But how could that have been possible? Surely he couldn't have been planning to move there? Not to the Soviet Union?

No, of course not. It would have meant losing touch completely with Joar and me.

Was she going to defect?

That sounded unlikely, too.

I went up to my room and brought the book back down with me. Not that I particularly wanted to read it, there was something about it that put me off, quite a lot, in fact, but I'd promised Krag and felt obliged, so I sat down in the living room with it and carried on from where I'd left off.

The old woman was detestable, greedy and self-seeking, but Raskolnikov was detestable too, because even if he was in the throes of feverish delusions he was still in control of himself, and what came up in him was evil. Didn't that rule out that he was a good person at heart? If he'd been good, then what came up in him would have been good too, surely?

It made my stomach turn. Squalor, drunkenness, wretchedness everywhere.

Could it really have been like that?

And why did the *pastor* want me to read it too?

I could understand where Krag was coming from. He was a socialist, this was Russia before the Revolution, and obviously something needed to be done about that society, if it was that depraved.

No, I couldn't be bothered with this, I thought. I put it down and went aimlessly into the dining room, stared out of the window at the road and the river beyond it that glittered between the trees, then turned and went into the kitchen where I opened the fridge to see if there was anything to eat. I found a carrot and bit into it without peeling it first, then picked up the phone book in the hall, looked up *Dønnestad* and rang the first number that was listed.

'Hello?' a woman's voice said. It wasn't Lisa, this was a woman in her fifties at least.

'Hello, is Lisa in?'

'Who?'

'Lisa.'

'There's no one of that name here.'

'Oh, sorry. I must have got the wrong number,' I said, and hung up.

I tried the second number, but there was no answer.

The third was a man. No Lisa there either, he'd never heard of her.

OK, I told myself, that'd have to do for now. At least I'd eliminated two. Now there were only three to go.

I heard someone on the gravel outside. A second later, Joar came in through the front door.

'How was school today?' I said.

'It was all right,' he said. 'I'm hungry, is there anything to eat?'

'Have a slice of bread with something.'

He dumped his bag and went into the kitchen. I wondered if I should wake Mum up. She wouldn't want to be asleep when Joar got home.

I knocked on her door.

'Yes?' she said.

She was lying on her side in bed, her head resting on her arm, and didn't look like she'd been asleep at all.

'Joar's home,' I said. 'I can make us something to eat. Anything you fancy?'

'No, whatever you feel like, it doesn't matter.'

I went in to get the breakfast tray she'd left on the bedside table. I took the empty aspirin packaging too, then noticed the waste bin from the bathroom. It was full, partly hidden under the bed.

'What are you after?' she said as I bent down to take it with me.

'Just thought I'd empty the bin for you.'

'No, leave it. I'll empty it later.'

'It's all right, I might as well take it down with me.'

'Didn't you hear me?' she snapped, raising her voice. 'Leave it where it is. I'll empty it myself.'

My heart nearly stopped beating. I straightened up, staring at her.

'I was only trying to help,' I said.

I turned round and picked up the tray, and went towards the door.

'I'm sorry, Syvert. I know you want to help.'

'Shall I take it with me, then?'

She shook her head.

'I'm getting up now, anyway. I didn't mean to get angry.'

'It doesn't matter,' I said. 'You weren't that angry.'

I wasn't sure if you could actually crumb fillets if they'd been frozen. In the forces, the fish we'd used had always been fresh, but I didn't suppose it mattered. Wasn't the whole point of freezing food that it was fresh once it thawed?

I got some potatoes on the boil, filled a bowl with flour, another one with beaten egg and another with breadcrumbs, peeled and grated some carrots, brought a bag of frozen peas up from the basement, divided a couple of lemons and set the table before turning another ring on full for the fillets, pouring a little olive oil into the frying pan and adding a knob of butter that slid away into the thick oil as it slowly melted, sprinkling salt and pepper onto the fillets and turning them one after another in the flour, dipping them in the egg and then turning them in the breadcrumbs. The butter in the pan browned nicely and started to fizz. I added two of the fillets. Steam and cooking odours filled the kitchen and I opened the window wide while thinking it was about time I fixed the extractor. After a short while I tentatively lifted one of the fillets with the spatula. It was brown verging on black along one edge, almost burnt.

Mum came in. She was looking better, a bit tired, that was all.

'Mm, that looks good,' she said.

'It's Sicilian blackfish, a navy recipe,' I said.

She smiled, got her smoking gear and went into the living room. I flipped the fillets, adding some more butter so they could really soak it up, I'd learned that was the only way to get them crisp even though you'd think the opposite was true, that all the butter would make them soggy and limp.

The water started boiling for the peas, I emptied the bag into it and turned the heat down, flipped the fillets again, then put them to one side a few moments later on some greaseproof paper before starting to fry the two that remained.

It smelled delicious!

I drained the potatoes and left them steaming in the saucepan, strained the peas and tipped them into a bowl. I arranged the fillets on a dish with the lemon wedges in between, and transferred the potatoes from the saucepan into a bowl. As I put it all out on the table, everything inside me went cold and still.

I realised why she'd got angry with me when I made to take the waste bin away.

For a few seconds, I stood transfixed.

Oh, Mum, Mum.

I went upstairs, opened and then closed the bathroom door so they'd think I'd gone to the loo, then crept quietly into her room. The waste bin was still there under the bed. I paused a moment without moving, staring at it. It looked like it was full of toilet paper, white, crumpled-up. It didn't have to be what I feared. And even if it was what I feared, I didn't have to know. *She* didn't want me to know.

Conceivably, it was nothing. And yet there I was in her bedroom, about to rummage through her waste. I felt stupid.

Delving into the bin, picking beneath the untainted paper she'd used to cover things up, I found the rest to be stained red with blood. At the bottom were two cloths, likewise soaked.

Without a thought, I stood and stared. Then, I covered it all up again, and pushed the bin back under the bed where I'd found it.

It could have been a nosebleed, or even menstrual blood. What did I know?

But why had she tried to conceal it?

She was embarrassed. Maybe she was afraid I'd be sickened by it.

I looked out of the window. The sky was open and blue, like an ocean of air above the green hills.

It was a lot of blood.

I opened the bathroom door quietly, pulled the chain, washed my hands under the tap and closed the door a bit harder behind me.

'Dinner's ready, Joar!' I said in a loud voice and went downstairs again. I filled the jug with water and then called for Mum.

They came in at the same time.

'This looks nice!' Mum said as she sat down. 'Doesn't it, Joar?'

'It does, actually,' he said. 'Are there bones in it?'

'No,' I said, putting the jug on the table. 'Help yourselves.'

'You'd make a good chef,' Mum said, looking up at me as she put a bite of fish into her mouth.

'Maybe,' I said without meeting her gaze.

'But you don't want to, is that it?'

'Not really.'

It felt like everything was inside me. Mum, Joar, the kitchen, the yard, the sunlit fields outside.

I sipped my water.

'Is something the matter?' Mum said.

I shook my head.

'No, nothing. I'm glad you like the food.'

'Who were speaking to on the phone?'

'Dag.'

She smiled.

'So why did you stop talking when I went past? Is Dag a secret now?'

'You think it was Lisa. But it wasn't.'

'Lisa. So that's her name.'

'There's a girl and her name is Lisa, yes,' I said. 'But we're not going out with each other, and we're not going to either. And it wasn't her I was talking to.'

'We'll see,' she said.

'See what?' said Joar.

'Nothing,' I said. 'Were you thinking of going over to Rickard's after tea, then, or what?'

'No. Why?'

'Just thought you might want to go out. It'd do you good, instead of sitting indoors all the time.'

'Mind your own business.'

'Boys,' said Mum.

'How come you never say anything to him?' I said.

'About what?'

'About him sitting in his room all the time and never going out.'

'It's not true!' said Joar. 'I go to Rickard's, or else he comes here. Besides, I'm at school all day.'

'What do you think, Mum? Is it good for a twelve-year-old to spend his life in his room? Isn't that just what nerds and failures do?'

Joar burst into tears. He put his hands up in front of his face like a shield.

'I hate you!' he sobbed, and jumped to his feet.

Mum gave me a furious look as he ran up the stairs.

'You'd never have let *me* get away with it,' I said with a shrug. 'It's for his own good.'

'What's wrong with you? You know Joar's not like you.'

'Oh, I know that.'

'How can you call your own brother a failure? No, I'm disappointed in you, Syvert.'

She got up and went after him.

I stayed where I was and poked at my food, but I couldn't eat anything now and tipped it all into the bin under the sink. It was true what I'd said, it wasn't good for a twelve-year-old to be cooped up in his room all the time, and I'd certainly never have been allowed to, not even if I'd wanted.

When they came back down again, Joar wouldn't look at me, he just sat down at his place and stared straight ahead. But Mum did look at me. Nevertheless, I couldn't return her gaze, even though I knew it would make her think I was ashamed of what I'd said. Rather than that I was scared of what I might see in her eyes.

They ate in silence.

'I'm sorry, Joar,' I said after a while. 'I didn't mean it. I was only trying to say it'd be good if you —'

'I know.'

'You're a good little brother. I couldn't ask for a better one.'

He said nothing, but pushed his plate away, drank the rest of his water and went upstairs to his room without a word.

'Do you want some coffee?' I said, and got up, taking his plate and two of the dishes with me over to the side.

'What's wrong, Syvert?' Mum said.

'Wrong?' I said, and poured what was left of the old coffee into the sink, rinsed the jug and filled it up with fresh water from the tap. 'I said I was sorry, didn't I?'

'You've not been yourself today. Is it that girl?'

'Stop going on about that!' I said. I was standing with my back to her, spooning coffee into the filter bag, so I couldn't really gauge what the ensuing silence meant.

I snapped the filter holder into place, took two mugs out of the cupboard and put them on the work surface next to the coffee maker, then got the milk from the fridge as the first drips splashed into the bottom of the jug.

When I turned round she was sitting with her elbows propped on the table and her hands held up in front of her, as if she'd been about to bury her face and had stopped in mid-movement. Her arms were trembling as they might if she'd been tensing her muscles. The look she gave me was furious, hateful almost.

She lowered her arms and her face fell back into repose.

I put a coffee mug down in front of her. The moment had been so fleeting I wasn't even sure it had happened.

'Thanks,' she said. 'I won't pester you about her any more. You're right, it's none of my business. You don't have to tell me anything you don't want to.'

'It's best that way,' I said. 'And the same goes for you. You don't have to tell me anything either. Unless you want to?'

'What would I have to tell?' she said with an abrupt laugh.

'I wouldn't know,' I said.

She made herself a cigarette. It cut through me as she inhaled, and I looked out of the window at the side of the barn, a glowing red in the sunshine. She'd never liked me criticising her for smoking, it had always irritated her if I passed comment, so it had been a couple of years at least since I'd said anything.

But now I couldn't help it.

'Do you think it's such a good idea to smoke when you're not well?'

'I've got a bad back, that's all. But thanks for your concern.'

She blew smoke out into the air.

'What are you staring at out there, anyway?' she said.

'Nothing. Spring's here now by the looks of it.'

'Let's hope so,' she said. 'Have you thought any more about what you're going to do?'

I shook my head.

'Don't you have to apply now if you want to get in somewhere in the autumn?'

'Not necessarily.'

'Oh?'

'I could take a foundation course. I've been thinking I might.'

'Where?'

'I'm not sure. Trondheim, maybe. Or Bergen.'

She nodded.

'What about until then? Have you asked at the factory?'

'There's nothing going at the moment.'

'No,' she said.

'But if it's money you're thinking about, I've signed on, so I'll at least have a small amount coming in.'

I regretted it straight away, I knew she didn't like it.

'I'll see how Joar's doing,' I said, putting my half-finished coffee down on the side and leaving her on her own. As I got to the staircase I heard her sigh. If the blood was an indication of anything serious, she'd have more important things to worry about than me and my trivial concerns, so maybe everything was OK after all.

I knocked.

'What do you want?' said Joar.

He was sitting at his desk with his back to me.

'I didn't mean what I said. It didn't come out right, that's all.'

'But it's what you said,' he said.

'Are you not coming with me to the swimming baths, then?'

'Now? Why?'

'It might be fun. I haven't been for ages. And we did talk about it the other day.'

'You're only asking because I cried.'

'Of course I'm not.'

'Yes, you are.'

'Listen,' I said. 'I need to get out a bit. And I'd rather not go on my own. Come on. We can get some sweets afterwards.'

'I've got homework.'

I gave a snort.

'You're way ahead of your homework, though, aren't you?'

'Yes,' he said.

'Are you going to come with me, then?'

'OK.'

The swimming baths were situated on a spit of land outside the centre of town. The building was right by the shore, with big panorama windows through which you could look out at the sea and sky. I'd always liked the feeling it gave, especially when it was windy and the waves outside were topped with white while I swam in the calm, clear pool inside, or when the clouds above the town were dark and pellets of rain fell all around. It was like being there and not being there at the same time, existing in one world while looking at another.

'They close at seven,' said Joar as we stood at the counter to buy our tickets.

'That's all right, it means we've got a whole hour,' I said.

I paid with the money Mum had given us, a hundred-krone note, and received two rubber wristbands, each with a little key attached, along with the change. Nearly all the lockers were taken, so the pool was probably packed, I thought to myself before finding two vacant ones at the end of a row, which was all right seeing as they were close to the showers. Four boys with wet hair, no more than ten years old, were chattering away as they dried themselves and got changed, while two elderly men sat at opposite ends of the bench that ran down the middle. One of them had a big belly that drooped to his thighs and a bloated face with wide bulging eyes, the skin underneath them yellow and fatty-looking, he looked like he could have a heart attack at any minute. The other was small and thin, ruddy-faced, most likely after his sauna, and his body, pubic area included, was almost completely hairless.

It was amazing how ugly people could be without their clothes on. An ape looked better than those two. At least apes had fur to cover them up.

Joar got changed at the bench, quick as lightning. I'd only just taken my sweater off and was bending forward to remove my socks, while he was already down to his underpants.

He was skinnier than I'd realised, all elbows and knees, and his vertebrae were visible all down his spine.

It was because he was growing, his body used up all its energy.

I undid my belt and stood up, pulling my trousers down to my knees. He got his towel out of the carrier bag and wound it around his waist before turning away from me.

'What are you doing that for?' I said, sitting down again to get my trousers off. 'It's a men's changing room, you know! No girls here!'

He said nothing and didn't turn round, but leaned forward and slipped his hand underneath his towel to remove his underpants.

'Joar! Bare bums are allowed here!'

'I don't care,' he said, and put his underpants down on the bench before picking up his trunks, stepping into them one foot at a time and wriggling them on under his towel.

'Are you embarrassed?' I said, and took off my own underpants, sitting then with my legs apart so he could see it didn't matter and there was no reason to be ashamed of being naked there.

He shook his head and removed his towel, then went to get showered.

'You're not going to *shower* in your trunks, are you?' I called out, finding my own towel and going after him with it tucked under my arm.

'Listen, mate,' I said when I found him standing under a shower head in his trunks, his arms behind his back. 'You're actually not *allowed* to shower in your trunks. It's for hygiene. Anyway, it looks daft, if you ask me.'

He turned away.

I'd forgotten. He was coming into puberty!

I stepped under the next shower and turned the water on.

'You're all right, though. I won't snitch!'

I laughed and lathered my hair, then held out the shampoo.

'I'll do it afterwards,' he said.

'OK.'

As I'd thought, the pool was busy. The three inside lanes were reserved for the swimming club. A dozen or so swimmers were doing lengths there, two trainers walking alongside, barking instructions, occasionally blowing whistles. Another group were sitting on the benches in tracksuits, presumably waiting their turn. With their tall, slender bodies widening into broad shoulders, they were like human trees. The ones in the water, in their goggles and caps, mouths ever-gaping, looked more like something transitioning between insect and otter.

The other lanes were teeming with kids and people swimming for exercise. The chairs over by the snack bar were occupied too, people with towels over their shoulders sitting at tables with soft drinks or coffee. Looking across, I recognised Renate in a white bikini with two of her friends drinking cola through a straw. She hadn't noticed me.

'Shall we jump in off one of the platforms?' I said.

Joar nodded.

'The three-metre or the five-metre?'

'The three-metre, I think.'

'Why not the five?'

'OK, you first.'

'No, you won't do it then. You first!'

I followed him up the steep staircase and stood waiting at the top as he went out to the edge of the little platform.

He turned and looked at me.

'I'd forgotten how high up it is,' he said.

'Go on, jump! Don't think about it!'

He smiled briefly and turned his back on me again.

'Do you want to go down to the three-metre?'

He shook his head.

'There's someone underneath, though. You'll need to wait a minute.'

Three kids who didn't seem to realise they'd ventured into the diving area were messing around down there. I was just about to climb down and tell them to get out of the way when Joar jumped. Like a spear he cut through the air, plunging into the water with barely a splash only an arm's length from one of the three kids.

'Hey!' one of them shouted.

Joar surfaced, gave me a thumbs up and beamed.

'You fucking idiot!' I heard one of the kids shout at him.

Joar said something to them and they all looked up at me before slipping back into the recreational zone.

If that kid had moved even slightly while Joar was in the air, he'd have landed on his head. Hadn't he seen him? He had to have done, it was impossible not to.

I stepped forward to the edge of the platform, glancing towards the table where Renate was sitting. They were too busy talking, she still hadn't seen me. Even so, I decided I was going to dive rather than jump. Jumping from the five-metre was what kids did.

Christ, it was high up, though!

My toes and fingertips tingled.

I told myself not to crouch first, it always looked so pathetic.

And I wasn't to hesitate either.

I launched myself, arms wide, gathering them just before I hit the surface and cut into the depths.

Joar was hanging from the side at the end of the pool.

'Didn't you see those kids before you jumped?' I said.

'Yes, of course I did,' he said. 'I judged it well, don't you think?'

'You could have hurt him!'

'No, I couldn't. I was in full control. Shall we swim some lengths?'

Without waiting for an answer he submerged and glided away, surfacing again in the next lane.

I did likewise.

He'd always enjoyed being in the water, he swam like a seal and could hold his breath for a surprisingly long time. I'd suggested more than once that he join the swimming club, but he didn't want to. There was something he didn't like about joining in with others.

We swam up and down a few times, and then he dived down in the deep end, passing over the tiles at the bottom like a flounder while I swam above him.

Afterwards, we hung from the side and got our breath back.

Renate and her friends were still at their table. I kept an eye open for a chance to wave, but none of them was looking in my direction.

'Did you ever see Dad's dick?' said Joar.

'What kind of a question's that?' I said, glancing round to see if anyone had heard him. It seemed not, and so I looked at him and grinned awkwardly. 'And why would you want to know?'

'Just wondered, that's all. If he had a big one.'

'Dad?'

'Yes, Dad. I was so little when he died.'

'But why do you want to know?'

He shrugged.

'Did you see it or didn't you?'

'You little crackpot,' I said. 'You don't talk about things like that.'

'Why not?'

'It's not done, that's all.'

'But it's only the body.'

'I know.'

'So why can't you answer me?'

'You don't ask other people the same sort of questions, do you?'

'No,' he said, turning his head and looking out of the big windows that ran the width of the hall, staring for a moment at the wide-open, darkening blue of the sea.

'I don't think I ever saw Dad without his clothes on, not that I remember,' I said. 'So I can't answer you on that.'

'OK.'

'Do you want a cola or something?'

'A Solo.'

'I'll have to get some money in the changing room. You can find us a table.'

'Get the towels as well.'

'Yes, yes, all right,' I said, hauling myself out of the pool and going back to the changing room where I unlocked the locker, got the fifty I'd put in my trouser pocket after we'd bought our tickets, and then took our towels, locked it again and was just about to go back in when I stopped in my tracks. Leaned against the bench in the corner was a leg. A leg with a foot and five toes. I knew immediately that it was artificial, a prosthesis, but I still jumped at the sight, it was that realistic.

It meant there was a one-legged man there somewhere.

A shower was on and I went over to see.

There he was with his back to the wall, on one leg, the other severed just below the knee. He saw me looking, and so as not to make him think I'd been standing there just to stare at him, I turned to go back, pretending I'd forgotten something.

Damn, I said to myself, realising that I actually had forgotten something, the towels, so I could go and fetch them without any pretence.

The stump had been round, a fatty blob of flesh and blood, and if the
human anatomy had been completely unknown to me, I thought, I'd
have supposed that was how everyone looked.

I found it unsettling, and I was glad to return to the pool area again,
where Joar was sitting with his arms folded at one of the tables, waiting
for me.

'There's a one-legged man in the showers,' I said, handing him his
towel.

'Is there?' he said without much interest.

'A Solo, was that it?'

'Yes.'

I went up and ordered a coffee, a Solo and two Lion bars. While I
waited, I turned to face the table where Renate was sitting, and when
she looked up in my direction I smiled and waved my hand without
lifting my elbow from the counter, an ironic sort of gesture of the kind
I thought James Bond might have been proud of.

She gave me a short reverse nod in return, tipping her head back and
lowering it again before looking the other way.

Two years ago, she'd been with Karsten. Girls liked Karsten, he was
big and brawny and quite good-looking, his eyes were gentle and
puppy-like. Renate had been quite a find, she'd only just started in the
first year at a different gymnas from us, no one had ever seen her
before. She was the type who looked ordinary in photographs and yet
was amazingly attractive in real life, with her little turned-up nose, a
spray of freckles across her cheeks, a sensual mouth and eyes that
nearly always seemed to mirror a smile. I'd told Karsten he had to make
sure to keep hold of her until they were old enough to get married.
He'd laughed and asked if I fancied her myself. I told him of course I
did. There was no point in denying it.

Then, only a few months later, it was 17 May and we were all hanging out together on the beach, he broke up with her. She didn't go
home, or anywhere else, but stayed and got drunk, sobbing and hiccup-
ing by turns. I sat down beside her to see if I could comfort her. It was
cold, already well past midnight by then, and it had started to drizzle,

but everyone was so drunk they didn't care, and anyway there was a bonfire still going at the shore where we could warm ourselves. She was shivering and I suggested we go down there, but she didn't want to. She just sat with a bottle of beer in her hand, drinking while the tears ran down her cheeks. I told her it wasn't the end of the world, that Karsten wasn't everything. I told her she was still only sixteen and had her whole life ahead of her, that she'd fall in and out of love loads of times yet. She looked at me then and asked if Karsten ever said anything to me about her. Yes, of course, I told her. Like what? she wanted to know. Like how fantastic you are and how lucky he was, I answered. But recently, she asked, what had he been saying then? He must have been thinking about it for a while, surely? I told her I didn't think he had, at least not as far as I knew, and he usually told me everything. Maybe he just thought it was a bit too soon to get so involved.

I smoothed my hand over her back. She didn't seem to notice, so I carried on, smoothing, smoothing.

I told her it was normal to get upset about that sort of thing when you're young. But it would soon pass. In a few weeks, things would be different.

She said nothing, but took another swig. She put her head on my shoulder.

She told me I was a good friend.

I asked if she wanted another beer.

If you're having one, she said.

She straightened up and I took my hand away. She looked down, and then screamed: *What are you doing? There's blood all over my jacket! It's everywhere!*

What? Where from?

It was from my finger. I'd cut myself on something and hadn't noticed. Renate's jacket was white and all my smoothing had left long red streaks all over it.

You stupid idiot!

And with that she'd jumped to her feet and marched off while shaking her head.

After that night she'd gone off the radar and had nothing to do with our group, no one ever saw her any more.

Thinking about her, and seeing her now in her bikini, I felt myself getting hard. It was OK as long as I was facing the counter, but it was going to be a problem as soon as I turned round to go back to the table.

The woman in the kiosk reached out and put my coffee down on the counter next to the Solo and the two Lion bars. I handed her the fifty kroner and then took a sip of the coffee in the forlorn hope it would make my hard-on subside.

I got an idea and beckoned to Joar.

'Can you bring me my towel?' I said, loud enough for him to hear me, at the same time as doing my best not to attract unwanted attention.

'What for?' he said, the little dope.

'Just bring it!'

Fortunately, he did as I asked.

He collected his Solo and the chocolate, I took my coffee in one hand and the scrunched-up towel in the other, holding it casually in front of me so as to conceal my predicament. By the time I reached the table it had died down anyway, the efforts I'd made to hide it obviously having been sufficient distraction on their own.

'There's that one-legged man,' said Joar with a nod in the direction of the pool.

'He's quite a fast swimmer for someone with only one leg,' I said.

'Mm,' he said.

'I wonder how he lost it.'

'Yes.'

'A car accident, perhaps?'

'People with diabetes have an increased risk of amputation,' said Joar. 'But I think it's usually a foot they lose.'

He bit into his chocolate bar and chewed methodically.

'Maybe you should be a doctor. I think you're quite knowledgeable about medical matters, is that right?'

'A bit,' he said. 'I find it interesting.'

'You've thought about it, then?'

'About what?'

'Becoming a doctor.'

He shrugged and took another bite, followed by a sip of his Solo.

'Remember when I taught you to drink pop from the bottle?'

'No.'

'Before that you used to just suck and never get anything out. So I taught you how to do it.'

'How old was I then?'

'Four or five, maybe. Five, I think.'

'I can't remember anything from before I started school.'

'Nothing at all?'

'No.'

Neither of us spoke for a moment.

I got up.

'Just going to say hello to someone,' I said, and went over to the table where Renate was sitting.

'Hi, Renate. Haven't seen you for ages,' I said. 'How's things?'

'OK,' she said. 'You?'

'Oh, can't complain. Just finished my stint in the forces. Sixteen months in the navy.'

'I see,' she said. 'Still hanging out with Karsten and that lot?'

'Of course. I can say hello, if you want?'

'Yes, why not?' she said. 'You can tell him how much better life is without him.'

'I'll pass it on. Sorry about your jacket, by the way. I don't think I ever got the chance to apologise.'

'What jacket?'

'The one that got blood on it that seventeenth of May?'

'Was that you?'

'Don't you remember?'

'No.'

'Well, that's all right, then,' I said, and laughed.

She didn't say who her two friends were, so I reckoned she didn't want me to sit down and join them. Anyway, I had Joar with me, so I said see you and went back to where I'd left him.

We swam a few more lengths, then sat in the sauna for a bit. Joar kept his trunks on, and then we went to get showered and changed. The artificial leg was still propped in the corner and I kept looking around for its owner. There was something weirdly fascinating about the thought of seeing him put it on. But he didn't appear, and after handing our keys in at the desk we went back outside. The wind that came sweeping in from the sea made my wet hair feel freezing cold. The shadows we cast as we went back to the car were long and thin. Some flags and pennants on the quayside a bit further away made snapping noises in the air.

'Do you realise you hardly ever say anything to me unless I ask you something?' I said as I got the car key out of my pocket.

'No,' he said. 'I hadn't thought about it.'

I got in and opened the door on his side.

'It's true, though.'

'OK.'

I pulled slowly away, then picked up speed as we turned onto the road.

'Do you remember when we went to that Åge Aleksandersen concert over there and they had to stop playing because of lightning?' I said as we passed the old fairground.

'Yes.'

'You used to like "Rio de Janeiro" — do you remember that one?'

'I still do like it.'

'*When thoughts weigh heavy and the road is long,*' I sang. '*When the mountain's too high and the valley narrows to quiet your song.*'

He laughed.

I looked at him. He looked back at me and smiled.

What would happen to him if Mum died?

But she wasn't going to die.

She wasn't even ill.

But what was all that blood?

And what about the pains in her back?

It was her lungs.

That was what it was.

It was her lungs.

Surely?

It wasn't that much blood, though. It could have been anything.

Throat infection. Tonsils. Glands.

Besides, she spent all day cleaning at work, it was bound to take its toll on her back. They weren't exactly robust in her family.

'Shall we get some sweets?' said Joar, bringing me round again. We were already at the bridge and I hadn't even noticed.

'Yes, I almost forgot,' I said. 'Do you think Mum will want some as well?'

The wind whirled up dust from the grit at the side of the road as we drove over.

'She might,' said Joar.

'Do you know what she likes?'

'I think so.'

'Get some for her as well, then,' I said, turning into the car park by the shop.

'How much can I spend?'

'Ten kroner each?'

There was a different smell in the hall when we came in, a faint whiff of aftershave, and I realised we had visitors. A moment later, I heard a man's voice in the living room. It was Oliver, Mum's brother-in-law.

What was he doing here?

'We're back!' Joar called out, kicking off his shoes.

Oliver got to his feet as we came into the room. He'd always worn a beard, only now he'd got rid of it and was barely recognisable. Younger, thinner, with a small pointed chin I'd never seen before.

Black jeans, black shirt.

'Hello, lads!' he said. 'Long time no see! Goodness me, Joar, you've grown! And you're not far behind yourself, Syvert!'

There was something else that was different about him, I just couldn't put my finger on it.

Joar ran up to him as if he was six years old again.

I was more restrained and put out my hand.

'This is a surprise,' I said.

'I was in the area and thought I'd pop round,' he said.

'How long are you here for?'

'Heading back up tomorrow.'

'Are you staying the night here?' said Joar.

Oliver looked at Mum.

He didn't wear glasses any more. That was it.

'If you've room at the inn for a poor traveller? I've never been fond of hotels.'

'Of course you'll stay. You must,' Mum said, and glanced at me. 'By the way, someone rang and was asking for you, Syvert.'

'Oh yes? Who was it?'

'A girl.'

Mum played the game, winking at Oliver as if to suggest how inundated I was.

'Did she say her name?'

'I think she said it was Lisa.'

She beamed.

I felt my cheeks go red and battled the urge to go up to my room.

'Did she leave a number, by any chance?'

Mum shook her head.

'She'll ring back, you'll see!'

Uplifted and gripped by a sudden impatience, I took the carrier bag with our swimming trunks and towels in it into the laundry room. Loading the wet things into the washing machine, I felt the mood of that first dream I'd had about Dad come seeping back into my mind. I closed the front, put some washing powder in the little compartment and started the cycle, pausing then and looking around me. I was fully aware that dreams were one thing and reality another, but still the stupid thought of him living on in my dreams wouldn't let go of me. Even so, everything about the laundry room was the same as it had always been. I decided to go upstairs to my room after all to spend a few minutes on my own.

I could hear the faint hum of their voices downstairs. Mum was invigorated by the unexpected visit, she was always like that when Oliver was around, there was something flirtatious about them when they were together, which I'd always disliked.

But Lisa had rung!

She actually had.

Most likely she just wanted to apologise for hanging up like that all of a sudden.

But why would she do that if she didn't want anything to do with me? Would she be that thoughtful?

I went into Joar's room. He was lying on his bed reading a magazine while eating his sweets.

'Are you hungry?' I said. 'I can make something, if you want?'

'No thanks.'

'OK,' I said. 'But thanks for going to the baths with me, it was fun.'

He looked at me without saying anything, as if waiting for me to add something more, or as if he hadn't quite grasped what I was saying.

I closed the door after me, and went downstairs into the living room. They stopped talking as I came in. Oliver smiled.

'Here he is,' he said.

I sat down in the chair next to his, opposite Mum who was sitting on the sofa.

'You got rid of the beard.'

'You noticed. Geir and Inge didn't recognise me. Frightened the life out of Inge, in fact. She thought there was a strange man coming down the stairs!'

'You look exactly like the first time I saw you,' Mum said.

He smiled again and looked at the floor.

There was something a bit feminine about him that I'd never seen before.

'How are Geir and Inge, anyway?' I said.

'Fine, as far as I know. Inge's still playing handball. Geir's studying at the Institute of Technology in Trondheim, as you know.'

'We must go up there this summer, Syvert,' Mum said.

'Yes, we should.'

'How are you, anyway?' said Oliver, scratching his thumbnail briskly against his thigh a few times. 'Did you enjoy your service?'

'I'm fine, thanks. Yes, it was great.'

Mum got up.

'I'll make us some supper, if you're staying the night.'

'No need for my sake,' said Oliver. 'I had something before I came.'

'I'll do it,' I said, and got to my feet. 'You sit here with Oliver, Mum.'

She sat down again and I went out into the kitchen as she told Oliver how good I'd become at cooking with being in the forces. I turned round in the doorway.

'Don't build your hopes up! It's only beefburgers.'

'Now you're talking,' said Oliver and laughed. Mum laughed too. As if he'd just told an amazing joke.

I got the beefburgers out of the fridge, the peas from the freezer, sliced an onion, cut some leftover potatoes into wedges and heaped them into the frying pan. All the time, I was expecting the phone to ring, it was like a tension in my body. But of course it didn't.

The sun went down in the distance, a yellowy-red haze, and gradually the light disappeared from the fields, lingering briefly on top of the hills before releasing them too and allowing darkness to flood the empty space it left behind.

The phone didn't ring.

I went in and asked Mum if we were eating in the dining room or the kitchen.

'The kitchen,' she said. 'It's only supper.'

Instead of serving everything on a dish for everyone to help themselves, I prepared individual portions, a beefburger on rye bread, with onion, tomato and cucumber on top, along with a little side of fried potatoes and peas. In case anyone wanted more, I made two extra ones I put out on a dish in the middle of the table. That done, I fetched three bottles of good Christmas brew up from the basement and a bottle of pop for Joar.

'Supper's ready!' I called out. Mum and Oliver came in, but when Joar didn't react I went up to get him.

'Food's on the table, daft lad.'

'I'm not hungry.'

'Please yourself,' I said. 'But the least you can do is come downstairs and sit at the table with us when Oliver's here.'

He closed his magazine and got up, placing it on top of his pile, adjusting it so it aligned exactly with the others, closed his bag of sweets, put it down on the desk and finally moved towards the door, only then to turn back and realign the bag with the edge of the desk.

'That'll do,' I said. 'It's all right being tidy, but there's no need to go overboard!'

He said nothing, as usual, but followed me down the stairs into the kitchen, where Oliver and Mum were sitting at the table waiting.

'This looks like restaurant standard, Syvert,' said Oliver.

'I wouldn't say that,' I said.

'It looks lovely,' said Mum.

I got the bottle opener from the drawer and opened the bottles before sitting down.

'Tuck in,' I said, picking up my knife and fork.

It was actually rather good.

'The simplest dishes are often the best,' said Oliver. 'Don't you agree?'

'Yes,' I said. 'It's a golden rule. The mark of a good cook is how well they can do an omelette.'

'Are you thinking of making it your living?'

I shook my head, tilting my glass to pour some beer into it.

He realised I wasn't going to say anything and turned to Joar.

'You look more like your dad every time I see you,' he said.

'Do I?' said Joar.

'I hear you're interested in computers.'

'A bit.'

'Well, that sounds very wise, if you are. They say computers are going to be used for everything in the future.'

'I can't see it myself,' I said.

'Mark my words, there'll be one in every home. It'll know everything, even how many eggs you've got in the fridge, and be able to tell you. And you'll be able to program it to regulate the temperature indoors and keep it constant.'

'And you'll be able to talk to it and tell it what to do,' said Joar.

'Will it do the shopping as well?' I said with a laugh.

And then the phone rang.

Lisa.

I resisted the urge to dash from the table. I didn't want to give them the satisfaction. Instead, I cut another forkful of food, put it calmly into my mouth and began to chew.

'Are you going to answer it?' said Mum, and looked at me quizzically.

'Mm,' I said, swallowing and getting slowly to my feet while my heart raced in my chest.

I closed the door behind me before picking up the receiver.

'Hello?' I said.

'Hello,' said Krag. 'Is that Syvert?'

'Speaking.'

'Good news,' he said. 'I've just about finished your letters.'

'Already? That was quick.'

'Yes. Couldn't stop once I got going, you see. It's interesting stuff. And of course there's the challenge of making it sound right in Norwegian. I can never say no to a challenge.'

'Excellent. Can I come and get them tomorrow, then?'

'Certainly.'

'Can you give me an idea how much it'll cost?'

'Oh, I won't accept money. A good wine, perhaps. We can share it, if you like.'

'Sounds good,' I said, even if it was the last thing I wanted to do. I'd be in the car, though, so I'd have an excuse not to.

'See you tomorrow, then,' he said.

'Yes, see you,' I said, put the receiver down and went back into the kitchen.

'Who was it?' said Mum.

'Just Dag.'

'Again?' she said with a smile.

If only she'd give it a rest.

'You may well laugh about computers,' said Oliver. 'But there's a huge momentum in that field now. In that respect, Geir's got his finger on the pulse.'

'Is he doing computer studies in Trondheim?'

'Yes,' he said, turning to Mum. 'Your dad always encouraged his grandchildren to get into oil. Do you remember?'

'I do indeed. He was a bit obsessive about that.'

'Lars was a very astute man. The oil industry's booming now. But that's not where the future lies! Oil will run out, and then what?'

So his own son had his finger on the pulse. And he was expecting *me* to work in a kitchen.

No one had touched the beef burgers in the middle of the table. I left them where they were, even though I was hungry. I wasn't going to sit there stuffing myself, not if the others had finished.

'That was delicious,' Oliver said, leaning back in his chair and draping an arm over the backrest as if he owned the place. 'Thank you very much, Syvert.'

Joar got to his feet and went back upstairs without a word.

I took my plate over to the side and started clearing away the rest of the things.

'I'll do the dishes,' Mum said. 'You did the cooking.'

'Anyone for coffee?' I said.

'Yes, please,' said Oliver.

'I've got some liqueur as well,' said Mum.

'Lovely,' said Oliver.

'A little snifter, Syvert?' Mum said as I filled the coffee maker with water.

'Perhaps he'd like something a bit stronger?' said Oliver.

'I don't think we've got anything stronger,' said Mum.

'Fear not,' said Oliver.

He got to his feet and went into the hall. His jeans were Levi's, I could see by the little red tag on the back pocket, far too young for him.

He came back with a flat black hip flask in his hand.

'I always have a little whisky with me when I'm away from home,' he said, winking at me. 'Are there any glasses?'

Mum took two from the cupboard and put them down on the table. Oliver poured some whisky into them.

'Feel free to go through,' said Mum. 'I'll be with you in a few minutes.'

I could see there was no way out of it, so I picked up my glass and went and sat down on the sofa. Oliver took one of the armchairs facing.

'Cheers,' he said, leaning forward to chink his glass against mine.

'Lagavulin. Best single malt Scotch in the world. Good, don't you think?'

'Very.'

We said nothing more for a while.

He sat with his legs crossed, arms on the armrests, glass held at a tilt.

'I ran into someone recently who worked with your dad,' he said eventually. 'He spoke very warmly about him. He was a highly respected man there.'

I said nothing, but sipped my whisky again. It was almost like drinking ashes, the taste was that smoky.

'You must miss him?'

None of your business, you creepy bastard, I thought to myself, and nodded in reply.

Mum's movements in the kitchen became all the more conspicuous in the silence. Oliver shifted in his chair. I looked through the window at the fields that lay colourless under the dark sky. It still had a faint blue tinge to it, whereas the trees on the hillside were a bank of black.

'What did he actually do at that place?' I said.

'He was involved in developing and manufacturing machinery for them, mainly for shipyards. Lathes, milling machines, that sort of thing. All with the newest technology. They were very leading-edge. Still are, in fact.'

'I didn't know.'

'What did you think he did?'

'Just that he was an engineer, employed by a workshop or something.'

'Well, that's true,' he said, turning his glass as he smiled, staring into it.

'But why did he need to travel around so much?'

'Did he? I'm afraid I don't know. But I can imagine he helped the shipyards they supplied install the machinery, and perhaps provided their workers with the necessary training. Your mother will know more about it. Fancy another?'

'Just a small one, then.'

He poured himself one first, then leaned forward and poured me one.

She wouldn't just ring once and then give up.

What was I going to say to her?

Ask her out for something to eat?

I'd never done that before.

It was a good idea.

I'd need to get my hands on some cash.

Maybe my dole money would come through soon.

'I actually came down to buy a boat,' said Oliver. 'It's a surprise, so don't tell anyone. Do you know much about boats?'

'Not really, no.'

'It's a Swedish sailing boat, a Storebro Sea Eagle, built in 1964. Lovely condition. I've got a picture of it here, if you'd like to have a look?'

I nodded. He pulled his wallet out, produced a picture he'd obviously cut out of a magazine, and handed it to me.

A sleek vessel with a gleaming white hull, beautiful deck and cabin.

'Thirty-two feet,' he said. 'Rather expensive, but worth every penny. Have you ever seen such a beauty?'

'No,' I said, and handed him back the picture. Mum came in at the same moment with a liqueur glass in one hand and her smoking paraphernalia in the other.

'Showing off your secret girlfriend, Oliver?' she said with a gleam.

'You could say,' he said, and laughed. 'Would you like to see her? Not a word to Jorunn, though! It's a surprise.'

He showed Mum.

'Are you buying it?'

'Already have.'

'And Jorunn doesn't know?'

'It's my present to us for our fiftieth birthdays.'

'I see,' said Mum. 'Do you think she'll be pleased?'

'That's the idea, yes. Do I detect a little scepticism here?'

'Not at all. But a boat like that must be terribly expensive?'

'It certainly wasn't cheap, I'll say that much.'

Mum got the liqueur from the cupboard, poured herself a glass, took a sip and then put it down on the table while she rolled a cigarette. All of a sudden, a cloud had come over her. I wondered if it was because there'd be no man in her life to shower gifts on her when she reached fifty. The bottle of perfume she'd no doubt get from me wouldn't really count, even if it cost me a fortune.

'We were talking about Syvert senior before you came in,' said Oliver, slipping his fat wallet into his back pocket. 'I ran into a chap who used to work with him, and he spoke very highly of him.'

'Oh, really?' said Mum. 'Well, he was always well liked.'

'What time's your flight tomorrow?' I said.

He looked at me.

'Just wondering how many I'll need to make dinner for,' I said.

He nodded a couple of times quickly before answering.

'No need to include me. The flight's not until evening, but I'll need to get back into town and check out from the hotel, so I'll have to be off in the morning sometime.'

I got to my feet.

'Thanks for the whisky,' I said.

'You're welcome,' he said. 'Nice to have a proper talk with you.'

While I waited for Lisa to ring I lay down on my bed and read the Russian novel for a bit. Every time I paused I became aware of their voices in the living room downstairs. They clearly had plenty to talk about. And the alcohol would be helping the conversation along.

He didn't just murder the old woman in the most brutal and horrifying fashion, planting an axe in her skull, he also killed her docile, downtrodden sister while he was at it.

The weird thing was that I could understand why he did it. To begin with, it had been no more than an idea. The kind of idea anyone could have. Once, while standing with a hammer in my hand, the thought had occurred to me that I could beat Joar and Mum to death with it if I wanted. It was as if the thought existed in the hammer itself and was transmitted to me when I gripped its rubber handle and felt its weight in my hand. A shiver had run down my spine at the realisation that such a deed was in fact possible, that I *could* actually do such a thing, and when I then used the hammer to drive in a nail I couldn't escape the idea that only a *thought* stood between me and such a hideous act. What if that thought *unravelled*? What if the thought no longer protected me? Thoughts are so fragile. And this was exactly what happened to Rasko, his thoughts stopped protecting him. Without them, that fanciful turn of his mind was free to encroach into the real world. When at last he stood there in the old woman's apartment, to all intents and purposes he had already killed her. Every barrier to the deed had already been crossed in his mind. All that remained were the formalities, like paperwork ensuing from a transaction.

But even if, like Raskolnikov himself, I knew what was going to happen when he stood in the apartment with the axe dangling from the designated loop he'd sewn inside his coat and conversed with the woman, who by now had become suspicious of him, I had to put the book down, it was simply unbearable.

It was a quarter past eleven and the darkness outside was dense. If she hadn't rung yet, she probably wasn't going to ring at all.

I might as well go to bed.

I saw Joar's door still framed by a crack of light as I went past into the bathroom. But I didn't want to keep on at him all the time, so I brushed my teeth and went to bed, avoiding the conflict.

After a while I switched the lamp on again and picked the book up off the floor to read the murder scene, not switching it off until Rasko was back out on the street.

I stirred when someone came up the stairs. It was Mum going to bed, I realised, and looked at the time. It was just gone two.

When next I woke, the room was full of light and Oliver was standing in the doorway.

'Sorry to wake you, Syvert. I just wanted to say I'm taking your mother to the surgery.'

I sat up.

'Why? What's happened?'

'It's not an emergency. But she's rather concerned about the back trouble she's been having, along with that cough of hers. We talked about it last night and so I offered to take her in and let the doctor have a look at her.'

He smiled and lifted his hand to his temple as if in salute before turning and going back downstairs. A few moments later, I heard the car start and pull away.

Why had she told him and not me?

I was the one who should be taking her to the doctor's, not him.

I lived here. I was her son, for crying out loud.

But no, not a word to me. Yet as soon as her smarmy brother-in-law turned up, she started confiding. All of a sudden there was something wrong and she needed a doctor.

But when there was no one else but me?

Nothing. Not a word.

I went downstairs to the kitchen, poured myself a coffee and drank it standing by the window. The weather was fine, at least. The sky quite as blue as the day before, the sun quite as bright, the trees perhaps that little bit greener?

I couldn't understand what she saw in him. The way he bigged himelf up all the time. Flying down to buy a sailing boat. Trying to look young and cool with the clothes he wore.

I only hoped he wasn't going to offer to come back and help out if she actually was ill.

I wouldn't be able to stand it. I'd rather move out.

Why didn't she tell me she was worried? I was perfectly capable of looking after her. She knew that.

Did she think I couldn't manage to phone the surgery and make an appointment and then drive her over there?

I fried two eggs and sliced myself some bread. I was stymied without the car. I couldn't do a big shop, couldn't drive into town, couldn't pick up Dad's letters. The moped wasn't an option, not when it was that far, and obviously not on the motorway.

I could get the bus, though.

But I probably needed to be in when Mum got back, in case it *was* something serious.

It was lung cancer she'd be scared of.

All that smoking.

I cleared the table and went down to fetch the post. There were some bills for Mum, some circulars and other bumf, and of course the newspaper. Nothing from the jobcentre.

When I dropped it all onto the kitchen table and went into the living room to read the paper, I felt a sudden impulse, opened the phone book at *Dønnestad*, and before I'd stopped to think about it dialled the first of the numbers I hadn't yet rung.

'Hello?' a female voice said at the other end.

'Hello,' I said. 'Can I speak to Lisa, please?'

'Lisa's at school. Can I give her a message?'

'No, it's all right,' I said. 'Thanks all the same. Or no, wait a minute. What school would that be?'

'She goes to the Cath, the Cathedral School. Who am I speaking to?'

'Tell her Syvert rang. Syvert Løyning.'

*

To pass the time until they came back, I sat down in the living room with the Russian book that after a while became impossible for me to put down, though at the same time almost equally impossible to read. I so much wanted Rasko to get away, out of town, into the countryside perhaps, at the very least to get away. But he did the opposite. Not only did he go to the police station and behave in a suspicious manner, he even went back to the apartment where he'd committed the double murder! He could just as well have stuck a note on his forehead saying *Guilty*. How could he be so stupid? The police had him sussed immediately and were circling, waiting for him to give himself away. They couldn't prove a thing, so in fact he was completely safe, even if he had no way of knowing it, but he had no idea how he came across, hadn't a clue where he was at.

Make yourself scarce! Get away from there, then everything will be all right!

But no. He hovered at the scene of his crime, hovered at the police station, digging his own grave.

Now and then I lowered the book and looked out of the window, seeking respite from the novel's claustrophobia, but also to keep an eye out for the car and to think about Lisa.

They got off at twenty to three most afternoons, or at least we did when I was at gymnasium school. If Mum and Oliver didn't get back late, I'd be able to get there in the car, and if I could catch sight of her among the students piling out on their way home, I might have a chance to talk to her.

I'd never have guessed she went to the Cath. If *anyone* wasn't the type, it was Lisa.

A fly took to the air from the windowsill and buzzed about a bit before heading into the kitchen. It was a sound I hadn't heard in a long time. I put the book down and went after it. There were several of them, and I opened the window and chased them out with the newspaper. Just as I closed the window again, Mum's car turned up the drive from the main road.

That hadn't taken long.

It couldn't be that serious, then?

I stood and watched the car approach and then pull up. The front doors opened, Oliver got out first and went round to the passenger side in case Mum needed a hand, and then they came towards the house, Oliver a few paces behind.

'How did it go?' I said when she stepped in through the door.

'It's too soon to say,' she said. 'I've got to go for some tests at the hospital next week. They'll know more then.'

'Tests for what?'

'Cancer.'

She hung up her coat and smiled at me fleetingly.

'They don't know anything yet. It might be nothing.'

Behind her, Oliver came in.

'Everything will be fine, I'm sure,' he said.

'I hope so,' I said. 'Does anyone want coffee?'

'Yes, please,' said Mum. 'That'd be nice.'

'I need to be making tracks, I'm afraid,' said Oliver, looking at me. 'You wouldn't know the number for the taxis offhand, would you?'

'Yes, of course,' I said. 'Do you want me to order you one?'

'If you wouldn't mind?'

While I dialled the number, the two of them went into the living room together and sat down. Oliver seemed restless and clearly wanted to be on his way. Mum was edgy too, I could tell, watching her through the open door as she brushed away some bits of tobacco after rolling herself a smoke, the way she glanced around as she inhaled, as if she didn't want to see what she saw and was compelled to keep shifting her gaze.

'Taxi's on its way,' I said.

'Excellent!' said Oliver.

I went into the kitchen and got Mum a coffee, put it down on the coffee table and smiled at her. Oliver stood looking out of the window.

'It's only coming from the shop,' I said. 'Three minutes at the most.'

'There it is now,' he said shortly afterwards. 'Anyway, thanks for putting me up. Lovely supper last night, Syvert. And very pleasant company.'

Mum got up. He gave her a hug, then put his hand out to me.

'Look after her, now.'

'I will.'

He turned to look back as he opened the door of the taxi, waved and got in.

'I thought his flight wasn't until this evening,' I said to Mum after he'd gone.

'He has some things to do first.'

'Yes, I can imagine,' I said as I sat down.

'We won't say anything to Joar about this,' she said. 'All right?'

'Of course.'

'He'd only be frightened. And we don't even know what it is yet. If it's anything at all.'

'What did they say, exactly?'

'That was about it, really. That they wouldn't know until the test results came back.'

'They must have said more than that? I mean, they must have told you why they wanted to run the tests?'

'Yes, of course. But they can't say yet.'

'Say what?'

'Whether it's cancer.'

We both went quiet.

'Everything will be all right,' I said. 'I know it will, I can feel it.'

She didn't say anything.

'But I think it's really important to stay positive,' I said. 'You've got to have faith. I read something about it once. There's a much better chance of getting well, if you believe you will. Really believe, that is. But then again, it might not be anything at all. And if it is, chances are it won't be serious. And even then, the treatment's really good these days.'

She gave me a smile.

'You've always been the optimist,' she said. 'I'm glad you're here.'

I got up and went over to the window so she wouldn't see that my eyes were moist. She'd never said anything like that before.

'When's your appointment at the hospital?'

'Monday, eight o'clock.'

'I'll take you.'

She nodded.

'That'll be a big help.'

For a long moment, neither of us spoke.

If I was going to pick up the letters and go and meet Lisa from school, I'd probably have to get going soon. But I couldn't leave her on her own now, could I?

Another fly had got in. It kept bumping against the pane, as if unable to understand why it suddenly couldn't get through the air any more.

It made a U-turn and settled on the back of the sofa.

'Are you hungry?' I said. 'I can fix you something, if you like?'

'No thanks. It's kind of you, though.'

'You didn't have any breakfast either, not as far as I could tell.'

'I can't remember if I did or not. Perhaps I didn't.'

'You've got to eat, Mum. Eat and rest. That's the way to get better.'

'*If* I'm ill.'

'*If* you're ill, yes. But food and rest will still do you good.'

With every little lull, she withdrew that little bit more. It was almost as if she wasn't there, as if she'd transported herself somewhere else instead.

It probably didn't make much difference if I stayed behind with her or not.

'Do you want some more coffee?'

'No thanks,' she said, and glanced up at me. 'You'll have things to do, I'm sure.'

'I do have a couple of things to take care of in town, now you mention it. And we need to get some shopping done. Will you be OK? It shouldn't take more than a couple of hours.'

'Of course. You do what you like.'

And then she laughed.

'I'm not dead yet, you know.'

I laughed, too.

She leaned forward and picked up her smoking things, then looked up at me again.

'I will stop,' she said. 'Only not today.'

'I understand,' I said. 'Anyway, I'll get going. Just one thing, though. I'll need some money if I'm going to do the shopping. Have you got any?'

'Have a look in my bag.'

I did. Four hundreds and two fifties, besides a lot of change.

'How much can I take?' I called out.

'As much as you need,' she said.

How much was that? Krag had said a *good* wine. What price category was that? I couldn't fob him off with something inferior, he'd spent hours of his time.

I didn't like the idea of paying him with Mum's money, but there was no other option.

'OK, thanks!' I called back, took three hundred and stuffed the notes in my pocket, picked the car key up off the table, poked my head round the door and said goodbye.

The hills in towards town were greener than they were only a few days before. The deciduous trees were coming into leaf and appeared light and luminous compared to the dark, heavy spruce, and the forest floor wasn't quite as drab and rain-sodden, its browns and yellows had taken on verdant hues. But the green had yet to prevail. It was as if the forest were on the brink, I thought, yet to decide. To burst into life or retreat once more into asceticism. For now, it had put feelers out, that was all.

Maybe this was Mum's last spring on earth.

For the first time, as if by some gust of insight, I understood what death was.

She wasn't going to leave the world. The world was going to leave her.

Oh, shut up!

It wasn't certain that she was going to die. It wasn't even certain that she was ill.

People survived cancer all the time.

You couldn't go around thinking the worst. The best could happen just as easily.

The road ran through a cutting that had been blasted out of the rock, the steep sides hemmed in behind heavy-duty wire mesh, and above, where the forest continued, I saw glimpses of grey-white that could only be snow.

It was almost like time was running slower here. As if it had only just got to March.

What if the spring really did retreat? What if the leaves and blossoms all of a sudden failed to appear one year? If it all stopped working and the system broke down?

We were so certain of that procession: winter, spring, summer, autumn.

But how did it arise?

Something to do with distance from the sun, I supposed. The closer we came to it, the warmer it got, the further away, the colder it got.

But wasn't the earth's orbit fixed?

I tried to picture its path around the sun as we'd seen it on posters at school.

Did the earth pass *behind* the sun?

It had to.

So we'd be looking at the back of the sun half the year and the front of it the other half?

Yes.

And the earth turned on its own axis, so that day became night.

But why was there a difference between summer and winter?

The road went over a short bridge and an inlet opened out to the right, enclosed by dense forest on both sides. I looked out at the sea that glittered in the sunlight. A ship that from its size could only have been an oil tanker lay motionless on the horizon. I glanced quickly to the other side, across the inlet that continued a hundred metres or so, to the little smallholding that lay a stone's throw from the shoreline. I'd always thought it looked so quaint. The perfect place to live, if it hadn't been so far away from everything.

I tried to imagine Lisa and me living there, but it was no use, she didn't come across as the type who could live such an isolated life. I didn't fancy it much either.

Maybe if we had kids?

Two girls and a boy?

Ten, seven and three years old.

Lene with the L from Lisa, Steinar with the S after me, and then little Merethe.

I couldn't believe I didn't know why summer came.

And did the earth really pass *behind* the sun?

What side were we on now?

A bus appeared up ahead and I slowed down a bit. There was a bend in the road, I could see there was nothing coming the other way, so I indicated and overtook. Not long after, the town lay stretched out before me. The clock on the dashboard said just after half one. I wouldn't have time to go to the off-licence as well as to Krag's before Lisa got off from school.

Krag could wait.

I found a parking space just behind the off-licence and after looking up and down the road to make sure no traffic warden was lurking, I left the car without paying, I was only going to be gone a few minutes.

There were two people in the queue before me, a man in his fifties with a boyish-looking face, it seemed at first, and an affable look, though his nose betrayed him somewhat: red, verging on purple at the bulbous tip, almost certainly an alcoholic. Behind him stood a lady in a beige-coloured coat with sunglasses pushed up into her hair and a thin green scarf wound around her throat, I was so certain that she was pretty it almost gave me a fright when she turned to go out and I saw her horsey teeth, sunken cheeks and close-together eyes.

'How can I help you?' the assistant said, fixing me with a severe gaze.

'That's just it,' I said. 'I'm a bit unsure. I'm looking for a red wine, a present for someone. Only I don't know much about wines, to be honest.'

'What price category were you thinking of?'

'I'm not really sure. It needs to be quite a good wine.'

He sighed, without even trying to conceal it.

'French? Italian? Spanish?'

'Which is best?'

'That depends on what sort you'd like.'

'Can't you just choose one for me that's OK?'

He nodded and disappeared into the back room, emerging a moment later with a bottle in his hand.

'A Rioja might be a good choice,' he said. 'So I found you a Faustino.'

'Excellent! What country's it from? Just so I can mention it when I give the present.'

'Rioja is Spanish,' he said, glancing towards the street before entering the amount into the till.

When I got back to the car again I still had more than half an hour before she got off. It wasn't enough time to go and see Krag, too early to drive by the school.

In the wing mirror I saw a traffic warden come ambling. He paused and bent forward at the windscreen of every car, like a hunter checking his traps.

The bottle of wine looked good and expensive with the old painting of the nobleman on the label and I put it down on the passenger seat with a feeling of satisfaction, turned the ignition and pulled away onto the road. There was a little supermarket not far from the school, I remembered, in the street behind the petrol station, I'd climbed onto the roof there once, I couldn't have been more than eight or nine as I remembered it, one Sunday when Dad's sister had been visiting and I'd been out playing with my cousins, Anne and Lisbeth.

It must have been the summer they moved to Bergen.

I stopped at a red light in front of the pedestrian crossing. The sun was shining straight at me and the straggle of figures that crossed over had a shadowy quality.

I thought about the other side of the sun again.

There was something disconcerting about the whole thing.

Why was that, exactly?

Maybe it was because *in front of* and *behind* made no sense in space. There was no *up* and no *down* there either. Just endless space, dark and empty, in which the earth revolved and rotated.

What was a human life in all that endlessness?

The pedestrian light turned to red and I threw the car into first gear in anticipation of green.

It was exactly what Rasko had thought.

There.

I drove quickly down the road, turning left to follow Dronningens gate down to the bridge, and then, a few minutes later, having sped past the big, sixties housing blocks, made a right and found a place to park outside the little supermarket.

They had quite an assortment, the small shops often did, they knew what people came in for. I grabbed a frozen chicken, some potatoes and broccoli, then some milk and bread, liver paste and a packet of ham slices. By the time I got in the car again after putting the shopping in the boot, it was twenty-five to three. The bus stop for those going east was just by the petrol station, whereas those going west or north, as I supposed she would be, waited across the road from the school. If I drove around the block, I'd pass the stop on the same side, just when she'd be standing there.

As I drew away I wondered what to say to her. Or what to do, even. I supposed I could pull up in front of her, roll the window down and shout, Hi! You phoned? — but how was that likely to pan out?

I'd think of something!

There were only three people at the stop as I approached, and Lisa wasn't one of them. But a bit further away, on the footpath leading up to the school, a whole gaggle was on its way.

I took the first left and carried on under the bridge, looping back towards town, past the petrol station and out onto the main road again.

She wasn't there then either. I couldn't be entirely sure, there were about twenty people waiting, but even if she'd been standing behind someone and only an arm and her hair, for instance, had been visible, I was certain I'd have recognised her, and so I decided to repeat the manoeuvre a third time. Left turn, under the bridge, back towards town, past the petrol station to the busy junction.

And then I saw her.

She was walking along the pavement under the tall chestnut trees, on her way towards town. Light blue denim jacket, white sweater, dark blue jeans. A fawn-coloured bag hanging from her shoulder.

I waved, but she didn't see me, so I took the next road left, made a U-turn outside some flats and drove back the same way I'd come, rolling the window down on the passenger side and glancing in the mirror to check what was behind me. Nothing, I was lucky.

There she was.

I slowed down and, coming up alongside her, tooted the horn.

She spun round.

I smiled and waved.

'Hi!' I called out. 'Do you want a lift?'

I stopped. Some cars came over the top of the incline behind me. She stared emptily at me.

'It's Syvert!' I called. 'The guy whose nose your boyfriend broke!'

She stepped closer to the car. I leaned across the passenger seat. The first car came up behind me, slowing down.

'Get in!' I said. 'I'm causing a jam here!'

I smiled my biggest smile.

She looked at me without reciprocating.

The car behind blew its horn.

She glanced back at it. Then she dropped her shoulder, allowing her bag to slide into the crook of her arm, opened the door and got in.

'Hi,' she said.

I set off even before she'd shut the door. The car behind pulled out at exactly the same time, slammed on the brakes and blew its horn several times in succession.

'Crikey,' she said. 'Just passed your test, have you?'

'I thought he was waiting for me.'

'He is now. Try the indicator next time. It's that little stick there.'

I looked at her and grinned, flicked the indicator and drew away.

'Where are you going?' I said.

'Home,' she said. 'Only it's a bit far.'

'It doesn't matter. I've got loads of time.'

'Not got a job yet, then?'

I didn't know if she was being funny or not, so I shook my head.

She smelled faintly of perfume, a light, summery scent, something I associated with dresses and skirts, not the denim she was wearing.

'How did you find me?'

'I saw you from the car as I was driving along.'

'Ha, ha,' she said, and stared out of the window on her side, her hands resting on top of the bag she'd put on her lap. 'I don't believe in coincidences like that. The town's not *that* small.'

'No use trying to fool you.'

'You can try,' she said. 'Only you won't succeed.'

'But it *was* a coincidence! Sort of, anyway. I knew you went to the Cath, I had an errand to run in the area and so I looked out for you on the way.'

I turned left and drove through the old residential area alongside the river.

'You live up at Eikelandsvannet, don't you?'

She nodded.

The sunlight gave her hair a reddish tinge. Her wrist, made visible by her jacket getting twisted and the sleeve riding up when she got in, was noticeably thin.

'You know a lot about me,' she said. 'It feels a bit creepy.'

'But I don't know *anything* about you!'

'You knew what school I go to, and where I live.'

'Your address is in the phone book. And it was your mum who told me what school you go to.'

'You rang our number?'

'You rang me. I wondered what you wanted.'

'And she told you I went to the Cath?'

'That's right. And that's *all* I know.'

'How could you say what you said, if you don't know anything about me?'

'Say what? Oh, right. *That.*'

'*That*, yes.'

'I was just being honest, that's all. It's the way it is. I can't help it.'

She smiled faintly, then looked out of the window again. But when she turned to face me a second later, her expression was more serious.

'I'll be honest, too,' she said. 'I'm not interested in you. I like you, you seem like a good laugh, but I'm not interested in you. Not like that.'

'That's fair enough.'

There was a silence.

I had to say something so as not to make her think she'd hurt me. So she wouldn't feel sorry for me.

The river that ran next to the road glittered and gleamed in the sunlight that came flooding from behind. She shifted her weight slightly, ran her hand through her hair and then rested it on top of her bag again.

'Do you like it at the Cath?' I said.

'It's all right.'

'What year are you in?'

'Second.'

'What line of study?'

'Society.'

'I chose Society as well.'

'At the Cath?'

'No, no. But some mates of mine went there.'

'Aha.'

There was a silence again.

Every time she said something, it was as if she then retreated into a default state. It was like a sadness.

Or maybe she was just bored.

'One of them works for the local rag now,' I went on. 'He was the one who tricked me into doing that interview, by the way. Dag, his name is. He's an albino. Good bloke.'

'You don't say.'

'He was the one I was with when we ran into each other at the Shell station.'

'I don't think I noticed him.'

The residential areas petered out around us, though we still weren't far from the town centre. Green hills, bluing ridges, black water. An occasional house, the odd smallholding, jetties where the river widened.

She looked out of the window as if I wasn't there.

'You live quite a long way from school, then,' I said. 'What time do you have to get up in the mornings?'

She looked at me.

'You're asking me what time I get up in the mornings?'

'No harm in chatting, is there? I mean, it's not as if we know each other that well.'

She smiled.

'Normally I get up at half past six. What time do you get up?'

'Not that early, not at the moment. Around ten. But I only just got out of the services. I was getting up at six every day then.'

'What service were you in?'

'Navy. I was a cook.'

'You'll make good dinners, then.'

'Better than I used to, anyway. Are you any good?'

'No. I can't fry an egg without burning it. I do a nice cup of cocoa, though.'

'It's as good a place as any to start,' I said. 'And it's by no means easy finding the right balance between sugar and cocoa powder. A lot of people use more sugar than cocoa. To the detriment of the chocolate taste. That little bit of bitterness. Which is the mark of a good cup of cocoa.'

'You're right there.'

'How many spoonfuls of each?'

'Two of cocoa and one of sugar per litre of milk.'

'Same here!' I said, and laughed. 'And you say you don't believe in coincidences?'

'I'm sticking to it. You might be just saying that, for all I know.'

'You don't think I'd lie about making cocoa, do you?'

'I don't know you, do I? I've no idea who you are.'

'You don't need to know a person to know who they are! Don't you agree? You know as soon as you start talking to them.'

'You reckon?'

'Definitely.'

'So who am I, then?'

She looked at me.

'You?' I said, buying myself a few seconds.

'Yes, me,' she said. 'Who you say you're in love with.'

'That's a feeling,' I said. 'Something you just *know*.'

She looked out of the window again.

'OK,' I said. 'But don't get angry with me!'

'Why would I get angry?'

'You can be surly and come across as stand-offish.'

'I know.'

'But you've got a good heart. You care about others. A lot, I think.'

'You think so, do you?'

'I know so.'

We drove a few minutes without speaking, passing through the hub that lay sprawled where the river valley widened and swept away into the great swathes of forest.

'Can I say one more thing?' I said.

'About me?'

'Not that it's any of my business. But it's like there's something you're sad about.'

'Maybe I'm sad about you.'

I laughed.

'That's a possibility that needs to be kept open!'

'So, if you go straight through the roundabout here and follow the road a few more kilometres.'

'Right you are.'

The sprawl thinned out again and soon we were surrounded by trees on both sides of the road, which was narrow with lots of bends. After a bit, the landscape opened out again and a long, inky expanse of water lay before us. Some farms came into view.

'Left here,' she said where the road forked.

We followed the line of a ridge, to some houses that stood scattered around the edge of a field.

'This is ours,' she said, indicating the first, a white-painted house from the fifties, run-down and with no garden. Junk strewn about outside, a rusting green VW parked in the drive.

She lived here? In this hovel? I pulled up behind the VW.

'Thanks for the lift,' she said.

'No problem! See you again, I hope.'

'Who knows,' she said, and got out. 'Bye.'

She went towards the house as I reversed out. I thought she'd have stood on the step and waved, but she didn't, she went straight in and closed the door behind her.

I drove back in the strangest of moods, excited at having been close to her for such a relatively long time, deflated by what she'd said, which I knew was true, that she wasn't interested in me. I couldn't blame her, the school she went to was teeming with lads who looked a lot cooler than me — nine out of ten probably wasn't wrong, maybe even more.

But this was me!

I liked her so much. I liked her so very, very much.

Everything about her.

I stopped off at a chippy in the nearest village, bought two sausages with mash and a cola and went back to the car with it all, eating with the door open as I gazed at the bridge, the sawmill on the other side, the forklifts that went back and forth outside, an articulated lorry, the forest rising up beyond, the outcrops of rock that here and there lay bare between the trees.

I thought about Mum.

It hurt so much I didn't know what to do.

She was going to die, and here I was eating sausage and mash.

I got out and dropped my rubbish into the bin, went back to the car again and headed back towards town.

Dad's letters felt even more tainted now. The right thing would be to leave them well alone.

But Krag had done a job for me, so there was no way out of it. I'd have to stop by and pick them up, pay him for his efforts. But I didn't have to read them.

It wouldn't do any good anyway. Dad was dead and Mum had lived on after him for nine years now. What had happened was in the past and it could stay there.

Satisfied with my decision, I drove to Krag's house, parked outside and with my free hand knocked on the door using his stupid little knocker, the bottle of wine gripped by the neck in my other.

He came to the door immediately, in a rather crumpled white shirt. He peered at me through narrowed eyes, a wry smile on his face.

'Syvert! I was beginning to think you weren't coming.'

'Sorry.'

'Come in!'

'Here, this is for you,' I said, handing him the bottle as I stepped into the hall. He turned it in his hand and looked at the label.

'It's Spanish,' I said.

'So I see. Thanks very much indeed! Come through, we'll have a little taste!'

'I'm driving, I'm afraid.'

'A glass won't do any harm!'

'It's not really convenient. My mother's ill. I need to be getting back.'

'I'm sorry to hear it. I've been looking forward to discussing social-ism and Dostoevsky with you!'

'That would have been nice. Another time, perhaps.'

He looked at me, but this time his smile had gone.

Was he gay?

Of course, that explained it.

Christ.

No photos of any kids on the walls. No wife. Only him.

'Yes, it would have been nice,' he said. 'But do come in, I'll show you what I've come up with.'

He beckoned with a small motion of his hand, fingers held together, as if I were a car reversing out onto a busy road.

'No need to take off your shoes,' he said as we went inside.

His desk was littered with books and papers. In the middle was a typewriter, next to it a near-empty wine bottle and a glass.

He took a sip from the glass, passed his index finger over his lips and picked up a bundle of papers.

'Here we are. As you can see, it ran to quite a few pages in the end. I've typed it all out this time, so it'll be easier for you to read. It's quite a story, I can tell you.'

He handed me the letters and I took them with a nod of thanks.

'Are you sure you can't spare five minutes? A glass and a smoke? To round things off?'

'I'd like to, really. It's just that it's quite serious with my mum. I've been gone too long as it is. I've got a younger brother to see to as well.'

'Joar?'

'How do you know his name?'

He indicated the bundle in my hand.

'It's in the letters.'

'Is it?'

'Yes.'

'I hope . . .'

The words trailed away.

'You hope I'll keep it all to myself? But of course, I've already promised. In fact, it's something of an affront to have to say it again! But I understand, of course, given the rather intimate nature of the content.'

'Thanks, I appreciate it,' I said, and then turned towards the hall to make it clear that I was leaving. 'And thanks for all the work you've put in. A bottle of wine isn't nearly enough reward!'

'No trouble,' he said. 'A shame we couldn't have that chat. I hope your mother recovers soon. You'll show yourself out, won't you?'

I made a point of not looking at the letters as I left. Once back in the car, I put them face down on the passenger seat.

She's dying, she's dying, was all I could say to myself as I drove home, but it was as if the thought was someone else's, not mine. And when I pictured her, she was skin and bone, sallow and haggard, with skull-like features, though I knew it wasn't what she looked like. Only when I pulled up in front of the house and saw her face peer over the top of the half-curtain in the kitchen, disarmingly normal-looking, did the skull image dissolve from my mind.

They were having their tea. I put the letters down on the telephone table and poked my head round to say hello before I went upstairs with them to my room. Joar knew nothing, I could tell straight away. Mum smiled at me and seemed in brighter spirits than when I'd left.

'Rissoles!' I said. 'Yum!'

While I was often tempted, and twice in the weeks that followed stood with the letters in my hand, I managed not to read them. I'd have been betraying Mum if I had. It was bad enough that I'd spent her money to pay Krag, I didn't have to read the letters from the woman Dad was going to leave her for as well, especially not now that she was ill, perhaps even dying.

I drove her to the hospital that Monday, and when the results came back the week after and she had to go and see the consultant, I waited outside in the car. In actual fact, the weather was fine and I was so restless that I went inside to the hospital cafe and bought myself a cup of coffee that I drank standing by the car, the saucer on the roof. In the days prior, her upcoming test results had been on my mind a lot, of course, and I knew it could go either way, though without it really sinking in until we were actually sitting in the car on our way there and something cold and dark and abyss-like opened up inside me, for she sat there without a word, with her best coat on and her bag in her lap, staring stiffly ahead, her face quite without expression.

'I'm sure everything's going to be all right, Mum,' I said. 'You'll see.'

'There's nothing we can do about it, one way or another,' she said.

She'd been in there half an hour as I stood with my coffee, and had probably already been told how things stood. Cars entered and left the car park, and over at the entrance the doors kept sliding open and shut, the glass gleaming in the sunlight. The hospital served the entire region and looked a bit like a cruise ship, with a landing pad for helicopters on the roof and everything.

I drained the last of my coffee, the dregs were tepid, and looked around for somewhere I could leave the cup and saucer. On the bin lid? No, best to go in with them myself.

Just as I reached the door, Mum came out.

It was impossible to tell from her expression how it had gone. And I wasn't going to ask her there, outside the entrance, with people coming and going.

'I just need to take these back,' I said, holding up the cup and saucer. 'Here's the key. I'll be with you in ten seconds!'

I hurried inside, put the things down on the nearest table, despite someone sitting there, then hurried out again to see Mum opening the car door. Something told me everything was all right, that the news was good.

I trotted over, slowing down to a walk as I got closer to the car.

Mum turned towards me as I got in.

'How did it go?' I said. 'What did they say?'

She shook her head and smiled faintly.

'Not so good, I'm afraid.'

'Oh, no?'

'I've got cancer. Lung cancer, as I thought.'

I didn't know what to say.

'So,' she said. 'It's serious.'

'But they're going to give you treatment. Aren't they?'

She nodded.

'At the Radium Hospital.'

'In Oslo?'

'Yes.'

She looked me in the eye.

'You'll have to look after Joar. Can you do that?'

'Of course. Of course I will. I'll do everything I can to help.'

'That's good.'

We sat in silence.

'Let's go home, shall we?' she said after a while.

I started the car and soon we were speeding home, the spring now warm and glorious and green all around us.

There was only one thing I wanted to know. Had the doctor said anything about her chances of survival? But I couldn't ask her that. The more frightened she was, the less chance of recovery.

Everything had to carry on as normal. Or as normal as possible.

She sat quietly in the seat next to me, her eyes fixed straight ahead, one hand holding the strap of her bag, the other resting like a claw on her thigh.

'When do they want you to go to Oslo? Did they say?'

'They'll try and get me in as soon as possible. In a couple of weeks, if I'm lucky. They'll do more tests there. The doctor thought they might be able to operate. That'd be best, he said. And then radiation therapy.'

'They'll be wanting to keep you in for a while, then?'

'A fortnight, I think. A bit longer, perhaps. And then perhaps another period of treatment after that.'

'OK. I'll look after things at home while they're getting you well again there.'

'That's good of you.'

'Maybe we can come and see you as well?'

'In Oslo?'

'Yes.'

'That'd be nice. But where would you stay?'

I shrugged.

'We could stay at a hotel. Joar would like that.'

'I doubt we can afford it.'

'Haraldsheimen's a none-too-expensive option. It's where we stayed on that school trip in ninth, do you remember? It's a hostel. It's cheap and quite decent.'

'We'll see.'

We drove past the factory, which looked even darker and more forbidding in the sunshine. Two ships were docked there, a crane swung something slowly through the air, and then we entered the sharp bend that led us onto the long stretch of road through the woods.

Radiation therapy — wasn't that radioactivity too?

Strange that radiation gave you cancer when it came from an atom bomb or a nuclear power plant, but cured cancer in a hospital.

I hoped they knew what they were doing.

Mum sighed.

I looked at her.

'It's Joar I'm thinking about,' she said, returning my gaze. 'That's all. I'll have to tell him now.'

'There's no rush, is there?'

'Yes, he needs to know. If I'm going to Oslo in two weeks, he'll need time to get used to it. I'm sure he realises already that something's not right.'

'Yes, he's not stupid.'

He'd known as soon as he had that dream, the bird that had flown out of Mum's mouth. He knew there was something wrong with her even then. Or something inside him knew.

A black cat was stretched out on the doorstep enjoying the sunshine so much that not even the sight of the car or the sound of the engine prompted it to move. I bent down and ruffled its fur before putting the key in the lock and opening the door. It stood up between my feet and stared into the hall.

'Have we got a tin of tuna we can give it?' said Mum.

'If we want it to stay, it'd be the right way to go about it.'

'I don't think there's much danger of that. It's so tame it's obviously got a good home somewhere.'

She put her bag down on the table and hung up her coat. The cat had slipped into the kitchen and stood watching us, purring audibly.

'I'll go and have a lie-down,' said Mum.

'Good idea,' I said. 'Is there anything you need?'

'No, thanks.'

She'd started taking long rests mid-morning, sometimes in the afternoons too. I didn't think she actually slept mid-morning, but lay in bed with the radio on. I'd thought maybe she'd somehow made herself believe she was worse than she was. But now there was no doubt.

I opened a tin of tuna, forked the contents out onto a tea plate, put a saucer of milk next to it and watched as the cat ate with its tail held high in the air. Its coat was short and well kept. A thickness of the neck and back suggested it was a tom.

She'd be off sick from work for months now.

I'd have to start earning money.

I went into the hall, got the phone book out and looked up the number of the cellulose factory. Terje had already asked for me, but that was a while ago now. If I was lucky, something might have come up in the meantime.

I closed the door so Mum wouldn't hear what I was up to, I thought it would be a nice surprise if I could tell her I'd got a job.

'Hello?' said the foreman.

'Yes, hello,' I said. 'It's Syvert Løyning here.'

'Hi, Syvert!'

'I was wondering if there might be a job for me at the factory? I'm up for anything, really.'

'I'm afraid not, not at the moment. Terje did mention it to me. You're going through a bit of a rough patch, I believe.'

'No, I'm fine,' I said. 'I do need a job, though. I can't just doss about.'

'I understand you.'

'No chance of just a bit of summer work?'

'No can do, I'm afraid. We're all sorted there, have been for a while.'

'OK. That's a shame.'

'I'll give you a ring if something turns up.'

'Thanks. I'd appreciate it!'

'Bye for now, then.'

'Bye.'

I hadn't been banking on anything, but I still couldn't help feeling a bit disappointed. A small hope, dashed.

Maybe I could phone Lisa while I was at it?

No.

Instead, I went back to the cat. It was still eating, and I smoothed my hand over its broad head.

It padded across the floor, stopped at the door and looked at me.

I went and opened it.

It strolled over to the car and lay down beside one of the wheels.

Signe worked part-time at the shop, Vidar had his job in town at the sports shop. I could ask them if they knew of anything.

I couldn't see myself on a checkout.

But a sports shop would be all right, I was quite knowledgeable when it came to sports equipment.

I went into the hall again and looked up the number. It was Arne who answered. I asked after Vidar and he went to fetch him.

'Hi, Vidar! Syvert here. How's things?'

'Syvert! Good, yes!' he said, sounding surprised.

'How did you get on at that shooting tournament?'

'Not bad.'

'You won, then?'

'Yes,' he said, and let out a giggle.

'Listen, I'm in need of a job. You wouldn't have an opportunity there by any chance? It doesn't matter what it is, I'll do anything. The hours don't matter either.'

'I don't think we have, no,' he said. 'I can ask, but I doubt it.'

'Would you? That'd be brilliant.'

'Of course. But don't get your hopes up .'

'Thanks a lot, Vidar. We'll have to see about that night out soon!'

'We will, yes,' he said.

We hung up and again the thought of ringing Lisa came to mind.

But I had to show some resilience.

I had to keep some pride.

I went outside with a mug of coffee and sat down on the step. The cat was lying motionless in the same place. Their behaviour was exactly

like a lion's. Their thoughts and instincts too, I imagined. Their crav-
ings and pleasures.

Mental hospitals were always short-staffed. Homes for the mentally
handicapped too.

It was such a glorious day.

How terrible for Mum.

She didn't look that ill.

It was inside her.

Cells out of control, spreading everywhere.

But they were so tiny. How could you die from that?

At least now she'd stopped smoking.

Fresh air into her lungs. Fresh air, light, healthy food.

I felt an urge to go upstairs to her room, snatch the curtains aside,
open the window, let the air stream in.

Cheer her up.

Light, fresh air, laughter and joy.

Who did you have to talk to to get a job at one of those institutions?
Presumably they had their own administrative departments. They'd
want people with qualifications, obviously. And for unskilled work
they'd take on the sons and daughters of those who worked there already.

I stood up and went back into the kitchen. I could faintly hear the
radio on in Mum's room.

She'd be scared out of her wits.

Mum was quieter than usual at the dinner table and I tried to compen-
sate by blathering on all I could. It worked, Joar didn't seem to detect
anything out of the ordinary, he ate heartily, and not only did he
answer my questions, he even contributed off his own bat, relating
something that had happened at the kiosk outside school that day. Two
of his friends had got into a fight, they'd been messing to begin with,
only it had turned nasty when one of them, Stian, had pushed the other
lad, Tor Arild, so hard he fell and scraped his wrists.

'Tor Arild went berserk and ran after him, and when he caught up
with him he kept shoving him in the chest, right until he was out by
the road. You know where Little Hawaii is?'

I nodded.

'He shoved him right out to Little Hawaii. And then when Stian tried to run away, he slipped and fell into the water.'

'He didn't?'

'Yes, he did! But that wasn't what I wanted to tell you about. Because afterwards he sat down on the bench —'

'Who did?'

'Stian. And then this man came and sat down beside him. He must have been about forty or something. He said he'd seen what had happened and if they were bullying him he could come home with him. He lived in the flats across from the school.'

'Really?'

'He was a pervert, of course.'

'How do you know that?'

'He was forty, at least! And he was asking a thirteen-year-old to go home with him!'

'Maybe he was just being kind,' I said. 'Maybe he got bullied himself when he was that age, you never know.'

'But what was Stian supposed to do in his flat?'

I shrugged.

'Drink cocoa with him?'

He turned to Mum.

'What do *you* think?'

'It's hard to say,' she said. 'But you're right to be sceptical. It's good that you are.'

He gave me a triumphant little smile.

'What do you think about my bread, then?' I said.

'It's good,' he said.

'How about the soup?'

'Good.'

'There's afters as well.'

'Is there?'

'Yes. Ice lollies.'

'Those little ones they sell in boxes?'

'No. Proper-sized. Yellow ice lollies.'

It struck me that I might have got him too worked up, that the shock

would hit him even harder than if he'd sensed there was something
wrong.

A breeze gusted through the open window, the curtain billowing
inside.

Late afternoon.

A gang of flies buzzed up into the room.

It was nearly summer.

'Joar, you know I had to go to the doctor's about my back?'

The instant she spoke, the light in her eyes went out and Joar's sudden vitality was likewise extinguished.

He knew.

'Yes?' he said, and carried on eating.

'Well, I got the results today and they say that I'm ill and that I'll
have to go to Oslo for treatment.'

'You've got cancer.'

Her eyes moistened as she nodded.

'It'll be all right,' I said. 'Mum's going to get better again.'

'Is it lung cancer?'

'Yes,' said Mum.

'Lung cancer kills you.'

'Listen, Joar,' I said. 'It's not as straightforward as that. A lot of people
get well again, a lot. The treatments are really effective now.'

He didn't say anything.

Mum and I exchanged glances.

What do we do now? her eyes said.

Strangely, I felt bolstered. She was acknowledging me.

'Thanks for dinner,' said Joar. He got to his feet and took his things
over to the sink.

'Where are you going?' I said.

'To my room.'

'What about your ice lolly?'

'I'll have it later,' he said, and went up the stairs.

Mum sighed.

'He'll be all right,' I said. 'He just needs some time on his own.'

'Talk to him about it, will you?'

'Of course I will. It won't be easy, though.'

'I know it won't. But he listens, even if he pretends he doesn't.'

I didn't say anything, but could only be doubtful.

'He never wanted to be cuddled or made a fuss of when he was little, the way you did. But I never gave up, because I knew he wanted to *really*. When I used to sing to him, he'd sit on my lap and drink his milk, but always facing away from me, and I'd stroke his back, it was the only physical contact he allowed. It's the same now, in a way. He wants us to try and get through to him. Do you understand?'

'Yes.'

She smiled and wiped her eyes quickly with the tip of a finger, first one, then the other.

'He needs me a good many years yet. You're grown up, Syvert, you can look after yourself. But Joar can't.'

'Don't think like that, Mum. The next couple of months are going to be a bit rough, but then you'll get better again and everything will be like it was before. I'm sure of it.'

Joar was sitting at his desk doing his homework when I went into his room. It looked like it was geometry, there was a pair of compasses and a ruler next to the two books he had open in front of him.

'I don't want to talk about it,' he said.

'That's all right, we don't have to,' I said. 'I just wanted to check how you were doing.'

'I'm doing fine.'

'Good. Geometry, is it?'

'Yes.'

'Is it difficult?'

'It's a piece of cake.'

I sat down on his bed. He threw me a disapproving glance.

'What do you want, exactly?'

'Nothing in particular,' I said.

He wrote something down in his rough book, then opened his exercise book, switched from pencil to pen and began to copy what he'd written. I could hear Mum's voice downstairs, she was on the phone to someone, probably Gro or Jorunn.

It felt impossible even to *talk* to him. I couldn't understand why. So much of what I said seemed simply to pass through him, diffusing without trace, and nothing ever seemed to come back the other way.

'When Mum goes into hospital, we'll be on our own here,' I said. 'I don't know how long it'll be, but a couple of weeks, at least. Is that all right?'

'Yes.'

'We can go to the swimming baths, you know that. And we can go out in the canoe. We can do a bit of shooting as well, if you want. I've been thinking about what we talked about, that you could join a club. I could have a word with Vidar about it. I think it'd be a really good idea.'

He sat in concentration while writing, then picked up the pair of compasses and drew a circle before placing the ruler on the page.

'We can rent some videos too. It doesn't have to be the weekend for that. And I'll make something nice for our tea every day. How does that sound?'

'I'm doing my homework,' he said.

I got up.

'Everything's going to be fine, you'll see,' I said. I stood still for a few seconds until realising he wasn't going to answer, then left him and went downstairs. Mum was sitting on the chair in the hall, the receiver wedged between her shoulder and cheek, uttering an occasional *mm*, *aha* or *I know* as she rolled a cigarette.

She glanced up at me. I wagged a finger at her. She smiled meekly, nodded and put the tobacco pouch down on the telephone table.

The dishes were done. The living room was tidied. The laundry bin was empty. I still had to finish my book, but I could read before I went to sleep.

The thought of the letters that ever since I'd hidden them away had glowed like burning embers in the cupboard, as if they were magic and had been drawing me towards them, now only made me feel like throwing up.

'Syvert?' Mum said from the hall. I turned round and went to see what she wanted. She held the receiver clasped to her chest now. 'Haven't you got football practice tonight?'

'Normally, yes,' I said. 'I just thought . . . well, I thought I'd give it a miss and make sure you're all right.'

'No, I'm all right. You get yourself away!'

'Are you sure?'

'Yes, of course.'

She put the receiver to her ear again and carried on her conversation.

Was she just saying it for my sake or did she mean it?

I'd have to take her word for it, I reckoned, packed my holdall and went out to the car. It was early yet, but that was OK, it felt good to be getting out for a while.

When practice was over, as we traipsed back to the changing room, I came up alongside Vegard.

'How's it going?' I said.

'Good. You? Not seen much of you lately.'

'I'm fine. A bit strapped for cash, that's all. I was thinking, that uncle of yours you mentioned. The one with the undertaking business. Is that job still going, do you know?'

'No idea. It wouldn't surprise me, though. He's always saying how hard it is to get hold of people.'

'I can see that.'

'Are you desperate?'

'I am a bit, to be honest. And it can't be that bad, surely? It'd only be for a few months.'

'I'll ask.'

'Or maybe you could give me his number? I could do it myself then.'

'It's in the book. Kristian Emanuelsen.'

I rang the next morning, while Mum was upstairs having a rest and Joar was at school.

I presented myself as a friend of Vegard and he knew who I was straight away. He was still a man short, and it was basically just a question of when I could start.

'It's the Whit holiday this Monday coming,' he said. 'How about Tuesday?'

'That'd be great,' I said. 'What time do you start in the mornings?'

'You can come in at nine. You've got a driving licence, of course?'

'Of course.'

'What about a suit? Have you got one?'

'I'm afraid I haven't, no. Do I need one?'

'It's what we wear. I'll have a look, I might have something lying about you can use until you get sorted. See you Tuesday, then.'

'There's no interview?'

'No need. I trust Vegard. He says you're a good lad. Not his words exactly, but that's what he meant. So it won't be necessary.'

It wasn't until I'd put the receiver down that I realised he hadn't mentioned how much I'd be getting. I assumed there was a standard rate they stuck to. And it couldn't be that badly paid.

I'd have money coming in every month for a while. I'd be able to help Mum out financially. But I didn't know what to say to her. It didn't feel right somehow, working for an undertaker when she was seriously ill. On the other hand, lying about it wouldn't feel right either. Besides, it'd never work. A thing like that would be impossible to keep secret.

I went up to the barn and got the garden table out, it was wrought iron and heavy as hell, but I managed to lug it into the garden, or more exactly the narrow strip of grass round the back where we'd always put it when summer came. The tulips stood brightly in the flower bed up against the wall of the house. The apple trees would soon be thick with foliage. And the fields, until recently a muddy black, were now tinged green beneath the blue sky.

I put four chairs out too, before going back in and getting some coffee on the go for her.

'Mum?' I called up when it was ready. 'Coffee's made!'

If she was asleep, it'd be quite annoying to be woken up like that. But it was better for her to sit out in the sunlight and fresh air than to lie festering in that dim and clammy bedroom.

Ten minutes later we were sitting in the garden, each with a mug of coffee and a plate of plain biscuits on the table between us.

'How are you feeling?' I said. 'Are you still in pain?'

'My back still hurts a bit, yes. But the good news is they're taking me in next week.'

'Are they? That's brilliant!' I said as enthusiastically as I could. The news wasn't that good at all, I reckoned. If they were taking her in that quickly, it meant she was a priority, which in turn could only mean she was bad.

'How are you going to get there?'

'Oh, I'll take the coach. That's the easiest.'

'Wouldn't it be better to fly? It only takes half an hour. I mean, if your back's hurting and everything.'

'It's too expensive, you know that.'

I snapped a biscuit in half and dipped one piece in my coffee before popping it into my mouth. Above the ridge a great cloud lingered, it looked like a snow-covered fell and seemed hardly to be moving. Apart from that, the sky was blue and empty.

Mum looked at it too.

A bird soared, outlined sharply against the white. A hawk of some kind, or a buzzard.

'The money situation might be looking up now,' I said. 'I've been looking for a job. There was nothing going at the factory, so I asked at the sports shop where Vidar works, only they had nothing there either. But it turns out Vegard's uncle has been short-handed for a while. I've just spoken to him and he says I can start on Tuesday. So that plane ticket won't be a problem. It won't cost that much, and it'll be a lot easier for you.'

'Well, there's good news, Syvert,' she said. 'What sort of work is it?'

'That's the thing. You might not like the idea, but his uncle's an undertaker. I don't know what I'll be doing there yet. He asked if I had a driving licence, so it might just be driving. The main thing is we'll have money coming in! Joar and I can come and see you for the weekend.'

'Do you think you can manage it?'

'What, coming to see you? Of course we can!'

'No, I meant working at an undertaker's. It sounds a bit bleak and horrible. We can always get by on what we've got, you know.'

'A job's a job, Mum. Can't be too choosy. Anyway, it's only for a few months.'

She looked at me and nodded almost imperceptibly. The big cloud seemed now to be balanced on the ridge. The spruce at the top stood outlined against it and took on a winter-like quality. The fire at the

Soviet nuclear plant was under control now, I'd read, so presumably there'd be no more radioactivity drifting on the wind. It was all on the ground. In the water, in the fields. In the animals and livestock, in the trees, in the flowers.

'It will be a big help, though,' Mum said. 'Thank you, Syvert. I can think of a lot of jobs a nineteen-year-old would rather have than that.'

'I'd have taken it on anyway,' I said. 'I could do with some cash myself.'

I got so drunk that 17 May that I slept under a rhododendron in the park and woke up shivering and confused, feeling sick and with a thumping pain in my skull. It was six in the morning and two figures were standing over me.

Two policemen in uniform.

'You can't sleep here,' one of them said when I peered up at them.

'No, no, of course not,' I said, and sat up. 'I'm sorry. I'll go home now.'

'Do you live nearby?'

'Outside town, a bit of a way. I'll be all right, though. I'll get the bus.'

The answer satisfied them and they went on their way side by side. A bit further along, one of them turned his head and looked back at me, presumably to make sure I hadn't gone back to sleep.

On my way to the bus station I discovered I had no money on me. I couldn't even ring anyone. I'd have to hitch it. Only there were no cars about, it was six o'clock in the morning, the day after the national day festivities.

As if that wasn't enough, it started to rain. No more than a light drizzle, but freezing cold nonetheless.

I walked down to the railway station and sat down in the empty waiting room, leaned back against the wall and fell asleep again.

When I woke up, it was gone ten o'clock and half a dozen others were sitting there too. I'd said to Mum I could stay the night at a friend's house if it got late, so I didn't suppose she'd be worried or angry.

If only I could get my hands on a coin so I could ring someone and get them to come and pick me up.

I went over to the phone box outside, checked the coin return, the

302

shelf, the floor. People often lost coins in a phone box, but I found nothing. I carried on towards the bus station. There was an empty cola bottle in a bin, and when I decided to have a scavenge around the ferry terminal I managed to find several beer bottles too. I got the money back for them at the Narvesen.

I tried Dag first.

'You owe me one,' I said, looking out across the harbour while trying not to breathe through my nose, the phone box reeked of piss.

'Do I?'

'The interview.'

'Ah, right. What do I have to do?'

'Come and pick me up. I'm stranded in town, I've got no money for the bus.'

'Pick you up in town? Now? You must be joking. I don't love you that much.'

'Come on. I'd do the same for you.'

'That's easy enough to say. Anyway, I can't. I had loads to drink last night and if the police are only out once a year with their roadside breathalysers, you can be sure it's going to be the morning after the seventeenth of May.'

'Thanks for nothing, you shit,' I said, and hung up.

There was no one else I could ask, not really. Karsten, Glenn, Vegard, Keith and Gjert had all been as drunk as me, or nearly, and none of them would be capable of driving now. Terje? I didn't know him well enough.

So I rang Mum, last resort.

She didn't sound pleased, but said she'd come.

To kill time, I wandered through the streets with my hands in my pockets, eyes scouring the pavement in front of me in case anyone had lost some coins or even their wallet.

We'd had breakfast at Tor Egil's and got started on the beer and spirits there, there'd even been champagne, before going into town to watch the parades. After that, we'd sat drinking on the grass by the old fortifications and then headed off to Sundown, eventually ending up at the trade-union penthouse Glenn had the keys to.

I'd been on the lookout for Lisa all day. Everyone was in town, so she was bound to be too. And then, suddenly, in the middle of a crowd on the other side of the street, I caught sight of her. I weaved my way towards her, stopping for a marching band, thinking I could cross the street after they'd passed, before the next one came, but then I saw she was with someone. She dipped her head to the lighter he held out in his hand, and when she straightened up again and took her cigarette out of her mouth, she smiled at him and he put his hand on her shoulder. He was a lot older than her, twenty-five or thereabouts. He was quite short and had a moustache and curly hair that looked like it had been permed, black cowboy boots with a heel. I ducked so she wouldn't see me, wheeled round and went back the way I'd come, to the corner of the street where the others still stood, easy to pick out with Karsten towering over everyone.

That was why she hadn't rung, obviously. She'd got a new boyfriend.

It was nothing to get depressed about, I had no chance with her anyway. Best just to get on without her and not look back.

So I drank and had a laugh with the rest of the lads. I remembered more or less everything clearly until we got to the penthouse, it was packed with people, but the time between then and waking up in the park was a blank.

I must have decided to go home or gone out looking for Lisa, the sort of thing you did when you were as pissed as that.

I only hoped I hadn't told anyone about her.

It was a futile hope. The mouth speaks what the heart is full of. Especially when you're pissed out of your mind.

I turned down towards the harbour again. It had stopped raining, but the ground was still wet. The cobbles were as if membraned by the light of the overcast sky. The Denmark ferry lay with its engines rumbling and the stern door gaping. Some lorries had already gone on board, I could see, while a handful of private cars were lined up waiting.

An idea I'd entertained a few times, to take the ferry to Denmark and pay to have sex with a prostitute, came back to me. There couldn't be that many nineteen-year-olds who were still virgins. I certainly didn't know any. It was Keith who'd put the thought in my head, he'd said that Norwegian prostitutes were all junkies, whereas in Denmark they were a different class altogether.

I followed the quayside to the bus station and sat down on a bench outside the kiosk. The harbour water was as grey and sleek as steel. The sky too was grey, but soft and gentle-looking, yellowing towards the horizon where the sun was. The cars had gone on board the ferry now and the whole area lay empty, apart from the gulls, of course, that stood perched on the tubular gangway, screeching, taking to the air, dipping to the water, taking to the air again, angling over the buildings on the other side.

Mum came half an hour later. The little blue car looked almost lost, like a cat among horses, as it pulled in at the far end of the station forecourt.

'Did you have a nice time?' she said as I got in.

'Yes, I did,' I said.

'Where did you sleep?'

'At Glenn's. His dad has the use of a flat in town, so we all dossed down there. Did you enjoy yourselves?'

'Yes. Joar's friends all came round.'

'And some of yours, too?'

'Oh yes.'

There was a short silence, and then, abruptly, I must have fallen asleep, waking up only when we pulled up in front of the house.

'I dropped off,' I said.

'You needed the sleep, I shouldn't wonder,' she said, and gave me a little smile. The reaction was so unlike her that I wasn't sure what to think.

'You must promise me not to go out drinking when you're on your own here with Joar,' she said, and the world fell back into place again.

Mum was going into hospital the next day and spent the afternoon packing and getting ready. She didn't want any help with anything, and she didn't want to fly either, I could take her to the bus stop on the main road where she would catch the coach. We hadn't spoken any more about Joar and me coming to see her in Oslo, but it didn't matter much, we could make it a surprise instead.

I made a macaroni gratin with sausages for dinner. I'd just put it in the oven and had started washing up the utensils I'd used when the phone rang. I expected it was for Mum, people had been ringing her all the time those last few days, so I shouted up the stairs — *Mum, telephone!* — and carried on with what I was doing. I heard her come down into the hall and close the door.

Her voice, and she opened the door again.

'It's for you,' she said.

I wiped my soapy hands with the tea towel and picked up the receiver.

'Hello?'

'Hi, it's Lisa.'

'Lisa?'

'Yes, I know. It's been quite a while. I was wondering how you were.'

'I'm fine. How about you? Everything all right?'

'Why didn't you come over and say hello yesterday? I know you saw me. Are you mad at me for what I said in the car? I wouldn't blame you, if you were. It didn't come out right.'

'No, not at all. I understand.'

'You're too nice for your own good, you know that?'

I didn't know what to say. All I could do was wonder why she'd rung, what she was about to say.

'I just keep talking all the time, me.'

'No, you don't,' I said. 'You've hardly said anything yet. You only rang up twenty seconds ago.'

'You did see me though, didn't you?'

'Yes.'

'But you want nothing to do with me, is that it?'

'No, that's not it at all. It's just that I could see you were with your boyfriend. I didn't want to interrupt anything.'

She laughed.

'You mean Erik? The one with the moustache?'

'Yes.'

'Erik's my big brother. I only ever see him once in a blue moon. He lives in America.'

'Ah,' I said.

'That doesn't mean I want to go out with you, if that's what you're thinking,' she said, and laughed again. 'I thought about you, that's all. Thought you might be angry with me.'

'Why would I be angry with you?'

'Exactly, why should you be? I've not done anything. You were the one following me around, wanting to give me a lift.'

'I wouldn't say I was following you around.'

'I've been thinking about what you said about me having a good heart. You're the one with a good heart, not me. You wouldn't have said so otherwise.'

'I'll stick to my words,' I said. 'I *know* I'm right.'

'That's what people say when they run out of arguments and realise they've lost.'

'What?'

'They just *know* they're right.'

'Sometimes the truth's so obvious you don't need arguments.'

'And what truth would that be?'

'Two and two makes four, for example. Water's wet. Night follows day. You've got a good heart.'

She went quiet a moment. I imagined her smiling.

'We don't actually know the sun's going to come up in the morning,' she said. 'So the night and day example might not be that good.'

'A hundred kroner says the sun comes up tomorrow. Are we on?'

'Of course we're not!'

'Why not? Because you *know* it's going to happen, that's why.'

'You think you've got me now, don't you? But it's not as simple as you think. The chances of the sun coming up tomorrow are pretty good, so I'd be stupid to bet against it. But it's still not an absolute certainty.'

'All right, but what if the bet's for the rest of your life? The chances of it not coming up will be increased then, if what you say's right.'

'Massively increased, yes. Do we have to keep ringing each other up the rest of our lives now, then?'

'I wouldn't mind,' I said with a laugh.

'You don't know what you're letting yourself in for.'

'I think I do,' I said, and felt myself filled with joy.

She went quiet again.

'I've got to go now,' she said, more restrained all of a sudden. 'I just wanted to know how you were doing. Bye.'

She hung up.

I didn't know what to think as I put the receiver down and went back into the kitchen and the smells of the baking gratin.

There'd been something different about her. She'd been so much more animated, and then she'd hung up.

'She's still phoning, then?' Mum said from the living room.

'Looks like it.'

'She sounds nice.'

'She is nice.'

Mum smiled at me and started setting the table. She'd been so agreeable the last few days, there'd been a faint glow about her. She was looking better than she'd done for ages. Even had a bit of colour in her cheeks.

It was hard to understand that she was seriously ill, that there was something in her chest that was growing uninhibitedly, killing her.

Are you afraid, Mum? I almost asked, but didn't. The question was too negative, too laden with everything I didn't want her to worry about.

'Do you want water or squash?' I said instead.

'Joar likes squash,' she said. 'So let's have squash. I thought I might make some waffles tonight as well. Seeing as I'm going to be away for a while.'

'Good idea. I'll make them, if you want.'

'No, you won't. I'm not dead yet, you know.'

She laughed and poured some undiluted squash into the jug, let the cold water run while testing the temperature with her finger, then put the jug under the tap.

It was raining when I ran her down to the bus stop the next morning. We dropped Joar off outside the school, and Mum got out with him to say goodbye. He hadn't shown any emotions since Mum told him she had cancer, but had seemed to be suppressing everything, only now he stepped close and wrapped his arms round her in a hug. She stroked his hair and told him everything was going to be all right, He let go of her

with tears in his eyes and hurried away. Mum got back in the car and I
pulled out onto the road again.

'Take good care of him while I'm gone,' she said. 'Promise?'

'I promise.'

'He's so special.'

'Yes, he is.'

The sound of the windscreen wipers reminded me of my own childhood, sitting on the back seat, Dad driving and Mum beside him, a
Sunday outing, an occasional holiday, visiting family or friends.

Now it was me who was driving. Dad was dead. Mum was ill. And the
windscreen wipers went backwards and forwards, backwards and
forwards.

The traffic got busier as we approached the junction. The bus stop
was on the other side of the road, so I had to carry on for a bit until I
was able to turn and drive back.

'What time was it due, again?' I said.

'Twenty to,' she said. 'Just drop me off, I'll be all right.'

'No, it's no trouble.'

She was wearing her best coat, the fawn-coloured one, and a green-
and-blue scarf. A brownish-red lipstick of some sort I hadn't known her
use before.

'Will you manage?'

'It's only the coach to Oslo, I'll be fine.'

'Do you want something for the journey? I'll turn in at the petrol
station, you've got time if there's anything you want to buy.'

'No, thanks. I've got a packed lunch with me and some coffee in the
Thermos.'

'The seasoned traveller,' I said.

I pulled into the bus lay-by, got out and took her suitcase from the
boot, then gave her a brief hug.

'Give us a ring tonight, then,' I said. 'Have a good journey!'

'I will.'

'Do you want me to wait until it comes? Or you could wait in the car?
It's raining, in case you hadn't noticed!'

She shook her head and got her umbrella out of her bag.

'OK, I'll get going,' I said, and waved as I got back in the car. I tooted the horn as I drove off and saw her wave in the mirror until I couldn't see her any more.

She rang that evening as she'd said she would. We never had much to say to each other over the phone, and this time was no exception. All she said was that she'd had a good journey and that they'd given her a pleasant room sharing with two other women her own age who both seemed nice, while all I said was basically that everything was all right at home and that we'd had chicken thighs with fried potatoes for dinner. She talked for some time with Joar, though he closed the kitchen door when he came to the phone, so I couldn't really catch what they were talking about.

I wondered why they found it easier to talk to each other than she and I did. We were the grown-ups, whereas he didn't understand irony and always said what he thought, and was obsessed with facts and everything he knew about computers.

Not that it bothered me. He was only twelve and needed his mother, whereas I was nineteen and living at home only because I had to.

I made cocoa and thought about Lisa the whole time. I imagined her being there with me, in the kitchen, sitting on a chair at the table. I imagined us talking about Joar, about Mum. But somehow it didn't work, placing her in the actual surroundings in which I was standing, it was as if it only became more apparent then that she was a fantasy, I just couldn't see her coming to visit me, sittting there in the kitchen with me, why would she?

The house seemed different without Mum. I was constantly aware of Joar, for instance, that he was upstairs in his room, while I was standing there in the kitchen. And the rooms were rooms all of a sudden, each with its own ambience, I noticed them now as if for the first time.

What kind of a phenomenon was that?

How could Mum's presence make the rooms disappear? It wasn't as if I went around focusing on her when she was at home.

I cut some slices of bread and put some ham and cheese out, poured the steaming hot cocoa from the saucepan into a jug and called up for Joar.

He came down at once and sat down at the table.

Was he in a mood?

It was hard to tell, his head was bowed, his eyes obscured by his fringe.

Maybe I could bring a smile to his face?

'I hear you've got a girlfriend now.'

He looked up at me immediately.

'Who said?'

'I met someone on the bus who was telling me about it,' I lied. 'What did they say her name was . . . Monica?'

'It might have been Merethe they meant,' he said.

'Merethe, that was it, yes.'

'She's not my girlfriend.'

I hadn't the heart now to tell him I'd been making it up.

'But she's someone you like?'

'Not particularly. But I think she likes me.'

'Well, that's a start!'

'Why should it be?'

'Come on! Girls liking you, that's brilliant!'

He didn't say anything.

Outside the rain had begun to pour again, slashing the air.

'Shall we drive up to Oslo at the weekend and visit Mum?' I said.

'Can we?'

'Yes, of course we can. It's quite a long way, but that's all right. We can make some sandwiches for the journey and drink Solo all the way there.'

He smiled.

'I haven't mentioned it yet, but I've got myself a job,' I said.

'Where?'

'In town. Starting tomorrow morning. I'll have to leave the house before you go to school. You'll be all right though, won't you?'

He nodded.

It was strange he didn't ask what sort of job it was, but I was glad he didn't.

He drained his cocoa and stood up.

'You'll remember to brush your teeth, won't you?'

He gave me an offended look. I was going to ask when he'd last had a shower, but decided not to, leaving him to go back upstairs to his room again while I cleared the table.

A sudden movement made me look through the window. Three deer were standing in the field with their heads raised, looking back at me. It made me feel happy. Mum always said it brought luck.

Threefold, then, if it did?

Me and Lisa would get together. Mum's operation was going to be a success.

What would the third thing be?

My share prices would go up!

Or perhaps something to do with Joar would be better.

No, he was doing all right.

I stood for a moment watching the three animals as they grazed in the dusk. They were in plain sight, you'd think they were running a risk being there, but they had their wits about them and were so quick they could run from any peril.

No one thought to get rid of *them* when *they* died. They would lie where they fell in the woods and be eaten up by scavengers, insects and worms. They couldn't bury each other even if they wanted to, not without arms and hands.

I smiled at the thought of deer with hands instead of hooves, digging graves for dead friends.

You ran fast, but now it's past. Deer today, gone tomorrow.

I dried the dishes, put them away in the cupboards and draped the tea towel over the oven door handle. When I turned and looked out of the window again, the deer were gone, and nearly all the daylight too. Only a shimmering band in the western sky remained, towards which the hills and the dark fields between them narrowed.

The undertaker's was in one of the side streets down by the river. The building looked like an ordinary house. Apart from the little black sign that said *Emanuelsen Funeral Directors* in yellow lettering, there was nothing to suggest the kind of business that was conducted inside.

I opened the door and stepped into a kind of reception area. A woman in her fifties with big earrings, red specs and short-cropped hair looked up at me as I came in.

Round face, droopy cheeks. Lips painted red. Kind blue eyes.

'Syvert?' she said, getting to her feet.

'That's right,' I said, and shook the hand she held out.

'I'm Unni. Kristian's wife. Pleased to meet you!'

'Same here,' I said.

'You didn't look like a customer, so I guessed it was you. So glad you'll be working with us! We're like a family here. Well, some of us actually *are* family! Do you know much about the undertaking business?'

'I'm afraid not.'

'Well, Kristian will be here soon to show you around. He'll have a little speech prepared, I shouldn't wonder.' She chuckled. 'He's busy just at the minute. But this is the first impression the customer gets.'

She made a little sweep of her hand.

I noticed there was a box of tissues on the counter and another on the table by the seating arrangement next to the window.

There were pictures on the walls, soft-toned photographs of birds, fields with trees, coastal landscapes, calm waters.

Vases of cut flowers on the counter and on the table.

'My job is to schedule all our appointments and receive the customers when they come in, organise for Kristian, keep all the records. A kind of secretary, you could call me.'

I nodded.

'Vegard has nothing but good to say of you.'

'I've nothing but good to say of him,' I said with a smile.

The phone rang. She indicated the seating arrangement over by the window as she picked up the receiver.

'Emanuelsen Funeral Directors. How can I help you?'

I sat down on the sofa, leaned back and crossed my legs, only then to check myself and sit up straight, both feet on the floor and a hand on each knee.

Unni winked at me and smiled before swivelling sideways on her chair and noting something down on a pad. A moment later a door opened to the left and a tall, thin man with a long, leathery face, creased and crinkled around the eyes, came out. He was wearing a black suit that was a bit too big for him, and a white shirt without a tie.

Unni gave a nod in my direction and he beamed at me.

'Syvert, is it?' he said. 'I'm Kristian. Nice to meet you!'

I stood up and shook his outstretched hand.

'Let's go in here, shall we?' he said, and ushered me into an adjoining room. There was a long table with three chairs on one side, an office chair on the other.

'How about a coffee?'

'Please, if there's any going.'

He popped out through another door and I gazed out of the window. Across a small cobbled yard there was a garage-like structure.

Tissues on the table here too.

He came back in, a cup in each hand.

'Have a seat!' he said.

I sat down and immediately took a sip.

'Right, then,' he said, looking at me now. His eyes were grey, his gaze keen, though his face appeared otherwise expressionless. 'Have you ever done drama, Syvert? Acted, been in a play?'

'No, never. Well, at school a few times. Just the usual end-of-term skits, though.'

'I'm actually an actor myself. Did Vegard tell you?'

I shook my head.

'It's true,' he went on. 'I went to drama school in Oslo. It was my profession for a few years, jobs here and there, but then when I started a family, I found we needed more money. After working as a teacher for a while, I took on the business here.'

'Interesting,' I said.

He leaned back into his chair, long and gangly, fingers fidgeting with a biro.

'Now you'll be wondering why I'd tell you such a thing. Well, there's a simple explanation. It's because a funeral is a play. A theatre piece. A funeral has to be dignified and solemn. No matter how we might be feeling, whether our love life has fallen apart or we were drunk the night before, we must deliver when the curtain rises. The moment the audience is allowed even the slightest glimpse of what we actually feel or think, the illusion will be destroyed and the funeral becomes a fiasco. Imagine if your own mother or father died. Or, God forbid, your child.

The last thing you'd want in that situation is to be made aware that the funeral is in fact theatre. That means we shoulder an enormous responsibility. Ours is not a prestigious job. No one's going to stand up and applaud. But sooner or later we must all sit in that chair, where you are seated now, to say farewell to someone we love. That's our curtain time. That's when we have to deliver. Are you with me?'

'Yes,' I said.

'Good! Are you nervous?'

'No, not at all.'

'I've had many assistants pack it in after a few weeks, you see. One only lasted a day. They found the work repugnant, unpleasant, creepy, whatever. To you, I'll say that everything you'll see here is natural. That's the best way of relating to it. Death is as natural as everything else in life. You must open your mind to it and everything will be fine. All right?'

'All right.'

'Good! Now, there are five of us here. Unni and myself, and our son Tor, and Johansen and Kjell, who've been here since my father's day. Out there we've got the reception and waiting area, this is the consultation room where I receive our customers and plan the funerals. My office is through there,' he said, indicating the door he'd left open after bringing in the coffee. 'There's a little kitchen next door to it, and outside we've got our storage and a garage. We've a small fleet, two hearses and a van.'

'What am I going to be doing?' I said.

'You'll be assisting Johansen. Lifting and carrying, basically.'

'Carrying . . . ?'

'The dead bods, yes.'

He looked at me and smiled, a smile that somehow didn't quite reach his eyes.

'We're backstage now, you see, in the green room. Here, it's our dignity we safeguard, not theirs. Make sure to keep the two roles apart. Are you ready?'

'Yes.'

He got to his feet. I followed.

'There's a suit and a shirt for you in my office, I hope they'll fit. And a pair of shoes, too. You'll need to buy your own, though, once your wages come through. Or borrow from someone, of course, if you'd prefer to spend your money on something else. Same difference.'

The shirt and jacket were a little snug across the chest, the sleeves and trouser legs slightly too long, but a reasonable fit all round, and quite serviceable.

Kristian smiled as I emerged from his office.

'You look like a farmer who's just won the pools!' he said and laughed. 'Splendid, splendid! Now, let's go and say hello to Johansen.'

I followed him out through a door in the passage next to the kitchen, across the yard and into the rear building. There were two rooms. In the first, where the only light came from the windows, a number of coffins were stacked on top of each other, while in the other, smaller and furnished with not much more than an old settee, a similarly time-worn coffee table and a desk over by the window, a man in a black shirt sat smoking with the radio on and a mug of coffee in front of him.

He put the cigarette out carefully in the ashtray and stood up as we came in. He looked to be in his sixties, a bit shorter than me and thickset. His head was large and heavy-looking, bald on top, a ring of yellow-white hair at the sides and back. His jowls sagged around a narrow mouth.

'Johansen, say hello to Syvert!' said Kristian. 'Syvert, this is Johansen.'

Thick-necked, double-chinned. No hint of a smile, nor any gleam in his eye as he shook my hand.

'Well, then,' said Kristian. 'I'll leave you to it.'

Johansen sat down again. I gave Kristian a quizzical look. He smiled, raised his hand feebly in a wave and went away.

'We're going out in twenty minutes,' said Johansen as the door closed across the yard. 'There's coffee over there. Do you smoke?'

'No.'

'You're allowed not to,' he said, and relit the cigarette he'd been smoking.

I didn't know where to put myself. I didn't want to sit on the grubby settee now I'd put the good suit on. I buried my hands in my pockets and walked around the room a bit, occasionally glancing down at my exceptionally shiny shoes.

'Have you worked here a long time?'

He said nothing, but moved his head slightly in what I took to be a nod as he stared out of the window, his cigarette held pinched between thumb and forefinger.

'Are you not a coffee drinker?' he said without turning round.

'Yes,' I said. 'Yes, I am.'

It felt like an obligation, so I went over to the small, square table in the corner where there was a jar of instant, three upturned mugs, a bowl of sugar and a handful of those little triangular sachets of cream.

'Where do I get the water?'

'The sink behind the door. On the left.'

'Is there a tea kettle?'

'I thought you were a coffee drinker.'

'A kettle, then. A kettle's what I mean.'

'Hot water's in the tap, if you let it run.'

I supposed it would do, shook some coffee granules into one of the mugs and took it with me into the passage. The sink was mounted at urinal height, white on the outside, the inside scratched dark, the sort you might see in someone's basement or an outhouse. I turned the tap on and let the water run, and it occurred to me I needed a piss. The water began to give off steam, I placed the mug under and filled it up. The coffee dissolved immediately, colouring the water brown, a scummy froth around the edge.

'Is there a loo in here?' I said, swallowing a mouthful of coffee as I went back in. 'Or is that in the other place?'

'The only one's across the yard,' he said.

I decided to wait a bit, it didn't seem right to be going back and forth when I'd only just got there. On the other hand, I couldn't stand around like an idiot for twenty minutes, so I ended up sitting down on the settee even if I didn't want to. It was hard and uncomfortable, and a little cloud of dust puffed from the upholstery as I plonked down. On the shelf under the coffee table in front of it, some magazines and newspapers were piled neatly. I put my mug down, leaned forward, lifted the newspapers aside that were on top, assuming them to be old, and picked up a magazine.

Aktuell Rapport.

I put it back hastily, at the same time glancing at the one underneath: *Cats.*

What sort of person looked at dirty mags in an undertaker's office?

I put the newspapers on top again, the way they'd been before, and
leaned back into the settee with my coffee in my hand and one leg
crossed over the other as if everything was normal, while my soul
burned with shame.

'They're the young lad's,' said Johansen from over by the table, again
without turning his head.

'Who would that be?'

'Tor. Here he comes now.'

I stood up and looked through the window to see a fat, red-haired lad
my own age come walking up to the passenger side of one of the
hearses, while a small, bearded man stood searching his pockets on the
driver's side.

'So that would be Tor and Kjell?' I said.

'Uh-huh,' he said.

I put my mug down on the coffee table and went out into the yard
just as Kjell unlocked the door and got in. Tor turned and looked at me.

'Hi,' I said. 'I'm Syvert. It's my first day.'

'So I heard,' he said, and got in. 'See you later.'

Kjell started the engine and reversed out slowly. I avoided looking at
Johansen who was no doubt watching me from inside, and instead
went to find the loo in the other building. As I stepped in, I heard Kristian's voice coming from the consultation room, and then a woman's
voice after that, before closing the door of the toilet as quietly as I could,
bolting it and pissing against the porcelain so as not to make a noise.

'Right, let's get going,' said Johansen when I got back.

'Was that twenty minutes already?'

'We can wait in the car at the other end.'

I followed him out, and felt once more the mild air on my face. The sun
gleamed in the vehicle's polished black paintwork. It was immaculate,
even if it was an old model that looked to be from the early seventies.

I felt strangely buoyant as I got in, which in part I put down to my
unfamiliar garb. The seat was like a little hollow, unyielding, yet
comfortable.

'I never imagined myself in a hearse,' I said with a smile to Johansen who'd turned the key in the ignition and now looked into the rear-view mirror as he threw the gear lever into reverse.

'Most people will see the inside of one sooner or later.'

'I meant while I was alive!'

'How do you know we're alive?' he said, and began to reverse out carefully through the narrow passage.

I looked at him. It was more words than he'd said in the last half-hour.

He wasn't smiling, but turned his head and looked without expression out of the side window as we rolled across the pavement and turned into the street.

'We can talk. We can walk. We can eat. We can drive cars. The dead can't do any of those things. So yes, I'm pretty sure we're alive.'

I gave a laugh.

He leaned across and opened the glove compartment on my side without removing his eyes from the road, took out a pair of aviators and put them on.

'One of the first things I learned in this job was that we were never to wear sunglasses,' he said.

'What happened?'

'I learned something else. To exercise one's own discretion.'

He indicated right, stopped at the junction and waited for a little convoy of four cars to pass.

'Some think we die twice,' he said. 'Did you know that?'

'No, I've never heard that before,' I said, and gave another laugh.

'This is the first death.'

'This?'

He nodded.

'The death *you're* thinking about is the second.'

'That's the daftest thing I've ever heard,' I blurted out.

'Is it?' he said.

I didn't answer him, and we sat quietly for a while.

We drove over the bridge in the centre of town, through the residential areas on the other side. An untroubled sky poured out its even light. The lawns between the housing blocks were a subtle green, the asphalt grey, the wooden cladding of the houses dull white. There weren't many people about, the morning rush to work and school was over, but the few I saw looked at us as we went past. Motorists did the same when we stopped at traffic lights.

Johansen drove sedately and seemed like nothing could bother him. His cumbersome-looking head was motionless, his movements slow and assured.

'Where are we going?' I said.

'Solsletta care home.'

'Where's that?'

'Solsletta.'

He must have thought I was thick, but I couldn't think of anything to say that would alter his impression. Anyway, I was there to earn money, not to be social.

I twisted round and looked through the glass pane behind the seat, but there was no coffin in the back.

We drove a kilometre or so along the E18 before turning right onto a minor road we then followed across the flatland. There were fields on one side that I supposed belonged to the old manor house we passed, then grassland that petered into woods; on the other a housing estate where little roads led between identical new wooden homes. Svaneveien, Måltrøstveien, Hegreveien, roads that were named after birds: swan, blackbird, heron. It struck me that the hearse would be more conspicuous here than in town, more ominous. But all was quiet and still in the mid-morning, and not a soul was about.

At the bottom end of the estate, a few hundred metres from the nearest house, tucking into the woods, was the old people's home. Johansen drove through the car park to the rear of the building and pulled up there.

He took off his sunglasses without a word, put them on the dashboard and got out. He stood for a moment, then leaned back against the vehicle and proceeded to roll a smoke between his thumbs and index fingers, tobacco pouch held firmly by his two middle digits. He put the finished cigarette between his lips with one hand, resealed the pouch and found his lighter with the other, bent his head forward slightly and lit up.

I opened the door and got out too, and stood by the other side of the
car. There was a skip next to where we'd pulled in, piled up with dis-
carded plasterboard, cables and leads, bits of rubble. An electric fence
enclosed the field the building backed onto, and some horses stood
grazing over by the woods.

Johansen stuck his tongue out and picked away a strand of tobacco
before pinching off the end of the cigarette he'd had in his mouth,
which presumably had gone soggy, and took another drag.

'What have we come here for, exactly?' I said. 'I'm sorry, but I've
never done anything like this, so I've no idea what to expect, to be
honest.'

'We're picking up a mors.'

'A *mors*?'

'A corpse.'

'Is that what you call them?'

'Yes. It's Latin.'

'Is there anything in particular I need to know or be prepared for?'

He shook his head.

'OK,' I said.

It was nearly five to ten.

Mum would be on the operating table in Oslo now.

Going to Oslo at the weekend would actually be doable. It'd be a nice
surprise for her.

If we went in the car, I'd only have to pay for the petrol. And just the
one night would be fine.

Drive up Saturday, back again Sunday afternoon.

Johansen dropped his cigarette end onto the ground and crushed it
under his foot. He opened the car door, leaned in and got something
out of the glove compartment. When he backed out again and drew
himself upright, I saw that it was a bag of carrots.

He tore a hole in the plastic and went over to the fence, clicking his
tongue loudly.

At the fringe of the woods, the horses, three in all, lifted their heads
in unison and came plodding towards him. They poked their muzzles
over the top of the fence. Great, dark beasts with muscular flanks. He
placed a carrot in the flat of his hand and held it out. The nearest of the

horses nipped it from his hand and crunched it between its teeth. Another snorted. Johansen leaned forward and put his arm around its neck, and said something to it that I didn't catch.

When the bag was empty, he scrunched it up in his hand and returned to the hearse, stuffed it back in the glove compartment, closed the door and went round to the rear of the vehicle. He opened the back door and pulled out a stretcher he managed to hold clamped under his arm as he closed the door again with his free hand.

'Right, then,' he said, lifting his brow as he looked up at me. 'Are you coming?'

He rang the bell. A tall, thin woman in her forties appeared and greeted us with a nod.

'On time as always,' she said. 'Come in.'

I glanced at my watch as I followed them along a corridor. Ten on the dot.

We came to a lift and the woman stopped and pressed the button. We waited without a word. Normally, I'd have said something to break the silence and I felt a desperate urge to make a disarming comment, but Johansen was in charge, he knew all the codes.

I studied the woman as she jingled the keys in her hand. Her hair was thick and curly, her face rather small, with round cheeks, a little turned-up nose. Long, slender neck, specs hanging from a cord. Flat-chested.

How much fun would that be?

She looked at me and gave a smile.

'Are you new?'

I nodded.

'Very new, yes.'

'I'm Jenny,' she said. 'Section manager here.'

'Syvert,' I said.

The lift came. It was a service elevator, much bigger inside than I'd expected waiting in front of the narrow door. I stared at my feet the few seconds it took to reach the second floor and took up the rear as we stepped out. The corridor along which we were led was empty. Somewhere, a radio was on and I heard faint voices too, from the far end, I thought, where I guessed there was some kind of common room.

Jenny stopped at a door and unlocked it.

The room was quite small. A white candle stood burning on a table, the flame flickering gently in the air from a window that had been left ajar. The deceased lay under a sheet in a bed that was pushed up against the wall. Only the face was visible. An old lady with fleshy cheeks, thin white curly hair. Her eyes were covered by two white squares. If it hadn't been for that, she'd have looked like she was sleeping.

It was the first dead person I'd seen.

It wasn't horrible at all.

Johansen put the stretcher down on the floor. I looked out of the window. The woods were a dark scribble underneath a bright, white sky. Where were the horses?

There. Heads lowered to the ground, tails flicking.

Jenny picked up a folder from a desk by the wall, put on her specs and sifted through the documents inside.

Johansen lifted the sheet. The old lady, in a blue-and-white floral-patterned gown, was barefoot. A tag dangled from a big toe.

It didn't look like she was sleeping any more. There was something about her body that wasn't right, and it had nothing to do with her not moving.

'Watch and learn. I'll need a hand in a moment,' said Johansen. I stepped towards him tentatively. He rolled the deceased onto her side and tucked the sheet underneath her, rolled her back in the opposite direction and then turned the sheet over the body from both sides, smoothing it carefully. Once she was covered, he produced some safety pins from his trouser pocket and pinned the sheet together in the middle. Then, he moved to the end where the woman's head was and slid his hands underneath the body, indicating with a nod for me to do the same at the foot end. I realised I'd have to grip the legs if I was to lift her. But I didn't know if I could, and hesitated with my arms outstretched.

'Take hold,' said Johansen, and so I gripped both calves through the sheet. They were oddly unyielding, and it startled me somewhat. It was like picking up a sausage without knowing it to be frozen.

We moved her carefully to the edge of the bed and paused.

'Now, lift on three,' Johansen said. 'One, two, three.'

She was heavy, but the stiffness made it easier and we transferred the body to the stretcher seamlessly.

A faint thundering sound came from outside the window. Johansen turned and looked out. It was the three horses, galloping away in the field.

'Everything seems to be here,' said Jenny, closing the folder and handing it to Johansen.

He put it on top of the body.

'Preferably not there,' said Jenny.

'Sorry,' he said.

I looked at him in surprise. He hadn't come across as a man who would apologise for anything.

'I'll send the lad back up,' he said, and put the folder on the desk.

'I've got a name, you know,' I said.

'I've forgotten it,' he said. 'What was it again?'

'Syvert.'

'*Syvert* will come up and get it,' he said, bending down then to grip the handles at his end. I did likewise at mine. He was rather smaller than me, so I stooped to keep her level as we went out.

Jenny stood in the doorway and watched as we slid the stretcher into the hearse. When it was done, both she and Johansen bowed their heads a moment. I took the cue and did likewise.

We stood in silence, then Johansen went round to the driver's side and opened the door.

'We left the documents,' he said.

I followed Jenny back to the room, where she handed me the folder.

'There you are,' she said. 'Thanks for your help.'

'You're welcome,' I said.

'Her name was Anna, by the way.'

I nodded, not knowing what to say. I glanced at the photos on the wall. An old wedding photograph in black and white, two more recent ones in colour: a gathering of people all looking at the camera, and two girls in what looked like a school photo.

The candle still burned, helpless-looking in the clear daylight.

Back at the hearse, Johansen put the folder on top of the body without a word, then put on his sunglasses, leaned over the roof and flipped up a little cross.

'Where to now, then?' I said when a few minutes later we turned back onto the main road.

'The cold room.'

'Where's that?'

'The chapel.'

'Aha,' I said. I had no idea what chapel he was talking about, but I couldn't be bothered asking either. We sat quietly all the way.

I'd wondered what it would feel like to have a body in the back.

Now I knew. There was no difference.

We came past the Cathedral School and I scanned the area in case Lisa was among the students who were hanging around there, but there were too many, a blur of shapes and colours.

What would she make of my job?

It wasn't the hippest of professions.

We turned right at the river, and then right again, and as we came back round on the other side of the school I realised what chapel we were going to, or not the chapel exactly, but the church and the cemetery at least.

How ironic, I thought, that I'd be working only a few hundred metres from where she went to school.

'With a suit, you unbutton the jacket when you sit down,' said Johansen.

'Is that right?' I said, looking down at myself to see my jacket buttoned tight. 'I didn't know. Why's that?'

'Because. Anyway, now you know. No excuse for doing it wrong the rest of your life now.'

We drove slowly along a narrow stretch of road before turning through a gateway that led us into the low-walled cemetery, carrying on towards the trees that scattered away at the far end, and three buildings of whitewashed brick.

'One more thing. Never, under any circumstance, do the bottom button up,' he said, and took off his sunglasses then, putting them down unfolded on the dashboard.

'OK,' I said. 'Why not?'

'Because.'

'But why's it there if you're not supposed to use it?'

He didn't answer and we rolled up on the gravel in front of the largest of the three buildings. He parked on the far side where we were hidden from view to anyone except whoever might be around at the bottom end of the cemetery, but there was no one there, which probably wasn't unusual.

He got out and leaned back against the bodywork, and began to roll himself a smoke as he'd done before, the pouch held in suspension while his thumbs and forefingers busied themselves. It didn't seem right to be sitting there, not with a dead person in the back, so I got out too.

'Is there anything I can do while you have your smoke?'

He shook his head and pinched away some surplus strands, dropping them back into the open pouch which he then closed and slipped back into his inside pocket before lighting up.

I ambled off a bit and looked over in the direction of the school, just visible between the trees, the sports hall next to it. The thought of her being there at that moment sent a tingle of joy racing through my body. She probably came outside for her breaks, being a smoker. I could go over and say hello.

I'd have to explain to her what I was doing there and why I was wearing a suit.

Maybe it wasn't such a good idea.

I went back and stood waiting for Johansen, who eventually stubbed his cigarette out in a flowerpot by the steps and unlocked the side door of the building without so much as glancing at me, lifted the vehicle's back door and began to remove the stretcher. When it was nearly out, he stopped and gave a nod, I stepped up and gripped the handles at the back, and together, Johansen leading the way, we carried the body up the steps and inside to a large, freezing cold room at the back where a bank of deep shelving racks stretched along one wall. We put the stretcher down on the floor, Johansen pulled a body tray from the racking and we lifted the corpse onto it. Johansen undid the safety pins and removed the sheet. I'd already got used to her being covered up and was startled to see the woman's face again, the slight wobble of the cheeks as he pulled the sheet from under her, the white squares that covered the eyes.

'They can make noises,' he said. 'Just so you're warned. It can give you a fright the first time.'

'OK,' I said.

He tossed the sheet into a big laundry bin next to the wall and put the safety pins back in his pocket.

'Was that it?' I said as he went towards a sink in the corner.

It was by far the most unsettling part so far. She was an object now. An object to be left somewhere.

'There's a viewing at twelve,' he said. 'But that one's already laid out.'

He washed his hands, then turned towards me.

'Will you do it?'

'Do what?'

'The viewing. You've done well so far. There's nothing to it. You receive the bereaved, lead them into the viewing room, then stand outside and wait until they're finished.'

'Yes, I can do that.'

He smiled at me.

It unnerved me almost. I didn't think he could.

'But wash your hands first,' he said, drying his own on a towel that was hanging there, before leaving the room without saying where he was going.

I turned round and stared at the four corpses that lay stored on the racking.

They didn't make me feel any less alone.

I heard the sound of an approaching car and went out to see where Johansen had gone. Probably for a smoke, I reckoned, and went towards the door just as it opened and he came back in. He turned left down the passage with a packed lunch in his hand. I followed him. There was a kitchen in the corner, just big enough for a small table, four chairs, a sink and worktop, some shelves on the wall for cups and dishes, and a fridge.

'Coffee?' he said as I went in. He'd put his lunch down on the table and was already filling the jug with water.

'Yes, please,' I said, and sat down.

There were some voices outside, a car door slamming shut. A moment later someone came in and walked past, their footsteps echoing away through the passage.

'Who's that?' I said.

He shrugged, picked up a tin of coffee from the worktop, opened it and filled the scoop before realising he'd forgotten to put the filter bag in the holder, dropped it back into the tin and got one out.

'Andresen's lot, probably,' he said, filling the scoop again.

'Andresen?'

'Andresen's, the funeral directors.'

'Ah.'

He sat down opposite me at the table and started rolling a smoke. The coffee maker began to tick and spit behind him.

'Is it always this quiet?' I said.

'Always quiet here, yes,' he said.

'The job, I mean. Is it always like this?'

'It has its highs and lows.'

With one arm laid flat in front of him, the elbow of the other propped on the table, he sat smoking while staring out of the window.

It felt like I'd been in the job for days. I could hardly believe it was only two hours.

'How many people actually die in this town per day?' I said. 'Roughly. Do you know?'

He shook his head slowly.

'But if you were to have a qualified guess?'

'A couple.'

'Is that all?'

'They don't die evenly. Sometimes there's more, some days none. When the weather's very cold, and when it's hot, that's when most of them go. And at Easter and Christmas.'

'Why's that, do you think?'

'You ask a lot of questions,' he said. 'My advice is get yourself an encyclopedia when your wages come in, then you can look things up.'

'Encyclopedias are expensive,' I said with a laugh. 'It's cheaper asking you.'

'You can pay in instalments. A bit every month.'

He didn't seem to be joking.

He got to his feet and filled coffee into two cups, handing me one before sitting down again and opening his lunch, which turned out to consist of three sandwiches made with brown bread.

'Haven't you got anything?' he said.

'I forgot,' I said.

He shoved the packet towards me.

'No, thanks,' I said. 'I'll pop out and buy something. How long have we got?'

He looked at his watch.

'You've got twenty minutes.'

'I'd better get a move on, then,' I said, and stood up as Johansen picked up a sandwich and began to eat.

Outside, another black hearse was parked next to ours, while in the cemetery itself, a red lawnmower trundled over the grass, following the line of the wall, a man in a white cap at the wheel. Across the main road, a group of students were crossing the lawns between the school and the sports hall. It looked like break time and I decided to go over.

How good it felt to be under an open sky, to breathe in fresh air.

And the trousers of my suit so nice and loose around my legs.

I passed through the birch trees, all now in leaf. The war memorial, a great stone with carved figures, had been vandalised, sprayed red, I suddenly saw, and stopped in my tracks. It could only be the work of final-year students from the gymnas, celebrating, as tradition required, the end of term before the exams. A red dick was what they'd thought to be fitting here.

In remembrance of those who gave their lives for the freedom of Norway 1940–1945, the plaque said.

The bloody idiots.

They got everything handed to them on a plate.

I was so ashamed I felt like vomiting.

They had no idea there were people to thank for all the privileges they enjoyed.

Beyond the trees, the school opened out in front of me on the other side of the road. People were streaming out through the doors. A rather large number were already outside. It was hopeless, of course, to try and find her in what little time I had. I thought maybe I should just pop into the petrol station and actually buy something to eat.

But then again, I could be lucky, and so I crossed over and onto the path leading up to the main entrance.

There she was.

It was definitely her. Light blue denim jacket, the slight curve of her back.

I was on the school premises now. My heart thudded uncomfortably in my chest. No reason for that, surely! She was just a person like me.

She was standing talking to three boys, a cigarette in her hand, gesticulating. They were standing quite close. One was wearing a green army jacket, another a blue cap with what looked like a red star above the peak, while the third was in a long black coat.

Was that who she hung out with? Socialists and new wavers?

Now they were laughing.

She took a drag of her cigarette and glanced up. As soon as she saw me she froze.

Immediately, I felt I'd made a mistake.

A huge mistake.

She said something to them and then came towards me.

I smiled as best I could.

'I didn't realise you were getting confirmed today,' she said when she came up.

'Ha ha,' I said.

'What are you doing here?'

'I was going to ask you out for a meal,' I said. 'I thought it'd be better to do it in person rather than on the phone.'

'To make it harder for me to say no?'

I laughed.

'I hadn't thought about that. But you don't have to say no! Not if it's that hard!'

She glanced back to where her friends were still standing.

Why did she do that?

Then she looked at me.

'A meal?' she said. 'Seriously? You mean like, in a restaurant?'

'Yes. Anything wrong with that?'

She smiled.

'No, nothing.'

'You will, then?'

'I didn't say that.'

Our eyes met. For a few seconds it was as if she filled me entirely.

I'd never felt anything like it ever.

She glanced back at the three boys again. They'd lost interest in us now.

'Of course I will.'

'Honestly? You've made me really happy now!'

She looked down and gave a little smile before looking up again.

'When were you thinking of?'

'Friday?'

She nodded.

'That suits me fine. I was thinking of hanging around in town after school anyway.'

A low, electronic hum came from the school building. Rather more advanced than the old-fashioned bell we'd had at our school.

'I've got to get back,' she said.

'Where do you want to meet?'

She extended her thumb and little finger in the air and lifted her hand to her ear.

'Give me a ring.'

'Already looking forward!' I said as she turned and began to walk away.

After a couple of steps she spun round again.

'What *are* you wearing a suit for?'

'It's a long story,' I said. 'Speak to you soon!'

Outside the mortuary, two middle-aged men were sliding a coffin into the other hearse while a third stood watching with a large wreath in his hands.

I went up to them and said hello.

The man with the wreath gave me a nod, the two others were too preoccupied to acknowledge me.

'You'll be from Andresen's, I suppose.'

'That's right.'

'I'm with Emanuelsen's,' I said. 'Just started today.'

'Aha.'

'Have you been in the job long?'

One of the other men turned his head and flashed me a look of annoyance.

'We're about to pay our respects to the deceased,' the one with the wreath said softly.

'Oh, sorry,' I said, lowering my own voice and smiling apologetically before going back inside.

Johansen was sitting where I'd left him. The only difference was that his lunch was eaten and the ashtray had filled up.

He got to his feet as I came in. It felt like he was an old acquaintance, and I smiled at him. He didn't smile back, but stepped past me.

'Am I late?' I said.

He appeared to shake his head as he went down the passage. I didn't know where we were going or what we were going to do there.

I wasn't bothered, not in the slightest.

She'd said yes.

And she'd looked at me, and kept looking at me for what seemed like a long, long time, with her big, dark eyes.

Johansen opened the door of the cold room. I followed him inside. He went over to the storage racks, pulled a pair of transparent gloves from a little box there and handed them to me. He put on a pair himself, went over to the tray where the old woman's body was stored, and pulled it out, looked at me, then nodded towards the table in the middle of the room. He put his hands under the shoulder blades and I gripped her legs as I'd now learned.

They were as cold as ice now, as stiff as two planks.

Once she was in place on the table, Johansen removed the white squares that covered her eyes.

He took hold of the chin and lifted it slightly.

'There's the chin collar, you see?' he said. 'You can just leave that. But if they've a support, you take it away before the viewing.'

'OK,' I said.

'I'll just make her up a bit, then we'll take her in. You see there's a slight discoloration now?'

He indicated an area of the cheek that was faintly purple in colour, and a similar patch at the throat. Fetching a small bag from a shelf beside the racking, he took out a powder case not unlike the one Mum used, and began carefully to powder the woman's face.

His movements seemed all too delicate for his bricklayer's stature and thick fingers.

He put the powder case back in the bag and we lifted her again, carrying her into the room across the passage and placing her on a low table that was draped with a white fabric.

He tidied her hair and arranged her gown.

'You take it from here,' he said.

'What about you?'

'I've got other things to do. But if anything goes wrong and you need help, you can come and get me.'

'Where will you be?'

'The cold room,' he said, and made towards the door.

'Wait a minute,' I said. 'What am I supposed to say? And who's coming, anyway?'

'The daughter and grandchild. They've flown down from Oslo and are coming straight from the airport. You say as little as possible. None of your chat, and no smiling.'

'OK.'

'Relax. They'll hardly look at you. You'll be invisible to them. Wait and see.'

And then he went out.

I stared at the deceased. She looked severe with her drooping cheeks. Perhaps she'd been a bit stern.

There was a small table with a candle on it.

Wasn't it meant to be lit, like in her room?

I looked around for a lighter or a box of matches, but of course there were none.

The curtains were drawn. They were beige, and the light from outside made them faintly luminescent. I went over and drew them aside.

For some reason, it felt uncomfortable having my back to the deceased, so I turned to face her again.

She was just as motionless as before.

Of course she was!

The daylight brought out every detail. The chin collar, the pasty hue of the skin. A blotchiness on the side of her calf, which was heavy-looking and purplish underneath.

Perhaps the curtains were meant to be shut, I thought, and went over to close them again.

I looked at my watch. Five minutes yet.

Enough time to find some matches in the break room.

Could I leave her here on her own?

It wouldn't take two minutes, I told myself, and darted through the door, hurried down the passage and into the break room.

A car pulled up outside.

I opened the top drawer in the kitchen. Knives and forks.

The next.

Bingo! Ten matches, at least!

I dashed back to the viewing room. She was lying as before, and no one else was there, thankfully.

I lit the candle, slipped the matchbox into my pocket, went over to the window, parted the curtains slightly and looked out.

There was a taxi out there with the engine ticking over. A teenage girl with a face red with acne, dressed in jeans and a dark cardi coat, stood beside it with her hands in her pockets, a woman wearing a coat was still in the back with the door open and one foot on the ground.

I went to the entrance, stepped outside and stood waiting on the step, my hands crossed in front of my lower abdomen.

My heart thumping in my chest.

What was I going to say?

I wiped my palms discreetly on my trousers.

The woman got out. She was wearing dark glasses and a headscarf. She closed the door, a handbag hanging from the crook of her arm. The driver pulled away, the vehicle describing a slack arc before parking at the far end, as the woman and her daughter came towards me.

'Welcome,' I said. 'My condolences.'

I put out my hand. The woman shook it, almost without realising, it seemed.

'Is this where she is?' she asked, pushing her sunglasses onto her forehead.

She was about fifty, but younger-looking and a bit fit.

I nodded.

'If you'd like to follow me?' I said.

Her heels clicked behind me as we went through. Reaching the viewing room, I opened the door and stepped aside, allowing them to enter first.

They went in slowly and halted beside the deceased, and the mother put her arm around her daughter.

'Take all the time you need,' I said. 'I'll be here outside the door.'

I closed the door carefully and leaned back against the wall.

What a bloody start this was.

Sobbing sounds came from inside. I assumed it was the girl.

Low voices.

After a few moments, the sobs were abruptly supplanted by laughter.

How strange that a lifeless bag of bones could trigger such emotions in them.

Well, not strange, exactly. She hadn't always been like that.

Obviously.

The laughter subsided, their voices became once more subdued.

It sounded like they got on well with each other, the two of them.

It couldn't be easy being that much plainer than your mother.

Maybe she didn't think of it like that.

Oh, Lisa!

The thought of her struck me like a punch and threw me into the most delirious frame.

Three more days.

How was I going to stick it out that long?

It had all gone quiet in there now.

Footsteps crossed the floor.

I straightened up and stood with my hands at my sides as the door opened and the woman emerged, her daughter behind her.

Was I supposed to see them out?

It felt like the right thing.

They went down the steps of the entrance and I stood in the open doorway for a moment, almost at attention, and watched as they went towards the taxi, before closing the door again and going back to Johansen in the cold room.

The door was locked. I knocked.

He appeared in his shirtsleeves, his hands in a pair of gloves.

'You're not of a nervous disposition, are you?' he said.

'I don't think so,' I said.

'Do you feel sick easily?'

'No.'

'Come in, then. I could do with a hand, as it happens. Maybe you can learn something as well.'

When he stepped aside, I saw there was a body on the table. Apart from the head, it was completely covered by a sheet.

The face was grotesquely swollen, its features all but erased. The beard that must have covered the cheeks and chin was as if pulled apart, leaving bare open patches between the follicles. The mouth was wide open, the eyes were open too, bulging and glistening with moisture, the orbs quite grey, the pupils distended and black.

It looked more like a seal than a man.

The skin was blue-white, mottled with great, dark blemishes.

The only thing that looked normal was the grey, tousled hair.

Johansen looked at me.

'What happened to him?' I said.

'Drowned. Then floated about a few days.'

'The poor sod.'

Johansen nodded.

'An old wino. Goggen, they called him. You'll have seen him around town, I imagine. They found him in the harbour. No one had reported him missing.'

He picked up a pair of scissors from the table and began to trim the hair. I realised I must have interrupted him when I knocked on the door, because I noticed now a few hair clippings scattered about the tabletop beside the corpse's head.

'What do you want me to do?'

'You can give me a hand in a minute.'

'OK.'

It was hard to look at the head without imagining it captured in a scream.

A trim did nothing to repair the impression.

'You can have yourself a coffee in the meantime,' said Johansen.

'Do you want one?'

He nodded.

'I think I might, yes. A drop of milk and three sugars.'

'Coming up,' I said, and went off to the break room. Waiting for the coffee to run through, I gazed out at the pale, mellow sky, the cemetery that extended from the old stone church, where the headstones stood close in the oldest part, the newer part stretching away towards the trees.

To the other side, the traffic passing along the main road into town.

What on earth had he meant when he said that we were dead? And what we thought of as death was only the second kind of death?

Where was life in all that?

Was there some other world in which we died, departing it to enter this one?

It was the wildest notion.

Though no wilder than the one that said we went to heaven when we died.

But no one believed that any more, surely?

The pastor came across as a man of reason. Did he seriously believe that?

I opened the filter holder and took the jug from the hotplate, even though the water hadn't fully run through, poured two cups, added milk and sugar to one, and took them both back to the cold room.

'Put it down there,' said Johansen, indicating the end of the table with a nod. He'd finished trimming the hair, now he was powdering the face.

'Normally I'd have shaved him,' he said. 'But the skin comes away when it's been in the water that long. So he'll have to meet his Maker unshaven.'

'Maybe it'll help a bit to close the mouth,' I said.

'You can try,' he said.

I smiled hesitatingly.

'Go on! But put some gloves on first.'

'It's all right,' I said. 'I believe you.'

'If the jaws aren't closed within an hour of death, you can forget all about it.'

'Why's that?'

'Like I said: get yourself an encyclopedia.'

He took a sip of his coffee.

'It's the rigor mortis, isn't it? It's a lot stronger than people realise. After a few hours you could stand them up against the wall and they'd stay there, upright.'

'I didn't realise that.'

'No, how would you know?'

He produced a lipstick from the little cosmetics bag and drew it meticulously over the lips of the deceased.

'That should give him something that at least resembles a mouth,' he said.

'Will there be a viewing for him as well?'

Johansen shook his head.

'He'll just be buried.'

'What, in an open coffin?'

'No.'

'So no one's going to see what you're doing now?'

He shook his head again, took another sip of his coffee, put the little bag back on the shelf, and returned with a pair of dark trousers in one hand, a pair of scissors in the other. He laid the trousers down on top of the deceased and cut them open, first the seat, then the two legs.

'He's had a post-mortem. Just so you're warned. Not the most pleasant of sights, exactly.'

He drew back the sheet. The body was bloated and balloon-like, so shapeless it was hard to even discern the knees or elbows. Large areas of the skin were blotched dark.

A thick, rough scar ran the length of the torso from the throat to the groin.

The penis lay like a little sausage above the distended thighs.

Johansen tossed the sheet into the laundry bin.

'How are you faring?' he said when he came back.

'Fine,' I said.

'Good. I'll need some help now. Put some gloves on.'

I did as he said. He laid the trousers out over the body and folded them around the legs.

'Lift here a bit.'

I took hold of a foot and did as instructed. It slid slightly in my latex-gloved hand. Some skin came away.

'That's it,' said Johansen, and proceeded to pin the flaps of the trouser leg together with safety pins at the back. 'A bit more.'

He glanced at me before we repeated the procedure with the other leg.

Then the white shirt.

When he started on the dark jacket, I couldn't help but ask.

'Why are we doing this, exactly? I mean, if no one's going to see him anyway? Couldn't he just be put in the coffin as he is?'

He didn't answer. Didn't even look at me. Just carried on working in silence. Perhaps five minutes passed without a word between us, and then he stepped back and considered the now besuited corpse.

'I think that's as good as we can manage,' he said. 'Now, come with me.'

I followed him into the passage to a room at the other end where some coffins were stored. We carried one back between us and with a bit of exertion put the body in place inside it.

Johansen stepped to the foot of the coffin and stood there completely still for a moment before performing a deep bow.

I did likewise, though it felt like an empty gesture.

Johansen removed his gloves and dropped them in the waste bin, then washed his hands thoroughly with soap. I washed mine. After that, we put the lid on top and carried the coffin out to the hearse.

Another bow, shorter this time, and he closed the door.

'Why do you think?' he said as we drove slowly over to the church.

I looked at him.

'Why do I think what?'

'What you asked about.'

'I know now,' I said.

'Good,' he said.

Driving home late that afternoon, I felt tired in a way I'd never known before. Not *tired* tired, the way I often was when I'd been doing my service, when all I'd wanted to do was sleep, and not the way you could be tired after hard physical exertion either. It was more like being filled to the brim with something, something that made everything else seem remote, and yet what filled me seemed at the same time to have no substance at all, it was just emptiness. The traffic on the road, the forest, the houses and buildings I drove past, were as if meaningless, insignificant fixtures in a landscape outside. And my own, internal landscape was just as divested.

I didn't get home until just before six. Joar was upstairs in his room, he'd made himself a sandwich, he said, and wasn't hungry, so I didn't bother with tea but went and had a long shower instead, after which I made myself a sandwich and then sat down in the living room with a coffee to watch the news.

Before it was finished, Joar came down and sat next to me.

'Did you have a good day?' I said, draping my arm over the back of the sofa behind him.

'Yes,' he said. 'I got A-plus for my science test.'

'Well done.'

I ruffled his hair, only for him to twist his head away.

'Have you heard from Mum?' he said.

'No. But we can give her a ring now, if you want?'

He nodded and got up.

Immediately, it occurred to me that we couldn't go to Oslo that weekend as I'd promised, I was taking Lisa out for dinner now.

It was no great disaster. We could go next weekend instead.

But if I told him now, the evening would be ruined.

I'd have to break it to him gently, drop the odd hint.

I looked up the number of the hospital with him standing next to me, dialled and was put through to the ward where she'd been admitted. A nurse answered.

'I'd like to speak to Evelyn Løyning, please,' I said.

'I'm afraid she's asleep at the moment,' she said.

'Ah,' I said. 'This is her son speaking. I was just wondering how things went with her surgery today?'

'The surgery went well. She's tired now, of course, so it's good that she's sleeping. I'm sure she'll be able to speak to you tomorrow, in the morning.'

'Good, that's a relief,' I said. 'Can you tell her Syvert and Joar rang?'

'I will.'

I put the phone down and turned to Joar.

'Did you catch that?' I said. 'She's asleep, but everything's fine and we can ring up and speak to her in the morning.'

He nodded.

'You did really well in that science test!' I said as we went back into the living room. Joar sat down next to me again.

TV Theatre was starting. More lofty socialist telly for people's licence money. *Curse of the Starving Class*, this one was called. We saw the inside of a house, a door being rattled, then a fist that punched through the wood.

'Since when did you start watching *TV Theatre*?' I said, and grinned at him.

'I was wondering the same about you,' he said.

A young man in a white T-shirt lay on his back on a bed, thinking. *I could feel this country close like it was part of my bones*, he said in a voice-over. *I could feel the presence of all the people outside, at night, in the dark. Even sleeping people I could feel. Even all the sleeping animals. Dogs. Peacocks. Bulls. Even tractors sitting in the wetness, waiting for the sun to come up.*

'Have you ever seen a tractor sitting anywhere?' I said.

Joar shook his head.

'I've never seen one waiting for the sun to come up either.'

'Shall we turn it off?'

'Can do.'

I got up and turned it off, then went to the kitchen for more coffee.

'Are you thinking about Mum?' I said when I came back in.

He shrugged.

'It's a shame we couldn't speak to her. But the nurse said it had all gone well, so that's the main thing.'

'Will I have to live with you when she dies?'

'Joar, she's not going to die. You mustn't think like that.'

'It's quite likely that she will, actually,' he said. 'Am I going to have to live with you then?'

'Listen,' I said, putting my coffee down on the table. 'Mum's ill. She's got cancer. Some people recover, some don't. You've got to battle it and not give up. If we go around telling ourselves she's going to die or wondering what we're going to do if she does, we'll have given up already. Do you understand what I'm saying?'

'Cancer's all about genes. Genes don't care what we say.'

'Not directly, no. But you've heard of the placebo effect, haven't you?'

'Of course.'

'It's when some people are given medicine, while others are given a dummy treatment, and then it turns out that the ones who've been given the dummy treatment get well too. And why's that? Because they *thought* they'd been given the proper medicine. So believing helps, you see? Not just psychologically, but physically as well.'

'The cancer cells are in Oslo. We're here.'

'Mum will know if we lose hope. She'll hear it in our voices.'

He fell silent.

Outside, the sky was blue again. The late sunlight drenched the trees across the field.

It was amazing how little of the world we could see at any one time.

Going somewhere else wouldn't help, all we'd see there would be another section, just as small.

All we could see was what the eyes could see.

It wasn't much.

A sort of duct in front of and behind us, with various things in it. Trees and bushes and hills. Or houses and streets. Or rooms and furniture.

That was the world.

'Anyway, we can't just sit here,' I said. 'We should do something.'

'Like what?' said Joar.

'I don't know. Is there anything you feel like?'

He shook his head.

'How about going for a drive?'

'Now? At this time?'

'We're on our own,' I said. 'Bedtime's for us to decide.'

'Where shall we go?'

'Wherever you want. The falls?'

'What are we going to do there?'

I shrugged.

'It'd be nice just to sit there for a bit. There'll be a lot of water in the falls now. Or we could go to the chippy? How about sausage and mash? A hot dog? Sausage and chips? A burger?'

'Sausage and chips.'

'Right, then. Let's go!'

The feeling I had of everything being small and condensed disappeared as, stepping over to the car, I felt the cool air of evening against my cheeks, the breeze somehow carrying with it the thought of Lisa, and everything then seemed to quiver and vibrate.

It was all in my head.

Nothing had changed.

The undertaker's job, that was in my head too.

Lisa was in my head.

Even Joar was in my head, sitting there next to me on the passenger seat, clicking his seat belt.

'It's a lovely evening!' I said to him, dropping the sun visor down with one hand as I turned the wheel with the other and pulled away along the road.

He smelled a bit, a faint odour of sweat mingled with something more pungent.

Did he use a deodorant?

Probably not.

It came all of a sudden, that smell of sweat.

I remembered Mum telling me. We'd been visiting her family over in the Vestland, it was summer and the weather was glorious, I was twelve years old, and one morning we were sitting out on the step in the sunshine waiting for Evert to come, and Mum said I'd grown up so much I'd have to start using a deodorant. She bought one at the supermarket that same afternoon, I could still remember it, a light blue Sterilan in a glass bottle.

I'd been embarrassed about smelling of sweat, but proud of myself at having reached the age when I had to use a deodorant.

I could buy him one without comment.

We followed the road through the woods and out onto the long flatland that was covered with strawberry plants on one side, sloping away to the river, while on the other tall spruce trees rose up like a wall.

The wino's funeral had not been well attended. I'd counted twelve in all, besides Johansen and myself, and Kristian, who was already there waiting for us when we came.

We'd rolled the coffin across to the church on a trolley, Johansen and me, Kristian walking in front of us with slow, solemn, measured strides, like he was a general or something.

General of Death.

Joar took a packet of chewing gum from his pocket, Juicy Fruit, and after removing the silver wrappers he folded two of the soft sticks together, popped them into his mouth and was about to put the packet back in his pocket when he changed his mind and held it out to offer me a piece.

'Do you want some?'

'Yes, please. Will you open one for me?'

He did so, and my mouth filled with the taste of artificial fruit flavouring.

The river ran green beneath us, dark, almost black under the trees. Glimpses of yellow where the sandy bed shone through. The road on the other side, hardly used any more, lay empty.

'We might have to wait a week before going up to Oslo,' I said.

He turned his head and looked at me.

'Why?' he said, a wariness in his voice and eyes.

'She's only just had her procedure today. She won't be feeling that good. Best to wait a bit until she's more up to it, I reckon.'

'I'd say it was the other way round.'

'How do you mean?'

'It'll do her more good to see us now.'

'Perhaps,' I said. 'But it'll be important for her to get as much rest and as much sleep as possible.'

How was I going to go out with Lisa now without him putting two and two together?

I'd have to cross that bridge when I came to it.

'Do you *want* to have a quick look at the falls?' I said.

He shrugged.

'Can do.'

I parked the car in front of where the bus pulled in. Even there, the air was a mist of tiny droplets from the falls. The roar increased as we walked along the path beneath the dark trees, the water here and there appearing to us in glimpses between the trunks, shapeless and greyish white.

My face was wet as we stood at the edge and peered across. In summer, the river often had so little water in it that you could venture out, stepping from rock to rock. One of them had runes carved in it, from the Viking age, I'd seen them many times, though without knowing what they meant. There were a couple more rock carvings there too, one from the fourteenth century, the other from the sixteenth century, something to do with the king having come past once.

We sat down on the bare rock. Further below us, we could see the faint glow of the factory windows. Some red forklifts stood lined up outside the main building. There was a row of dark green containers, too. A lorry trailer with a blue tarp. Three cars.

We sat for a while without speaking. I stared at the plunging falls, the way they seemed to force the near-black waters of the pool below onwards into the river channel.

Joar stared too.

It was impossible to tell what was on his mind.

'What are you thinking about?' I said after a bit.

'What?'

'What are you thinking about?' I said, louder.

'Nothing.'

'I don't believe you,' I said. 'You're always thinking about something. Things nobody else thinks.'

'Am I?'

'You know you are!'

'OK.'

'Go on then, what are you thinking about?'

'Nothing in particular. Just looking at the water.'

'Without a thought in your head?'

'Yes. Or rather, I was thinking that the form's always the same, but the contents keep changing. How strange it is. What difference is there, exactly, between form and content, if you look at the water there?'

'There, you see,' I said.

He looked at me.

'See what?'

'You *were* thinking about something.'

'What were *you* thinking about, then?'

'Not that!'

'What, then?'

'Nothing. I was just looking at it all. The falls and the factory, and the hill over there. I wasn't really thinking about anything.'

'How come you thought I was?'

'I could tell. Besides, you're a person who thinks a lot.'

'You think as well, you know,' he said.

'Oh, thanks!' I said, and laughed.

'But if you don't think about what you're thinking, your thoughts just drift away, because there's nothing to tie them down.'

'There's a word for people like you.'

'What?'

'Precocious.'

'I have reached puberty, you know.'

'I've realised,' I said, and laughed again, wiped the mist droplets from my brow and cheeks and got to my feet. 'Shall we go back?'

Among the cars outside the chippy I immediately recognised Gjert's black Ascona, and once I'd parked I ambled over. Gjert, with a carton of chips in his lap and a sausage in one hand, rolled his window down. Bente was sitting beside him, struggling with a big hamburger.

'All right?' said Gjert.

'All right,' I said. 'Sausage and chips, is it?'

'Has to be done.'

'I'm with you as far as the ketchup goes, but the mustard you've got there's a different matter. Chips and mustard, it's not on. Tastes horrible.'

'Have you come all this way just to criticise?'

'It's not a criticism. I'm merely sharing my experience. You should be grateful. Don't you think, Bente?'

'Yes,' she said, gripping her burger with both hands like it was still alive.

'How's things, anyway?' I said, glancing then at Joar, who stood studying the menu in the window.

'Not bad,' said Gjert. 'Busy, which is good. How about you?'

'I'm OK.'

'I hear you've gone into the funeral business?'

'Who told you that?'

'Vegard. What's it like?'

'OK. Not much to talk about.'

'I can imagine,' he said, and laughed.

'It's only to tide me over. I'll be packing it in after the summer.'

'It's all money.'

'That's the way I look at it.'

'You coming to practice tomorrow?'

'I reckon so.'

'See you there, then.'

'Yes, see you,' I said, and went over to where Joar was standing.

'What's it going to be, then?' I said. 'Flat fried cow or ground pig with flour, herbs and preservatives in a casing of intestines?'

'Hamburger and chips, please. And a cola, if I'm allowed.'

'Course you're allowed.'

I stepped up onto the little veranda-like platform and ordered Joar's hamburger and chips and a sausage and mash for myself. When the food came, we took it over to one of the tables that had been put out on a patch of grass next to where the trees started. We were quite high up the valley, the hillsides were steep and tall and the air between them chilly now that the sun had retreated and shone only on the trees that stood uppermost on the slopes. Most of the young people who hung out

here were from the town a few kilometres further up the road, so neither the cars nor the faces inside them were familiar to me.

Below the road, on the flat ground beside the river, was a camping
site. Whenever I saw it, I always wondered who on earth would come
camping here. Midges, forest, youths cruising around in cars, what
kind of a holiday would that be?

Nevertheless, the place was packed with tents and caravans all
summer.

I squirted a long line of ketchup into my carton and handed the bottle to Joar. Pressed the sausage into the mash and tried to gouge some
up with it, but either the mash was too firm or the sausage was too soft,
so I picked up the plastic fork instead, ridiculously small though it was,
hardly bigger than a toothpick, and scooped some mash into my mouth
before dabbing the sausage in the ketchup and biting the end off.

'Your hamburger all right?' I said.

Joar nodded with his mouth full.

'Since you do so much thinking, what do you think's the meaning of
all this?' I said, indicating the situation, the general surroundings.

He rolled his eyes.

'I'm not joking, I'm asking you seriously. Have you thought about
it?'

He swallowed, then drank some cola.

'No,' he said.

'Fair enough,' I said. 'But don't you think it's strange that everything
we can see around us here is the result of an *explosion*, and that before
that there was nothing?'

'Are you talking about the Big Bang now?'

'Yes. How can something as complex as a cat emerge out of
nothing?'

I'd run out of patience with the little fork and used my fingers to
pick up a big mouthful of mash.

'Is this something you've been wondering about?' he said, looking at
me with his mouth half open.

'What if I have?'

'There's nothing strange about it,' he said, his voice suggesting
puzzlement that I could even ask. 'Matter accumulates into great

clouds. The clouds become stars and planets. On the planets, matter crams together and forms systems. In some of those systems, life emerges. Some of that life develops and becomes a cat.'

'Simple as that?'

'No, it's not simple at all,' he said. 'It took science thousands of years to work it out.'

He dipped the end of a chip into his little blob of ketchup and popped it into his mouth.

'How come *you* know?' I said.

'It's something I learned at school. Didn't you?'

'I suppose I must have done,' I said, and licked my fingers before taking another bite of sausage. 'What about God, though?'

'That's just superstition.'

'Are you sure about that?'

'Now you're being stupid.'

He bit into his hamburger again.

'You're not getting confirmed, then?'

He shook his head, his mouth still full, swallowed, then gulped some more cola.

'Does Mum know?'

'No.'

'What do you think she'll say?'

'She can say what she wants. I can't get confirmed just for Mum's sake, can I?'

'I did.'

'I thought you did it for the money?'

I laughed.

'That as well.'

We finished eating. I went and got some serviettes from the dispenser next to the serving hatch and wiped my mouth and fingers, but the dry paper wasn't enough, so I gave the car key to Joar, crossed over to the petrol station toilet and washed my hands in the sink there. It wasn't until I stepped outside again that I realised how dark it was getting. The lights had come on at the side of the road and the light from the petrol station windows suddenly seemed a lot brighter.

'Can we give Mum a ring when we get home?' Joar said as I got in the car. 'She might be awake now.'

'Where's the key?' I said.

'You're sitting on it.'

I lifted my backside and felt around until I found the key, then stuck it into the ignition.

'It'll be too late now. We'll give her a ring in the morning, OK?'

'OK.'

I reversed and swung round, waited for a car to go past, then turned onto the road. Soon we were sweeping through the valley in the dimming grey of dusk, the beam of the headlights reaching out in front of us.

'That was nice,' I said as we pulled up outside the house. 'Instead of staying in.'

He smiled fleetingly before opening the door and getting out. By the time I got inside, he was already up the stairs.

I knocked on his door and opened it.

'You can have a shower now,' I said. 'I'll have one in the morning.'

'OK,' he said, lying on his bed with a magazine.

'Use my deodorant, if you want. I'll buy you one tomorrow.'

He looked up at me.

'I don't need one.'

'I think you do. You're turning into a young man. A young man needs a deodorant.'

'OK,' he said, reverting his attention to the page in front of him.

'Go on, then.'

'Don't fuss.'

'I won't,' I said, and closed the door, went into my own room, lay down on the bed with my hands clasped under my head and stared at the ceiling. The same marks and knots in the wood that I'd been staring up at nearly all my life. The motorbike and sidecar, the fairy-tale man with the stubby nose, the owl's head, the boat with the full keel.

Mum was in Oslo. Joar was in his room. I'd got a job. I was going out for a meal with Lisa.

Was there any real reason not to read those letters?

What was written in them was written, whether I read them or not. All of a sudden it felt right.

I got up and went over to the cupboard, lifted up the boxes I'd hidden them under, took them out and went back over to the bed. Switched on the bedside lamp, angled it so I could see. Placed the pillow up against the headboard, sat down, leaned back and began to read, my heart now thumping.

Sivertik, my very dearest!

You must excuse the name I have given you, I am unsure whether you will care for it, as silly as it sounds, but I love it and cannot wait to whisper it into your ear. Sivertik, I love you, is what I shall say.

When are you coming?

You were unable to tell me with any certainty last time, and you have not yet replied to my letter.

If only you knew what torture it is not hearing word from you, you would surely have engulfed me in letters.

Engulf me in letters!

As I wait to hear from you, life goes on here as ever. Mama helps me as best she can with Sasha, nearly every day, so much so that he becomes almost more attached to her than to me. I see that she relishes it, which angers me occasionally, yet I can do nothing about it, and of course cannot bring the matter up with her. You know my theory as to her kindness.

I know that she will like you.

She will be sceptical of us, but she will like you.

And now the spring has arrived. Not with sunshine and blue skies, for that is not the kind of spring we have here, where the season brings with it rain and mist, mist and rain. But then one day the birch trees will all of a sudden be green and the woods white with anemones, and before we know it summer will have come.

Without you, it will be but half a summer.

I pester you. I badger and beleaguer you. I know I do. Sometimes I'm afraid it will turn you against me.

I have never felt this way before, not with anyone. I have never been afraid of being abandoned. I protected myself against it. I didn't realise at the time (I knew no other way of being with a person), but my heart was never in it, I was never really there, not with my full emotions, not with all my heart and soul.

I am now. Not an hour passes without my thinking of you.

You hold my heart in your hands.

Dear Syvert, if you do not feel the same about me, you must say so.

Promise me that.

Yours for ever,

Asya

Syvert

(Does your name not appear more distinguished like this, prouder and more splendid, unadorned with my clinging 'dears' and 'dearests'?)

Syvert,

I have just read your letter. How glad I was to see your handwriting and realise that it was from you! I had not abandoned hope, but all kinds of thoughts have been milling in my mind, as indeed you know. I ought to wait before writing back, wait several weeks as you made me wait. But why? It would only punish you – and that would be the last thing I wanted!

How lovely to read about your boys. They are fortunate to have such a considerate father. That Joar hasn't yet begun to speak is nothing to be concerned about as I see it. He is strong and healthy, and from what your letter tells me he seems to have no problems communicating! I recall how Mama went on at me during Sasha's first year, for there was something slightly unresponsive about him, as if we weren't quite getting through. Have I told you this already? I felt certain there was nothing to be worried about. A parent knows such things. I was right, but do you think Mama would accept it? She, who has never been wrong in all her life!

I smiled when reading about Syvert who talks to everyone and is afraid only of the headless man! Who knows, perhaps one day I will meet your sons, though of course circumstances in my country dictate that it is easier for you to travel than me. I've been thinking I'd like to introduce you to Sasha the next time you come. It feels strange to me that he is unaware that you exist – you, who are so important to me in my life.

I recognise what you write about restlessness being the body's expression of longing. I'm fine when I'm at work and there's lots to do (always the case, as you know), as well as when I'm with Sasha, but once he's been put to bed I become unsettled and can find nothing with which to occupy myself. I might pick up some knitting, watch the television, or talk to my friends on the telephone (reading seems not to be an option any more, it's as if my ability to concentrate has simply evaporated!), but whatever I do it is without enthusiasm.

You know what I mean, and described it so much better than I can manage!

That sense of longing, that is so good and so painful at the same time.

August is such a long way off.

Please, don't get me wrong. I'm very, very, very happy that you're coming! My fear is only that one day you will not. That you never will again. Sometimes I think it's unfair. I'm stuck here, while you come and go. Everything is up to you, in other words. But of course I know, dear Syvert, that it can be no other way. I know that you cannot live here and that I cannot live there. Not the way things are. And if anything does ever change, it will not be in our lifetimes.

But what is our relationship then worth, if we cannot live and share a life together? Are we to go on living apart with our longing? Year in, year out? How long will we endure it?

This isn't what I wanted my letter to be about. But when you're here, I don't want to waste our precious time discussing problems, and do not even think of them then, at least not until the final hours before you leave again. Still, it must be vented.

Must it? I hear you say.

You, who would sweep every problem under the mat and believe everything to be well with them being out of sight.

But I adore you for that.

I adore you for your equanimity.

And for your awkwardness in intimacy.

Are you offended now?

But I adore it!

I adore you for your beautiful body.

I adore you for your blue eyes.

I adore you for the way you speak Russian. When life is difficult and my mind is dark, I need only think of something you said in that delightful accent of yours, and a joy comes streaming.

I hear the lift outside the door now. It'll be Mama and Sasha. I'll write more later this evening!

At last Sasha is sleeping, and I am alone again. We had borscht with cabbage rolls for dinner and Mama had brought with her a rhubarb pie we had for pudding. After we'd eaten, Sasha went outside to play football with the other children from the flats, while I washed up. The boy wants always to be outdoors, whatever the weather. Rain, snow or storm, he

cannot be kept in. But he can be pensive and quiet too, and so immersed in
something that nothing else will matter to him, though only ever one thing
at a time – as with all men! It's nice to think that you have a son who is
almost exactly the same age. It seems like they share many of the same
interests. I'm thinking of what you wrote about Syvert and the poster of an
English footballer he got for his birthday. Sasha has a poster of Oleg
Blokhin on the wall above his bed. He was devastated and quite
inconsolable when our national team lost to Czechoslovakia and failed to
reach the finals in Yugoslavia.

I've always been fond of the noise of the great sports championships in
the summer when all the television sets are on in the evenings in all the
flats, their sounds drifting in through the open windows. The same voices,
the same roars of the crowd everywhere.

I don't know how I shall manage to wait until August.

Whenever something unusual happens, whenever I see something that
captures my imagination in some way, I tell you about it in my mind. It's
as if I see things for your eyes too. If only Syvert could see this, I think to
myself, when I draw the curtain aside in the morning and the sun is
shining down on the forest that stretches away in all its green behind the
housing blocks. Or when I've baked a good cake. If only Syvert could taste
it too, I think then. When something out of the ordinary occurs at work,
what I miss when I get home is you being there for me to tell you about it.
Today, for example, I met an elderly woman, I suppose she was seventy
years old or thereabouts and had not long since undergone surgery because
of a heart attack. Now one of her feet had gone numb and she'd been
suffering headaches for some days, all of which caused her discomfort. She
was rather matronly, I can tell you. The lenses of her glasses were so thick it
made her eyes look enormous. She sat on the chair with her feet planted
firmly apart, upright in posture, her skirt pulled up so that I could
examine the enlarged veins on her thighs. I like to talk about all sorts with
my patients during such examinations – often, the cause of the affliction
lies somewhere else in the body (longing presents as restlessness, but what
does restlessness present as? It settles in the body) – but this lady made me
rather frightened! Nevertheless, I managed to get something out of her. She
was a widow, her husband having been killed in the war, she had three
children, all girls, and lived with the youngest, her son-in-law and their

two children in a small village, now all but depopulated, some distance
from the town. There was nothing wrong with her. Her blood pressure was
normal, the numbness she felt was in all likelihood down to little more
than a trapped nerve, and there was nothing to indicate that her
headaches were anything other than just headaches. And of course varicose
veins are very common in people that age. So I told her she had many good
years ahead of her yet. She contested that they would be good, but agreed
with me that her remaining years would be many. As you know, she said,
soon life will know no end. Soon we shall live for ever. I see, I replied. That
sounds good, at least. And not just those who are alive now, she said. But
all the dead as well. Are you talking about the Resurrection? I said. When
the Saviour returns to judge the living and the dead? At this she snorted.
I'm talking about the common task, she said. The common task? What's
that? I naturally asked. It is the physical resurrection of all who have lived,
she said. Not only our parents, but their parents too, and their parents'
parents before them, all the way back to the very first humans. As the great
Fyodorov has written it.

Just another day at the hospital.

The notions people come up with, it beggars belief! I for one have never
heard of this 'great' Fyodorov before, and I'm guessing neither have you!

I should have asked her about it and at least found out how she thought
the dead were to be revived, but of course there wasn't the time for it and
off she went, presumably for good.

I miss you so very much, Syvert. I hope you're all right, wherever you
happen to be when reading this, and that you will not delay your reply but
will sit down and write back as soon as you can. It needn't be a long letter!
If you think I'm being too insistent, please know that I will manage and
always will. I am not your responsibility (that's just about the worst that
could happen, that I become your responsibility), but what we have
together is so precious and seldom that it would be a crime to squander! A
crime against us.

It's still light outside, though it will soon be eleven o'clock, and now I
must get some sleep, tomorrow will be a long day.

Write!

I love you.

Your Asya

Dear Syvert,

This will be my last letter to you. I have put off writing it for several weeks. All I have been able to do is to try and get through the days, to hide my pain and sorrow from Sasha. Something died in me when I read your letter. I have lost not only you, but also the future. At first I refused to accept it. Then I became indignant, more so than I have ever been before. Now only sorrow remains. The longing for something that will never transpire. I hope you will not think that I am writing this to burden you. I still want us to be together. I love you, and always will. I understand your arguments. They are rational and reasonable. You cannot come and live here without losing everything you have. Your two sons, you mustn't lose them. At the same time, I cannot leave here. To go on seeing each other only once in a while, to never be together more than a few days a year, would sap the life out of us in the long run. I understand all that. It's rational and reasonable. But something in me would not give up after reading your letter, something in me wanted only to go on hoping. That something was love. Could love not conquer these practical problems? Practical problems surely cannot be greater than love?

There is something I wonder. I want your honest answer.

Did you know it was over when you visited last time?

I think you did. I think the reason you wanted to meet at the hotel rather than at mine was because you didn't want to meet Sasha. You knew it was over.

But I'm not certain.

What difference does it make now?

It was the last time we were together. Was I alone then, and you already somewhere else, or were we really together?

You were quiet when we left the room and went out to eat. You're often quiet, but this was a different kind of quiet, I remember thinking.

You already knew, didn't you?

Perhaps you were thinking of telling me to my face instead of putting it in a letter, and your courage then failed. Was that it? Were you prevented from speaking by cowardice? Or perhaps you wanted our last hours together to be as good as possible.

They were. Apart from the slight unease I felt at your silence.

You smiled and we raised our glasses to each other. The climbing roses that covered the brick wall were blood-red and beautiful, the sky above us was deep blue, and the voices that drifted up from the water came as if from another age. I was so happy then. It was such a joyful moment.

Was my happiness without foundation?

There was something else in your letter I still can't understand that you could write: 'I would never be able to live up to you or your expectations.' Do you really know me no better than that? It disappoints me. I've never expected anything of you but have loved you for the person you are, even your weaknesses. As for living up to me, I simply have no idea what you mean. What is it about me that you feel you must live up to? Or perhaps the question should be put differently: what is it in you that makes you think like that? The first time I saw you, you were part of a large group. I wasn't looking for anyone. I wasn't watching out. My eyes must have seen thousands of men over the past ten years, but I saw only you. My eyes stopped at you. You, and only you, wakened my heart. When I got to know you, I found that my intuition had been right. You are a highly intelligent and many-sided man. The thought of you being unable to 'live up to' me is either self-deception or something you're saying in order to cover up the real reason, which is that you do not love me.

I think the former. And if the latter is true, you would never admit to it anyway.

Is this how my life is to be, endless speculation as to why you left me?

Of course not. I have Sasha, I have my job, I have my friends. And I have the memory of you. It will always be good, and it will never leave me. Now it is like a wound, hurting, hurting, hurting. But wounds heal, time passes, and love, Syvert, love will always prevail.

Yours for ever,

Asya

Dear Syvert,

Today it is two years since we met that first time. I still think of you, but more about what was than what could have been. I no longer look for your face wherever I go. I hope that all is well with you and that you are happy where you are. I know that I shouldn't send this letter, but I want you to know that I am fine. You need not reply.

With warm wishes,

Asya

Dear Syvert,

Last night Mama died. Sasha is inconsolable. Thankfully he is sleeping now. You never met her, fate would not have it thus, but she knew who you were, I told her everything about us. It feels right to put this in a letter to you. I am still in shock, her death came unexpectedly, but unlike Sasha I am not inconsolable. She was a complicated person. So when I cry, I am perhaps crying a little for myself. She was a witness, as all parents are their children's witnesses. Who shall be mine and Sasha's now that she is gone? I must learn to live without — as she did herself.

Peace be with her.

I hope all is well with you, Syvert, and that your two boys are thriving. With love,

Asya

Dear Syvert,

I don't know what to believe or think. Do you mean it? If you really mean it, I will come.

Asya

Sivertik, my own dear beloved!

I write this on the train in a carriage full of people and smells and sounds. It is only a few hours since we said goodbye at the station. I fell asleep immediately, completely exhausted after our two sleepless days and nights together! When I woke up I did not know quite where I was at first, but then everything came back to me, thoughts of you and us, and I was again uplifted with joy.

It is a wondrous feeling. It is as if I am protected from everything. Nothing can harm me. I am filled with light!

On one side of the carriage people are sitting or lying in the berths, eating or sleeping. On the other, the tables beneath the windows are fully occupied. It is so crowded in here that one should not be surprised to bump into the dangling bare foot of a sleeping passenger as one passes through the carriage. Next to me sits a family of four, the father playing a game of cards with his two sons while the mother nods off with her knitting in her hands.

The smell of you is still in my clothes. Had I been sixteen years old, I would surely have believed I would never wash them again. In fact, I almost feel like a sixteen-year-old, the same tremendous love of life that could come over me then (not that I knew what it was at the time!) has come over me now. And were we not rather like teenagers this time? I feared we might be thrown out of the restaurant the way we kept leaning across the table to kiss each other, not just once, but time and again. You electrified me, in case you didn't know it.

I fell asleep again! The dusk is falling outside. In the endless cornfields, the threshing machines move slowly like boats, their headlamps shining now in the dimming light. Before I slept, I could see the dust as it clouded around them. Now all details are erased. And as the windows darken, life inside the carriage becomes more conspicuous. The two boys in the bunk next to me are sleeping, their parents sit beside each other without speaking. They are young, no more than in their twenties. As I write, you have begun your journey home. Soon you will be giving your sons the presents we bought. Thank you for bringing the photographs of them, it was such a joy to see what they look like! You are fortunate in having them, and it is only good that they are so different. Syvert so carefree and uncomplicated, Joar so sensitive that he must protect himself. They have each inherited a different side of you!

And now it hurts.

Not even the light inside me can stave away the pain.

I know it hurts you too.

Is there no other way we can be together?

There must be!

You must divorce, you say. You can't live like that any more. But coming to live with me means that you will lose them.

Can you live with that?

Is it really what you want?

I know you don't want to lose them.

My own feelings are firm. There is nothing I want more than to share my life with you. I doubt only on your behalf. You understand that.

Perhaps we could wait a year or two? You could talk to her, move to a place of your own. You'd be free then and things would be easier for me too, knowing that you were free – knowing that you were mine alone! – even if we still wouldn't be living together, not even in the same country.

It's too big a sacrifice, Syvert.

If you came now, we would risk everything coming apart, the loss you felt would eat away at you, would it not? And if everything came apart, would the damage not be irreparable?

Know that I will always wait for you.

Always, always.

Write soon, for God's sake!

I long for you so much.

I love you with all my heart and all my soul.

Your Asya

Syvert, my dearest beloved man,

Something fantastic has happened, something that will change everything for good!

I shall tell you what it is when we meet!

I long for you, and I love you, everything about you.

Your Asya

I read the letters and read them again. It felt like a wind had blown through me, tearing up everything that wasn't secured. I didn't know what to believe, what to think.

Dad had been planning to leave us high and dry.

He wanted to be with her instead of us.

It was all there in writing.

I could forget about going to sleep.

I put the letters back in the cupboard and went downstairs. Everything was still and vacant.

Something fantastic that would change everything for good.

It could only have been a child.

But chances were she never had it. Dad had died shortly afterwards.

Did she know?

She must have written. There must have been letters, lots more than these.

Where were they?

They'd have been sent here. Mum must have opened them.

She wouldn't have understood what they said. Could she have worked it out? Put two and two together?

I stood in front of the living-room window and looked out into the murk.

How terrible it was, everything.

Mum's cancer. Dad's betrayal.

I needed to talk to someone about it. Get it out of my system.

But who?

Dag?

Lisa, Lisa. Can I phone you at this hour?

I went into the hall and switched the light on, then the light in the kitchen to see what time it was.

Quarter past eleven.

It was impolite to phone anyone before ten in the morning and after ten at night.

Anyway, she was probably asleep.

Did I have a brother or a sister in Russia?

Born in 1977.

Nine years old now.

She wouldn't have had it. No way.

How could she have been so in love with *Dad*?

She must have been really good-looking if he was ready to give every-thing up for her sake. A stunner.

Carefree and uncomplicated.

What the hell did she know?

What business did she have in my family? In my head?

Fucking cow.

And now Mum might be dying.

I put my shoes on and went outside. The air was chill against my bare arms.

He used to go about here.

Lived here most of his life, in fact.

Above the ridge the moon was a blur of yellow and almost full. The light it shed on the fields was faint. A reflection of a reflection.

I was just about to go over to the barn to see if her letters might be there somewhere, when the door opened behind me.

Joar was standing in his underpants, his hand on the door handle.

'What are you doing out there? Is it Mum? Is she dead?'

'No, no, it's nothing,' I said, moving towards him instantly. 'I couldn't sleep, that's all, so I stepped out to get some air.'

'Are you sure?'

'Of course I'm sure. No one's rung, I haven't spoken to anyone. Come on, let's go back in.'

I closed the door behind us and put my arms around him. Instead of pulling away like he usually did, he held me.

I ran my hand through his hair.

'Do you want some cocoa or something?'

He shook his head.

'Couldn't you sleep either?' I said.

'I fell asleep straight away,' he said. 'I woke when I heard the door.'

'Sorry about that,' I said. 'I wasn't thinking.'

'No.'

'Shall we go back to bed, then?'

'Yes. But don't go out again.'

'I promise.'

I followed him up the stairs. He went into his room and got into bed while I stood looking at him.

'Everything will be all right, you'll see,' I said.

'It's not exactly up to you.'

'True,' I said, and smiled. 'We'll talk to Mum in the morning, OK?'

'OK.'

'Night night.'

'Night night.'

I closed his door and went into my own room. There was nothing for it now but to lie down and hope for the best. It worked a treat, only I forgot to set the alarm and didn't wake up until Joar knocked hard on my door.

'I've got to go soon,' he said from the landing. 'Aren't we going to phone Mum?'

'Yes, yes, of course,' I said, hurriedly pulling on my clothes that I'd dumped in a heap on the floor, before going downstairs to the kitchen where he was sitting waiting with his shoes and coat on.

'Have I got time for a coffee?' I said.

He shook his head.

'Not even if I drive you to school?'

'I like walking best.'

'All right,' I said, and went into the hall with him following on behind me, dialled the number of the hospital and was put through to Mum's room.

'Hello?' she said in a faint voice.

'Hello,' I said. 'Your elder son speaking. Syvert Løyning. On behalf of my brother and myself, I'm phoning to ask how you're feeling.'

It gladdened me that I could sense her smiling.

'I'm feeling fine,' she said. 'The doctors say the procedure went well.'

'Does it hurt?'

'A bit, yes. But nothing to go on about.'

'Oh, that's good! Everything's fine here. Joar's eager for a word. Here he is,' I said, and handed him the receiver. I stepped into the kitchen to get some coffee on the go and closed the door behind me, not wanting to listen in or inhibit him in any way.

They were on the phone at least ten minutes before they hung up and he came back in.

'Sounds like she's doing fine,' I said.

He nodded.

'Are you off now, then?'

He nodded again.

'What do you want for dinner?'

He shrugged.

'Don't know. You choose.'

'What are your three favourite dishes?'

'Kebab, hamburger and pizza.'

'In that order?'

He shrugged again.

'See you later,' he said, and went out.

I filled a cup halfway with coffee from the pot even before the water had fully run through, poured some milk up to the brim, though I didn't normally take milk in my coffee, gulped down the lukewarm blend, splashed my face with water, pulled on the trousers from my suit, wriggled into the same shirt as the day before, squirted some washing-up liquid on my shoes and wiped them with the dishcloth before going out to the car with my suit jacket over my arm, the good shoes in my hand and my trainers on my feet. It was much better driving with them on, so I'd already decided the day before that was what I was going to do.

I was late. Needed to get a move on.

It wasn't good, only my second day on the job.

Oh no! I'd forgotten to switch the coffee maker off!

But the pot would be full now. So the bottom wouldn't get burnt, would it?

Sod it, then.

If I put my foot down until hitting the rush-hour traffic, I'd gain a couple of minutes. Or maybe I was running so late the tailbacks had already eased?

It was five past nine by the time I pulled up outside the premises. Changing my shoes in a hurry, I then checked my hair in the rear-view mirror, smoothing it flat at the back as best I could. It'd have to do. The gateway at the side of the building was open, so I went through, reasoning that if I went that way and straight round the back they wouldn't know what time I'd got there.

Johansen was sitting on his chair smoking.

'Morning,' I said.

He looked up at me and gave a nod.

'Thanks for showing me the ropes yesterday!' I said as I sat down on the settee. 'What time do we start today?'

'Same time.'

'Same place as well?'

He shook his head. Kristian came across the yard. The same suit, on the short side. He stopped in the doorway and looked at me.

'We start on time here,' he said. 'Understood?'

'I got stuck in traffic,' I said. 'And I was only five minutes late. The dead can't be in *that* much of a hurry, can they?'

I laughed tentatively.

Kristian didn't laugh at all.

'I hear you did a good job yesterday. I'm pleased. Keep it up,' he said, then turned and went back, a march across the cobbles, to his office.

Johansen got to his feet and I followed him out to the hearse, catching a glimpse of Kristian through the window, telephone held to his ear.

'*He* was in a good mood,' I said to Johansen after we got in.

'Word of advice,' he said, twisting round to look out the back as he started to reverse. 'Don't speak ill of your boss when talking to someone you don't know. You've no idea how loyal I might be to him.'

'I wasn't speaking ill! Everyone's entitled to be in a bad mood every now and then.'

Johansen gave a faint smile, threw the gear lever into first and we rolled slowly out onto the street. Just as the day before, people stared as we went past. I decided to be as quiet as Johansen. Asking questions all the time was hard work when all you got were single-syllable replies.

We crossed the bridge and carried on along the old main road that after a bit was lined with great chestnut trees, all in blossom. I'd always thought they looked like epaulettes from a distance, but now I found that conception silly. Not even the most self-applauding of dictators would pile such flowery towers on his shoulders.

Johansen slowed down as we approached a set of lights. The woman behind the wheel of a small car in the next lane threw a glance at us.

It felt like I'd dreamt those letters. As if they weren't a part of the same reality I was in now.

They weren't either. It had happened ten years ago.

It was all in the past.

'Where are we going?' I said as we headed along the main artery out of town, remembering then that I wasn't going to ask him anything else.

'A house,' he said. 'On one of the new estates.'

'Right,' I said.

Reading her letters, I'd formed a picture of her in my mind. I saw her as still youngish, with dark shoulder-length hair and delicate features that you hardly noticed on account of her eyes, which were immensely expressive. I realised the chances of her actually looking like that were minimal, or more likely non-existent, but every time I thought about her, that was the picture I got.

She hadn't written anything about how they'd met. Only that she'd noticed him among a group of other people.

It was odd. He wasn't the sort who turned heads.

And then a memory flashed back at me out of nowhere. We'd just got out of the car. It was the post-office car park. There was only Dad and me there. He walked ahead of me and didn't notice the woman he passed on the way. I did, because she wheeled round and looked at him.

I remembered wondering why.

That must have been the reason it came back to me.

Why would a strange woman turn round to look at my dad like that?

I must have been about eight or nine. Too young to understand such things. Old enough to be puzzled.

Wait a minute.

He'd had a post-office box!

That was why we were there, to pick up his post. No one else I knew had a post-office box, they all got their letters delivered at home. He said it was to do with his job.

But it was because of her!

Mum must have cancelled it when he died. I'd never heard it mentioned since.

'You're quiet today,' said Johansen. He gave me a quick glance, his big mitts resting on top of the steering wheel.

You'd be the one to know, I thought.

'A bit tired, that's all,' I said. 'Didn't get to bed until late, and then I overslept.'

'Out on the drink?'

'No, it wasn't that. Why, were you?'

He gave a laugh.

'Can't say I was.'

The strait came into view up ahead, and the sea it strove towards. Some cars were parked below the bridge, and by the anchorage blocks a few people were fishing.

Crossing over to the other side, we turned right and soon there were houses all around.

The road we followed wound its way up the hill. There was no one about, presumably the kids were all at school, the grown-ups at work. The house we were going to turned out to be nearly at the top. It was a big place, with a veranda running its width at the front, affording a panoramic view of the sea.

'You'd need to be well heeled to live here,' I said as we pulled up on the white gravel in front of the house.

'Reassuring in a way, that death doesn't care if you're wealthy,' said Johansen, engaging the handbrake and opening the door.

'Don't tell me you're a socialist,' I said as he got out.

He turned and put his finger to his lips.

He was right, but I was still a bit offended as I stood beside the hearse and watched him ring the doorbell and then wait, his big, heavy head bowed.

A woman aged about forty came to the door. Thin and pale, without make-up, eyes swollen from crying, she had on a pair of light blue Levi's and a white T-shirt, and her hair was gathered in a tight bun.

Johansen bowed discreetly and shook her hand while saying something I didn't catch. She smiled faintly and nodded a few times. After a moment, she stepped back into the hall while Johansen returned to the hearse and opened the rear door. He drew out the coffin as I stood there. I waited until the other end emerged into view before stepping forward, and together we lifted it out.

A woman stood watching us from an upstairs window in the house next door. When I looked up at her, she stepped away.

'He's in here,' the woman said as we went through the hall holding the coffin at either end.

We followed her into what looked like an extra living room that had been turned into a sickroom. The deceased lay on a double bed in the middle of the room, underneath a white duvet. The face was so withered I at first took it to belong to an old person, but as we came closer I realised it was that of a much younger man. We put the coffin down carefully on the floor. Straightening up, I noticed there was someone else in the room. A girl was sitting on a sofa that was backed up against the wall behind the bed. She looked to be about sixteen, seventeen. Spiky peroxide hair. Black make-up around her eyes, giving her a panda-like appearance. Black trousers, black T-shirt, studded belt.

A punk.

'Perhaps you should leave the room now, Marie,' said the woman, who I supposed to be her mother.

'I'm fine here.'

I looked down at the floor. Johansen stood with his hands folded in front of him.

'No, come with me,' the mother said. 'The gentlemen need to be left alone to do their job, I'm sure you understand.'

The girl shook her head defiantly.

Her mother looked at Johansen.

'It's all right,' he said.

'Are you sure?'

'Yes, of course.'

He gave the girl a little nod.

She didn't react, but looked out of the window as if we weren't there.

When her mother left the room, a boy came and stood in the doorway. He couldn't have been more than ten. His face was expressionless. But when his staring eyes met mine I could see he was very angry. He turned and went away again. Johansen went out as well, leaving me on my own with the girl. With no task to perform, all I could do was stand there next to the bed where the deceased lay and wait for Johansen to come back.

I sensed her looking at me.

I felt I should say something. I could ask if the man was her father. But he was right there. Was I supposed to use the past or present tense? Either way would be strange.

She stood up and came over to the bed. Placed her hand on the duvet where his chest would be. Leaned forward and put her cheek to his. When she drew herself upright again, she turned and looked at me. Tears were streaming down her cheeks.

'I was talking to him *yesterday*,' she said.

I nodded.

Fortunately, Johansen came back in at the same time. He had the little black case in his hand. The girl sat down again on the sofa, drew her legs up and wrapped her arms around them, then rested her forehead against her knees. Sobs ran through her body. Johansen took a razor and a small packet of wet wipes from the bag, closed it again and began to shave the deceased.

'Is there anything I can do?' I said as quietly as I could.

But not quietly enough.

'You can sing a hymn,' the girl said, unfolding her arms and putting her feet down on the floor. 'You look like a God-botherer. I'm sure you know loads of hymns. You can sing one for my dad.'

I didn't know what to do and looked at Johansen for help, but he was too occupied to offer me a lifeline.

'"Oh Mighty Lord, Thy Precious Name and Glory" would be good.'

'I'm afraid I don't know it,' I said.

'*For God is God, though earth no fruits were giving,*' she recited. '*God is God though mankind ceased from living.*'

Johansen drew the razor upwards under the chin a few times, gently turning the head and then cleaning the skin carefully with a wet wipe before glancing over at the girl.

'Would you like to help get him ready?' he said.

She shook her head and Johansen carried on with what he was doing, the girl looking on in apathy. Behind us the mother came back into the room with a suit and a shirt draped neatly over her arm. She put them down on the chair next to the bed and went away again without having spoken.

'Oh God, is that what he's going to be wearing?' the girl said, rising and stepping forward to snatch them up again. 'Mum?' she called out. 'Mum!'

She strode from the room and a moment later I heard her voice upstairs, loud, though the words were muffled.

Johansen glanced up at me before returning the razor to the bag. He was humming softly and took out a small pair of scissors. The boy went through the hall, the front door opened and closed, and a moment later I saw him through the window as he biked off down the hill.

Johansen drew the duvet aside, gripped the fingers of the deceased with his left hand, lifted them slightly and proceeded to cut the nails. The scissors looked ridiculously small in his big fist.

The girl marched in with a pile of clothes in her arms.

'These were his favourites,' she said. 'He wore them all the time.'

'Good,' said Johansen. 'If you could just put them down on the chair?'

A pair of worn-out jeans, a dark blue sweatshirt, a green hiking jacket.

She buried her face in both her hands and stood quite motionless, sobbing for a few seconds before turning and leaving the room again without removing her hands from her face.

Johansen moved on to the other hand.

'Outdoor type, by the looks of it,' he said, nodding towards the opposite wall where some framed photographs hung. A young man boiling coffee over a campfire, a little fair-haired girl in a red anorak snuggled up next to him. The man, the woman and the girl, a baby in tow on a pulk sledge, standing with skis and poles before a great white plain under an immense blue sky.

'But she went punk,' I said.

He put the deceased's hand down gently, and dropped the scissors into the bag.

'Give me the trousers, will you?' he said.

The girl and her mother watched from the hall as we carried the coffin out to the hearse. The boy was nowhere to be seen. We slid the coffin inside and stood with our heads bowed for a moment before Johansen went up to them, exchanged some words and shook them by the hand while I waited beside the vehicle.

As we reached the bottom of the hill, the boy came cycling towards us in the other direction and was seemingly caught unawares, his eyes suddenly wide with fright before he stood up on the pedals and accelerated away as fast as he could.

'My father died when I was eleven years old,' I said.

'I'm sorry to hear it,' said Johansen.

'No, it's all right,' I said. 'It just occurred to me when I saw the little lad there.'

'A bit out of the ordinary, this one,' he said after a pause. 'Normally when we pick them up we take them away on the stretcher and don't get them ready until they're in the cold room. But she asked for him to be made ready at home and taken out in the coffin.'

'How come?'

'I had no reason to ask.'

No more was said until we sat ourselves down in the break room an hour later. For the second day in succession I'd forgotten my lunch and when Johansen realised he shoved his own towards me again as he'd done the day before. This time I thanked him. I was starving.

Brown bread with cheese and a little squirt of cod roe from a tube.

'What you said yesterday,' I said. 'That we're actually dead and what we think of as death is what you called the second death.'

'Yes?'

'Where did you get that from?'

'Glad to have made an impression,' he said, his tongue then darting to remove a bit of butter from the corner of his mouth.

'It's still nonsense, of course, but it did make me think.'

'The ancient Egyptians weren't afraid of dying. To them, death just meant you went somewhere else instead. But there, in the realm of the dead, they *were* afraid of dying. *That* death was definitive.'

'Ah,' I said. 'So that's why you're not out drinking at nights. You stay in reading about ancient Egypt, is that it?'

'Now and again, yes.'

'But the Egyptians didn't believe *this* was the realm of the dead, did they?'

'No.'

'So who does?'

'I do.'

'What makes you think that?'

He looked at me without speaking for a moment, chewing his food slowly and methodically.

'It's something I feel,' he said at last.

Behind us the coffee had run through into the pot and I got up and poured two mugs, one with milk and lots of sugar.

'Are you being serious or messing me about?' I said as I put them down on the table.

'What do you think?'

'I don't know. I don't know you well enough.'

'But you've got intuition?'

'I think so.'

'What does it tell you?'

'That you're being serious.'

'Always trust your intuition. It's never wrong.'

We drank our coffee in silence for a while. He crumpled his sandwich paper, but instead of taking aim at the waste bin, as I would have done, he got to his feet and went over with it, sweeping then the few crumbs he'd made to the edge of the table and into the palm of his hand before dropping them too in the bin.

Everything he did was performed as if it were part of a ritual. Meticulously, with measured movements.

He glanced at the time as he sat down again.

'Have you ever seen a newborn baby?' he said, turning his attention to the tobacco pouch his hands were now opening.

'My younger brother, I suppose. But I was only a kid, so I can't really remember.'

'You'll have kids yourself one day, I shouldn't wonder. You'll see it then.'

'See what?'

'There's something in their eyes. Something old. Ancient.'

He shook his head a couple of times, as if confounded by the thought.

'It's very strong right there at the beginning,' he said. 'Then it gets weaker and weaker, and eventually, after a few weeks, perhaps, it's gone completely. It's almost as if their lives don't begin until then. As if *that's* the starting point. But what was going on *before*? That look of the old. Where did that come from?'

We sat in silence again.

I sipped my coffee and watched as he nipped the strands of excess tobacco from the ends of his cigarette before putting it between his lips. He shielded the flame in his cupped hands even though we were indoors.

'Have you got kids of your own?' I said.

He nodded.

'A girl. Camilla. She's grown up now. But I'll never forget what I saw in her eyes that time.'

'Hm,' I said.

He glanced at me, took a deep drag and exhaled. Dry grey smoke scudded across the table.

'Is there a shower here?' I said.

He shook his head.

'It's just that I'm going out after work on Friday. I think I can make it home and get changed there, only it's a bit of a bind if I've got to go back and forth in the car.'

'Can't help you with that, I'm afraid,' he said.

There was a ladder leaned up against the wall when I got home. My first thought was we'd been burgled, but when I saw where it led, to Joar's window, I realised he must have forgottten his key.

'Joar?' I shouted up the stairs.

'Yes?' he shouted back.

'Come down here a minute, will you?'

'What for?'

'Just come down here, that's all.'

A minute or so passed before he appeared in the kitchen doorway.

'Hi,' I said. 'Did you have a good day at school?'

He nodded.

'Did you bring me all the way downstairs just to ask me that?'

'No. That ladder outside . . .'

'I forgot my key. Sorry.'

'That doesn't matter. The ladder was a good idea. But what isn't such a good idea is leaving the window open!'

'I always leave it open,' he said. 'Mum's never said anything.'

'It goes without saying, not to leave the window open when we're not in! She probably never realised it's what you do.'

He rolled his eyes.

'Anyway, just remember your key next time. But that wasn't what I wanted to say. I'm meeting someone tomorrow after work. What am I supposed to do about you?'

'I can stay here on my own, can't I?'

'But you don't like being left on your own in the evenings, do you?'

'I'll be fine.'

'How about going over to Rickard's? Stay the night there? That'd be fun, wouldn't it?'

'You're going out for my sake, then, is that it?'

'Not exactly,' I said, and laughed. 'Only partly.'

'Sounds like it.'

'You could ask him now, if you like.'

'*Now?*'

'Tonight.'

'OK.'

Once he'd gone upstairs again I fried us some eggs and cutlets for our dinner. Thinking about Dad now, I couldn't see him *here* at all, suddenly it was as if he'd never known the place. I couldn't picture him in any of the rooms or even connect him with the house.

He'd grown up here, he'd lived here all his life, apart from the few years he'd spent away in the forces. I knew that, only it didn't alter anything.

One day I'd have to tell Joar what Dad had been up to.

I'd have to show him the letters.

But not tonight, exactly.

After we'd had our dinner, he phoned Rickard. It turned out they were having visitors the next day, so he wouldn't be able to go. He had no other friends he could stay the night with at such short notice.

'I can stay in on my own,' he said. 'It's not a problem.'

Mum had told me he was scared of the dark, and only the night before when I'd stepped outside he'd come out in his underpants he was so frightened.

But if he said it was all right?

It needn't be that long.

'If you're really sure you'll be OK,' I said. 'Just don't tell Mum. She wants me taking good care of you.'

'I won't tell,' he said. 'But I'll want some sweets.'

I laughed.

'I'll buy you some sweets, of course I will.'

The phone rang.

'Will it be Mum?' he said.

'I shouldn't think so,' I said, and went to answer it.

It was Lisa.

'I thought you were going to ring?' she said.

'I was just about to,' I said, waving away Joar who was standing there looking at me.

'I bet you were,' she said. 'Are you having second thoughts?'

'You must be joking!'

She laughed.

'Where do you want to meet then? What time?'

'Seven o'clock outside the library?'

'OK.'

There was a silence.

'Do you want me to do myself up?' she said then. 'I mean, if you're going to be wearing a suit as usual.'

'Ha ha.'

Another silence.

'I'll see you there, then,' she said. 'Seven o'clock outside the library.'

'Yes, see you there.'

Before I'd even hung up Joar asked who it was. He'd been standing behind the door where I couldn't see him.

'It was Lisa,' I said.

'Is that who you're meeting tomorrow?'

'As a matter of fact, it is.'

'Have you had sex with her?'

'Joar, you don't ask people things like that. Not even your own brother.'

'Why not?'

'You just don't, that's all.'

'Have you had sex with anyone?'

'Joar. That's enough.'

'You haven't, then. Otherwise you'd say.'

'Of course I have. Now stop being silly. Haven't you got homework to do or something?'

'I did it before you got in.'

'Do you want to watch the telly, then?'

He shrugged.

'There's nothing on.'

'You're right there. Oh well.'

He went back to his room. I left the dishes where they were and had a long shower. When I turned the lights off and went to bed, it was only a quarter past ten. That was when I remembered the dream I'd had about Dad, the one where he'd been down in the laundry room. The feeling I'd had then was the opposite, that it was *his* house and no one else's. The rest of us were hardly more than guests.

Should I tell Lisa about him?

Yes.

It was a good card to play. A father, now dead, who'd had a secret love affair with a woman in the Soviet Union.

The undertaking job, on the other hand: not so good.

Best not to mention it.

Mum having treatment at the Radium Hospital likewise.

How could my dream know Dad was unhappy here?

Could I have sensed it at the time, for the dream then to spell it out?

With a nine-year delay.

It was a bit far-fetched.

I'd never understand how the picture of him could remain inside me, and so vividly.

Lisa Dønnestad, will you take Syvert Løyning to stand beside you, as your husband?

No, that wasn't right.

Lisa Dønnestad, will you take Syvert Løyning, who stands beside you, as your husband?

Ha ha.

She knew nothing about me.

I knew nothing about her.

A fit-looking girl with a nice line in repartee, a bit trashy in the way she dressed. That was it.

Trust your intuition, Johansen had said.

Look how far it had got him!

After lunch the next day, while Johansen and I were having a break in the back premises, Kristian came over and said he wanted a word with me in the office.

'Thought we might have a chat. Let's call it employee development planning,' he said, indicating for me to take a seat as he sat down behind his desk.

He was in a different mood from the day before, more like he'd been on my first day, chatty and smiling, but eyes cold and dispassionate.

'Well, Syvert,' he said. 'How's your first week with us been?'

'Good,' I said.

'Any difficulties?'

'No. Not really.'

'A touch unpleasant, I'm sure, seeing all those dead people all of a sudden?'

'A bit, perhaps. But it's been fine.'

He nodded a few times, his grey eyes fixed on me.

Glad he wasn't my dad.

'Johansen has given you a glowing report. He speaks very highly of you. You've made the job your own, he says, and he's been impressed by the intuitive way you've acquitted yourself even when the situation has been demanding.'

'That's kind of him.'

'We agreed that the first week would be a trial period for us both.'

Did we? I couldn't remember, but nodded anyway.

'I've drawn up a contract of employment here. In practice we're talking about a summer job. You're heading off to university at the end of August, is that right?'

'I don't actually know yet. My mum's ill, so it depends what happens there. But probably, yes.'

'I'm sorry to hear of it,' he said. 'Anyway, as it stands the contract runs to August the fifteenth. That's a Friday. How does that sound?'

'Fine.'

'In that case all you need to do is sign.'

He pushed the document across the table and handed me a pen. I signed my name at the bottom.

'Make sure to give Unni your bank details on Monday.'

'Will do,' I said.

'Well, have a nice weekend!' he said.

I looked at him quizzically.

'Yes, you can go home early today.'

'Thanks,' I said, and got to my feet. 'Have a nice weekend yourself.'

He pushed back from the desk on his swivel chair and opened a drawer in the filing cabinet, looked up at me and gave me one of his zippy smiles before turning to flick through the files. I lifted my hand and sent a wave in the direction of Johansen, whose figure I could see behind the window, then I crossed the yard and went out through the gateway to the car I'd left parked on the other side of the street.

As on the other days when I'd got off work that week, I felt an urge to run. Kilometre after kilometre along the road, through the forests, over the fields. There was something stifling about the job. It had nothing to do with what I actually did, because there was a fair amount of physical activity during the course of a day, certainly a lot of carrying, and a lot of going about from one place to another. No, it was more one's thoughts that felt confined, as if they had to be minded all the time when someone dead was involved. If I could only look at the deceased as objects, my thoughts wouldn't have to bounce off the walls all the time and the job would be more like a removal man's.

But three months wasn't a problem, I could manage that.

I stopped off at the petrol station, filled up and bought some sweets, some crisps and a few bottles of Solo for Joar. Lucky I'd got off early, now I'd have time to shower, get changed and make Joar something to eat before it was time to go. We needed to give Mum a ring, too.

As I stood frying some fish fingers and onions, potatoes boiling in a saucepan, the phone rang. For some reason I thought it was going to be Lisa ringing to call it off, but fortunately it was only Terje wondering if I was still available for the match tomorrow seeing as I hadn't been to practice.

'Yes, count me in,' I said. 'Sorry I couldn't make it yesterday. My mum's in hospital and I'm on my own looking after Joar. And I've got a job now, so it was all a bit much, one thing and another.'

'Sounds fair enough to me,' said Terje. 'Mads was a bit pissed off, though. He wants us to let him know if we can't come.'

'I'll bear it in mind.'

'Any plans for tonight? Been a while since anyone's seen you in town.'

'I'll have to see. First priority's looking after Joar. But nothing's chiselled in stone. Where are you lot going?'

'Nowhere in particular. The usual watering holes, I imagine. See you there, hopefully!'

I upended a bag of peas into the boiling water, prodded one of the potatoes with a knife, decided they could do with another couple of minutes, scooped the fish fingers and the onions onto a dish and called for Joar, who came listlessly down the stairs shortly afterwards.

'How did you get in today?' I said, pointing the spatula at him as if to give him the third degree. 'Down the chimney?'

'Through the front door,' he said.

'You do know that when someone says something funny you're supposed to be funny back?'

'Yes.'

'So?'

'You're not as funny as you think.'

'Is that your honest opinion?'

'Yes,' he said again, and sat down at the table. I lifted the lid of the saucepan aside and poured the water out through the crack, put the saucepan down on the hotplate for a few seconds so that the moisture evaporated, transferred the potatoes into a bowl and put them out on the table.

The phone rang again.

'Can I get it?' said Joar. 'It'll be Mum.'

'Go on, then.'

'Joar Løyning speaking,' I heard him say in the hall, an echo of Mum when she answered the phone.

'Yes, I'll go and get him.'

I got to my feet.

'It's for you,' he said and sat down again. 'Lisa.'

I closed the door behind me before picking up the receiver.

'Hello?'

'Hi, it's Lisa. I'm afraid I can't come tonight after all. I'm really sorry. It's not because I don't want to.'

'What a shame,' I said. 'I've had a shower and everything!'

'Don't you normally?'

'Only on special occasions.'

She laughed a bit, then went quiet.

'I don't usually let people down like this.'

'What's got in the way? If you don't mind me asking?'

'My little sister. She was meant to be staying with her dad this weekend. Only he just cancelled and my mum's out. So I've got to stay in and look after her.'

'I understand,' I said. 'I'm looking after my own little brother for a couple of weeks at the moment. How old's your sister?'

'Ten. How old's your brother?'

'Twelve. Old enough to be left on his own.'

'Sølvi isn't, not yet.'

'No. Ten's not old enough.'

She went quiet again.

'I could come up to yours, if you want?' I said.

The silence persisted.

'It's not really convenient,' she said at last.

'That's all right,' I said. 'Maybe we could see each other tomorrow instead? Same time, same place?'

'I've got to look after Sølvi tomorrow as well. I'm really sorry.'

'OK. I understand.'

'You're really nice.'

'Nice? Me? That's what you think. I'm seething inside. I'm going to have to beat my brother up after I put the phone down.'

'The way you beat Kjell up, you mean?'

'I *could* have beaten him up, if I'd wanted. You do realise that?'

'Right,' she said.

I felt annoyed. She took me for a weakling. I wasn't. But I didn't want her to know, so I just laughed.

She went quiet again.

'When do you think we can see each other, then?'

'Not next weekend, but the weekend after would be good,' she said. 'I'd understand if you gave up on me.'

'I'm not giving up, not ever,' I said. 'Same time, same place?'

She laughed.

'Yes.'

'Have a nice evening, then. And say hello to Sølvi from me!'

'I will. Say hello to your brother.'

We hung up and I went back into the kitchen where Joar's dark eyes looked up at me.

'Good news! Looks like I'm staying in tonight anyway!' I said as I sat down. Joar lifted two fish fingers onto his plate, then a couple of onion rings, a potato and some peas.

'Has she chucked you?'

'Not at all. We just rearranged, that's all. But seriously, Joar, *five* peas!'

'I don't like peas.'

'You've got to eat. Two fish fingers and a potato aren't going to fill you up.'

'I'm not hungry.'

'Well, I am,' I said, and shovelled some onto my plate. 'You know the brain uses up fifty per cent of the body's energy, don't you? So the less you eat, the poorer your thinking's going to be.'

'Is that why you eat like a horse? To improve your thinking?'

'That's right, yes.'

'I'm sorry to have to disappoint you, but it's a myth. The correct figure is around twenty per cent.'

'You speak for yourself. *My* brain uses up fifty per cent!'

He smiled, though mostly to himself, without looking at me.

Did he really think I was stupid?

It annoyed the hell out of me.

But why should I care what a twelve-year-old thought about me?

I cut into a potato and pulled away a piece of the skin with my knife. Joar had put a knob of butter on his, which had already begun to melt.

Her excuse seemed genuine enough. She had to look after her little sister. Whether she was sorry about it was another matter.

Everything told me she was.

A tingle of joy ran through me.

It felt like I'd got closer to her.

She had a younger sister, I knew now.

She was at home looking after her at the same time as I was sitting thinking about her.

Why hadn't it been convenient for me to go round and see her?

It wouldn't have felt right, not with her sister there.

'By the way, our class are having a party tomorrow,' said Joar.

'Oh?'

'At Elise's.'

'How come you didn't say?'

'I forgot.'

'Do you want me to take you there in the car?'

He shook his head.

'Are you going to go on your bike?'

He nodded.

'Will Monica be there?'

'Merethe, you mean?'

'The one who fancies you.'

'That's Merethe. Everyone will be there. So she will be too.'

'I see!' I said.

He grimaced as he got to his feet and took his plate over to the side.

'Joar?' I said before he went up the stairs.

He turned round.

'What do you want to do tonight? I bought some sweets thinking you'd be on your own. We can share them if you want, and watch the telly.'

'Can do,' he said.

I went and got the paper and looked at the TV page to see what was on. Nothing to get worked up about. Light entertainment and a bit of jazz. Then there was something called *Right Now* with special guest Dario Fo, whoever he was.

Italian playwright.

I might have known.

If they'd had Dino Zoff instead, I might have watched it.

Zoff. Scirea. Gentile. Collovati. Bergomi. Conti. Tardelli. And of course Paolo Rossi.

If I ever had a son, I'd call him Paolo.

Paolo Løyning.

OK, maybe it wasn't that good.

Pål?

Pål Løyning. That wasn't bad. I could tell him he'd been named after Paolo.

I did the dishes and swept the crumbs up off the floor, took the rubbish out and looked around to see if there was anything else that needed doing. I was tired, it had been a long week, but I was restless too, and the thought of staying in just didn't appeal.

What was it Dad had said?

Restlessness was the body's expression of longing.

He wanted away from here. I didn't.

The restlessness I felt was different. I longed only for Lisa.

What a bloody idiot he'd been. Letting himself get taken in by that Russian woman. He'd lost his head.

I decided to go over to the barn to see if Mum had kept the letters that must have come after Dad had died, and put them among his things. Not that I thought she would have done.

I stood for a minute in front of the house and looked at the sky in the west, where the sun was a reddish glow. All was still. The evening light embraced the trees. Here and there, columns of insects swarmed between the boughs. The fields and the slopes of the ridge seemed almost luminous.

How perfectly organised it all was.

The sky was a roof above us, so that we didn't have to think about the cold and dreadful void beyond. The earth was the floor beneath us, so we didn't have to worry about the burning core of metal below. And all we saw was a single room at a time.

The field, the hills, the horizon, the sky, the sun.

And if I turned round, the house.

But how did we get in here?

Into this room?

Out in the field, the deer appeared, emerging one by one from the edge of the woods, pausing to survey the landscape, walking on, pausing again, grazing on whatever it was they ate. I went over to the barn and rummaged through the boxes again without finding anything. It was as I'd expected. Mum would have cottoned on to what the Russian letters were all about. She wasn't stupid.

Poor Mum.

I went back in and rang her up. After being put through to first one place, then another, I eventually heard her voice at the other end.

'How are you doing?' I said.

'I'm doing fine,' she said. 'It's like a hotel here. Breakfast in bed and coffee whenever you want.'

'It's not as if they can do things any different though, is it? Breakfast in bed, I mean. Are you feeling any pain?'

'A bit, when I sit up. Are you both all right?'

'Yes, we're fine.'

'Is Joar in?'

'He's in his room as usual. Do you want a word?'

'Yes, that'd be nice.'

'OK, hang on a sec.'

I held the receiver against my chest and shouted his name up the
stairs.

'What?' he shouted back.

'Mum's on the phone!'

The next instant he came bombing down. I poured myself some coffee and took it with me outside, dragged the bench into the sun and sat
down.

Funny how he could be so independent and yet such a mother's boy
at the same time.

A new tingle of joy went through me.

Lisa.

She was out there somewhere, at that very moment.

I ambled over to the garage, found some shooting targets and hung
them up in the trees behind the barn before going back to the house to
get the air rifle. Joar was still on the phone and turned his head to look
at me when I came in.

It seemed like they had a lot to talk about, the two of them.

Passing through the hall again on my way back out, the rifle in my
hand, I waved for him to come with me. He nodded, indicating that
he'd come when he was finished on the phone.

I carried on, lay down prone behind the barn and took aim at a
target.

The smell of warm grass in the sun — was there anything better?

It felt good, too, to lie on my stomach on the ground, to feel my own
weight, a sense of place.

Pop!

Pop!

Pop!

I got to my feet and went over to see. How was I going to get through
the next two weeks? I examined the target against the dark blue sky.

A two, top right. Two misses.

Joar appeared.

'Your go!' I said.

He nodded.

I handed him the rifle and he lay down and took aim.

Pop!

Pop!

'Nice,' I said. 'Let's go and have a look.'

He got up.

'I remember Dag and me shooting with Dad one time,' I said. 'It was the only time I saw him get angry.'

We walked up to the target.

'Why did he get angry?' said Joar, the gun pointing at the ground.

'I was lying down, about to take aim. Dag got the idea he wanted to look down the barrel. Dad was standing over by the barn there. When he saw what was happening, he *screamed* and came running.'

'It's only an airgun,' said Joar.

'But still dangerous at close quarters! He could have lost an eye.'

'He didn't, though.'

'No, he didn't, fortunately. I'm glad I've not got that on my record!'

We stopped and studied the target.

'Wow,' I said. 'An eight and a nine.'

'That's a ten,' said Joar. 'Can't you see? It's just nicked the white.'

'So it has! You should start doing this properly, join a club. You're really good.'

'It's boring.'

'No, it's not. It's fun!'

'Now, maybe. But not after ten thousand shots.'

'For all you know, it might be the other way round. You might get hooked.'

'I doubt it. What did you get?'

'A two and two misses.'

He looked at me and beamed.

'Maybe it's you who should join a club. You could do with the practice!'

'Ha ha.'

From the other side of the barn, a cat came sauntering. It was black, so it was probably the same one that had been here before. It stopped and looked at us with its narrow yellow eyes.

'Puss, puss, puss,' I said, crouching down with a hand outstretched.

It sat down, licked its paw and began to wash behind its ears.

I stood up again.

'Do you want another go?' I said.

'Not really,' he said.

'It's a shame to be cooped up inside in this weather. How about going for a drive somewhere?'

He shook his head and handed me the rifle.

The cat trotted after us as we went round the barn. It was probably after some food. We crossed the yard and sure enough it sprinted ahead of us to the door.

Joar pulled up.

'Black cats are bad luck,' he said.

'Don't be daft! It's only a cat! It's not its fault it's black.'

It lay down and luxuriated on the step.

'Besides, it's only when a black cat crosses the road, isn't it? And this isn't a road!'

'I don't like it,' he said, but walked on nevertheless. The cat darted in as soon as I opened the door and I gave it a fish finger on a plate. It sniffed at it, then straightened up without touching it.

'You're a bit picky, aren't you?' I said, and opened a tin of tuna instead. It started purring and rubbed against my legs.

'Can I have a Solo?' said Joar, who was standing in the doorway.

'Course you can.'

The cat set about the tuna. Joar took a Solo from the fridge, opened it and gulped down a mouthful while standing by the worktop.

'So you don't believe in God, but you do believe that black cats are bad luck?'

I laughed.

'It's two different things,' he said.

'No, it's not,' I said.

I got myself a Solo, too.

'Do you want some crisps?'

He nodded.

'Come and sit outside, then,' I said, taking the bag with me. I moved the table to where there were still some rays and we sat down and crunched in our separate chairs, occasionally sipping our pop.

This was what it'd be like if Mum died, I thought to myself, though of course I said nothing. He was much closer to her than I'd ever been.

SYVERT391

He hadn't asked me a single question about my new job.

'It's a fine evening,' I said. 'Don't you think?'

'Yes,' he said.

The deer had gone. The field lay empty and still. Here and there, the soil had taken on a reddish tinge in the last of the sunlight.

What would Dad have done if it had been him and me sitting here?

He'd have done something, and I'd have watched or done the same next to him.

Hang on. The moped!

I looked at Joar as he sat with the bottle in one hand, his other arm draped over the back of the chair as he gazed lazily in the direction of the road and the river.

'Do you fancy a go on the moped?'

He turned his head to face me.

'Drive it, you mean?'

'Yes.'

'Am I allowed?'

'You are on the property here, yes. You can drive the car as well, if you want.'

'But I don't know how to work the gears or anything.'

'You can learn, then, can't you?!'

'It would be fun . . .' he said, though rather tentatively.

'What, the moped or the car?'

'The car?'

'OK. Come on.'

Awkward and uncertain he sat in the driver's seat next to me while I explained to him what to do. Press the clutch down, turn the ignition, put it into gear, then release the clutch slowly at the same time as pressing down gently on the accelerator.

I handed him the key.

'Is this where it goes?' he said, glancing at me inquisitively.

'That's right. Now turn it. But remember the clutch!'

He started the engine and looked at me again, this time with a smile on his face.

'Now put it into first gear, release the clutch and press down gently on the accelerator.'

'OK.'

He did as instructed and the car lurched forward and stalled.

'Try again,' I said. 'Easy on the clutch.'

He gave it another go. This time he was too heavy on the accelerator, the rev counter's pointer leapt as the engine whined. He panicked and stepped on the brake, and we stalled again.

'That's all right!' I said. 'Try again.'

'I don't think I want to,' he said.

'You've only just started! Practice makes perfect, you know. We'll be whizzing around here before you know it.'

'I don't want to.'

He removed the key, handed it to me and got out.

'Joar!' I said.

But he went back inside without turning round. I went after him, stepping into the hall just as his bedroom door closed.

He must have been frightened by the noise of the engine, the feeling of not being in control.

Just because I thought it was fun didn't mean he had to.

I went back out and got the crisps and the two bottles of pop, switched the telly on and sat myself down on the sofa.

The news had just started. The main story was the strike. They were interviewing a woman taxi driver and asked if she'd been busier since it started. She said she hadn't. It sounded like she was from Risør, somewhere round there. The next story was about Chernobyl. The first pictures were already familiar. A convoy of red lorries driving through forest, on their way to the nuclear plant. So it was still on fire! Incredible. Firemen stood hosing water onto the reactor while the reporter said they were digging a tunnel under the buildings so as to seal them off with cement. There was an interview with one of the workers. A face mask dangled under his chin, it looked like the kind surgeons used.

They had to be crackling with radioactivity, all of them.

What was happening?

A fire that couldn't be put out, what did that mean?

Asya could be living somewhere near there.

Her son Sasha would be about twenty now.

No chance she'd kept Dad's baby. Or was there?

If that was what she'd meant by something fantastic having happened.

Joar's door opened and I heard him come down the stairs into the kitchen.

He rummaged in the cupboards.

'What are you looking for?' I called out.

'The sweets,' he said. 'Have you hidden them?'

'They're in the fridge!'

A moment later he came into the living room.

'Who puts sweets in the fridge?' he said, sitting down next to me clutching the big paper bag full of pick and mix.

'There's chocolate in there, too. Didn't want it to melt.'

On the television, Margaret Thatcher came down the steps of a plane in the dark. She was on an official visit to Israel. The first British prime minister to have been there since the Israeli state was established, they said.

'Are we going to see Mum next weekend?' he said.

'Yes,' I said. 'Don't I get any of those?'

He gave me one of his dark looks. He didn't like sharing, but he couldn't get away from the fact that I was the one who'd bought them, so he held the bag out reluctantly.

We watched the light entertainment programme, but after a few minutes we exchanged glances and switched it off.

'Give me a shout if you want some supper later on,' I said. 'I think I'll go upstairs to my room.'

Lying on my bed with my hands clasped behind my head, the window open to the evening, I thought about Lisa as I listened to the birds that still chirped now and then, the distant swoosh of occasional cars going past on the road. Or perhaps I felt her more than thought about her. What filled me weren't thoughts, but the most compelling emotions. Yet there was an undertow too, something that pulled in a different direction. It said she didn't feel the same about me, that the flow of emotions went one way only, from me to her, not from her to me. She liked me, she'd told me so, and I felt it too, but she didn't want to go out with me. She'd told me that as well.

Was I meant to be just a friend? A puppy dog that wagged its tail whenever I was around her?

I didn't know.

Dad had known. There was no doubt about what Asya had felt for him.

What about Mum?

She wasn't exactly the type who waved her feelings around in front of people.

She'd more likely shoot herself than say she *loved* anyone.

Once, she told me she liked me.

I supposed she did.

It was hard to tell.

Did I like her?

Go on, Syvert. You can say it.

I got up and went over to the window, stood with my hands on the sill and looked out. The sunlight had crept over the hillsides, but still seeped into the valley. Not a breath of wind. Not a cloud in the sky.

I found myself thinking of horses in a meadow next to a wood and couldn't remember where the image was from at first, whether a film or some memory of childhood, but then it came to me, it was the horses outside the old people's home.

Their movements, fine and highly strung.

Perhaps death created a disturbance in the air, a soulquake, or whatever you might call it, the smallest of tremors that they detected without knowing what they were, causing them suddenly to quiver and toss their heads and bolt away across the field.

But there wasn't a single reason to believe it!

Death was the extinguishing of life. It was what happened when a body could no longer do the job of a body and therefore ground to a halt.

I drew myself upright and breathed deeply a few times to still my trembling chest.

I should go out. Meet up with Terje and that lot.

Joar would be all right on his own.

He was meant to be on his own tonight anyway.

But everything would still be intolerable, even if I went out.

I went downstairs into the kitchen, opened the fridge without knowing what I was looking for, then closed it again. The cat was lying on the sofa in the living room, asleep with its head on its paws, the cheeky thing. I put the telly on again and ran through the frequencies to see if I could pick up the Danish channel. In periods of atmospheric high pressure we'd often get a decent picture from Denmark.

There it was.

Two women were sitting in a restaurant speaking English. The colours were a bit blurred and the picture gave the odd shudder, but it was certainly watchable.

I went and got the paper to see what was on. A TV movie called *Ann and Debbie*. It didn't look like it was up to much. But after that there was a proper film called *The Detective*, starring Frank Sinatra.

'Joar?' I called out.

'What?' he called back.

'Come down here.'

I could almost hear him sigh. But he came down all the same.

'There's an American film on Danish TV in a bit. Do you want to watch it with me?'

'Couldn't you have come upstairs and asked me that?'

'Don't be so irritable.'

'I'm not irritable. It's logic, that's all. You've dragged me down here, now I've got to go back up and come down again when the film starts. If you'd come upstairs and asked to begin with, you could have called when it started and saved me the bother.'

I laughed.

'What are you talking about? It's not like you live at the North Pole, you know!'

Just then, a car came up from the road.

It could only be Terje or Gjert.

I went to the window and looked out.

A white Escort pulled up in front of the house.

I'd never seen it before.

'Who is it?' said Joar.

'Haven't a clue,' I said, and went to open the door. Joar came after me.

It was Lisa. Lisa, stepping out of the passenger side with a big smile on her face.

What was this?

'It's not inconvenient, is it?' she said. 'If it is, tell me and I can get a lift back straight away!'

'No, it's not inconvenient at all!' I said.

She leaned into the car and said something to whoever was driving, a girl, as far as I could see, took out a small rucksack, closed the door and came towards me as the car reversed and Joar retreated up the stairs.

She was wearing a dark blue-and-white-striped T-shirt under her pale blue denim jacket. She held the rucksack in her hand.

'Hi,' she said, and gave me a hug.

She was bubbling.

And how gorgeous she smelled!

'Hi,' I said. 'I wasn't expecting this, I must say. What a lovely surprise!'

'I hope so!' she said. 'People have gone out of their way! Aren't you going to ask me in?'

'Oh, yes, sorry!' I said, and stepped backwards into the hall. 'I'm a bit flabbergasted, that's all.'

'Flabbergasted?' she said, taking off her jacket now and hanging it up on the peg.

'At seeing you here all of a sudden.'

'I realise that. It was more the choice of word I meant. I don't think I've ever heard anyone actually say *flabbergasted* before.'

'Oh, we say it all the time here,' I said. 'It's a local thing.'

We stood and smiled at each other.

'So this is where you live, is it?'

'Correct.'

There was a little silence.

'Can I get you something? Coffee? A beer?'

'A beer would be nice,' she said as she bent down to undo her shoelaces.

'Beer it is, then,' I said. 'Make yourself at home in the living room and I'll go and get us some.'

I went down the stairs into the basement and switched the light on, then stood for a moment to get my head round what was happening.

She'd come to my house.

No one had forced her.

She was *here*!

It looked like she was planning to stay the night. Her lift had gone and she'd brought a rucksack with her.

I couldn't ask her. All I could do was take it for granted.

But what did she want exactly?

I couldn't ask her that either.

I undid the top button of my shirt and straightened my hair a bit before picking up two bottles of beer, one in each hand, and hurrying back up the stairs again.

She was sitting on the sofa stroking the cat that lay with its eyes closed and its head tipped back.

'Nice cat you've got,' she said. 'Very affectionate.'

'Actually, it's not ours,' I said, putting her beer down on the coffee table. 'It just comes round every once in a while. My brother thinks it brings bad luck.'

'Was it your brother I saw go up the stairs just before?'

'That was Joar, yes.'

I sat down and was about to take a swig when I realised the cap was still on.

'Need to get a bottle opener,' I said, getting to my feet again.

'Is it all right if I smoke?'

'Yes, of course. I'll bring an ashtray as well.'

Should I sit down beside her when I came back?

It would be a bit unnatural if we were going to talk.

'You're not an alcoholic, I see,' she said after I opened her bottle and handed it to her.

'How do you mean?'

'You'd have drunk your Christmas brew by now, if you were.'

'Ha ha! You're right there. No, I'm not an alcoholic, not me.'

I laughed again.

She took a packet of Prince Mild from the bag she'd put on the floor next to the sofa, lit a cigarette and looked at me with a smile as she blew out the smoke.

'So, what happened?' I said. 'Didn't you have to look after your sister?'

'I did, but I managed to bring in some help. I've got two cousins who live just down the road. They're twins, the same age as me. I felt so guilty after I'd talked to you on the phone. You'd had a shower and everything! So I rang them up and asked if they could do me a favour. Luckily, they didn't mind at all.'

'I'm glad,' I said. 'But you'd no reason to feel guilty. I could quite understand you having to look after her.'

'It wasn't just that. I really wanted to see you as well.'

We looked at each other.

The same thing happened again. It was as if her eyes swallowed me up completely.

She looked down, and smiled a bit self-consciously.

'Cheers,' I said, reaching across the table with my beer in my hand.

'Cheers,' she said, and chinked her bottle against mine.

'Are they identical twins?'

'No. They hardly even look like sisters.'

'What about your sister? Does she look like you?'

She shook her head.

'She looks like her dad. And I look a bit like mine, I think. That's what they say, anyway. What about your brother? Do I get to meet him?'

'He's a bit shy. Or not shy, exactly. He just likes to keep himself to himself. But we can go upstairs and say hello, if you want. He could do with learning some social conventions.'

I got up, grasping the chance of an interlude, something pragmatic to ease the tension. Lisa stubbed her cigarette out and came with me.

'That's the kitchen,' I said as we went past. 'The bedrooms are upstairs.'

'It's a nice house you've got,' she said as we went up the stairs.

I knocked on Joar's door. Lisa stood beside me, so close I felt myself getting a hard-on.

'Come in,' his voice said.

I stuck a hand in my pocket and opened the door with the other.

'Say hello to Lisa,' I said.

He was sitting at his desk, his head turned towards us.

'We've already spoken on the phone,' he said and came over, shaking her hand with a smile. 'Nice to meet you, Lisa.'

Where on earth had he learned to behave like that?

'Nice to meet you, too,' said Lisa, smiling back. 'You're in seventh, is that right?'

He nodded.

'Enjoy it while you can. I'm in second at the gymnas, and we're up to our ears in homework.'

'Joar finds school easy,' I said. 'You don't really need to do homework, do you?'

Immediately, I realised it sounded like I was assuming Lisa *didn't* find it easy.

I laughed awkwardly.

'You must be good at school as well,' I said. 'Going to the Cath and all!'

Joar and Lisa exchanged glances.

'Not that it's *that* special, of course,' I said. 'I mean it's still just an ordinary gymnas, isn't it?'

'No need to backpedal any more,' said Lisa.

'Your chain's already come off,' said Joar.

'Is it that obvious?' I said.

'Not at all,' said Lisa, and placed her hand gently on my forearm. 'Is the bathroom in there?'

'Yes,' I said.

'Just need the loo,' she said. 'Nice meeting you, Joar. See you later!'

She closed the bathroom door behind her and I went into my room.

All of a sudden I could see what it looked like.

A lad's room.

I snatched up the items of sports clothing I'd dumped on the floor and tossed them all in the cupboard, then opened the windows.

The toilet flushed.

'This is my room, by the way,' I said, stepping out onto the landing again as the bathroom door opened and she came out.

She went and stood in the doorway and looked in.

'I'm a bit too old to be living at home,' I said. 'I know that. Only I was in the forces a while and I'm starting at uni in the autumn.'

'Oh, where are you going?'

'I'm not sure.'

'Haven't you got in anywhere yet?'

'I'm going to do the *Ex.phil.* first. You can do that anywhere. Are you hungry?'

'Not particuarly.'

'OK. Just say the word when you are and I'll rustle something up.'

We went downstairs into the living room again. Outside, the light was getting dim.

'Your brother's nice,' she said as she sat down on the sofa.

'He is, yes.'

'Where have your parents gone? You said you were on your own a couple of weeks?'

'Yes, well. My dad's dead. And my mum's in hospital.'

'Oh no,' she said.

'No, no, it's all right, really. It sounds terrible, I know. But Dad died when I was little. And Mum's just had an operation. So it's like that. But everything's fine.'

'Glad to hear it,' she said.

'Yes. Yes.'

She'd been effervescent when she first got here, so vibrant and brimming with joy, I'd never seen her like that before.

Only now she wasn't. It was obvious.

I had to do something in a hurry.

She'd put her hand on my arm. That had to mean something.

But she'd never taken back what she said in the car that time, about not being interested in me like that.

I glanced at her. She was sitting with her legs drawn up underneath her at one end of the sofa. Her tender face with its blue eyes that sometimes didn't seem to belong there, hard and derisive as they could be.

Why had she come?

She put her bottle down on the table and I saw that it was empty.

'Do you want another?'

'If you're having?' she said, and reached for her cigarettes.

I took the two empties into the kitchen and fetched two more beers from the basement. That left only one. There was nothing else to drink in the house.

'What was that suit about, anyway?' she said when I came back into the living room. 'You said it was a long story.'

I opened the beers and handed her one.

'Ah, that,' I said. 'Not sure I want to go into it, really.'

'You've got to now!' she said. 'What is it you don't want to tell me?'

'You saw that piece they did on me in the paper about being unemployed, didn't you?'

'Yes?'

'Well, it was like this. I had no money and no job. Then Mum got ill and it was like from bad to worse, if you know what I mean? I was going round looking for work everywhere, a sports shop, the factory up here, only there was nothing doing. That's when this friend of mine, Vegard, tells me he's got an uncle who's . . . well, he runs a business in town and was looking for someone. So I phoned him up and got offered a job there until after the summer. That's why I was in a suit.'

'What sort of business?'

'Just a business, you know . . .'

'No, I don't! You haven't said yet. What does this uncle do that's such a secret. Is he a contract killer or something?'

'Not far off.'

'You're being really annoying now, you realise that, don't you?'

'OK, so I've got a job at a funeral director's.'

She looked at me while slowly blowing out smoke.

'Blimey,' she said. 'I'd never have guessed that. A funeral director's?'

'I know, it doesn't come across that well. Not at all, in fact. But that's what it is.'

'It sounds like a hard job. Is it?'

'Not really.'

'So you've seen a lot of dead people now?'

'A few, yes.'

'Blimey,' she said again. 'I never thought I'd be going out with an undertaker . . .'

'I wonder what your cool friends are going to say about it.'

'What do you mean?' she said, her eyes fixing me with a stare.

'The lads I saw you with outside the school. They looked pretty cool.'

'They are pretty cool, as it happens. But what's it to you?'

I shrugged.

'Nothing.'

She didn't say anything.

Now she was more like the Lisa I knew from the first few times I'd seen her. Sneering and cold as ice.

But she said *going out with*.

Probably just being funny.

For the first time in my life, I wished I smoked.

'There's a film on Danish TV,' I said. 'I was going to watch it with Joar. Shall I switch it on?'

'If you want,' she said. 'What kind of film is it?'

'It's called *The Detective*, with Frank Sinatra. I haven't seen it, so I don't know if it's any good. But we could give it a go?'

She didn't say anything, so I got up and switched it on.

It was slightly blurred and a bit flickery, but not enough to stop us watching it.

'Aren't you going to fetch Joar?' she said when I sat down again.

'Oh yes, I forgot,' I said.

He was lying on the bed reading when I opened his door.

'Lisa and I are going to watch that film,' I said. 'Do you want to watch it with us?'

'Yes,' he said, and was on his feet so quickly it was as if he'd only been waiting to be asked.

Downstairs, I sat in the armchair again. But when Joar sat down next to her on the sofa it felt all wrong. Still, it was too late to do anything about it. I couldn't exactly ask him to swap places.

'Have you listened much to Sinatra?' I said as the film started.

'Sinatra, no,' she said. 'Why, have you?'

'No.'

Nothing else was said for a while. Normally, I'd be passing comment all the time when watching a film with others, but I knew some people found it annoying and I guessed Lisa would be one, sitting quite still as she watched, so I did the same.

If it had just been Joar and me, I'd have wound him up about all the half-naked women in the film, but with Lisa there he'd have died of embarrassment and I certainly didn't want to make him feel bad, the little know-all.

About halfway through, Lisa stood up and left the room, I assumed to go to the loo again. With her out of earshot, I turned to Joar.

'I'm looking forward to me and Merethe sitting on the sofa watching a film with you here,' I said.

'Ha ha,' he said. 'Very funny.'

'What do you think of Lisa?'

'She seems nice.'

I laughed.

'That's not what I meant!'

Lisa came back in and sat down on the sofa again.

'What do you reckon so far?' I said. 'Any good?'

'Yes, it's good,' she said.

'Are you hungry yet?'

She shook her head and gave a little smile.

I turned back to face the telly and we carried on watching the film in silence.

Something about her told me she didn't want to be here any longer.

How did that come about?

It was only me and her and Joar!

The thought uplifted me slightly. It wasn't exactly magic that was required. All I had to do was get a bit closer. Make her laugh and feel more at ease.

If only there was something we could do together.

Instead of sitting here.

It was all going to fall apart.

I turned and glanced at her. She pretended not to notice.

What was she thinking?

Had she changed her mind because of the undertaker's job?

Had she?

She could have done.

But it was only a summer job! It said nothing about the person I was.

At last the film finished. Joar said goodnight and went up to his room. Lisa and I stayed where we were in the living room. I angled my chair towards the coffee table. It'd be too obvious if I got up and sat next to her. She lit a cigarette.

'Can I cadge one off you?' I said.

'Of course. I didn't know you smoked?'

'Just the odd one now and again, that's all.'

'I'm impressed,' she said. 'I'm more the all-or-nothing sort myself.'

I took one from the packet, put it between my lips and lit up with the lighter she handed me.

I'd only ever smoked once before. Round the back of the barn with Dag when I was eleven. It was a lark until we inhaled. We felt so ill we ended up throwing the whole packet away.

I coughed as the smoke caught the back of my throat, and my mouth filled with the most disgusting taste.

Lisa sat watching me.

'I haven't had one for a while,' I said. 'These are good and strong.'

I inhaled again, convulsing once more into a coughing fit. This time it brought tears to my eyes.

She laughed.

'Who do you think you're kidding?' she said. 'You've never smoked before in your life, have you?'

I shook my head and coughed again.

'It's horrible,' I said.

'Why don't you put it out, then?' she said. 'You don't have to smoke just because I do!'

'I think you might be right,' I said, and followed her suggestion.

At least it had made her laugh.

'Have you got any music?'

'My record player's in my room. I don't think you'll like my records much, though.'

'Don't underestimate me, thank you very much. What do you listen to?'

'Heavy metal.'

'Is that all?'

'Yes.'

'Hm. You don't look the type, if you ask me.'

'Because I don't wear black and haven't got a studded belt and long hair?'

'That too.'

'Do you like heavy metal? Or am I overestimating you now?'

She smiled.

'A bit.'

'So you don't, then?'

'Not much. But I grew up with power ballads.'

'At home?'

'You must be joking. No, in cars and at parties.'

'Sounds just like here. What *do* you like?'

'All sorts.'

'Such as?'

'I'm quite into Pink Floyd. That one with "Shine on You Crazy Diamond" on it. *Wish You Were Here*. And I like the Doors. And Janis Joplin.'

She got up and went over to the window. Stood there for a bit, staring out into the dusk.

'What are you looking at?'

'Nothing in particular.'

Even the thought of stepping up behind her and putting my arms around her was enough to give me the first stirrings of a hard-on.

She'd be able to feel it pressing against her.

'Do you run this place as a farm?' she said then, turning her head to look at me.

'No, most of the land was sold off years ago. We've still got a bit of our own, but we let it out.'

'No risk of me ending up a farmer's wife, then?'

I laughed.

'No. Not if you don't want to.'

She turned to look out of the window again, her hands flat on the windowsill.

I went up and stood next to her.

'The river's just down there, across the road,' I said. 'Joar and I go canoeing quite a lot. There's a stretch of rapids a bit further upstream, which is fun.'

'Aha,' she said, glancing at me.

'It's OK for me to stay the night here, isn't it? I forgot to ask.'

'Of course! Where do you want to sleep? You've seen most of the house now.'

'Your room?'

I nodded.

'There's a spare mattress over in the barn. I might as well go and get it now. It's quite late already. Are you tired?'

'A bit,' she said.

'OK,' I said. 'I'll be back before you know I'm gone!'

I slipped my feet into my sandals, switched the outside light on and crossed over the yard, conscious of myself and all my movements, assuming she was watching me from the window.

Ending up a farmer's wife.

She'd been joking, but the underlying assumption had perhaps been genuine enough. The idea that we were going to stay together.

I went up the ramp and opened the big doors, turned on the light and picked up the mattress that stood leaned on its end against the far wall with a rug underneath. I clamped it under my arm, switched the light off and closed the doors again before lugging it back to the house.

'I'll get you some bedlinen as well!' I announced, stepping into the hall, then dragging the mattress up the stairs and putting it down on the floor in my room.

She came up after me.

'Do you need any help?' she said.

'No, I can manage.'

'I'll go to the bathroom then and get ready.'

'Great!' I said.

I shoved the mattress a bit further from the bed so there was a gap in between, and put the sheet on. That done, I stuffed one end of the duvet into the cover, and once the corners were in place I gripped them from the outside and gave it all a shake until the cover dropped down and I was able to put the other two corners into place too.

The linen smelled fresh and gave me a feeling of satisfaction.

I could hear her brushing her teeth in the bathroom as I closed the windows and then sat down on the edge of the bed to wait until she was finished.

She came in wearing a big white T-shirt and smiled at me.

'I'll go and brush my teeth,' I said.

She'd left her little rucksack up against the wall. Her toothbrush was in the glass along with ours.

I reckoned it'd be better to get undressed in the bedroom instead of going in in my undies. I didn't have *that* much control.

She was sitting on the chair by the desk when I went back in, with her legs crossed.

'Shall I turn the light off?' I said.

'If you want.'

Her white T-shirt stood out in the murk.

I smiled at her as I sat down on the edge of the bed and started getting undressed the way I always did, while she turned slightly away and stared out of the window in the direction of the luminous ribbon of the road lighting.

Instead of dumping my clothes in a pile, I folded them neatly before getting under the duvet and lying down on my back with my hands clasped behind my head.

'Aren't you going to lie down?' I said.

'Yes,' she said.

I gazed at the ceiling as she got to her feet, sensing her movements from the corner of my eye, the way she drew the duvet back, sat and then lay down.

'Is the mattress OK?'

'It's fine. Thanks.'

A motorbike roared in the distance, tearing through the flatland.

I should have taken a chance and put my arms around her before she got into bed. She might have said no, but it could have gone either way.

Too late now.

'Can I use the phone in the morning?' she said. 'So they can come and pick me up?'

'Yes, of course,' I said. 'But I can take you home, if you want?'

'I've already arranged with them,' she said. 'We just didn't say what time.'

'OK,' I said.

We lay there in silence.

I couldn't think of anything more to say. At least, nothing that wouldn't sound stupid given the situation.

'Goodnight, then,' I said after a while.

'Goodnight,' she said.

Even though I was acutely aware of her presence and every little movement she made seemed to transmit itself to me, I must have fallen asleep straight away, because the next thing I knew the sun was pouring in through the window and her bed was empty.

I jumped to my feet, put my trousers on hastily and pulled on my shirt.

She wasn't in the living room or the kitchen, and she wasn't in the bathroom either when I went back up to check. Her toothbrush and rucksack were gone.

But the coffee maker was on, the pot was half full and the little lamp shone red.

Maybe she was sitting outside in the fine weather?

I poured myself a cup and went out to see.

There she was. Sitting at the garden table with her mug in front of her, a cigarette in her hand and her rucksack leaned against the table leg.

'Been up long?' I said, and sat down on the chair next to her. 'Thanks for making coffee! Did you sleep all right?'

'Not that long, and not really,' she said. 'But I'm going home now. They should be here soon.'

'OK.'

She said nothing more, and I sipped my coffee.

'It's not just cocoa you know how to make,' I said.

At the same moment, a car slowed down on the main road and turned up the drive, the sound of its engine rising as it approached.

'That'll be them,' I said.

She stubbed her cigarette out in the ashtray and got to her feet, put the packet in her pocket and picked up her rucksack.

I went with her round to the front. The white Escort pulled slowly up. Lisa waved to the driver, the same girl as before, by the looks of it, and then turned to face me.

'Look after yourself,' she said, and gave me a quick hug before opening the passenger door and getting in.

I followed the car with my eyes until it turned onto the road and drew away. I went back and got her coffee mug, then went quietly inside to make some breakfast.

YEVGENY

The young man who could only be the new helper was standing outside the office building when I came into work that morning. I turned into the parking area, and although it was as good as empty, I picked a space at the far end just so I'd have time to give him the once-over. He didn't know who I was yet.

The snow still lay heaped up along the verges, packed hard after the long winter, glittering in the sunlight. The asphalt was wet, and behind the trees the ice on the river was retreating, the water gliding green and full through the wide channel that had already opened in the middle, and here and there what looked to be chunks of ice came bobbing.

I slammed the door shut and went towards him. He looked to be twenty at the most. Small and well built. Shaven-headed. Blue jeans, black boots, a grey hoody under a blue jacket. He stood staring at the ground with both hands buried in his pockets. As I came closer I noticed his throat was tattooed. His face was pale, not yet that of an adult, his cheeks a blotchy red.

I walked past him and went inside to the office, still barely a shed, where Stanislav was standing at the printer gathering the sheets of paper it was spitting out into a pile, while Natasha sat with the phone clamped between her cheek and shoulder and chewed her fingernails.

Stas turned round.

'Yevgeny Pavlovich,' he said.

'At your service,' I said, and sat down on his swivel chair. A grimace of annoyance passed over his face, but he said nothing.

'What's the plan for today?' I said.

'You've got a new man. He's waiting outside. Viktor. You're going to Kazan. I take it you knew.'

I smiled at Natasha, who smiled back.

'I suppose I did, now I come to think about it,' I said.

'Then Moscow on Monday.'

'Parquet staves?'

'That's right.'

'Anything to bring back?'

He shook his head.

'Just yourself and the lad.'

'Where did you find him?'

'He phoned the same day as Seryozha quit.'

'And you just took him on?'

'No, of course not. I interviewed him here last Friday. He came with some good references. Seems like a decent lad.'

'You're not the one who's going to be sitting next to him every day.'

I stood up, took the documents Stas handed me and went back out. The lad took no notice even when I went up to him.

I lit a cigarette. Held the packet out.

'Want one?'

He shook his head.

'I'm Yevgeny,' I said. 'You'll be with me.'

'Pleased to meet you,' he said, without sounding like he meant it.

'I hear you're a good worker. I like that. But what's with the tattoo?'

'Nothing in particular,' he said, his eyes still fixed on the ground. 'It's just a tattoo.'

'Of what?'

'The FC Rubin crest.'

'Ah!' I said. 'The lion that's a swan! A football fan, then?'

'Yes.'

'Of course you are. Do you play yourself?'

He shook his head, then turned aside and spat.

Crude and angry, the way short men often were.

'But you go to the matches?'

'Yes.'

I took a final drag and flicked the end away.

'Right, let's go,' I said.

The lorry was where I'd left it the night before. There had been several then, and I'd parked between two others. Now it was on its own in the middle of nowhere and looked like it had been abandoned by a drunk.

'Have you been in one of these before?' I said after we'd climbed into the cab.

He shook his head.

'Have you got a licence?'

Again, he shook his head.

I started the engine and threw it into gear before pulling away towards the exit.

'I used to deliver cars for Lada,' I said. 'From Tolyatti to the nearby towns, often to Kazan, occasionally to Yekaterinburg or Moscow. After five years I was sick of doing the same every day, so I packed it in and came to work for Stas. It's a bit more varied.'

I turned onto the main road and slowly picked up speed.

'What about you?'

'What about me?'

'Where have you worked before? And why did you stop?'

He shrugged.

'I worked in a storeroom. Got sick of it. Wanted to get out a bit more.'

'Who told you about Stas?'

He shrugged again and gazed out of his window. Not much to look at there. Trees, trees and more trees.

I yawned and put the radio on.

'It's six hours there and six hours back,' I said. 'Were you thinking of staying quiet the whole time?'

'I wasn't thinking anything one way or the other.'

'It's OK with me if you're not the talkative kind. What isn't OK with me is if you're just going to sit there in a sulk. You'll appreciate the difference, I'm sure.'

'I do,' he said.

'Good!' I said. 'Who told you about this job, then?'

'I know someone who knows Sergei. He said he was packing it in and that I should ring and see if I could get his job. And now I'm here.'

'Now you're here, indeed. Do you live with your parents?'

He gave me a look like I'd made him fume, then crossed his legs as we crawled up a long, gentle incline.

'Not seen them since I was sixteen.'

'I left home when I was sixteen as well,' I said. 'Couldn't stand living in the same house as my dad, so I moved in with my grandfather. He was a giant. His fist was as big as both of mine together. Four of yours! He was giving water to a calf once out in the byre. The weather was hot and there were flies everywhere. The calf was bothered by them and tossed its head, catching him hard as it did so. He was so incensed he actually punched the creature, killed it dead on the spot. Can you imagine that?'

He shook his head.

'Anyway, I moved in with him. He was old by then and no longer the man he used to be. But I liked him. Six months later he had a stroke. I found him on the floor in the passage, he'd collapsed while he'd been putting his boots on. He was still alive. I called the ambulance and went with him to the hospital. He'd gone into a coma and they were saying it was a matter of days. But then that same night I had a dream. Three strange men dressed all in black, with black hats on, came into the house where we lived. They looked like Georgians, I remember thinking. My grandfather was there, sitting in a chair by the window. It was completely dark outside. We lived in a village, not far from here, as it happens. Fields and meadows all around. The men went past me as if I wasn't there and went straight up to him. One of them grabbed him by the shirt and hauled him to his feet. He didn't resist, but I did. I clung to him as they dragged him outside into the darkness. I couldn't save him, even though I'm strong myself. It was no use. I was screaming and shouting. One of the men spun round and said, *Who's that making such a racket?* He saw me then. *How long's the old man got left?* he asked. *A year*, said one of the others. *For a few good deeds.* And then they went away.'

I said no more. The lad stared at me.

'What happened?'

'What happened? I'll tell you what happened. It was just as the strange men in the dream had said. My grandfather woke up from his coma and lived one more year exactly.'

'I don't believe you,' he said.

'Are you calling me a liar?'

'No. But you're spinning tales.'

'So you don't believe dreams can be true?'

'No.'

'In that case I'm sorry for you.'

We passed through the last of the villages on the way, crossed over the bridge and followed the road down the hill until we came to the factory where they made the parquet staves. The river ran fast on the other side of the buildings, its waters white with foam, and snow lay heaped between the trees.

The lad worked hard and didn't flinch as we loaded the heavy oblong cases into the trailer in their hundreds.

We each bought a coffee from the machine in the works canteen and sat down on top of some pallets in the spring sunshine before we got going again.

'Any more tales to spin?' he said after a while.

'What, are you bored already?'

'I'm never bored.'

'That's a positive attribute. But yes, I've got tales. Have you heard the one about the second-rate KGB officer who came to rule over all of Russia?'

'Ha ha.'

'You think I'm making it up? Well, my mother says we belong to the Romanov family, so by rights I should be claiming the throne. Her grand-mother, my own great-grandmother, got pregnant when she was sixteen years old. Do you know where she was working then? The Winter Palace. They made her chuck it in, though not without handing her a very generous redundancy payment. All her life she refused to say who the father was. And what does that suggest? Someone paid her to keep her mouth shut. And in whose interest would that be? I'm asking, that's all.'

'So why don't you claim the throne, then?'

'It's too hard to prove.'

'No, it's not. You could take a DNA test.'

'But I've already got a good life as a lorry driver.'

He grinned, but turned his head quickly to look out of his window so as not to give me the satisfaction.

'You do know they can cut and paste DNA now?' I said. 'This friend of a friend of mine breeds dogs. He's started experimenting with it. One night we were out at his place. He showed us how far he's got. As soon as it went dark he took us outside to the pen and called the dogs. They all came running, but only one stood out in the murk. It was luminous. He'd made a luminous dog.'

'I don't believe you.'

'Haven't you heard about it? They take the genes from a luminous microorganism, then put them in the dog's semen and the pups all light up in the dark.'

'That's the stupidest thing I've ever heard.'

'I saw it with my own eyes. I can take you there, if you want, so you can see for yourself.'

'So he's a scientist as well as a dog breeder, is he?' he said with a sneer.

'You don't need to be a scientist. It's all simple now. You can order everything you need off the internet and do it yourself.'

He looked at me, raised his eyebrows, then looked out of his window again.

Clearly those endless plains were more interesting than me, I thought.

Yellow and sodden and uninspiring though they were.

Huge, factory-like farm structures here and there, then suddenly the Volga. Wide as a lake, chopping in the wind, glittering in the sunshine.

Nineteen years old and as angry as that. It didn't bode well for the young man's life.

'Tell me, Vitya,' I said. 'Have you got a girlfriend?'

'None of your business,' he said without looking at me.

'So you haven't then.'

He said nothing and I decided to leave him alone. It was almost better not talking at all than talking to him.

After unloading at the facility in Samara we stopped at a roadside cafe and had some dinner before carrying on home as darkness fell. It was just gone nine by the time I parked the lorry, locked it and went over to the car having asked him first if he needed a lift, an offer he blankly refused. I'd got nothing on for the weekend, so I drove straight to Kalashnikov's and got well and truly drunk. My lights went out around three, I can't remember anything after that until waking up with a thumping headache around twelve the next day.

What did it matter?

I lay on the sofa watching old movies one after another until it got dark again and I fried myself some potatoes and boiled some spaghetti for my dinner. Maks didn't care much for being at mine, so in a way it was OK not seeing him. I looked forward to the weekends when it was my turn, but there was no getting around the fact that it was a strain having to keep him happy the whole time.

With a good bit of ketchup on it and a beer to wash it all down it was a fairly decent meal that at least filled my stomach ready for another night out. Out of habit I pressed the button for the lift even though it had been out of order for three weeks, and when suddenly it started up from one of the floors below it still took me a moment to realise it was working. Someone must have been and fixed it, unlikely as it sounded.

A gang of youths were sitting leaned up against the wall of the landing, drinking and playing tinny music on their phones. Once I got outside I understood why. The temperature had plummeted, the asphalt was a glassy film of ice from all the water that hadn't run off after the big thaw. I decided to leave the car and walk it instead. It wouldn't take more than half an hour. The jacket I'd put on was too flimsy, but if I walked briskly enough I'd stay warm, so I didn't think it was worth the effort going back up to change.

The pavement was so slippy I had to walk on the soil of the verge. Above my head the starry sky was like a frozen eddy, cold and clear. I got the feeling I often had as a kid, that I wasn't looking up but down. That I was standing on the edge of a huge dark well whose frozen water had captured all these tiny air bubbles.

I hadn't been born when Gagarin went into space and I'd been too young to remember when he died. Nevertheless, it was like he was everywhere when I'd been growing up, and all I'd wanted was to be a cosmonaut, nothing else would do.

I lit a cigarette as I got down to the main road. I was looking forward to the pub more than usual. The warmth, the smoke, the thrum of voices that would hit me when I stepped inside, like walking into a wall. A bit of vodka to get going, then a few rounds of billiards and take it from there. All in the hope that it was going to be one of those nights that kept on giving, when it seemed like door upon door kept opening in front of you, so by the time Sunday came round you could spend your entire day reconstructing each and every room you'd entered, and the order in which they'd presented themselves.

The journey to Moscow was fourteen hours if you didn't stop. Normally I did it in sixteen, so in order to get there before the facility closed for the night I'd told Viktor we'd be making an early start Monday at five o'clock. I wasn't sure he'd turn up, I had to admit.

But then just before five he came walking in the haze of the road lights. I was already in the cab with the engine running. He climbed up, opened the door and got in. His face was half hidden by his hood, but I could tell straight away that something was wrong.

'What's happened to you?'

'Nothing,' he mumbled, looking the other way.

'Have you been in a fight?'

'Thlipped on the ithe,' he said.

'Let me have a look at you.'

He didn't move for a second, but then grudgingly he turned towards me.

Christ almighty.

He was sporting a great big shiner, a swollen, bloodied nose and bulging lips. He looked a right mess.

'What the hell happened to you?' I said. 'Someone's given you a beating. Who was it?'

'Some ulthrath,' he said.

'What?'

'Ulthrath, for fuckth thake!'

'Ultras?'

'Yeth!'

'Let's have a look at that mouth of yours. Have you lost a tooth?'

He nodded, but kept his lips together.

'Have you seen a doctor?'

'Betht do without.'

'You could have a concussion. And if you've lost a tooth, you'll need to see a dentist.'

He turned away again and stared into the empty parking area.

'Have you got the money for that?'

'No.'

'I'll lend you some, if you like?'

'No.'

'You should go to the doctor's at any rate. Apart from the concussion, that nose looks like it's broken.'

'Are we going to Mothcow or not?'

'You, my friend, aren't going anywhere, not like that. You can't be doing heavy lifts if you've got a concussion.'

He looked at me with something like fear in his eyes.

'I'll lothe my djob.'

'I won't tell anyone. You get back home. I don't want to see you again until you're fit and ready. Anyway, it's my lorry, so what I say goes.'

He mulled it over a few seconds, then opened the door, climbed down and disappeared in the same direction he'd come.

It was a long day on the road. By mid-morning it had started snowing, big wet gobs of the stuff that to begin with didn't stick but held up the traffic nonetheless. I was all right, the cabin was warm and cosy, and as ever the radio was a good companion. I listened to a long programme about Rurik, the Viking who founded the federation of Kyivan Rus, and after that another one just as long about the scientist Vladimir Vernadsky, before switching over to a music channel that mostly played stuff from the seventies. I sang along, my eyes glued to the red tail lights that glowed through the blur ahead, though without really being aware of them at all in the semi-absent state that was so typical of such long hauls. The only problem was the time. As the day had worn on the snow had got heavier and the last couple of hours the traffic moving into Moscow had been stop—start. There was no sense in pressing on, so I made for a truck stop I knew with the idea of spending the night there. There was only one other vehicle and it pulled out again a few minutes after I came in. It was gone midnight and I felt tired, the week-end had taken its toll, so I put the kettle on straight away and got undressed while waiting for it to boil. The radio was on, so I didn't hear them come.

Suddenly, the window on the passenger side was smashed in. Before I could even react an arm came through and a hand unlocked the door from the inside. The next thing I knew, the door was flung open and a man wearing a balaclava climbed in. I put an arm up to protect myself and started the engine on instinct. He looped a cord around my throat.

I pressed back in the seat so he couldn't get the purchase he needed, fending him off with my left arm as I threw the gear lever with my right hand and stepped on the accelerator. Another man climbed inside, this one with a knife. The lorry lurched forward. I needed to get it out onto the road, stop the traffic. The first intruder wrenched my arm away, I couldn't keep him at bay, he tightened the cord and suddenly I couldn't breathe. I let go of the wheel and lunged at him with all my body weight, pressing him back. The guy with the knife was trying to come at me, but the other one was in the way.

'Give me the knife!' the first one said.

If he did, I'd be done for. With all the strength I could muster, I rammed my elbow back in the hope of hitting something vital and gave out an almighty roar as I wrenched away. My hands fumbled to open the door and he jabbed the knife into my back. I lashed out, the door opened and I tumbled out, hitting my chest on the cab steps before smacking onto the asphalt, the lorry rolling away. I scrambled to my feet and ran as fast as I could the other way. For a minute or so I kept on running, and then I stopped and looked back to make sure they weren't coming after me. They weren't. The lorry had come to a stand-still, but the engine was still running. I felt wet all down my back and reached inside my T-shirt, discovered I was bleeding rather badly.

The lorry was then thrown into gear and pulled slowly away onto the road, picking up speed and disappearing from view.

I crouched down.

Christ, I'd been lucky.

If it'd been the first guy who'd had the knife, I'd be dead.

Fucking bastards! Fucking idiots!

I stood up and felt pain. But it couldn't be anything serious, like vital organs, or I wouldn't be standing there.

A lot of blood, though.

I'd have to get help.

I walked towards the road. It was still snowing, it lay thick on the ground. I started shaking. I'd hardly got any clothes on! Underpants and a T-shirt. What would my mother have said?

I walked along the hard shoulder. A car approached and I waved my arms in the air. It slowed down, only to veer over onto the opposite carriageway before accelerating away. Thanks for nothing. I carried on walking. Another car came from behind. I crossed over and waved my arms again.

This one didn't even slow down, I had to jump out of the way.

There was no decency in the world.

My underpants were wet. It could only be blood. I'd have known if I'd shat myself.

I was shaking badly by then. I realised I was in serious trouble. It was night, below freezing, I was practically naked and bleeding heavily from a knife wound.

The lorry had been hijacked. Stas wasn't going to be pleased. Or else he wouldn't care that much. It wasn't his money. Vladimir Leonidovich, he was the one who wouldn't be pleased.

Wasn't there a police post not far from that truck stop?

Yes, I was certain of it.

I could see it in my mind's eye. On the other side of those trees.

Not a single vehicle came past as I made my way. Then when it came into view I could see even from a distance that it was unmanned. No police car, no light on in the little Portakabin. But still I went towards it, right up to the door, where I stood and knocked for a while and waited in case anyone should turn up.

I wasn't that lucky.

Across the field, lights shone from a house. They wouldn't just see a man in his underpants, they'd listen to what I was telling them and help me.

It was heavy going, I wasn't sure if I'd make it. It wasn't the cold, it was the bleeding. I felt myself weakening, as if somehow I was getting thinner. Was it all in my mind? Probably it was.

But I took off my T-shirt, rolled it up and pressed it against the wound to try and staunch the blood. It made no difference as far as the cold was concerned. My whole body was shaking, from the pituitary gland to the little hollow behind the knee.

Music came drifting. I could see cars parked up in front of the place and through the windows people inside the house, figures moving about. There was a party going on. Most likely they'd be so drunk they'd laugh at me.

Or else so drunk they wouldn't notice.

I went inside into the hall, still with my T-shirt bundled against the wound. I opened a door on the left and found the room it led into to be a combined bathroom and utility room. A bit of luck at last. I tossed my T-shirt into a pile of clothes in the corner, soaked a towel with hot water from the tap and washed my back as best I could. There was a first-aid kit on top of the medicine cabinet. Another stroke of luck. I fashioned a kind of compress out of some gauze, pressed it to where the blood was coming from and wound a length of bandage round my midriff to keep it in place. There was a clothes horse with some dry clothes still on it. I took a shirt and a pair of trousers and put them on, then a fleece jacket from the peg inside the door and a pair of sturdy boots from the shoe rack in the corner. I'd only just stepped into them when the door opened. Distracted by my unreasonable fortune, I'd apparently forgotten to lock it.

A big bloke in his thirties, bald and bearded, stared at me in astonishment.

'Who are you?' And then, when it seeped in: 'And what the hell are you doing here?'

'Let me cut a long story short. I've borrowed some clothes, and thanks a lot for that! I didn't mean to disturb you. I was just leaving!'

I stepped past him and went out again into the snow. I felt like I was full of vitality, even if the cold did go right through me, and walked away as briskly as I could without breaking into a trot, while the guy stood in the doorway and shouted after me.

That was better!

Now I needed to find a phone, get word to Stas and talk him into shelling out for a hotel and a ticket home. The chances of someone stopping to give me a lift had to be a lot better too, now that I wasn't half naked and covered in blood.

But there was hardly any traffic on the road and the few cars that did go past obviously didn't fancy picking up a lone hitchhiker. After half an hour or so walking along the side of the road in the direction of the city, a blue light came flashing towards me. A patrol car with its siren turned off. They pulled in on the other side of the road before I even had time to flag them down.

Then they put the siren on! They jumped out of the car, two young officers, and came running. One of them didn't look to be a day over sixteen. I stood calmly with my hands in the air, palms open towards them, but still they twisted my arms round my back and snapped a pair of cuffs on me.

'Steady on, lads, what are you doing?' I said. 'I've just been stabbed and robbed! They took off with a whole fucking lorry full of parquet staves!'

They bundled me over the road and into the back of the car. One got in beside me, the other behind the wheel. We turned round and sped in the direction of Moscow.

'You've got it all wrong!' I said. 'I've been robbed! If it's the clothes I'm being nicked for, I had no choice. I was in my underpants out there!'

'You shut it,' the sixteen-year-old said.

'I'm a law-abiding citizen and I'm telling you I've been robbed,' I said. 'You're not going to throw me in the nick for that, surely?'

'Not another word, do you hear?'

'But don't you get it? I've been R-O-B-B-E-D.'

He still didn't get it, even if I did actually spell it out for him, because the next thing I knew he punched me in the face. He didn't even turn his body to do it, just lashed out with his fist clenched, hit me right on the nose. There wasn't much I could do with my hands behind my back, apart from bleed and let my eyes water from the sudden pain.

VASILISA

Dear Daniil

Here at last is my foreword. I'm sorry it's taken so long. The reason has not been want of words or even laziness, but rather the opposite: the piece simply took on a life of its own, eventually growing out of all proportion. I have worked hard to pare it down and make it more stringent. But editing is not my strongest suit, as you know! However, it is yours. Please have a look and see if it might be saved. By all means be brutal. Also: it became more personal than I had envisaged, more about people than books, life more than theory. To be honest, I'm not sure if you'll even find it suitable. The commission you gave me was for something else entirely.

Read, think and let me know!

Warmest wishes from
Vasya

Vasya!

You're right: the foreword you sent me is unsuitable. In all haste, I've passed the job on to someone else. I do hope you won't be offended or, God forbid, angry with me! The fact is, it's a brilliant piece. My thought is this: how about expanding it so that we can publish it as a book in its own right? It'll mean a good deal of work, obviously, but if what we have is a *shortened* version, as you indicate, the task might not be *quite* so demanding.

Just a thought.

Daniil

ALEVTINA

S eva's alarm was ringing in his room as I came from the shower. He couldn't even be bothered turning it off so he could sleep on undisturbed, because it was still ringing when I sat down in front of the mirror.

'Sevastyan! Turn that alarm off and get up!' I said loudly, thumping my fist against the wall.

The ringing stopped.

I removed the towel I'd wrapped around my head and dabbed my face with it before blow-drying my hair and turning to my make-up.

He didn't need to do any of that, so I left him alone for a bit. I finished putting on my face, went over to the wardrobe and took out a pair of blue jeans and a white blouse. The jeans might have been a bit informal, but the blouse was smart and elegant. With a nice pair of shoes, the black suede ones, perhaps, I thought I'd look all right.

I put the radio on in the kitchen and filled the kettle, then stood and gazed out of the window while it was boiling. The sky, black as night only half an hour earlier, was now dissolving into greyer tones, as if someone had lifted an enormous lid up there and a little crack of light had escaped and percolated down.

It was snowing again. But now a wind had got up as well. Snowflakes whirled in the air, so fast it was almost impossible to distinguish them as flakes at all, they looked more like white lines.

The people in the street below walked with shoulders hunched, heads down against the wind, their thick coats and jackets, their scarves, hats and mittens padding their figures and making them look more like a species of animal, small, round and fat.

From higher up they'd resemble trilobites at the bottom of the sea.

It was the kind of thought only someone in my job would have, I thought to myself with a smile, spooning some instant into a mug and adding the boiling water.

The radio was tuned to a station that played only classical greats. In other words, I'd been feeling sorry for myself the night before. It was the only reason I ever listened to it.

What was that piece again?

Bam bam bam bambambam, bam bam bam bambambam.

Beethoven.

Come on, it was one of his most famous.

I opened the fridge and took out the milk. I poured some into my coffee, where it came together in little clumps.

For goodness' sake.

What date was it?

Still two days until the best-before date. It must have been left out, a whole day, perhaps.

Why couldn't he think of others once in a while? When was he going to pull himself together?

I poured the coffee away in the sink and made myself some more, finding some cream in the fridge that I used instead.

Moonlight Sonata.

That was it.

A bus pulled out of the flow of traffic into the lay-by at the stop. About ten people stood waiting.

I looked at the time.

Five to.

'Seva!' I shouted. 'You'll be late!'

There was no response. I put my mug down and went to his room, knocked and opened the door.

The air inside reeked, a boozy fug.

His big hockey bag was dumped in the middle of the floor, his kit spilling out like some frozen geyser.

'You'll have to get up now if you're not going to be late.'

He stirred, though his eyes didn't open, his only communication a deep grunt that escaped his throat.

'Are you just going to lie there?'

'Mm,' he said.

'Well, you can't. You do realise, don't you? You're throwing your life away like this.'

'Not now, Mama.'

He opened his eyes and peered at me with a little smile on his lips.

How could he smile?

'It's your life,' I said. 'I can't force you. But I can kick you out, you know I can.'

'You're wicked,' he said, and turned over onto his other side.

'Please yourself. But if you're not at the station this afternoon, I will kick you out. Do you understand what I'm saying?'

'I'll be there, I promise.'

I finished my coffee, dropped my good shoes into my rucksack, grabbed my bag, put my coat on and left without switching the radio off, just to annoy him.

It wasn't until I was on the bus that I realised of all things I'd forgotten the suitcase. I sent him a text.

Forgot the suitcase! It's beside the wardrobe in my room. Will you bring it with you? No, delete that. You MUST bring it with you!

He didn't reply, but then I hadn't thought he would.

I sat with the rucksack and bag on my lap and with the back of my hand discreetly wiped away some of the condensation so I could look out of the window. Not that there was much to see: broad avenues, high-rise flats, the occasional little park, desolate with leafless trees. People like shadows, characterless, almost erased in their winter garb.

The man next to me, who had made room for me as if I were old, infirm or pregnant, kept glancing at me, wanting me to turn, I sensed, so that he could strike up a conversation.

He smelled faintly of sweat and garlic.

I texted Oksanka to confirm that I could meet her the next day. I asked if it was snowing there too.

'You work at the university, don't you?' the man next to me said after I'd put the phone in sleep mode and again sat staring out of the window.

I gave him a cursory look.

'None of your business,' I said.

'I've seen you there a lot. So either you're a perpetual student or you work there.'

I woke my phone again without responding. Oksanka had already replied. They were knee-deep in snow there now and the river was freezing over. She said she'd posted some new photos of her daughter on VK, but I'd be seeing her tomorrow in any case.

I logged on and looked at the photos.

In the first she was looking straight at the camera while sticking her tongue out. How old was she now? Not even one yet.

Her eyes were like the darkest lanterns.

I felt a surge of longing. Then its companion, sorrow.

But it was easy enough to shake off. I had Seva, and if there was one thing there was no room for in my life now, it was a baby.

It was ridiculous to even think it.

But my goodness, how gorgeous she was!

I texted back, the same words. *My goodness, how gorgeous she is!*

'I work there too,' the man next to me said.

I dropped my phone into my bag without answering him, then stared out of the window again. Only a few more minutes and I'd be getting off.

'No reason to be disdainful,' he said. 'I was just trying to be friendly.'

I looked at him.

'Perhaps you can find someone else to be friendly with.'

He smiled. His teeth were yellow. Skin pasty, dark under the eyes. Two-day stubble. Ashen eyes.

'Understood. I'm Pavel, by the way. In case you're wondering. Faculty of Mechanics and Mathematics.'

The bus pulled in and I stood up to get off, though the next stop was closer. A few more minutes of fresh air would only do me good. Especially if it meant I could get away from Pavel.

As I stepped into the office, a splashy internet page disappeared in a flash from Marta's screen, leaving her staring at a Word document.

'You don't have to pretend to be working just because I'm here,' I said, hanging my coat and scarf up inside the door and putting my mittens and woolly hat on the radiator.

'Sorry?' she said, removing an earbud.

'I said, what are you listening to?'

'Coldplay.'

'Mm,' I said. 'Coffee?'

'Please, if you're getting one yourself, that is?'

'I am, yes.'

'Then I'll have a latte, if you don't mind.'

What a hopeless individual she was, I thought to myself as I went down the corridor to the canteen. Had it been me in that situation, I'd have gone and got them myself and been quick about it.

Then I'll have a latte, if you don't mind.

There was only twelve years between us, but it felt like a whole generation.

The snow fell densely outside the windows of the canteen. It could snow for weeks with this kind of weather, layers of cloud smothering the city. Not like a lid, because a lid would protect. This gave only seemingly constant precipitation.

'A small latte and a large cappuccino,' I said to the woman behind the counter. When she turned away to prepare the order, with all that the task involved in the way of swift, purposeful movements, clattering metal and hissing steam, my eyes wandered. The murk of outside, the descending snow, the thick wet overcoats and the dampness they brought in with them, reminded me of school, the classroom, first period in winter.

'Why are you reading that when you don't have to?' Sevoshka would often say to me whenever I sat down with a book on some subject or other that was completely alien to him. 'You were the sort who actually *liked* school, weren't you?'

I explained to him then that I liked learning and that it had to do with the world, not school.

He didn't understand.

I took the two coffees back to the office and put the latte down on Marta's desk. She looked up at me and smiled fleetingly before taking a sip and returning to whatever it was she had immersed herself in, whether it was the music in her ears or the article she was working on.

Sevoshka had replied.

OK, his text said.

I sent him a heart before sitting down at the computer and opening the document containing the notes for my lecture. Not that I needed to look at them. This was the fifth year running I'd given the same series of lectures, and to the first-year students, so it was all basic stuff. But I enjoyed the experience. The mystery of life became no less mysterious however many times it happened to be regurgitated in a lecture hall, and anyway it wasn't for my benefit but theirs, the students who for the most part were hearing it all for the first time.

My phone began to vibrate on my desk. I could see it was Papa. It was unlike him to call, and I was gripped by a sudden unease.

'Papa,' I said. 'Is everything all right?'

'Has it ever been?' he said, and my unease dissolved as quickly as it had arisen.

'Is it important? Only I'm lecturing in . . . nine minutes.'

'The electricity's gone,' he said. 'It's cold as hell. I just thought I'd let you know, seeing as you'll all be here this evening.'

'Can't you light the fire? That'll be one room warmed up, at least. And isn't there a wood burner in the kitchen as well, come to think of it?'

'Yes. But no wood in the house. And I don't want to be burning the furniture, not just yet.'

'How about buying some, did that occur to you?'

'Of course it occurred to me!' he said irritably.

'But what?'

'I'm not so mobile at the moment.'

'Oh?'

'It's nothing.'

'Can't you go out?'

'Yes, I can go out.'

'So what's the problem?'

'I just told you!'

'Right. You're not so mobile.'

'Exactly.'

'But you can go out?'

'In theory, yes.'

'Papa, why haven't you said anything? Can you walk?'

'Yes, I can walk.'

'Is it your foot?'

'Yes.'

'Did you turn your ankle?'

'Not exactly.'

I sighed.

'All right. I've got to go now,' I said. 'But I'll order you some wood and get them to deliver this afternoon. Tell them to take it into the living room for you, and I'll see you tonight.'

'Thank you, Alevtinka.'

I turned my phone off, put my shoes on, put my laptop in a tote bag and hurried to the lecture hall, finding it almost full when I entered, buzzing with chat and laughter, the rustle of coats and bags, books and paper.

Eyes followed my every movement as I got ready to start. It was their privilege and it didn't bother me any more. The same applied to all the emotions that at any given time were present in the auditorium. They reflected back at me as I looked out and surveyed the faces, some uninterested, others impassive and focused on learning, others admiring, envious or annoyed, and always one or two who were clearly infatuated.

I moved to the lectern and the room quietened.

'So, to recapitulate,' I said. 'The earth is approximately 4.5 billion years old. The first life emerged something like 3.8 billion years ago, in the shape of single-celled organisms drifting around in the oceans. Those organisms, believe it or not, have evolved into the life forms we see all around us today. Birch trees, trout, deer, blackbirds, spiders, mushrooms, lions, whales — and, of course, human beings. The question we're posing in these lectures is how such development can be possible. What sort of conditions are necessary for it to occur? By what factors is it governed? How can the human brain, the most complex phenomenon known to us in the universe, have developed out of those first primitive single-cell organisms? Our first thought would surely be that such a process would have to be highly complex indeed. But no, it is in fact incredibly simple, and therein lies the beauty of the theory of evolution.'

A bead of sweat rolled from my armpit and I pressed my arm to my side at the same time as I moved from the lectern and sat down on the edge of the desk beside it. Only a few of the students were already taking notes, I could see. They hardly ever did until hard facts and figures were introduced.

'In fact, it's so simple, we could almost say that only two conditions are required: *time* and *variation*. Of course, the further we delve, the more complicated it becomes. Still, for present purposes it's a simplification that will serve us well. Now, the *time* perspective that's involved here is particularly important for us to grasp. When we look at the various stages of evolution, what we see is a taxonomy covering different periods of time, all of course scientifically established. But when we consider that the Ediacaran organisms, for instance, which we're going to be talking about today, emerged some 635 million years ago and died out around 541 million years ago, the notion of time becomes somewhat abstract to us, all we see are the figures. Yet the Ediacaran Period lasted almost a hundred million years. A hundred million years! Think of everything that's happened in human history since the Roman Empire, and that was only two thousand years ago. Twenty thousand years ago we were living in caves and hadn't even invented the wheel. But in the theory of evolution, twenty thousand years is nothing. It's a drop in the ocean. So that's one thing we need to bear in mind. That life has had this huge amount of time in which to develop. The second is *variation*. Individuals, as we know, reproduce. Now, if what came out of that were only identical copies of those selfsame individuals, nothing basically would change, there would be no development, everything would stay the same. But the offspring always differ from the parent organisms, and are as good as always more *numerous* too. However, if *everything* about the offspring were different, that would likewise stand in the way of development. As we know, though, this isn't the case, the offspring will always inherit *some* of the parent organism's traits. The fact that the offspring are almost always greater in number serves of course to increase diversity. Which is to say, greater variation. Think in terms of choice. The individuals that make up a given population are alike in one respect in that they belong to the same species. But they're also different from each other, which allows for still new combinations to emerge. Greater leaps become possible by way of mutations in the genome. And this is where natural selection comes into play: the most suited individuals will pass on their genes to more individuals than those less suited. But suited to what? you may ask. The answer is: suited to the environment in which they live. And of course that's something that's in a constant state of flux, constantly changing across the dizzyingly enormous spans of time we're talking about here. Again: without variation, nothing would ever have occurred.'

I moved on from the slide of the red starfish on the green seabed that until then had filled the screen behind me to a schematic outline of organisms belonging to the Ediacaran Period which I remembered I'd drawn up late one evening a few years previously.

'Mutation, adaptation, reproduction, heredity, variation, time. These are all vital elements in the theory of evolution. Easy to learn, easy to understand. But in order to really grasp the magnitude of all this — how that development actually took place, from a simple single-celled organism floating around in the world to the creatures who sit here now, us, in this room — we need to get specific. And that's what we're going to do now, by taking a look at Ediacaran life.'

I stood up, ran a hand through my hair and registered at the same time a movement at the back of the room to my right. A young man with a sparse beard and glasses had put up his hand. He still had his coat and scarf on.

I pointed at him.

'Yes?'

'You're talking as if there's no doubt as to the veracity of evolutionary theory. Wouldn't it be fair to point out to us that not everyone is in agreement about it? Isn't what you're doing here a form of brainwashing, in fact? No contesting theories? Really? Wouldn't it be more honest to make it clear to us that all you're doing here is pushing a theory?'

'I think you've come to the wrong place,' I said. 'The philosophy department is across campus. Or perhaps you study religion? We do science here.'

There was a ripple of laughter, and heads turned to look up at the young man and see his reaction.

'I'm not so sure what you do here,' he said. 'Your science can't explain how life emerged in the first place. The kind of reductionist materialism you all stand for can only point to physical and chemical laws, but there's nothing in those laws that can explain how life arose out of non-life. Is that science? And as for the theory of evolution, is it able to explain how the genetic code emerged, not to mention how it's actually read? The theory has to be able to do that in order to be valid. Only it can't. Is that science? Or is it orthodox faith?'

'What you're saying isn't true,' I said. 'In the hundred and fifty years evolutionary theory has existed, new evidence in its favour has been piling up all the time, whereas nothing, and I mean nothing, has been put forward that can refute it. The discovery of DNA, the whole science of genetics, has, contrary to what you're suggesting, significantly bolstered the theory of evolution. So to put it bluntly, we can't be wasting our time on your objections. However, I'm sure you didn't think all this up yourself? So just for amusement, perhaps you could tell us what you've been reading that has led you so sadly astray?'

Again, laughter filled the room, and the poor fellow blushed visibly.

'I've read various things,' he said.

'Thomas Nagel, perchance?'

'Nagel too, yes.'

'To all of you, I will say, by all means, read Thomas Nagel. But at the same time be aware that he is a philosopher, not a scientist. He understands little, if anything at all, about what's been going on in science over the last, well, fifty years. He is critical of evolutionary theory, yet presents no alternative, save for some vague teleological musings to the effect that developmental processes are goal-directed rather than haphazard and a suggestion that there are factors we've yet to discover. And though he claims to be an atheist, what he actually writes about is God. So there you have it. Now I should like to continue my lecture. We'd got to the Ediacaran Period, beginning some 635 million years ago. Probably the most dramatic time in our entire evolutionary history. Not, however, dramatic in the sense of a lot of things happening in a short space of time, because, as we've said, we're talking about a period of something like a hundred million years. But dramatic in the sense that what happens in this period is so crucial and has such an enormous impact on the way in which life develops on earth.

'So what happens?

'The life that emerged 3.8 billion years ago consisted, as you now know, of microscopic single-celled organisms. They remained unchanged for two billion years. Then, suddenly, on the cusp of the period we're now talking about, these single-celled organisms start clustering together. Why? The conditions in which they existed changed. The oceans became more nutritious, more oxygenated, presenting thereby a whole new set of possibilities.'

A girl on the first row put up her hand.

'Yes?' I said.

'What was it that caused conditions to change?'

'An important question. For a few million years the earth had been locked in a total ice age. The whole planet was covered in ice. But then it melted, releasing enormous amounts of nutrition and oxygen. For evolution, this was like a kick in the backside — a kick-start, if you will. Now, if this window had only been open for a short time, let's say twenty thousand years, and then closed again, probably nothing would have happened. But again, with the huge time spans we're talking about, what *can* happen *will* happen, sooner or later. Yes, it's down to accident,' I said, looking up at the Nagel proselyte with a smile, 'but given enough time, the accidental will sooner or later become the imperative.

'So, first two billion years of single-celled organisms, then they cluster together into colonies. And now this.'

I moved on to the next slide.

'Say hello to your ancestors. This is Charnia, a life form that existed at the bottom of the sea seven hundred million years ago. It looks like a plant, right? A kind of fern, perhaps? Yet it lived at such great depths that it can't possibly have been a plant. It was just too dark there to enable photosynthesis. It's got nothing resembling limbs, no digestive system, no circulatory system, no nervous system. It hasn't got a head or a mouth or anything else even vaguely familiar to us from the animal world. It can't think, obviously, and it can't feel anything or move either. But it's alive, it takes in nutrients and it grows. So as you see, it's not just a lump of cells but an organised body. Organised, that is, according to the fractal principle whereby an object is made up of identical parts that are just smaller copies of the whole. That means that each element basically is a building block, which makes expansion easy.'

The Nagel proselyte raised his hand.

'Yes?'

'How does this organism know how to build itself?'

'That's encoded in the DNA.'

'But how does the DNA know?'

'The DNA doesn't *know* anything, any more than an instruction manual knows it's an instruction manual.'

'But if DNA is a plan, where did the plan come from?'

'That would lead us into molecular biology, which isn't what this course is about. But it's an interesting question, certainly. The principles of evolution apply also at the level of cells, so it's by no means irrelevant. We don't know if DNA was present in the very first cells, in all likelihood it developed out of RNA, a rather simpler replication mechanism. In any circumstance, it's old technology, and by *old* I mean something like 3.8 billion years, as old as life itself. But if we're going to discuss mysteries today, I'm not sure the emergence of life and the development of DNA is the biggest one we could find. It's not that big a leap from dynamic self-organising systems, structures and currents present in nature to a cell. A system of that kind in nature — a tornado, for instance, or bathwater eddying down the plughole — keeps going only as long as it's induced with energy. When the energy runs out, it dies. We might posit that the first cells *harnessed* one of those self-organising systems by somehow hemming it in and inducing energy into it. At the molecular level there's an absolute frenzy of activity going on in a cell, and what the cell does is to give order to that chaos, to direct the currents in directions that are specific and unvarying, in the same way as a whirlpool in a river. So the cell basically is a form of order. But if it hadn't been for DNA, or some other similar mechanism, the structure would just have been trapped there a short time and then died out, the way a tornado dies out after a while. What the DNA does is enable the structure harnessed by those first cells to be passed on to a new generation. And that's what's been happening now for nearly four billion years. As you'll recall, it's likely that all existing life can be traced back to one and the same cell, which, using an acronym from English, we call LUCA: the Last Universal Common Ancestor. We might say that a torch was lit back then that cells have been carrying in relay ever since. DNA is what makes it possible to pass the flame on to the next generation, as it were. That's its function. But the biggest mystery, and what today's lecture is actually supposed to be about, once we get round to it, is what happened within the cell after some two billion years. In all probability this was something that occurred only in a very small number of cells. Nevertheless, we can confidently say that all plant and animal life as we know it today stems from that small handful of cells. Every other cell in existence at that time lived on as if nothing had happened and are all around us to this day. *That's* the mystery. *That's* the big leap. Although Charnia, as we've seen, is a very simple life form, it represents something radically new compared to what went before it. Its cells collaborate, they communicate with each other, and they come together to form something that is greater than the sum of its individual parts.

'Some might say that life at that time sounds rather boring. There was no sex, not even any movement. All these things did was lie at the bottom of the sea. They didn't involve themselves in each other's lives, there was no interaction. They were a bit like babies, you could say, lying side by side without yet having learned to play with each other. And maybe they didn't have much of a career, existing only for twenty million years before becoming extinct. Because, as we know, twenty million years is the blink of an eye in the history of life. Why did they die out? Perhaps their fractal-modular architecture effectively ruled out their chances of developing further. At any rate, after them, though still in the Ediacaran Period, a quite different group of creatures emerges, among them this.'

I moved on to the next slide and glanced at the time. Only a few minutes left.

'This is Dickinsonia. It looks like a doormat, right? This thing could be up to a metre and a half in length, or as small as a coin or a button. Quite a number of fossil imprints have been found of it, and for many years they were something of a mystery. Is it an animal? Is it a plant? In the world of evolutionary biology, we're talking about the Holy Grail here. But a few years ago the mystery was finally solved, and by a Russian doctoral student. It could have been me, it *should* have been me . . .'

I smiled as the comment elicited some laughter.

'Unfortunately for me, however, the student in question was a young man by the name of Ilya Bobrovsky. He found a fossil of Dickinsonia here in Russia that was something more than just an imprint in stone, it actually contained organic remains, molecules. Ilya managed to analyse them. They turned out to contain cholesterol, which is found only in animals. Like Charnia before it, Dickinsonia had no eyes, no mouth or limbs, but the evidence suggests that it could move about on its own. It's the first animal life form we know of that could do this. But there was something else about it, too, perhaps even more significant: bilateral symmetry. Meaning that its right and left sides were the same. And this of course is something that has turned out to be an incredibly efficient body form. Every animal now living on earth is made in the same way, and most of those living in the sea.

'Why did life suddenly become so advanced?

'That's what we'll talk about next time.'

I closed my laptop, pulled out the cables and put everything into my bag, making sure not to look up and encourage attention. Students were always coming up to me after the lectures to ask questions or discuss a matter, even to give me compliments. Often I'd stay behind, however tedious it was to me, but now all I wanted was to get back downstairs to my office and wind down a bit.

I could see the troublemaker out of the corner of my eye, making his way forward, and so I slipped out through a side door that led into a corridor, at the bottom end of which was a lift. I wasn't happy with the way the lecture had gone, it had been too messy by far and I hadn't got round to saying half the things I'd wanted. It was supposed to have given a systematic outline of the Ediacaran Period and how it began, and then presented the various life forms that had been present. Instead, it had been incoherent, all over the place.

The lift door opened at once and I stepped inside and pressed the button before checking myself in the mirror. In the glaring light, the line between my foundation and my natural skin colour was clearly visible. The difference was at least a couple of shades.

How annoying. I'd be aware of it the rest of the day now.

I rubbed my thumb across my throat a few times. I'd have to remember that firewood for Papa. I could just as well get it done straight away.

The lift stopped and the door opened. I got my phone out as I went down the corridor. No sooner had I turned it on than it pinged with notifications, one after another. Sasha had called. Oksanka had sent another six texts. Whatever she had to say, she always divided it up, which sometimes had me scared that something terrible had happened when I saw how many she'd sent. There was something from Aeroflot, then a text from one of my private students, Gregori, to say he couldn't make it on Monday. And one from Vasilisa.

How about coffee?

I stopped in my tracks and wrote back.

Great. When?

Now? she replied straight away.

Where are you? I typed.

Canteen, she wrote back.

I didn't know whether to laugh or cry. It was so typical of her. I hadn't heard from her in over a year and now all of a sudden here she was.

I stopped by the office and dumped my bag before going down to the canteen, where I caught sight of her immediately, though she was sitting facing the other way. Her big, round figure was easily recognisable, as was the fur coat.

'Vaseshka,' I said.

She jumped up and we hugged. She stood as if to take me in for a moment with her hands on my shoulders.

'You're looking good as ever,' she said.

'You too,' I said.

'You don't *have* to lie,' she said. 'But I shan't complain.'

I smiled and sat down.

'How are you?' she said.

'Good,' I said. 'And you?'

'Oh, not bad.'

She took off the big coat and draped it over the back of the chair next to her, pushed up the sleeves of the thin white lambswool jumper she was wearing, then planted her elbows on the table, her hands clasped in front of her. Staunch, and yet not entirely unquivering. She looked so robust and healthy, but the body deceived, I knew. The soul inside it was erratic, inconstant.

'So, where have you been all this time?' I said. 'This last year? Have you been here in the city?'

'My grandmother died last year, did I tell you? No? She was as old as the hills, so it was no great tragedy, but took its toll nonetheless. Did you ever get to meet her?'

I shook my head.

'I only heard about her.'

'Well, anyway. She kept a dacha outside Bogorodsk.'

'I remember. You went there once in a while.'

'Yes. I moved in. That's where I've been this last year.'

'You could have phoned or replied to my texts, even so.'

'There's no internet there. I had no mobile phone either. I should have told you I'd be going away, of course. That it would be hard to get in touch with me. But I didn't.'

'No, it's OK,' I said. 'It's just like you, that's all.'

'Is it?'

'It's not the first time you've disappeared off the face of the earth.'

'No, perhaps not,' she said, and laughed.

I turned and looked at the clock on the wall behind me.

'Are you in a hurry?' she said.

'No. Not at all, in fact. I've just given a lecture and thought I might go into town. It's Papa's eightieth birthday tomorrow and I haven't got him a present yet. Why don't you come with me? We could have lunch.'

'That sounds like an excellent plan.'

'Let me just pop up and get my things first.'

Back in my office, I called Oksanka as I wriggled my coat on.

'Alya,' she said. 'Hi.'

'Hi,' I said, now putting my feet into my boots, phone clamped between shoulder and chin. 'I was wondering if you could do me a favour.'

'Of course.'

'Papa needs some firewood, only I don't know where to get it. Can you find out for me, then send me the number?'

'No problem. I'll order it for you, if you like? It won't take a few minutes.'

'Do you mind? That'd be great, if you would.'

'It's no trouble.'

'You're an angel. Looking forward to seeing you tomorrow!'

I hung up, wrapped my scarf around my neck, grabbed my woolly hat, my tote bag and rucksack and went down to the canteen again. Vasya was standing waiting by the door.

'Are we taking the metro?' she said.

'I was thinking we might,' I said.

The snow was still falling outside. Everything was white and grey.

'I wasn't entirely sure you wouldn't be angry with me, to be honest,' she said as we crossed the concourse, heads lowered against the weather.

'Why would I be angry with you?' I said. 'It's not as if we're married. It's up to you if you don't want to be in touch. I don't own you. That's not how friendships work.'

'Not everyone would look at it like that.'

'But I do.'

'I know. And I'm glad. However, a lot of people might be inclined to think you didn't care enough about your friends.'

'What people? Who are you talking about?'

'In general, I mean. A person who asks nothing of those around them, but lets them get on with it and do as they like. One could easily think it was down to lack of interest. It's no big deal, though.'

'You don't get in touch for over a year and then you come here and criticise me for not caring? Is that it?'

'So you are a bit angry.'

'I wasn't to begin with. But now I am. I don't understand why you'd say such a thing.'

'It didn't come out right,' she said.

'No, it didn't.'

The figures coming up the stairs of the metro across the park were dark and shadowy in all the grey and white. A bit further away, red tail lights shone from the traffic that had come to a halt at the junction.

'You'll be going to Samara tomorrow, then?' she said after a while. 'For Yegor's birthday, I mean.'

'Yes, we're going this evening.'

'You and Seva?'

'Yes.'

'Yegor throwing a party?'

'You must be joking. He's still as misanthropic as ever.'

'He's very fond of *you*, at least.'

'He puts up with me. Admittedly, that's saying a lot by his standards.'

We went down the steps into the underground. The grey-and-red stone beneath our feet was awash with slush melting into puddles. An elderly woman had forgotten to close her umbrella and held its protective canopy over her head as she walked in front of us. I saw the annoyance in people's eyes when they had to dodge her.

'What were you doing at the dacha, anyway?' I said. 'Were you writing?'

She nodded, and her eyes lit up the way they so often did when she got the chance to talk about herself.

'Writing, yes. A lot. And working in the garden, weeding and planting. She'd done nothing with it for ten years at least, so it was very overgrown. Apart from that, reading.'

'Were you on your own the whole time?'

'Yes.'

'It sounds marvellous, if you ask me,' I said, standing back against the wall on the platform and putting my bag down between my feet. A minute and a half until the next one came.

'It was. But it was cold as well. The place is hardly insulated at all. The walls are little more than the bare planks.'

'I've no idea how you manage. I certainly wouldn't be able to.'

'A basic matter of wrapping up warm, that's all. I'm used to sitting with my coat and scarf on indoors.'

'Financially, I meant. I'm assuming your books haven't made you rich.'

She laughed.

'God, no. But I do odd jobs for various publishers. A bit of translating here, a bit of proofreading there. And I hardly ever buy a thing.'

She looked at me.

'How about you?'

'I do buy things, yes,' I said with a smile. 'Not much, though.'

I recognised a face in a group of young people standing a bit further along. A student of mine. Then I realised the others were familiar too. They'd all just come from my lecture.

I turned away from them and gave Vasya a smile as our eyes met.

'I've started writing prose,' she said. 'Not a novel, more like a very meandering essay. You know the way a dog goes sniffing off, distracted by every scent?'

'Sounds interesting,' I said. 'What's it about?'

'I'm not sure, really. It's not finished yet. But the part I've just been working on is about Fyodorov and his *Common Task*.'

'Fyodorov?' I said, my eye drawn by the group of students again. The troublemaker had joined them now and was already holding forth. He saw me and sent me a snide-looking smile and a little nod. A couple of the others turned to see who he was looking at.

'Haven't you heard of Fyodorov?'

'I don't think I have,' I said as the light in the tunnel came on and a faint rumble grew to a crescendo, the train sweeping then into the station like one of the sandworms in *Dune*. I picked up my bag and stepped forward.

'He was a philosopher, very reclusive, though he worked for a period as a librarian at the Rumyantsev Museum in the late nineteenth century. He believed that humanity needed to work together and channel all its resources into bringing back to life every person who ever died.'

The train came to a halt and we got on. We found two seats next to each other. Thankfully, the students had gone into the carriage in front.

'I've definitely never heard of him,' I said. 'He sounds like a proper lunatic. Why are you writing about him?'

'He turned up.'

'And now you're having a sniff?'

She laughed.

'That's it, yes!'

The train pulled away. The passengers on the row of seats facing us all sat with their heads down, staring at the phones they held out in front of them in the palms of their hands. It looked like it had been choreographed.

'I think you might be able to help me out,' she said. 'Fyodorov didn't just think it was possible to revive the dead, he also of course believed in eternal life. What sets him apart there though is that he wasn't coming at it from a religious angle. For him, it was nothing to do with God or Jesus. He believed science would make it possible. So naturally I thought you might enlighten me a bit. I'm thinking of the practicalities. I know there's a lot of research into ageing and that a lot of scientists think it's quite feasible that we can halt the processes of ageing, am I right? Genetically, I mean.'

'Is this why you came to see me?'

She laughed sheepishly.

'Not entirely,' she said. 'But it gave me an excuse to see you.'

'Does it need an excuse?'

'No, of course not. Only now it's two birds with one stone, isn't it? All I need really is a few suggestions for reading. I could get there myself, eventually, but that would take time, I'd have to sift through all sorts of rubbish first.'

'I can send you some links,' I said without looking at her.

'Would you? Thanks ever so much,' she said. 'You're a good friend.'

I first met Vasya when we were in our first year at university studying philology. It was impossible not to notice her. Rather more difficult to actually like her. She gave off a strange blend of uncertainty and pre-eminence, as introverted as she could be overbearing, and once I got to know her I discovered her to contain many more such dichotomies, of which perhaps the most obvious, or obtrusive, had to do with a complete lack of boundaries and extreme self-regulation. She could have periods where she would eat just about anything she came across in quite unbridled fashion, and from there go to the opposite extreme entirely. I remember once she came to dinner at some friends of ours and produced a set of scales from her bag, having decided, she announced, that from then on she was going to weigh everything she ate. She seemed not to notice the general astonishment this gave rise to at the table, but set up her scales as if it were the most natural thing in the world. It was much the same when it came to parties: either she'd be drunker than anyone else by far, or else she wouldn't come and instead would stay in on her own, drinking tea and wallowing in her solitude the way she often did, when she'd refuse to open the door if the bell rang, even if it was one of her friends who'd come to see her.

I noticed her on our very first day, in clothes that looked like an old person's, not their drab everyday garb, but the sort of thing someone old would wear for a special occasion, someone's seventieth birthday, perhaps, or even their own: a floral-patterned blouse, a navy-blue skirt, a bead necklace, pearl earrings, flat black pumps. She was heavily built, with oddly unpronounced features and a thick head of dark, shoulder-length hair, her thin lips accentuated with bright red lipstick, her eyes blue, at times strong and dazzling, at others timid and unassertive.

It wasn't enough for me to want to approach her, rather it was reason to stay away. But then I saw she had a book in her hand, Rilke's *Duino Elegies*. Until then, I'd never met anyone besides my father who had actually read Rilke. Rilke had been the reason why I'd chosen philology. Not necessarily to meet others who read him, but at the very least to meet people who *read*.

So when I saw her sitting on her own in the canteen one day, I took my tray over and asked if I could sit down.

'Be my guest,' she said. On her plate was a salad and several slices of bread piled up at the side. If the salad was because she was on a diet, the bread wasn't going to help much, but of course I kept my thoughts to myself.

'You do literature as well, don't you?' I said.

She nodded, her gaze wandering around the room as if she were looking for someone.

'What did you make of the lecture just now?'

Without answering, she got to her feet, picked up her tray, went over to another table and struck up a conversation with the people sitting there.

I was gobsmacked.

She'd turned everything around. She was the weird, unattractive one, not me. And yet she had rejected me?

I started eating, sitting on my own didn't bother me for once, and before long some people I knew came and joined me anyway.

In the lecture hall the next morning, she found a seat in the row in front of me and after putting her things out on the desk turned and said:

'I don't accept charity from good-looking people.'

And then she turned away.

Again, I was speechless.

Who did she think she was?

What did my appearance have to do with anything?

She didn't know a thing about me, the person I was.

From then on, I did my best to avoid her. I took pains never to look in her direction. Why would I? And of course I would never sit down at the same table, not even if people I knew happened to be sitting there too.

Then one night in some basement club or other, she suddenly appeared and came charging up to throw her arms around me.

'How lovely to see you, Alya!' she said. 'I'm so glad you came!'

She was as pissed as a newt. I swivelled towards Lev, the boy I was with, told him I was just going to the loo and suggested he get the drinks in while I was away.

He nodded and I leaned in and kissed him before making my way to the toilets.

'Who was that?' said Vasilisa. She was following me. 'Have you found yourself a boyfriend?'

'Who are *you*?' I said. 'That's *my* question. Because I don't know. So why are you asking if I've got a boyfriend?'

She stopped in her tracks, her face all of a sudden drained of expression. When I came back she was nowhere to be seen.

It was after that we became friends. She came up to me in the library one day and apologised for her behaviour, said she was sorry for the way she'd thrust herself on me. She'd been very drunk, she said.

'Not that it's any excuse.'

'Well, it is in a way,' I said. 'We do all sorts of stupid things when we're drunk, everyone knows that.'

'I saw a familiar face and got carried away,' she said.

'That's OK.'

'Thanks for taking it so nicely.'

'You like Rilke, don't you?'

'Not unconditionally, no. He's often too sentimental for my liking. I find there can be too much beauty in his work, it can be too soulful. That said, there's no doubting the quality. Every now and then he does hit the very pinnacle.'

'You should meet my father. He was obsessed with Rilke for a time. When I was around ten years old, he used to read me his poems at bedtime.'

'What about you? Do you like Rilke?'

'I do, yes. I feel he speaks to me. And only to me.'

'I know what you mean. Do you write poetry yourself?'

I laughed and shook my head.

'I leave that to the poets. But you write. I'm sure of it. Do you?'

She gave me a suspicious look that seemed to come out of nowhere.

'What makes you think that?'

'Something in the way you asked me. You thought you'd found a companion. Anyway, do you?'

She nodded.

'Or rather, no. I can't profess that I do. I mean, I can't bring myself to say, *I write poetry*.'

'But you do?'

'Yes.'

We laughed.

Not long after that, she came round to mine with her poems. She sat in the chair and looked at the floor, while I sat on the edge of my bed and read them. The situation would have been awful if she'd been talentless, because I'd promised her I'd give her my honest opinion, and it was a promise I was intending to keep. But she wasn't talentless, far from it. Even I could tell.

She published her first collection two years later. Most of the poems I'd read that evening were in it. I didn't really understand them that first time, I couldn't work out what she was trying to do, where she was going with them, but I did realise at once that they were of a very high quality. There was something severe about them, something contrary, as if the world outside them was something she couldn't accept and was therefore unable to put into language. Or else it was the other way round, that what she'd put in them was the sum of everything she *could* accept. The lines were hard and compact, with big spaces in between, they looked almost like the bars of a cage. Later, I found myself thinking they alternated between keeping something in and keeping something out. The reader could be the tiger in the cage, staring out at the crowd, or she could be the crowd looking in at the tiger from without.

I remember putting the last page back on top of the others and neatening the pile.

'What do you think?' she said. 'Do you like them?'

'Vasya, you're a genius.'

Her eyes moistened and tears ran down her cheeks.

After that, I enjoyed her complete confidence, with all that it involved in the way of windows being opened on her chaotic emotional life. It was more than I'd asked for, and something that after a while I had to make efforts to constrain. I liked her, even became fond of her, so whenever I backed away I took pains to do so as considerately as possible, so that she wouldn't feel I was rejecting her.

A short time after that poetry evening, Lev and I became an item. To begin with we were together day and night, utterly consumed. Everything else was put on hold. We lay in bed well into the mornings and would then pop out for breakfast, yet as soon as our eyes met across the table we'd hurry back home and dive into bed again. Afterwards we'd sleep, and then carry on where we left off. We spent the evenings drinking, listening to music, dancing, making love. He was the only thing I wanted, nothing else meant anything at all. Everything that didn't involve him was vague and possessed no outline.

After a week or so, I decided I needed to go home and get some clean clothes. Lev came with me. We held hands all the way to the metro, or else walked with our arms around each other. We kept stopping to kiss. And when we carried on walking, he slipped his hand inside my back pocket, as I slipped my own into his.

'Let's go back,' I said. 'I want you.'

He laughed.

'We can do it in your room as well as mine, can't we?'

'But I want you now.'

He put his arms around me there at the entrance to the metro and we were like an island in the stream of people pouring into and out of the underground. I was hot with arousal and pressed my body against his.

Hand in hand we hurried back. As soon as we'd closed the door behind us, he kneeled and buried his face in my crotch, it was so heavenly I could hardly bear it. I shoved him away and unbuttoned my trousers to allow him inside me, it was all I wanted.

'I wonder how far we'll get this time,' he said, when eventually we went back out.

I smiled and squeezed his hand.

The communal room was empty. On the kitchen worktop was a large paper bag with my name on it. Opening it, I found it contained coffee, chocolate, sweets, and a couple of bread rolls, as well as a packet of aspirin.

'Who's it from?' said Lev.

'No idea,' I said. 'There's no note or anything.'

But I knew it could only have been Vasya. She must have thought I was ill when she hadn't seen me at lectures or in the library.

Lev said nothing when we stepped into my room, but sat down on the chair and waited while I found some clothes and a bag to put them in.

He didn't hold my hand on the way back either.

'What's the matter?' I said as we sat on the metro.

'Nothing,' he said.

'It's like someone turned your electricity off,' I said.

'It's nothing,' he said.

I realised he was jealous, and it quite appealed to me too, the thought that he cared so much about me that even the tiniest suspicion of there being someone else could darken his mind like that. I sensed he wasn't going to admit it if I started probing, so I left well alone and eventually brought him back round by employing other, more physical means.

'Where have you been?' Vasya said when I ran into her outside the lecture hall a few days later. 'Have you been ill? I've been worried sick!'

I nodded. I hadn't the heart to tell her the truth. It would only have made her kindness seem misplaced.

'A bit of flu, that's all,' I said. 'Was it you who left that goodie bag?'

'Yes, I thought you might need cheering up.'

'Thanks ever so much, Vaseshka, it was really kind of you.'

'But where were you? You weren't there.'

'I was with Lev,' I said reluctantly.

'Nearly two weeks?'

I didn't reply.

'Are you two serious now?'

I looked at her and couldn't help but smile as I realised we actually *were*.

'It might not be any of my business,' she said. 'But he's not good enough for you.'

'You're right,' I said. 'It's none of your business.'

I went inside and found a seat. Though several rows were practically empty, I sat down between two other students for the sole reason of stopping her from coming after me with her apologies.

It was no surprise to me that she knew about Lev, everyone did. Dashingly handsome, it was hard to keep your eyes off him when he walked into a room. He had a reputation, of course, and the rumours were many. The first I heard of him was that he was modelling for an agency alongside uni and that he was a real skirt chaser. The next was that he was involved in petty crime. Someone even said he was a junkie, so they'd heard.

Rumour debases the elevated, sullies the pure, and its function is to tell us that the best are no better than us and in fact are inferior.

I had no problem understanding that Vasya was jealous. Not because Lev was a threat to our friendship, but because someone like him was way beyond her reach. She probably didn't realise it herself, at any rate I was in no doubt that she believed what she said about him not being good enough for me, and that she said so because as a good friend she felt she could, indeed ought to, say things as they were.

By the time the lecture began, I'd decided to forgive her. Not being able to talk to her about everything Lev and I did together and how ecstatically happy it made me didn't feel like much of a loss. I'd never been one for confiding anyway. I liked to savour life's joys on my own, to let them glow inside me. Perhaps it was because I was practically an only child, perhaps because I read so many books when I was growing up and was used to not being able to share the strong emotions they evoked in me. I so remembered the singular joy of looking up from a book and knowing that no one else had any idea what world I was in as they went about doing whatever it was they happened to be doing at the time.

I went over to Vasya after the lecture and we went out and sat on a bench with coffees in the autumn sunlight. She apologised, just as I'd thought she would, told me I was right, that it was none of her business, and could I ever forgive her?

'There's nothing to forgive,' I said. 'You're blunt, it's the way you are. I like you for it. Not what you said, maybe, but the fact that you said it.'

'You're so in control all the time. How do you do that?'

'I wasn't in control when I walked away like that.'

'You were, in a way. You were controlling the situation. All I could do was stand there with the shame.'

I looked at her. She smiled at me.

'No harm done,' she said. 'Shame and me are old friends. You don't know her that well, though, do you?'

'So shame is feminine?'

'Didn't you know? No, of course you didn't, how could you?' She laughed. 'If we suppose that the masculine is all action and doing, and the feminine inaction and comtemplation, then shame is definitely feminine. It prohibits action, that's what it's there for.'

'Why would we suppose that the masculine is action and the feminine inaction?'

'We don't need to. We can call it something else. If doing is *kakaji* and passivity is *kakajo*, then shame is *kakajo*. Better?'

I smiled.

'You're funny,' I said.

'We complement each other.'

'There, you see. You *are* funny.'

Often there was something naive, childish almost, about Vasya, she could be like a little kid sometimes, and thought like one too. But in the poems she wrote all trace of that side of her was gone, they were advanced, sophisticated, controlled. In her course essays, and her contributions to our seminar discussions, she was incisive like no other. It was strange to witness how such maturity could coexist with its diametric opposite, seemingly without the two sides of her in any way impacting on each other. Yet the phenomenon was by no means unfamiliar to me, for Papa likewise had always had two very different sides to him. Although in his case it was not a matter of maturity versus immaturity, I nevertheless found the similarities striking. In Vasya I recognised Papa. Often disgruntled, often alone in his room, and then all of a sudden in the finest of moods, though always on his own terms, never one to bend down and meet me at eye level, so to speak. Even when he was being nice, it was always top-down. Papa was his own man, clear-cut and uncompromising, often spiky and abrasive in his interactions with others. And yet, when he began to play and filled the room with his music, one found oneself perplexed as to how something so wondrous could possibly emanate from him. That a man of such pent-up emotion moving a bow across the strings of a wooden box could even be associated with the ethereal richness and beauty their coming together produced, and which touched one's soul, was, if not unfathomable, then at the very least hard to grasp.

Something of the same applied to Vasya's poetry. Although she and Papa were as different as two people could be, they shared that same dichotomy between the people they were and the art they produced.

Lev, too, had a certain naivety about him, albeit well concealed behind his handsome, confident appearance, and something of the child would come over him whenever he was in the grip of his emotions, whether they were positive or negative.

After we'd been together three weeks he introduced me to his mother. We had dinner at hers one Sunday along with his sister who was three years older than him and did all she could to ignore me. His mother though was friendly, showed an interest and was very chatty. She had her hands full preparing the food in the kitchen and I understood then from the way he let her get on with it, without lifting a finger to help, that Lev was used to being waited on. When I got to my feet myself to offer a hand, she wouldn't hear of it.

As we drank our tea in the parlour afterwards, she told me about her brother's twelve-year-old son who was so good at playing the guitar that he'd just won a talent contest.

'I'm good at playing the guitar too,' said Lev. 'Or had you forgotten?'

I couldn't believe it. Was he unable to give credit to a child without feeling outdone? Didn't he realise how it came across?

It wasn't because we were soulmates that we were together, and it wasn't for the sake of profound conversation either. We were together because such things melted away and became unimportant as something else more primary consumed us — and because it felt so good! It was such a compelling force and brought with it a light so strong that everything else was erased in its glare. I'm not sure Lev ever thought of it like that, but I've no doubt that his feelings were the same. He wanted me as much as I wanted him. And he was proud of me, too, and liked to show me off.

It couldn't last. But then I never thought it would. I never went around thinking Lev and I had a future together, even if I never went around thinking we *didn't*, at least not as far as I remember. It was all about the here and now, about the longing I felt when he wasn't there, the joy that surged in me when he was.

He was expecting me to take him home to my parents. I procrastinated, kept putting it off, making up excuses.

I'd never had a boyfriend before, so bringing one home would have been a big thing for Mama and Papa, a significant event.

I should have done it, of course, taken him home with me and not cared about what they were going to think, stood up for my right to choose, but I wasn't that independent, wasn't that free. I envisaged with horror Papa probing him about his reading preferences, his opinions, his thoughts. Mama would have received him with open arms, an open mind, and would never have said anything at all critical about him to me, but she'd have had her own ideas, and the last thing I wanted was to disappoint her like that.

It ended predictably. The overpowering lust, the thrill and the joy of it all, diminished, and then there was little else left. Lev became draggy, nothing interested him, all he wanted was to hang out with his friends, strum his guitar, play his computer games. He saw nothing wrong in staying in bed all day smoking hash if that was what he wanted. He didn't like me going out without him either, on several occasions even insisting on going with me to wherever it was and then returning to pick me up when it was time to come home.

So I ended it. He made it more difficult than I'd envisaged. Hadn't he realised how different we were? That there was a gulf between us? Apparently not. He just stared vacantly at me as I told him I thought it best for us to split up.

'What are you saying?'

'I think it's best we split up.'

'Why?'

The astonishment in his voice was genuine. He seriously didn't get it.

I explained my thoughts to him. *But we're so great together!* he said more than once. When eventually I moved towards the door, he almost shouted at me:

'Don't go! Do you hear me? If you go out that door, we're finished!'

'I'm sorry, Lev,' I said, and left.

I didn't share those last words of his with anyone for years. What he'd said was comical, and I didn't want people to think of him like that. Not least because I was pregnant by then. I hadn't known at the time, but a week later the signs got me wondering. I took a test and was hurled into a turmoil of confusion, joy and despair when it turned out positive.

Every argument spoke in favour of an abortion. I was only twenty years old, had only just moved away from home, only just started at uni, and was no longer in a relationship with the father.

The fact that I chose differently had to do, I think, with Lev and what I'd experienced with him. Before we met, I'd had a certain picture of myself, the sort of person I was, and thought that was what I was going to be like for the rest of my life. I'd never had a boyfriend, and the two times I'd gone to bed with someone before Lev it had been awkward and a bit painful too, with only the slightest flare of gratification, like a match struck in the dark, and so that's what I thought it was like, the real thing didn't seem at all comparable to the eruptive sexual experience I'd read about. But then along came Lev and we were together through all those fantastic weeks, a time filled with so much desire, so much joy, and through it all the recurring thought: Is this me? Is this really me? I love this new me!

Becoming a mother at the age of twenty wasn't a prospect I'd ever entertained. Faced with the choice, my first thought was a tentative: Why not? Why couldn't I? Why not now?

'You must complete your education first.' That was Papa's stance. 'You want a rich life, don't you? An education will give you opportunities that won't come your way otherwise. Have a child now and your life will be seriously restricted. You realise this, surely?'

'If it's what you want, then we'll help you all we can,' said Mama, bless her.

I took my exams heavily pregnant, went back home to Samara, had the baby there and lived with Mama and Papa, with Seva, for a year before resuming my studies. Seva stayed behind with them then. Mama's mother had done the same for her, with Sasha, so it was almost a family tradition, she joked. I'd had to give up my student accommodation, but Papa had lots of connections in Moscow, one of whom got me into a small flat I could rent at well below the going rate, one and a half rooms and a kitchen, where first I lived alone, then with Seva.

Lev couldn't understand why I wanted to have the baby when we weren't together any more. When Seva was born, Lev seemed oddly unable to grasp the situation, to see the child as anything separate from its mother, and at first invested nothing. Later, when Seva was about five years old, Lev's paternal instinct was as if awoken and the two of them spent more time together, the father finding great joy in his son from that moment on.

My life of course became so much richer with Seva, in no way as restricted as Papa had warned. The year I'd supposedly *lost* made no difference one way or another. I went back to uni, if not to literature. This in part was down to Vasya. Literature was just about everything to her, it was something she lived and breathed, providing her with a space in which to grow and infusing her life with purpose. At least, that's what it looked like from where I was standing. I was in a different place. I'd grown up with books, and Papa had fed me with the finest works from an early age, sometimes even with volumes that were banned, impressing upon me that while he, for some reason, was allowed to own them, it was of the utmost importance that I not mention to anyone that I was reading Akhmatova, Whitman, Cervantes, Tsvetaeva and Hamsun, to name but a few of the authors whose work he made sure came my way while I was growing up. And yet gradually literature became more of a supplement, something extraneous, not the be-all and end-all I'd thought it was. This became clear to me when I met Vasya.

So what *was* the be-all and end-all?

What did I want?

Or more exactly: what did I want to *know*?

Everything I'd wondered about ever since I was little, things that had never let go of me and which nonetheless I'd never given a chance, kicking them into a corner where the rest of my childhood lay collected, came back to me once I started thinking these very foundational thoughts. Why faces looked the way they did, that was one thing I used to wonder about, seeing them as somehow detached from the people they belonged to, a bit like the way one might consider a strange animal. Why did trees look the way they did? They too were different from one another, every one was unique. What was life exactly? Once, while on a class excursion, I suppose I was about nine years old at the time, I lifted up a large flat stone under which a snake lay curled, giving me such a fright that I immediately dropped it again. When a few moments later I plucked up the courage to lift the stone once more, I found the snake had been chopped in half. The front part with the head slithered forward, it looked a bit like a lorry without its trailer, while the rear end lay wriggling. It was alive, no question, but what sort of life could it be without a head? Life stripped back to its purest form, perhaps? Life as life and nothing else?

I hadn't cared for maths at school, I had no aptitude for it, the same with physics, but I was good at chemistry and biology. I didn't give it any thought at the time, it was just the way it was, but going back to uni after Seva it suddenly became clear to me: maths and physics were abstract, chemistry and biology were concrete. That literature studies hadn't really worked for me, even though I loved reading, had nothing to do with abstract versus concrete, however, more with it being so sub-jective and concerning itself so little with fact: the most important thing in any text about literature was not a question of right or wrong but of persuasive force. And that always led back to whoever wrote it.

Wherein did the persuasive force of such a text lie? This was a matter of rhetoric, a cultural phenomenon that was partly acquired, partly to do with individual personality, qualities and traits you either had or hadn't. Vasya had them, I didn't. What did that mean? If we were writ-ing about the same text, we'd be doing so on the basis of our different experiences and backgrounds, naturally, that was why what we wrote would be different regardless that we were writing about the same thing. But in what way were those differences articulated inside us? The brain wasn't abstract, even if the thoughts it produced were. The question of what a thought actually *was* seemed more interesting to me than any thought itself, whatever its nature. The head slithering away on its own, the body left wriggling behind, was something long since past, yet it remained in my mind to be repeated at will. That too was something concrete, a physical event. All this appealed to me. The body, not the book. Nature, not culture.

The same logic that had led from Lev to Seva — *this too could be me* — caused me to take these childlike musings seriously, holding them up to the light to see what happened to them then. Did they belong to childhood or to me?

I switched to biology. It was like coming home. In every room I entered, doors led off into other rooms. Eventually I found my own. Not the tree, not the animal, but the forest and all its correlations. I delved into the interplay between fungi and trees and wrote a thesis on the subject. It was enthusiastically received throughout the department and for a while I was regarded as a highly promising talent. After that I made a couple of less fortunate choices, I had big ideas about myself and went against some very good advice thinking it didn't apply to me, I'd seen something they hadn't, I thought, and by the time Vasya turned up out of the blue in the canteen that day all that was left of my career were my lectures to the undergraduates, which I assumed would soon be given to someone else more promising than myself. In all likelihood my peers saw me as a rather esoteric character, a kind of hippy biologist who talked to trees. Nothing could have been further from the truth, or further from my nature. But the truth was nobody's friend, not even mine.

Vasya for her part had left university, but not literature. After finishing her degree she founded a literary journal. When circumstances forced her to close it down she found a job working for another one, alongside translating books of varying quality from French and English, though she continued writing her own poetry even if her name remained unknown to all but a small audience of the initiated.

She knew practically nothing about what I was doing with myself, apart from that I worked at the university, so the fact that I felt so tormented by feelings of stagnation, both professionally and in my private life, wasn't something I particularly wanted to get into as we sat together in the restaurant on the top floor of the shopping precinct. She was so full of herself. It's what happens to a person when they spend a whole year on their own, I told myself.

She munched her salad while I sat prodding at my salmon. We'd been lucky to get a table by the window. The snow was still falling into the streets below, the great belly of the sky pressing down on the tallest buildings across the river.

'No new man in your life?' she said, a dribble of white salad dressing poised in the corner of her mouth, a bit of green leaf stuck between her front teeth.

'None to speak of,' I said. 'How about you?'

She shook her head.

'Who wants a fat, pasty poet?'

'Firstly, you're not fat. But even if you were, I'm sure someone somewhere will be fantasising about it as we speak.'

'What a bizarre fetish!' she said, and laughed.

'You've got some salad dressing, just here,' I said, putting an index finger to the corner of my own mouth to indicate the spot.

'Here?' she said, dabbing with her napkin.

'No, other side.'

She wiped it away and returned the napkin to her lap.

'Really nice to see you, Alya,' she said.

'Same here,' I said. I couldn't mention the salad leaf too, one had to be careful not to be fussy with people, so when she smiled at me I smiled back, turning my head to look down into the street below so as to avoid the issue altogether.

'Would you like to read what I've written so far?'

'Of course!' I said emphatically. I knew how sensitive she could be when it came to her writing.

'Oh, that's marvellous! You're the best reader I know.'

'I've already agreed. No need to flatter me now.'

'But you are! You're as sharp as a knife. No one cuts through the nonsense I write like you.'

'What's it called?'

'I don't know yet. Either *The Wolves* or *Eternity*, I think.'

'*The Wolves*.'

'Sure?'

'Yes. *Eternity* is too abstract. But what kind of wolves are they?'

'The wolves of the dense forest of Eternity.'

'Ah, Tsvetaeva. Aren't you done with her yet?'

'*However much you feed a wolf, it always looks to the forest. We are all wolves of the dense forest of Eternity*,' she quoted. 'Isn't that splendid?'

I nodded.

'I thought about you, actually,' she went on. 'I always do when I read about the forest. That wasn't the only reason though. She touches on Rilke in that essay, too. He was obsessed with Russia, as you know. *There is such a country called God, and Russia borders on it*, he wrote. Do you remember?'

I shook my head.

'It does sound like Rilke, though.'

'Yes, doesn't it just?'

'Was that before or after the Revolution?'

'Before. But I don't think it mattered that much to him, he considered the Revolution to be something temporary, something that got in the way of what he thought to be the true Russia.'

'How wrong can a person get! He was certainly no prophet.'

'Funny you should say so, because Tsvetaeva is writing about time there. Past, future, present, eternity. She believes Rilke to be the

counterweight of her time, its antithesis. Wherein lies his contempo-
rality, as she writes.'

'So there's a time that's time as we know it, marching on with revo-
lutions and wars and inventions and the like, and then there's Rilke's
time, which is outside of time as we know it, and where everything
stays the same?'

'That's it.'

'It's all a bit *kakajo* and *kakaji*, don't you think? On the one hand
action, doing, change, and on the other inaction, passivity, immutabil-
ity? It's politics and religion, isn't it?'

'It's what I'm writing about. About something having happened to
time.'

'Like what?'

She gave a shrug and shifted on her chair. I took a sip of wine and
surveyed the room in search of our waiter, sending him a discreet nod
once I'd located him and he caught sight of the hand I raised.

'It sounds a bit silly, I know,' said Vasya. 'But not in the essay, not in
its context.'

'Then tell me.'

'The idea is that eternity has begun. That's what's changed. The
future is no more, and eternity has begun. So what you called politics
has become what you called religion, in the sense that it oversees the
immutable. And awaits the immortal.'

'The immortal?'

'Yes. It's no longer just the Church that talks about eternal life. Science does too.'

'I'd like to give myself time to read this, Lisa,' I said. 'But now I really
must buy that present for Papa before Sevka comes.'

'Was it that silly?'

'Silly? No. No, not at all. Quite the opposite, in fact. I get what you're
saying completely, about eternity having begun. And I'll really look forward to reading about it. But the fact is we're stuck in real time right
now, and I've a flight to catch . . .'

Fortunately, she smiled, then drained her wine glass.

'I'll pick up the bill,' I said, waving a hand to fend off any false protest and avoiding looking at her for the same reason, rummaging in my

bag and taking out my wallet. 'I won't hear of anything else, this is on me,' I added before she had time to reply.

I looked up at her, card in hand, and she gave me a little nod.

'Thanks awfully, Alya.'

Once outside, we paused to say goodbye, and then, after we'd done so, she suddenly asked me about a book.

'Have you read Aitmatov, *The Day Lasts More than a Hundred Years*?'

'It sounds familiar,' I said. 'I'm not sure that I have, though. What's it about?'

I couldn't resist the urge to glance at my watch.

That did it. She got the message.

'You're in a hurry,' she said. 'Thanks for lunch. It was really nice seeing you again, Alya!'

She gave me a quick hug and then started off in the direction of the metro over by Red Square, whereas I hastened in the other direction. I didn't have much time, but as long as I could find a book in a hurry, I'd be all right.

The antiquarian booksellers had been there for as long as I'd lived in Moscow, but I'd only been inside a few times. They specialised in first editions, which had never been my interest. What was in a book interested me, not books themselves. The same was true of Papa, only his eightieth birthday called for something a bit more than the usual.

Two German tourists were browsing in the otherwise empty shop. They looked to be academics, or perhaps that was just me stereotyping, thinking you had to be an academic to take an interest in books. The proprietor, bald with a white beard and a bulbous nose with wide open pores, was sitting behind the counter staring at his mobile phone.

I went over to a row of glass cabinets and passed my eye over their contents.

Pasternak's first poetry collection, *My Sister, Life*, how much could that cost?

Papa would like that.

I approached the counter, and the man looked up at me.

'The Pasternak you've got there, *My Sister, Life*. How much are you asking for it?'

'Eighty thousand, my dear,' he said with a smile. 'Do you want it?'

'Eighty thousand?'

He put up his hands.

'Eighty thousand and it's yours.'

'But that's madness.'

'It's dedicated to Lermontov.'

'I think I'll read it in paperback!' I said, and gave him a disarming smile. 'I'm looking for a present for someone who's very interested in literature and whose eightieth birthday is tomorrow. Only he's not worth eighty thousand.'

'He likes poetry?'

'Yes.'

'I have a first edition of Tsvetaeva's final collection, *After Russia*. Would that be of interest?'

'I'm sure it would. But of course it would depend on the price.'

'Thirty-five thousand,' he said. 'No?'

'Do I look like the sort of person who can afford to pay thirty-five thousand for a book?'

'Yes, as a matter of fact,' he said. 'But how much do you have at your disposal? That might be the sensible approach. Then we'll see what we can find.'

'Call me naive, but I was thinking maybe two thousand, three at the most.'

'Ah,' he said. 'In that case I think we must disregard the first editions, at least those of the well-known writers. Would it have to be a first edition?'

'Not at all. It just needs to be something special, that's all. I'll have a look round on my own, if you don't mind.'

I had to be making tracks soon to meet up with Seva. But I couldn't just swipe any old thing off the shelf.

I should never have gone in. Papa had so many books as it was.

When I was a child, I got him the same aftershave year after year. A square green glass bottle. That would probably touch him more than any poetry collection.

'I've a Tolstoy's collected works, not in the first edition, but it's old and as good as untouched,' the owner said, coming towards me. 'It would make a fine gift.'

'No thanks. He hates Tolstoy with a passion.'

I lifted my gaze and straight away something caught my attention in the window. A man was standing outside looking in, and our eyes met.

My blood ran cold. It was the troublemaker from my lecture.

Had he been following me?

It couldn't have been coincidence. Moscow was a huge city and I was a long way from the university.

He turned and walked away.

Should I go after him and confront him?

He'd only deny it.

I turned back to the bookseller and smiled apologetically.

'I'm afraid it looks like I'm going to have to find something else,' I said. 'But thanks for your help!'

'My pleasure,' he said. 'I could put you on our mailing list, if you like?'

'Thanks all the same,' I said. 'But I only came in for the present.'

Outside I paused on the step and looked up and down the long street before satisfying myself that the troublemaker had gone.

Why had he been following me?

Was he a madman who'd become obsessesed with me and thrown caution to the wind?

He was nothing more than a big kid, I couldn't be scared of him.

But I was.

I'd been planning to take the metro, the nearest station was only a couple of blocks away, but instead I ordered a taxi using the app and stood waiting outside the bookshop for it to come. There'd been something about his face that frightened me. It hadn't shown a trace of surprise. He must have known I was there. And he'd smiled as if he owned me.

How old could he be? Twenty? Twenty-two?

The taxi pulled up at the kerb. I opened the door and got in. Took off my hat and gloves and put them down on the seat next to me. It was like an oven in there.

The driver looked at me in the rear-view.

'How long will it take approximately?' I said.

'Half an hour, give or take,' he said.

In that case, I could remove my coat as well. I began to unbutton it, then changed my mind, sensing that I'd feel naked in just my blouse. Unprotected.

I leaned back in the seat and gazed out the window. I liked few things better than travelling, even short rides such as this. I was unbound to anything I saw, buildings and people appeared in my field of vision and disappeared out of it again while demanding nothing at all of me. How different it would be to be *there*, inside one of those buildings, for example. Buildings always required something of you. People did too, of course.

We turned onto Tverskaya and the driver picked up speed. I got my phone out and saw that Vasya had sent me a text.

Great seeing you! And thanks for lunch!

I hesitated, feeling I'd had enough of her for the moment, and texted Papa instead.

Did the firewood come?

Outside, a huge crater of a building site came into view through orange mesh fencing. Behind the fencing, yellow diggers, men in over-alls and hard hats. A new shopping precinct, perhaps.

Papa replied:

YES. THANK YOU.

Good, I typed back. *But why the capital letters?*

GOT A NEW PHONE. IT'S ONLY GOT UPPER CASE.

I smiled.

I'm sure it hasn't, I typed. *Seva can show you when we get there. Upper case looks like you're shouting!*

PERHAPS I AM.

What could I get him in Samara?

Maybe the aftershave wasn't such a bad idea. If you could still get it.

What else?

Books.

But not antiquarian.

Something he'd never heard of before.

A collection of poems by some new poet?

It wouldn't be enough.

Ten collections by ten new poets? Now that would be good! He'd be pleased with that.

I got my phone out again and texted Vasya.

Great seeing you, too. Looking forward to reading your essay! Question: the 10 best poetry collections of the last 5 years?

There was no reason to be annoyed with her, not really. She was only being herself. Needy as ever. But she was a giving person as well. At least sometimes she was. Mostly she seemed unaware of how she came across, how her behaviour could affect people. It was an aspect of human life she appeared never to have noticed. Other people's feelings.

Seva was sitting with a beer in front of him and his headphones on when I walked into the cafe. Although I came up to him from behind and touched his shoulder before he'd had a chance to see me, he didn't jump but calmly took off the headphones, lifted his phone out of his inside pocket and switched off his music, smiling before asking if he could get me anything.

'No thanks,' I said. 'And you know what I think about the hair of the dog, don't you?'

'It's not the hair of the dog, Mama. It's just a beer. We're on holiday now. You don't need to be so tense.'

'I'm not tense,' I said, sitting down to face him at the table. 'I just don't want my son ending up an alcoholic. Did you remember my suitcase?'

He nodded, indicating the two cabin cases he'd tucked out of the way under the table next to him.

'Maybe I will have something,' I said. 'A latte, perhaps.'

'Do you want milk in that?' he said, getting to his feet.

I looked at him.

'Joking,' he said. 'How stupid do you think I am?'

He went over to order. The girl behind the counter, slight of frame, her forehead inflamed with acne, threw him a bashful glance before immediately looking away, then another as she began to prepare the coffee. Seva turned his head towards me and smiled.

The unease I'd felt on seeing the troublemaker from my lecture had evaporated now that I was with Seva. My son, as tall as a house, with all the build and bearing of an ice-hockey pro. How strange it was that I, who had looked after him ever since he was an infant, should now seek protection in his company.

But it wasn't like that really.

He said something to the poor girl, who looked up at him again as if from the depths of shyness. He probably didn't realise the power he had, or that he was exercising it now. In all likelihood he simply thought it was how the world was arranged. For his benefit.

'A latte with milk,' he said as he put the coffee down on the table.

'Thanks,' I said.

'It's ages since I was there last,' he said.

'Are you looking forward to it?'

'Yes, I suppose I am.'

'I'm glad you wanted to come.'

'Good. Is he doing all right?'

'I think we can be reasonably sure that everything's the way it's always been as far as your dedushka is concerned. He has been having some pains in his leg, though. A bit of trouble walking, by the sounds of it. That's about all I could get out of him. He's too proud to tell me about it.'

'What's pride got to do with it?'

'He doesn't want to complain. There was a time, you know, long ago in a faraway world, when it wasn't the done thing to complain.'

'I don't complain.'

'Did I say you did?'

'No, but it was what you meant. I know you. Besides, you're the one who complains.'

'I am not. What do I complain about?'

'Me.'

I laughed.

'That's different!'

'Complaining is complaining.'

He drained the rest of his beer in a single gulp and put the empty glass down with a little thud on the table.

'The next train leaves in eight minutes,' he said. 'We can catch it, no problem. Better to hang around at the airport than here.'

As we left Moscow behind and darkness descended outside, Seva sat playing a game on his phone, which lit up and flickered intermittently, small in his big hands. It looked like it was a children's game, a figure on some endless journey, obstructed continually by all sorts of hindrances. I sat with a book in my lap, dipping into it every now and then. It was a Christmas present Papa had given me a few years back, one that I'd left untouched until for some reason the previous evening I'd decided to take it with me. *A Journey Round My Skull*, it was called, by Frigyes Karinthy. He must have been prompted to get it for me after a discussion we'd had late one evening on the subject of the human mind, which presumably had left an impression on him, because normally he wasn't the kind who would buy anyone a present on the basis of that person's own interests or preferences. Nearly everything he'd bought me in the past had been something he was excited about himself. Usually something that tied in with his reading projects. He would read progressively, theme by theme or author by author, and could be absorbed in his endeavour for weeks, months or even years, according to how wide a frame he'd given himself. The seventeenth century was one such frame, the Greek dramas another, J. W. Dunne a third. Mama had once told me how at the age of fifty-something he'd panicked completely at the realisation that his days were numbered and that life was never going to allow him time enough to read and study everything he was intending to. I'd asked him often what he wanted with all that knowledge. *When you're dead, it'll all be gone!*

He'd laughed at the notion, and had even returned to it several times since with the same amusement.

But he hadn't answered.

I sensed someone staring and when I turned my head I found myself looking straight at a young dad in the seats across the aisle. He held my gaze for a long moment before looking away. His wife was holding a baby in the crook of her arm, rocking the child to sleep, while a boy of about four sat watching something on a phone that lay on the table between them. He'd been throwing a strop when they got on, his dad shoving him along in front of him with a suitcase in each hand while the mother had taken up the rear with a rucksack and the baby, it too screaming, a blobby shape in its padded snowsuit.

I returned to my book. A few minutes passed, and then I felt him staring again.

It was pathetic.

I felt an urge to ask him what he wanted, why he kept looking at me all the time, so that his wife would know what she was married to.

She probably knew already.

I stared at the page for a long time without taking in anything it said. It was the same whenever I started reading something new, it was as if there was a glass wall between it and me that I had to make an effort to smash before I could get into it.

I wasn't happy.

Why not?

I was going home, to celebrate my father. I'd be seeing Oksanka, and Seva was going to be there.

A glass wall between me and that too.

I stood up, put the book down on my seat, picked up my bag and went through to the next carriage where there was a WC. The floor inside was wet and stained with footprints. Some bits of toilet paper lay floating in a little puddle.

At least I didn't look as tired as I felt. I refreshed my lipstick and put some more eyeliner on, then washed my hands. The paper towel dispenser was empty and as I reached for some toilet paper instead someone rattled the door, pressing the handle down hard several times in succession.

What was wrong with people? Why couldn't they look and see if it was occupied first?

There was no toilet paper either.

I pulled the window down as far as it would go, which wasn't very far, and let the cold air assail my face. Some housing blocks lit up the darkness a few hundred metres from the tracks, and behind them a ribbon of light where a road went.

Whoever it was now knocked on the door.

For crying out loud, have some patience.

I pushed the button to flush the toilet and a rush of noise filled the small space, drowning out all other sound for a moment.

'About time,' the man outside grumbled as I opened the door.

Thickset, with a fleshy face, youthful-looking curls, round glasses.

'Yura?' I said.

He didn't reply but squeezed past and locked the door behind him.

It *was* Yura, I told myself as I went back to my seat. I couldn't be wrong about that, surely?

Seva didn't look up as I sat down next to him again.

'Are you winning?' I said.

'I'm always winning,' he said.

'You don't want to talk to your mum, then?'

'In a minute.'

The train's loudspeaker system chimed, followed by an announcement saying we'd be arriving in a few moments. I dropped my book into my bag and stood up.

'We don't need to be first out, do we?' said Seva, still without looking up.

'Come on,' I said. 'Put that phone away, now.'

He looked up then in surprise. *Seriously?* his eyes said. *You're mad at me for this?*

But he did as I said. Slipped his phone into his inside pocket, stood up and took our two cases down from the luggage rack.

I saw him again in the departures hall, Yura, he was standing at the check-in desk next to the one where we were queuing up. He turned and tucked his boarding card into his coat pocket, and then he recognised me.

'Alevtinka!' he said, coming across. 'So it *was* you! I'm sorry, I didn't mean to —'

'Ignore me?'

'No, no, I wasn't ignoring you, I just didn't *see* you, that's all! I heard a voice, yes, and my name, perhaps, but it was too late by then, I'd locked the door. What could I do? I had a rather urgent matter to attend to, if you follow my drift!'

He laughed disarmingly.

'Are you going somewhere?' he said. 'Stupid of me, of course you are. But where? Where are you off to?'

'We're going to Samara,' I said. 'This is Sevastyan, by the way. Seva, this is Yuri Sergeyevich.'

They shook hands.

'Yura and I were in upper secondary together,' I said.

'Twenty years and twenty kilos ago,' he said.

'Do you still live in Samara?' Seva said.

'Samara? No. No, I live and work in Moscow these days. Or work and live, I should say. In that order.'

The man in front of us turned away and we stepped forward. I handed our tickets and passports to the woman at the desk and she began checking us in while I carried on talking to Yura. He was just as amiable as I remembered him, though the sensitivity that had always been such a part of his make-up, not immediately detectable but somewhere beneath the surface, a guardedness in his eyes, was no longer evident, supplanted now by something more compliant. Perhaps it was down to the weight he'd put on. It lent his face an almost puppyish appearance.

'Baggage?' the woman said.

'Hand luggage only,' I said.

She handed me back the passports with our boarding cards tucked between the pages.

'It was really nice seeing you,' Yura said. 'You haven't changed a bit!'

'Nice seeing you too,' I said. 'You were one of the few people I actually liked back then.'

To my surprise he blushed.

'Now she tells me,' he muttered. 'Couldn't you have said so at the time instead of waiting all these years?'

He laughed and produced a business card.

'I'm off home for the weekend as well. Perhaps we can have a drink together for old times' sake, if you can find a minute.'

'I doubt if I can,' I said. 'We'll have our hands full. But if there's an opening all of a sudden, I'll give you a ring.'

'Great,' he said. 'I'll be saying goodbye then, for the time being. See you at the security check in a few minutes!'

He laughed again and walked away. I glanced at his business card before putting it away in my wallet. He was managing director of a car import firm.

Who would have thought it?

'What a dork,' said Seva.

'That's easy for you to say,' I said with a smile. 'But remember before you judge him that he's got twenty years more life experience than you.'

'I read somewhere that men reach their peak between the ages of eighteen and twenty,' he said. 'It's all downhill after that. You get slower and slower, and weaker and weaker.'

'It's true. But a person is more than just their body.'

'Says the biologist?'

'Yes. Says the biologist.'

When we went through to the security check, Yura was already at the conveyor. He took off his beige-coloured coat, folded it neatly and placed it in the plastic tray, turned his pockets out and put his loose change and keys on top. Then, in white shirt and blue tie, rings of sweat under his armpits and his belly bulging over the top of his trousers, he stepped into the little cage-like structure with his arms in the air, as if giving himself up to someone we couldn't see.

He'd already gone by the time we got through ourselves and I found it rather disconcerting knowing that he was somewhere out there in the departure area; on the one hand I'd hardly be able to ignore him if we ran into each other, on the other I had no desire at all to sit down and talk to him.

'What did you get Dedulya for his birthday?' Seva asked as we ambled through the shopping area.

'I couldn't find anything. I'll have to go into town tomorrow and get something. Any ideas?'

He shook his head and ran a hand through his short dark hair.

'How about a bottle of cognac? He likes cognac.'

'It's his eightieth birthday!'

'Eighty bottles, then.'

'I was looking at a book I thought he might like. Do you know how much it cost?'

'No.'

'Eighty thousand.'

'For a book?'

'Yes. Not just any book, though. A famous one.'

'Who'd pay eighty thousand for a *book*?'

'More people than you'd imagine. Not me, though.'

'I'm hungry. How about you?'

'No, I'm all right. But you go ahead.'

'There's a burger place over there.'

'We'll go there, then.'

I caught sight of Yura again, standing at a coffee-shop counter. He lifted his hand in a wave and smiled when he saw me, then immediately turned away. No doubt he was thinking the same as me, that we couldn't keep saying hello to each other all the time.

While Seva placed his order I checked my emails. Vasiya had sent me a list of twelve poetry collections and attached her essay. I'd also received a reminder about a faculty meeting, an invitation to a colleague's fiftieth-birthday reception and a word from Regina, my therapist, saying I owed her for three sessions and could I pay for four at my next appointment.

Nothing that could give me a lift.

Seva came over with a tray gripped between his hands. In his black leather jacket and black jeans he looked even more like his father than usual, if that was possible.

He put the tray down and handed me back my card.

'Forgot the ketchup,' he said, and went up to the counter again.

I switched my phone to flight mode while I remembered, and then got my book out of my bag.

'You don't want to talk, then?' Seva said after a couple of mouthfuls.

I put it down and smiled at him.

'Yes, that would be nice.'

'What do you want to talk about?'

'Conversation is supposed to be something that happens, you can't plan it.'

He took a swig of beer and dipped a couple of fries into his blob of ketchup.

'All right,' he said, biting then into his hamburger. 'We could talk about ice hockey. We never talk about ice hockey.'

'There's a reason for that.'

'Football, then?'

'Same.'

He threw up his arms.

'That's it, then. I've run out of topics now.'

'What about girls?'

'I'm not going to talk to you about girls. You understand, I'm sure.'

'Is that something you talk to your father about?'

He gave me a look I couldn't gauge.

Then shoved the rest of his burger into his mouth.

'Is it all right if I get another one?'

I nodded and handed him my card.

Fortunately, the flight was only half full. Classical music came through the speakers as we boarded. I'd got a window seat and Seva thoughtfully shifted to the aisle seat so I'd have plenty of room. Or else he was making sure he could stretch his long legs. I picked out Yura's curly mop of hair in one of the seats up front, expecting him to turn round and wave at any minute, or at least look to see where I was sitting, but he didn't.

The blinking lights outside were oddly soothing, perhaps it was because I was so patently, so inextricably in the hands of others. I closed my eyes and absorbed the music. The darkness allowed it to come forth inside me, like a figure almost, wispy and thin, with unseeing eyes it felt its way around, mingling at first with my thoughts, then, for a brief moment, in the seconds before I fell asleep, quite on its own.

When I woke up, we were airborne. Seva was asleep with his mouth wide open. The two heavily made-up flight attendants had reached our row with their trolley. It must have been that that woke me.

I asked for a coffee and put it down on the tray in front of me, then gazed out into the darkness that was punctured here and there by little dots of light, ribbons where the roads were, clusters where there were villages and towns. The taiga from which they shone seemed so endless when traversed by car or train, a landscape that was part forest, part plain, fields stretching away with the roads, monotonous and unspectacular. Bitterly cold and lashed by winds in winter, blazing hot and dry in summer.

I opened the little sachet of milk and tipped its contents into my cup.

Those few minutes of sleep had done me the world of good. For the first time all day, I was actually looking forward to going home.

How strange that I still thought of it that way, as *home*. It was more than twenty years since I'd left the place.

I glanced at Seva, who was well away, a dribble of spit bubbling in the corner of his mouth. I got my book out, but after only a couple of pages put it down in my lap again and leaned my head back. I thought about my lecture earlier in the day. I would never have dared disrupt a lecture the way he'd done. Interrupted, perhaps, to ask a question, but certainly not to query the very foundations of the discipline.

What was it he'd said?

That evolutionary theory needed to explain where DNA came from before it could be taken as valid.

It certainly did not.

I almost wished he'd known what he was talking about. It could have been interesting. But evolution started with DNA. That was the mechanism that made it possible.

Why hadn't I said so?

Listen, I should have explained, *DNA does two things: it replicates itself so that life can be passed on to the next generation. But not without the occasional error, mutations, as we call them, which are what make variation possible. Both are crucial to life's continued development. Therefore, evolution starts with DNA.*

But where did DNA come from? he would have asked. *If DNA is something separate from evolution? Was it just chance? A fluke? How can such a sophisticated technology, a biological coding language, arise out of chance?*

Oh, go to hell with all your stupid questions! I could hear myself respond. *Get out of here, go on!*

That would have been something.

I could have taken my shoes off and hurled them at him. My laptop, too. Screaming and shouting.

Then, when called to explain myself to the faculty executives: *He was asking questions of a heretical nature! He believed God was behind all life!*

What? they'd say. *You mean, he didn't believe life to have emerged all by itself? Well, in that case, we understand your behaviour, Alevtina Yegoryevna! You have our full support!*

All creatures were limited in their scope of understanding. We were continually impressed to learn how much animals and insects could do. Bees, for instance, could take instructions from signs. But the most striking thing about animals was that they had no conception of how tethered they were to their respective worlds. There was no reason why human beings should be any different in that respect. Like animals, we possessed a horizon of understanding within which our thoughts could freely move, and the space in which they moved was our reality. The edges of that horizon were mists where everything blurred, and beyond the mists was a wall, everything after that was unreachable to us. The nature of the mind was something that lay beyond our horizon of understanding. The nature of the universe and the atoms: beyond. Time: beyond. Death: beyond.

What would my twenty-year-old self have said about that?

Come on, you don't really believe that, do you? It can't be right. I know you! And as you well know, human beings have always existed within their horizon of understanding, and what lay beyond it once had a name: God. And we don't believe in God. Do we?

No, we don't. But we believe in the mists, and in the wall at which everything stops.

Speak for yourself!

The noise of the engines altered pitch and I realised we'd started the descent. One of the flight attendants came up the aisle with a bag for rubbish. The other one stood with her back towards us in the space between the seats and the door of the cockpit and took a handset down from the wall. A moment later her voice came over the intercom.

Seva opened his eyes.

'Are we there?' he said, wiping his mouth with his forefinger and thumb.

'Not long.'

'Have you got any snacks with you?'

'Are you hungry again?'

'Low blood sugar. It's always the same if I sleep during the day.'

'Sorry. Or rather, wait a minute. I think I might have an apple somewhere.'

I reached between my feet and felt around inside my bag until my fingers encountered the round, smooth surface of the fruit.

'There you go.'

He devoured it within a minute.

In the lights that lit up the tarmac I could see it was snowing. A bit further away, snowploughs with flashing beacons were hard at work.

'Are you going to see Gena while we're here?' I said.

'I hadn't thought about it. Maybe.'

'I think you should.'

'Mm.'

The plane wobbled from side to side and then the wheels touched the ground and we hurtled along with the flaps up, the engines roaring with reverse thrust. The snow blew horizontally in the floodlights.

'Are we getting a taxi?'

'Mark's picking us up.'

'Who's Mark?'

'Oksanka's husband. You know Mark.'

'Oh, him. What sort of car has he got?'

'How should I know? And what does it matter?'

The aircraft came to a halt outside the terminal building and Seva jumped to his feet.

'We're not in a hurry,' I said.

He sat down again.

'You're only saying that because you don't want to see that old friend of yours again.'

'His name's Yura,' I said. 'And of course I'm not. I don't like being rushed about and getting worked up, that's all. We've plenty of time.'

Seva smiled to himself.

'What are you smiling at?'

'Nothing. You don't like getting worked up. OK.'

He got his phone out and started playing his game as the passengers began to shuffle past. He couldn't sit still for even two minutes without entertainment. I said nothing, but stared out of the window at the great mounds the snowploughs had piled up outside the terminal building, a plane that came slowly towards us, lights blinking from its wings that swayed in the wind. He wasn't stupid. He saw right through me sometimes. But he wasn't curious about anything. He was like his father in that respect. The way he'd rather sit back and enjoy rather than make an effort for the future, it infuriated me. And when occasionally my exasperation got the better of me and I confronted him with it, he'd simply say life was happening now, in the present, and what else was life about than enjoying it while it lasted? He knew how much it got me going.

The last of the passengers from behind us had now vacated their seats and I gave him a nudge.

'Wait a minute,' he said. 'I just need to finish this.'

'We're going now.'

'I thought you didn't like rushing about?' he said, slipping the phone back into his pocket with a look of annoyance.

He took our two cabin bags from the overhead locker and handed me mine. One of the flight attendants looked at him as we came past. He returned her gaze and she smiled warmly, her colleague putting on a light blue coat she'd taken from a cubbyhole.

'Thank you,' said the one who'd smiled, narrow eyes with powdered skin and bright red lips, closer to thirty than twenty.

'Look after yourself,' said Seva, his eyes fixing her again before we left the aircraft and went up the ramp.

'She was at least ten years older than you,' I said once we were out of earshot.

'Who? What are you talking about?'

'The flight attendant you were smiling at. She was at least ten years older than you.'

'Am I not allowed to smile now?'

'You don't need to flirt with *everyone* you see.'

He didn't respond, but strode on ahead when we got inside the terminal proper so I wouldn't be in doubt as to what he thought about my interfering. Carrying only hand luggage, we could pass straight through into arrivals, where Mark stood waiting over by the exit in a thick blue puffer jacket and a sheepskin hat with ear flaps.

He gave me a hug of sorts, his face expressionless, shook Seva's hand and led us out to the car park on the left where the cars stood like silent furry animals in their coats of snow, apart from the ones that had just been in use, which by comparison looked like they'd been sheared.

'Journey all right?' said Mark.

'Yes, pleasant enough,' I said. 'How's the little one doing?'

'Sleeping, I hope.'

'She's so delectable. I saw some new photos of her today.'

'Yes, she's a lovely baby,' he said, holding out his arm and pressing the key he held in his hand. A short distance ahead, the indicators of a car lit up and flashed.

'It's really kind of you to come and collect us, Mark.'

'No problem.'

When we got to the car, he turned to Seva.

'You'll want to sit in the front for the headroom, I suppose?'

'Yes, if that's OK? Or do you want to, Mama?'

'No, you can,' I said. 'There'll be more room for your legs as well.'

Mark put our cases in the boot, opened the back door and removed one of the child seats, which he then put in the boot beside the luggage before shutting both doors again and letting us get in.

It felt demeaning in a way to be sitting in the back, as if I'd been demoted to child status. There was a doggy smell too. The whole seat was probably covered in dog hairs. I was only thankful it was dark and I couldn't see them.

'Are you all right if I move the seat back a bit, Mama?'

'Yes, fine,' I said.

It was a small car and he pushed the seat back so far I had to sit with my legs to one side. Mark turned the ignition and the heater and radio came on.

I was regretting having accepted Oksanka's offer. It would have been so much better to have taken a taxi. It was always worth it, no matter the cost.

We left the airport area with a cloud of snow whirling in our wake.

'Which way were you thinking of going?' I said.

'E30,' he said.

'Do you think we could follow the river instead?'

'If you want.'

'It's what I miss most in Moscow, I think. The Volga.'

'I can understand,' said Mark, indicating right at the roundabout. He was a man of few words and in that respect I was glad to be sitting in the back where I didn't feel obliged to choose between trying to drag words out of him and enduring the ride in uncomfortable silence.

He worked at a timber suppliers just off the road we were now on, though he didn't care much for the job, or so I gathered from Oksanka. It was the dog and his fishing and hunting trips he lived for, besides his wife and their two children, that is. From what she'd told me, he was a good husband, loyal and trustworthy, and I had no reason to disbelieve her. But I did often wonder what stirred in him, if anything stirred at all.

Seva tried to strike up a conversation about the local ice-hockey team, CSK Samara, who as far as I could grasp from what he was saying played in the second tier with no chance of getting promoted any time soon. Mark muttered a few non-committal replies and soon it petered out, supplanted by the hum of the heater and engine.

Not long after, we could see the Volga stretching into the darkness ahead of us. In places it was as wide as a lake, elsewhere it narrowed, but the Volga was never anything but mighty. Ice covered its shores, extending well into its waters, but still there was more open water than ice by the looks of it. I remembered winters when the river froze almost completely and the entire town would go out onto the ice on Sundays. Even cars had been known to venture out, and that sight, motor cars on the Volga, had made such an impression on me that it sometimes returned to me in dreams.

I snuggled down, the side of my head against the lip of the backrest, my forehead pressed gently to the window, but it occurred to me this was too much like the way a child would sit, and so I straightened up again, picking up the gloves I'd put down on the seat beside me and turning them in my hand as I stared out, the river coming in and out of view, its black water glistening like oil in the open channel.

Seva barely ever noticed his surroundings, never had done. But what about Mark, was he curious about the world around him, behind that silent exterior? Could silent men be curious? If so, how did they express it?

I thought maybe I'd give Yura a ring when I got back to Moscow. He definitely wasn't silent. He'd always had a zest about him, interrupted now and then by moments of self-consciousness that blushed his cheeks. I remembered how I'd liked him for that, for being so sensitive. I'd liked his idealism too. And now, his body, his face, weighed down by middle age, his eyes so adrift. How could an active conservationist like him end up importing cars? I'd be intrigued to hear what he might tell me about it.

Gradually, the sprawl condensed around us, factories at first, and warehouses, the industrial parks, then the concrete blocks of the sub-urbs that led us in an unbroken line towards the city centre whose buildings were quite as grey, quite as brutal, quite as neglected. But on this particular evening everything appeared softer, dreamlike almost, because of the snow that had fallen: every street, every square was white and hushed with snow.

Looking between the high-rises on the right I caught sight of the Soyuz rocket, harshly illuminated under grey-black sky. A few minutes later it was the promenade that came likewise into view, fleeting glimpses as the buildings allowed.

I leaned forward between the seats.

'Can you remember where it is?' I said.

'Yes,' said Mark.

The old town, that we were now about to enter, was a different place altogether, a town within the town. The buildings there were old, many of timber, and along with the river and the promenade, this was the part of Samara of which I was most fond. Because of the snow the streets were almost empty, but the bars and restaurants we passed looked like they were packed.

Mark pulled into the side and drew up onto the pavement.

'There we are,' he said, unclicking his seat belt and opening the door with the engine still running.

'Thanks ever so much,' I said, and got out the other side, buffeted by the wind that whistled down the street.

Mark got our cases from the boot, put them down on the ground and extended the handles the way a taxi driver might have done.

'Give Oksanka our best for now,' I said. 'And drive safely.'

He nodded and got in again, pulled out into the street and was gone.

*

The apartment in which Papa lived had been in his family since the early 1900s when his great-grandfather had married his great-grandmother, the daughter of a German merchant by the name of Walser, who purchased the property on their behalf. At that time, it had been huge, several hundred square metres in floor area, and while it had since been divided up, it remained a very spacious dwelling. Sasha and I had both had our own rooms when we'd been growing up there. No one else I knew then had known such luxury. But Papa was well connected, I was aware of that, though quite who they were, these connections of his, was a mystery. I never saw them, they belonged to the life he conducted outside the home, a life that had been going on since before my time, into which he now and then would recede when I was a little girl.

The rooms were as we once had left them, and this always filled me with a faint sense of discomfort, it was as if we were dead, and the rooms were our museum. But Papa had space enough. Now that he was on his own, he barely used the living room, and confined himself largely to his study and bedroom.

I unlocked the front door and went up the staircase with Seva behind me. The air was freezing cold, my breath condensing into a vapour, illuminated by the naked bulb that dangled from the ceiling.

'It's open!' Papa called out when I rang the bell for politeness's sake.

Fortunately, it was warm inside. I had no idea how poorly he actually was, but he'd managed to get the stoves going, at least.

The smell. It was so distinct and reminded me of my childhood, though strangely I hadn't ever been aware of it at the time.

Cigarettes and books, those were Papa's smells. But underneath was a much older smell, thick and heavy, it pervaded everything: cabbage, boiled fish, cooked meat.

I hung up my coat, tucked my scarf into one of the sleeves and put my gloves on the hat shelf. Seva removed his shoes, levering each from the heel with the toe of his other foot.

'You'll ruin them like that,' I said.

'They're old anyway,' he said, and tossed his jacket on top of my coat. I didn't want to annoy him and put him in a bad mood now that we were at Papa's, so I waited until he went down the hall before hanging it up on a peg of its own.

'Have you fallen asleep there?' Papa called out.

'Hey, Dedulya,' Seva said as he stepped through the door. I followed him in. The place was surprisingly tidy, apart from where Papa was sitting; the floor in the corner where his chair stood was littered with empty yogurt containers, used plates, juice cartons and orange peel, besides a large number of books, mostly lying open and face down, like birds stopped in flight.

He was slouched in the chair with one foot stretched out in front of him and a cushion behind his head. A woollen blanket lay dumped on the floor at his side.

Did he sleep there?

'Hello, Papa,' I said, going over to him.

'Alevtinoshka,' he said, and put out his hand. I crouched down and took it in mine, stroking my thumb over the skin a few times before he withdrew it again.

'Nice of you to come,' he said. 'I ought to have done you something to eat, but with this leg of mine . . . Can you sort something out for yourselves?'

His white hair, always cut short, now curled down his neck and over his ears, and his beard, scant as ever, was longer too than I remembered seeing it before. Besides that, he'd grown thinner. He still had a little paunch, but his legs and arms, his upper body, were a skinny old man's.

He was eighty, and eighty was old, but I'd never thought of him as old before.

It pained me to see it.

I got to my feet.

'What's the matter with your leg, anyway? You wouldn't tell me on the phone.'

'I don't know what it is. It hurts, that's all. I can't put my weight on it. Can't walk.'

'Do you want me to have a look?'

'You? Since when did you become a doctor? Anyway, there's nothing to see. It looks fine from the outside. Not a mark, not a sore, nothing.'

'Have you twisted it, do you think?' said Seva. 'Or pulled a muscle?'

'Who knows,' said Papa. 'It'll get better on its own. But we can't starve to death in the meantime. Can you have a look and see what I've got, Alyushka? And how about you, young man, do you want a drink?'

'I wouldn't say no,' he said.

'There's a bottle of cognac on the sideboard in the kitchen.'

Seva got up, but Papa motioned for him to sit down again.

'Your mother will get it. You sit here and keep me company.'

'I may not be a doctor,' I said. 'But I'm not your servant either. I'm pleased to help, but I won't be bossed about.'

He looked at me in astonishment.

'But you were going to the kitchen anyway, my dear,' he said. 'And I'm stuck here unable to walk!'

Seva smiled. An anger rose up in me abruptly. I concealed it, turning away and going to the kitchen, where fortunately it disappeared as quickly as it had come. Papa was from before the war, another world, one in which the attitudes he voiced had been natural, as natural as mine were to me. And whether I chided him or not, he was hardly likely to change now. He was eighty, for goodness' sake!

Seva was another matter.

I found the cognac where he'd said it would be and took two glasses from the cupboard. The kitchen was freezing cold. The worktop was a clutter of used plates, cups and pans, with various items of plastic packaging thrown in, but nothing I couldn't clear away in less than twenty minutes. The rest of the kitchen was spick and span. I assumed that was down to Katya coming in to help him, because I couldn't imagine him paying someone. Not that he was miserly, it was more that he didn't care for strangers, especially in his home.

I went in with their drinks. Seva was relating something to Papa, who sat with his head turned, looking out of the window, seemingly engrossed in a world of his own, but I knew, and Seva did too, that he never missed a trick.

From what I could glean, Seva was telling him about all the broken legs he'd witnessed.

Papa turned to look at me when I came in.

'Aren't you having one?' he said.

'I'm not that keen on cognac, you know that.'

'There's some vodka in the freezer. Will that do?'

'Perhaps,' I said. 'I'll see if I can rustle up something for us to eat first, though.'

It was easier said than done. The fridge wasn't exactly empty, there was just very little in it that I could actually use. Three six-packs of yogurt that looked like his main source of nutrition, a carton of milk and a pot of sour cream, some eggs, butter, a jar of roe, several of beetroot, some pickled cucumber, sauerkraut, a couple of onions and as many carrots, so soft they wilted in my hand when I picked them up, and a whole row of home-made raspberry jam someone must have given him, presumably Katya, the only relative he had left in Samara.

I took the eggs out and checked the sell-by date. Four days past. They'd be all right, though. I could make us some pancakes.

He'd like that. Pancakes had always been my mother's speciality.

Had he got any flour?

Yes, he had. An unopened packet of wholemeal flour in the cupboard, probably ancient, but flour couldn't go bad, could it?

Before I got started, I swept up the bits of bark from the floor where the firewood was stacked and tipped them into the stove along with some sticks of kindling, placed a couple of small logs on top, stuffed in some crumpled newspaper and put a match to it all. The thunderous noise it made when it got going was pleasing and I stood for a minute watching the little firestorm through the open stove door until it died down and the only light inside came from some glowing bits of bark and the sticks that had now begun to burn nicely. I melted the butter then, whisked it together with the eggs and a pinch of salt, tipped in some flour and a packet of dry yeast, then added milk and more flour by turns until I'd got enough batter for perhaps a dozen pancakes. I left it to stand for a few minutes while I washed up and then ran a cloth over the work surface.

It made me feel good, coming here and taking over. I only hoped he wouldn't think I was trying to emulate Mama.

Was I?

I turned the old cooker on, dropped a knob of butter into the frying pan and waited for it to sizzle before pouring in some batter.

A bit, perhaps? But I was a completely different person, we were nothing like each other, a few pancakes weren't going to alter that.

Once I'd used up all the batter I set the table in the living room and put the little pile of pancakes in the middle, flanked by roe, onion and sour cream.

'Shall I help you to the table?' Seva said.

'I'll manage on my own, thanks all the same,' said Papa, leaning to one side to pick up the walking stick he'd put down next to the skirting board. As he shuffled across the floor, I returned to the kitchen, poured some fruit syrup, it too home-made, into a jug and filled it up with water, then took it back in with me along with three glasses.

'Who's the jam and the fruit syrup from?' I said as I sat down.

'Katya,' Papa said.

'Does she come in a lot?'

'Once a week.'

'That's good.'

'Yes.'

'Don't you think we should ask her to come tomorrow?'

'Not on your life.'

He rolled up a pancake and ate it without bothering to use his knife and fork, shoving it into his mouth. I'd never seen him do that before.

'Why not?' I said.

'She's got nothing to say. Absolutely nothing.'

'I'm sure she has.'

'Never stops talking, but nothing to say. If she's not prattling on about her children and grandchildren, then it's her friends and their children and grandchildren. Everyone bar the devil and his grand-mother. Now, if she could only talk about the devil! I might listen then. But she bores me to tears every minute she's here. No sooner has she come through the door than she's pulled up a chair and off she goes.'

'Who are we talking about?' Seva asked.

'Yekaterina, Papa's niece.'

'Ah, I see,' said Seva.

He was eating as if his life depended on it. Papa and I barely got a couple each, the rest he scoffed.

'Do you want to go back to your chair?' I said after we'd finished.

Papa shook his head.

'I've come all this way, I might as well stay for a while.'

'I think I'll go out for a bit,' said Seva.

'Now? It's nearly half past ten!'

'I won't go far.'

'Let the boy go out and have some fun.'

'I'm not a kid, you know,' Seva said, and got to his feet. 'I won't be that late.'

'Are you meeting someone?' I said.

'Maybe,' he said. 'Have a nice evening!'

I heard him put his shoes and coat on in the hall, the latch clicking shut behind him as he went out. Only then did it occur to me that he didn't have a key. I dashed to the door, snatched it open and called down the staircase after him.

'Seva! Key!'

I heard him pause and then saw him look up as I leaned over the banister.

'The small one's for the front door, the big one's for the flat, I said, and handed them to him as he came trudging back. 'It's the opposite of what you'd think.'

'OK,' he said. 'Don't wait up.'

'I wouldn't dream of it. But give me a hug before you go.'

When I went inside again, Papa was sitting with his head in his hands staring at the table in front of him. He straightened up as soon as he saw me.

'Thank you for coming,' he said.

'I thought you didn't care for other people,' I said with a smile. 'I thought you preferred being on your own.'

He didn't smile back but swallowed a mouthful of his cognac. A drop of it dribbled down his chin and he wiped it away indifferently with the back of his hand.

'I'm no humanist,' he said. 'I'm not sorry for people, in case anyone should think so. They get what they deserve, most of them. Small-minded. Can't see further than their own noses.'

'Don't you consider yourself a person?'

'Hm?'

'You referred to *people* as *them*.'

'Ah. Figure of speech, that's all. *We* get what *we* deserve, then. I'm no better myself. But at least I know so and won't go bothering others with it.'

'There you are, you *are* a humanist,' I said, and smiled at him again. 'You think of others and so you don't see anyone.'

'And when did you become such a people lover, if I may ask?'

He laughed, only to convulse in a coughing fit.

'Let's put some music on, shall we?' he said after it subsided.

'Yes,' I said. 'What do you want to listen to?'

'You choose.'

'All right, but where's the record player?'

'In the study, where else?'

'So we leave the door open, is that it?'

'No, no, that won't do. Bring the speakers out here. They're on long leads. Put one either side of the door, well apart.'

I went into the study. The room was freezing and even more of a mess than I remembered. Books were piled up everywhere, on the desk, on the chairs, and of course on the bookshelves, but also on top of the books that were on the bookshelves, and all the way along the floor in front of them. Where there were no books, there was art, big and small works, old paintings, prints, icons, as well as some fossils, a number of ashtrays, and a few ancient artefacts such as a large and elaborate Roman brooch he'd been given by an Albanian musician he'd performed with once. And then there were the records, shelf upon shelf of them.

I carried the speakers out and put them either side of the door as he'd said.

'What shall I put on?'

'Like I said, you choose.'

'In that case, you must try and guess what we're listening to,' I said, passing my eye over the spines of the LPs.

Papa was a discerning listener, never afraid to say so if he didn't like a piece, but this was his own collection, so presumably everything would be to his taste.

I opted for one of Mozart's violin concertos.

The crackle from the old vinyl filled the room as I went back into the living room, and then the first notes were struck.

'Mozart's Violin Concerto No. 3,' he said immediately.

'Yes,' I said. 'But who's playing?'

I went into the kitchen and got some matches from the odds-and-ends drawer, came back in and lit the candles on the table.

'Leonid Kogan,' he said.

'Correct. I'm impressed.'

'No need to be. He taught at the conservatory when I went there. Possibly the finest violinist of his time. Of *our* time.'

'Is he still alive?'

'Died in the 1980s.'

'Did you know him well?'

He shook his head and said no more as he listened attentively to the music.

I stood up and went to the stove, opened it and saw that the fire had burned down to the embers. I put three logs on and took Papa's empty glass with me to the kitchen where I filled some more cognac in it, found the bottle of vodka in the freezer and poured myself a drink.

We raised our glasses to each other and sat without speaking as the music played.

For the first time in ages I felt content. The music, the warmth, the smell of smoke, the vodka. Papa and the apartment.

He looked at me. I returned his gaze and smiled.

'How are you, Alevtinushka?' he said.

'I'm fine.'

'You don't look it.'

'I'm fine, really.'

'Hm,' he said, and let it drop.

I gazed at the candle flames that flickered in the draught, heard the low rumble of the burning logs in the stove, lending to the music a deep, underlying tone.

'The most difficult years of my life were when I was your age. Then I met your mother. Nothing in my life at the time could have predicted it. I hadn't wished for it, nor even considered the possibility. But everything was at once changed.'

'So what you're saying is that I'm not doing fine, but that something will come along and put things right?'

'Did I say that? No.'

'But it was what you meant. The only reason you had for saying so was the comparison between your life and mine.'

'It wasn't until I was in my forties that my life became a life at all,' he went on, as if I hadn't said anything or as if it were of no consequence. 'Before that, it was all merely a series of possibilities, of what might be. And that shift, from living in the what-might-be to living in what actually *was*, turned out to be rather painful. I suffered a kind of mental whiplash, you might say — everything that had happened in the past came charging up and hit me full force from behind. It would be no exaggeration to say that I was damaged by it.'

'You started drinking.'

'Yes, that too. I didn't want to live the life I was suddenly living. I didn't want to be the person I had become. Learning to accept that took some years. But after that my life became my own.'

We sat for a moment in silence.

'That was when I stopped composing,' he then said.

He'd never spoken of it before.

It felt like a confession.

I didn't know what to say.

'Was it?'

He nodded.

'It unburdened me. Once I'd made the decision, it was a relief.'

Again, there was a lull.

I'd heard the story so many times of how Mama and Papa had met that it had become almost mythological. Presumably it held the same status for them. Papa had been giving a recital in Kazan, Mama had been sitting in the third row, it was in the aula of the university there, and he'd noticed her several times during his performance. When the recital was over, Mama remained in her seat as the space emptied. Papa saw this, of course, and approached her. It was the music that had moved her, not him, she hadn't even looked at him, only because of the music had she remained seated, it was as if it had transported her to some other place, she told me many years later when I was old enough to understand, and she had not wanted to leave it but wished to stay there for as long as possible.

'It was a place of great sorrow, yet also of beauty,' she told me. 'Those emotions were in me, not in the music, but it was the music that took me there and illuminated it all.'

Papa knew nothing of this, all he saw was an attractive woman who sat waiting for him after the concert. She had cried, but composed herself, smiling when thanking him for the performance, nodding when he suggested they meet outside the entrance twenty minutes later and find somewhere they could go for a drink.

It had been snowing then, too, the air was glitteringly cold under a starry sky. I wasn't there of course, but I've stood outside the university building in Kazan several times and have no difficulty imagining them there that night in 1981. Papa, the forty-four-year-old violinist with his thick dark hair and beard, blue eyes and sensitive mouth, a scarf almost certainly thrown elegantly around his neck. Mama, the forty-year-old doctor, her own dark hair cut into a pageboy, her beautiful neck, her warm hazel eyes, her powerful aura, filled with the love of life.

The university was situated on a low-lying hill outside the centre of town, so the lights of the city would have twinkled below them. A tall statue of Lenin stood there then as now, perhaps more appropriate in that place than so many others, given that Lenin in fact attended Kazan's university.

I lay sleeping in our apartment across the city. Mama's sister Anna was there to look after Sasha and me. I was four years old and would have known Mama had gone to a concert, but of course I remember nothing. Nor do I remember exactly the first time I met Papa, for in a way he has been with me always, though I know it not to be the case.

They strolled down the hill to the Hotel Soviet where Papa was staying and enjoyed a few drinks there. Mama insisted on going home alone, though of course he offered to accompany her. He phoned, he wrote, and returned several times to Kazan with no other reason than to see her, and eventually she gave in to his relentless will. They married in 1982, and we moved to Samara.

If I was to believe their stories, what they wanted to tell me by telling me them, they rescued each other then. Mama rescued Papa, and Papa rescued Mama. I'd grown up with them both, so I knew how things had been between them, but while *rescue* was probably the last word that came to mind when I thought about how they'd got on together, they never wavered from that basic narrative. It governed the way in which they looked at their lives. Maybe it even shaped them. Could a story really be stronger than life itself?

'Perhaps we should turn the record over?' Papa said, and only then did I become aware of the little click repeating with every revolution of the LP, the needle now having reached the run-out groove.

'Perhaps you mean I should,' I said with a smile.

'I wouldn't want to boss you about.'

'Papa, do you want me to apologise for saying you were bossing me about?'

'No, it's quite sufficient that you know I wasn't.'

I stood up and went behind his chair, leaned forward and gave him a hug. He moved his head slightly away, never one for close contact.

'No need to go overboard,' he said.

'I wasn't,' I said, and smiled at him before going to turn the record over. It was as if being with him made me younger in a way. All of a sudden I was behaving like I was nineteen again.

The music that streamed into the room was quite different from before. Bright and romantic, but also hectic, and yet without substance, even though the whole orchestra of wind instruments and strings, was involved.

'This can't be Mozart, can it?' I said as I sat down again.

'No, it isn't,' Papa said. 'You can hardly get further from Mozart than this. Can you hear it? — there's no melody. No theme to carry the piece and propel it onwards. Can you guess what it is?'

I shook my head.

'But you can tell where it's coming from? The period and the country?'

'I'd say Russian. There's something folkish about it.'

'Not bad at all. When do you think it's from?'

'Pass.'

'It's rather interesting as a matter of fact. It's a violin concerto by Tikhon Khrennikov. From the fifties, I think. He wrote it especially for Kogan. Khrennikov was the same generation as Shostakovich, the one after Prokofiev, that is. There's something in the tonal language that's

very similar. Can you hear it? There's a part of it that's alive, horizontal, multifarious. But then you have the romantic aspect and that
folkish theme, as you call it. The two things don't go. Every time I listen
to it, it has me gnashing my teeth. He's hedging his bets! Either draw it
towards the romantic and take the consequences, pursue a melody,
onwards, onwards, and see where it takes you, or else get rid of the sentimentality altogether and lay life bare. Melody wins you emotion, but
only at the expense of complexity. Romanticism is for the one, the individual, and is vertical. Romanticism is a matter between you and God,
whereas Shostakovich, now that we've mentioned him, and in fact his
name suggests itself here, is horizontal, complex, alive. Not without
emotion, of course not, but the feelings in Shostakovich's work are not
concentrated, they are, as it were, out there, among the people, rather
than within the composition. Khrennikov didn't understand that, he
wanted the best of both worlds. And do you know why?'

He looked up from the tabletop he'd been staring at and held my
gaze.

His eyes were the most sensitive I'd ever seen in anyone. It was as if
they left his soul wide open, and whenever he was unaware of himself,
as now, he became quite defencelesss, there was nothing between him
and the world.

'No,' I said, and looked down.

'Imagine you're the youngest in a family of ten children in a small
godforsaken town in the hinterland. They're poor, the father deals in
horses. But you have a talent. Someone in the family, your uncle let's
say, owns a guitar, you're allowed to borrow it and you teach yourself
to play. Someone else has a mandolin, you learn to play that, too,
because it all comes so easily to you! The music flows in and out of you,
you command it, you master it, and are able to create it. And such a
gift, such a talent, will always be admired by those around you, regardless of how musical they may be themselves. Because where does it
come from? When music suddenly emerges from a child? So you sing
in the local choir, and in the local orchestra you learn to play the piano.
You're still a boy! You have already become your talent, do you understand? Your talent is you. They send you off to Moscow, of course. At
the age of sixteen you begin to study composition there, and at

nineteen you enter the conservatory. The work you compose for your final exam is performed in public, it wins great acclaim and popularity. In Moscow! Now you are considered one of the country's most promising composers. And you become *that*, too. But since you are talented, since the music is inside you, since it flows in and out, you know too that Prokofiev is a step above you. You can handle that, perhaps, because he is older than you, whereas Shostakovich is the same age and doing things you know immediately to be superior not only to your own work so far, but also to what lies within your capabilities. Shostakovich is out on his own, and in art this is the highest elevation. So what can you do?'

'Carry on with your own work?'

'Ha ha! In the knowledge that what you are doing is mediocre? No, certainly not.'

He picked up his cognac and drained the glass. The music, which in the meantime had drifted into the background, came back and filled the silence between us.

'An artist cannot be mediocre, it's impossible. How then to explain that the world is full of mediocre artists? To that end we must resort to psychology. Defence mechanisms, projection, self-deception. All artists, even the few who are good, are driven by such.'

He paused.

'Do you want another drink?' I said.

'No thanks. You have one.'

He sat gazing into space in front of him, elbow propped on the table, chin in hand, forefinger pointing upwards along his cheek. If I had to choose one posture that was typical of him, it would be that.

With a crackle and hiss, the needle came to the end of the record again.

I went and took it off, and found some Shostakovich to put on instead.

'He wrote this when he was eighteen,' Papa said. 'It was his graduation piece from the conservatory in Leningrad. Astonishing how already he has found himself. And what mastery! He frolics! Listen to this. The beginning is so simple and tentative. It's almost nothing. As if the instruments are feeling their way. First here, now there. And yet it has this epic quality, don't you agree? It's so often said about him that he's ironic. Perhaps he is, the way he always plays on one's expectations, building up to something that never comes, but still there's a little world here, of tones and moods, very vibrant, and now the strings come in with a quite different solemnity, and then in a moment the flute on its own, not a hint of irony there. Oh, but yes, there's the march after that, which is pure comedy. Not really my thing. But then, you see, he takes it further and weaves it back into the theme from the beginning, the lightest of touches, turning the comedy in on itself. Do you understand? Remember, he was eighteen when he wrote this.'

I nodded. It had been years since Papa had let me inside his world of music.

'By rights we should play Khrennikov again, you'd really grasp the difference then.'

'What did Khrennikov end up doing? You were talking about psychology?'

'Oh, that. He allied with Stalin. After persecuting writers in the 1930s, Stalin turned his attentions to composers and musicians when the war ended. A congress was held in the Kremlin in 1948, an infamous event. More than seventy composers and musicians attended. They were there to learn how to compose music the way Stalin wanted it, in the true Soviet spirit. Khrennikov gave a speech in which he attacked — well, guess who?'

'Shostakovich?'

'No less. And Prokofiev and Khachaturian. He accused them of being elitist and anti-populist — which of course they were! — and denounced their music as neurotic, escapist and repulsive, pseudo-philosophical and formalistic, Western and decadent. He held that they were betrayers of the Soviet Union. As a result, they were forced to distance themselves publicly from their own work. Khrennikov was appointed general secretary of the Union of Soviet Composers and held the position until 1991. You'd have to be improbably pragmatic to manage such a feat. He was the most powerful man in Soviet musical life, and he had Stalin's ear. Naturally, all his works were widely performed in public and he was awarded medals for them. What's interesting, though, is that it's Khrennikov who ends up the lackey, not

Shostakovich or Prokofiev. Or Mandelstam, for that matter. Why? Why didn't the good ones lie down, when the lesser ones did? The answer lies in their art. It is unique. Only Shostakovich could have composed what Shostakovich composed, only Mandelstam could have written the poetry Mandelstam wrote. The uniqueness of their art is already so strong that it simply *cannot* be given up. It's not a matter of courage, nor a lack of it, it lies far beyond that. Shostakovich did lie down in one sense, when agreeing to publicly acknowledge his purported guilt, but never in his art. What do you make of that as a theory?'

'It sounds plausible.'

'There's that story about Pasternak and Stalin, too. Have you heard it?'

I had, but shook my head anyway.

'You see, Pasternak was a very good writer. At the time of his debut he was looked upon as a genius. Tsvetaeva was full of admiration for his poetry. He wasn't a genius, but he wasn't mediocre either. He was, indeed, a very good writer. They were friends, or acquaintances, all of them. So, Mandelstam writes his Stalin Epigram, and he recites it for Pasternak, who is scared witless by it. He tells Mandelstam, *I didn't hear this*. A month later Mandelstam is arrested and deported. Pasternak, to his credit, goes to Bukharin and asks for his help in securing Mandelstam's release. Then one evening the telephone rings in Pasternak's apartment. It's Stalin. Stalin is phoning him at home! He is probed as to what's being said about Mandelstam in literary circles. Pasternak, the poor fellow, is terrified for his life and tells Stalin no one mentions Mandelstam and that Moscow's literary circles are as good as non-existent. So Stalin asks *him*, Pasternak, what *he* thinks about Mandelstam. Now, you have to remember that Pasternak and Mandelstam are friends. Pasternak replies that he and Mandelstam are at variance in their views on literature. That's when Stalin says: *I see. You cannot stand up for a friend.* And then he hangs up. Ha ha ha! You see? Mandelstam was a great writer and he died in a concentration camp. Pasternak was a very good writer, and he kept himself alive, a little bit in opposition, a little bit not. Whereas Khrennikov was mediocre and became a lackey. He was a dreadful human being. He hadn't the courage to confront his own mediocrity, but made others suffer for it in the most inhuman manner.

How he must have believed in himself! He must have convinced himself that Shostakovich really was decadent and repulsive, and that he
himself was a brilliant star.'

He sat as if in silent reflection.

'Did you know him?' I said cautiously after a moment.

'Khrennikov? No, he was upper echelon, far too important. But I saw
him on a few occasions. We went to the same conservatory, he a good
many years before me, of course. It's not that long ago that he died, in
fact. 2004, if I'm not mistaken.'

'That *is* long ago, Papa. I was twenty-six then.'

'Perhaps it is. He was a Stalinist until the end, though. I read an
interview with him shortly before he died, in which he attacked Gorbachev and perestroika and claimed Stalin was a genius and knew more
about music than any of us! Ha ha ha!'

My room was freezing cold and I had to fetch an old electric heater
from the big cupboard in the hall that was crammed with all sorts of
things that were no longer in use. There was a smell of burning dust
almost as soon as I plugged it in and the bars came on. It was a small
appliance, green down the sides, shiny metal on top, and its shimmery
red glow made me feel good inside. Perhaps because it was an object
from my childhood, perhaps because it was actually beautiful. But who
knows if an object has its own beauty?

I opened my suitcase and unpacked, hanging my clothes up in my
old wardrobe as the room grew warm. It was gone midnight, but I
wasn't that tired. I put the case to one side, upright in the corner, and
sat down to remove my make-up in the mirror that stood leaned against
the wall on top of the desk. It had been nice talking to Papa, it had been
ages since the two of us had spent an evening together like that. He
didn't like talking about himself — what he'd said about being in his
forties had been an unusual disclosure — and he didn't like me doing
it either, but he did like to talk, and on almost any subject. It was his
way of keeping the world at bay. I realised this when I was still a teenager, that there was a connection between the supersensitive look in
his eyes and his at times near-constant talking.

His own family had been anything but horse dealers — his father was a professor of history at the university in Samara, his mother taught Russian at upper-secondary level — but the story of the gifted youngster whose talent astonished and enthralled could easily have been his own.

He'd given recitals all his life. When he and Mama got married, he declared that he would cease performing and earn a living from teaching instead, contending that he could no longer go on with it on account of all the travelling that was involved. But he never managed to stop completely. It was something he'd become addicted to. He'd be away for a week every now and then, and when he came back he'd be brimming with energy. He fed on his audience the way a vampire feeds on blood. It wasn't as strange as it sounded, that he, at heart so misanthropical, would bathe in people's adoration, an audience being more than the sum of its individual members, music something other than words. In all probability he wasn't even aware of who was sitting there when he performed, I thought to myself now, more likely he was simply absorbed in the music, aware of neither the audience nor himself. But then wouldn't it suffice to simply play here, at home in the study? Of course, he'd done that all along, several hours a day, sometimes into the evening and night as well. Always with the door closed, alone with his work, but what we heard then were only traces.

I'd have to ask him about it in the morning, what the difference was between playing on one's own and in a packed concert hall.

Not that I was all that curious to know the answer. But it was a way of getting closer to the person he was.

Why had he thought I wasn't doing fine?

It was what he'd implied when he'd talked about being forty-something.

I lowered my hand with the cleansing wipe in it and looked at my face in the mirror. A person would have to look closely to see the fine, threadlike lines around the corners of my eyes. With a bit of concealer they were invisible. But I still looked different from how I'd done ten years before. It was impossible to put a finger on it, but I saw it immediately when I looked at old photos. When I was thirty there'd been a freshness to my face that wasn't there any more, or was less obvious now. It was almost as if my face had grown bigger, too, though I hadn't put on weight, at the same time as it had become more distinct, more severe. The younger face had been well defined in its features, but there'd been nothing like the same severity about it.

This wasn't something you saw, it was something you felt.

Some of the girls from school looked like they were in their fifties now, so I was lucky.

And I was doing fine.

Wasn't I?

It was like I was still waiting for something that never happened.

Waiting and waiting.

And as I waited, age altered my face in its image. As if somewhere far off in the future there was a picture of an old person it kept resembling more and more.

Only the picture of that old person wasn't in the future at all, it was already stored in my genome and had been there ever since I was conceived, in a capsule outside of time. The picture was timeless, the old person was not: time seeped into the capsule and released the old person bit by bit, cell by cell, until she was fully emerged with her bony, wrinkled face, wispy hair, trembling hands, moist eyes, and a brain that became less and less efficient with every day that passed, dulled and blundering.

Oh, for goodness' sake. I was forty, not sixty.

I had all the time in the world to worry about that.

Putting the cleansing wipe once more to the skin under my eyes, I was startled to hear a loud and repeated knocking from somewhere in the apartment. I went into the hall and realised it was coming from Papa's bedroom. I opened his door cautiously and looked in.

He was sitting on his bed, thumping the floor with the end of his walking stick. He'd never worn pyjamas or any kind of nightshirt, always slept in only his underpants, so his upper body was naked as he sat there, his chest skeletal-looking, a cage of ribs with a thin covering of skin.

I went inside. Immediately, he stopped and let go of the stick, which dropped to the floor with a clatter. Without a word, he lay down again and pulled the cover over himself.

'Would you get me my sleeping pills?' he said. 'They're in the drawer over there.'

He pointed. I pulled out the top drawer to find several packets of the tablets neatly stacked in the corner. I took the one on top and held it out to him.

'That's them, yes,' he said, and sat up again.

He pressed one from the blister pack, popped it into his mouth and threw his head back as he swallowed.

'Don't you take them with water?'

'Apparently not,' he said, and pressed out another.

'Are you taking two?'

'As you see. Any more stupid questions?'

'Isn't one enough?'

'I wouldn't be taking two if it was!' he almost shouted back at me.

The white hair and beard, his flaming eyes, made him look utterly deranged for a moment.

I said nothing and he seemed to calm down.

'Normally I take only one. But when there are people here, I take two. There's never anyone here but you, so it's only when you come. Otherwise I wouldn't get a wink all night.'

'All right,' I said. 'Goodnight.'

'Goodnight,' he said, and switched off the bedside lamp.

Returning to my room, I sat down at the mirror again and applied some La Prairie moisturiser to my face and neck, my greatest extravagance. I undressed and put my pyjamas on, lifted the curtain and stood for a moment, staring into the empty street below, where the wind flurried the snow, before turning off the light and getting into bed.

The bed was too narrow, but the mattress was hard, the way I liked it. It was a preference that must surely have stemmed from all the many nights I'd slept in that same bed. I'd become familiar with it, and it had shaped me.

Or was that stretching it a bit? Could a person be *shaped* into a penchant for hard mattresses?

I remembered I'd been given it the year of my thirteenth birthday. I'd grown too big for a child's room, Mama said, so that summer she'd given away all the furniture that had belonged to it and then painted the walls and the wardrobe in colours I chose myself, at least in principle, the fact of the matter being that she rejected my pale blues and pinks, which according to her I'd quickly have outgrown. Instead, she talked me into white walls with the concession of pale blue for the wardrobe. The desk and the bed were a swap she made with one of her colleagues, and she painted them too.

It was the first summer I could actually distinguish from others, the ones before all merged together in a jumble of more or less sun-drenched recollections. I started menstruating in June. I was doing my homework, I remember it down to the smallest detail. My physics book lay open on the desk, the chapter was about electricity and batteries, the window was open, the air outside hot and still and smelling of car exhaust. Several of the girls in my class had already had their first periods, so I'd been waiting for it, and longing too, but when finally it came it was awful. I bled like mad, and of course I had to be wearing my white trousers, which were ruined before I could get to the bath-room. Mama was at work and I was never in a million years about to ask Papa for help with such a thing, and anyway he was giving a lesson to one of his pupils. I cleaned myself up as best I could, found a cloth in the cupboard and put it between my legs, put a clean pair of knickers on and changed my trousers, black this time, before trying to wash the blood out of the others. We never threw anything out, everything that came apart would be repaired, Mama would sew and darn and apply her endless creative skills to every mending. The white trousers were my favourites. I stood at the sink, washing and scrubbing, and hung them up on the rail above the bathtub before going back to my room in tears. I felt dirty and contemptible, stupid and ridden with shame.

'What is it, my little star?' she said, having opened the door of my room to look in on me, always the first thing she did when she got home. 'What are you doing in bed?'

'My stomach hurts,' I said.

She put her hand to my brow.

'You've not got a temperature. Have you got diarrhoea?'

'No,' I said. 'I think I've got my period.'

'Oh, but that's marvellous, Alevtinoshka! Come on, I'll help you get sorted out.'

She led me to the bathroom, I showered and when I was finished she received me with a big towel and showed me how to insert a tampon.

She'd taken them from work, she said, in readiness for when it happened, and had long been thinking the time was ripe to give me some
instruction, only for some reason she'd left it too long and now events
had caught up with her.

'Typical me,' she said. 'Forever putting things off, and then all of a
sudden it's too late.'

'It doesn't matter, Mama,' I said. 'My trousers are ruined though.
They were my best pair. I'm sorry.'

'Nonsense. We'll soon have them as good as new.'

'Do you mean it?'

'Yes, of course. Now, you go and have a lie-down and let me take care
of it.'

I lingered a moment.

'Go on, off you go,' she said, turning the trousers in her hands as she
examined them.

'You won't tell Papa, will you?'

She looked at me and smiled, an absent look in her eyes, as so often.

'Of course not.'

'Do you promise?'

'Mm.'

But when I came into the kitchen for dinner, Papa winked at me, so
obviously she'd already told him. I glared at her as she put the frying
pan with the hunks of fried fish in it down on the table between us, but
she didn't look at me, and turned round again to fill the jug with water.

She cared more about him than me.

Until that summer I'd been quite the tomboy. I was wholly uninterested in clothes; as long as they did the job and covered me I was
content. I never gave a thought to how I looked, wore my hair short, the
practical option, and often I'd come home with my knees and hands
scraped after being out playing. I went away with the pioneers and
loved our camping trips, the outdoor life, chopping wood, campfires,
cooking food on the Primus, even our long tramps into the forest in
rainy weather. I learned to play the piano too, though not from Papa.
He was a good teacher, but declined to teach me, so instead I took lessons at the arts centre after school, and what drove me to learn there

was the thought of winning Papa's recognition. I played at the parents'
evenings, and at the little concerts that were put on at the end of term,
and I was good as well, not because I had any real talent, but because I
was diligent and stuck at it. Papa was measured in his compliments, so
a *well done* or a *fine job* was something I treasured. I would tell him, too,
about the books I was reading and he would always take the time to
listen, and whenever we did something together, however seldom, for
instance when we went berry-picking in summer, I would stick closest
to Papa. I never reflected on why that was, but I think possibly an
important factor was that he often wouldn't have time for me. It was an
obstacle I had to overcome, whereas Mama was always there for me.
She worked long hours at the hospital, and had private patients too, so
it wasn't in any literal sense that she was always there for me, but more
generally, in the sense that she was caring and mindful, and there was
no hard surface to come up against in her as there was in Papa.

All of this changed that summer. I don't know why or how it happened, but almost from one day to the next it was as if everything had
to be different. I became interested in the way I looked and started
using make-up, borrowing from Mama to begin with, experimenting
with different looks. I started wearing tight T-shirts that accentuated
my breasts, it made me tremble with excitement inside, and with something else whose nature I didn't quite understand as yet, but which had
to do with expectation. Yes, the expectation of being seen filled me to
the brim, altogether a new feeling, and it was as if a whole new space
was opening up inside me. It was painful in a way, too, because it was
something I wanted, yet didn't, but more important than the ambiva-
lence was the sheer power those feelings had. It was almost as if they
were leading the way, and all I could do was follow. I wore heavy black
eyeliner at school, and just as much lipstick, and butterflies fluttered in
my stomach the first time I went through the gate like that. But no one
laughed, in fact I was rewarded: boys looked at me.

Papa, who'd still been asleep when I went to school that morning,
was infuriated when he set eyes on me after I came home, and told me
to wash it off immediately.

For the first time, I defied him.

Mama must have spoken to him about the psychology and

vulnerability of adolescent girls, because while he didn't apologise for the harshness of his words, he did come to my room later that evening and gave me a book, my first adult novel: Hamsun's *Victoria*. Soon, he would come with Dostoevsky's *Crime and Punishment*, as well as an old volume that had belonged to his own grandfather, Goethe's *Wilhelm Meister's Apprenticeship*.

I made friends with Oksanka, who I'd never talked to before, and became a part of her crowd. We hung out together at the shopping centre after school, sometimes we'd go to the arcade, something Sevka many years later would ask me about, it was almost the only thing from my childhood and youth he was curious about, what kind of games there were then, how they worked and what they looked like. We hung out on the prom too, in the evenings that autumn, and I remember the sun sinking into the forest across the river, the groups of boys who'd be there too, all ages, some from school, some we'd never seen before. Nothing much happened, but it was exciting nonetheless. Mama and Papa would have noticed the change in me, of course, because that summer it was as if I stepped out into a life of my own. At the same time, they let go of me, whether it was intentional or simply because of what was happening during those months, I still don't know. They would sit glued to the television set in the evenings, talking politics whenever I saw them, like everyone else, I suppose. No one knew how it was all going to pan out, what it was we were actually looking at. The weekends saw big demonstrations in town. I'd seen parades and marches many times, but there'd always been an atmosphere of control and regulation about them. These gatherings were different altogether, pervaded by nervous unrest. At the same time, there was a clear enthusiasm, something exultant about them. People chanted and sang, arms in the air, flags waving. Fear, joy, uncertainty, this was the mood of that autumn and winter. Mama's pay stopped and Papa's pupils were unable to keep up their lessons, which meant we had no income and were able to buy only the basic essentials.

'It's only material things,' said Papa. 'Unimportant in the wider scheme.'

'There is no wider scheme,' said Mama. 'What could be more important than food and clothes, family and friends?'

Papa had no answer. Instead, he said:

'We are a country of hypocrites. If they were really against the state all these years, how come they didn't speak out until now, when everything's fallen apart and protesting comes without a cost?'

'Look who's talking, Yegor Fyodorovich,' Mama said. 'As if you weren't here all that time yourself.'

I didn't really know what they were talking about, what they stood for, or what it was exactly they wanted. But I agreed with Mama. No one could get by without money. The teachers at school were quiet about what was going on. None of my new friends talked about it either.

Sometimes, usually when Papa wasn't speaking to Mama after one of their long arguments, he would call for me from his study, wanting to talk, and I would sit down obediently and listen to whatever it was he had to say.

One such evening he produced an old album of photographs to show me. He pointed at one of the first: four young men, two seated with their arms folded and legs crossed, two standing behind them. Their faces were solemn, and oddly dark.

'That's my great-grandfather,' Papa said, indicating the one sitting on the left.

'How old was he there?' I said.

'I'm not sure,' said Papa. 'Nineteen or twenty, perhaps. He didn't live very long. He was hanged on the square down there in 1876.'

He threw a nod in the direction of town as he spoke the words.

'Why? Had he killed someone?'

The thought of having a murderer in the family was rather bracing.

'He was part of a revolt against the Tsar. He was arrested by the Tsar's police and hanged. His name was Grigoriy.'

He turned the pages, stopping at another photo.

'And this is my grandfather, Sevastyan, Grigoriy's son.'

The picture had been taken on a summer's day. Seva, he too a young man at the time, was sitting on a grassy bank wearing a white shirt that was unbuttoned to his chest and dark trousers, he was smiling and his hair was tousled and unruly.

'He fought in the civil war on the side of the Reds. They put him in charge of a village in Simbirsk where he was taken prisoner by the

Whites, a company of Cossacks who killed his staff and threw him in a cell. He was supposed to have been executed, but the Red Army came and saved him at the last minute. And this, Alya,' he said, pointing at another photo, this one of a small, smiling baby swathed in white, 'this is my father. He was with Komsomol, who quelled anti-Soviet uprisings in the villages and fought the kulaks. The party gave him the choice of leading his own division or taking an education. He ended up a professor of history at the university here. Do you see where all this is leading?'

I smiled cautiously and nodded.

'And?'

'You want me to know your family.'

'Yes. But I also want you to know that they fought for what they believed in. Some of them risked their lives for it.'

'Like Lenin,' I said.

'Like Lenin, yes.'

'He lived here too.'

'Indeed. But the country Lenin fought for is not the country we have today.'

Papa then closed the album, stood up and put it back in its place on one of the lower shelves.

'Why not?' I said.

'Why not what?'

'Why is the country today not the same as the one Lenin fought for? I mean, he won, didn't he?'

'That's a long and complicated story,' he said. 'And you're still too young to understand it.'

'I'm thirteen,' I said.

Papa smiled.

'Yes, you're a big girl.'

'Then tell me.'

He sat down again, leaned forward and folded his hands, with his elbows propped against his knees.

'A hundred years ago, Russia was still immeasurably poor, ravaged by want and misery, and a few very rich people decided everything.'

'I know.'

'Yes, of course you do. A lot of people wanted to change all that. Lenin was one of them. The question they asked themselves was how they could go about changing society. How could power be passed from the few rich to the many poor? One thing was certain, the rich weren't going to give up power of their own accord. You'll know too that the country was in the depths of crisis at that time, Russia had been at war, there was a famine, people had no food, and on top of that ninety per cent of the population were still uneducated. Something had to give. And so there was a revolution, following which a power vacuum arose. The Tsar stepped down, but those wanting to take over were many, with many different opinions as to how the country should be run. That's when Lenin intervened and seized power. He was a political genius, you see. Incredibly strong-willed, incredibly resilient, and he could outmanoeuvre anyone. Lenin held that the people weren't ready for freedom yet, they needed someone who could make decisions on their behalf. It was the only way to implement change. So basically Lenin ruled everything. Which meant that when he died, a new power vacuum arose! From then on, the interests of the people meant less than the quest for power.'

'So Lenin wasn't really a good person, is that what you're saying?'

'Not entirely, no. He *wanted* to do good, and carried out a lot that *was* good. People were given schooling, for instance, and electricity. People's lives were changed for the better.'

'In that case, I don't get it,' I said.

Papa laughed.

'History doesn't really exist,' he said. 'All we have are versions of history. So what you must ask yourself is, who is telling the story, and what do they stand to gain from it? Look then for another version. And ask yourself the same two questions. Who is telling the story, and what do they stand to gain from it?'

'But Lenin won, didn't he?'

'In Lenin's version he did, yes. But there are many others. One I find interesting is Bogdanov's. You won't have heard of him. He was Lenin's friend and comrade-in-arms. He believed it would be a fatal mistake to centralise power once it was won. And he believed that the new society had to be allowed to emerge from below, rather than be run from above. Lenin had to split with him then. But the interesting thing about Bogdanov is that he basically predicted what would happen to the Soviet Union. We can ask ourselves how different it all might have been had we followed his path. Without centralisation, the Revolution would probably have failed, so perhaps the answer is that nothing much would have changed. Would that have been any better? There would have been no civil war, which of course was a bloodbath without precedent, Russians murdering Russians, famine arising in its wake, millions of people losing their lives. In fact, one of the worst places to be then was here, in Samara. People were in such need they had to eat the dead. Cannibalism. Here, in this very city, only seventy years ago.'

I stared, eyes wide.

'Perhaps that was more than you needed to know,' he said. 'But it's a version of the same story. What got me started telling you all this, anyway?'

He scratched his head and blinked.

'No matter. The important point is that we have a new power vacuum now. The power has dissolved, no one has it, and the question is who's going to grab it. We don't know.'

'Is that good or bad?'

'That depends on what follows! Now, off to bed with you, I'll see you tomorrow.'

No one could accuse Papa of having a way with children, but him talking to me like that, as if we were equals, was something that had always endeared him to me, even if a lot of it naturally went over my head. He didn't underestimate me. I suppose the truth is that he didn't *estimate* me at all, I was just a small person who happened to be in the same place as him. But he made me stretch myself. It was the distance between us that made that possible, which is something I've since thought about a lot, how distance as an element of childhood can be unappreciated. In later life, too, for that matter. Nearness is undemanding and therefore unproductive in a way. What we know is near to us — no effort required. What we don't know is remote from us, at a distance, we're not in the same place as what we don't know, and so we have to traverse that distance in order to learn. Longing requires distance — longing for another place, another state, another person, another set of things we know — and if there's one thing that drives us, individually and collectively, it's longing.

Mama would have smiled at such reasoning.

If you were left in the forest as an infant, naked and quite alone, what do you think would be most important to you, nearness or distance? she might have said.

But I wasn't left in the forest, I'd have replied.

I don't mean literally, it was a metaphor.

For what?

If a person is without nearness in their life, they'll want to strive to overcome the distance that separates them from it.

She'd have had a point.

There were a lot of things about Mama that I didn't understand until after she was dead. I'd wished so much in that first year she was gone that I could have shown her I at last understood, until it struck me that she'd have known I'd get there eventually, or perhaps it hadn't even mattered to her. That was her talent, letting you be the person you were, and seeing the best in everyone. All of us have shortcomings, nothing can ever change that, certainly nothing from outside, so why condemn a person, why not simply try and understand them instead?

I don't think Mama would ever have formulated it for herself as such, she wasn't a person who would try to define her way of thinking or identify reasons why she was the person she was, who thought the things she thought, felt the things she felt. She was impulsive, though not excessively so, because she was also unflappable, unruffled by what went on around her. As a teenager I remember thinking, rather aggressively, that she was too simplistic in her outlook, and therefore rather superficial.

Why had I been aggressive? She'd never gone against me, had always been there for me. And why superficial?

It was the last thing she was. She could talk to anyone, and everyone liked her, not just because she paid attention to them, but because the interest she took in people was clearly so genuine, and also because she was so full of life — yes, vivacious too.

Or no, vivacious isn't the right word.

Vibrant?

Not that either.

Warm, attentive, with something scintillating in her eyes?

Scintillating is too cold.

A glow?

No, there was no fire in her as there was in Papa.

But a light.

A light, like in a house one passes by in the dusk, a house on a hill-side as you drive past along the shoreline of a lake and which makes you think how lovely it would be to live just there.

God knows why I'd been so irritated by her, and occasionally so angry. Was it because I thought she always paid such attention to every-one, instead of just me? Was that why I distanced myself from her? Or was it because we were so different?

Could I have been jealous of her, the qualities she possessed, the per-son she was?

It's not implausible.

For Sasha it was different. He was close to Mama, but couldn't abide Papa. He moved out as soon as he could and wouldn't ever come back as long as Papa was here. He referred to him only as *the violinist*. He was very angry, Sasha. Mama and I went to see him a few times in Moscow, we'd take the train and stay with Mama's aunt. It couldn't have been easy for Mama, but I didn't think about it much at the time, Sasha was grown up and led his own life.

The first time I got drunk, Mama had to come and fetch me. She didn't comment and when suddenly I had to be sick she put her arm around me as I stood vomiting at the side of the road. Not a word of reproach did she utter, not even the next day. All she did was smile and carry on as if nothing had happened.

I was fourteen.

A few years later it was the other extreme. I sat in my room in the afternoons and evenings revising for exams or reading for pleasure. I had no close friends at school and didn't want any either, at least that's what I told myself. I wasn't interested in boys, wasn't interested in par-ties, wasn't interested in clothes.

By the time I moved into student halls in Moscow I had no idea who

I was, what made me *me*. Those months with Lev were a revelation. And Seva, the fact that all of a sudden I was a mother myself, that changed everything.

At least Mama got to be there for the first four years of his life.

She told us her diagnosis, calmly and objectively. But even though she only had months to live, I still didn't move back home. Her condition worsened rapidly, however, and Papa phoned one night and said I had to come home as quickly as I could.

She was still alive when I got to the hospital the next evening. Seva had fallen asleep in the taxi from the airport and cried when I woke him, working himself into a fit until he threw himself screaming to the floor inside the hospital entrance and a security guard appeared out of nowhere.

'You can't take him in here,' he said.

'I know,' I said. 'But my mother's desperately ill, she's a doctor herself, she's worked here for years. It's the last time she'll see him.'

'Rules are made to be followed,' he said, and stared emptily in the direction of the reception desk.

'I appreciate that,' I said, and kept looking at him until he turned his head towards me again, my eyes imploring him, until he looked away once more. 'Please.'

'He'll have to behave, then.'

'Oh, thank you so much,' I said, and crouched down beside Seva, who was now lying quite still, his cheek to the floor, with eyes wide open.

'You heard the man,' I said. 'You've got to be on your best behaviour now, so we can go and see Babulya.'

'Yes,' he said.

I lifted him up and carried him on my hip to the lifts, his head heavy against my shoulder. We went up to the floor where Mama's room was, stepping out into a small waiting area with a reception desk at one end, two rows of chairs at the other. There was no one behind the desk, but people everywhere else. Patients on trolleys all the way along the corridor, nurses going about with weary faces after long shifts, the families and friends of those being looked after on the ward, who had descended all at once now during visiting hours.

Sasha was standing over by the window. His face, deflated and expressionless, lit up in a smile as soon as he saw us. I put Seva down on the floor. Sasha put his arms around me and held me tight.

'So good to see you, Alevtinka!' he mumbled.

'Damn you, you idiot!' I said, pulling myself free immediately. 'Couldn't you have stayed sober, just for today? For Mama's sake?'

He threw up his arms.

'So there he is, the little Master Sevastyan!' he said, bending down and lifting Seva into the air.

Seva grizzled, and Sasha put him down again.

'How's she doing?' I said.

He shook his head, unable to say anything at first.

'She's in there,' he said then, indicating the nearest door with a nod. 'He's in with her.'

'Can you manage to look after Seva for two minutes? Or are you too drunk?'

'I've only had a couple.'

I stared at him until he looked at me.

'Mama, Mama,' said Seva.

'Yes? What is it?'

'Where's Babulya?'

I crouched down.

'She's in there,' I said, and pointed at the door. 'I'm going in to see her now. You have to wait here with Uncle Sasha. I won't be long.'

I looked up at Sasha. 'I've got some nuts here you can give him, if he wants any.'

I unzipped the pocket of my case.

'You'd like some nuts, wouldn't you, Seva? And there's still some pop left in your bottle.'

He was happy enough with that, and so I went over, gave a little knock on the door and went in. It was a room for four. Papa was sitting beside the bed nearest the door. He looked up at me with exhausted eyes.

'Thank goodness you're here, Alya,' he said, getting to his feet and putting his arms around me. 'She's sleeping at the moment, God bless her. You can sit here. I'll go out and stretch my legs.'

He stepped past me and I sat down on the chair. Mama's eyes were closed, her shoulder-length hair dark against the white pillowcase, her face pale and without make-up.

'Dearest Alevtinoshka,' she said softly, without moving. 'Give me your hand.'

I took her hand in mine.

'I'm going to die tonight,' she breathed, the faintest smile on her lips, eyes still closed.

'Of course you're not, Mama,' I said, and tears welled in my eyes.

'Don't be frightened,' she said. 'And don't be sorry. I've had a good life.'

I didn't know what to say, but squeezed her hand tightly.

'I want you to know I'm proud of you,' she said. 'Remember that, when I'm gone.'

She paused a moment.

'Alya?'

'Yes, Mama?'

'You don't need to be against everything all the time. Try saying yes once in a while. It'll help you.'

'Yes,' I said. 'I'll do that.'

'Is Seva with you? Is he here?'

'Yes.'

'Will you bring him in?'

'Yes. But he's tired and a bit stroppy.'

She said nothing, and so I got up and went back out into the corridor. Papa was at the window looking out. Sasha was standing next to him with Seva on his arm. I reached out for him. He just looked at me.

'Come here, Seva. You can come in and see Babulya now.'

'I don't want to,' he said, and clung instead to Sasha.

'You must,' I said. 'It won't take long.'

I stepped forward and took hold of him, he kicked his legs and started screaming.

'No, no, no, I don't want to! I don't want to!'

I held him tightly and went back towards Mama's room. A nurse appeared with a stern look on her face. Seva struggled and squirmed, and although I held him to my chest with all my strength, he slipped through my arms and I had to put him down on the floor again. He made to run back to Sasha, I stopped him, this time gripping him by the midriff, and picked him up again.

'What's he doing here?' the nurse demanded. 'Children aren't allowed. Take him away.'

'Two minutes, that's all,' I said. Sasha opened the door and I went inside with Seva dangling in front of me, arms and legs flailing. The nurse put a hand to my shoulder to hold me back, but I ignored her.

'No! No! AAAAHHH!' Seva screamed. 'AAAHH! AAAHHH!'

It was impossible to get through to him. Mama, who had now opened her eyes slightly, smiled her benevolent smile as Seva struggled to extricate himself from my arms, not even looking in Mama's direction.

'Thank you,' she said. 'You can take him out now.'

In the corridor again, he settled immediately and walked on his own back to where our suitcase stood.

'Thanks,' I said to the nurse. 'We'll be leaving now.'

'Have you got a key?' said Papa.

'Yes,' I said. 'Phone, if there's any development.'

Seva adored his grandmother, so it was strange that he'd been so angry when I'd taken him in to see her, I thought as we sat in the taxi on our way home through the darkness. It couldn't just have been down to him being tired, because he'd been fine in the waiting room both before and after.

Had he sensed death? The way animals do?

I doubted it. And yet he was quite still as he sat there next to me, looking out the window. I patted his head and he put a hand up to shove mine away. I leaned towards him and kissed his cheek, and my eyes were filled with tears.

Early the next morning, Papa phoned and told me Mama had died that night, just as she'd predicted.

We stayed on a couple of days after the funeral, my thinking being that Papa needed someone there with him, but the opposite turned out to be the case, which I realised from the way he asked me, on the third morning, how long we were thinking of staying, his tone of voice suggesting casual interest, the look in his eyes telling me otherwise. He wanted to be alone with his grief. Perhaps Seva was getting on his nerves too, the daily round of having a child about the place no doubt taking all the focus from Mama's passing.

My life in Moscow allowed for little else but Seva and my studies. I'd started on my thesis by then and immersed myself in the work over the months that followed. The subject was mycorrhizal association, specifically the relationship between fungi and trees, the way the roots of the fungus, the mycelium, penetrate the cells of the host tree's root tissue, helping them take in nutrients they wouldn't otherwise be able to access, the mycelium receiving sugars from the tree's photosynthesis. As such, the fungus does the tree a favour it then returns. It's what's known as facultative mutualism, a form of symbiosis on which neither interacting species is dependent, yet which benefits both. In late summer the previous year, Mama had looked after Seva while I spent a few weeks at the Pushchino scientific centre some hundred kilometres south of Moscow, where along with my supervisor and six other students I'd carried out fieldwork in the forest there. In one area the trees had been cleared completely and new ones planted in their place; in another a few trees had been left standing among the saplings, while in a third area large clusters had been left untouched. We set out to investigate how mycorrhizas were impacted in each case. Our work proceeded slowly, we had to be as patient as we were methodical, and the tools we used on our digs were as finely calibrated as those employed by any palaeontologist or archaeologist, the mycelium threadlike and delicate, dehydrating quickly if left exposed. One would think it to be the most tedious work, digging in the earth on one's hands and knees with a little trowel, carefully brushing soil from the roots, photographing them and taking samples back to the laboratories there, all under the watchful eye of our supervisor, Vasily Bochanov, who would allow no individual initiative of any sort, our place being so firmly at the bottom of the hierarchy, academic navvies as it were, licensed only to dig — and yet I soon discovered that I loved it. The smell of the dark soil, of pine needles dried by the sun, of everything that grew and flourished. The sound of rustling leaves, the creaking of branches and boughs gently swaying, the drumming of a woodpecker in the distance, the birdsong, their flappings and flutterings in the crowns above. The richness of new smells released when it rained, heavier and darker in a way. The pandemonium of sound and movement in windy weather. But also the emotions I felt for the tree at whose foot I kneeled as I exposed its roots, towering perhaps twenty metres above me it would become increasingly an individual in my thoughts. When I brushed the soil from the roots it was almost like scraping the hooves of a horse, I sometimes thought. But whereas a horse was a fickle creature whose patience would soon be unnaturally tried, quivering with unspent energy, the patience of a tree belonged to its very nature, to such an extent that the word hardly sufficed, presupposing as it does a conspicuous yardstick of some sort. A horse had a lifespan of perhaps twenty years, whereas a tree could live for hundreds, in some cases even a thousand or more years. Everything took place slowly in a tree, every process occurring over long, long periods of time, certainly compared to the nervous twitches that would shoot through a horse's shoulders and forearms. Bochanov, who was something of a tree expert, had spoken of this in his lectures, that in order to understand a tree — those were the words he used — we needed to be aware that trees lived in a different time dimension from ours, and that this was something that defined their entire existence. What took place in minutes or hours or even days did not exist to them.

All organisms lived in such pockets of time, whose settings differed from species to species, in which their life cycles ran their course, complete for every individual, filled to the brim with life in time. The trees had no brain either, nor any central nervous system, and this of course defined their existence too, the way systems of sensory perception defined the existence of all things living on earth, meaning that the world looked quite different to a fly than it did to a cow or a tree. *Different animals inhabit radically different realities, as do different insects, plants and trees*, I wrote in my notes from one of his lectures. I'd never thought about it in that way before, certainly not when it came to trees. But during those days I spent on my hands and knees, uncovering the subterranean tree, Bochanov sitting with his back against the trunk of another, perhaps ten metres away, in his green wellingtons, smoking, his hand curled around the cup of his Thermos flask that was filled with coffee, elbow propped on his knee, this was indeed my experience: that what rose up above me was a living organism, and while it might not have registered me as such, it certainly registered that something was going on.

I glanced at Bochanov, and he glanced away, as a person does when they've been observing someone and don't want them to know. He was in his early sixties then, and I hoped the reason for him looking away was that he realised his behaviour was inappropriate.

Shortly afterwards he was standing over me, still with his cup in his hand. He said nothing, but watched me work for a few moments before moving on to one of the other students. I liked him, he was mild of nature and highly knowledgeable. There was something resigned about him too. It was as if that resignation in some way had to do with the knowledge he possessed, though of course I wasn't sure. He was almost bald, only a few wisps of hair remaining at the sides and the back of his head, his face large and heavy-featured, apart from his eyes, which were so narrow they made him look like he was perpetually squinting.

Whenever he sat down with us at lunch or dinner, I felt uplifted. Often he would have something thought-provoking to say, but his apparent interest in me, little glances in my direction when he thought I wouldn't notice, occasionally holding my gaze a second too long, made me ill at ease. It meant I had to be careful, that even the smallest sign of enthusiasm or interest on my part could be construed as leading him on, and that I had to watch out not to end up on my own with him in situations unrelated to our professional work.

After dinner times in the big canteen, I would phone home and speak to Seva, exchange a few words with Mama, though never many — she was interested mainly in how I was, not so much in my thoughts, and I hadn't really a great deal to say about how I was. I worked, ate, slept, and was fine.

Seva thrived, he enjoyed all the attention he was getting from Mama, her warmth and nearness. Of course, he was quite oblivious to the fact that Mama and I had our own relationship, and when he said one day that it had been *the best day of his life* it meant something else to me than it did to him, though naturally it made me happy for him.

There was a river where we were staying and in the evenings

sometimes I'd walk along beside it until coming to one of the forest roads and following that instead. They nearly all led back to the university buildings or to the places where we carried out our field studies. It was as if I needed all that space to sort out my thoughts, as if the landscape opened itself to them and offered them room, when usually they were crammed together and forever piling up.

The trees were silent and tall, the birds and animals fluttered and rustled, flitted and stole about, around the trees, on them, in them. Darkness spread itself, a murk between the trunks, the moon shining far above in a sky as yet blue.

Bochanov had once said there were indications to suggest that the trees slept at night. I was sceptical. It would mean that they woke up too, but how could you wake up if you weren't a sentient being?

I spent the first two years of the course ingesting the terminology and the particular ways of thinking that belonged to hard science. I'd come from the humanities and most of my fellow biology students had more of a scientific ballast than me. Presumably that was the reason I didn't care much for Bochanov's speculations about trees sleeping and the questions they gave rise to about whether trees were sentient beings or not, these were issues that broke down the walls between natural science and the humanities, thereby reducing the distance I'd put between my former and present disciplines. As a new science student I'd been more Catholic than the Pope, everything had to be as scientific as possible, which is to say quantifiable and amenable to formalisation. The fieldwork I was taking part in was of the simplest kind, all we had to do was register, map and compare our data in order to discover in what ways, if at all, the fungi present in the soil interacted with the new saplings that had been planted, and whether it made any significant difference if a few or all of the trees of an area had been left unfelled, and if so what kind of difference. But what I discovered, and have since found to be the case in a great many instances, is that it doesn't matter what you focus on, where you zoom in, and that regardless of how small and restricted an area may be, it will always open up into something bigger. The first time I really considered mycelium with my own eyes, I was struck by how wispy and insubstantial it looked, particularly against the thick dark mass of the soil, and although there were such a great many of those white filaments, they were so delicate that it was hard to grasp they could in any way be important to the enormous tree to which they had attached themselves. But they were. Mycorrhiza occurred in around eighty per cent of all plants on earth and had in all likelihood arisen as far back as in the Devonian, something like four hundred million years ago. At that time, land-based plants were a relatively new phenomenon and the first trees, *Archaeopteris*, date back to the same period. In other words, mycorrhiza could be assumed to be an important reason for the great spread of trees and plants after that time. We might posit that it happened by chance the first time, that these blind, dumb and unfathomably slow organisms bumped into each other as it were in the soil and that the spindly threads of the fungi grew into the cells of the tree roots without purpose or meaning, and that the first exchange of nutrients was a simple fluke. With no brain or central nervous system involved, such an occurrence obviously couldn't have been planned or in any way intended. The question that then arose was how that collaborative relationship managed to spread to other fungi and other trees and plants, both geographically, to all four corners, and temporally, over the course of the four hundred million years that followed. If it was knowledge – and what else could it be? – then it had to be transmitted. In any case, the behavioural pattern was inside them, it couldn't just occur by chance every time, it had to be passed on from generation to generation. The question wasn't so much one of how the information was passed on – that happened by way of the DNA molecules replicating themselves – but rather how the information was first identified and captured in code. What was it that identified the information and by what mechanism was it encoded? And, by extension, what *was* the information?

This was the crux, it was what separated the non-living from the living. Venturing into that space would be a bit like asking a first-year theology student to write a thesis proving the existence of God. I left it alone, of course, not possessing the language, the knowledge or the insight required to even consider it, but once the question had been posed it turned out impossible to ignore, and all of a sudden I was seeing information and communication wherever I turned. All organisms living in or close to the tree read and decode the information in their own way, from their own starting points, and they read and decode each other too. What else was the forest but a teeming collection of signs? It was the same as with any physical body. If DNA was a language, then each individual could be seen as an expression of that language, an expression in turn to be read and decoded by other organisms, the forest being a level above. If the individual was a sentence, the forest was a book.

When I returned to Moscow from Pushchino, Mama and Seva were there to meet me at the railway station. They'd come on the train the day before. What I didn't know then, but which transpired later on, was that Mama hadn't just come to make things easier for me, but also because she had an appointment with a gastroenterologist. She told me she was going to see an old colleague of hers. Papa knew nothing of it either.

The evening before she went back I told her she spoiled Seva too much and that he was always quite impossible after he'd been staying with her. She didn't argue with that, but said only that it was quite likely she did. I felt guilty about it, the way I often did about one thing or another when we were together, so it was a relief when she boarded the train home the next morning and I could finally get Seva off to nursery school on my own again.

I'd decided to write my thesis at home, so apart from the trips it involved to the university library, and a few meetings with Bochanov in his office, that was where I spent the next few months. It came easily to me, so the problem wasn't so much what to write as what not to.

That everything was language, to be read and decoded, the world a book, was a medieval conception, easy to dismiss, and little to do with science. But in the Middle Ages it had been understood that signs were meant for us, that it was we who could read and decode them and thereby gain insight into God's plan for us, as well as the meaning of His work of creation. The kind of signs I was now reading about weren't meant for us at all, they belonged to processes to which human beings were not privy, even if they took place in our own cells.

These were alluring thoughts. Secret languages, codes, strange forms of cognition, visible, and yet incomprehensible signs. Everything that lived was pervaded by information and communication, from the very smallest components of a cell to flocks of birds, shoals of fish, crowds of people in the streets during a revolution or on any normal day. The problem was that life wasn't *at all* like that, an abstract, fantastic system, and that I was too quick by half to have pursued such trains of thought. Because down on my hands and knees in the moist soil of the forest, meticulously teasing forth a white thread of the mycelium, *that was all it was*, a white thread. It connected with one of the roots of the tree and absorbed nutrients. What it knew was in *itself*, quite literally. It had to possess some form of perception, and a form of memory, too. Everything living had that, it was almost a definition of what was alive. And what we were investigating was at the functional level, how the symbiosis *worked*, as seen from a practical forestry perspective.

But although that wasn't the way I went, my fascination must nevertheless have been considerable, because during one of our meetings Bochanov took the matter up.

'It's important to distinguish between information and knowledge,' he said as we sat in his office. I can't remember the exact context in which the words came, but I do remember what he said next: 'All we're doing now, in all our research, is accumulating information. We can keep on doing that for ever, but it won't take us anywhere.'

He sat smiling with his arms folded over his chest, his eyes fixed on a point somewhere near the top of my forehead.

'I don't agree,' I said. 'The enormous technological leaps we've seen over the last fifty years, weren't they the result of scientific research?'

'What technology are you talking about? Information technology? But all we're doing is using information to make machines capable of handling more information!'

'But maybe everything *is* information,' I said. 'Maybe that's what it's all about.'

He rolled his chair a bit closer to his desk so that he could reach his coffee. The cup was stained brown along the rim and looked like it hadn't been washed up for ages. He hadn't drunk from it either since I'd come in twenty minutes earlier, so the contents could only have been lukewarm at best. Nevertheless, he swallowed a good mouthful, wiped his mouth with the back of his hand, put the cup down on the desk again and rolled back to where he'd started.

There were two photographs on his desk. One of a young woman, one of a young man. The woman I took to be his wife when she'd been younger, the man their son. The odd thing was that they looked to be the same age.

'And what do you mean by that?'

'I don't know. It just came to me.'

'You must have meant something by it?'

I shook my head.

His eyes found my forehead again and he smiled.

'Something you might not know is that there was a working group in the field of theoretical biology here at this university back in the 1970s. They held meetings and ran what they called a winter school. It was quite the thing, around a hundred and fifty people took part each year. I didn't, but I remember it well. It was all wound down in 1978, for political reasons. It didn't sit snugly enough with the Soviet ideology, one could safely say. They held courses in mathematics and semiotics, among other things. In 1988 the work was resumed when Alexei Sharov ran a series of weekly seminars in biosemiotics here.'

'Biosemiotics?' I said. 'Is there such a thing?'

'Yes, it sounds like it's right up your tree, doesn't it?'

'Perhaps.'

'I don't know how good an idea it is, to be frank. What they're doing isn't really science but speculation really, nothing else. And those involved are looked at askance by most scientists. Besides, you're young, you've got no track record. You wouldn't get anywhere. No one would touch you.'

I said nothing, but continued working on my thesis which contained not a word about biosemiotics. But the fact that there was actually a field *called* biosemiotics aroused my curiosity, which was by no means diminished by it having started at my own department in what at the time was still the Soviet era. From the library I took out what I could find in the way of articles and other material based on the seminars. They turned out to contain a wild cross-pollination that traversed all sorts of disciplinary boundaries. Someone called Sedov wrote about what he called genolinguistics, a Chebanov about biohermeneutics, an Ogryzko and an Igamberdiev applied quantum mechanics to explain biological phenomena, Ogryzko also considering language to be a part of the epigenetic system. There were semioticians, linguists, mathematicians, molecular biologists, quantum physicists and palaeontologists involved. And while all this was taking place in Moscow, I soon realised, similar thoughts had been occurring elsewhere in the world, and what they had in common was that they were all in one way or another pushing at the boundary between nature and culture, whether they were looking at culture's biological roots or investigating linguistic dynamics at the molecular level.

Vasya loved the idea of life's core consisting in signs, communication and relations, of course she did, to her it was a fantastic thought, that the whole world was basically language. She lived, as Papa lived, in the world of literature. I didn't care for her inclination to dissolve the world into language, that was when it became too abstract for me, because it wasn't like that at all, that wasn't the point, the point was the exact opposite, that language was matter, language was flesh and blood. Mind was not a product of the brain, mind *was* the brain. There was no gap between the abstract thought and the concrete matter that produced it. The problem was, as Wittgenstein noted, not the phenomenon itself, but how we spoke about it.

And then Mama phoned.

She asked after Seva first, then she asked how I was, and I asked her how she was, and Papa, and some friends of hers too. And once we'd been through all that and were silent for a moment, she said:

'I've some rather bad news, I'm afraid, Tinoshka.'

'Oh?' I said. 'Has something happened?'

'It appears I have cancer.'

'Mama, no. Is it serious?'

'Quite serious, yes. It's in the pancreas. It's been discovered rather late, so apparently there's no way back now.'

She gave a little laugh.

'Such things are notoriously hard to predict, but it won't take more than a few months, six at most.'

'Oh no,' I said. I had no idea what else to say.

There was a lull, in which she said nothing, before I spoke again:

'Do you want me to come home? We can stay with you, Seva and me. I'm just sitting here working, I can just as easily do that there.'

'Thanks, it's thoughtful of you. And it would be nice, of course. But when I get poorly, which I will soon, it won't be such a good environment for Seva.'

'Perhaps not,' I said with relief. I hadn't imagined only a few short weeks would pass before she was taken into hospital and Papa called to say she hadn't much time left. If I'd known, I'd have gone back home with Seva and stayed with her those last weeks of her life. Of course I would.

Only I didn't. A few minutes was all I got with her before she was gone. After that, three days with Papa in the apartment, during which he spent most of his time on his own in his room, but I was used to that, so the only real change I noticed in him was that he hardly spoke. Sasha had gone home, he didn't want to be there with us, he refused to share his grief with Papa and didn't appear again until the morning of the funeral. Seva screamed through the entire ceremony. He was too little to understand what death meant, but old enough to register the emotions it involved. The white coffin with all its wreaths appeared so distressing when I tried to look at it as if through his eyes, and the hush of those in attendance would have unsettled him too, the stifled sobs now and then, the cold and solemn mood. Of course I, his mother, was not my usual self either. And Sasha, his beloved uncle, breaking down like a child after stepping up to say a few words. I'd urged him not to speak, nothing would be worse than him turning up drunk, standing there swaying at the coffin. But he insisted and promised he wouldn't touch a drop. He kept that promise and was sober as a judge in the church. Stepping up, he took his speech from his inside pocket and unfolded the pages with trembling hands, only for grief to overwhelm him, his face contorted, his mouth opened and closed a couple of times before he went and sat down again, his shoulders heaving, a look in his eyes that was part terror, part distress.

He wasn't a strong person, Sasha, never had been. It was I who had to take care of the arrangements, for the funeral and afterwards, I who took it upon myself to welcome those who came. Papa was even more distant than usual, his face was like a mask and he almost shoved me away when I put an arm around his shoulder to give him a hug after the coffin had been lowered through the floor to be taken away for cremation and we were on our way outside.

Sasha looked after Seva, it was kind of him, but I couldn't help hoping when I saw them together in the function room afterwards that Seva wouldn't turn out like his uncle.

The reaction didn't come until a few weeks later. When I'd collected Seva from nursery school one afternoon, the staff told me they'd noticed a couple of small blisters on his body that they were worried might be chickenpox, they'd had a couple of cases only recently, and they asked me to keep an eye on it. As soon as I got home, I took his clothes off and could see immediately that he was now developing a rash, even in the short time it had taken us to walk back it had broken out visibly. I counted three blisters on his tummy, five on his back, two on his thigh, one on his arm, two on his cheek.

'I think you've got chickenpox, little man,' I said, and put his trousers and top back on. 'Shall we give Babulya a ring and ask her what to do?'

'Is Babulya *alive*?' he said.

'No, she's not. Of course she's not,' I said, horrified, and turned the television on for him, then fetched him a glass of milk and a biscuit while he curled up on the sofa.

Standing at the window I bit my lip as my eyes filled with tears. I wiped them away with my sleeve and thought I could control myself, but then my whole chest started heaving, a sob escaped me and when I tried to breathe in I just broke down. I stepped into the kitchen so that Seva wouldn't notice, but it was too late, he came after me.

'What's the matter, Mama?' he said, looking up at me. My face crumpled, my mouth quivered, and when I tried to answer him, my voice would emit only a wail.

'Why are you crying, Mama?'

I kneeled down and hugged him tightly.

He patted my back like a little man.

I got to my feet and turned the tap on, splashing cold water onto my face as I tried to regain control of my breathing.

I knew I mustn't break down in front of him, but although I did all I could to pull myself together, I couldn't help it, all I could do was stand there weeping at the sink, aware between every sob that he was watching me.

'Mama's a bit upset, that's all,' I managed to say eventually. 'It's all right. Come on, let's go and watch the television again, shall we?'

I'd settled a bit by the time we sat down, letting out only the smallest sob, the occasional sniffle, a kind of afterquake, until eventually that too subsided and I was able to ruffle his hair and smile at him through still teary eyes.

At bedtime, I read *Vasilisa the Beautiful* for him. He loved fairy tales and this one was his favourite. I liked it too. This evening it seemed apt, with all the grief the little girl felt when her mother died. Seva lay as always with his head back on the pillow, looking straight up at the ceiling as I read, never at me. The story was a world of its own, beyond the world we knew. He liked the fact that he knew someone called Vasilisa, too. That she could hardly be called beautiful wasn't something he gave a thought to yet.

'Sleep tight, my little star,' I said, switching the light off by the bed and drawing the curtains before going for a shower.

The strange thing was that there hadn't been a thought in my head while I'd been crying. I puzzled over it as the hot water streamed over my body. Not a thought about Mama, about death, about myself, about anything. The thoughts came now.

I knew she was dead, yet she was still near to me, that connection hadn't been broken. I could think about her.

But she couldn't think about me.

She couldn't think about Seva.

She'd never know what was to become of him, or me.

And I'd never be able to tell her it didn't matter that she spoiled him like that. I'd never be able to apologise for all the barbed comments I'd aimed at her, never be able to say, I'm really sorry, Mama, for behaving so badly towards you then. I took everything you gave, but gave nothing back, I know, and I'm so very sorry.

She'd never be able to say, it's all a part of life, my love, that's what it's like having a daughter, you must lead your own life, you understand, and sometimes it's hard.

I'd never be able to put my arms around her and thank her and tell her, you're the best mother anyone could ever have.

I want you to know I'm proud of you, she'd said.

Oh, Mama, Mama.

I started crying again, but this time it felt good, and my tears mingled with the water that washed everything away.

Not long after that, Papa started phoning me. He'd never done that before. He'd call once a week, always at the same time, 7 p.m. on the dot. Mostly he talked about what he'd been reading or thinking about since the last time we spoke. If he was on form, we could end up talking for perhaps an hour. Gradually, I learned to handle it, making it more dialogue than monologue. If I ignored his lack of interest and talked about whatever I wanted to talk about, regardless, he would eventually start listening and engage himself in a conversation, however half-heartedly.

What struck me around that time, something I'd never thought about before, was that everything Papa concerned himself with was an abstraction. Books, music, ideas, concepts. He had no interest at all in nature or his surroundings. His only physical activity was to go for a walk every day, but only so that he could think without being disturbed, not to exercise. Apart from that all he did was sit in his chair or behind his desk. Everything went on inside his head, that was where he lived his life. That it hadn't occurred to me before had of course to do with all that abstraction going on *inside* him, invisible to anyone but himself, whereas what we saw, Mama and I, was him, his physical being and all its various expressions, that was as concrete as things got with him. Only after I'd moved away and he became a voice on the phone did it occur to me at all. Words, sentences, thoughts, opinions — these were things that didn't exist on their own, only as parts of a system that referred to itself. So when I told him about mycorrhiza, he couldn't just let it be a phenomenon I was studying and listen to what I had to say about it, he would have to compare it, typically, to Deleuze and Guattari's concept of the rhizome, thereby turning it into something else, a model for alternative ways of thinking and understanding, horizontal and branching, centreless, non-linear.

'But, Papa,' I said then, 'mycorrhiza isn't an example of anything! It's a thing in its own right! It's there in the soil, you can dig it up and look at it with your own eyes, feel it in your hands. It's not a concept!'

'Now, now,' he said, back to his most patronising. 'I understand, I understand. But when you write about it, it becomes a concept whatever you say, whether you like it or not. You can't just present these roots at your exam, now, can you? It's your understanding of them the examiners are after, and that's something other than the thing itself. That's the whole problem with the natural sciences. Language about the world isn't the world. Even mathematics — no, mathematics *especially* — is culture, it belongs to our human sphere. What the natural sciences are really about is our relationship to the world, not the world itself. And that relationship exists in language.'

'So evolution isn't something that actually happens, it's just something that's inside our heads?'

'The theory of evolution describes our understanding of what we observe, yes. There's nothing wrong with that. I've nothing against your subject, if that's what you think.'

'What about DNA?'

'Inside our heads, as you so succinctly put it.'

'But, Papa,' I said again, 'we know exactly what DNA is composed of, as well as how it works. It's not a theory, it's validated every single day in laboratories all over the world and in the most tangible of ways, in animals and insects, plants and bacteria, and everything else that's living. I really don't understand how you can deny it.'

'It's not that hard to understand, is it? A lot of things in nature repeat themselves, so if you observe and describe a phenomenon in a certain way and understand it that way, you're bound to understand it in exactly the same way the next time it occurs, even if it's in a different place, in a different context.'

'You're incorrigible,' I said. 'You know nothing about natural science, nothing about biology, not a single jot, and yet you set yourself above it and claim to know better!'

'A little opposition can do no harm, surely? There's enough whooping self-congratulation as it is in the world of science.'

'I'm actually trying to learn something by it. Your opposition is the

last thing I need. How about some support instead? Oh, that's fascinating, Alya! Amazing what all those little roots can do there under the
soil!'

I laughed, because even the thought was absurd.

'It is rather amazing, of course, you're right about that. But amazing
from what perspective? For the fungus it's quite banal.'

'Papa!'

He chuckled.

'I do think what you're doing is interesting. Just don't take everything at face value, that's all.'

Neither of us spoke for a few seconds.

'Thanks for the chat,' he said then. 'Take care.'

And with that he hung up.

After one such discussion I found myself thinking I was getting to be
like him. Apart from the staff at Seva's nursery school, shop assistants
and librarians, and Bochanov once in a while, I hardly saw anyone at
all during those months of reading, writing, working. I looked after
Seva too, of course, but it couldn't have been good for him living somewhere no one visited, with only his mother for company. It was shaping
him, I could tell. He became more used to playing on his own and had
turned into something of a little grown-up. At nursery school he was
different, more unbridled, more physical, and the thought that he felt
perhaps he had to be compliant when he was with me, that I was suffocating him in that way, the part of him that was him, was enormously
unpleasant.

On the other hand I was doing what I wanted to do. I didn't miss
anyone, wasn't longing for anyone, Mama's death had been a lot easier
to cope with than I'd feared. After my little breakdown that day I hardly
even thought about her. Only occasionally did I feel a jolt of grief and
would pause for a moment as if before an abyss, a void that was her
absence, but all I had to do then was turn away and it would be gone.

I really didn't want to be like Papa. I wanted what I did to have consequence, to mean something. In literature, the tangible world was
blown to pieces, whereas the opposite happened in biology, where the
abstract took on substance and form and became concrete. The rough,

hard bark, the lattice of veins when the sun shone through the delicate leaves, the dark, moist earth. The swarms of midges, the pink maggots, the woodpeckers, the blackbirds. The thing about it was that there was no doubt — what was, *was*. The stringency and logic, too, the clarity of the natural sciences were aspects that had drawn me to them, that their abstractions weren't just speculation but were verifiable. DNA was no abstraction, its signs were proteins, matter, and its code was transformed into concrete actions. The abstraction was in the language employed about them — *signs*, *code* — not in the phenomena themselves. Papa was right about that, but the conclusion he drew from it was wrong.

My thesis was well received, my supervisor told me he had support in urging me to apply for a doctoral scholarship. I would, of course. But what would I specialise in, what would I research and write about? I thought about it all through the summer, which was unusually hot and dry that year in Moscow, I remember it almost as a colour, the colour of grass everywhere after months of blazing sun, almost white. I'd never known anything like it before, the way the heat made it seem as if the landscape stiffened and became unpliable, usually it was the cold that had that effect. Seva spent some weeks with his grandmother in the country, it was good for him, while I lay reading in the daytime under shady trees in the park next to the student halls, going out in the evenings, guzzling vodka and tonics in bars and clubs, often ending up with quite different people from the ones I'd gone out with, those casual encounters in the night, when all of a sudden anything can be said and anything done, the alcohol turning even complete strangers into confidants. I liked it, as long as it was only for a short time. Years and I would have been one of those who glitter in the night-time and fade in the daylight, one of those flickering shadows without a will of its own any more. But for those few weeks it was a release to let go for a while and just drift.

The first day after Seva's return, I felt the longing to be out there again, enveloped in the darkness, with all its anonymous faces, that compelling, all-or-nothing desire that coursed through my body. And perhaps I even toyed with the thought of going out after I'd put him to bed, given that he always slept through until morning without waking, but it was never a serious thought: the two worlds excluded each other.

In the evenings we made dinner together. Which is to say that he would sit on a stool in the tiny kitchen and watch me as I heated the food in the microwave and sliced some tomato and cucumber. I'd hand him two plates and he would put them out in that solemn little way of his on the table in the living room, then glasses, knives and forks. I always tried to make an effort and keep things together when we were on our own, even though the flat was so small that I slept, ate and worked in the same room. Seva had his own little room, barely more than an alcove, and there was a minuscule bathroom next to the kitchen. We didn't have much space, but the place was ours, and we each had our ways of making it work.

Once Seva had been put to bed, I washed the dishes before settling down on the sofa, which doubled as my bed, with a cup of tea and a book. Although the windows faced south and had seen only shade for several hours, the room was so hot it felt like the sun was beating through. It didn't help much to open them, but I did so anyway, filling the room with the sounds of the city: the rumble of traffic across the park, chatter and music from those who were still sitting out on the grass there, the sudden roar of a motorbike tearing the air apart and then dissolving into the distance in seconds, a sound I'd heard in every city, every town I'd ever been; footsteps on the pavement two floors down, the voices of those they belonged to, if they happened to be talking, now and again so very clear, almost as if they were walking in the air right outside the pane.

I stood there, tea in hand, and looked out over the park where a man at that same moment threw a ball and a dog set off to chase it. A bit further away stood another man, holding a bulky remote control in his hand, and all of a sudden I picked out a high-pitched whirr that presumably had been there all the time without me having noticed it, it came from a radio-controlled car that was speeding bumpily over the bone-dry and uneven grass.

Tea was too hot in such weather, what had I been thinking?

I went into the kitchen and tipped it into the sink, filled a glass with water instead and drank it standing beside the worktop, and when it was drunk, I reached up for the bottle of gin on the top shelf, opened a bottle of tonic water, took two ice cubes from the tray in the freezer and sat down in front of my faintly humming typewriter.

The application deadline for my doctoral scholarship was more than a week away, so I still had time. Earlier in the summer I'd outlined a project for myself, but I was rather uncertain about it. I had another, much safer, that hardly required any work at all, tacking onto a pre-existing and comprehensive research project under the name *The European-Russian Forest* which had the participation of universities from all over the country and which was to culminate in an extensive multi-volume book publication, as those things did in those days. It would give me a niche and bring me into the fold. My own project, on the other hand, was more left-field. Perhaps it was hardly a project at all, little more than a few loosely connected thoughts I'd scribbled down. That was the problem with it. The application needed to be stringently formulated and underpinned, and the project itself had in some way to be useful.

I sipped my drink, which was now ice-cold, and opened my note-book at the outline for my project description. I'd written it down in one go on the train, just to get something on paper, all those loose thoughts of mine. The moment I saw them again, my face flushed warm and I knew it was the other option I had to choose.

I closed the notebook and took another sip of my gin and tonic, then looked in on Seva, who was lying on his back in just his underpants, fast asleep. I dialled Vasya's number to ask if she fancied coming over for an hour or so, only there was no answer, so I went and had a shower instead, as cold as I could bear, before plonking myself down on the sofa again and reaching for the notebook.

It felt good to have come to a decision. I was in no doubt.

And it really was flimsy to say the least, the idea I'd sketched out for myself. Unanchored in anything of substance. Just a thought that had occurred to me and then grown out of all proportion. When we'd been away on the field trip to Pushchino and I'd seen the thin threads of mycelium, the way they spread out in patterns that in places resembled dendrites, they not only appeared clearly to connect with the roots of the tree, they looked as if they could reach out to the roots of the one next to it too. The tree roots as well could be entangled, the roots of one criss-crossing those of another, so the connections went this way and that, something that in my imagination became a great subterranean network, not unlike one of the old telephone systems whose cables went from house to house. I hadn't read anything about the mycelium connecting with more than one tree at a time, so when the opportunity presented itself, I asked Bochanov about it, careful to do so in the most casual manner, as if it didn't matter one way or another.

He was sitting opposite me at the table in the canteen, eating his lunch, his fork in his right hand, left forearm resting on the tabletop.

'I was wondering about something,' I said.

'Yes?' he said, looking up at me as he chewed his food.

'Can the mycelium connect with several trees at once? It looks like it could.'

'Yes, certainly,' he said.

'What practical function would that have?'

He swallowed, picked up the salt cellar and sprinkled some salt onto his boiled potatoes.

'Taking up nutrition from two sources rather than one is bound to be preferable, wouldn't you say?'

'Yes,' I said.

'Also, it would establish a channel between individual trees,' he went on. 'Allowing them to exchange nutrients, the fungus being a kind of intermediary, so to speak. But that's just speculation.'

He looked at me and held my gaze, as if he now had the right.

I smiled at him. He smiled back, then returned to his meal, forking up another mouthful of food as meticulously as if meals too were a part of his work.

I said nothing about the idea that had come to me, neither to Bochanov nor to my fellow students, friends or Papa. There was nothing in it. A few thin white filaments attaching themselves to the network of tree roots under the soil. That the trees thereby became connected didn't necessarily mean anything. Certainly not that they had to be communicating. What the roots did, those of the fungus, the trees and the plants, was to take up water and nutrients, and since they had different properties, the idea of collaboration naturally came to mind. On the other hand, if anything characterised evolution, it was that life forms that had evolved for one purpose would sooner or later be exploited for another. The most familiar example was perhaps that the human auditory system, the highly complex organ of the ear, began life as the jawbone of a reptile. Before that, life had been deaf. But that jawbone came into being, and since evolution will never fail to exploit the opportunities present in any living organism, it eventually developed into an ear. Hearing wasn't planned, it just came into being by chance. It's easy to imagine that evolution picked up a scent, as it were, and followed it. In a way that's just how it works, some developments are rewarded, advantages coming to light that serve to reinforce the process, whereas a development that leads nowhere, or brings about something negative, will be abandoned. It was from that perspective I saw the notion of those subterranean connections, that they would at the very least make possible a form of communication between trees, and that the chances of it actually happening were as good as those of it not. In which case there had to be some kind of consciousness at work. But if there was, how did it manifest itself? A tree had no brain, no nervous system, nothing even resembling. Yet it possessed knowledge, it grew of its own accord and took on a certain form, it strove towards the sun whose energy it converted, it sucked up water and the nutrients it needed to stay alive, and it delivered them to its various parts. A tree could have no awareness of that knowledge, but it was there anyway. Human consciousness existed somewhere above cellular level, though no one knew exactly where. Thought took place in the cells, or by means of them, but could not be localised there, in the individual cell, what occurred was something different, it was all in the interaction, the relation, the space in between, not the single cell itself.

Could some similar form of interaction take place in the tree, above the level of the cell, but below the level of our own human consciousness?

And could it be the case that a tree, like that single cell, was merely a locus, unconscious of itself, as the human brain cell too was unconscious of itself, and that the level above, where consciousness unfurled, was actually the forest? Could the forest possess a form of consciousness, vastly different from our own, so alien to us that we didn't even know it was there?

These were thoughts that burned in me. They went against every-thing I believed in, perhaps that was why I found them to be so strong. Reason told me it was mind spin, but there was something else in me that opposed such a viewpoint, a part of me that proposed new argu-ments, the most important of these being that the fantastic, the inconceivable, the unfathomable belonged not to the peripheries of reality, outlands attended only by the most fevered and self-suggestive of minds, but rather to the very midpoint. The more I read about evo-lution, for example, the greater its mysteries became. Not that an organism mutated and developed a property that made it better suited to its environment, and that its progeny would then be hardier and more numerous, the property thereby slowly spreading through the community, because that was logical and easy to understand. What I was grappling with was what went on above all that: what *was* evolu-tion? Or rather: *where* was it? All information had to be somewhere, in some or other form of matter, whether it be waves in the air, chemical reactions in the cells, words on a newspaper page or electrical signals in a transistor. Even though information in a certain sense was abstract, it couldn't exist without physical form. So far so good. But where was the information about the system of which it was a part, the pattern all life followed, which is to say the principles of evolution? I'd put that ques-tion to perhaps the brainiest of my fellow students, Seryozha, one of those pale, gangly young men who are so good at everything involving numbers — mathematics, computer programming, chess, and some-times, albeit in a more mechanical kind of way, music — but who can be so helpless when it comes to anything that goes on between people that often it's hard not to think of them as verging on the autistic. He said it was the simplest thing imaginable, that it was like a computer program, you fed in a few rules and off it went, in particular, though not always completely predictable, directions. He was enthused and flattered by my interest, and presented me with some examples.

'You've seen great flocks of birds, flying together as if they were one?'

'Yes,' I said, standing behind him as he sat hunched over his computer.

'It looks highly complicated and very advanced. How do all the birds know how they're supposed to fly at any given point in time? They're in perfect formation! But look at this.'

On the screen in front of us a swarm of dots started moving. They were coordinated, each following the other, sweeping waves of movement across the screen, exactly the way a flock of birds would move across the sky at dusk.

'The rule they follow is that every dot has to do the same as the dot that's adjacent to it. That's it. And now look,' he said, showing me another pattern, some dots moving along what looked to be a corridor with an open door in the middle, each waiting its turn before going through the door.

'You see? It looks like they're being polite. As if they've a thousand years of civilisation behind them. But the only rule here is that they have to maintain a certain distance to the others.'

He swivelled to look at me, with a big grin on his face.

'Cool, don't you think? I know another program I can show you tomorrow, the simulation's on a slightly bigger scale, but it's quite amazing. It has a *little* bit to do with evolution, too. It's called the Game of Life. Have you heard of it?'

I shook my head.

'You've got something to look forward to, then,' he said.

And it really was fascinating, when he demonstrated it to me the following day.

The screen was divided up into a grid of square cells. He activated a few and they turned yellow.

'To begin with the cells are dead,' he said. 'So before you start, you have to enter in a configuration of living cells. That's the yellow ones, you see? So now they're alive. Let's stick with seven. The rules are really simple. If a living cell only has one or zero living cells adjacent to it, it dies. If it's got more than three, it dies too. If it's got two or three living cells for neighbours, it'll go on living. And all the dead cells that have got exactly three living cells adjacent to them are given new life. Ready?'

'Yes,' I said, with no idea what to expect.

The seven cells quickly multiplied and started to form patterns. Some looked like stars, others fireworks, but there were simpler crosses and rectangles too. Then some of them split off and stayed where they were in blocks without moving, while some others began to move across the screen in formation, a bit like a caterpillar.

'Hey, where's it going?' I said.

Seryozha laughed.

'Now it's reached a kind of ideal state. It's got five cells, perfect when it wants to move. It's called a glider. Do you see? It gains as many new cells as it loses, and off it goes, up, down, sideways.'

Another pattern stood quite still, blinking, one instant it was a cross, the next a rectangle. More patterns appeared, blocks of still life again. Some chains of three flashed from horizontal to vertical.

'If you hang on a bit, you might see what they call a spaceship. Bigger, mobile patterns. There. Beautiful, don't you think?'

'Beautiful probably isn't the first word that comes to mind,' I said.

He sniggered.

'You can't predict what patterns are going to form, even if you know the rules and the exact starting point. That's a bit like evolution, wouldn't you say? I see beauty in it.'

'How long does it go on?'

'In principle, for ever. Shall we try another combination?'

He configured some more cells and set the game off again. This time it was like an explosion, the cells then splitting into two camps, forming patterns that were identical, as if there was a mirror between them, at the same time as they occasionally came together to form a ring or a block with a hole in the middle.

'I can sit and watch this for hours,' he said.

'I don't doubt it,' I said. 'Thanks, Seryozha. See you later.'

There'd been something unnerving about the way the game unfolded, the cells behaved so much like they were alive and seemed to be in possession of an own free will. Especially the caterpillar that crept away from the others and disappeared off the screen, only to reappear again, still crawling. There were four rules that made it do that. But those rules were programmed by someone and were a physical part of the game. I could accept that evolution too followed only a few simple rules that determined everything that happened. But where did they come from, and where were they? Were they in each and every organism? It was a bit like the laws of nature, which had no existence as such either, but which every natural life form nevertheless followed.

The greatest difference between what was living and what was not, was that what was living was driven from within, whereas what was not was governed from without. Even a bacterium strove to do something, even a bacterium had a will. What must have happened was that some of the self-generating chemical processes that in all likelihood had arisen not long after the earth was formed, and which perpetuated in a kind of loop, in some way separated away from their environments, the establishment thereby of a within and a without, whose relative imbalances had to be equalised, being constitutive of the very life force itself, the urge to live. The mystery was how such a lifeless, wholly material chemical process could develop memory. Because that's what the DNA code is. Some of the codes in my cells stemmed from that same time, they were almost four *billion* years old. So these self-generating chemical systems kept themselves going by fencing themselves in and making use of a code that, put simply, told them exactly what they were, and what they could do, and which furthermore could be reproduced, so that what they were could be replicated somewhere else. But how did that code arise? And, no less importantly, how did it get to be decoded? Wouldn't that have to involve some form of consciousness or will? At the same time, wouldn't it be the code that gave rise to that consciousness, that will?

Life emerged when something was held firm, and whatever did that has never let go. That something was information, in the form of a very particular language in a code that had remained unchanged ever since. It had happened at the very lowest levels of life known to us. But the information and the language in which it was encoded were just as essential at all levels of life. Most notable were the information processes in the brain, because of their dizzying complexities and minutely calibrated nature, but also clearly because of the mysteries of cognition. And those ideas, that all life is centred around information and communication, and that the consciousness of any being cannot be localised to individual cells in the brain and the electrochemical processes that take place there, but may be understood only as a function of the sum of all cells and all processes, made the thought that trees communicated with each other appear utterly reasonable, and the thought too that local communication could come together into something greater, the forest and the consciousness of the forest, so different from our own that we would never be able to fathom it, was also altogether less fantastic than it had originally seemed.

That was how far those wispy white threads in the soil had brought me.

It was ironic, because I wanted so much to be down to earth, and now I was burrowing into it!

When I told Papa about what I was working on and reading about, without of course mentioning communication between trees with even a single word — the idea of the forest as a sentient being was something I hadn't yet dared to formulate even to myself at that stage, dismissing it rather with an unvoiced grunt of disapproval and a shake of the head at my own folly — he suggested I take a look at Bogdanov, he would interest me, he said.

'Bogdanov the revolutionary?' I said. 'The one Lenin ostracised?'

'That's him, yes. But he was also an economist, philosopher, sociologist, culture theorist, doctor and psychiatrist. He even wrote two novels of science fiction. In his final years he ran the first blood transfusion clinic in the Soviet Union. A universal genius, you could say. His genius though was not a blaze, it was more low-energy than that. Maybe that's how you end up if you spread yourself over as many fields as Bogdanov did.'

'Hm,' I said. 'Why should I read him?'

'He developed his own science, which he called *tektology*. It's about systems and organisations. He was far ahead of his time, in many ways. What he wrote back then is employed in cybernetics today. What was particular about it was that Bogdanov equated all systems, looking at the principles that unite them, so in his view there's no difference between what occurs between atoms and what occurs between people. It came to mind when you were talking about the living and the non-living, you see.'

'I'll look into it,' I said.

'Everything he wrote is available again now. Read his science fiction. *Red Star*! It takes place in a communist society on Mars. Brilliant, brilliant. And then you might cast an eye on Vladimir Bibikhin too.'

'Who?'

'Bibikhin, the philosopher.'

'Never heard of him.'

'Alyushka! You can't be serious. I thought everyone had heard of him. Or you, at least, a person of letters.'

'Sorry to disappoint you.'

'He worked for years at your own university. They kicked him out in the nineties, I think, probably because he wasn't positivist enough, or perhaps his style was too messy for them. Who knows what they found wrong with him. But what he did then was to pitch up at the university in civvies, so to speak, find himself an empty lecture room and start lecturing. He packed them in, all the students wanted to be there. One of his last, and this is my point, one of his last lecture series was about the forest.'

'I see,' I said.

'That *is* what you're interested in, isn't it?'

'Yes. Though maybe not from a philosophical angle.'

'It never hurts to read philosophy. Heidegger wrote about the animal world in his *Fundamental Concepts of Metaphysics*, you know.'

'So you've told me, many times. You don't miss a chance to get me started on him. The same with Lucretius.'

'There are certain things an educated person needs to have read,' he said, quite without irony.

'You're not offended by my ignorance, I hope?'

'Me? Offended? Of course not.'

I hung up with a bad feeling in my stomach. It was so easy to forget how sensitive, how touchy he was. It had always been well hidden behind his gruff facade and endless monologues. But he'd changed a bit those past months, and when I climbed into bed that night it suddenly occurred to me that he actually looked forward to our conversations. Sometimes it even seemed like he'd read up in preparation.

Was there really so little in his life that an hour on the phone with me was something he lived for?

The thought saddened me. I wanted him to be strong and independent and not need anything, the way he'd always been.

But perhaps he'd never been like that? Perhaps it had only come to light now that Mama wasn't with us any more.

I read Bibikhin first, but found only an endless series of speculations and associations, sparked by the fact that the ancient Greek for matter, *hyle*, was the same as that for forest. Bogdanov turned out to be something else entirely. He belonged to that area of philosophy that believed the only thing we could have knowledge about was what we could observe and experience, and that we were unable to say anything meaningful about what lay beyond. That did away with metaphysics, which appealed to me greatly. He called metaphysics *false thinking*, as opposed to *real thinking*, which concerned itself only with what was experienced. I shared his antipathy, it had to do with the scepticism I'd always felt towards abstraction, though I'd never got round to formulating it. Metaphysics departs from concrete reality in two ways, according to Bogdanov — by assuming firstly that elements exist which aren't a part of our experience, for instance the *thing-in-itself*, and secondly that relations exist that aren't based on experience, such as *the absolute* or *the timeless*. The dismissal of metaphysics wasn't exactly a new phenomenon, it had been separated from science since the 1500s, banished to another sphere from that which dealt with our concrete material reality, but that dismissal was reductionist and applied to everything that could not be measured or weighed or in any other way formalised. Bogdanov's dismissal was different. Firstly, his critique of non-experientially based relations had to apply not only to metaphysics, but also to the natural sciences, which operated with both the absolute and the timeless, not least in conceptions about natural laws. Secondly, his dismissal of metaphysics was not reductionist, since an experientially based understanding of the world, where what we can talk about emerges in the encounter between experiencer and experienced, which is to say in the relation, radically heightens complexity. Bogdanov was therefore naturally concerned with the relation between the mental and the physical, or the internal and the external, or the subjective and the objective, which he brought together on the basis that both were experientially based, whereas the difference between them was in the way the various experiences were organised — the mental was organised individually, the physical was organised socially. Natural laws, which cannot be experienced, were something he believed to be a product of thought that had come into being as a way of organising experience.

I liked that idea very much.

Natural laws are our way of organising experience.

Organisation was indeed a key concept of Bogdanov's thinking, and essentially it was what I took from it, and not without a certain quiet enthusiasm. An organisation was any unit in which the whole was greater than the constituent parts, and what was liberating about that was that he didn't discriminate between the structures of material, biological or social realities. If the individual parts became greater than the whole, the organisation came apart. An organisation or a system existed exclusively by virtue of the relations within it — indeed, the organisation *was* those relations, not only the internal relations of which it was comprised, but also the external relations with which it coexisted, by which it was influenced, or which it influenced itself. The elements of a system were themselves systems, and one could begin with the social sphere, with its groups of individuals, continue with the individuals themselves, and move on to the brain and the brain cells — ever downwards as if descending a staircase, until reaching the very smallest elements in the depths of the strange world of quantum physics, where the insight that nothing exists in its own right, only in relation to something else, presumably had to be taken literally, at least according to certain physicists who believed that such particles simply did not exist at all until the moment they entered into a relation. They are nothing in themselves, however strange it may sound. They possess no properties of their own, and they exist only in their relation to others.

That was the end of the line.

Everything is nothing.

It was barely comprehensible. That staircase wasn't for me. But I had no reason to be there either. It was trees I was interested in, and the forest.

Communication between trees. The forest as a sentient being.

Who would support such a project? Or even see a project at all.

It was as vague as mist, wind, water.

Was there a project in there somewhere?

What thoughts supported it?

Could they even be called thoughts?

On the one hand our concrete reality, its physical organisms, I could grasp that, it was tangible, the idea that the world and life were there and that even the abstract had to have physical form. On the other hand the opposite, where everything was about relations, the space in between, of information and communication.

I asked Bochanov for a meeting in his office. He lit up when he saw me, and beckoned me in. I wasn't thinking of telling him that much, only of indicating the basic direction and asking him if he had any good advice he might care to impart, but when I sat down and he looked at me in anticipation of me taking the initiative, as if he were a therapist and I his client, I realised it made no sense to be cagey, it would only mean that what he had to say in reply would be similarly vague and consequently of little help.

'This PhD project . . .' I began.

'Yes?'

'I'm wondering if I should carry on with mycorrhiza.'

'Really?'

I nodded.

'In what way?'

'I'm not sure. But maybe looking into whether there's more going on than just the exchange of nutrients between fungus and tree.'

'What might that be?'

'I don't know. I'm not clear about anything yet.'

'You're back with biosemiotics, is that it?'

'Not necessarily, no. No, not at all.'

'What could go on down there other than the exchange of nutrients?'

'That's what I was thinking of looking at.'

He laughed.

'You must pinpoint your object and define the problem as clearly and as stringently as possible. I'm afraid *looking into* something isn't enough, Alya.'

'Thanks, but I'm painfully aware of that already.'

'If you want me to help you, I'll need to have more of an idea as to what you're actually thinking.'

'I realise that.'

'So, mycorrhiza.'

'Yes.'

'Does the connection between fungus and tree allow trees to communicate with each other, something like that, perhaps?'

'That could be the gist, yes. But I don't want to get stuck with anything yet.'

He laughed again.

'You can't get stuck with nothing.'

'I'm sorry to bother you with so little,' I said, and got to my feet. 'I'll come back when I've got something more substantial.'

'No, wait,' he said, lifting a hand. 'Do you know where Belomorskaia is?'

'Yes,' I said.

'I'm teaching there for three weeks later in the summer. You could come with me. You wouldn't need to take part in the classes. It's a big place, you could even have your own office. Work fully focused. And I'd be on hand if you needed any assistance.'

'I don't think so,' I said, and gave him as friendly a smile as I could muster.

'I happen to know they're running a course on mycology, too,' he persisted.

Couldn't he take no for an answer?

'It'd be perfect for you, now I come to think of it.'

'I really can't,' I said. 'I've got a little boy to take care of.'

'I understand,' he said, and stood up. 'Just a thought. Enjoy your summer, all the same.'

'Same to you,' I said, and smiled again to soften the snub before leaving and going to collect Seva from nursery school.

Belomorskaia was on the White Sea, about a thousand kilometres north of St Petersburg, beneath the Kola Peninsula, not so very far from the border with Finland. I'd thought the research station the university ran there was dedicated to marine biology, but obviously not. There were courses there on cellular biology, microanatomy and comparative physiology, for instance, as well as in comparative embryology, immunology and something they called eco-immunology.

The more I thought about it, the more appealing it seemed. The forests up there were vast and untouched, and the place was so far north that the nights would be as light as the days. It was a big facility, too, so I wouldn't exactly be stuck on my own up there with Bochanov.

The next time Papa phoned I mentioned it to him.

'The White Sea?' he said. 'What do you want to go there for?'

'For peace and concentration to write my application for the doctoral programme. There's a very stimulating scientific environment up there. They've all sorts of things going on.'

He sniffed.

'A *stimulating scientific environment*? Are you training to be a bureaucrat now?'

'You know what I mean.'

'Oh yes. I just don't know what you'd want there.'

'I told you.'

'But there's nothing there that you haven't got here, surely?'

'There aren't that many forests in Moscow.'

'Ah, so it's forests now.'

'It's always been forests. Trees, you know, they grow in forests.'

'Have your read Eliade's book on shamanism?'

'I really can't say I have, no. Shamanism?'

'You want forest, don't you? Well, give it a click. You'll find it useful, it'll give you another angle than the purely scientific one. The forest is so much more, you know.'

'I tried reading what Bibikhin wrote on the forest.'

'And?'

'Not much use to me, to put it mildly.'

'I see,' he said, and went on to talk about Robert Walser, whose books he'd been ploughing his way through for the second time, wondering even if he might be distantly related to him, his great-grandmother's maiden name having been Walser too. Walser's microscripts led him on to some musing about the difference between notes and letters of the alphabet, one of his favourite topics. I let him talk.

The following day, I bought Eliade's book in the university bookshop and took it with me to a nearby pavement cafe. It wouldn't harm to give it a scan, and I'd be able to tell Papa then that I'd read it the next time he rang. I was sceptical, not because I supposed it to be a poor book, but because of its subject matter. Superstition was perhaps interesting from a psychological or sociological viewpoint, but not on its own terms, it was vacuous and silly then. In something I'd read not that long ago, the author had suggested that religion was something we used to fill in the gaps. The transition from non-life to life, which we knew nothing about, was one such gap, and we filled it by positing God as the agent of creation. Likewise the transition from life to non-life: God again. It was reasonably put, and it was true. But shamanism turned out to be something else. It wasn't a system of any sort, and its primary purpose wasn't to explain the world or fill in the gaps, it had to do with another *experience* of the world. And after reading Bogdanov, experience was a word I liked. The concept was simple: the shamans used hallucinogenics, brought themselves into a trance, experienced something other than what they normally experienced, and perceived it to be just as real. That was shamanism. The strange thing was that the experiences the shamans described, from many different places in the world, and from many different times, were all similar. They would be in contact with the dead, with demons and spirits of nature. They would travel to the underworld, and to the upper world. The rites of initiation were all about suffering, death and resurrection: the prospective shamans would be taken to the underworld, to remain there for three days while their bodies were dismembered, their heads put on a stake, their flesh cooked, and then they would be reassembled and the candidate resurrected as a shaman. Although there were clear elements of psychosis in what they described, Eliade distanced himself firmly from any attempt to cast them or their activities as sick. For me, the most interesting thing was that they were conversant in a secret language, the language of nature itself.

If only!

That perceptions of reality could be altered by means of chemistry was of course natural, given that the only way we could experience reality at all was down to chemicals. What was less obvious was that what those shamans experienced while under the influence apparently wasn't arbitrary, since what they reported was the same in so many instances. The gods and the spirits could appear in the shape of animals or birds, owls, for instance, lynxes, crows, eagles, snakes, or in human form, or a combination, such as horses with the heads of men. At the centre was the world tree, from which unborn infants hung like leaves. Birds were messengers from the spirit of night.

It was impossible to be any further from my own experience of the forest and nature. To me the forest was silent and unforthcoming, with a presence I sensed, yet was unable to penetrate. The plants and trees, the animals, birds and insects had their own lives, as if arched above them, like belljars. The animals and birds observed me from a distance, from another world, another reality. The trees were even further removed, as if from another age.

That this solemn, unfathomable world, in which such slow and patient processes occurred, could in some way be accessed, somehow seep into us and become amenable to communication, open up, as it were, into something tangible, was an immensely intriguing, if rather frightening thought, but at the same time one that was so removed from reality all you could do really was shake your head. As an expression of man's yearning to connect with existence: yes. As an expression of genuine connection with existence: no.

I felt almost like I was a pioneer again as I boarded the train to St Petersburg with my rucksack on my back and a carrier bag with some food and drink in my hand. It was the high season, and although it was gone midnight the train looked like it was going to be full, mostly with tourists. I found my seat and took my Discman, headphones, a book and some CDs out of my rucksack, sensing out of the corner of my eye a man looking at me, and guessed immediately that he would offer to give me a hand as I pulled the drawstring tight, flipped the top cover back into place and snapped the buckles shut.

'Can I give you a hand?' he said.

He was in his forties, small and sinewy, full of pent-up energy, dressed in long army-green shorts with lots of pockets, and a white T-shirt.

'Thanks, I can manage on my own,' I said, as I lifted the rucksack aloft and shoved it onto the luggage rack before sitting down and opening my book. The journey, in several stages, would take some twenty-four hours in all, so I could just as well get myself into travel mode from the off: read, sleep, listen to music, with no clear-cut boundaries in between, a flow to mirror that of the landscape through which we passed.

Seva was with his paternal grandmother and Oksanka was borrowing my flat while I was away, so there was nothing for me to worry about.

'Are you going to St Petersburg?' the man said, having sat down across the aisle.

'Yes,' I said, glancing up at him before returning to my book.

'Holiday, perhaps?'

From the corner of my eye I saw him bend down and take a clear bottle and a glass from the little rucksack between his feet.

I pretended I hadn't heard. He poured himself a drink and put the bottle back in the rucksack.

'Sorry, do you want one?' he said.

I put my finger on the page to mark my place, looked up at him again and shook my head before going back to the sentence I'd already read.

He sipped the clear alcohol and leaned back with the glass resting in his hand.

'I'm going all the way up to Karelia,' he said. 'My brother's getting on at St Petersburg, we're going up there together. Fishing trip. We've got an old cabin up there. Haven't been for years. The place will be falling down now.'

I sensed him staring, but kept my focus on my book.

'You want to read,' he said. 'Don't mind me. I won't disturb you.'

'That's all right,' I said. 'But I do want to read, yes.'

The carriage filled up. A mother and her two boys came in, the mother, in her thirties, sat down opposite me, the two boys, ten and twelve, perhaps, in the window seats. As we pulled out of the station, I put my headphones on and switched on my Discman. There was a CD already in it. Beethoven's late string quartets.

I couldn't read with my music on at the same time, so I sat looking out the window as I listened, at vast, run-down satellite towns, then gradually fields and woodland, scattered houses, villages. Under the grey summer-night sky everything was beautiful, even the wonky sheds that here and there stood behind wooden fences alongside the tracks, the clustered shopping outlets on the edges of the towns, empty, shining their yellow light into the grey. Or perhaps it was the music that imparted some of its beauty to what passed by outside the window.

The mother produced a loaf of bread and some plastic containers of food that she opened on her lap before handing one each to her sons along with a hunk of bread she tore from the loaf, before she herself began to eat from the one that was left. Chicken and potatoes, glistening with fat. The boys, dark-haired with identical fringe cuts, tucked into their meal without a word. They hadn't spoken at all since they came in, it occurred to me now. The three of them clearly belonged together, a family unit, and yet their togetherness seemed so very different from Seva's and mine.

Once they'd finished eating, the mother gathered the containers together and put them back in her bag, handed them each a paper tissue for them to wipe their mouths and fingers, and then a bottle of water that was passed between them before it too was tucked away into her bag.

The boy sitting next to her leaned his head against her shoulder. She put her arm around him and closed her eyes. The other one sat with his forehead against the pane, staring out without moving.

Why did I envy her?

I knew nothing about her. I even had a little boy of my own.

And, not least, my freedom.

The music was sorrowful, but not cheerless. There was such movement in it. When I listened properly, as I did now, it was as if it reached into something that never moved in me otherwise and that was quite unfamiliar to me. It wasn't hard to think that the music was drawing a map over my inner being, following its every rise and fall, all its hills and valleys, flatlands and forests, in such a way that I only then became aware of them, but as I sat looking out into the still and pale night, it struck me too that perhaps there was nothing there before the music ventured inside, that it was the music that created it.

I closed my eyes and fell asleep, the music as if far above me for a moment, growing more and more distant, like a boat you've fallen out of that remains floating on the surface, while you slowly sink to the bottom beneath it.

I woke up as a voice over the loudspeaker announced that we'd be arriving at St Petersburg in a few minutes.

'Good morning,' said the man across the aisle. I got the unpleasant feeling he'd been watching me while I'd slept. He looked to be rather drunk, his face stiff and expressionless.

I gave him a weary smile and got up to go to the lavatory, wondering for a second whether to get my sponge bag out of my rucksack so I could brush my teeth and do myself up a bit, but there was something ever so slightly intimate about it that I didn't want him to see, so I didn't bother. But then there was a queue, so I went back and sat down again. The washrooms at the station would be better anyway.

'That was quick,' he said.

I flashed him a look of annoyance. He held both hands up in the air and leaned back in his seat.

Then he laughed.

'If looks could kill, I'd be dead now.'

The mother on the other side of the little table was still asleep, her cheek resting against the head of the boy next to her, who was awake and sitting awkwardly by the looks of it. I assumed he was reluctant to move in case he woke her up. The other boy, next to me, was sleeping too, his head tipped back, mouth wide open.

There was something about the two boys that reminded me of animals. Perhaps it was because I hadn't heard them speak, but saw their dark eyes peering out warily at the world. The way one of them had curled up to his mother.

People started getting to their feet, taking their luggage down from the overhead racks in anticipation of our arrival.

I felt so miserable. There was no reason to, quite the opposite, I had two whole weeks ahead of me at a research station in the forests by the White Sea, with all the time in the world to concentrate on what I enjoyed best.

The train slowed into the station. Through the windows I could see the platforms teeming with people. I'd been expecting the annoying little man to pipe up with some parting remark, or at least say goodbye, but to my relief he disappeared without a word. I waited until the carriage was almost empty before making my way out. I washed my face in the station washrooms, put some lipstick and eyeliner on, brushed my hair and put on a clean T-shirt, then bought myself a cup of tea on the concourse and went and sat down with it on a bench on the platform while I ate the sandwiches I'd made the evening before.

The people boarding the train for Chupa were quite different from the passengers that had come from Moscow. Their clothes were cheaper-looking, their bodies more unshapely, faces wearier. I saw the annoying man again, walking along the platform with another man who looked almost identical. Each carried a fishing rod and a rucksack with a sleeping bag rolled up under the top cover. He'd said he was going to Karelia, so I'd no reason to be surprised. Fortunately, it looked like their reservations were at the other end of the train.

The mood in the carriage was quite different on this leg of the journey, the people around me chattering and laughing as if they hadn't a care in the world. Perhaps it was just down to the different time of day, but something told me it was something else. People made as if they were at home, some produced food and drink, not clutched to their chests, but spread out almost like a picnic, while others played cards or listened unabashedly to the radio.

The journey would be sixteen hours, arriving at Chupa just after four the next morning. Bochanov had promised to lay on transport for my onward journey from there, he'd said there'd probably be several more coming on the same train, but the driver wouldn't be there until seven at the earliest, so there'd be a couple of hours to kill at the station.

He'd been surprised when I'd called him and asked if his offer still stood, but he said yes without hesitation. I'd thought he would, knowing he'd always go to some lengths for me, and felt rather guilty about it afterwards, as if I was taking advantage of him.

But of course I wasn't, I told myself now. I'd never promised him anything, and it was he, as my supervisor, who'd invited me.

The first stop wasn't for four hours, a small station in the middle of the forest. There was nothing else nearby, only this long, single-storey brick building on one side of the four tracks that were separated by concrete platforms. There was a cafe at one end, the air inside thick with cooking smells, a little shop at the other that sold everything imaginable, and a waiting room in the middle.

Like most of the passengers, I stepped out to stretch my legs and get some fresh air. The platform milled with people, most had a cigarette in their hand. Some pedlars moved between them with baskets filled with cheap samovars, dolls, plates, embroidered tablecloths, napkins and scarves. I crossed the tracks and joined the queue at the cafe, where besides a cup of tea I bought some pirozhki and a bottle of water, a yogurt and a packet of biscuits.

The sun beat down, the air was hot and dry, the forest, so close to the building, was motionless. My skin was sweaty and horrible. I began to feel uncomfortable in the midst of so many people, so I went away from the station building, towards the end of the platform. Once I was on my own, I stopped and put my bag down, and sipped my tea for a moment while staring down the tracks that ran ruler-straight through the forest. The air shimmered above the sleepers and steel. Nothing else moved.

A dreadful feeling of emptiness came over me.

Turning to look back at the crowd of people, the feeling only intensified, I saw their frames to be lumpy sacks with arms and legs sticking out, hair that grew like grass from their skulls and faces, they were creatures, as alien to me as beetles or mites.

It lasted only a short moment, then everything was as before. But the sense of meaninglessness remained. Sitting in my seat again and staring out at the wall of trees that now, as the journey continued, sporadically opened out to reveal plains, fields or villages, I felt a cold, slow-burning panic that I tried to force back by clinging to clear and rational thoughts, because what I felt was indeed irrational, completely irrational, it was something that didn't belong in me, something unfamiliar that had suddenly taken me up in its clutches, unconnected to any reality of mine, unconnected to the truth of my life.

But what I told myself didn't help.

I was scared.

All I wanted was to shut myself in and be on my own in a room somewhere.

But I had to sit here, in the open.

What was I scared of?

Not that they were going to harm me.

It was just that they were there.

I felt every thud of my heart, and what came with it, a rising sense of tension and dread, pumping into my organism with every beat.

Nothing had happened.

Nothing had changed.

No one wanted to hurt me.

And yet, my heart, and yet, that terrible feeling, coursing through me.

It was a panic attack, I told myself, and clutched at the thought. It was a panic attack, it wasn't me, I was the same as before.

It would pass over in a minute and everything would be all right again. All I had to do was sit still and wait. Look out the window and not think about anything.

A few hours later, the strange feeling began slowly to ebb away. The hours in between had been awful. When they were over, the terror I'd felt seemed inconceivable. It was as if I'd been poisoned by something.

If it was a panic attack, it could happen again. But I could do something about that, not just wait until the next one.

I decided to get in touch with a therapist as soon as I got home again, and with that I took out the food I'd bought and began to eat while gazing through the window at the trees that stood close to the tracks, pine and spruce mostly, awash in the sunlight that still flooded into the forest, the lakes we occasionally passed glittering and glistening.

After I'd eaten, I fell asleep, utterly exhausted by the enormous tension that had clenched me so tightly. When I woke up, it was still light outside, though it was nearly eleven at night. Many of the other passengers around me had gone to sleep, though a group at the rear of the carriage were wide awake, four young students drinking beer, in front of them three women in their fifties playing cards as I went past on my way to the lavatory. This time, I had my sponge bag with me, and washed and tidied myself up as best I could, imagining that I wouldn't sleep again before we got there and reasoning that I could just as well do it now.

The last couple of hours I simply sat looking out, listening to the CDs I'd brought with me. The sky had gone cloudy, a greyish-white wash, and where its light met the darkness of the ground a wispy opaqueness materialised, veiling the landscape, duller between the trees than above the lakes. The night wasn't dark, but it wasn't light either. The feeling it gave me was quite the opposite of what I'd experienced at the station in the forest, when all meaning had vanished and left only emptiness. Now it was life I saw, and depth. Everything out there was living. The swaying trees, the low ferns, the thick heather, the soft moss. Into the soil their roots strove, into the air their leaves. Life upon life, stretching away into the distance.

I don't know why that white night brought such a feeling out in me, only that it did. Perhaps it was because of the way its refracted light had enveloped the forest and revealed it to me at the same time. I saw its secret, though only as that: a secret.

Of course the birds were messengers. Not from the spirit of night, but from the forest. Birds were the forest in flight. Ants were the forest as they teemed. When they died, they decomposed and became soil into which the trees slowly sent their roots. If you filmed that, an injured or sick animal that crept away to hide, died and rotted, and then ran that film backwards, the soil would pull apart to become an animal that rose up and slunk away. If you could do the same with the forest itself, the soil would pull apart everywhere, as if under a bombardment, and animals would rise up and slink away wherever you looked.

The soil was dead life that made new life possible. The forest was self-sufficient and self-creating, it took on ever-new forms, in slow, unpredictable shifts, such as that which led four-legged mammals to climb the trees, where they swung about as apes, and to climb down again onto the plains, where they rose up as human beings. Or the butterflies, the butterflies. The beavers. The badgers, the pines, the wolves, the birches, the hawks. The bark beetles, the heather, the owls, the dragonflies and damselflies, the oaks, the lichen, the lichen.

How could I get inside it all?

Make a small section, perhaps. Two, three trees. Observe and analyse everything that went on there, from the microlevel upwards. In the trees, among the trees, beneath the trees, in the soil.

Even that was way too big, and way too vague. What they wanted was a simple, well-defined research-worthy problem. One that had to do with the uptake of inorganic phosphate compared to organic phosphate, for instance, or the relationship between *Serpula lacrymans* fungus and mycorrhiza, or investigations of mycorrhiza in relation to various specified plant species.

But what if I could join forces with someone? A joint project, in which different clear-cut research problems came together?

A small organisation in which the whole was more important than its constituent parts!

I'd have to speak to Bochanov about it.

The train arrived at Chupa at ten minutes past four. The station building was grey, rather small and neglected like the rest of the area in which it was situated, where low, barrack-like structures were dotted about, surrounded by tall grass and scrub of the kind that might grow at the side of a road, though here it was everywhere. Rain drizzled as I stepped out onto the platform. The air smelled of wet concrete, wet grass. Most of the twenty or so passengers who got off soon disappeared in cars that had either been waiting to pick them up or else had stood parked and ready for them to drive away on arrival. The little man and his brother were among them, dumping their rucksacks and fishing tackle in the back of a pickup before getting in and driving away. I hadn't seen him at all during the long journey and assumed he hadn't even known we were on the same train. And even if he had, he probably wouldn't have given it a thought.

I pulled the hood of my anorak up and tightened the cord under my chin. I felt quietly excited, the way one always did when staying out all night, when the idea of sleep would become increasingly hostile, as if the body somehow identified all sorts of other possibilities and suddenly regarded a life without sleep as an option to be seriously considered. At the same time, there was something good about sitting quite still and not succumbing to restlessness.

The drizzle became steady rain. The four students from the train went past me into what I supposed was the waiting room. Shortly afterwards, I did likewise, pulling my hood down, getting my book out and settling down to read. Sleep exerted its pull, as if tugging on my conscious thoughts, wanting to drag me away. I didn't give in to it, but didn't fight it either, and soon dozed off, waking again when my book dropped to the floor, picking it up and tucking it away in my rucksack, before leaning my head back and sleeping once more. The next time I woke it was because the students were leaving, and I got to my feet, befuddled, hoisted my rucksack onto my shoulder and hurried after them in the direction of a white minibus that had parked in front of the building. As the driver loaded their luggage into the back, I went up to him and asked if he was going to BBS. He nodded.

'You too?' he said.

'Yes,' I said.

'Give me your bag.'

I dropped my shoulder and left the rucksack in his charge, then climbed in, the four others already seated.

'Hi,' I said.

'Hi,' they said.

'We thought you might be going the same way,' one of them said, a fair-haired girl in a yellow anorak.

'What course have you signed up for?' another said, a guy with a high brow and a shaved head.

I sat down by the window on the back seat.

'None, actually,' I said. 'I've got a doctoral project I need to think about.'

'Oh?' said the girl. 'What's your research on?'

'Fungus,' I said, hoping it sounded sufficiently uninteresting for the conversation to die out before it began.

'Magic mushrooms?' the guy said with a laugh.

'I'm afraid not,' I said.

'It's rumoured they're very abundant up here,' he said.

'I'm sure,' I said, as the driver started the engine and we swung away from the station area. We didn't talk any more after that. The road was dead straight, leading us through monotonous landscape, sparse forest on both sides, birch and pine, no buildings anywhere to be seen. We hardly saw another vehicle. But after an hour or so, it was as if there was a transition of some sort, something about the surroundings changed, though I couldn't say in what way to begin with, until between the trees I caught a glimpse of water and realised we were close to the sea. Not many minutes later, we pulled up in a parking area in front of a pier that reached out into a bay, land fairly close on the other side, an island or a peninsula, I assumed, where the forest ran all the way down to the shore, a sombre, jagged wall of trees stretching away as far as the eye could see.

With the engine still running, the driver opened the back door and unloaded our bags as we climbed out, dumping them unmindfully on the ground before slamming the door shut again and driving off without a word as I followed the others down to the pier. Two boats were moored there, but there wasn't a person in sight.

It was a silent place. Not a sound, not a ripple on the water.

A smell of brine, pine cones and something faintly rotten.

'Where are they?' the bald student said. 'Wasn't someone meant to be meeting us here?'

One of the girls pointed across the water.

'Can't you hear it?' she said.

He shook his head.

I couldn't either.

'A boat engine. That'll be them, I'm sure.'

We walked to the end of the pier. Only then did I hear the faint thrum of a high-powered outboard. The girl in the yellow anorak took out a packet of cigarettes and held it out to me. I shook my head.

'My name's Yelena,' she said, pulling one from the packet. 'This is Igor, Maksim and Anna.'

'Alevtina,' I said. 'How long are you here for?'

'A month.'

'Have any of you been here before?'

They all shook their heads.

A boat now came into view, rounding the point in the distance, the sound of the engine growing louder. A man in orange bib and braces, almost luminous against the sheeny greys and blacks, was standing up in the middle of the boat, steering. I'd been half expecting Bochanov to come and collect us, but of course as it came closer I could see it wasn't him.

The surface was so calm the wake of the vessel trailed hundreds of metres behind it, an elongated grey-white V stretching back into the bay. The man steered towards the pier without slowing until he was almost in front of us, throwing the motor abruptly into reverse so that the boat near-miraculously halted with only a few centimetres to spare, rising and falling then on its own swell.

'Hop in!' he said. I made him out to be around my own age, with spiky, sand-coloured hair and pockmarked cheeks.

Once we'd sat down, he reversed out, and then, as he thrust the engine into forward gear, the bow rose slowly up out of the water until soon we were skimming across the surface, the wind peppering our faces with spray and ruffling our hair. Behind the point, we cut across the bay and soon a cluster of buildings came into view, some near the shore, others in between the trees, and a pier at which several boats were moored, one relatively large in size, almost a small ferry, I thought, while poking up above the trees a bit further back were what I assumed were the blades of a wind turbine.

A figure came down the gravel track from one of the buildings. He was still too far away for me to be able to pick out his features, but I could tell it was Bochanov himself.

He waved as we came nearer, and I waved back.

The girl whose name was Anna kneeled down in the bow, put a hand against the jetty as we came alongside and threw Bochanov the mooring line with the other. He was in a pair of khaki shorts, a blue T-shirt and wellingtons. At his hip, a knife dangled in its sheaf.

'Welcome to BBS,' he said with a smile. I stepped onto the pier and he gave me a hug.

I would have wished he hadn't been so happy to see me.

'What an incredible place,' I said, sweeping my hair away from my forehead before picking up my rucksack and slinging it over my shoulder.

'Yes, isn't it just? How was your journey? OK?'

'Fine, yes.'

'But long!' he said with a laugh. 'Come on, I'll show you your accommodation.'

I walked beside him along the pier. When I turned to see where the others had got to, I saw they were following the man from the boat, who I took to be the odd-job person around the place.

A large, three-storey building with a mast on the roof occupied the middle of the site, its satellite buildings, scattered among the trees and connected by a network of narrow unmade tracks, were smaller and made of wood, most painted red or yellow.

'This way,' said Bochanov, leading us left. 'I've found you a nice house. The best, I'd say!'

Here and there, washing had been hung out to dry on lines that drooped between trees, or between a tree and a house. There was a small-sized football pitch of grass and sand, and outside one house a deck with tables and benches.

'It's like a little village,' I said.

'It *is* a little village,' he said. 'There's about a hundred and seventy of us here at the moment.'

He was like a different man altogether, bouncier somehow, in body and mind.

We passed a small log cabin, the timber grey with age. Foxgloves, meadow grasses and slender young saplings encroached on its grounds, as if reclaiming the site after a fire, while the forest itself rose up perhaps twenty metres away, a delightful blend of deciduous trees — I saw rowan, aspen and birch — pine and spruce.

'We've our own botanical gardens here,' said Bochanov. 'Across the site, on the other side. But the forest here is as good as untouched. Hunting's banned, and commercial forestry too. And there are seals in the bay!'

The track we were following narrowed into a sliver as the houses became more scattered.

'That's where we've put you up, over there,' he said.

A large house with stained wooden cladding stood alone among the trees a bit further ahead. Two sets of stairs, one on each side, led up to a first-floor veranda.

'Your room's the one with the sea view,' he said, leading me up the stairs, opening the door and standing aside. I stepped past him, entering a small living room where there was a sofa, a table and a bookcase. A hallway led us further, with rooms on each side. Mine was at the far end, flooded with light from the window from which the sea indeed could be seen between the trees. In front of the window was a desk, while the bed stood slightly away from the sloping wall. Everything was made of wood.

I dumped my rucksack and gave Bochanov, who was standing in the doorway, a smile.

'Thanks a lot,' I said.

'Do you like the flowers?'

He nodded to indicate a vase of blue and yellow wild flowers on the desk.

'They're lovely.'

'I picked them myself.'

'That was kind of you.'

He stepped over to the window and looked out.

'You'll be fine here, I think,' he said, glancing at me before withdrawing to the doorway again. 'You've got the upstairs to yourself, so it should be quiet enough. Anyway, I'll let you get settled in. You must be exhausted after the journey. Lunch is at one o'clock. Dinner's at six.'

'Thanks,' I said. 'And thanks for sorting it all out for me.'

'No problem,' he said, and glanced at me again, this time with a smile. 'See you around!'

He closed the door as he went.

I sat down on the bed with my rucksack between my knees and surveyed the room again. There was a low chest of drawers beneath the sloping wall opposite and I put my clothes away in it before standing for a moment and gazing out of the window, the water a metallic sheen between the trees, the sky lighter, but duller. I wondered whether to go for a little walk now or have a sleep first. I decided on sleep, pulled the roller blind down, lay back on the bed and closed my eyes.

By the time I stirred it was well into the day. The cloud had broken up and blue pockets of sky were now visible above the forest across the bay, but the trees were still dripping, I could hear the sound it made against the roof, so it couldn't have been that long since it stopped raining. I was hungry, but I'd missed lunch and dinner wouldn't be served for another few hours. I put my denim jacket on, and my wellingtons,

and went out to see if there might be a little shop somewhere. A boy
came cycling up the track, the gravel grey and leaden-looking in all the
fresh, rain-drenched greens. He couldn't have been more than ten years
old, zigzagging between the puddles that were considerably bigger now
than before. Behind him came a woman in her thirties who I took to be
his mother, jeans and a T-shirt under a transparent raincoat. I gave her
a nod and she nodded back. There was something of the holiday camp
about the place, I thought, and imagined get-togethers in the evenings,
bonfires at the shore. My project, if I could call it that, seemed even
more indiscernible to me here than it had done at home.

What was I doing here?

I stopped at a map of the area that was nailed to the side of a house.
Most of the buildings near the pier turned out to be laboratories and
offices, whereas the accommodation spread out like a fan. There was a
clinic, I noticed, and an aquarium. The botanical gardens were over in
the other direction, where Bochanov had indicated. A shaded area said
Graveyard, but that couldn't be right, surely? Unless the place *had* been
a village once.

No shop, at least none that was marked on the map.

Some students stood chatting at the shore, a couple of them holding
life jackets. A man on the pier was attending to some fishing nets. Outside one of the houses a woman sat knitting on a stool, while a group
of middle-aged men were gathered on the decking I'd noticed before,
where all the tables and chairs were, drinking beer. On the tables in
front of them were plates of leftovers. Obviously they'd been eating, so
perhaps I could still get something?

As I went over I could see Bochanov was among them. He waved as
soon as he set eyes on me.

'Alya!' he said.

I halted at the railing.

'This is Alevtina Yegoryevna, one of the most talented doctoral students I've ever had,' he said, before introducing everyone by name. I
nodded at each in turn. They all wore a beard or glasses, if not both, a
checked shirt or else a T-shirt with something or other printed on it,
and cheap jeans worn high and secured with a belt that was buckled
too tight, the look of all natural scientists.

'Are you out for a wander?' Bochanov said.

'Yes,' I said. 'This place is amazing!'

I put the thought of food to the back of my mind, thinking he was going to ask me to join them and it would be awkward to decline and then sit down at another table to eat.

'What's the best way to go for a longish walk?' I said instead.

He swept a hand out in front of him.

'Any way you like, dear Alya,' he said. 'There's a path that leads off that way behind the wind turbine,' he said, indicating with the same hand. 'And another one from your house, in the opposite direction. Or you can just follow the shoreline, if you prefer.'

'OK, thanks a lot. I'll see you later, then!'

It was a relief to get away. The faces, the looks, the voices felt like they'd clutched at my very soul, or whatever that most defenceless part of me was called. All I wanted was to be on my own. But I didn't want to sit in my room, the only thing I could do there was work, and that was the last thing I wanted now. A long walk was what I needed most.

He must have been a bit drunk to say what he'd said about me being so talented. And flattery always came at a price.

I should never have come.

On the other hand, I'd only been there a few hours, so it was a bit early to be giving up just yet.

The site wasn't exactly crowded, but there were still quite a few people flitting about between the buildings, mostly students a bit younger than me.

My panic attack must have affected me more than I'd realised, I felt myself trembling at the mere sight of another person, as if the photons weren't just forming images for me but were actually bombarding some kind of sensitive membrane that was inside me.

Out at the point, I went down to the bare, sloping rock at the shore, following it until I jumped down onto the narrow ribbon of sand that appeared after a while. It was soft and wet, and my boots sank in at every step. Reeds grew in a thick belt at the foot of the forest, and although the air smelled strongly of brine, I couldn't get away from the thought that I was following the shoreline of an inland lake, the way the trees too grew right down to the water.

After a hundred metres or so I came to a small inlet where a boggy clearing was edged by a cluster of birch whose leaves winked green and white in the sunlight. As I got nearer, I discovered a stream running between the trees and began to follow its course, struck by the way these fringes of the forest were so airy and delicate, drenched with light and moisture, which was what made the foliage and the trunks so bright in appearance, whereas only a stone's throw away it took on a different character altogether, spruce prevailing, shutting out the light, casting the forest floor into such darkness that in many places the soil lay bare, covered only by a thin carpet of yellow and brown needles, directly above which thin, twiggy branches reached out, grey and dry and cobwebby. There, where I was barely able to proceed unhindered, it was as if the forest consumed me. Some hundred metres on, it opened up into another kind of space, a bank rising up to my right from the stream, along its length surprisingly tall deciduous trees, their crowns a canopy through which light filtered down, and on the open floor grew mosses and ferns. Ancient, fractal, greedy. Here, all connections to the sea were as if severed, this was a world all of its own, but then, after I'd climbed the slope and emerged onto bare rock, between the trunks of spruce, the waters of the bay once again came into view.

The trunk of one spruce had split into two close to the ground, one running a metre or so almost horizontally before angling upwards, and I sat down on it, pulled away a strip of bark, which was flat and almost shell-like, and sniffed it. Resin.

Mm.

Even that was something no one knew: how molecules were turned into smells.

As if we needed to know!

Earth warmed by the sun. Resin, and a faint smell of the sea. My own sweat.

In the distance a boat was approaching. I turned my head to the west and saw two more, one quite still, the other cutting across the bay.

I'd never even considered marine biology, but I thought now how exciting it must be, diving and all that. Or maybe it was a bit claustrophobic.

I reminded myself that I had to phone Seva before his bedtime and tell him I'd arrived and how lovely it was here.

What could the time be?

The light was certainly no reliable indicator. Normally I had a fairly good idea what time it was, give or take an hour, perhaps, but here it was impossible to tell.

I'd never thought about it before, that I oriented myself according to the light in that way.

The boat came closer and I could see it was a small ferry that soon disappeared from view behind the point.

Back at the research station, there were still plenty of people around. I stopped a man who was on his way into the main building and asked if there was a payphone anywhere. He said there was one in the reception area. I didn't even know there was a reception area, so I asked him where that was and he pointed in the direction of the pier and said first building on the left.

The phone was mounted on the wall under a perspex bubble next to the reception desk. Like on a campsite, they had various items on sale there, soaps, deodorants and shaving tackle, chocolate and biscuits.

His grandmother answered.

'So, you thought you'd phone at last?' she said.

'I've only just got here,' I said. 'How is he? Can I talk to him?'

'He's gone to bed.'

'Already?'

'He's had a busy day, he's tired.'

'Are you sure he's asleep?'

'Yes.'

'How's he been?'

'He's been fine. He misses you, he says.'

'Tell him I miss him, too. Lots. And that I'll ring tomorrow.'

'But will you? That's the question.'

An anger rose up in me and I had to breathe in deeply before saying anything.

'Of course I will. I told you, I just got here. I couldn't get to a phone until now.'

'So you say.'

'Thanks for looking after him for me.'

'I'm not doing it for your sake.'

'Well, thanks anyway,' I said, and put the phone down before I got myself into an argument. It wasn't worth it. I was responsible for him every single day of the year, I fed and clothed him, made sure he was washed, took him to nursery school and picked him up again, bought him toys to play with, and everything else he needed. Her son did nothing, he didn't even pay me any child maintenance.

She had to look after him for two weeks and was acting as if she was lumbered with him all year round.

I walked briskly back along the track. Here and there, big swarms of insects hung sacklike in the air. The sunlight, angling low across the landscape, was full, the shadows long. Cheerful voices, laughter, drifted up from the pier, it sounded like people were swimming. Or perhaps not. Wouldn't it be too cold for that?

But she was good with Seva. Adored him, even.

Maybe her insults didn't mean much.

I knew the way things were, so it didn't matter what she thought.

Passing the log cabin from before, I saw a man bent over by the trees at the back. He held a white carrier bag in one hand while picking something from the ground with the other. I paused, not to stare, more on instinct, and he sensed me there, turned and looked at me. I nodded, he nodded back, but returned immediately to whatever it was he was doing as I started walking on.

I was really hungry.

Should I go back and see if the cafe was open? Or maybe get something from the shop?

But going without wasn't such a bad thing, if you could. And the hunger would pass.

I saw some figures through the ground-floor windows as I approached the house and heard the faint sound of music as I went up the stairs outside. Upstairs in my room, I sat down at the desk and tried to collect my thoughts. Sunlight glanced off the water in glittering shards and haloed the trees outside the window.

I was here now and would have to make the best of it.

Or actually I didn't. I wasn't bound by anything, I could go back tomorrow, if I wanted.

Would that be weakness?

In whose eyes?

My own?

No one else would think so.

But weakness it would be. The smallest displacement and I lost my grip on everything.

Was it really just my life at home with Seva and all our routines that kept me grounded?

So what?

It worked, we had a good life together, Seva was thriving.

But I couldn't just turn round and go back. Two weeks at a research station, I *had* to be able to cope with that.

It had never been a problem before.

Having meals with others, forging new professional relationships, working on an application, walking on my own in the forest. Why on earth shouldn't I be able to handle that all of a sudden?

I went over to the bed, got my book out and put my headphones on. But I couldn't concentrate on reading, all I could do was listen to the music, and so I lay back and followed it, to that place in us where no thoughts exist.

Then suddenly the door opened. I jumped up, my heart nearly stopping at once.

Bochanov poked his head round.

'Oh, sorry to barge in, Alya. I did knock. Twice, in fact. Didn't you hear me?'

I shook my head.

'A few of us are going down to sit on the rocks at the shore. I was wondering if you'd like to come? We've got beer and vodka, and probably a lot more besides. They're all good people.'

'It's nice of you to think of me,' I said. 'But I'm still really tired after the journey.'

'It's all very relaxed. There's a fire going, and —'

'It sounds like a lovely evening. Only I really need to sleep, if I'm going to be able to do anything at all tomorrow.'

'Of course, I understand,' he said. 'See you tomorrow, in that case!'

He went away again and I heard his footsteps disappear along the hall. It was impossible to go back to my music now I knew the door could open at any time. To do so again would feel almost like inviting danger.

I looked around the room for a key. There had to be one somewhere, I thought, opening the top drawer of the desk. And there, indeed, was a key. It even fitted the lock, turning without a problem.

But it wasn't enough, I could still be disturbed.

And I was hungry now like never before.

I put my jacket on and stepped into my boots, found my water bottle in my rucksack and filled it up at the tap in the bathroom, drank until I could drink no more and then filled it up again before going out. This time I went up the path behind the house. After leading me a few hundred metres through the forest it turned towards the sea and again I found myself following the line of the shore, over the sweeping bare rock, through soggy sand, the saturated belt of reeds. The sun was now almost completely hidden by the jagged tops of the trees across the water, only here and there did the occasional bundle of rays break through the cloud. The sky had a faintly red tinge to it. The walking was doing me good, I felt better now, pressing on through the undulating terrain whose constant variation asked for my keen awareness and attention. In some places the forest reached down so close to the water it forced me to veer away between the trees, at one point leading me to stumble upon a narrow path knobbled with roots and carpeted with pine needles, which I followed further inland.

Now and then, I stopped and gazed up at the crowns above me, but I could never stand still for very long, the air around me teeming with midges in seconds. It was as if they'd been waiting to ambush me, pursuing me then along the path for a short time before giving up.

It gave me something to think about, connecting with my project. Tiny, sentient creatures of the forest inhabiting a totally different reality, orienting themselves exclusively towards any smell that promised blood, the smallest wafts of air that told them where trees were and where the ground was, the hum of other wings in the swarm. Mapping that out descriptively wasn't a problem from the outside. But it was impossible for us to know how that same reality looked from the inside. And if we were unable to get inside the world of the mosquito, which after all was a fairly close relative of ours in genetic terms, possessing eyes and a brain, then trees would surely always have to remain a puzzle.

The problem with language was that it anthropomorphised everything. All we had to do was say the word *communication* and what we thought about was *human* communication.

Hey, birch, my old friend. How's tricks?

Oh, not so bad. Been a bit dry lately, but we'll manage. How about you?

Well, the drought has been a bit of a bind, but they say the dry spells tend to be followed by downpours, so that's something to look forward to, at least.

What about those caterpillars there, have they been bothering you?

A bit, but we've plenty of leaves, so a few less here and there won't make a difference. They need to support themselves too, I suppose.

Now that's where I beg to differ, you see. They've no right to eat us. They think they can do what they want, just because we can hardly move.

You may have a point there. But what can a poor birch do?

Could we even imagine another language? A non-human language? A non-human thought? Another way of existing in the world than our own?

I put my hand against the smooth stem of the birch.

It was alive. It was here. And it had brought itself into being. Stretched towards the sun, striven to maximise its surface area in order to capture the light, but also in the other direction, downwards, into the soil, there to come up against all manner of obstacles: stones, rock, other roots. Surely all of this required some form of sentience?

The trees were so clearly open to the world, allowing it to pervade them, exploiting it and assimilating it.

If they were in touch with everything around them, there was no reason for them to be in touch with each other.

We had to be careful not to personify them, individualise them, or even think of them as separate from one another, but rather as parts of a greater whole, as limbs and branches were parts of the tree's greater whole. We needed to consider communication at the cellular level as belonging to the same processes as communication between plants and species. We needed to observe mycorrhiza under different conditions.

I looked up at the tangle of leaves and branches.

What was it I saw?

What did it express?

The will to live.

Where did that come from?

From within.

Everything that was living possessed that will. Perhaps that was even what life itself *was*: the will to live.

Why? What was the point of such a will?

It moved life on.

But why? Why did life have to go on? Why had this birch tree brought itself into being? What did it want?

Life. Life. Life.

But life couldn't just be the will to live, it had to be something more besides, something in itself! An eddy or a tornado, or any similar mechanical system, possessed no inner will, these were phenomena that simply occurred under certain external circumstances, they knew no meaning, because they had no self.

The tree had a self.

Not like my own, obviously, just as the body of the tree wasn't like mine either. My body was symmetrical, an arm and a leg on each side of a frame, whereas the branches of the tree expressed a looser, more random architecture.

The self of the tree had to be a lot looser too, more outspread, more all over the place, and much, much weaker, verging on nothing, perhaps only a vague reverberation of the processes that took place inside it.

Something that was consolidated by dint of the tree's connections with other trees and to the forest.

But it didn't matter, we'd never know, I thought to myself, and patted the trunk a couple of times before carrying on along the path, crestfallen now, sensing that such thoughts led nowhere, could never lead anywhere.

Though it was late evening, it was still as light as it was in the middle of the day. I no longer had any idea in what direction I was going, but I wasn't in the slightest bit tired, my hunger had disappeared, and I reasoned I could just as well keep walking a while yet, then simply turn round and follow the path back.

After a few minutes I saw what looked like a clearing in the trees ahead. It was, and when I got there a small, weathered log cabin was revealed, badly run-down. I could tell there'd been a field there once, or a pasture perhaps, long since abandoned and now overgrown.

But in the middle of the forest?

In the same instant, I saw the blades of the wind turbine above the trees and understood that it wasn't the middle of the forest at all. I'd come full circle and was back where I'd started, at the research station.

I crossed through the clearing, went in between the trees and emerged onto the little meadow at the rear of the cabin.

The man with the carrier bag was no longer there, of course. But what he'd been picking was.

Mushrooms!

Small and slender, with a bell-shaped cap. An abundance of them.

Magic mushrooms, if I wasn't mistaken.

Funny there should be so many of them here, with all these biologists around.

Did they eat them?

I was certain they did. The guy from the minibus had mentioned it. And the man with the carrier bag had been picking them.

Typical naturalists.

I walked on, following the track up to the house, solid and still beneath the trees, went quietly up the stairs and pressed the door handle down. Fortunately, it was open. I passed along the hall, careful not to make a sound, and unlocked the door of my room, finding it filled with strange nocturnal light, took my jacket and boots off and flopped back on the bed with all my clothes still on. I'd have to start the day with a shower in the morning, then breakfast, and I'd have to get hold of Bochanov, too, and see if he had time for a talk about my project. If I could only pluck up the courage to really tell him what I'd been thinking, he'd be able to help me, either give me a *yes, it's an idea worth pursuing*, or a *no, it's a complete non-starter, give it a swerve.* But if all I came with were nebulous musings, I might as well forget it.

The problem was that nebulous musings were all I had.

But it was his job to give me guidance so that I could turn it all into something precise and scientifically doable, was it not?

Bochanov was nowhere to be seen at breakfast the next day. I went down there as soon as they opened and sat almost alone in the canteen at a table by the window, looking out at the rain that was falling, eating porridge and wondering whether to go home or not.

Back in my room I got my notebook out and sat staring by turns at its blank pages and the grey sky whose sodden clouds hung low across the water.

When I got to my feet again a couple of hours later, all I'd written was:

THE FOREST
THE TREE
MYCORRHIZA
COMMUNICATION
THEN WHAT?

Not exactly anything I could present to Bochanov, I thought, and lay down on the bed. If we got rid of all the romantic stuff and all the meta-physics, removed all that from the idea of the forest and simply addressed the observable reality, which was what I needed and wanted to do, there was still more than enough left — in any square metre of forest, there was enough going on to fill a whole lifetime of scientific research, generations of lifetimes, in fact, so that wasn't the problem. It was more the point of it that I'd started to doubt. Where it was all meant to lead.

What I wanted to achieve by it.

There was something so crystal clear about science. The systems it revealed to us, as in quantum physics and molecular biology, could be as complex as you liked, but in science they were always pure and clear, stringent and precise. Its dizzying magnifications of miscroscopic life shared that same clarity. I'd been attracted by that, and still was. But the question that had arisen in me, especially after I'd read Bogdanov, was whether the reason we saw it that way — that microscopic reality, right down to the subatomic particles that teetered on the very knife-edges of being and not being — was that we could see only what we were able to see, because we were us. Whether what science was actually mapping was the human gaze, human reason. If it was, it would mean there'd be no real difference between a verifiable scientific theory and metaphysical speculation. And, perhaps more fatally, that we would never be able to get through to the other side.

Science saw everything from without. As if the world were a little house and we stood peering in at its windows. Or else it saw everything from above, like through a microscope. But we were in life's midst! Electrons were inside us. Atoms were inside us. Molecules were inside us. Cells were inside us. Evolution was inside us. The forest was inside us. Even the sea was inside us!

This didn't just apply to science, it was something all humans did. And of course what removed us from the natural world was our capacity for thought.

Without our thoughts we'd be at one with everything.

But then we wouldn't be us. We wouldn't wonder about anything then, would never pose a single question.

What was worse, to be totally unknowing and yet belong to the natural world, or to wonder about that world and remain excluded from it?

I stood at the window and looked out across the water, the clouds hanging low over the forest, blanketing it completely further inland. Today, too, there were boats out there. I could see two rather small dinghies with outboards, as well as the little ferry on its way into the harbour beyond the point.

The forest I surveyed was where the taiga began, its westernmost extremity. Away to the east it stretched, thousands of kilometres, with barely a human being known to it, only wolves, bears, foxes, beavers, elk, ravens, crows. The animals of the shaman. Indeed, the taiga was the shaman's forest. Not here exactly, but further east, that was their habitat. The word itself came from there, derived from the Tungus word *saman*, so I'd gleaned from reading Eliade.

Imagine if it were true that the shamans spoke the language of the forest. That they were connected with it, from the inside, as a part of it, not from the outside, as mere observers, like I was.

But they were nothing but wretched, semi-deranged con artists.

The only reason they saw things we couldn't was they manipulated the chemistry of their brains with hallucinogenics, so reality altered before their eyes.

Their testimonies lent credence to nothing.

On my way to lunch I stopped by the reception area and rang Seva's grandmother again. This time Seva did come to the phone, so beside himself with excitement and joy that his words tumbled from his mouth. They'd been to the zoo and he could hardly contain himself, telling me all about the monkeys, penguins, bears and wolves he'd seen. I could barely get a word in edgeways, but was glad to hear that he'd had such a lovely outing. Before he ran off, I asked him to hand the phone to his grandmother, and I must have thought he did, because I started talking to her, only for her to hang up immediately.

It was probably a misunderstanding, I told myself, without really believing it was. She'd heard my voice, but hung up in the hope that I'd think she hadn't realised I wanted to talk to her.

In the canteen, I nodded to the girl in the yellow anorak who was standing in front of me in the queue wearing a T-shirt with a sweatshirt tied around her waist. She nodded back.

'How's things?' she said. 'Work going all right?'

'Fine, yes. How's your course.'

'Really interesting. It's like being on holiday as well, though, isn't it? Come and join us tonight, there's a whole gang of us.'

'I might just do that.'

She smiled at me before going to sit down outside at a table packed with people. They looked like they were already fully socialised. It was often the way at places like this, it happened so alarmingly quickly.

I sat down at one of the tables by the window and began to eat. Fried meatballs with gravy and potatoes, pickled cucumber and cauliflower. Shouldn't they have been serving fish with the sea being right outside the door?

She'd never had anything against me until I broke up with Lev. Not that she probably cared much about that, she'd never exactly invested in us. It was the fact that I had sole custody that did it. She hated me for that.

Hated was perhaps too strong a word.

Disliked intensely.

The person I was didn't matter, it was what I'd done that she couldn't forgive.

On the other hand, I didn't like her either. She was a rigid, self-righteous woman.

I parted a meatball in two, the knife cutting through the dark crust to reveal the grey-looking meat, then turned the piece on my fork in the gravy before putting it in my mouth. As I ate, I looked across at the table where the girl with the yellow anorak had sat down. Yelena, was that what she'd said her name was? She was in high spirits, vivacious, in the very midst of her group, if not its midpoint. The bald guy — Aleksander? — kept looking at her. I may have been imagining things, but wasn't there a sadness in his gaze? But he was definitely interested in her.

Mama had been the opposite type. It was hard to imagine anyone less rigid than her. And if anything she'd been more self-effacing than self-righteous. But not boundless. It would be absurd to call her that.

It was my mother Seva should have been with now, not Lev's mother.

She was the one who should have seen him grow up.

I scraped my leftovers into the big bin in the corner, put my tray on the rack and went out to look for Bochanov. He hadn't said anything about where he might be, so my plan was to go over to the main building and ask around, but as it turned out there was no need, I happened to see him as I was making my way over there, he was standing talking, with three girls in attendance. He always spoke so softly, Bochanov, and I'd always thought it to be a technique of his, rather than his nature, a way of ensuring that all was quiet around him, so that what he said was accorded more weight.

I didn't want to interrupt, so I hovered a short distance away, intending to wait until he was finished and the little group dispersed. But as soon as he saw me he waved me over.

'How's it going, Alya?' he said. 'Are you settled in?'

The three girls looked at me inquisitively.

'Yes, I'd say so,' I said. 'But I was wondering if we could have a meeting about my project. If you've got time, that is?'

He nodded.

'Of course. I'm a bit tied up just at the minute, but I've got the whole evening free, if that's any good?'

'How about tomorrow?'

'Yes, I'm sure I can fit you in. Ten o'clock?'

'Ten o'clock's fine.'

'We could go for a walk, if you like? My office is a bit cramped, and anyway it doesn't feel right sitting indoors out here.'

He laughed.

'Indoors out here!' he repeated.

I smiled.

'Meet you here?'

'Fine, yes,' he said. 'See you then!'

I left them and he turned to the three girls again. The gravel had dried in the sun, whereas the bushes still looked drenched. A man in a wetsuit was walking along the pier, a pair of running shoes on his feet. It looked odd, as if two different worlds had been cobbled together. A horse with the head of a man. He was lugging a yellow oxygen tank in one hand. A wind had picked up, a pennant on the boat he looked to be heading for flapped briskly, and the surface of the bay was roughened with small, white-edged waves. Everything was making a racket down there.

I wondered what to do the rest of the day. There was no point in working on my application before I'd spoken with Bochanov. Not until I'd isolated a specific focus and formulated my objectives precisely would I be able to begin any kind of work at all.

Should I take Yelena up on her offer? Go down to the shore with them tonight, loosen up? Get to know some of the others, socialise a bit?

It wasn't that I couldn't, it just didn't appeal.

Perhaps I'd feel differently after a few hours alone in my room, I thought, pausing to look at the old cabin, thinking about the night before, the mushrooms that grew there.

It only occurred to me then that what my thoughts were actually striving towards were *mushrooms*, fungi.

Magic mushrooms, I'd thought dismissively, like a layperson.

But they were *fungi*!

And hallucinogenic!

My heart thumped in my chest as I started walking again. Everything I'd been trying to think about had suddenly come together. The shamans ate mushrooms in order to alter the chemical balances in the brain and access other realities. They partook of the forest, they ingested the forest. It was the forest that altered everything they saw.

In a way, it was the forest that spoke in them then.

I'd written about mushrooms and the trees and the forest. Why shouldn't I eat the mushrooms, eat the forest, and see it all in a whole new way?

A wall of protest rose up in me. I didn't believe in shamanism, I shunned everything that was irrational, and the thought that one might be able to think like the forest if only one ingested it wasn't just abominably irrational, it was also utterly idiotic, shamefully idiotic, in fact.

And then Mama came to me. The memory of her as she lay in her sickbed filled me for a short moment, accompanied by the sound of her voice.

You don't need to be against everything all the time. Try saying yes once in a while. It'll help you.

But this isn't what she meant! I nearly shouted at myself. Say yes to life, say yes to other people, that was what she'd meant. Not say yes to hallucinogenics!

On the other hand, I thought, once I'd got back to my room, calmer, though still strangely enthused, why not? What harm could it do? None.

I was filled with the most powerful feeling of freedom. No one needed to know, I didn't have to tell anyone, I could just go out into the forest on my own, eat some mushrooms and see what happened.

A few hours later I filled my bottle with water, slung my rucksack over my shoulder and went down to the cabin. I met no one on my way, though I heard music from the pier area, rising and falling in the light summer night, drifting cries, laughter. While I wasn't doing anything wrong, I was nervous and apprehensive, as if I actually was about to commit a crime.

After first making sure no one was coming, I searched the area at the side of the cabin where I couldn't be seen if anyone happened to come past, but finding hardly any meant I had to venture then into the open, and I crouched down with my rucksack next to me, picking the mush-rooms I discovered there as quickly as I could. I had no idea how many I'd need, but they were only small, so I gathered perhaps thirty or forty, dropping them into a pocket of the rucksack before closing it, getting to my feet and passing through the cluster of trees to emerge into the meadow on the other side. I had to force myself to walk without haste, as if I was simply out for a stroll. Glancing over my shoulder, I could see I was on my own. I found the path from the night before, and as I walked along I scanned for a place where I could be reasonably sure I wouldn't be disturbed. After a while, I left the path and wandered among the trees, pine mostly, that stood well apart, the forest floor, now bare soil, roots and pine needles, now mosses, heather and scrubby mulberry bushes, soft and good to walk on. Here and there, bare rock protruded, mottled with lichen, patterns of yellow and bluey greys. At one point, I came to a steep rocky incline which I scrambled up, discov-ering that it sloped gently away on the other side, the bare rock occasionally peeping up out of the ground, before the trees became denser, latticing together, still mainly pine, but also spruce and birch. Further on, at the far end of a small clearing where the trees stood side by side like an army, lay a toppled tree, some thirty metres in length, which resembled a bridge in all its surrounding verticality.

Here, perhaps?

The wall of the forest with the toppled tree on one side, the clearing opening out on the other.

Yes.

The ground was uneven, mostly covered with heather and mosses, and I made myself comfortable in a little dip, my back against a smooth outcrop of rock, opened my rucksack and took out the mushrooms, making a small pile next to me.

Just because I'd picked them and come here didn't mean I had to eat them. I could sit and relax a while, then cut down to the sea and follow the shore back.

Why did the thought of that feel like such a defeat?

There was only me, no one else.

I put three mushrooms in my mouth, chewed them well and washed them down with some water.

No going back now.

I took a few more, then some more again.

How many were you supposed to take?

They were so small. The hallucinogens would be only a microscopic part. And they were organic, not concentrated, the way laboratory-produced drugs were. I should have been worrying about taking too few, not too many. In case they didn't work.

I ate them all, drank the rest of my water and leaned back as I looked up at the sky that was still blue above the trees.

I had the forest in me now.

All I had to do was wait for it to start talking to me!

I smiled at my own stupidity, but felt nothing other than the slight apprehension that had come and gone ever since the idea of taking mushrooms had first occurred to me. Something faintly tremulous and fluttery, good and bad at the same time, exciting and disquieting.

Perhaps it would help if I moved around a bit? Got the circulation going.

I stood up and started tramping around the little clearing, up and down, over the mounds, the moss-covered rock, over to the fallen tree and its upended roots. When I sat down again, my pulse was beating quickly in my neck.

But nothing had happened.

Everything was the same as it had always been.

I must have taken too few. Either that or I was immune to them in some way. I had to have extra anaesthetic when I was at the dentist's, it had always surprised them. Somehow it didn't affect me like it did others.

I decided to walk around some more.

As I got up, I felt a wash of nausea. My forehead and the palms of my hands were sticky. A few moments later, I was so dizzy I couldn't walk.

I leaned forward and propped myself against a tree, pressed my fore-head against the trunk. I opened my mouth, tensed my stomach muscles to vomit, but nothing came up.

It was horrible.

I dropped to my hands and knees.

Oh, oh, oh.

All I wanted was to be sick. Or die.

I reached two fingers as far down my throat as I could and gagged.

But nothing came up.

I did it again. Dry vomiting.

Sweat ran from my brow, I shivered, hot and cold.

Please God, let me throw up. Please, please God, let me throw up.

Suddenly, swimming with nausea, the thought struck me that I might be seriously poisoned.

I *had* to throw up.

I rubbed my face against the heather, lay down on my side, got to my knees again, put my fingers down my throat, repeatedly. My stomach convulsed, and this time a swill of watery vomit, bile and semi-digested food, gushed from my gaping mouth.

Oh, thank God.

I remained on my hands and knees for a moment, the nausea not yet releasing, and then I spewed again, yellow bile, and once more again.

I wiped my mouth with the back of one hand, the tears from the corners of my eyes with the other, and got to my feet, resting my fore-head against the trunk of the tree once more.

Oh, thank God. Thank God.

That was it! I must have vomited all the mushrooms. A reflex reac-tion to the poisoning.

Maybe it was all for the best.

I glanced around to see if anyone had seen me, but all I saw was grass, branches, leaves, tree trunks and sky.

All right.

I went over and picked up my rucksack, hoisted it onto my back and started walking. All I wanted was to brush my teeth and have a shower, put some clean clothes on. Perhaps go down to the pier and see what was happening there?

The sun was lower now, the sky above it a blush against the deep blue that arched over the forest and everything there was. The pine trees above my head, upstanding and majestic, took in the last rays.

I was on a sphere. It was turning slowly, in such a way that the place where I stood was on a downward trajectory, moving away from the sun, which was another sphere, suspended out there in emptiness, encompassed by flame.

I'd always known, but now I understood.

The thought overwhelmed me.

It was insane.

Two spheres in empty space.

One was our own. The other burned for us.

A gust of wind passed through the forest, I heard it before I felt it against my skin, the leaves of the trees rustled and shook, hundreds, no, thousands of them, rustling and shaking, and I felt that too, against my skin, the lightest and tenderest of touches, before it was gone. It was the trees on the other side of me that whispered then. The wind ran like a river of air through the forest, and the forest stirred and liked it so much, wished only to be shaken by the wind, the harder the better, there was nothing like a good sway, a waving of branches, leaves fluttering in the currents. It was good for them, the trees. And the sun, yes, the sun when its rays found and warmed the leaves, how very good it felt. All those tiny, invisible molecules that were set in motion and began to work, converting the light into themselves, more leaves, more trees, more and more, because leaves were so fond of being many, they so much liked to be in abundance, the leaves, and they liked the light and the water and the wind, and everything that came up out of the dark, dark soil, they liked that especially, the heaviness of the earth, the warmth of the sun, the light and the darkness. Such a murmuration there was of frolicking leaves, and the trunks stood proud while the roots were afraid. For they weren't the same, no, they were not the same, they belonged to different species. The leaves were light of heart, the trunks were proud and upstanding, the roots were cautious and afraid, wary in their subterranean darkness. What was that? That hard thing, what was it? That very soft thing? Too soft, far too soft. What's happening up there, you're tugging and straining. But the leaves were not afraid, they loved it up there in the air, on their airy perches, bathed in sunlight, drenched by rain, they wished only to be plentiful, that there should be more and more and more of them.

The bark in front of my eyes flaked open, orange, and I broke off a piece and sniffed it, because the tree had no feeling in its bark, which was akin to our nails or the hooves of the horse or the shell of the snail.

Up through the branches I peered with my eyes, the green tassels of the pine, and although the tree couldn't feel it, I put my arms around its trunk, because I could feel, the hard wood, the moisture that rose in it, through the roots and up, all the way to the leaves of the furthest, thinnest branches. A quivering of life, water rising, air and sunlight and rain, all this the tree took in, all this was inside it. Tree after tree, mile after mile, all open to the world, not at all as aloof as I'd always thought them to be, but open. They were the very entrance to life! They allowed light and air and water to stream through them and become life, more and more life, it was why they strove upwards, strove downwards, strove to extend themselves, they captured matter and turned it into life. Transformed it into leaves and boughs and branches, into ants and midges. Into worms, into hands and arms and faces. Into me, as I lay with eyes closed on my back in the heather with one arm stretched out behind my head, my hand against the tree trunk, as it might have been placed to stop a lover from leaving. They had transformed the world into me. And in me too the fluid ran, red, pounding in my neck, pounding in my chest, pounding in my head, pounding even in my fingers.

Cautiously I touched one. It was as if the joints had been oiled, every little movement felt so good and travelled through my body, filling me with delight. Behind my eyelids everything was red, but I didn't have to go there, I could remain with what felt so good, the finger moving back and forth, the little bones, delicate as a bird's, the tendons that were attached to them, the blood rushing by.

How the heart strove. How the heart beat.

And the blood rose.

Full of iron from the ore, salt from the sea, air from the trees.

Rising and rising.

The ore, the sea, the trees.

Rising and rising.

The sea, the forest, the sun that burned.

The blood that rose and rose.

The blood that sang.

All is good. All is well.

Say yes, say yes.

Yes.

Yes.

Yes.

I sat up, eyes still closed, but the movement devastated me, accompanied by a torrent of emotions, and so I lay back again and allowed myself to go with them wherever they would take me, they lapped the shore of the land, were slurped up by the sand that edged the rock, which was folded and creased and was the brain. That was where I lived. Or was held captive. Now I was free. Now I could see my prison from the outside. The sand onto which my emotions washed lay around it like a ring of Saturn, and over its surface ran hundreds of thin veins, pulsing faintly as the blood ran through them, while inside, in great caves, bolts of moist lightning flashed.

Far, far from there, away in the realm of the hand, something crept across the skin. The minuscule, gossamery movements grew, and as they entered the brain I heard them resonate, loud and heavy. How far was it to the hand? With its five points it lay like the reaching rock of the shore. Far, far removed. But for me it was no distance. I contained great rivers running this way and that, through the land, through plains and valleys, bounded by banks and dams, into caves and halls. The land rolled and pulsated, for it was alive, but not in the way the animals were alive, no, no, not as the animals were alive, for the animals lived as life in itself lived, without a face, rolling and pulsating.

I opened my eyes and sat up, meticulously moving my hand over which the ant was crawling, holding it up in front of me, and I understood that it too was a rolling, pulsating land of rivers and plains. And grass. And heather. And trees. Land, within land, within land. And deep, deep inside, as far as we could reach, atoms and electrons raced about, with vast spaces between them, I saw it now, and I saw how the distances between them grew smaller and smaller the further away from them we got, until they not only began to come together in patterns, but also became firmer, and firmer still, until the frantic flood of atoms seemed to have stopped, at the same time as a new and different movement began, in the firmness of the patterns, and this was the cells, and the same thing happened with the cells, they stiffened, became as if unmoving, in forms now larger, and in those forms another movement began, the feet of the ant! Walking over my hand!

I leaned back against a tree trunk and was so happy it almost hurt.

Everything was surface. Depth only surface upon surface.

And everything was movement. Inertia didn't exist.

Everything that existed was patterns, whirls, streams.

I was too.

Immensely satisfied, filled with a hitherto unknown warmth of thought, with the knowledge that never again would I need to wonder about anything, never again need to question anything, I stood up.

I was so huge it almost frightened me. My hands were slabs. Heavy as rock.

My footsteps pounded against the ground.

What was happening?

Was that the sun rising again now?

How long had I been here?

Had I slept here?

The mushrooms.

They must have worked.

I turned and looked back. There was the clearing with the fallen tree, in the midst of the army of spruce. I couldn't remember going there.

But I must have done.

It was no ordinary light that fell upon the forest. It bore a reddish tinge. Like the sun of another planet.

Everything looked different. As if . . . *visible*?

I felt afraid.

There was only me. In all that was strange and silent.

It was all around me.

I had to get back.

I went towards the clearing. A flapping sound came suddenly from one of the trees. I stopped and looked up. Two crows arguing. One came arrowing out, the other after it. Their movements were so alarming I had to look away, it was as if they were fighting inside me.

This was where I'd thrown up.

There wasn't a trace left.

How could that be?

It had happened, I was sure of it.

The moss must have absorbed it.

Everything was the way it was supposed to be. Everything was good.

I really had to get back now.

I went through the lattice of trees. My movements sounded unnaturally loud, the forest around me unnaturally still. My breathing. My pulse, beating in my neck. My thighs, rubbing together as I went. My boots, tramping the ground, the snapping of twigs underfoot. Branches that slithered over the body, whipping back with a rattle and a sigh.

The ground became increasingly moist, soon a boggy mire dotted densely with birch. The light, a low-hanging blush. Not a movement anywhere. Sodden earth. Yellow, with eyes of black water. Spruce.

Motionless.

Unacknowledging.

Hostile.

A shallow slope, space between the trees, rowan, pine, spruce, shrubs of bilberry. Steeper now, surfaces of bare rock. There was nothing in the landscape I recognised, but I knew the direction I had to go, and carried on down the other side.

A sound broke the silence.

A horrid sound, and a cold shiver ran through me. I looked around. Nothing.

There it was again. A hissing sound, as if from a reptile.

It came closer.

I started to run, crashing through the trees, heaving soon for breath, until abruptly I stopped in my tracks.

The mushrooms were still at work. There was nothing there. The sound had been inside me.

There, all quiet now.

I carried on walking.

But the fear wouldn't go away. Instead of subsiding, it grew, radiating out, proliferating. Everything around me was alien and cold, empty and blind. And I was all alone in it.

I kept turning round to see if anyone was following me, but saw nothing, and strode on with tears in my eyes, up a bank, between branches of spruce that scraped my cheek, in the hope that the sea would come into view when I got to the top, perhaps even rooftops, but there was nothing to be seen, only trees, trees, trees. The monotony of that, life repeating itself into infinity, was terrible. What was living had no value as long as life went on no matter what, covering every centimetre of the earth, and such ravenousness was all it possessed, the ravenousness to grow, grow, spread, spread, spread, cover, cover, cover, without aim, without meaning. The empty ravenousness to fill in emptiness, that was life.

From somewhere, music came, so faint it drowned in the small sounds of my own movements, but when I stood still I could hear it, there was no doubt. It could only be from the research station.

If it wasn't something imagined.

I followed its direction and a few minutes later emerged onto rock above the shore, the sea almost flaming red in the light from the low sun. I recognised the place, I'd sat there on my first day.

I scrambled down and followed the shoreline around the point, and there ahead of me was the research station, touched by that same red light, making it look like something in a dream.

The water was calm as a millpond.

What time was it?

I'd completely forgotten I had my watch on.

Just after one o'clock.

How long had I been gone? I couldn't work it out.

I walked slowly. There wasn't a person in sight. But the music grew louder, and seemed to be coming from the shore by the pier.

A young man came out of a house with a bottle in his hand. He turned and looked at me.

His eyes were white.

He bared his teeth at me.

I started to run, not stopping until I got to the track that led to the pier, leaning forward with my hands on my knees to get my breath back.

A fire was burning on the shore and there were lots of people there, thirty, forty. Sitting on the rock, standing in front of the fire, wandering about.

Loud voices, waves of laughter, music.

I looked back and saw him coming towards me, and hurried down to the pier, to the shore, to where the people were.

Everything looked so strange in the midnight sun.

The nearest member of a group of five, sitting with her legs tucked under her, a bottle of beer in one hand, a cigarette in the other, turned her head and looked at me.

'Alya!' she said. 'So good you came!'

Her eyes were white and blind.

'Come and sit here! Do you want a beer?'

The young man beside her tipped his head back and opened and closed his mouth a few times like a fish. His eyes too were white.

Another figure came towards me over the rock. Where their face was meant to be there was nothing.

Then they had the face of my mother.

It was Mama.

She touched my arm and gave me her warmest smile.

'My dear child,' she said.

I recoiled and ran. Up the hill and to the house I ran, up the steps, along the hall, into my room.

And locked the door.

The feeling of having rejected Mama was so strong that I screamed.

Once I'd stopped shaking I lay down on the bed and tried to sleep, but it was impossible to keep my eyes closed, I had to keep looking to see what was in the room.

I got up and sat down at the desk.

The sea was calm, the sun burned in the sky, the night was filled with light.

Some people came out of the forest, dressed in white, as if they belonged to a religious sect. At the same time, small boats came sailing from the trees, laden with people. I closed my eyes. When I opened them again they were all gone.

I circled about the room, sat down on the bed, sat down on the chair, sat down on the floor with my back against the wall.

The lamp cord trembled when I looked at it.

I stood up, went to the bathroom and drank from the tap.

When I looked up into the mirror, it was Mama's face I saw.

I was woken by a knocking on the door. I drew myself upright, realising I'd slept sitting up, slumped across the desk.

'Alya! Are you there?'

It was Bochanov.

'Yes, I'm here,' I said. I stood up and went to the door.

'Ah, there you are,' he said, standing in his shorts and a T-shirt, his feet in a pair of wellingtons. 'I was bit worried. You weren't answering.'

'Sorry. I was asleep. Bit too much to drink last night.'

He nodded solemnly.

'I saw that.'

'You did?'

'I saw you come down to the beach and I saw you run away, yes.'

I looked down at the floor.

'You won't be feeling up to a walk, then?'

'No, not really.'

'It doesn't matter. We'll do it later.'

He touched my arm.

'Tonight, perhaps?' he said with a smile, his eyes narrowing.

I nodded.

We agreed to meet outside the canteen at seven, even though I'd already decided I was going home. It was too difficult to explain in person, so I left him a note.

I packed my things together, left my rucksack in the room and went out to ask about getting to the railway station. The woman at the reception desk said the boat sailed twice a day, the first departure was in twenty minutes. I made it just in time after hurrying back to pick up my bag.

I tried not to think about what had happened, and apart from a couple of times when it all came flashing back, I managed to keep it from my mind. Nothing had happened, I hadn't seen anything, or understood anything, it had all been inside my head, unconnected with the world outside.

But I was dreading the train journey, thinking it would be harder not to dwell on things then. As the train pulled away from the platform, I decided to take the opposite tack, to confront my thoughts, explore them and try to disarm them in some way. I took out my notebook and wrote down what I remembered, the good part first, the feeling of gaining insight into life's most inscrutable mystery, then the bad part, the forest expelling me, the students with their white eyes, Mama.

The chemical balance in my brain had been altered, every thought and emotion radically upended. It was as simple as that. And since nothing had happened, there were no real consequences either.

It was like a dream, and dreams are without consequences.

I slept the whole night, drafting an application with surprising ease during the course of the day that followed, buoyed by the feeling of no longer having anything to lose, and arrived in Moscow that night. I took a taxi home, rang Seva's grandmother first thing the next morning and told her I was coming to collect him.

'You can't do that,' she said. 'The agreement was that he was to be here with me for two weeks. It's not even been a week yet.'

'You were only looking after him while I was away,' I said. 'I'm home now, so I don't need your help any more.'

'He's having a wonderful time here, and he's expecting to stay a fortnight. You can't just snatch him away.'

'I am actually his mother.'

'You should think more about what's best for him, instead of what suits you.'

'THAT'S QUITE ENOUGH!' I yelled. 'HE'S MINE!'

She hung up.

When I turned up at her door an hour later, she let me in without a word. Seva was standing next to her with tears in his eyes. She bent down and gave him a squeeze. 'Be a good boy now and go home with your mother,' she said in a low voice, and he nodded bravely. She handed me his suitcase and closed the door after us, and only then did I get to hug him myself.

'It's so good to see you!' I said. 'Have you had a nice time?'

He nodded.

'I want to stay,' he said.

'I'm glad you've had fun,' I said. 'But we're going home now.'

'I want to live with Babushka for ever.'

I smiled and ruffled his hair.

'You can come and see her again soon. Come on, let's go! You can have an ice cream, if you want. How does that sound?'

He nodded once more and I took his hand in mine, we went down the stairs and out into the street.

I'd suspected my notes from the train journey would be useless, but as long as I didn't look at them there remained a hope in me of sorts, a kind of unarticulated, totally unsubstantiated optimism that was shattered completely when eventually I returned to them, for there was nothing there, my great insight was reduced to emptiness. I may have been a talented student, but I wasn't talented enough to find my way through such problems on my own, and there was no one else I could turn to, so the decision I came to was right, I was convinced of it as I went about the flat tidying up after Seva had been put to bed and lay sleeping in his little alcove.

I ended up applying to join Bochanov's project instead.

'Welcome aboard!' he said when I told him the news. The project was almost the antithesis of everything I'd spent so long thinking about, taking in politics, sociology and history. Bochanov thought it suited me well with the background I had, and it wasn't long before I'd written two chapters, one concerning the conclusions drawn from some research work I'd become involved in, about deforestation in the Soviet Union between 1982 and 1992 as compared to deforestation in Russia from 1992 to 2002, while the second was more history than biology really, a project I did on my own, a study of attitudes to the forest in the Stalin era seen from industrial, conservational and cultural angles. Papa approved. He was still feeding me with inspiration, directing me for instance to Shostakovich's first oratorio, *Song of the Forests*, premiered in 1949, as well as to the Soviet-loyal and highly acclaimed Leonid Leonov, in particular his novel *The Russian Forest* from 1953.

*

Papa still had all the books from the project in his study. I supposed he was proud of me, although he had no reason to be. I hadn't stood the distance, I'd given up, and now look where it had got me, I thought to myself as I lay staring at the ceiling of my old room, every now and then hearing a car go past outside, the occasional voice in the street, while Papa snored in his room.

Assistant lecturer to first-year undergraduates. That was what I was. And mother to a student son. Though hardly that, the distance between us was increasing with every day that passed. But then that was only natural.

Did I wish it to be any different?

Yes, I did. And it wasn't as if it had just happened on its own and was now out of my hands. The march of nature could be steered, that's what culture's for. Seva grew up without me even noticing. What else could that mean but that I hadn't been there? And the older he got, the more he looked towards his father and his father's family. There was barely anything of me in him, he hardly cared at all about the things I was interested in. It was all ice hockey, football, computer games, his mates. He kept up at school, but no more than that, putting in a minimum of effort, even less if I passed comment on the matter. It wasn't a teenage backlash, he was always amiable enough in our interactions, and so I consoled myself with the thought that he was fine, that it was just the way he *was*. He was wrapped up in the things that interested him, and the fact that he never talked to me about them, never shared his thoughts with me, never told me what he was doing, wasn't something intentional on his part, a strategy he was employing to get at me for whatever reason. But it tormented me nevertheless, perhaps not on a daily basis, but in the bigger picture.

He was drifting away, it had been years since he'd been here in Samara with me, with his mother.

My therapist, who I'd consulted ever since that first panic attack, wanted me to talk about my relationship with Mama, and clearly saw Seva's relationship with me in that same light. There was something in it, of course. I'd shut myself off from Mama, I could see that now. I hadn't let her in. Hadn't let anyone in, not really.

But how could that transmit to Seva? He was only four when she died and knew nothing about my relationship with her. It was easy to think I'd been unresponsive with Seva, too, but that wasn't the case, I'd never been like that with him at all, quite the opposite.

He'd be moving out soon and it'd be too late then.

No, it had been too late for years already.

Perhaps it would change things for the better. That was possible, too.

Did I believe that?

A bit.

He was a young man and immature, the way young men were, but that wouldn't last for ever.

I sat up in the narrow bed, lifted the curtain and looked out as I'd done so many times at night when I was a girl.

Snow was still falling into the street below. But the wind had dropped, and great flakes of white descended slowly now through the air, vertically, without disturbance. The footprints on the pavement had been covered by a thin, linty layer that concealed all traces of any pedestrian bar the most recent.

I let go of the curtain again and lay back.

Papa's snoring had stopped.

Should I go and check up on him?

No, he lived here on his own and took care of himself, why should that be any different just because I was here?

I patted for my watch in the pile of clothes I'd placed on the chair next to the bed, found it and turned the luminous dial towards me.

Nearly half past two.

And Seva was still out.

I only hoped he wasn't too drunk.

He couldn't sleep all morning here, especially not when it was his grandfather's eightieth birthday.

But they liked each other, as different as they were, so that was something.

I'd have to do the shopping for the dinner tomorrow. There'd be a lot to buy, he had hardly anything in. Sturgeon, salmon, more roe. Mushrooms, fresh, as well as pickled and salted. Meat for the stuffed cabbage rolls. Bacon. More onions. Turnip, carrots, cabbage, potatoes. White bread, rye bread. Champagne, of course. He probably had enough vodka, I'd have to check. Flowers, perhaps two bunches. Oh, and his dratted present. But the bookshop here wasn't bad, I was sure I'd find something.

How old he'd become now.

How unbelievably old.

I couldn't be sure he'd be around more than another couple of years. Sooner or later, the phone would ring.

It looked like it was going to be one of those long nights. Not the slightest bit of sleep in me. My eyes opened again, as if of their own accord, and I peered into the dim light, the room illuminated faintly by the street lamps outside.

I got up and went to the bathroom. Perhaps my body would agree to sleep once I was under the covers again, recognise the routine and go along with it.

My pasty face in the mirror, its shadowy sockets. No wrinkles in my brow yet, only around my eyes, and even they weren't particularly conspicuous.

I turned side-on and dropped my head, which gave me a double chin. I'd always had it, it was nothing to do with age. The skin was saggier there, but a person would have to look hard to notice.

I splashed my face with water and was about to dry my hands with the towel next to the sink when I saw that it had toothpaste on it. It was stained with something else too, something brown and indeterminable, so I took a fresh one from the small chest of drawers that had always been there and which wobbled on its wonky legs every time you opened one of them.

Going back to my room I paused, opened Papa's door gently and looked in. He was lying on his back with one eye open, the other half shut. Mama had often complained about it in jest, saying she felt like she was being monitored even when he slept. *Count yourself lucky you've a husband who still looks at you*, he'd quip back.

In actual fact, it was he who felt himself monitored by her, though his mumblings to that effect, as far as I could glean, were baseless. Yet the feeling had been strong in him. I remembered a few outbursts, always when they thought I was asleep. *You're suffocating me*, he could say in that angry voice of his. To which she might respond: *Have I ever denied you anything?* Papa again: *It's not a matter of what you say. It's what you do that counts! You always have to know where I am, who I'm with, what I'm thinking. And that eternal question of yours – why! Why this, why that!* Mama: *Now you're being unreasonable.* Papa: *Maybe it's because I'm sick and tired of being so damned reasonable all the time! Maybe that's what I want, to do some-thing unreasonable for once! Something that escapes your attention! You check up on everything I do, do you realise? You always have to know everything.* And then Mama, close to tears: *I'm sorry that's how you feel.*

That was how she won, always. Not by being close to tears, but by sympathising with his feelings and understanding them. But that was exactly what was suffocating him!

I looked at him as he lay there with his open, unseeing eye.

Their strengths and weaknesses had been unevenly distributed. He never managed to rid himself of what tormented him, because he never really understood what it was. He formed his own theories, though never that accurate, regardless that he allowed them to steer his behaviour.

It was impossible to say anything negative about Mama. She was a wonderful person. Cheerful, enthusiastic, sympathetic, always under-standing. Nothing but good, all the way through.

So why had Papa felt so hemmed in? And what about me, why had I always kept her at arm's length?

I closed the door again quietly and went back to my room. Again, I lifted the curtain, sat down on the stool and gazed out at the myriad snowflakes descending through the electric light, so densely that now and then it looked like they weren't moving at all, but hung suspended in the still air.

Yes, it was one of those nights.

But I needed to sleep. I had so much to do in the morning.

I lay down again, turned the pillow over onto the cooler side, nuz-zled into it and drew my legs up.

Ten minutes or so later I heard the front door bang downstairs.

It would be Seva.

I resisted the impulse to get up and see if he was all right. Letting the door slam like that suggested he was drunk. I didn't want him to feel I was checking up on him if he was.

Footsteps on the stairs. Loud voices, laughter.

He wasn't alone.

Had he brought someone home with him, *here*?

To his grandfather's house?

I pulled the duvet aside and sat up on the edge of the bed.

His voice outside the door of the apartment. A key that wouldn't go in the lock. A thud as something or someone, probably him, fell against the wall.

I got up and went into the hall just as the door opened.

Seva stumbled in with his arm around a girl. She looked to be around sixteen or seventeen, with so much make-up on it was hard to pick out her features.

I was so angry I was speechless.

'Oh, hi, Mama!' he said. 'I thought you'd have gone to bed ages ago! Ha ha ha! This is Kira, by the way. Kirusha, say hello to Mama!'

'Hello, Mama,' she said.

They giggled.

'Sevastyan! What do you think you're doing? This is your grand-father's house. If you want to bring someone home, you must ask him first.'

'If you say so. Where is he?'

'He's asleep! It's the middle of the night. And you're drunk. Now send this girl home and get yourself to bed. You should be ashamed of yourself.'

He looked at me and his face went white.

He let go of the girl and stepped up close to me.

'Don't you tell me what to do,' he said. His voice was low, yet full of aggression. 'Don't EVER tell me what to do. Do you understand?'

He gripped my wrists and squeezed very hard, glaring at me.

'What's got into you?' I said. 'Let go!'

'Don't EVER tell me what to do,' he said again, and released me. 'Do you understand me now?'

'I think I'd better be going,' the girl said, and turned towards the door.

'No, no,' said Seva. 'Don't mind her. Come on, you've only just got here!'

He curled his hand around her neck and smiled ingratiatingly.

'Come on,' he said. 'Come inside. She doesn't decide over me, even if she thinks she does.'

The girl hesitated.

He pressed himself against her and kissed her, throwing me a sideways glance before putting his arm around her waist and leading her past me, through the hall, into the living room.

I followed them.

'Think about what you're doing, Sevastyan,' I said. 'There'll be consequences.'

'Don't be so neurotic, Mama,' he said. 'Go back to bed. Leave us alone!'

He went into the kitchen. The girl sat down in Papa's chair, crossed her legs and gazed lazily up at the ceiling as if I didn't exist.

'You're not welcome here,' I said.

She turned her head as Seva came back in with two glasses and the cognac in his hands. His eyes met mine and widened with anger. He put the bottle and the glasses down on the table and stepped up close to me.

'Get out,' he hissed. 'Just get out, will you?!'

I slapped him.

The girl spluttered a laugh.

As furious as I'd never been in my life, I turned and went back to my room. I couldn't lie down, would never be able to sleep now anyway, and so I sat on the chair, distraught and stunned at the same time.

If only he'd kick her out now and just go to bed and apologise in the morning.

If he didn't, I'd never forgive him.

His voice was a low hum through the wall, punctuated by the girl's occasional laughter.

What had I done to be treated in such a way?

What had gone wrong for him to be like this?

I buried my head in my hands.

Thank goodness Papa had taken his sleeping pills.

They came out into the hall again and I heard them go into his room. They were whispering now, as if it made any difference. They sniggered and crashed about for a moment or two.

Silence.

A rhythmic creaking of the bed. Her low moans.

The shame was unbearable.

And I was powerless.

I pressed my hands to my ears like a little girl.

After a few minutes, I jumped up and went to the bathroom, found a box of sleeping pills in the medicine cabinet and took two, went into the living room, the packet still in my hand, snatched the blanket from the chair, lay down on the sofa and covered myself up with it.

I couldn't ever forgive him for this. Even if he was my son.

It was light outside when I woke up. Papa came into the room with his walking stick for support.

'What are you doing sleeping there?' he said as I blinked up at him.

I sat up. The sky outside the windows was blue, the snow on the rooftops glittering in the sunlight.

'I couldn't sleep,' I said. 'I sat here most of the night.'

I pulled the blanket off me, got up and folded it.

'Worried about the young man?'

'No. No, it wasn't that.'

'What time did he get in?'

'Around three.'

'Drunk, I suppose?'

'A bit, yes. Shall I get you some breakfast? Oh, and happy birthday! How could I have forgotten! You're eighty today!'

'Thank you,' he said. 'Never thought I'd see the day, to be honest.'

He hobbled over and plonked himself down in his chair.

'I never partake of breakfast, as you surely know. A cup of tea would be nice, though.'

I put the blanket down on the sofa and went into the kitchen, put the kettle on and dropped a tea bag into a cup. Anger welled in me again. I only hoped he'd had the presence of mind to send her on her way.

He was out on his ear now. I didn't want him living with me another day.

How dare he.

Abusive and violent to his own mother.

Being drunk was no excuse.

He had to go. The sooner the better.

I poured the boiling water into the cup, stirred the tea bag round with a teaspoon, then pressed it against the side a few times to squeeze the excess liquid out of it, before dumping it in the bin, adding two sugars and a drop of milk, and taking it in to Papa.

'Right, I'll have a quick shower and get dressed,' I said.

He nodded and took a sip, his head half turned towards the window as he looked out.

If the clear sky was anything to go by, it would be rather cold outside.

'I can't remember all my birthdays,' he said. 'But I do remember the mood of them. It's the same every time. Isn't it strange?'

'Not really. It's always the same time of year, the same light outside.'

'I suppose that would be it, yes,' he said absently, then turned to look at me. 'Can you do me a favour?'

'Of course.'

'In the top drawer in my bedroom there's a packet of cigarettes. Would you fetch it for me, and bring me an ashtray, too? And a lighter, if you can find one?'

'I didn't know you'd started smoking again. How long's that been?'

'I'm starting now,' he said. 'It's been my intention for a long time. I was sixty-two when I stopped, and I said to your mother that I'd start again when I was eighty. She thought it was a good idea. It can't hurt me any more. And it's been something to look forward to all those years.'

'That sounds just like you,' I said, and went to get them for him. He tapped one out of the packet and lit it as I sat down on the sofa and watched him with a smile.

He glanced up at me with a look of irritation.

'Can't you pretend it's not my birthday?' he said.

'Why should I do that?'

'That loving look. Your usual self will do, if you don't mind.'

I laughed and got to my feet.

'No one's going to accuse *you* of not being your usual self.'

On my way to the bathroom, I gently opened the door of what I still thought of as Sasha's room. Seva was asleep on his side. Fortunately, he was on his own.

I would let him sleep.

But when he woke up, I wasn't going to speak to him. Not a word would I say. I had to make him think about what he'd done. He had to understand that he couldn't behave like that without there being repercussions. Serious repercussions.

After showering I went back to my room in my dressing gown, dried my hair with the hairdryer, put some make-up on and laid some clothes out on the bed so I could decide what to wear, eventually opting for the black wide-leg trousers and a black top with loose-fitting sleeves. Around my neck I fastened the necklace with the turquoise stone in it that Mama had given me after I finished school, and which she had been given by her mother before her. I put on the earrings I had with the same turquoise stones in them, only smaller, which I'd bought some years later to go with the necklace.

I decided to put it all from my mind. There was no reason to let him ruin his grandfather's birthday too.

In the living room, Papa was already smoking what I supposed was his second cigarette.

'I've got a lot to get done today, so I'll go into town now,' I said. 'Not sure what time I'll be back. Are you going to be all right?'

He snorted.

I put my boots and coat on in the hall.

'Alya?'

I went back in to see what he wanted.

'Could we go and visit the grave today, do you think?'

He didn't look up at me, but ran his fingers up and down the handle of the walking stick he for some reason still held in his hand.

'Yes, of course,' I said. 'This afternoon sometime?'

He nodded and I left him, closed the door of the apartment behind me and went down the stairs, stepping out into the street just as a snowplough with a flashing beacon came slowly by with an infernal scraping of metal against asphalt. The whole street was in shadow, as if it were a valley tucked away in a landscape, and sunlight danced on the rooftops high above my head, my breath puffing out in little clouds of vapour.

I hadn't visited Mama's grave since the funeral. He knew that. Where she'd been put to rest didn't matter. She was dead. He probably thought the same way. Sentimentality wasn't a part of his make-up.

So why go there today?

The cold air wrapped around my face as I walked. It felt like a mask.

I didn't know how I'd manage the shopping without a car, I'd just have to see. There was only the three of us, so it wasn't that much, not really. Not much at all.

Food. Flowers. Confectionery.

I'd have to remember his present. And I was supposed to be meeting Oksanka.

I halted.

All of a sudden it all seemed so insurmountable.

How was I going to cope?

It wasn't just the shopping and making dinner, I had to make sure he enjoyed a memorable evening too.

The cars that went past whirled up tiny particles of snow that prickled my face. The ruts they made were already stained with dirt, but everywhere else I looked the snow was as white as one would see in the forest or on the ice.

It wasn't the energy I lacked, it was the will.

I stopped in front of the old tea rooms. I'd often hung out there with my school friends. Through the windows the place seemed so unchanged. I felt a strong urge to sit down and collect myself, so I opened the door and went in. I took my gloves off as I walked through, and put them down on a table that was free at the back of the room. It was warm inside, with a vague smell of sweet pastries. I draped my coat over the back of a chair, tucked my scarf into the sleeve, then went up to the counter and bought myself a cup of tea and a piece of chocolate cake.

Returning to my table, I was surprised to see a ghost from my past. Someone I'd gone to school with, he was seated at one of the tables by the window staring at his phone. I couldn't for the life of me remember his name.

He'd been rather shy.

His father was a teacher.

Maksim. That was it.

He'd have to swivel round to notice me, so I was quite safe at my table, I thought, putting my cup and plate down before sitting down myself.

I just had to pull myself together. Do what was required of me.

It wasn't much.

I pressed the edge of the spoon through the cake. The chocolate was thick and smooth, with pieces of biscuit in it. As the taste melted into my mouth, I was almost overcome by a sudden and ravenous hunger. I could have eaten a horse.

I thought about calling Oksanka and making an excuse.

Or maybe she could come to the tea rooms instead?

I took my phone out, wiped my mouth with the napkin and tapped her number.

'Are you calling to cancel?' she said.

'No, I wouldn't dream of it. But I was wondering if you had time now instead?'

'Yes, that would work. Where were you thinking of?'

'I'm at the tea rooms.'

'OK. Let me get Sonya ready and we'll be right with you!'

I dropped the phone back into my bag and finished my cake, then sat with my elbows propped against the table, the cup between my hands, as I gazed around the room and out through the window, the road outside a narrow white band visible here and there between the bobbing heads at the tables in front of me. I wondered what Oksanka would say if I told her about Seva. But I wouldn't. I wouldn't ever tell anyone. But if I *did* tell anyone, it would have to be Oksanka.

She possessed such remarkable composure, Oksanka, took everything in her stride no matter what. When I first got to know her, she was wild and adventurous. I'd been all boundaries, there'd been so much that had been unthinkable to me before I met her, without me even knowing that my boundaries *were* boundaries. Why not? she would often ask. It could almost have been the motto she lived by. Why shouldn't we go to bed with a boy, if that was what we wanted, even if we were only fifteen? Why shouldn't we get drunk? Why shouldn't we smoke joints? Or sniff petrol for that matter, if we ever wanted to know what *that* would be like? It would be easy to think that the reason for her pushing against all those boundaries was that she didn't want to be in the place she was, didn't like herself, and was doing it because she wanted to either get away from herself or destroy herself. Mama probably thought so, she never cared for me spending so much time with her. But twenty-five years had gone by since then, and it was obvious now, at least it was to me, that it had always been about the opposite, not of getting away from her life, but of accepting it for what it was and throwing herself into it with all her abandon. *He* was like *this*, *she* was like *that*. If you did *that*, *this* happened, if you did *this*, *that* happened. Not that she thought ahead, she wasn't a person who planned or calculated, it was more that she accepted the consequences when they came back at her, regardless of their nature. And it wasn't something she thought about either, not as far as I could make out, it wasn't a strategy she employed, it was just Oksanka being OK with the way she was. She knew what was her, and what was everyone else, what she could change, and what she couldn't.

When I got to know her, I wanted to be like her. But only a few years later, when she started training to be a hairdresser, I about-turned and was ashamed of her. I didn't want to be seen with her by my new classmates. We read books and studied, full of big ideas and plans. She never read at all, she wasn't inquisitive in that way and had no plans other than to settle down, start a family and work in a job she liked. My old and new lives were incompatible, I broke with the former, and Oksanka disappeared out of my life. I studied philology in Moscow, she worked in a hairdressing salon in Samara, and the chances of us ever getting back together again were slim to say the least. But when I had Seva and moved back home for a while, she was the one who was there for me, no one else.

She adored Seva. Sometimes I found myself thinking it was he she would come to see rather than me. She loved to change him and talk to him. I'd almost go as far as to say that it was she who taught me to appreciate him fully and made me understand how lucky I was. She was married by then, they were trying for a baby, but hadn't yet succeeded. After a while, it turned out she couldn't have children at all. She took up night school, they got divorced. She trained as a social worker, that was in the evenings too, after work, it took five years. Then she met Mark and married him. They went through fertility treatment, and she got pregnant, though not without complications — her waters broke and she had to lie in a hospital bed for three months. But eventually the child was born, and before long she was pregnant again, without the fertility treatment.

That it would be she who laid out a plan for her life, worked hard and achieved what she set out to do, while I ended up in a vacuum both professionally and in my personal life, was hardly conceivable when we'd been teenagers. And yet it was what happened.

The thought was a painful one. It wasn't that I didn't wish her all the best, it was the feeling of not having done well myself, and of being unhappy where I was now.

Or not unhappy, exactly, that would be coming on a bit strong.

I couldn't allow myself to see everything in the light of Seva's behaviour.

The door opened and I looked up. A thickset man in a sheepskin coat had come in and stood now with his back to the room as he held the door open for a woman with a pushchair. It was Oksanka and little Sonya. I got halfway to my feet and waved. She waved back, picked Sonya up, and with the child on her hip pulled the strap with her free hand to fold the pushchair. The man, in a white woolly hat and a thin burgundy scarf wrapped around his neck, stamped the snow from his shoes as he stepped past her, and I saw at once that it was Yura. He didn't see me but stopped at the table where Maksim was sitting. It seemed Maksim had been waiting for him. Oksanka, who in the meantime had tucked the pushchair away by the wall, came towards me with the baby.

'Oksanochka,' I said, and gave her a hug. 'So good to see you! And little Sonechka! How fine she is!'

She lay on her mother's arm in her white puffer suit and stared at me with her lovely dark eyes. Her features were so small and delicate and a strand of dark hair could be seen peeping from under her hat.

'Say hello to Alya,' Oksanka said, holding her out to me.

'Hello, little one,' I said, beaming at her. 'How fine you are!'

I looked up again at Oksanka.

'What would you like? Coffee? Tea? Cake?'

'Tea would be nice,' she said, sitting down as she began to undo Sonya's suit.

On my way up to the counter, Yura caught sight of me and I went over to say hello.

'Fifteen years without seeing you, and now twice in two days! You remember Maks, don't you?'

'Of course,' I said. 'Hi!'

'Long time no see, Alya,' he said with a smile.

'Maks had a bit of a crush on you, I think, didn't you, Maks?' said Yura.

'I did not,' said Maks, blushing as he laughed. 'You're speaking for yourself there, I think.'

Good grief.

'Got to go,' I said. 'I'm with a friend. Nice to see you both, though.'

I bought two cups of tea and a piece of cake and took it all back to our table on a tray. Sonya was propped up in Oksanka's lap, her soft spine against her mother's tummy, Oksanka holding her little hands in hers.

'Do you know Maksim?' she said as I sat down.

'No, not really. But I do remember him from the old days. Do you?'

'No. I just know who he is, that's all. He runs a little association that works to preserve the old buildings here. They restore some of them, too. Without permission. Restoration activists, I suppose you could call them.'

'Really?'

'But I think he's actually an estate agent.'

'Someone has to be,' I said. 'How are you, anyway? You look radiant!'

'I feel radiant, too. She's so good.'

'What about Anya? Has she been jealous?'

'A bit to start with. But she's got used to her now. She loves her baby sister. But how are you?'

'I'm good. A bit stressed out just at the minute, though, with Papa's birthday today. I haven't got a thing ready yet.'

'What do you need to do?'

I shrugged.

'Get the shopping in for the dinner. Buy his present. *Make* the damned dinner. Be in a good mood all evening.'

'It does sound a bit stressful,' she said, lowering her head to kiss Sonya's scalp. 'But I can give you a hand, if you want.'

'No, no need. You've got your hands full as it is.'

'We could go to the shopping centre? Get everything done in one go?'

'That would be fantastic,' I said. 'Are you sure?'

She was, and not long afterwards we were walking along the pavement on our way to the car she'd parked a couple of streets away, Sonya staring up at the blue sky as her mother steered her pushchair. Oksanka was just as calm as ever, only in a different way now, I thought. She seemed so perfectly poised, invincible almost. Impervious to all that was bad and could hurt a person, as if there was simply no room for such things inside her.

'I'm afraid you'll have to sit in the back,' she said when we got to the car and she lifted Sonya out of the pushchair into her car seat.

'I'm almost used to it now,' I said. 'Seva sat in front last night.'

She threw me a brief smile, concentrating on the baby, talking to her as she gathered the safety straps and clicked them into place.

She didn't really care about me, I found myself thinking as I got in and she turned the key in the ignition and flicked the indicator to pull out.

But why should she? And what did it actually mean to care about a person?

Or for a person to care about you?

What did *that* mean?

Or no, that wasn't the question. The question was what *good* was it.

What *good* would it do for someone to care about me? What would it help?

In the tea rooms I'd wondered what I could do to get what Oksanka had. Find some kind, well-intentioned man and have a baby with him?

It wasn't too late, and it wasn't impossible either, even if it felt that way.

Yura, perhaps? I wouldn't be able to love him, but I'd be able to like him and have as good a life with him as with anyone else.

He had a decent job, and probably more than enough money. I'd be able to pack mine in at the university and look for something else. Maybe retrain in a different field. It wasn't too late for that either. I was only forty. I could still start again.

I could start from scratch.

Although these thoughts were meant to be optimistic, I found they only dampened my spirits as I sat there in the car, gazing out of the back window at the snow that whirled in our wake, the sunlight glittering in the frost wherever it broke through. The smoke that rose up in thin unmoving columns from the buildings, white against the blue of the sky, glimpses of the river through the side streets that ran down between the housing blocks.

'What are you giving your father?' Oksanka asked.

'Some books, I think. Only I don't think I've got the energy for it today. Maybe I'll just tell him his present's on its way.'

As I turned round again, I saw she was looking at me in the rear-view.

'Thanks for doing this,' I said.

She snorted.

'I'm just glad to see you, that's all.'

'Why?'

'What do you mean, why?'

'Why are you glad to see me? What part of me is it that would make you glad?'

'Oh, Alyushka! Are you so unhappy with yourself?'

The sudden solicitude in her voice made my eyes moist. I swallowed and looked out of the window.

'I'm not unhappy with myself. Not exactly.'

'*Something's* the matter. I do know you well enough to tell.'

I shook my head.

'It's nothing. At least nothing in particular.'

We sat for a while without saying anything, the heater blowing its warm air out.

'When we became friends — how long ago is that, twenty-five years ago? — I wanted to be like you. Have I ever told you that?'

'Why would you want to be like me?'

'You were so beautiful. And you always knew what to say, and how to behave. You were always so annoyingly smart as well. You still are, of course!' she said with a laugh.

'It's funny, because I wanted to be like you.'

'You're just saying that.'

'No, seriously. I even thought about it at the tea rooms just before.'

'Now it's my turn to ask why.'

'Because you were so wild, so brave, so exhilarating. You didn't give a damn what other people thought. You did what you wanted. I never could.'

'Hm,' she said, and went quiet for a moment before looking up at me again in the mirror. 'I never saw it like that.'

'But that's the way it was.'

She turned into the big car park in front of the shopping centre, a glaring white expanse filled with gleaming cars, many of them mantled with snow and ice. Sonya woke up as Oksanka lifted her into her push-chair. She grizzled a bit, but by the time we went inside she'd already fallen asleep again.

Back home, I put the shopping bags down in the hall as I took off my coat and boots. The place was quiet.

'Hello, anybody in?' I called out.

'We're in here,' Seva's voice replied from the living room.

Normally I'd have asked him to help me carry the things in, but I'd decided not to speak to him, so I lugged them through into the kitchen myself.

Papa was reading in his chair, Seva sitting on the sofa scrolling on his phone as I went past.

'Did you get everything?' he said with a smile, as if nothing had happened.

I didn't answer him, but put the bags down on the worktop, found a chopping board and cut the ends off the stalks of the two bunches of flowers I'd bought, got two vases out of the cupboard, filled them with water and arranged the flowers in them. One with red roses, one with white. Blood and snow. Life and death.

I put the food items away in the fridge and cupboard before going into the living room again.

'Are you ready?' I said to Papa.

He put the book down in his lap and took off his glasses.

'What for?'

'You wanted to go to the cemetery.'

'Oh, so I did.'

'I've borrowed a car. We'll have to go now, I've got the dinner to get ready when we come back.'

'I'll come as well,' said Seva.

'You and I will go on our own,' I said to Papa.

'But I want to come,' said Seva.

Papa looked at me quizzically.

'Let me help you,' I said, stepping up to him and holding my arm out for him to take.

'I usually put my shoes on here,' he said. 'It's easier. And my coat out there.'

I went into the hall. Apart from my own winter shoes and Seva's, I saw only summer shoes there. And a pair of wellingtons. But his feet would be cold in them.

Perhaps if I found him a thick pair of socks.

I checked the drawers under the mirror, finding a pair of green woollen ones which I took with me along with the wellingtons.

'I couldn't find any winter shoes,' I said. 'Will your wellingtons do, with some thick socks?'

He nodded and took the socks from my outstretched hand.

'Your mother knitted these for me,' he said. 'Rather fitting, I suppose.'

'Mama?' said Seva.

I was standing with my back to him and did not turn to look at him.

'You're still angry with me, aren't you? But I want to go to Babulya's grave. You've no right to deny me that.'

My anger, until then subsiding, rose up again.

'Here, let me give you a hand,' I said to Papa, who was having difficulty reaching his feet in the position he was sitting, and took the socks from his hand.

There was something uncomfortably intimate about dressing him, and rather demeaning for us both, but now I didn't care, all I wanted was to get out of the house and away from Seva.

Once he'd got his boots on, Papa gripped my arm and pulled himself upright, dismissing me then with a small movement of his hand, clearly intent on walking by himself, at least while we were still in the apartment.

Descending the stairs in an old black woollen overcoat that had seen better days, he decided he needed my support again, his long, strong fingers gripping my upper arm tightly.

'Who lent you the car?' he said as we walked along the pavement.

'Oksanka,' I said.

'Who?'

'Oksanka.'

'Never heard of her.'

'An old friend of mine from school. You never took an interest in who I was friends with, so I'm not surprised if you can't remember her. She's a social worker now.'

'Is that it?' he said, indicating a black Mercedes.

'No, the one behind.'

He sat with his walking stick between his knees, his hands resting on the crook of the handle as we drove through the city, whistling softly every now and then, looking out, attentive to what he saw.

'Is it a long time since you were at the grave?' I said.

'Yes.'

The cemetery was next to one of the main traffic arteries. It covered quite a large area that sloped gently away, and usually it was rather a depressing sight, not only because it was where the dead were laid to rest, but also because it was so neglected, all rusty wire fencing and dilapidated sheds, quite apart from the thundering traffic that never abated even at night. But on this particular afternoon it was almost a wonder to behold. Everything was blanketed with snow, the only exception being the footpaths that had been cleared and now lay bare and twinkling with frost, the snow scintillating in the light of the sun that even now hung low in a vast, clear sky that seemed to become a deeper and deeper shade of blue with every minute that passed.

And then the cold, that put an edge on everything, sharpening every sound, sharpening every outline, sharpening even the senses. At least that's what it felt like.

Papa took my arm as we left the car, and held it all the way to Mama's grave. He was seldom quiet more than a couple of minutes at a time, but now he was. Silent, we walked arm in arm along the path, the thin snow creaking underfoot, the nearby traffic a rumble in the background.

We halted at the black headstone that bore her name.

It wasn't Mama the grave made me think about, but the day we buried her. All the people who'd stood there then, many I'd never seen before, many I knew only vaguely, besides relatives and her closest friends. I remembered the overwhelming feeling I'd had then that she'd never belonged to me, that I'd been sharing her all along with those other people, and that they'd all been just as important to her as me. It hadn't been resentment, but it was what I felt. My therapist had pointed to the obvious fact that it was Papa who'd never been fully mine, thereby opening up the idea to me that the feeling I'd had was a simple case of projection.

Papa stood leaning against his walking stick as he stared at the headstone in front of us. I glanced at him to gauge his emotions, not exactly expecting tears in his eyes, but the look on his face was quite impassive.

He sighed.

'Do you miss her a lot?' I said.

'I've got used to her being gone.'

He turned his head and looked at me.

'Do you?'

'Sometimes,' I said. 'I wish I'd known her better. I wish I'd understood things better while she was still alive. But somehow I wasn't interested.'

'Nothing odd about that. She was your mother. Mothers are invisible.'

'Do you think she knew?'

'Knew what?'

'That I took her for granted.'

'Of course she did. That's what children do.'

Neither of us said anything, but stood staring at the grave.

'Why did you want us to come here today?' I said.

He hesitated for a moment.

'I wanted to talk to you about her. And it struck me that it would be more obligating in a way, to do so here.'

'Obligating?'

'Yes.'

'Why would it have to be obligating?'

He didn't reply, but took something out of the pocket of his coat. It was an envelope.

'This came in the post a few weeks ago,' he said, handing it to me. 'It's addressed to Asya. You should have it, not me.'

'Who's it from?' I said, glancing down and seeing Mama's name written in an unfamiliar hand.

'It's from your father's son. Your half-brother.'

'What?' I said, and stared at him.

'Read it,' he said.

I took the letter out of the envelope, unfolded it and began to read.

Dear Asya,

I am Syvert's son. I have been thinking about writing to you for a long time, but only now am I able to collect myself and do so. My father died in a car accident in 1977. Some years later I found letters from you among his belongings. Before that, I had no idea you even existed. I have been thinking a lot about you and what you meant to my father. I would really like to meet you. I understand if you don't want that. But if you do, I am able to come to Russia and meet you there.

Yours sincerely,

Syvert Løyning (Jr)

My eyes filled with tears.

'He doesn't know Mama's dead,' I said, lowering the letter in my hands.

'Not only that,' said Papa. 'He doesn't know he has a sister.'

I wiped my tears with my index finger.

He looked at me.

'What will you do?'

'Oh, Papa, I don't know,' I said. 'Shall we go now?'

He took a few slow and unsteady steps with his stick before halting.

'Can you help me, do you think?'

'Of course I can,' I said, taking his arm at once.

'It's rather slippery here.'

'You must see the doctor about that foot of yours. I'll go with you.'

'You're going home tomorrow.'

'I'll put it off.'

He nodded and we said no more until reaching the car.

I couldn't understand why the letter had made me cry. Perhaps it was because I'd felt Mama's presence so strongly there at the grave as I'd read it, and everything about her that I had no control over had welled up in me then.

Why had he sent it? Couldn't he have left the past alone? He didn't even know I existed. And he'd never met Mama.

I opened the door for Papa, waiting until he'd made himself comfortable before closing it again and going over to the driver's side.

'How long did you say you'd had the letter?' I said, turning the key in the ignition, throwing the gear lever into reverse, turning the wheel and backing out in an arc.

'A few weeks.'

'Why didn't you say?'

'I didn't want to tell you over the phone. I wanted you to read it for yourself. He's your brother.'

I shifted into first gear and drove slowly back up to the road.

'What do you think I should do?' I said, indicating right and looking left to see what was coming. A lorry as big as a small house came thundering in a cloud of snow.

'I don't know, Alevtinoshka. What do you want to do?'

'Forget about it.'

'In that case, I think you should forget about it.'

'Yes. If he's gone twenty-five years without knowing about me, I'm sure he can go another fifty.'

But I knew I couldn't do it. Papa knew so too, I was certain.

I turned onto the road and so eager was I to pick up speed that the rear end skidded, first to one side, then the other, before I managed to straighten our course again.

Papa said nothing, but I could see him grip the handle inside the door.

'Sorry,' I said. 'Not used to this car.'

I'd thought visiting the grave would impart some kind of clarity, that Papa's grief, and mine too, would be made plain there in front of the headstone. Instead, the opposite was the case. Everything had gone muddy.

If the letter had opened a door to a place I'd never set foot in, I couldn't just close it again as if nothing had happened, something had got out.

'She never got over him,' said Papa all of a sudden. 'She claimed she had, but she never did. I was only the reserve.'

'You were not!' I said.

'I knew the score. And I went into it with eyes open. So I've only myself to thank.'

'That's not true.'

He gave me that ironic look of his.

'We can just as well be truthful,' he said. 'It wasn't for love that she married me. She needed a father for you and Sasha. It was that simple.'

'I don't believe in love. And I didn't think you did either.'

He laughed.

'Of course you don't believe in love. You grew up with your mother and me.'

He laughed again, though more feebly this time, and then coughed, before withdrawing into himself and saying nothing for a while.

The sun was huge as it went down into the forest, far away in the distance, the sky above it flaming red and orange. At the roadsides, the air hung dismally over the snow, as if the sun had sucked up all the light there in order that it might blaze above the world one final time.

'She barely even knew him,' I said. 'They were only together a few weeks. You and Mama were together for twenty-five years.'

'Love is not amenable to quantification.'

'Do you want me to tell you what I think?'

'Yes, I do.'

'I think *you're* the one who never got over him. I think *you* kept him alive in your marriage. I think Mama loved *you*, and that you couldn't handle that.'

'Couldn't handle what?'

'Being loved. Not everyone can handle being loved.'

Neither of us said anything for a bit after that.

It felt wrong, talking to him about his and Mama's relationship. On the other hand there was such a lot that felt wrong in my life that one more thing was hardly going to matter.

When we came back into the centre of town the sky above us was the darkest blue, the forest across the river as if dipped in melted gold by the setting sun. The people in the streets were dumpy figures in their thick winter coats, hats, scarves, mittens, exhaling little fountains of frosty breath.

Entering the old part of town, I cast a glance at Papa.

'Are you OK if I just drop you off and take the car back?'

'Of course,' he said.

'And you'll manage the stairs all right?'

He didn't condescend to answer that.

He didn't say a word. Not even when he got out a few minutes later. I watched him go through the front door and close it after him.

I got off the bus down at the promenade and instead of going straight home decided to walk for a bit and then cut up into town just after the hotel.

The ice, topped with snow, reached towards the open channel in the middle of the river. Some huddled, tent-like figures were visible further upstream, anglers who hadn't yet packed it in for the day.

The sun had set almost completely now, the sky was dark save for a narrow strip of crimson light above the trees at the horizon.

My shoes squeaked against the snow, the cold air tightened the skin of my cheeks.

I wondered what to do about Seva. What had happened the night before no longer seemed quite so important. I knew it would all melt away at some point and find a place for itself within the bounds of acceptability.

I just hadn't thought it would happen so quickly.

But I didn't want it to. I wanted to still be angry. I wanted to punish him. He'd abused me. And the way in which he'd done so was unforgivable.

Even so, the letter Papa had shown me at the grave had put everything in a new light. Seva and I weren't on our own. We were part of a line, and he was at the end of it. I came before him. Mama before me. Her mother and father before her. In that perspective, what he and I did somehow seemed less important.

I could live with him having defied me. But not with him being abusive to me. I couldn't live with that.

I stopped and sat down on a bench. The slats were icy cold, even through my trousers and tights.

The crimson light had narrowed to a sliver.

It was like an eye closing.

I gazed at the sky. A large number of stars already shimmered in its darkness.

I saw the look in his eyes as he shoved his face into mine, gripped my wrists and spat out his words. Hatred, sheer hatred.

He'd been drunk, but that meant only that he'd been able to let go and give vent to something he normally held back.

I'd never done anything against him that could give him reason to hate me.

That hatred was his, it had nothing to do with me.

I got my phone out and sat with it in my hand for a moment, wondering whether to text him. It wouldn't be talking to him, a text was more detached.

Why were you so abusive to me? I typed.

I read the seven words to myself over and over again.

They couldn't hurt. It wasn't like talking to him.

I sent the message.

The reply came swiftly.

You're the one who was abusive.

I took a deep breath. How dare he.

The insolence.

He sent another.

You don't tell me what to do.

And another.

No one tells me what to do.

And another.

I'm a free person. I do what I want. Not what YOU want.

A wall of self-righteousness.

If that was the way he wanted it, he could get out of my flat. It wasn't negotiable now. He could live with his father or his babushka. Or one of his girlfriends.

What had I done wrong?

I stared vacantly. The snow was a glittering arc beneath the lamp posts that ran along the promenade, dulling beyond their pools of light, dulling, dulling towards the ice, until the massive barrier of inky trees loomed up on the other side. The light above them, deep red, narrow as a pencil line, was unfathomably beautiful, stretching away into the darkness.

Syvert Løyning Jr.

My unknown brother.

I took the letter from my inside pocket and read it again, in the light from my phone.

Why was he getting in touch now, so many years after?

His father hadn't told him about Mama, and died before he could.

It was so hard to understand that he was my father too.

When Mama had told me about him, it had sounded almost like a fairy tale to me. A man from the north who died before they could get married. Was he nice? I asked. Yes, she replied, he was very nice. Was he handsome? Yes, he was handsome. Why did he die? It was an accident, nobody's fault, it just happened. And then you married Papa? Not straight away, but a few years later I met Papa and grew fond of him.

I knew it had all been real, that my father had belonged to the real world, not the world of fairy tales and myth, yet it was all so far away that it felt unreal to me when I'd been growing up. Reality was Mama and Papa and Sasha and me.

If I wrote to him and agreed to meet, everything would become so much more complicated. I'd be invaded by a past that wasn't mine, by people I didn't know and might not want to.

He wouldn't know if his letter had been received or not.

He was my brother, but what did that mean if we'd never met? It was in the blood, yes. The genes. Which meant it was a bodily thing, at the animal level, and how many animals cared about their siblings? Kittens from the same litter were separated and given different homes. Did that bother them?

Not that we were to be compared to cats, not as such. But we shared nothing of what made us human beings. All we shared were blood and genes.

I saw us in a flash with feline faces and human bodies, and felt myself smile. At the same time, a shiver ran through me.

It was too cold to be sitting there.

But I didn't want to go either.

The crimson line at the horizon, thin as a hair now.

And then gone.

The eye had closed.

I got to my feet, flapped my arms across my body a couple of times for warmth and started walking. On my way up the hill after passing the hotel, everything suddenly went dark around me, and quite still. All the sounds I'd barely noticed stopped. All the lights in all the windows, which I'd likewise been unaware of until then, went out at once.

A power cut.

Looking up at the sky, it was as if it had come closer. The stars were bigger, and more numerous. It seemed like all of a sudden everything below became connected with everything above.

The darkness brought everything together.

It was a good thought.

I went down to the promenade again and saw that it wasn't just the buildings around me that had been hit, it was the whole city. Everything was silent and dark.

People would die that night. The temperature was down to minus twenty at least outside.

Only then did it occur to me that I wouldn't be able to make dinner without electricity.

As I went back up the hill my phone rang.

It was Sasha.

'Hey, sis!' he said. 'Has your power gone, too?'

'Are you *here*, in Samara?' I said.

'Yes, just having a drink. A bit of Dutch courage, if you know what I mean.'

'But I thought you weren't coming? You said you weren't coming!'

'A person can change his mind, can't he? Don't be so angry. You're always so angry, sis. It's the violinist's eightieth. Let's celebrate him like he's never been celebrated before.'

THE WOLVES OF ETERNITY

VASILISA BARANOV

E very night I fall asleep to the sound of the trains. There is something so very calming about them, even when they are noisiest
(and some indeed are like a whole factory, with their clattering empty
wagons, squealing brakes and wheels that clunk and pound like thudding canon — da-dum-da-dum-da-dum!). As I lie in my bed with eyes
closed and wait for sleep, the line that separates me from my nocturnal
surroundings becomes all but erased, and the first sounds of the trains
reach into my inner being, the distant provinces of the mind. As those
sounds grow louder, it is as if they rattle through my very self. My first
nights here were not calming at all, quite the opposite in fact, my soul
as if wrenched open in the flashing glare of a strobe, or pierced by such
metallic clamour. But then I became accustomed, and those sounds
were then my friends.

While of course I know that these trains of the night are prosaic too,
hauling all manner of worldly objects — great tank wagons, refriger-
ated wagons of fish and meat, containers filled with consumer items,
open wagons laden with metal girders, scrap, sand, motor cars — they
nevertheless exist in my mind as dark, obscure and forbidding, already
half belonging to dreams. And the sounds that escape from them belong
not to the moment alone, but stretch away into the future (as dreams
themselves do), laden with notions of unfamiliar places, unfamiliar
lives. Dubrovnic, the trains sing within me, Odessa, Trieste, Vladiv-
ostok. Seville, Genoa, Madrid. Vienna, Budapest, Berlin. Indeed, even
when I am almost asleep and only faintly aware of these sounds as they
rise and fall in the night, they carry with them the clang of the world,
picked up and understood by the emotions and transmitted then out
into my being as gentle waves of something good and full of promise.

But there is more to the train than longing. Although the first railway in Russia opened as late as in 1837, the train is utterly enmeshed in the country's culture, and like almost everything else here, it is a thing of ambiguity. As a symbol of modernity, mechanisation and alienation it has been associated with our human demise, a horseman of the Apocalypse, as well as with hope and the future. The Revolution arrived by the railway: Lenin's sealed train, rattling its way through war-torn Europe in the spring of 1917, all the way from Switzerland, north to St Petersburg, where he, that sinewy, badger-like man, stepped out and as good as single-handedly seized power over this entire vast empire. The Revolution was sustained by the railway: Trotsky, leader of the Red Army, used a train as his headquarters. The Revolution was propelled by the railway: trains laden with flyers, pamphlets, newspapers, red flags and speakers, some carrying whole libraries and printing presses, propaganda to every corner of the land. And neither the Bolshevik victory in the civil war nor that of the Soviet Union in the Great Patriotic War would have been conceivable without the railway, without trains.

For as long as the trains have stamped their pistons, trundled, rattled and raced along the 125,000 kilometres of railway lines by which Russia is criss-crossed, they have been sung and written about: hardly a Russian author has not penned a word about trains. Prince Mishkin makes his entrance into world literature while seated on a train. Anna Karenina throws herself to her death in front of a train. Pasternak wrote of trains and train journeys all his life, and the first time he saw Rainer Maria Rilke was on board a train, when Pasternak was ten years old and a young Rilke was on his way to Yasnaya Polyana to meet Tolstoy together with Lou Andreas-Salomé. Marina Tsvetaeva wrote 'The Train of Life', Mandelstam wrote 'Concert at a Railway Station', Yerofeyev wrote *Moscow-Petushki*, and the main character in Chinghiz Aitmatov's *The Day Lasts More Than a Hundred Years* works at a remote railway station in Kazakhstan, at the very periphery of the Soviet empire. Those who live there ride camels like their nomadic ancestors, but they see too the rocket launches that take place on the barren steppes in the far distance; a striking encapsulation of how different ages exist beside each other in this land, as they have done always. Another encapsulation of the same thing: the embalmed Lenin. The leader of the workers' Revolution preserved like an Egyptian pharaoh, a human deity. His face, icon-like everywhere. A third encapsulation: the underground metro stations, as splendid as ballrooms.

When Lenin died, his corpse was transported from Gorky to the centre of Moscow, not by car, not by horse-drawn carriage, but by train, pulled by an engine called the Red Locomotive, of which Lenin, in a ceremony the previous year, had been made honorary first engine driver. After that the embalming, after that the mausoleum, and a hundred years later he lies there still.

And Tolstoy died at a railway station. In the middle of the night, 28 October 1910, he left his wife, Sofia, to whom he had been married forty-eight years, and his estate, Yasnaya Polyana, where he had been born eighty-two years earlier. He took the train south, to his sister, Maria (a nun of the convent at Shamordino), planning to spend what remained of his life in a hut there. But after only two days he worried that Sofia would learn of his whereabouts, and took the train onwards towards the Caucasus. During the journey, he fell ill and was taken to a room in the stationmaster's house at Astapovo, where he died a few days later of pneumonia. His last words were by all accounts: *But the peasants . . . how do the peasants die?* Tolstoy of course wished to be a man of the people, but was one even less than Lenin, and there was nothing at all reminiscent of the peasantry about his final days, for the news that he lay dying at the railway station spread on the winds, and soon the place was teeming with journalists and reporters who followed every hour of his death and wrote about it in all the newspapers of the world. He was even filmed, on his deathbed there in the stationmaster's house. Russia's most famous physicians hastened to the scene, and his children came too. Sofia also arrived, but was not admitted for fear that the shock of seeing his wife would be the end of the great man. There is a photograph of Sofia as she stands peering in at the window of the room where he lay dying.

The night he left home, she wrote in her diary: 'Lev Nik. has left! My God! He left a letter telling me not to look for him, as he had gone for good, to live out his old age in peace. The moment I read those words I rushed outside in a frenzy of despair and jumped into the pond, where

I swallowed a lot of water; Sasha and Bulgakov dragged me out with the help of Vanya Shuraev. Utter despair. Why did they save me?'

Two days later: 'I cry day and night and suffer dreadfully. It's more painful and terrible than anything I could have imagined. Lev Nik. did visit his sister in Shamordino, then travelled beyond Gorbachevo — who knows where. What unspeakable cruelty.'

Four days after that: 'I received a telegram from the *Russian Word* first thing this morning. "Lev Nik. ill in Astapovo. Temperature 40." Tanya, Andryusha, the nurse and I all left Tula for Astapovo on a special train.'

And then, 7 November: 'At six o'clock in the morning Lev Nikol. died. I was allowed in only as he drew his last breath. They wouldn't let me take leave of my husband. Cruel people.'

What a story. We carry our death within us, as Rilke held. Children to a small extent, old people to a large extent. And everyone's death is their own. Tolstoy died trying to escape his life, in the full, blitzy glare of the public eye. It was a death that fitted him as a hand fits a glove; it was almost too good to be true. If one reads Tolstoy's diaries (as I think one should), the novels and the short stories and the religious writings, he comes across almost more like a place than a person, a place where the greatest contradictions meet. Or alas, more human than most. Akhmatova did not care for him much — to Isaiah Berlin she opined that the morality of *Anna Karenina* was the morality of Tolstoy's wife and his Moscow aunts. Why did Anna Karenina have to be killed? She is punished by the same society whose hypocrisy Tolstoy never tired of denouncing. Tolstoy lied, he knew better than that. He gave in to the pressures of conformity: 'When he was happily married he wrote *War and Peace*, which celebrates family life. After he started hating Sofia Andreevna, but was not prepared to divorce her because divorce is condemned by society, and perhaps by the peasants too, he wrote *Anna Karenina* and punished her for leaving Karenin. When he was old and no longer lusted so violently after peasant girls, he wrote *The Kreutzer Sonata* and forbade sex altogether.' There is much truth in this. Tolstoy was a hedonist who longed for asceticism, an aristocrat who wished to be a peasant, a proud and arrogant man who wished to be humble, a writer who wished to be in the world, not in his writing, a lascivious man who wished first to be a family man, then to live in celibacy, a fabled man of worldwide fame who wished to be a hermit. He battled these forces within him all his life, and he died as he lived, with all his contradictions laid bare. But we must not be led to believe that his attempts to reconcile them were not genuine, for indeed they were. When he first met Nikolai Fyodorovich Fyodorov, librarian of Moscow's Rumyantsev Museum, in 1878, it was not so much Fyodorov's thinking Tolstoy admired as his way of life: Fyodorov gave away almost everything he possessed and practised the strictest frugality, living in a small room without furniture, owning not even a bed or linen, sleeping on top of a chest or on the floor with newspapers to cover him, a book for a pillow. 'Nikolai Fyodorovich is a saint. A tiny room . . . He doesn't want payment. No linen, and no bed,' Tolstoy writes in his diary in October 1881. And in a letter to a friend: 'It is very hard for me in Moscow . . . But there are some real people even here. And God has granted to me to make friends with two of them: one is Orlov, and the other and principal one is Nikolai Fyodorovich Fyodorov. He is a librarian at the Rumyantsev Library . . . He has devised a plan for a common task for humanity, the aim of which is the bodily resurrection of all humans. First, it is not as crazy as it sounds (don't worry, I do not and never have shared his views, but I have understood them enough to feel capable of defending them against any other beliefs of a similar material nature). Secondly, and most importantly, because of these beliefs he leads the purest Christian life . . . He is sixty, a pauper, gives away all he has, is always cheerful and meek.'

Tolstoy and Fyodorov were born in the same year, 1828, but their personalities and lives were so different that their friendship contained an imbalance from the start and came to an end after a few years, Fyodorov breaking with Tolstoy following the latter's series of articles concerning the famine in Samara and Kazan and the rest of the Volga region, which Fyodorov found to be infused with socialism (they also prompted Tolstoy's exclusion from the Orthodox Church). Fyodorov was a complete and undivided person, his morals and his way of life were as one, a uniquely consistent and monophonic man, and his philosophy may be condensed into a single thought. Yet it was a thought so grand and so bold that his name lives on to this day.

It was this: *we must resurrect all persons who have ever lived*. This must be our common task and duty. And we must invest everything that is ours, the complete resources of science, culture and finance, to ensure its fulfilment.

In other words: we must conquer death and eradicate it.

Yes, I know. It is an idiotic thought, ridiculous and dull-minded. For death is of course final. Death is invincible. From death's continent no one may return.

But think again . . .

What if . . .

Fyodorov was of course ridiculed — when Tolstoy put forward Fyodorov's name in proposal of his membership of the Moscow Psychological Society, and one of its members, a Professor Trotsky, asked how it would be possible to find room on earth for all those who would be returned to life, Tolstoy's reply being that Fyodorov in addressing that very issue had suggested human beings might colonise other planets, he was met only with roars of laughter. Still, many others took Fyodorov more seriously, among them Fyodor Dostoevsky, who in a letter wrote that he was in complete agreement with Fyodorov's ideas and had read them as if they were his own. (An early draft of *The Brothers Karamazov* is peppered with references to them.) Vladimir Solovyov, the wunderkind philosopher who in the 1870s gave a sensational series of lectures to thousand-strong audiences in St Petersburg, went even further. In a letter to Fyodorov he wrote: 'I accept your project unconditionally . . . I have much to say to you. But for the time being I will say only that since the emergence of Christianity your project is the first step forward of the human spirit along the path of Christ. As to myself, I can only recognise in you my teacher and spiritual father.'

Solovyov was a Christian thinker, Dostoevsky a Christian writer. The notion of resurrection is of course a central tenet of Christianity, particularly in the Russian Orthodox Church, so the thought of overcoming death was by no means remote to either, indeed it had already occurred with the resurrection of Jesus, and would happen again, on the Day of Judgement.

However, Fyodorov's grand idea is not a Christian one, insofar as his own notion of resurrection is conceived as taking place within our human world, outside the realm of the Divine. It is a rational conception, not a mysterious one, facilitated by empirical knowledge and scientific method. And he criticised both Dostoevsky and Solovyov for their mysticism and irrationality.

The starting point of Fyodorov's philosophy is that death belongs to nature and life belongs to humans. Nature is a destructive force we permit to control us. Death is a result of our passivity towards nature: we allow nature to kill us. But this is by no means a necessary outcome. Whereas the forces of nature that tear everything asunder are blind processes taking place according to laws and systems of which nature itself is unknowing, we human beings possess consciousness, will and emotions. As such, we are more than nature. And what makes us more than nature, that which separates us from it, is moreover that which allows us to separate ourselves from death. The mistake we have made is that we have submitted to death, accepting it passively and without question. What we must do is to intervene actively in nature: steer it, control it, conquer it. As yet, we remain at the very outset of human life, ignorant still of the true powers of reason and rationality.

Humans die for two reasons, Fyodorov wrote. The first concerns the body itself, its susceptibility to illness and its inability to restore itself. The second concerns the unpredictable nature of the bodily environment. Both forms of death may be prevented by regulation, of the body and nature respectively.

But death's cancellation, in effect eternal life, is not the most important element of Fyodorov's philosophy. That is the resurrection of the already dead. We must resurrect our fathers, it is our duty, and our fathers, as they are resurrected, must resurrect in turn their own fathers, it is their duty, and thus it must continue, generation by generation, backwards in time, until all persons who have ever lived are returned to life. And the resurrection of which he writes is not to be understood in any metaphysical sense, but as a concrete, physical, bodily phenomenon.

How this is to take place in purely practical terms is something Fyodorov discusses in his *Philosophy of the Common Task*, written in the latter part of the nineteenth century, an age when science and technology were taking giant leaps. Fyodorov sees no reason for such progress not

to continue, in fact it seems as if he sees no limits at all for what it may
be possible for human beings to achieve by such means. Man is the very
culmination of evolution, and we have arrived at such a point that we
are ourselves able to grasp hold of the evolutionary processes and steer
them in any way that may be desirable to us. The inherent call of the
title is important: if we *all* subscribe to this, if we put *everything*
else aside, eternal life and resurrection will both be real options to us in
the future. One notion is fundamental: the universe wastes nothing.
People die and their bodies decompose, but their matter, which is to say
the atoms of which they consisted, remains, entering into new affilia-
tions in a never-ending loop. Thus, Fyodorov suggests, at some point in
time it will be possible to trace every atom that once belonged to a person and to put them all together again. Physical distance and time will
be of no hindrance: in the future man will go into space, and as Tolstoy
noted in his meeting with the Moscow Psychological Society, if we can
resurrect the dead, we will surely also be able to colonise other
planets.

What a thought!

But Fyodorov would not have been Russian if his utopian vision had
stood alone. Instead, in the same manner as the later utopia of the communists, it drags with it a huge undergrowth of notions, Slavophile,
patriarchal, Orthodox and autocratic. Important to both visions, albeit
in different ways, is the ancestral cult. Fyodorov saw the movement
from generation to generation as a form of parricide — our parents give
life to us, and yet we shove them aside and seize all that they have
worked to achieve, without gratitude of any kind, all they are given in
return is death. (This was to a large extent what interested Dostoevsky
about Fyodorov when he wrote *The Brothers Karamazov*, in which the
sons kill the father and all that resonates in that kinship.) They give us
life, and we take their lives away from them. The least we can do would
be to resurrect them and return to them what we took. But we kill our
parents in another sense too: if the atoms of which they were composed
are everywhere, then they are also in the food we eat. Or, put differently: we consume our ancestors in order that we ourselves may live.
For that reason, Fyodorov wished us to change our bodily make-up in
such a way that would allow us to take up nutrients from sources other

than organic matter. Once this occurred and was fully evolved and everyone who was ever alive on the planet had risen again into eternal life, it would no longer be necessary to propagate and have children, sex would die out, and men and women would be equals, as brother and sister are equals. History too would emerge to us in all its fullness, nothing would be hidden to us any longer, since all who were there, in history, would be with us as witnesses. We would then have attained the perfect world, a world without death, without hunger, without war, without sex, without hatred, without conflict, without secrets. As Fyodorov writes: *the world* is a fact, *the perfect world* our task. Nature is imperfect, and we are imperfect insofar as we are mortal — nature tears us asunder — for which reason we must create ourselves in our own image and be endlessly renewable bodies in a meticulously regulated and controlled world.

If we ignore all local and epochal peculiarities, and all the philosophical shortcomings of the layperson in Fyodorov's work, we are left with a recognisable core: human beings have always existed at the mercy of nature, as if tossed among its raging forces, hurled this way and that, battered and beaten by its reckless ways. Disease, famine, storms and floods have ever determined the quality and extent of human lives. Millions upon millions have died in childhood, millions of mothers perished in childbirth, man's lifespan has been short, and life itself filled with pain and suffering. Fyodorov's message to us was that it doesn't have to be like that. Mankind is life, nature is death, but man thinks and reasons, man invents, man is not blind but *may assume control of nature*. And in the hundred years or so that have passed since Fyodorov himself died, this is indeed the path we have taken. We have assumed control of nature. We can clone animals, we can modify genetic material so that plants become more robust and more suited to our needs, we can replace failing organs and body parts with new ones, we have wiped out diseases and illnesses, and we have extended our lifespan by several decades. Throughout the world, research is conducted into the human genome and the processes of ageing, our insights into what causes us to age, and what we can do to stop it, accumulate year by year. And while we cannot yet revive our ancestors, we will surely soon be able to clone them.

Another cause championed by Fyodorov was the struggle against gravity. In his article 'Falling worlds and the being that counteracts the fall', he writes: 'Under "falling stars" we mean to include all the worlds, from cosmic dust particles and bolides to the largest planets and suns, which seem unmoving, but in actuality are also falling, differing only in the time and manner of their fall. Nature is an aggregate of falling stars (or worlds), whose slow falling is taken for stability. The falling of the world is thus taken for the state of the world, world destruction for world order! But falling is connected with death and dying . . .' Fyodorov conceived the use of a massive configuration of so-called 'aerostats' that like lightning rods could capture the sun's energy and utilise it to nudge the earth from its celestial course, releasing it from the bonds of gravity and recasting the planet in the form of 'a great electric boat', allowing us in effect to steer it wherever we wished as we sailed through the cosmos.

Again: What a thought!

Yet its premise is anything but far-fetched, Fyodorov was well aware that man has always striven against the gravital force, from the time when he raised himself from a four-legged, horizontal orientation to a two-legged, vertical posture, to our own age with all its upreaching monuments and edifices, its houses, bridges, churches and skyscrapers. The horizontal is the realm of the beast, nature, death; it is the corpse in its grave. The vertical belongs to man. 'Man's vertical position itself is already a counteraction to falling. All construction erected by man, all architecture and sculpture are expressions of that same act of arising, of an intellectual or a material (aerostat) lifting up,' he writes.

Because of these ideas of interplanetary travel and the colonisation of outer space, notions that predate by far the invention of the aeroplane, Fyodorov has been hailed as the seminal figure of Russian cosmism, considered by some to be the founding father of the Russian space programme. By dint of his work as a librarian, it is a documented fact that Fyodorov met the celebrated rocket scientist and pioneer of astronautic theory, Konstantin Tsiolkovsky, the formalist literary critic Viktor Shklovsky even claiming in his memoirs that Fyodorov was

Tsiolkovsky's mentor. Tsiolkovsky, in his later years an eccentric who shunned all company, derived from his theories the equation that allowed him to perform practically all the calculations necessary to send rockets into space flight, his work influencing greatly the Soviet engineers and rocket designers Korolyov and Glushko, masterminds of the Sputnik programme that was to send the first human into space: Gagarin, the greatest Soviet hero of all. But then, in 1957, all mention of Fyodorov's name, any reference to his philosophy, became forbidden in the Soviet Union.

In an interview, Tsiolkovsky described his first meeting with Fyodorov at the Rumyantsev Library thus (he was sixteen years old and newly arrived in Moscow):

It happened on one of my first visits. I dropped in and here's what I saw: a dozen or so people, mostly students, were crowding around the librarian. I was shy. I stood there waiting for the librarian to get free. I had time to look him over: a bald head, around it white curls sprinkled with grey, coal-black eyebrows and surprisingly young eyes. He looked about fifty, but he had youthful movements — quick and sharp.

When the last student had left, the librarian noticed me and motioned for me to come to him. Apparently, I looked nervous, because he smiled encouragingly. If you could only have seen his smile! It changed him and brightened him up at once. It was so affable and open, the way a father smiles at a son, or one brother at another. But this was the first time he had seen me. I was immediately filled with affection for him, and, having forgotten my earlier shyness, walked up to him. He cheerfully asked:

'What do you want to read?'

'Give me, if you can, *The History of the Peasant War*.'

'That book is forbidden.'

'Please speak a little louder — I don't hear well.'

'The book is for-bid-den!'

The words sounded so harsh, as if to say: 'See here now, with the kinds of readers we have — give out forbidden books indeed!' But his eyes were merry and smiling. Still, I hadn't been around

people much and didn't know what to say. He went off somewhere, quickly returned, and handed me a book. I asked:
    'What's this?'
    The History of the Peasant War.
    'But isn't this book forbidden?'
    'Take it!'

From that day on, Tsiolkovsky visited Fyodorov almost daily and
would later refer to the library as his university. I like this anecdote
very much, not only because it connects Fyodorov to Gagarin in such
a way that the heroic cosmonaut emerges as it were from the feverish
worlds of Dostoevsky, Tolstoy and Solovyov, but also because it gives
us such a very different picture of Fyodorov than what may be gleaned
when reading his own writings. In his own work he is brazen, aggressive, monomaniacal, derisive, his thinking often short-sighted and
riddled with prejudgement, a recurring failure to distinguish between
mythical and actual realities, with no trace of self-insight, a man
whose sights are fixed in one direction only. Herein, of course, lies the
originality. To read Fyodorov is like watching a man break loose from
his chains only to discover that he remains in his dungeon. Or, put differently: Fyodorov is like a character in a novel by Dostoevsky. But
outside the writing: generous, accommodating, sympathetic, insight-
ful, warm-hearted. Once, Tsiolkovsky appeared at the library in a coat
too light for the cold weather, Fyodorov told him he had some spare
money all of a sudden and took him out to buy him a new one more
suited to winter. As a young man Fyodorov had worked as a teacher in
several small villages, the pay was a pittance and yet he gave his earn-
ings away. When the father of one of his pupils fell sick, Fyodorov
used up all his money to pay for a doctor. Later, when the man died,
Fyodorov sold his teacher's uniform to cover the burial costs. Returning to the school in his own shabby clothing, he was reprimanded by
the school inspector who demanded an immediate explanation. Yet
Fyodorov refused to provide one. Such stories about him abound, and
resonate too in the way he passed: the Moscow winter that year was
particularly severe and his friends managed to persuade him to invest
in a warm overcoat and to start taking a cab rather than walking to

work; yet, despite following their good advice, he contracted pneumonia and died.

We carry our death within us. Fyodorov's death came when he relin-
quished his strict ideals in favour of a sudden luxury. His thoughts
were perhaps not entirely his own, but came from all corners, most, if
not all, were ancient indeed — but he shaped them into an arrowhead
he then shot into the future.

Into this present now, where his arrow quivers still.

I once saw a demonstration on one of the squares in Moscow. It was a
grey Saturday in November. Perhaps sixty people were assembled there.
Some held up placards and I went over to see what they were protesting
against. AGE IS A DISEASE, one of them said. DOWN WITH DEATH,
said another. The people passing by shook their heads, some laughed
and pointed. I did neither, but lingered, immensely curious. Who were
these people? What kind of belief could bring them out in protest
against death?

A woman began to speak through a megaphone. She said ageing was
the biggest problem of all faced by society and that the authorities were
not taking it seriously. She said it was possible to put an end to death
and that doing so ought to be the foremost task of government. Once it
was achieved, it would furthermore be possible to resurrect the dead.
Soon, we would have the technology to do so. Animals had already
been cloned, and there was no longer any obstacle to humans being
cloned too. We didn't have to submit to getting old, we didn't have to
submit to dying.

Why did I not shake my head, why did I not laugh and point, as
other passers-by were doing?

The world is full of conceptions, full of theories, ideas, models of
explanation, flights of imagination. Some we accept and make our
own, the rest we discard.

What is it that prompts us to accept one explanatory model and discard another? What prompts us to say yes to one theory, no to another?

In this particular instance the answer is simple. I once had a baby
brother who died, and I would have given anything — *anything at all* —
to get him back.

Of course I knew that what was said that afternoon was absurd, just as I knew that the Church's notion of resurrection too was absurd.

But the tiny, microscopic possibility that it just *might* be feasible, even though every part of me told me it was not, turned those ideas into allies of mine.

Because it might *indeed* be feasible.

God might exist, and to an existing God nothing was impossible.

Yes, such was my frame of mind at the time. Perhaps I was disposed to such ideas, knowing they were untrue, knowing it was the comfort they provided that made me embrace them, even though I never believed in them.

Might I concede that after that those thoughts began to occupy me as a phenomenon?

That they were the reason I started going to church, the reason I began to delve into Fyodorov and cosmism, the reason I started reading up too, after a while, on the research into extending life and arresting ageing that is conducted now across the world, though especially in the USA?

The music, the incense, the chanting, the icons and the vestments bring forth feelings in us that we have no idea we even contained, and they uplift us. The Orthodox service erases the boundary between the worldly and the Divine, suddenly the Divine embraces us in the worldly realm, and the exceeding of that boundary, one might think, or more accurately *feel*, is akin to moving from death to life.

In the case that one has been attentive to one's feelings for a while without anything happening, one may be inclined to turn things around and seek progression not from the worldly to the Divine, but from the Divine to the worldly — this is the dissection of the miracle, the wrestling from nature of its secrets, it is physics, chemistry, biology. And in this domain it is not feelings that are set asway, as in the Church, but life's tangible matter.

Nothing can bring my brother back, I know that. But his death is alive. It lives in me. And the insight that came to me that grey afternoon on a city square in Moscow was that this pertains not only to me, but to all of us, and is our cruel condition: all who live, live with the deaths of us all. And then we die.

Why not rise up against it? Why not crush death, that great oppressor? Why not organise a revolution of life? Why not let our dead be the last to be dead, and from now on become the eternally living?

Yes, I know: impossible.

But what if it isn't?

There exists only a single image of Nikolai Fyodorov, a drawing by the artist Leonid Pasternak (father of Boris). Apparently, he just happened to be at the library and was so intrigued by one of its reading-room staff that he began discreetly to sketch him. However, when the old man realised what he was doing and sent him a look of reproach, Pasternak retreated behind a stack of books, glancing only infrequently at Fyodorov while continuing what he was doing in secret. The surviving sketch shows an old, high-browed man with a full beard, surrounded by books at his desk, his eyes seemingly gazing inwards. The sketch was later used as the basis for Pasternak's portrait of Fyodorov, Tolstoy and Solovyov together at the same library. In it, Fyodorov's gaze is directed towards Tolstoy and is brighter now, no longer turned inwards, while Solovyov, considerably younger than the two elderly, white-bearded men — indeed, with his own dark beard, his impressive black mane and piercing dark eyes he is a handsome man, something that could never have been levelled at either Fyodorov or Tolstoy — rests his arm on a pile of books and likewise has his attention fixed on Tolstoy. It is an unmistakably Russian painting, one that could never have been produced anywhere else. Exactly wherein that Russianness consists, however, I have no idea. There are many portraits of Tolstoy, Repin painted him on a number of occasions, seated at his frugal desk in his peasant garb, ploughing a field behind a team of horses in his peasant garb; there are many photographs of him too, and several minutes of film footage. From the funeral procession in November 1910, a few seconds: a great crowd in a field, fog hanging in the background, the forest dark behind a muddy earth. A coffin carried aloft by arms outstretched, like a small boat in a human sea. The mood is charged, as if with bridled violence. These images are not unmistakably Russian in the same way as Pasternak's painting. The clothing, the faces and the quality of the film suggest to us the early twentieth century, though not necessarily Russia. If, as I have done, one has given time to reading novels, poetry, letters and essays from that period, these twenty or so seconds of moving images are a veritable shock of reality. Reading, or beholding a work of art, is all about thoughts and conceptions, even letters of correspondence concerning the most prosaic of matters, for the simple reason that we translate words into pictures, and where do those pictures come from? They are created out of our existing conceptions and slot neatly into their schemata. Reading Sofia Tolstoy's words about her rushing from the house and jumping into the pond after reading her husband's letter of farewell, I picture a woman in a white crinoline dress come running from a manor house into the moonlit open and without pausing continue her flight to a rather shallow fishpond into which she throws herself forward, landing face down in the water while lights go on in the house behind her and people in nightshirts appear and come dashing to her aid. In other words, I read her diary entry as if it were a scene in a novel, and nothing in Sofia Tolstoy's brief account can correct it. Any correction is up to me. This may occur by way of gaining more information — by looking at photographs of her and of the house in which she lived, finding out what kind of clothes she wore, the identities of those who helped her, perhaps even by going to Yasnaya Polyana and seeing the place with my own eyes — yet the series of events she describes will still be confined to my imagination, and no matter how finely calibrated my imagination may be, what happened will of course never break through the page into our present reality. Sofia Tolstoy's account of her husband's funeral, which took place three days after his death, leaves almost everything to the imagination: 'Back in Yasnaya. Crowds of people at Zaseka. We lowered the coffin on to the station and they came to pay their last respects. Masses of young people and delegations. They all followed the coffin from Zaseka to Yasnaya Polyana. We buried Lev Nikolaevich.' The twenty seconds of moving images of the same event require less imagination, the degree of detail being that much greater, the sense of being there likewise magnified, hence the shock of reality to which they give rise. But still we are not *there*. It is a place to which we can never travel, a lost land.

Now, returning to Pasternak's painting, the occasion it depicts never occurred in the real world, Pastnerak was never in the same room at the same time as Fyodorov, Tolstoy and Solovyov. The imaginary nature of the situation raises the question of why Pasternak would bring these three men together, and the answer, which has to do with their being such important figures, directs our attention to what they stood for, more than to who they were, and as such we are led into the realm of ideas. Moreover, all three are portrayed with clearly iconic features, which is to say that the figures are more than their faces, representative of something more than themselves. What could that be? The Russian idea? The Russian spirit? One of the three believed in resurrection and eternal life in the human domain, achieved with the aid of science, a second believed in resurrection and eternal life as part of God's plan for mankind, the third wished to live the simple life of the earthly Jesus. All three were deeply reactionary, albeit in widely differing ways, and two of them — Fyodorov and Tolstoy — moreover entertained the most radical and utopian of ideas. They lived in the Russia of the Tsars, in what was, in every respect, a turbulent and violent age, and all three died before the Revolution, but what they represented, and what Pasternak depicted, lived on, assuming other forms, wearing other masks. We may hold up their ideas, but not the lives they led, in which those ideas were conceived and unfolded. And now we are on treacherous ground, for it is easy indeed to believe that our ideas are representatives of our lives, the shadows of history that may be brought forth by the imagination representatives of reality.

In a cupboard in my parents' home are two shoeboxes of letters, postcards and photographs, relics of life, left by ancestors and relatives of mine. A few postcards from European cities and Black Sea holiday resorts in the decades before the Revolution, photographs of people outdoors, in gardens, picnics in the countryside. Letters from husband to wife, wife to husband, during various periods of absence, descriptions of children and the stuff of day-to-day lives, expressions of love and longing, some passionate, some less so. One or two came from the front during the Second World War, where my father was a medic and his younger brother, a lieutenant, perished. And then there are letters from someone who has always been talked about in my family as being different in some regards, Alexei, who in the 1920s was a young journalist in Moscow, later the author of two blockbuster novels. All these mementos are of course in one way or another bound up with the great events of their time — revolution, civil war, world war, the Soviet Union's growth and demise, the purges, the prison camps, the oppression, the food shortages, the ban on travel, the censorship — the history occasionally making itself known, though most often only in glimpses, such events and states of affairs being to the people in these letters and photographs not history but circumstance, the set of conditions under which life took place. History writing seeks out the junctures and points where those conditions came to prevail, the centres of power from where their ramifications radiated out to impact ordinary lives to a greater or lesser extent depending on how far away they were from the epicentre. The Kremlin, and the edicts and decrees that issued from it: the Soviet Union. Pasternak's depiction of Fyodorov, Tolstoy and Solovyov: Russia. Both worlds are gone now, approachable only by way of ideas and conceptions (which of course have never been real, not now, not then) — and although the latter was old and the former not only new but also established by the overthrowing and annihilation of the latter in the most violent ways imaginable, the two were nevertheless enmeshed. For the young Soviet Union, in the feverish, quivering decade that ran from Bolshevik victory in the civil war in 1921 to Stalin's first purges in the early 1930s, was obsessed with scientific experiment on the border between life and death, pushing and occasionally exceeding it in a baroquish exploration of bodies, cells, tissue, blood. The aim was to extend life and thereby counteract death. This may appear strange to us insofar as resurrection and eternal life were so closely tied to religion, which the Bolsheviks shunned more than almost anything else, and yet it is logical: without the soul, man is but body and mind, and the totally new beginning for which communism stood, in which all the old institutions and structures were to be torn down and new ones risen in their place, was completely dependent on reason and planning, and that same mindset, its enormous, thrusting optimism and materialism, was applied quite naturally to the body as well. The following passage by Leo Trotsky is illuminating:

Man at last will begin to harmonise himself in earnest. He will make it his business to achieve beauty by giving the movement of his own limbs the utmost precision, purposefulness and economy in his work, his walk and his play. He will try to master first the semiconscious and then the subconscious processes in his own organism, such as breathing, the circulation of the blood, digestion, reproduction, and, within necessary limits, he will try to subordinate them to the control of reason and will. Even purely physiologic life will become subject to collective experiments. The human species, the coagulated *Homo sapiens*, will once more enter into a state of radical transformation, and, in his own hands, will become an object of the most complicated methods of artificial selection and psycho-physical training [. . .] Man will make it his purpose to master his own feelings, to raise his instincts to the height of consciousness, to make them transparent, to extend the wires of his will into hidden recesses, and thereby to raise himself to a new plane, to create a higher social biologic type, or, if you please, a superman.

Scientists became engineers of the flesh and experimental biology the new frontier of enquiry. In 1925, for instance, a series of public lectures took place at Moscow's Polytechnic Museum under the title 'The Problem of Life and Death', audiences numbered some two thousand at a time and the speakers, an ichthyologist by the name of Petr Shmidt and the surgeon Fedor Andreev, delivered talks on the most recent scientific advances in the field, taking in themes such as 'apparent death', 'suspended life', 'revival' and 'resurrection of isolated organs taken from cadavers'. Some months later, during a lecture to a congress of pathologists in Moscow, a young doctor named Sergei Briukhonenko demonstrated an apparatus he had constructed to keep alive the severed heads of laboratory animals. He had already succeeded in keeping one such head alive for one hour and forty minutes before it ceased to exhibit reflexes. The following spring, in May of 1926, at a congress of physiologists in Leningrad, Briukhonenko presented further results. An article suggests he kept a dog alive for two hours after its heart and lungs had been removed. In another experiment a year later, a dog's head remained alive for twenty-four hours. A number of photographs of these experiments may be found. The dog's head lies on a metal plate, the eyes are open, giving it a rather unsettling appearance, for the head is without body, attached to a machine from which all manner of wires and tubes extend about a metal container only slightly larger than a Thermos flask. Blood from the head is extracted with the aid of an electric pump and led through a system of rubber tubing into a vessel where it is oxygenated and warmed slightly before being pumped back into the head. Briukh-onenko's experiments were a sensation in the Soviet Union and news of them soon reached abroad, British scientist John Bernal considering them to be a first step on the way to human immortality.

Other researchers experimented with anabiosis, the revival of animals and insects in suspended animation after having been either frozen or desiccated. A Bulgarian-based Russian biologist, Porfiry Bakhmet'ev, was the first to note the strange phenomenon that frozen insects returned to life when warmed up again. The freezing of the bodily fluids of course halted all blood circulation, respiration and metabolism, so the insects were clinically dead, and yet not, since all these processes were resumed as soon as the body temperature was returned to normal. Could the same thing be done with warm-blooded animals, or even people? Could they too be frozen, perhaps for years, perhaps hundreds of years, then to be revived? This was the question Bakhmet'ev posed. He performed the same experiment with a bat, reducing its body temperature from 26.4 degrees Celsius to minus 4. When subsequently he put the creature out on a table to thaw, it was utterly lifeless and as hard as stone. Within five minutes it began to breathe, and before long its behaviour was exactly as before. Bakhmet'ev's research was furthered in the Soviet Union itself, notably by Petr Shmidt, who experimented with desiccation rather than freezing. He succeeded in drying out earthworms, which could shed up to seventy-three per cent of the water in their bodies — sixty-one per cent of their total body weight — and then be revived forty-eight hours later if during that time they were frozen too. In 1923, Shmidt published a book on the subject, *Anabiosis (The Phenomenon of Revival)*, towards the end of which he broaches the possibilities of desiccating and deep-freezing humans. 'Of course, so far this is only a dream that, though possibly realisable, would require long and consistent labours,' he wrote.

Another, related phenomenon in the 1920s' Soviet Union was the research conducted into rejuvenation and the extension of life through experiments with hormones, gland transplantation and blood transfusion. Following the work of the Austrian physiologist Eugen Steinach who had transplanted the testes of young rats to older individuals with remarkable results — weak, hairless, impotent individuals would be transformed, now strong, hirsute and virile — gonadal transplantations were performed on cockerels, guinea pigs, dogs and humans in Moscow. Working at Tver, Leonid Voskresenskii performed thirteen transplantations of testicles from human to human — and would no doubt have carried out more such experiments had willing donors been easier to find — and while results varied, he nonetheless recommended his operations as a means of rejuvenation. Krementsov writes that such procedures were later performed in humans at Petrograd, Kharkov, Smolensk, Baku, Kazan, Tashkent, Omsk, Arkhangelsk, Tbilisi, Irkutsk and Odessa, biologists experimenting similarly with horses, dogs, rabbits, rats, guinea pigs, cockerels and cats.

Rejuvenation by means of blood transfusion, older individuals receiving the blood of younger ones, are also a part of this picture. The Moscow Institute of Blood Transfusion was founded in 1926 under the directorship of Alexander Bogdanov. Bogdanov was a social economist, physician, teacher, writer, philosopher, and for a long time a leading light of the Bolshevik movement — as is well known, he vied with Lenin for the leadership, only to be ostracised and then expelled a few short years before the Revolution. Bogdanov was the unflappable revolutionary, the level-headed utopianist whose egalitarian conscience was of such abundance it compelled him to challenge the power-hungry Lenin's elitist centralisation strategy, prophetically realising not only that it would end in disaster, but also how. Bogdanov was arrested, though not for long, and was soon at liberty to concern himself with other matters: he pursued now the study of blood transfusion, a notion that had absorbed him since before the turn of the century. In a science-fiction novel he published in 1908 under the title *Red Star*, set in a utopian communist state on Mars, members of the collective there are rejuvenated by means of regular blood transfusions. 'Immortality Day', a short story from 1912, describes a future society in which cities no longer exist, thanks to the ease and availability of air travel and a

device called the *spectrotelephone* that connects homes with the wider
society and shows images on a glass screen, allowing people to enjoy
the songs of performing artists, theatre shows, political speeches or
simply conversations with friends. More importantly for present
purposes, everyone is young and sustains eternal youth, due to a physi-
ological immunity formula injected into the blood. The story is set one
thousand years to the day since this great breakthrough took place and
humans became immortal.

Bogdanov's primary philosophical work was the three-volume *Tektology: Universal Organization Science*, published between 1913 and 1922.
Here, Bogdanov construes the world in terms of its various organisa-
tional elements, from the level of the atom to the social sphere. One of
its chapters is entitled 'Tektology of the Struggle Against Old Age' and
deals with the transfusion of blood and lymph as a means of delaying
the body's ageing processes. Or more precisely: the *exchange* of blood
and lymph. Bogdanov found blood transfusion in itself to be limited in
all its unidirectionality; what he truly believed in were the potentiali-
ties that lay in mutual exchange and the blending of blood, a form of
biological socialism as it were, the blood of young and old being
exchanged and blended to the advantage of both. He considered too the
issue of the inheritance of acquired characteristics, which is to say
whether worldly experience could be transfused from one life to
another, believing that the blood or lymph would be the medium by
which such characteristics would be carried towards the new cells.

Bogdanov's contemporaries were long deaf to his ideas about the
potentials of blood transfusion, and after twenty years, in 1917, he
writes in an essay that he has decided to undertake experiments himself. With the help of a few sympathetic doctors he arranges almost a
dozen blood transfusions. The results were encouraging: 'Out of eleven
participants in the first experiments (four seniors, seven young
people — some of whom were subjected to the procedure more than
once), approximately ten reported an increased sense of vitality and
energy. The most consistent influence was on the nervous system — we
observed a marked boost in productivity and improvement in overall
well-being.'

Bogdanov, then, was eminently qualified to head Moscow's new transfusion institute. Only two years after his appointment, however, he died when the blood of a student infected with malaria was given to him in a transfusion experiment.

We carry our death within us. Bogdanov's was a result of his idealism, which was overarching, though always grounded in its practical orientation. Indeed, it was this unflagging belief in the utility of his ideas that eventually cost him his life, for if the notion was pure, that blood should flow between us all, young and old, men and women, to keep the processes of ageing at bay, the blood that ran in his own veins was tainted and carried with it his demise.

Bogdanov's body would not be embalmed like that of his former friend and fellow revolutionary Lenin. His brain was sent to Moscow's Brain Research Institute for investigation and preservation, but now, nearly a hundred years on, the thoughts it produced are advancing and gaining traction.

That the idea of immortality should become revitalised in the Soviet Union of the 1920s is perhaps hardly surprising: the country had emerged out of a violent and brutal civil war that had cost millions their lives, as well as a catastrophic new famine that ravaged the Volga region, far worse than the one in which Tolstoy engaged himself, with reports even of cannibalism, citizens feeding on the dead flesh of their fellow humans. In such times, life is cheapened, while its physical nature is brought to the fore, and this physical, bodily aspect, the severed limbs, the broken chests and skulls, the blood that streams from them, will overshadow everything else in human life, which more than ever before will be construed as little more than a destructible biological construction — and therefore one that may also be repaired, perhaps even improved. In addition, of course, comes the cause that was fought for: a total overhaul of society that would utterly eradicate the order of old; no more a society that had developed gradually through hundreds of years, but one that was planned from the outset, stained with blood, but also charged with hope and visions of the future. Why does it have to be like this, just because it's always been like this? The idea that such a thought could apply not only to societies but also to human beings themselves became tantalising. Why accept ageing?

Why accept death? These were ideas that did not come sweeping into currency in the manner of those that sought to radically reconstruct society, there was nothing unified about them, they existed as it were in small pockets — some worked with glands, some with blood, some with dogs' heads, some with freezing and desiccation, while alongside them ran small networks of artists, philosophers and poets, who came together to present manifestos for the times, against death, against ageing, clarion calls in the name of eternal life. They knew of Fyodorov, but were not his disciples, they had their own agenda. Alexander Svyatogor, founder along with the poet Aleksandr Yaroslavsky of biocosmism under the slogan 'Immortalism and Interplanetarianism', published journals and lectured on themes such as eugenics, anabiosis and rejuvenation, part of a nascent movement that spread to Kharkov, Pskov, Kiev, Omsk and Irkutsk, counting among its members such poets as Grozin, Anist, Ivanitsky, Zikeev, Degtyarev and Lidin. In a declaration, they claimed 'the right to exist for ever, and the right to unimpeded movement throughout interplanetary space', while Yaroslavsky penned his 'Poem of Anabiosis'. They were revolutionaries for whom the struggle against nature and death was a logical extension of the Revolution's struggle to overthrow bourgeois society. As Svyatogor stated: 'The struggle for social justice leads necessarily to the struggle against death'. Unlike Fyodorov, the biocosmists were individualists, wholly uninterested in the 'dust of the fathers'. Svyatogor was deported to one of Stalin's labour camps in 1937, where he perished like so many other Russian immortalist thinkers and prophets of eternal life of that time, among them Valerian Muravyov, who in the 1920s had been a diplomat of the Soviet foreign commissariat and in 1924 published a book under the title *Control Over Time*, also concerning the notion of conquering death, and much inspired by Einstein's relativity theory, before being sent to his death in the 1930s. But their thoughts died not, living on unheeded until surfacing once more in the 1990s after the Soviet Union's demise, since when they have remained in plain sight. In 2012, the Longevity Party was founded in Moscow, its supporters considering the extension of life to be a human right, the party committing to fight politically for scientific development in the field. The most central figure in this movement is Mikhail Batin, perhaps the most prominent of all Russia's transhumanists. His vision is a world without ageing, and he says this: 'When we think about tackling ageing, we find ourselves between the world of uncertainty and the world of endless tools and possibilities. The next step is to choose which of these tools we can use. However, before we begin trying to change the world for the better, before we create a world without illness or suffering, we must first answer one question: who is this "we" exactly? We all have different capabilities and skills. Who exactly will tackle the issue of longevity? If we don't decide on the "we", this issue will remain in the realm of ideas and good intentions.' For Batin, it's all a question of organisation, coordination — individuals or individual organisations on their own won't hack it. No single talent or initiative would ever be big enough. But together, collectively, we enter the realm of the doable. This is Fyodorov's idea, but unlike Fyodorov Batin inhabits a world whose science can clone cells, organs, whole bodies, and edit DNA, a world in which microbiology, genetic engineering and epigenetics have made such inroads that we can now extend the lives of mice, for instance, by thirty per cent. Our insights into the mechanisms that govern our ageing are increasing by the day, and as Batin says, no one doing serious work in the field has any doubt that life extension is possible. And if life extension is possible, immortality should be too. What's needed in order to achieve it is a major lift, financially to begin with, but also in the form of a shift in public opinion and mentality. What Batin calls the 'Great Wall of Death' is something all of us, sooner or later, will encounter, and the idea of overcoming it runs against all our traditions, rituals and stereotypical behaviours. As he says, it's easier to take the familiar beaten path of death than to struggle against it. It's not a question of faith, because it's already possible — it's a question of attitude. And financing. The absence of any major government-backed programme to counteract ageing and put an end to death is down to lack of vision, while the work proceeds elsewhere, for example in Silicon Valley, whose tech billionaires and the companies they run have begun to engage in the science. The foundation set up and run by Peter Thiel, PayPal founder and the world's fourth-wealthiest individual, is investing heavily in life extension and artificial intelligence, Thiel himself regularly has young people's blood transfused into his veins at a Californian clinic in order to stay young, while Google has invested billions in Calico, a biotech company whose aim is to combat ageing and advance life extension. Batin estimates it will take ten years before we see any kind of megaproject emerge in the form of a private, non-commercially financed research programme, and another ten for the first results to be extracted from the big data. Which takes us forward to somewhere between 2040 and 2045 — coinciding with forecasts of the possible emergence of a strong AI, Batin says.

Another Russian eternal-life pioneer is the neuropsychologist Timour Shchoukine, who in 2011 partnered Dmitry Itskov in launching the Russia 2045 movement to promote ideas about radical life extension as well as to lobby the Russian government into adopting the project of constructing artificial bodies. Their aim is to transplant human brains into robotic bodies by 2045. One step towards that goal is the transplantation of a brain into a living body. Shchoukine has involved Aleksandr Kaplan in this work, a professor of biology who headed the division of neurophysiology and neurointerfaces at Moscow State University. This was the same institute to which Briukhonenko belonged, he who cut the throats of dogs and kept their heads alive in the 1920s. Mikhail Batin too believes in brain transplants as an alternative, alongside artificial blood and the cyborgisation of organs. 'We would get rid of half of the problems if we learned to artificially deliver oxygen and nutrients to the brain. I think a head transplant, or rather a body transplant, is a good alternative. There is a rather important stage here: the maintenance of the vital activity of the head of a large mammal outside the body [. . .] A simpler step is the exchange of circulatory systems between animals, so that the heart of one pumps blood for another. I wonder what would happen if these animals were clones.' Asked if he sees such experiments as unethical, Batin replies: 'If we make the value of human life absolute, then inaction, missed opportunities to prolong life, becomes the true evil. Religious figures often hide behind talk about bioethics in order to slow down progress. Just look at the ban on human cloning. Naturally, we should not clone a person if we are not sure that the clone will be healthy. But to prohibit cloning because of the assumption that a clone will not possess a soul is going too far.'

The most important single doctrine of Christianity, at least in Russian Orthodox Christianity, is the Resurrection of Christ. The apostles saw the resurrected Christ with their own eyes: Thomas even poked a finger into his wounds, satisfying himself thereby of the corporeal nature of his Lord's return. In subsequent centuries, the story of Jesus's bodily resurrection has been central to Christian belief, which since that time has spread to all corners of the world. But that belief followed another, which was that all people would one day be raised from death, not merely in a spiritual sense, but physically: your body, although it has lain and rotted through hundreds of years, will be revived on Judgement Day and be restored to its former state. Augustine of Hippo, who struggled with Platonic impulses in Christianity, made his views crystal clear on this point, in his writings about how exactly such resurrection would take place — for instance in what form an unborn child that died in the womb would be raised into life, or what would happen in the case of people whose limbs had been torn off and devoured by beasts. All would be resurrected, not necessarily into the body as it had been at death, but as it had been at the peak of its development, or as it would have been had it been allowed to reach that point.

In classical Judaism too, the notion of resurrection was a central belief. The Tanakh contains but small mention of it, though the Book of Ezekiel has the following passage:

The hand of the Lord was upon me, and carried me out in the spirit of the Lord, and set me down in the midst of the valley which was full of bones, and caused me to pass by them round about: and, behold, there were very many in the open valley; and, lo, they were very dry. And he said unto me, Son of man, can these bones live? And I answered, O Lord God, thou knowest. Again he said unto me, Prophesy upon these bones, and say unto them, O ye dry bones, hear the word of the Lord. Thus saith the Lord God unto these bones; Behold, I will cause breath to enter into you, and ye shall live: And I will lay sinews upon you, and will bring up flesh upon you, and cover you with skin, and put breath in you, and ye shall live; and ye shall know that I am the Lord. So I prophesied as I was commanded: and as I prophesied, there was a noise, and behold a shaking, and the bones came together, bone to his bone. And when I beheld, lo, the sinews and the flesh came up upon them, and the skin covered them above, but there was no breath in them. Then said he unto me, Prophesy unto the wind, prophesy, Son of man, and say to the wind, Thus saith the Lord God; Come from the four winds, O breath, and breathe upon these slain, that they may live. So I prophesied as he commanded me, and the breath came into them, and they lived, and stood up upon their feet, an exceeding great army. Then he said unto me, Son of man, these bones are the whole house of Israel: behold, they say, Our bones are dried, and our hope is lost: we are cut off for our parts. Therefore prophesy and say unto them, Thus saith the Lord God; Behold, O my people, I will open your graves, and cause you to come up out of your graves, and bring you to the land of Israel. And ye shall know that I am the Lord, when I have opened your graves, O my people, and brought you up out of your graves.

Perhaps it's precisely because of the Resurrection of Christ that resurrection as a trope has nevertheless been so downplayed or is ambivalent in Jewish faith. As important and influential a figure as Maimonides, who worked in the twelfth century in what today is Spain, became embroiled in a major controversy on the resurrection of the dead, which was accorded a rather unclear position in his philosophy. Maimonides ignored the body, it was the spirit that mattered to him, and although he explicitly stated in his writings that he believed in bodily resurrection, almost everything else he wrote contradicted the standpoint, hence the controversy.

His students saw the Resurrection as an allegory. Rabbis closer to our time, such as Abba Hillel Silver, held that resurrection of the dead was a late and degraded development in Jewish thought, borrowed from neighbouring cultures. Yet there are many traces of belief in resurrection in ancient Jewish texts outside the Tanakh, for instance in the Amidah, the core prayer of the Jewish liturgy, which includes the words: 'You are the one who revives the dead.' The prayer is to be recited three times each weekday, four or five on holy days. Nineteenth-century translations began to modify its text, and a near-seamless shift occurred, highlighting the spiritual aspect at the expense of the physical. Something similar occurs in the Christian faith, where the Day of Judgement and resurrection of the dead become increasingly downplayed, the concrete issues relating to it, so hotly debated in the Middle Ages, now completely absent. Eternal life sounds indeed so very vague and spiritual, relatable not to the muscle of the heart, the pressure of the blood, the lungs, the liver, the hair and the nails, but to the soul, which cannot be concretised either, such that everything, the entire core of the faith, dissolves into nothing, or at best a pearly and indistinct light. In Jewish writings of the late nineteenth and early twentieth centuries, one detects a sense of shame over belief in bodily resurrection, as if there were something immensely primitive and perhaps rather infantile about it. This is so, of course, because the world and our culture within it have become rational: we live and have lived now for a long time in an age governed by the paradigm of science, in which all that contradicts rational thought is gradually expelled. Thus, religion has issues with miracles and with the resurrection of the body, and elects to tone them down and attach weight to other aspects of divinity instead. What is paradoxical about this, fantastic even, is that belief in resurrection and eternal life then reappear in the world of science! Religion has become too rational to sustain it, but the conception would seem to be too important to us to be allowed to vanish out of our culture, and so it seeps forth again, albeit in a new form, pertaining no longer to notions of the Divine, but on the contrary to the rational itself.

It was in this very schism that Fyodorov operated: he was ridiculed for shifting resurrection and eternal life from God's domain into the human, but now, some hundred and twenty years on, hardly a trace remains of such ideas in Christian faith, whereas science teems with them. Scientists today do not venture as far as Fyodorov — his idea of bringing together the parts of rotting corpses, identical with Augustine's own conception, is still too wild, too irrational, too steeped in religion for anyone but a few fanatics to take seriously — but their vision, of fully commanding the body and nature, conquering disease, discovering the causes of ageing and counteracting them, extending life so that one day we may live for ever, is something they share with Fyodorov. And why not? one might ask. No law of nature stands in the way. It *is* feasible. We know of other organisms that can live for hundreds of years, some even for thousands. They consist of cells containing DNA, the same as us.

*

But the new can never get away from the old, never shake it off or run away from it, it will be there always, like a shadow. It's not just death we carry within us, but the past, too. Never has that appeared clearer to me than when I visited a premises belonging to RusKryonic on the way out to Samara earlier this autumn. RusKryonic is a company that preserves human and animal corpses in cryotanks filled with liquid gases at temperatures down to minus 250 degrees Celsius. Their website had an appealingly modern design, and the woman I spoke to on the phone was courteous, obliging and professional. I didn't want them to know I was planning to write about them, so I told them my mother was terminally ill and that she wanted to . . . That was all I said, but the woman, whose name, if I'm not mistaken, was Anna, seemed used to such matters being difficult to air. At any rate, she told me immediately that she understood, and when I asked if it would be possible to view the facilities, she was most accommodating, and I booked an appointment for the following day.

That night, the first snow fell, and when I woke up everything was white. It felt like a good sign. Apart from weekly outings to do my shopping, I hadn't been among other people in almost two months, and as always when I've been on my own for such a long perod of time, it was as if my surroundings positively screamed. People on the platform screamed, their clothes screamed, the trains that came in and out screamed. The pigeons underneath the roof screamed, the hatch of the kiosk was a mouth that screamed. It was all so unpleasant, almost like when you're ill with a fever and your skin can't bear to be touched by even the flimsiest cloth. I sat down in my seat, took out a book and read all the way in to Moscow. There, I changed trains, seemingly acclimatised, for the world felt like a milder place, near and more benevolent. The premises I was visiting were quite far away in the outlying sprawl south of Moscow. I imagined a modern, lab-like facility with lots of glass, plush carpeting and sliding doors. But it was very different, an abandoned farm on a bare patch of land. The buildings were run-down, the spaces in between them littered with barrels and scrap, a rusting tractor, probably fifty years old, some car tyres, while hens stalked about, a dozen at least, pecking in the debris.

A small, snazzy black Peugeot that was parked there stood out, and I guessed it belonged to the woman I'd spoken to on the phone. Sure enough, the door opened and she got out, smartly dressed for business, she could have been an estate agent.

We shook hands and she led me into the shed where the tanks were. Oh my word.

Big and metallic they stood in the great, empty, dusty shed where straw could still be seen on the floor.

'The premises themselves may be a bit low-tech,' she said with a smile. 'But the technology itself is cutting edge. That's the important part.'

She told me about the liquid gases and the minus 250 degrees.

'How many . . . are there in each?' I asked.

'Eight to twelve bodies. They're stored in suspension, upside down. We can arrange cryofreezing of the brain only, as a cheaper alternative. We have a few of those. And a number of pets, too.'

'How . . .'

'Your mother would have to sign an agreement. We have our own medical section to take care of all the practicalities once death has occurred.'

I walked around one of the tanks and looked up at the top. It was hard to believe there were dead bodies suspended inside its metal casing.

'The liquid gas preserves the bodies for ever. For all time,' she said.

'May I take some photos to show to my mother?'

'You may, but I wouldn't advise it. She might find the reality of it disconcerting, you understand. We do have some brochures you can take with you, that would probably be better.'

'Yes,' I said.

On the train back into the city, I couldn't let go of the thought of those dead people hanging upside down in a shed on the outskirts of Moscow, in that frozen environment, nor that they would continue to hang there, unless someone intervened, for all eternity. It was as if they were floating in outer space. Yes, that made sense. Space was black and cold and eternal. Space was death. Fyodorov had coupled them as well, outer space and the dead, but he had coupled them wrongly. Aitmatov hadn't. He too had put them together. That long day when Yedigei rides his camel through the desert, heading a small procession comprising an excavator, a tractor and a lorry, in which lies the body of his best friend. They are to bury him at a cemetery in the sand. The journey is filled with recollections, arguments, grief and despair. When at last they arrive, they find the cemetery closed, fenced off now inside a designated military area, a rocket base. They must bury Yedigei's friend elsewhere, in a deep grave dug by the excavator, placed with his head towards Mecca as prayers are spoken. Then, a number of rockets are launched into space. I think Aitmatov's novel is about life never really being modern, but always new. And that the death we carry within us, which Rilke compares to a fruit, grows inside us until ripe, and is in other words alive, belonging to life itself. Death in thought is death without life, it is cosmos, it is eternity, it is nothing. Our death is something.

I slept in my own apartment that night, gripped by a fear I hadn't known in a long time. The next day, I went out to the university to meet a friend who is a biologist there in the hope that she could provide me with some more detailed information about the research that is conducted all around her every day, concerning identification of the cellular processes that have to do with ageing. We talked about Rilke and I was suddenly put in mind of something Marina Tsvetaeva wrote about him in an essay of hers, which may carry this book by its nape:

However much you feed a wolf, it always looks to the forest.
We are all wolves of the dense forest of Eternity.

SYVERT

As always when I went up the escalator and saw Gardermoen's great departure hall loom above me in all its light-coloured wood, its glass and steel, it struck me how magnificent a place it was now. Flooded with sunlight, and so high-ceilinged it made all the people in it look small, like in a cathedral.

Who would have thought it, after all that noise about fog and Hurum and Fornebu, not forgetting that furniture dealer from Jessheim with all his lobbying against the site?

What was his name again?

Nesset?

No, that was the serial killer. The care worker. Arnfinn Nesset. He was from Orkdal, not Jessheim.

But what was the furniture dealer called?

I paused, put my bag and cabin case down, got my phone out and googled it.

Arvid *Engen*. That was him, yes.

I opened the camera app, tapped to switch to the front-facing camera, grinned and took a photo before texting Lisa and attaching it just to annoy her a bit.

Off to Moscow now. Where was it you were going again?

She replied straight away, a middle-finger emoji, no text.

Birkeland? I typed. *Or was it Øyestad? Lots of excitement there!*

She didn't react, but had probably smiled. She hadn't wanted to come anyway, always the stay-at-home.

The sky outside was sheer blue, the trees beyond the car parks lush green. The air trembled above the asphalt like petrol fumes. I'd been avoiding the heat all day, the air conditioner on full in the car, and not until I crossed the car park did I feel it bearing down on everything, while the asphalt was soft under my feet. The news sites I checked showed people splashing about in fountains in cities across Europe.

Being from the Sørland, there was hardly anything I liked better than hot, lazy days of summer. And today was one of the hottest yet. A day for the beach, cool dips in the sea, a wafting breeze.

I checked the weather in Moscow: 35 degrees, blazing sun all day.

No chance of seeing the sea there! It would be like an oven, in the middle of the plains.

I picked up my case and bag and scanned the departure board to find out the gate. It was right at the other end. Hardly a surprise, it probably wasn't the most popular route.

I was only going to be away three days, so all I had was hand luggage, and I was so early that there were only two people in front of me when I joined the queue to check in and get my boarding pass.

The sight of the Aeroflot sign made a shiver go through me with all its associations: the Soviet Union, Brezhnev, Gorbachev, Chernobyl, Red Square, the Russian bear. Not to mention Putin's Russia.

And Dad, too. He must have flown with Aeroflot. Or Aeroflop as witty souls had dubbed it then.

Was there a flight from Moscow to Fornebu in those days?

There couldn't have been. The Soviet Union was hermetically sealed.

Maybe he'd flown from Berlin or some other city on the continent.

Or taken the train?

It was terrible really, how could I know so little about him?

A couple in their late sixties or thereabouts stepped up to the desk. The man lifted the first of their heavy suitcases onto the conveyor and put two passports down on the counter. He was kitted out for the journey in a pair of beige chinos, a pale blue shirt with white stripes and a white cardigan. All either brand new or just washed, the cardigan so glaring you almost needed sunglasses just to look at him.

She'd stepped aside so as not to get in his way as he grappled with their luggage, and was dressed too young in tight jeans and a lightweight grey coat.

Dad would have been over eighty now.

But it was impossible to imagine that he could be alive. His life was completed, and complete in itself, it couldn't have contained any more than it did. What more *could* it have contained? Forty more years of what?

If there was one thing I'd understood, it was that. A life is always complete in itself, always whole, no matter how long or short. Joar had once tried explaining to me that infinity wasn't just infinity, there were different degrees of infinity. He said it had to do with set theory. I hadn't a clue what he was talking about, surely infinity was unbounded, so how could there be different kinds, with different extensions? Exactly the opposite applied to life, it had occurred to me afterwards. Life was finite, not infinite, but even if it was bounded in time, time didn't determine its boundaries — every life was complete in itself, none more complete than another.

It wasn't something I went around talking about. Thoughts that in the mind could be so revelatory, and feel so momentous, became so tiny and inconsequential as soon as I tried to put them into words. The only person I mentioned it to was Lisa. She, so grounded in all life's aspects, argued that I was wrong. I couldn't seriously believe that the life of a stillborn infant was as complete as that of an old person who had died full of years, she held. But that was exactly what I meant. Put into words it sounded absurd, but instinctively I knew it was right.

The service agent handed the passports back to the man in front of me, the couple's boarding passes tucked between the pages, before leaning over and tagging their cases. As they turned to go, the man gave me a nod.

'Russia, is it?' he said. 'You are Norwegian, aren't you?'

I nodded.

'Ellen and I are off on a river cruise on the Volga,' he said in a lilting Stavanger dialect, glancing down for a second to slip the passports into his pocket.

'Sounds good.'

'Yes, doesn't it just!' he said, beaming. 'Not exactly Gran Canaria! We'll see you on the plane, no doubt. Bye for now!'

'Yes, bye for now,' I said and stepped up to the counter with my passport already opened at the ID page.

'It is me,' I said, as the service agent studied first the photo, then me. 'The photo's from a bit of a down period. I think I may have had a depression at the time. Hence the beard.'

He said nothing, but turned to the visa page as if I hadn't spoken to him, then after a moment ran the passport through the reader, typed something on the keyboard, turned to the printer next to him, and the boarding pass slid out into his hand.

'Luggage?' he said, closing the passport around the boarding pass and handing it over without even looking at me.

'None. Travelling light, as the Brits say. Thanks a lot!'

He was efficient, I'd give him that much, his every movement impeccably smooth and practised, but surely the only reason he was there instead of a robot was to give the check-in process a human touch?

It didn't matter.

Passing through security, I bumped into the couple from Stavanger again. He was gathering their things together at the end of the conveyor, while she stood passively by and watched him as before.

'Staying in Moscow, are you?' he said, threading his belt back through the loops of his trousers while I stood waiting for my tray to come through.

'That's right.'

'Been there before?'

'No, first time.'

'Same here,' he said, just as the ringtone sounded from my phone, the riff from 'Enter Sandman'. I stepped over to the conveyor and located the phone where it lay vibrating with the display lit up, next to my Mac in one of the trays that was on its way along the conveyor. It was Jarle, I saw right away as I picked up the tray and took it over to one of the little tables to answer his call.

'Yes?'

'A small problem here. Vidar's taken ill and had to go home. Sander's off sick as well.'

'And?'

'We're short-handed, basically. We've got three funerals tomorrow, and if they can't come in, there's no way we can cope. The nursing homes are keeping us busy in this heat as it is.'

'Can't you run down the list and find someone?'

'Done that. No one's available.'

'How about Lillesand? I'm sure they'll lend us someone in a crisis.'

'Already asked them. Nothing doing, I'm afraid.'

'Rubbish. Let me give them a call myself.'

'Thanks. One more thing, though. A bigger problem, actually.'

'Come on, Jarle. How long have you been left in charge? Five hours?'

'There's a mors gone missing.'

'What do you mean, gone missing?'

'It came in yesterday. I was just about to prepare it, only it was gone.'

I sighed.

'Who brought it in?'

'Vidar did. He swears he put it in the cold room. And now it's not there. We've got the family coming in two hours.'

'It can't have gone off on its own. Have you checked the vehicle? Maybe Vidar forgot to take it out.'

'I'll do that.'

'What about the others? Have you mentioned it to them?'

'Only to Helge and Brita. They knew nothing about it.'

'Check the hearse. Check with everyone, someone's bound to know something. If you're still none the wiser, get on the phone to the family and postpone the viewing. OK?'

'OK, thanks a lot.'

I ended the call. Jarle wasn't the sharpest knife in the drawer, but he was capable enough and would always put in a shift, he could empathise and knew how to behave, and I'd always been able to trust him.

Now maybe I'd have to think again about that, I told myself, heading for a quiet corner where there weren't so many people, to phone Erling in Lillesand. His mobile was switched off, so I called the main number instead.

'Remembrance Funeral Homes, Elin Bjelland speaking.'

'Hello, Elin. Syvert here. Listen, I can't get through to Erling. Do you know where he is?'

'He's in a meeting at the moment. Shall I ask him to call you back?'

'No, I'm just about to catch a flight. You can give him a message, though. We're two pairs of hands short for tomorrow. Can you get him to send someone over? Two, preferably. I know it's short notice, only it's an emergency. Can you do that for me?'

'Will do. Are you going somewhere nice?'

'Are you flirting with the boss now?'

'No, of course not! I was just wondering, that's all.'

I could almost hear her blush.

'Only joking,' I said with a laugh. 'I'm going to Moscow. Back in three days. Say hello to everyone.'

I went over to the newsagent's and bought a couple of newspapers, *Dagens Næringsliv* and *Klassekampen*, before going over to sit down at the nearest cafe with a coffee and a pastry. For some reason I'd always liked checking the share prices in the printed newspaper rather than online. Maybe it was something to do with keeping the excitement the few moments it took to scan the page. Not that it mattered, the shares I'd invested in barely moved anyway. But checking them still gave me a sense of satisfaction. They'd earned me more than the funeral homes. Which was all right by me, getting rich out of burying the dead would feel wrong somehow. Earning a living, that was OK. But not accumulating wealth, not on the backs of the dead.

I read *Klassekampen* to keep abreast with what the loony left were up to, what opinions Lisa would be likely to hold about this and that.

We'd learned what not to talk about, though sometimes we clashed anyway, and she could get so angry with me she often wouldn't speak to me for a day or two.

You're so stubborn, you're so blinkered, you're so rigid, it's unbelievable, she could almost yell at me when things got going. *I can't stand it! Do you know what I mean? I can't stand it!*

No, I could say then. *I don't know what you mean. We've got differing views. Nothing wrong with that.*

My composure would get her even more riled.

But it's my opinion! It's not just words!

And what I say is my opinion.

That's just it! How can you have an opinion like that? It's completely beyond me.

I liked the way she was still idealistic after all these years. I just wished she could like the way I still wasn't.

I looked up at the big departure board that hung suspended from the ceiling in the middle of the hall, though my flight wasn't for another three hours.

Only then did I realise I'd gone through into the area for domestic flights. But I wasn't going to Bergen or Trondheim or Tromsø, I was going to Moscow, for God's sake!

I folded my newspapers and put them in my bag, got to my feet, drained my coffee and meandered towards the doors at the other end, scanned my boarding pass and was let through with a little beep. I thought I might as well sit somewhere close to the gate, so I looked around to see which way to go. Everything was less familiar to me here. The restaurants, the shops, the cafes and bars were as if unanchored, scattered about at random, but then after I'd walked about a bit, everything mapped out again: the tax-free shopping, the row of eating places, the shops, the aisles leading this way and that, more shops, more eating places.

I sat down at one, bought myself a pint and sent Lisa a text.

Can you call me when you've got a minute? The flight's not for another three hours.

She answered straight away.

Do you miss me, or are you just bored?

Miss you, of course, I typed back. *We've been apart more than seven hours!*

Counting the hours, how sweet! I'm in my meeting now, call you when there's a break.

I sat and people-watched for a while as I drank my beer. Then I phoned Jarle.

'What's the score?' I said. 'Have you found it yet?'

'Yes, all sorted. A misunderstanding, that's all. It wasn't our fault. The body had to go for post-mortem. Sander had taken it over last night and forgotten to tell anyone.'

'Post-mortem? What for?'

'Died alone in his flat. The doctor was a bit inexperienced, didn't really know what she was doing, so the mors got sent straight to the hospital, where we picked it up. Only then she realised it should have been sent for post-mortem. I think it was her father who told her. He's a doctor too, apparently.'

'I see,' I said. 'What a botch. But you postponed the viewing?'

'Yes.'

'OK. All's well that ends well.'

I bought another pint and attended to some emails to pass the time. I was still hoping the kids would ring and wish me a good trip, or at least text me. But they had their own lives, and not being that interested in mine was only natural, and probably a good thing. It didn't bother me that they would ask me for money, apart from when Astrid especially would phone for a cosy chat, buttering me up before calling again a couple of days later to casually ask for a handout. How funny that she didn't realise I saw right through her! On the other hand, it demonstrated that she at least had a modicum of decency, even if it was only for show.

No, the kids were great, all of them.

The fact that I had an unknown sister in Russia obviously meant less to them than me. And they'd never met Dad, so his clandestine relationship with a woman over there was no more than a story to them. The Soviet Union was something they'd only heard about, something that had existed in a time before they were born, and they would never really be able to understand what it was, what kind of shadow it had thrown over our lives.

The evil empire, Reagan had called it.

My phone came to life, 'Enter Sandman' again. Some people at the tables nearby looked up. Maybe it was a bit loud, that ringtone, I thought to myself, and turned the volume down before taking the call.

'Hi,' said Lisa. 'Are you in departures now?'

'Yes,' I said. 'Chilling with a beer.'

'Sounds good. Is it busy?'

'It could be a lot worse. Where are you?'

'Having a smoke outside.'

'Outside where?'

'The hospital in Arendal, where else?'

'That's right, I'd forgotten that was where you were going.'

'Obviously.'

'How's your meeting?'

'It's OK. Not exactly thrilling. Plus it's so bloody hot. It's almost scary. I can't remember it ever being as hot as this.'

'The summer of 1982, do you remember? Twenty-six degrees.'

'Twenty-six degrees is nothing.'

'That was the *water* temperature. Do you remember that summer, though? How old were you then? I was fifteen, so you'd have been thirteen.'

'No, I can't remember it. I hardly remember anything from when I was that age.'

'I remember being out in a sailing boat with a friend of mine. It's one of my very fondest memories, I think. There wasn't a sound from the boat, just the odd creak and the water against the side. We went ashore on one of the outlying islets. I'd never been there before. The sea was open in front of us. Calm as a millpond. And boiling hot!'

'Anyone would think you'd never told me before!' she said with a laugh.

'Maybe we should get a sailing boat?'

'I wouldn't mind.'

'Seriously?'

'If it'd make you happy.'

'I hadn't seen that coming,' I said.

A waiter came past clearing empty glasses from the tables. He took mine, too, and I managed to catch his eye and raise a finger in the air before he turned away with a nod.

'Anyway, I thought I was *always* happy,' I said.

She laughed again.

'Self-insight was never one of your strong points.'

'What do you mean?'

'What I said.'

Neither of us spoke for a moment. I heard her light another cigarette.

'Are you nervous?' she asked then, and sounded like she was catching her breath as she inhaled.

'About meeting my sister?'

'Yes.'

'No, not at all. I'm looking forward to it actually. It'll be interesting to see if there's any family resemblance, how much Løyning she's got in her. And of course I'm wondering what she might be able to tell me about my dad.'

'Have you got the letters with you?'

'Yes, they're in my bag.'

'I wonder what that'll be like for her? Rather a powerful experience, I imagine, letters like that from your own mother.'

'She's a grown woman. And unlike me she's always known about it.'

'Why wouldn't she send any photos of herself, do you think?'

'No idea. Maybe she looks like the Elephant Man.'

Another laugh.

'I'd best be getting back,' she said. 'The meeting's starting again in two minutes. But give me a ring when you get there.'

'I will.'

'Have a safe journey!'

We hung up and I leaned across to the table next to me, where a tall-looking woman with curly hair and ruddy cheeks was studying her phone while a little girl sat beside her, dangling her legs and chewing a croissant.

'Could you do me a favour and keep an eye on my luggage for a couple of minutes?'

'Yes, no problem,' she said, and smiled fleetingly.

Leaving the restaurant area, I saw the waiter approach my table with three pints on a tray. I waved to catch his attention and jabbed a finger at the table. He nodded and put one of them down, and I headed for the toilets.

My bladder function had deteriorated in the last couple of years, at least I suspected it had. I hardly ever needed to go before, not even when I was on the beer, but now I'd be bursting for a piss after only a couple of hours, sometimes I wasn't sure I'd even make it. I could find myself wondering if I had prostate cancer, but there was no history of it in the family, and I'd never seen traces of blood or anything, so I wasn't really that worried. Still, it was annoying, especially if it was a sign of ageing.

Mum had had cancer, but survived, tough as she was. She'd knocked back a heart attack as well.

I stepped up to the urinals in between two other men, both rather short, and pissed while staring at the wall in front of me. Pissing with other people was a bit like taking the lift, I thought. You couldn't say hello, couldn't talk to anyone, all you could do was stand there as if you were the only person in the world.

I washed my hands and dried them under one of the fierce dryers Pål had been so terribly scared of when he was little, ran a hand through my hair, which for a change I'd just had cut, and messed it up a bit before going back out again.

'Thanks,' I said to the woman as she glanced up at me.

'No problem,' she said.

'Are you travelling far?'

She hesitated a moment before answering, no doubt wondering what sort of intentions I had.

'We're going to London,' she said.

'Lovely city,' I said. 'On holiday?'

She shook her head.

'We live there,' she said, without looking at me. I took the hint, leaned back in my seat and sipped my beer, taking care then to look in every direction but hers.

The Moscow route wasn't exactly prioritised — not only were the check-in counters as far away from the entrance as you could get, the plane was parked way out on the apron, meaning we had to be bussed out there to board. The heat that greeted me as I stepped from the bus and made my way towards the steps of the aircraft felt almost solid, but I was never going to complain about hot weather the way some of the women I'd grown up with would do as soon as the first days of summer were upon us — despite having moaned all year about the cold winter and the rain in spring.

No, hot weather was good, hot weather was brilliant.

Not that there was anything wrong with cold weather. I liked that, too.

I'd asked for a seat right at the back, I always did if it was possible, it was an old habit from when I used to get the bus to school. I used to sit at the back of the classroom as well, come to think of it.

We'd boarded early, so there was still twenty minutes until departure after I'd put my case in the overhead locker and sat down in my seat. Twenty minutes of phone and internet connections.

Maybe I should text the kids after all?

It wouldn't be a sign of weakness, and I'd hardly be ingratiating myself either, if I sent them a text before going away.

Hi Pål, hope all's well! I'm off to Moscow now, as you know. Back in three days. I'll keep my phone on over there, so if you need me just call!

Or maybe it *was* a bit ingratiating?

I deleted the last sentence and typed another: *Enjoy the weather and say hello to June!* That was better. I sent it, then copied the text into two new ones, changing the names to Astrid and Cato in one and Tor and Åsne in the other before sending them too.

I leaned back in my seat and looked out at the tarmac that shimmered in the heat.

Lisa grew up further from the coast than me, so if I did buy a sailing boat, it'd most likely be my own project. But half the fun was in sharing the experience. Gliding along in stillness together.

Maybe she'd get hooked on it, if I could get her out on the water with me a few times.

You never knew.

I googled sailing boats for sale and scrolled down. A lot of nice ones there. Nice, but expensive.

A text message dropped down in front of the internet page. It was from Astrid.

Have a nice trip, Dad! And good luck! she wrote.

Bless her.

I should have bought that sailing boat when they'd still been kids. I could have taught them how to sail, we'd have had fun together. But we'd bought the cabin at Åmli instead. Forest and midges, lakes in summer, wet snow and fog in winter. Lisa liked it and I didn't mind, not that much anyway, but still we used the place less and less. Hardly ever at all now.

'Now there's a coincidence,' a voice said. I turned my head towards the aisle, where the man from Stavanger stood with a holdall and two carrier bags from the tax-free shop in one hand, the other gripping the handle of a cabin case.

'Hello,' I said. 'What coincidence would that be?'

'It turns out we're sitting next to the only person we've spoken to!'

'He did come across as rather methodical, the agent at the check-in desk,' I said. 'He'll have done everyone seat by seat and row by row, I imagine. We did check in at the same time.'

'But still!' he said, turning his attention to the overhead locker into which he crammed his two carrier bags before reaching a hand underneath the panel and pressing one of the buttons there. It gave a low-pitched chime that sounded through the whole aircraft. He smiled at me.

'Locker's full,' he said.

One of the cabin crew appeared, and he indicated the locker, threw his hands in the air and shrugged, a little pantomime.

'I think there's some space further forward,' the female attendant said in English. 'Just let me check.'

'I'll sit down while you sort it out,' he said in Norwegian, edging into the seat next to mine as she began to rearrange the contents of a locker a couple of rows in front.

I felt like telling him she probably expected him to lift his own case into the locker, but stopped myself. It was none of my business.

His wife, if that was who she was, sat down in the aisle seat.

'Moscow, you say?' he said.

'That's right,' I said.

'Business, is it?'

'No. A little getaway, that's all.'

He craned his neck to look at the flight attendant, who gave him a thumbs up, though with no indication that she was intending to store his luggage for him.

He beckoned to her.

'Could you help me with these, please?' he said, in English now. 'My back hurts, you see.'

'Of course,' she said, smiling stiffly before taking the two items and lifting them into the locker. She probably didn't believe him either, but what else could she do?

He clicked into his safety belt and made himself comfortable, an arm on each armrest. His wife put her hand on his. It looked out of place.

'So what line of work are you in?' he said, and turned his head to look at me.

It didn't normally bother me, telling people what I did. But in this case I didn't really want to. He looked like the judgemental sort, and we'd be sitting next to each other for three hours. A lot of people saw undertakers as unscrupulous shysters making money out of people dying, and I'd never, in almost forty years in the business, met anyone who actually found it an interesting or in any way worthwhile profession. It annoyed me, it was important work and I was good at it. The local paper had once referred to me as *the funeral magnate*. I'd phoned the editor straight away and told him he'd overstepped the mark. I owned four small funeral parlours in four small towns, and one bigger one in a bigger town. I employed a large number of staff and took out what by any standards was a modest salary. The paper's wording made it sound like I was running an empire. He understood, he told me, and apologised. It wasn't something that warranted a retraction, of course, but that wasn't the reason I'd phoned. All I'd wanted was to put him straight and make sure it didn't happen again. To make up for it, he offered me a profile interview, which I declined without hesitation. One bad experience with journalism was more than enough for me, and if there was one thing a funeral business needed to abstain from, it was publicity. Discretion was its first imperative.

'I work in the service industry,' I told the man from Stavanger. 'And you?' I added before he could ask me to elaborate.

'I was a science teacher,' he said. 'Many moons ago.'

'It's not *that* long ago,' his wife said.

'Secondary school?'

'No, gymnas.'

The aircraft started its pushback. I got my phone out to check my emails before take-off. Nothing important or even interesting, so I switched it off and put it away in my bag between my feet.

He'd been to university, then. Who'd have thought? He must have had a brain somewhere, after all.

'Do you know Stavanger?' he said.

'Quite well, yes.'

'I taught at Kongsgård, in the centre of town. Forty years. I can hardly go down the street without bumping into former students of mine.'

'I imagine not,' I said. 'It must be a good feeling, having left a mark

like that. There's nothing more important than education. It's a crying
shame teaching isn't better rewarded.'

'You said it there,' he said.

The tug that was pulling us out onto the tarmac had been uncoupled
and the aircraft began to taxi forward under its own power.

'What are you going to see in Moscow?' the woman said, leaning forward slightly to look at me as she spoke. 'We're staying there ourselves
to begin with, two days.'

'I haven't really decided yet,' I said. 'Red Square, of course. Lenin's
Mausoleum. Apart from that, I was thinking I'd just wander about.
Take it all in. How about you?'

'Ellen has an interest in art, so knowing her there'll be museums,' he
said. 'She dabbles a bit herself, as it happens. Her work's very good, if
you ask me.'

'No, no, it isn't at all,' she said, blushing at the same time as she
began to scratch her forearm. 'I'm very much the amateur.'

'We're not talking Rembrandt, that's not what I'm saying,' he said.
'But it's good work, nevertheless.'

He turned to me again.

'Sometimes it's like looking at a photograph, do you know what I
mean? I'm no art buff, but I know what's what. We've been to the Lou-
vre and that other place, in Florence, what's it called?'

He looked at her.

'The Uffizi,' she said.

'That's it, yes. Bit of a slog, that was. But you liked it, didn't you?'

'Oh yes, I loved it.'

'How about you?' he said. 'Do you know much about art?'

'Can't say I do,' I said. 'I'm more of a beer and football man, I think.'

'You don't say,' he said, his voice suddenly toneless and without
interest. His mind had switched to something else now, I sensed, and
his eyes, staring at the seat in front, began to gleam.

'I'm a philatelist myself. Been collecting since I was a boy.'

'Oh, really?' I said, sounding far too eager, his eyes now keener as he
fixed me with a gaze.

'Are you a philatelist, too?'

I shook my head.

'Only when I was a kid. I used to steam the stamps off the letters my parents got.'

'Yes, that's right.'

Neither of us said anything for a moment. I realised he was getting ready to tell me all about his collection, so I slid down into my seat and closed my eyes. I wasn't pretending that much either, the three pints I'd drunk had made me rather drowsy.

The aircraft came to a halt and the engines began to roar.

'I started collecting from all over the world,' he said.

I opened my eyes and sat up slightly again, nodding to indicate that I was listening. The pilot gave it full thrust and we hurtled along the runway, rattling and shaking, faster and faster.

'I found it so exciting with all those faraway places, foreign countries. Helvetia, do you remember? Switzerland, to us. I remember a blue stamp showing a train running along the side of a mountain and Helvetia written across the bottom. A whole world in a few square centimetres.'

The aircraft left the ground and rose obliquely into the sky before describing a wide arc towards what I supposed would be the east.

'It's no exaggeration to say I'd collected thousands of stamps before I was into my teens,' he went on. 'But there was no value in them, because there was no system. It wasn't a collection, you see. When I started at gymnas I joined the local philately club in Stavanger. That's where I found out what a collection was. I hadn't much money to speak of, but I started collecting properly then. I worked at a garden centre at the weekends and in the summer holidays, and everything I earned went into my collection. Well, not everything, of course, I did need money for other things, but most of it.'

'Not most,' his wife said. 'A third, perhaps.'

'Yes, all right,' he said. 'The point is, I built up a magnificent collection. Gold medal in Stavanger, bronze in Oslo. Do you know what I did with it?'

You sold it, you idiot, I guessed, but said nothing, continuing to look at him with feigned interest.

'I sold it! And do you know what I spent the money on?'

Stamps, I said to myself, and smiled.

'A stamp! *One* stamp!'

'Really?' I said. 'A rare one, I suppose?'

He said nothing for a second, but looked at me with eyes that scintillated with glee.

'A Soviet specimen from 1964. I first became aware of it because it features a Norwegian flag. Right there alongside the Soviet hammer and sickle are the Danish, Swedish and Norwegian flags. The pictorial shows a ship sailing on the sea. The script of course is Cyrillic.'

'How come it's so rare?'

'Well, I'll tell you. Nikita Khrushchev visited the Scandinavian countries that year, and so they printed a commemorative stamp — it's known by some as the "World Peace Cruise" stamp. Only they never issued it. Do you know why?'

'No, go on.'

'Khrushchev was given the boot shortly afterwards. So there's only a very few specimens left in the world, the rest were destroyed. And I've got one of them! Have a guess how much it cost me.'

'Give over, Odd-Einar,' the woman said.

'It's all right, he can take it,' he said, and lowered his voice. 'Two hundred thousand!'

'But it's worth more than that now, isn't it?' she couldn't help adding.

'I should certainly think so,' he said. 'So there you have it. I'm a stamp man. I won't be buying anything in Moscow, though, even if I will have a look.'

'Is it the Soviet Union you're collecting now, then?'

'The whole shebang. Tsarist Russia, Soviet Union, the Russian Federation.'

'And now we want to see the place for ourselves, don't we?' she said.

'We do,' he said.

We appeared to be approaching our cruising height, the aircraft was levelling out.

'I've had a very early start today,' I said. 'I think I'll have a snooze. But don't mind me! I always sleep like a log.'

'You do that,' he said.

'It'll be nice to be rested when we get there,' she said.

I twisted slightly away in my seat, so they wouldn't be able to see if my eyes were open or shut, and stared for a while at the landscape below, until eventually my eyelids closed of their own accord and I fell asleep.

When I woke up to the voice on the tannoy announcing that we'd started our descent into Moscow, it was with a feeling of disappointment. I'd been looking forward to seeing the Russian landscapes, the forests, the steppes, the rivers and cities, but now I'd slept through it all.

'Welcome to Russia,' said Odd-Einar as I sat up.

I didn't answer, but smiled faintly.

'We didn't know whether to wake you when the food came,' he said. 'But you were well away, so we thought it best not to.'

'Thanks,' I said, immediately feeling a pang of hunger.

The landscape below us was flat as far as the eye could see. Forested plains, drenched in sunlight. We were already flying at low altitude, so the airport could only be a matter of minutes away. I felt unprepared.

But what was there to prepare?

I'd go to the hotel, wander around for a bit, have dinner and then go to bed. Tomorrow I'd be meeting with Alevtina. We'd agreed to meet for lunch at her suggestion, but I was hoping we'd have more time together than that. Maybe she could show me the sights.

It was as if my heart stopped beating.

I had a sister. Dad's daughter. In Russia.

Of all places in the world.

What was she like?

I'd never met a Russian in all my life, only seen them on TV. They didn't have as much equality as we did, so I'd read. Everything was a lot more traditional.

Her emails had been a bit reserved. But it was only to be expected, we were writing in English, and the whole situation was weird, to say the least.

She probably thought the same.

Below, I could see cars now, making their way along a road, the shadows cast by the trees. So where was Moscow? It had to be here somewhere.

I craned to see through the window across the aisle, and there, a few kilometres away, dense, grey-white tower blocks. Almost certainly from the Soviet era.

A flight attendant came past, checking we'd got our safety belts on and mobile phones weren't in use.

'What hotel are you staying at?' said Odd-Einar.

'I can't remember what it's called,' I said. 'But it's near the Bolshoi Ballet.'

'Right in the heart,' he said. 'That must have set you back.'

'I've no idea what things cost here. I just went for something central and picked one out at random. What about you?'

'A place called the Aroma. It's a little way out.'

'It looks nice, though, and it was very reasonable,' said Ellen.

We were just above the trees now, and when the wheels touched the ground a few moments later, some passengers applauded. I did too, then reached down and got my phone out of my bag and switched it on. All around me, text messages pinged into other people's phones. Mine came on, but couldn't find a network, and as the plane taxied towards the gate, I tried to find one manually. I'd got the most expensive package from Telenor, so I wasn't expecting there to be a problem. But there was. As a new collective surge of activity went up around me, safety belts being clicked open as the plane came to a halt, I still had no connection.

Lisa was a nervous soul and she'd be worried sick if she didn't hear from me. She knew approximately what time I'd be landing, too.

Could I ask them if I could borrow theirs?

No, I didn't want to be indebted to them, I was looking forward to them disappearing into Moscow and never seeing them again.

Something could happen at work as well. I had to be available.

I switched it off again and dropped it into my inside pocket, leaning my head back to rest a minute before trying again. Sometimes that was all it took.

Odd-Einar and Ellen got up and moved down the aisle. He reached up and got their cases out of the locker. The Aeroflot seat had obviously worked wonders for his back.

I followed them out of the aircraft, coming up alongside them as we left the gangway and emerged into the terminal, then standing behind them at passport control. They were waiting for me after I got through.

'Enjoy your cruise,' I said. 'And have a lovely time in Moscow as well!'

'Thanks a lot,' said Odd-Einar. 'Don't you want to share a taxi, though? With three of us it won't cost much more than the bus.'

'No thanks,' I said. 'There's something I need to sort out first.'

'We're not in any hurry. We'll wait for you.'

'It's kind of you, really. But I'm afraid I can't.'

'We're going to different ends of the city,' said Ellen, touching her husband's hand.

'Well, it was nice meeting you, anyway,' he said. 'Perhaps we can swap photos at some point, if you give me your number?'

I threw out my hands.

'My phone's dead. I can't get a connection. But have a good holiday and we'll bump into each other again somewhere, I'm sure!'

With that, I gripped the handle of my cabin case, gave them a smile and walked off in the opposite direction. I didn't like giving them the cold shoulder, but they really hadn't given me much choice. I was sure they didn't believe what I'd said about my phone, which only made me feel worse, dishing up what was only a half-truth like that, but what else could I have done?

I followed the signs to some toilets, emptied my bladder and washed my hands before heading in the direction of the shops and eating places. The terminal looked like any other in Europe, apart from the strange lettering that was everywhere. It was hardly the standard of Gardermoen or Kastrup, but nowhere near as shabby as I'd been expecting.

I sat down on a bench and switched my phone on again.

Still no connection.

I wasn't bothered for my own sake, it was Lisa I was thinking about. And knowing she'd be worried was going to stress me out.

Wait a minute.

There'd be internet here at the airport. I could send her an email.

Or even better, I could FaceTime her. That worked over the internet, didn't it?

I opened my laptop and clicked Settings and then Wi-Fi. It turned out that all I had to do was connect up, there was nothing to fill in first, just immediate connection.

I sat up straight, found her number in my contacts and clicked the FaceTime icon. When it started to ring and the picture of me appeared on the screen, I shifted my position a bit so that she'd see the planes outside the windows.

She was sitting in a bikini top and shorts on the bed in the bedroom. She smiled.

'So you do FaceTime now, do you?' she said.

'Not really,' I said. 'It's just that I can't get my phone to work. And I wanted to let you know I've landed safely and that everything's all right. So far, at least!'

'That was nice of you.'

'What are you doing?'

'You can see what I'm doing. Trying to stay cool in the bedroom. It's boiling hot outside, I can't stand it. Thank God for air conditioning!'

'Remind me who it was who said we didn't need it.'

'Yes, I know. I can't be right *all* the time.'

Neither of us spoke, and she smiled at me again.

'Lovely to see you,' she said. 'I wasn't expecting to.'

'I love your tits,' I said.

'I'm sure you do, you old lech,' she said. She moved the camera phone to her breasts so they were all I could see.

'I loved them when I was a young lech, too,' I said.

She laughed and her face reappeared into view.

'You're not sorry you married me, then?'

'I didn't marry you, you married me. You married down, I married up.'

She got to her feet and went over to the big patio door.

'That's your version.'

'It was how it felt.'

'It wasn't how I felt.'

'A person has to get lucky sometime,' I said. 'Show me the view.'

She turned her phone again. There was the rock, sloping towards the sea, deep blue, the sky light blue above it.

'Aren't you having anyone over?' I said when she appeared again.

She shook her head.

'What are you having for dinner?'

'I think I'll skip it. It's no fun eating on my own.'

'You could go down and have a dip tonight.'

'I might.'

'I'll just eat at the hotel, I think. Not much fun either.'

I smiled, and she smiled back.

'Give me a ring tonight, then,' she said. 'If you FaceTime again, I might not have anything on.'

'It's hot enough here as it is,' I said. 'Moscow would burn down.'

'Ha ha. See you later.'

'Yes, see you,' I said, and ended the call.

I left it a while before going towards the exit, wandering around for a bit instead, then buying myself a burger with fries and a cola at a fast-food outlet and sitting down to eat. The ketchup sachet was hard to open, my fingers couldn't get any purchase, and when I squeezed it hard to see if it was going to give, the contents spurted onto my shirt. I wiped the ketchup off with the napkin, but the stain remained.

Typical, but because of the hot weather I'd packed several shirts, more than I'd normally have taken with me on such a short trip, so it wasn't that big a problem.

After I'd finished eating, I headed past the baggage carousels, all of them in use, though fortunately the Oslo flight looked to have been completed. I passed through customs into a small arrivals hall where a crowd of drivers held up signs with people's names on them, and went towards the exit, where a man, big and burly, with a pale, fleshy face, stood loitering and looked at me as I came towards him.

'Moscow city centre, sir?' he said in English.

Behind him, two more appeared, shorter in stature, one wearing glasses, dark-haired, his cheeks thick with stubble, while the other had a moustache and had pushed a pair of sunglasses up onto the top of his bald head.

'Moscow city centre, sir? Good price! Very good price!'

I smiled and shook my head as I went past them through the door.

The heat hit me.

The two men came after me. I didn't trust them and looked around
for something more legitimate, but couldn't see anything even resembling a proper taxi.

'How much?' I asked them.

'Good price!' one of them said.

'How much is that?'

'Good price.'

I saw the first man still standing calmly in the shade of the entrance
and went over to him.

'How much to the city centre?' I asked.

'Five thousand,' he said. 'Cash only.'

I had no idea how much that was. But he didn't know that, he'd have
given me a price on the asumption that I'd be reasonably clued up, so
on that basis it probably wasn't too extortionate.

'OK,' I said. 'But I've only got a card.'

'Cash machine inside.'

'Will you wait?'

'Of course. I take the luggage, you go.'

'No, no, it's only a small suitcase,' I said, and wheeled it after me into
the arrivals hall again, hanging my bag on the handle when I found the
cashpoint so I could wipe the sweat away that had started to run down
my forehead and cheeks.

I withdrew ten thousand to be on the safe side. He was standing
there as before when I came out again. Pale and solemn, in a white
shirt, slacks worn high around his waist. Not a drop of sweat on him.

'Follow me,' he said, leading me over to a row of cars close by. He
stopped at a white Mercedes, took my suitcase and put it in the boot.
Then, with a glance at my shirt, he stepped towards me, and, with a
gesture as intimate as it was unexpected, began to rub the ketchup
stain with his thumb.

'It's not going away,' I said. 'But thanks all the same.'

He nodded and stopped, smiled faintly and got in behind the wheel,
and soon we were heading away from the airport.

The road was wide and new, the asphalt quite black, and alongside
it buildings were under construction. Then, in what looked like the
middle of nowhere, a big shopping centre came into view with a giant

TV screen, on which, as we sped past, a female face loomed in close-up.

Shortly afterwards, the driver left the motorway and we turned onto a much narrower road that led us several kilometres through a built-up area. I wondered if he was taking me on a detour, but having agreed a fixed price I couldn't see how he'd gain anything by it.

With that small reassurance, I leaned back in the seat and looked out. Everything was different from back home, but not quite in the way I'd imagined. It all seemed so normal, despite the contrast. Fields with long, flattened grass, parched yellow here and there, in places almost white. Signage with Russian lettering. Old, unpainted shacks. A man in camouflage trousers watering a vegetable patch. The detached cabin of a lorry left on the ground next to a house. A small blue car with what looked like firewood piled on the roof, squeezed in between a rusting lorry bed and a sagging wooden shed. An old woman in a white head-scarf leaning on a fence, watching the traffic.

'Nice and cold, yes?' the driver said, glancing at me in the mirror.

'Yes, very nice,' I said.

Dad would have come along these roads, too. If not here exactly, then somewhere close by. To see the woman he was having an affair with. While Joar and I were at home.

Did he like it here? Or did he come just for her sake? And what sort of procedures did he have to go through to be allowed entry back then in the seventies?

I'd have to ask Alevtina about it. What it was like here at that time. How the authorities viewed visitors from the West. Wouldn't they have been under surveillance by the KGB?

How did that work when he was staying with her? Did their agents sit in a car outside?

Did he think about us then? Or was he too wrapped up in her while he was here?

I wonder what Syvert's doing now. Did he ever think such a thought, on his way into Moscow?

My own children were grown up now. But Joar and I had still been little kids at the time.

A large compound came into view up ahead on the left, surrounded by high fencing. Several towers loomed up from inside the perimeter with what looked like CCTV cameras mounted on them. I peered out of the window as we passed, and decided it was a prison. Then trees appeared on either side of the road, and everything plunged into shadow. As we emerged into glaring sunlight again a few moments later, the driver slowed down and turned off into a petrol station.

'I need gasoline,' he said. 'I'm sorry.'

'That's OK,' I said. 'As long as I don't have to pay for it!'

He glanced at me in the mirror, expressionless.

'Only joking,' I said.

He pulled up at the pumps and got out. I got out, too. Traffic rushed by on the road. The sun was perhaps even more scorching here on the plain. Flecks of dust danced in the still air. The sky was a relentless blue. I was parched, and went into the little shop while he filled up. The place was dark and stuffy. The items on sale had been put out haphazardly, everything was all over the place, like a jumble sale, nothing like the streamlined displays of service stations back home. But they had cola! I took a can from the battered old fridge, then another in case the driver wanted one. I noticed toy army helmets for kids, stacked up in a corner, and toy guns too, frisbees and those plastic cones we'd had when we were kids, where you press the trigger on the handle and try to catch the little ball that pops out.

The girl behind the counter sat idly chewing gum, watching my every movement. She was all puppy fat, probably not a day over fifteen.

I put the two cans down in front of her and pulled out a thousand-rouble note. Two small racks of chewing gum were stood on the counter. Gum for boys in one, gum for girls in the other.

'And a packet of gum for boys!' I said, taking a packet from the rack and putting it down next to my cans.

Maybe some biscuits, too?

'Just a moment,' I said, and went back to take a packet from the shelf next to the fridge. She deleted what she'd already entered into the till and started again without batting an eyelid.

Patient people, these Russians. Weren't they supposed to be temperamental?

The driver came in as I was going out. He held the door for me. I thanked him and opened one of the cans on my way over to the car, stopping to drain the contents almost in one go before tossing the empty can in the bin next to the pumps and getting back in.

'Do you want one?' I asked the driver when he came back.

He shook his head and held up a bottle of water.

'This is more healthy!' he said. 'But less good!'

He even smiled before turning the key in the ignition. I got my phone out to give it another go and see if I could find a network. This time I was more methodical, trying them all instead of just the first. And lo and behold, all of a sudden there was a connection and messages pinged in. From Pål: *Have a good trip*, simple and to the point. From Tor, a bit more effort: *Hi Dad, hope everything works out over there in Moscow. Enjoy yourself. All fine here. Åsne says hello!* Two from Lisa: *Have you landed?* and *Call me when you read this*. And one from Jarle at work: *Five more so far today. It's the heat. Have we got enough staff?*

I started typing a reply to him, but realised it wouldn't do: it wasn't a staff shortage that was the problem, it was his lack of confidence in himself. I called him instead.

'Just got your message, Jarle,' I said. 'Listen, all you need to do is stay calm. One thing at a time, all right? The care homes aren't a problem, they can hold on to their departed overnight, you know that.'

'But we've got three funerals on tomorrow. And the way things are going, there'll be more coming in. Not to mention the bereavement consultations.'

'Make a list of priorities and tick things off as you go along. The important thing is to keep a cool head. And remember, the bereaved are always your first concern.'

'OK,' he said. 'But I still think we're short-handed.'

'Have you heard from Sander and Vidar? Are you quite sure they can't come in?'

Ahead of us on the right, a clearing opened out in the trees. My eyes were drawn to it as we went past, it was like a small park with a big wall of granite in the middle, in front of which a flame burned, almost transparent in the sunlight.

'Sander's definitely not coming. I don't know about Vidar yet.'

'See if you can get hold of him,' I said. 'Tell him you're in a bind. He can't be *that* ill.'

'I think it's a stomach bug.'

'If that's all it is, tell him to go to the chemist's and take something for it. He should be able to drag himself in tomorrow.'

'I'll see what I can do.'

'And lean on some of the names on the standby list. Say it's critical, or they won't want to come in in this weather.'

'Will do,' he said. 'Are you in Moscow now, then?'

'On my way in from the airport.'

'Is it just as hot there?'

'Hotter. But listen, call me if you need me. I'm available any time.'

'OK, thanks.'

I ended the call and leaned forward.

'What was that on the right just now?' I said. 'The monument back there.'

'The Great Patriotic War,' the driver said without taking his eyes off the road.

'What was that, the Revolution?'

'No, no, no!' he said. 'No. The big war. Stalin.'

'Ah,' I said. 'World War Two.'

'You call it that, yes.'

I leaned back and opened the biscuits as quietly as I could, unsure of whether he'd care for crumbs in his Mercedes. I wondered if I should text the kids again. The best thing would be to send them some photos now and then. I could phone them when I got back.

Industrial estates began to appear, with storage facilities and light industry, and the road widened seamlessly into a dual carriageway. Tower blocks rose up on both sides, and soon we were cruising along a five-lane ring road, surrounded by traffic as we smoothed through the outlying suburbs, passing railway stations, shopping centres and dense housing developments.

We turned off and approached the centre of the city. Crossing a bridge, I saw an enormous skyscraper reaching up in the distance.

Moments later, we were driving along wide avenues lined with trees,
winding through narrower side streets, until without warning we
pulled in and stopped.

'Your hotel, sir,' the driver said.

As I counted out the money, a man in uniform opened my door.

'Welcome, sir,' he said.

'Thank you very much,' I said, handing the driver seven thousand.

'This is too much.'

'There's a tip included.'

'Thank you, sir,' he said, raising an index finger to his forehead in
salute.

Being called *sir* all the time made me uncomfortable, but I supposed
it was all just part of the package. I smiled at the driver and got out,
though a moment too late to prevent the porter picking up my case and
carrying it inside. Did that mean I'd have to give him a tip now? Not
that the money mattered, it was more the act itself, slipping a note into
his hand as if I was superior in some way.

And how much would he expect?

I followed him into the foyer, a grand, imposing space with a marble
floor, all glass and gleaming surfaces.

The only Russian word I knew, apart from *da* and *nyet*, was *spasiba*.
But I wasn't sure if it meant *thanks* or *please*. Or maybe even *hello*. There
were some words and phrases in the guidebook I'd brought with me,
and as I put my passport down on the counter I made a mental note to
have a look before I went out again. An elegantly dressed receptionist
who looked more like she worked in a perfume department, with long
eyelashes and green eyeshadow, came towards me with a big smile, her
eyes fixed on mine.

'Hello,' I said. 'I've booked a room here.'

She picked up my passport and opened it. Her long nails were
painted pink and a cloud of scent surrounded her.

'Welcome, Mr Løyning,' she said, and began right away to type my
details into her computer. 'You are staying for three nights, is that
correct?'

'That's right, yes,' I said.

What on earth had possessed me to book such a posh hotel?

In a surprisingly short time, the check-in formalities were completed. Room on the first floor, key card slipped into a little cardboard folder, breakfast between seven and eleven o'clock.

She smiled at me with lips closed and fixed me with a warm gaze again. I couldn't help but feel a flutter in my chest.

Turning away from the desk I scanned the foyer for the porter who'd taken my case. He wasn't there.

'Excuse me,' I said. The receptionist looked up. 'Do you know where my suitcase went?'

'It is in your room, sir. Enjoy your stay with us.'

At least I wouldn't have to give him a tip, I thought to myself as I went up the stairs, following the plushly carpeted corridor to my room.

It was luxurious, but fortunately on the small side, so I wouldn't have to feel quite so embarrassed. It was nice and cool, too.

I parted the heavy, dark yellow curtains to let some light in. The street outside, baking in the slanting sunlight, was deserted, only the odd car came slowly past. After a sleep, I opened the minibar and took out a beer and a bag of crisps, sat down on the bed and unfolded the map from the guidebook I dug out of my bag.

The hotel was indeed right next to the Bolshoi Ballet, which in turn was just across the road from Red Square. The restaurant where I was meeting Alevtina for lunch the next day was a bit further away.

Should I text her to say I'd arrived?

I'd added her details to my list of contacts in my phone, so I scrolled down to find her number.

Hello, sister! I typed. *Arrived in Moscow now and very much look forward to seeing you tomorrow! Syvert.*

I sent the message and then decided I'd have a shower, but seeing how big the bathtub was I took a bath instead, leaning back and lying immersed for some time with a beer in my hand as a sense of well-being spread through my body. Not that I'd been tense or anything, it was more fatigue, travelling was always more strenuous than I anticipated for some reason.

I heard my phone chime and supposed it to be Alevtina replying to my text. If it wasn't Jarle having another panic attack.

Almost six years passed from me sending my letter until she replied. I'd put it all behind me by then, so her email had come as something of a shock. A total shock, in fact. I'd been chopping vegetables for a fish soup, it was a Saturday and we were having Lisa's sister and her family round for dinner. Radio Sør was on in the background and I'd been checking the Premier League live scores, and now and then my inbox, too. And all of a sudden there was an email from a Russian sender.

It could only have been her.

I put the phone down and dropped the finely chopped onion into the pot with some butter. Lisa was sitting on the sofa with her glasses on the tip of her nose as she read through some documents.

'Everything all right over there?' she said.

'Yes, fine,' I said. 'Why wouldn't it be?'

'You stopped humming.'

'Just had to concentrate a moment,' I said. 'It has to have the right balance between butter and onions. Shall we open a bottle of wine?'

'Yes, let's.'

I opened the fridge and took out one of the two bottles of white I'd left to chill for a couple of hours.

'Haven't we got any red?' she asked.

'Yes, of course. Would you rather have red?'

'No, it's all right. White's fine.'

I opened the bottle, poured two glasses and took one over to her.

'There's something on your mind,' she said.

'Maybe,' I said, taking a sip. 'It's rather nice, this.'

I went over to the cooker again and added a good measure of the wine before filleting the fish and cutting it into chunks, then melted a big knob of butter in a saucepan along with some cream.

'I just got an email from Russia,' I said. 'That's what's on my mind.'

'What does it say?'

I gave a shrug.

'I haven't opened it yet. But it can only be from Asya or someone in her family. I don't know anyone else in Russia. Maybe she's died and they've found some letters or something. Who knows.'

'Wouldn't it be better to read it than guess?' she said.

'It would, yes, only it's thrown me a bit. I don't want to sit thinking about it over dinner either, really.'

'We could cancel?'

'No, no.'

I poured fish stock into the saucepan, added the vegetables — carrot, celery root, leek and fennel — and turned up the heat. Before it began to boil, I turned it down again to simmer, put the lid on and went to the bathroom, sat down on the toilet seat and opened the email.

Dear Syvert,

My name is Alevtina, and I believe you are my brother, that we have the same father. My mother Asya died twenty years ago, and the letter you sent her was received by my stepfather. He showed it to me, but I didn't have the strength to contact you then. I'm truly sorry about that. I would love to meet you, I really would. I have been thinking a lot about you and Joar and our father throughout the years. But when I grew up, my country was separated from the rest of the world, as you know, and in a way that separation also influenced my relation to you – you were distant, part of another world, forever out of reach, and later I never questioned that, strange as it might sound. Your letter moved me greatly, and I tried to write a reply many times, but in the end it was too hard. But now, dear unknown brother, I finally have! Please forgive me for not having done it before. And please be braver than me and write a reply soon!

Yours sincerely,

Alevtina Kotov

I cried when I read it, and for a long time afterwards. There were no thoughts in me then, only emotions and tears. I cried and cried. I had a sister. Dad had had a daughter.

Eventually, I stood up, breathed deeply a few times, splashed my face with cold water and was about to go back out when it all welled up in me again. I grabbed a towel and pressed it to my face until I was quite sure I'd stopped shaking. I splashed my face again, dabbed my eyes and cheeks dry, breathed deeply once more, and paused for a moment before deciding I was all right. Then I went back into the living room.

Lisa looked up at me as I came in.

'I've got a sister,' I said.

She took her glasses off, her mouth open.

'Seriously?'

'Yes,' I said.

'In Russia?'

'Yes.'

'So your father did have a child over there.'

'Yes.'

'Yikes,' she said.

'Yikes indeed,' I said.

She stood up and put her arms around me.

'How does it feel?' she said.

'I'm not sure,' I said. 'A bit crazy.'

'Stupid question.'

'No, not at all,' I said. 'Do you want some more wine?'

'Yes.'

I fetched the bottle and poured us some more. She sat down again.

'What does it say?'

'It says she got the letter I sent to her mother, only she couldn't muster what it would take to write back. She apologises for that.'

'*She* got the letter?'

'Yes. Asya died a long time ago.'

'She could at least have given word that she'd received it. It sounds a bit weird, if you ask me. All that time and you didn't know she existed! Your own sister.'

'She must have had her reasons,' I said. 'You can read what she's written, if you want.'

I handed her my phone and went to the kitchen, where I added the cream and butter and the chunks of fish.

'Do you want me to go with you?' said Lisa.

'Go where?'

'To Russia. You'll have to go and see her.'

'Will I?'

'Don't be silly. Of course you will.'

'I suppose you're right. You could come if you wanted.'

'No, actually I think you should meet her on your own at first. Then you can invite her to come and see us all over here.'

'I think I need to digest the whole thing first,' I said. 'Anyway, where's that sister of yours? The soup's almost ready now.'

I wrote back to her the next day, attaching a photo of me, Lisa and the kids down on the jetty the previous summer, along with an old one of Joar when he'd come to Astrid's confirmation. She replied straight away, telling me she had a son who was twenty-six and another only five, that she was originally a biologist and had taught at the university for a number of years, but had then retrained and was now a doctor and worked at a hospital. She didn't send any photos of herself or her children, but it was OK, I didn't want her to feel obliged just because I'd done so. We arranged to meet in Moscow.

And now I was here, only hours away from seeing her for the first time.

I still couldn't understand why I'd cried like that. Before then, I hadn't cried since I was a kid. I realised it wasn't to do with Alevtina as such — learning you'd got a sister at my age was nothing to cry about. But hearing from her out of the blue like that had dislodged something inside me and everything had come avalanching down.

It didn't take much self-insight to understand that.

I drained the last of my beer, put the bottle down on the floor next to the bath and leaned forward to remove the plug, only to find it stuck fast and unattached to any chain I could pull it up with. There was no other mechanism either, as far as I could see, so eventually I climbed out, dripping wet, and went and got the corkscrew from inside the room, prising the big metal plug out of the plughole so the water could run away. After drying myself and putting a pair of clean underpants on, I checked my phone. I was right, it was Alevtina, replying to my text.

Dear Syvert. Welcome to Moscow and enjoy your evening. I hope you like it here. I'm very much looking forward to seeing you tomorrow too. A xx

She seemed really nice, my sister.

I pictured her with dark hair and kind eyes, and quite without resemblance to anyone in my family. Even if I knew she shared Dad's genes and probably did look a bit like him, or a bit like me and Joar, it was impossible for me to imagine.

I put on a light blue short-sleeved shirt, my beige cotton trousers and my deck shoes without socks, put the key card in my wallet, slipped my wallet into my back pocket and left the room.

The uniformed porter was standing at the bottom of the stairs. He turned to face me and nodded. I went up to him.

'Thank you for your help with my suitcase,' I said as I pulled my wallet out. Of the three notes I had left, I handed him one. To my relief, he accepted it. He even gave a little bow.

The heat wasn't quite as stifling now, though the air was just as still as before and the sun hadn't yet gone down fully. Everything cast long shadows, including me.

The shops along the gently sloping street were the exclusive kind, many with French names. Clearly, this was where the wealthy did their shopping. At the bottom, I crossed over and followed a pedestrian street. It was busier there, but relaxed all the same, people ambling around, half of them seemingly with an ice cream in their hands.

Who would have thought it would be so pleasant here?

Normally, if anyone said Moscow, the first thing that came into my mind would be grey buildings, grey skies and queueing for food. Coming at it from another angle, I might have imagined an irrepressible, warm-hearted people who never said no to a vodka. Then there was the secret police and the surveillance of ordinary citizens. Censorship and oppression. It was a long list.

But being there in person, seeing it all with one's own eyes, was something else entirely.

Of course things could be good here too.

I stopped and got my phone out, opened the camera app and held my arm up to take a selfie with the street in the background.

The photo didn't do it justice, and so I looked around for someone who might oblige. A young couple, both with rucksacks on, were standing in front of a statue a bit further away. I went over to them.

'Hello,' I said. 'Do you think you could take a photo of me with my phone? It's for my family. If you could get the street in the picture too, that would be great. So they can see how nice it is here. My arms are too short!'

'Yes, of course,' the guy said, taking my phone as I held it out to him.

'If you stand there, maybe?'

He stepped back a bit and held the phone up in front of him.

'Take a few while you're at it.'

'OK,' he said.

'Thank you very much!' I said, when he handed it back. 'Where are you from?'

'Portugal,' he said, and for some reason looked at his girlfriend, who nodded.

'Lisbon,' she said.

'Do you like it here?'

'It's a very exciting city,' she said.

He asked me if I could read Russian.

'You must be joking!' I said.

'We were wondering who the statue is. Do you know?'

I looked up at it. A man hurrying along with a newspaper under his arm.

'No idea,' I said. 'All I can say is it's not Lenin or Stalin!'

They smiled and exchanged glances, and I sensed they wanted to go.

'Nice to meet you!' I said, and carried on up the street, stopping as I reached the top to look at the photos they'd taken. They were quite decent.

Moscow's answer to our Markens gate! I typed and sent them to all three, as well as to Lisa.

A bit further down, the street opened out into a wide avenue and the relaxed, convivial atmosphere evaporated. The buildings rose up tall on both sides, the traffic rattling along the road in front of them.

At the end of the avenue was what looked like a palace of some sort, resplendent in the light of the sinking sun.

Wow.

It was imposing, to say the least.

It could only be Red Square.

I followed the road down and came to a halt at a big, chaotic intersection where there wasn't a pedestrian crossing anywhere in sight. How were you supposed to get over to the other side?

I took some pictures of the palace in the sunset, even though sunset photos were never any good, and then realised that the stairs down to the metro station also led into an underpass. It was run-down and teeming with people with prams and bulging shopping bags. Two escalators slid into the depths, both attended by security guards. Moscow's metro stations were famed for their beauty, so I'd read, but this one could only have been the exception, unless the beauty made itself manifest further underground in the station proper.

I crossed through the open area on the other side, walking towards a double-arched gateway at the base of an ornate red building with twin spires. People were milling about there. A drone with a flashing blue light descended from the sky behind them. A man picked it up, lifted it above his head, and then, like a tame falcon, it took off again. Over by the wall a bit further along was a temporary-looking swimming pool from where music blared. Above it, I could hear a monotonous loudspeaker voice, and as I approached I saw a man standing at the entrance, speaking into a microphone he held in his hand. No one seemed to care what he was saying, people just streamed past, in and out of the big gate, where three soldiers stood staring vacantly straight ahead.

I went past them up a cobbled incline and emerged onto the square itself. It was big, but still smaller than I'd imagined. A high wall ran the length of it on one side, conspicuously red. Behind it lay the Kremlin, I knew that, where all the Soviet leaders had resided, and where Putin now reigned. Below the wall were some low, bricked terraces I assumed were for the great military parades I remembered from my childhood, columns of goose-stepping soldiers, rocket launchers, Brezhnev looking on, as motionless as if he were embalmed, until lifting a hand in a ponderous wave, revealing there to be life in him after all.

That Mathias Rust had been able to land a plane here was mind-boggling.

I walked slowly on towards the middle of the square. It all looked like something out of a fairy tale. A great church with colourful onion domes at one end, the palace at the other. The long, red wall.

How strange to think that Putin might be in there at that very moment, while I ambled about just outside.

Maybe he was having his dinner.

What would he be having today? Borscht?

I stopped and looked around. There was something strange about the mood here. What could it be? People posed and took photos of each other, smiling and laughing, pointing, chatting. Was it something to do with ordinary life going on so close to this centre of power?

No, that wasn't so strange.

And then I realised.

It was so quiet here. The ever-present rumble of traffic was almost absent. All I could hear were people, their sounds amplified by the cobblestones. Their footsteps, their conversation, their laughter, all lifted into the air, more sonorous than was usual in a big city.

I got my phone out and filmed the square from one end to the other.

No sooner had I slipped it back into my pocket than it chimed. It was Lisa.

Looks lovely! she wrote. *Call me before it gets late, OK?*

At Red Square now, I typed. *Smaller than on TV. Quite amazing. What are you doing?*

Watering the garden. Doing the washing.

OK. Call you after I've eaten. You OK?

Yes, fine. Speak to you soon.

She probably wasn't, I realised that. She didn't like being on her own. It was to do with when she'd been a kid and growing up. A father who'd left them, a mother who often wasn't there and couldn't be trusted.

She didn't introduce me to her mother until we'd been together a couple of months. I could tell she was ashamed of her and the way they lived.

She'd been very protective of her younger sister.

It had touched me, but it had been hard to deal with, too. She was extremely defensive when it came to her family, and words had to be carefully chosen, at least to begin with. The last thing she wanted was for people to feel sorry for her. Fortunately, I'd understood that from the start.

At the far end of the square, down by the fairy-tale church, a man in his late twenties was sittting on a bike that was all flashing lights and flags, smiling at a camera that had been set up on a tripod on the ground a bit further away. He kept changing his pose, then climbed down, fetched the camera and started showing the photos to

passers-by. He went back and set the camera up again and began jumping up and down, performing split leaps in the air, an unflinching,
wide smile stuck to his face.

I hadn't seen a grin like that in ages, it was just a shame he was an
idiot, I thought as I left the square at the opposite end from where I'd
come in. I was seriously hungry now, but the restaurants in the vicinity
would be expensive tourist traps, so I decided to carry on walking and
trawl the streets that were a bit further away.

The sun had just about gone down, peeping now to throw the last of
its rays onto the roofs of the buildings on top of the hill. I walked up,
passing a small park, grey in the dusk, nestled among trees, and then
turned downhill again to the right. There was hardly a soul about here,
so I'd obviously left the tourist area. At the bottom was the river, and I
turned left, following one of the streets that ran parallel.

The last daylight had been sucked from the sky and everything cast
into greys and blacks, but the air was still so hot it felt like walking
around in a sauna. The buildings became increasingly run-down, and
suddenly there were people again. Two wiry men, both the worse for
wear, each with a bottle in his hand, stood loitering on the pavement.
One of them swayed and staggered forwards as I passed them by. On
the corner further along was what I discovered to be a bar as I peered in
through the windows. A small, chaotic room packed with people. Some
of them looked out at me. The place was too full to go inside and so I
carried on along the street. The building on the opposite corner looked
like a bomb site, one wall missing, a bevy of men and a couple of
women standing drinking on the open concrete foundation, they too
wiry and broken-down. Two of them had their arms around each other
as if in the middle of a dance, only they weren't moving. The others
laughed.

I pulled up as I passed the front of the building. Some steps led down
into a basement and above them was an illuminated sign.

PIOMOYHAR, it said.

HAR, would that be a bar?

I decided to give it a try. The gaggle I'd passed looked like they could
be junkies, the basement maybe the place they hung out, but the sign
seemed to indicate it was a proper establishment.

The door was open and I stepped into a bunker-like space so crammed with stuff I wasn't sure where I was at first. The walls were decorated with old newspapers and car number plates, vinyl records and photographs. A big, old-fashioned radio sat on a shelf along with an old dial phone. There were posters with the hammer and sickle, military memorabilia, cassette tapes, medals and trophies. But there was a counter at the other end, and there were tables and chairs, so it was definitely a bar.

I went up and saw from the corner of my eye an adjoining room as a young man with a severe buzz cut appeared behind the bar and stared at me.

'Hello,' I said. 'Do you serve beer here? And some food, maybe?'

'Beer, *da*,' he said, and pointed at the taps. I chose one at random and he started to fill a glass.

'Food?' I said.

He looked at me vacantly as he pulled my pint.

I opened my mouth and gestured.

'Food?' I said again.

He nodded, put the pint down on the counter and went away into the back room, returning with a packet of beef burgers he showed me.

I gave him a thumbs up and put a note down in front of him. He took it, entered an amount into an old-fashioned till, handed me back some smaller notes and a few coins and gave me a thumbs up of his own.

With the pint in my hand I went into the adjoining room. A man and a woman were sitting in a corner, but apart from them the place was empty. The walls were covered in what looked to be diplomas. An old postbox hung there too, and a big oil lamp stood on one of the tables.

I suddenly realised that everything was from the Soviet era. I'd stumbled on a Soviet nostalgia bar.

I gulped a mouthful of beer, which was good and cold, and discreetly studied the couple in the corner. She was blonde and looked to be in her mid-forties. The man, with his back to me, was about the same age, heavily built, close-cropped hair, a round-looking head. They'd just eaten, their plates still on the table, a pile of empty prawn shells on his. A night out.

The woman glanced at me and I smiled at her before sipping another mouthful of beer, passing my eyes over the photos that adorned the beams under the ceiling. I supposed they were film stars from the fifties and sixties, presented as they were in exactly the same way as American movie stars of the era, glamorous people with gleaming white teeth — the photos looked like they were coloured in. It was strange to look at them as stars, when I didn't recognise a single face among them.

The man shifted his chair to sit beside the woman. He put his arm around her and looked at me.

I didn't know what he wanted, so I raised my glass to him. He did likewise, while she looked down at the floor and seemed rather ill at ease. The next minute, she was looking up at him warmly.

The guy from behind the bar came up with a small glass in his hand.

'Free,' he said, beaming a smile.

'Thank you!' I said.

The glass was ice-cold. It could only be vodka.

Some music came on, and over in the corner, the woman took the man by the hand and led him out onto the floor. They started to dance. The woman danced as if she was twenty again, leaning her upper body forwards and walking backwards, shimmying, straightening up again, stepping close to him and placing the flats of her hands against his broad chest. His own moves were more restrained, but he too seemed comfortable. It was like watching a couple dancing at a school disco.

I didn't know where to look, there was something intimate about it, and I drained the vodka in one go. My shoulders gave a shudder, the alcohol glowing inside me for a moment. The couple's dance became wilder.

I realised I felt a bit sorry for her. It was as if there was so much she wanted.

Another couple came into the room. They were young, in their early twenties, and went over to the table football at the far end. When the first couple stopped dancing and went and sat down again, the woman looked at me and smiled, her cheeks flushed.

'Nostalgia!' she said. 'We here because nostalgia.'

Then she said something in Russian.

'She wants to know why you are here,' the young guy at the table football said.

'I'm a tourist from Norway,' I told him.

He nodded and translated into Russian for her. She raised her glass to me.

'*Na zdrowie!*'' she said. I guessed it meant *skål*. I lifted my glass in return, while she again spoke in Russian.

'She is saying her name is Nina and his name is Alexei. She is wondering what your name is.'

'My name is Syvert,' I said.

They both raised their glasses.

The bartender came in, this time with a plate of food — hamburger and chips, a lettuce leaf and a couple of slices of tomato. Fortunately, they allowed me to eat in peace, sitting next to each other at the same side of the table and holding hands, while the younger couple had sat down at a table nearer the middle where they talked quietly over their beers.

Another eighties hit came on, and Nina and Alexei danced again. I'd finished my meal and didn't fancy another beer, so I got up to leave. Nina stopped dancing and came over.

'Real life,' she said, her hand to her heart. 'Humanity. Direct contact.'

She put her hand fleetingly to my own heart.

'You understand?' she said, looking me directly in the eye. 'Reality.'

Alexei stood politely at her rear, swaying to the music, a tooth giving a metallic flash as he smiled.

'Very nice to meet you, Nina and Alexei,' I said. 'I like eighties music, too!'

They each shook my hand. The bartender as well wanted to shake my hand before I left. I paused outside to check my phone, but no one had called, and I stepped out into the street. The junkies, if that's what they were, had gone, and the street was empty.

Everything was bathed in the strangest light. I looked up at the sky. A great star shone from on high. Or maybe it was a planet.

I got my phone out again and tapped Lisa's number, FaceTime as before, so that she could see where I was.

'Hi,' she said when she answered, standing at the patio door in the bedroom.

'Hi,' I said. 'How are you getting on?'

'I'm so glad you called,' she said. 'Have you seen the light in the sky? Can you see it where you are? It's so scary I think I could die.'

'I think it's a planet,' I said. 'And it's not half as scary as the streets around here. Can you see?'

I turned the phone and showed her my surroundings as a car drove slowly past.

When I looked at the screen again, she was looking up at the sky.

'Hello! Anyone home?'

'What do you think it is?' she said.

I looked up.

'Mars or Venus,' I said.

'But they're never as big as that.'

'It's probably just something atmospheric.'

'Perhaps you're right,' she said.

'I can give Joar a ring in the morning, if you want. He'll know all about it. How are you, anyway?'

'I'm fine. What have you been up to?'

'I've just been to this crazy place. A Soviet nostalgia bar. People dancing between the tables, that sort of thing. I had a hamburger and chips, and now I'm on my way back to the hotel.'

'Sounds like you're enjoying yourself.'

'I am. No need to feel sorry for me!'

I heard the door of the bar open behind me and so I walked on in the direction I'd come from, Lisa's face lighting up the dark in front of my own.

'What was that?' she said suddenly. 'Did you hear it?

'Hear what?'

'Something in the loft.'

She held the phone towards the ceiling. I couldn't hear anything.

'There's someone there,' she said, her voice hushed into a whisper now.

'How would anyone get in the loft? It'll be a squirrel,' I said. 'They can be really noisy when they want. If we're really unlucky, it's a rat. I don't think it'll be a rat, though. The house is too new, it's rat-proof.'

She shook her head, her mouth open.

'It's bigger than that,' she said.

'It'll be a badger, like in that kids' song!'

'It's not funny, Syvert. I'm actually scared.'

'I wish I was there with you,' I said. 'But there's nothing to be scared of. It's just a planet in the sky and a squirrel in the loft.'

She didn't say anything, but stood staring at the sky, her phone as if forgotten in her hand.

'Why don't you get Sølvi to come over?' I said. 'Or go over to hers?'

'No,' she said. 'I'd only be making a fool of myself.'

'All right, but promise you'll call me if you need me,' I said. 'I'll be getting back to the hotel now.'

'I will,' she said.

'I can call you when I get back there, if you want?'

'No, I'll be all right. I think I'll just go to bed.'

'OK. Sleep well, then.'

'Thanks. You too.'

I ended the call, put my phone back in my pocket and began walking back to the hotel.

YEVGENY

There was no air conditioning in the lorry and it was so hot outside it was almost worse with the windows wound down. If the air wasn't trembling in all its heat, it was motionless beneath the baking sun. Typically, this was my busiest day all summer. We'd picked up three wooden huts for a building site on the outskirts, as yet little more than sand and dust, where a new sports hall was going up. After that we had a load of prefabricated roof trusses going into the centre of town. I got into the swing of it all quickly enough, though, and was only happy Viktor had so much work for us. I was never going to complain about that. It was just this sapping heat that made everything such hard going, even if it was just operating the hydraulic crane.

Maksim straightened up on the bed of the lorry and gave me the thumbs up. I started lifting, cautiously to begin with, and once the load was clear and dangling there, Maks jumped down onto the ground and then climbed the scaffolding to guide me in setting the thing down again.

My phone rang. It was Viktor, and so I took it while slowly steering the heavy truss towards the construction.

'Yes?' I said.

'How's it going?'

'Soon be done here.'

'Listen, something's cropped up. Can you deal with it before knocking off?'

'Give me a break, Viktor. You do realise how hot it is?'

'Forty-two degrees here. Don't know what it is where you are.'

'The asphalt's actually melting. I could fry an egg on the lorry.'

'This won't be until later on this evening. It'll be cooler then. I've already agreed, so it's not as if you've got much choice.'

The truss was almost there, swaying slightly. Maks leaned out, it looked like he was going to fall, but even though I hadn't got a full view he obviously had a good hold of the scaffolding with one hand, and with the other he grabbed a corner and swung the whole thing into place.

'Hello?' said Viktor.

'What are we shifting then?'

'A tank. Pickup at the railway station. Twenty kilometres, if that. You'll be done in an hour.'

'A gas tank?'

'A tank, that's all I know. Empty, too, as far as I can gather.'

'Send me the specifications, then.'

'Will do.'

A couple of hours later, we'd finished the unloading and headed off to a service station to get something cold to drink. Maks bought himself an ice cream as well. We sat down at a table underneath a parasol, the traffic thundering past next to us. It wasn't often I reminded myself that he was only a fifteen-year-old lad, he was as big as me now, but as he sat there licking his ice cream there wasn't much of the adult about him at all.

'Ice cream good?'

He nodded, a bit embarrassed, I sensed.

'We've got another job yet,' I said. 'A small one, though.'

'I thought we were finished,' he said, and looked almost despairing.

'I can do it myself. You've done a grand job today. I'll drive you home to your mother, if you want.'

'No need.'

'What, are you going to walk?'

'I'll go with you,' he said.

Oh, come on, lad, show me a will of your own!

'It's OK, you can knock off now,' I said, tapping out another cigarette from the packet and putting it between my lips. 'Get off home with you and have a nice cold bath.'

'Thanks,' he said. He wiped his mouth with the back of his hand and got to his feet. 'I'll wait in the lorry.'

He didn't like the smoke, not even outside, never had.

I sneezed violently three times in quick succession. It was the dusty air, I reckoned, squeezing my nostril between thumb and index finger to get rid of the excess snot, wiping it off on the underside of the table while checking to see if anyone was watching. But apart from a sun-scorched guy in khaki shorts who was filling up with petrol, there was no one else around.

I stubbed out my cigarette, downed the rest of my cola out of the can and traipsed back over to the lorry.

Maks was sitting in the cab, fiddling with the pistol.

'What the hell are you doing, lad?! Put it down, now!'

He blushed and did as he was told.

'It's not *loaded*, is it?' he said.

'Of course it's loaded! That's the whole idea, so you can shoot people with it.'

'I didn't even know you had one.'

'No, because if you did, you'd start fiddling with it, wouldn't you?' I said, starting the engine. 'What were you doing rummaging, anyway?'

He shrugged.

'I was bored, that's all.'

'Well, now you know,' I said.

He jumped out at the railway station to catch the train home. I carried on to the goods terminal on my own. The buildings threw long shadows across the soft asphalt. The tank was huge. It was standing outside, conspicuous among all the pallets and containers. I signed the forms and hoisted it onto the back of the lorry with some help from a forklift driver I managed to shanghai.

'What's it for?' he wanted to know when he came over.

'No idea,' I said. 'Looks like a recompression chamber, if you ask me.'

'The sort divers use?'

'Something like that, yes. Do you know what they look like?'

'No.'

'Me neither,' I said.

We laughed and he gave me a hand securing it before I headed off, following the ring roads to the outskirts on the far side of the city. It was a lot further than Viktor had said. When I got there, it turned out to be little more than a village, the sun had just about set, only the rim of the flaming sphere still visible, and the dusk had already come creeping.

I couldn't find the premises. The satnav led me to a sloping field surrounded by trees. The properties across the road belonged to a different address.

I climbed out and lit a smoke as the sun disappeared behind the forest in the distance. The field looked like it had just been mown. An old woman was pottering about, picking up sticks in a wheelbarrow she kept shoving on ahead of her.

I phoned Vika. He asked for the address I'd been given. It turned out there was a discrepancy, the one he'd got was slightly different, and when I plotted it into the satnav it said I was thirty kilometres off. I got in again, and as I pulled away I could see the darkness was really setting in. When I got there, it was pitch-black.

It was an old farm by the looks of it, and quite secluded. There was plenty of room out front, so I pulled up and parked, no need to go and knock, they'd have heard me come, if they hadn't seen me.

A fat guy my own age appeared in the door of the main house and came towards me. Sweat had soaked through his T-shirt. His face was round, with a small mouth, his skin red with sunburn.

'A tank for you,' I said. 'Where do you want it?'

'Ah, good,' he said. 'It's to go in the shed there.'

I turned my head in the direction he indicated.

'It won't go in there.'

'Put it down in front of the doors. They'll take care of it.'

I wondered who *they* might be, and backed the lorry as close as I could get.

When I got out, the man had gone. Looking at it again, maybe it would go inside, I thought. The shed doors looked both wide enough and tall enough.

I drew the bolt back and opened them, then threw the light switch on the wall inside.

The space was nearly empty apart from three tanks the same as the one I'd brought, standing next to each other at the far end.

What could be in them?

I went and stared up at them, put my hand against the metal, which was nice and cold. I tapped my knuckles against the side. Solid.

I went outside again. The air was completely still, so hot it felt almost unreal now that the sun had gone down. Some distance away, a bird sang. It sounded like a whistle. A reply came immediately from a different place.

The trees surrounding the property loomed like giants in the dark, as if bending forwards to examine something I couldn't see.

I went up to the house and knocked.

The man came to the door.

'Yes?' he said. He wasn't hostile, he just wasn't that friendly.

'I think I can get it inside for you after all. Do you want me to do that?'

'That'd be fine,' he said.

I hesitated.

'Can I ask you something?'

He looked at me and blinked three times in quick succession.

'What's in those tanks?'

'Dead bodies,' he said.

'Dead bodies?' I said.

'Yes. Human corpses. Six in each tank. Plus a few heads.'

'Are you having me on?'

'No. They're frozen. People pay a lot of money. And I'm paid a lot of money for having them here. Was there anything else?'

'Jeez ... I mean, no. Do you want me to let you know when I'm done?'

'No, not necessary.'

'I'll need you to sign for it now, then.'

He nodded and I went over to the cab to get the documents and a pen. He signed his name with a sigh and asked if that was all. I said it was, and he closed the door in my face.

I set the stabilisers and hooked things up, raised the tank a couple of metres, then went over to guide it as I swung it over the side. As I began lowering it to get it through the doors, I became aware of a bright light at the edges of my vision. I put the remote down on the ground and stepped away from the shed so I could see what it was.

It looked like the forest was on fire over there.

Hardly surprising in this weather.

Only then I realised it wasn't a fire at all, the light was rising into the sky. It looked almost like the sun had decided to come up again.

What on earth was it?

A sphere of some sort. And it was ascending with great speed, already clear of the trees.

Was it something to do with the military?

The field and the premises I was standing on were illuminated now as if by the most powerful full moon.

It was so quiet I could hear myself breathing.

Without taking my eyes off the sky, I picked a cigarette out of the packet in my shirt pocket and lit one.

It was like being the last person alive on earth. As if there was only me and the star, or whatever it was. It felt like it was looking back at me, as intensely as I was looking at it.

I'd be able to read about it in the morning, I told myself, crushing the end of my cigarette under the sole of my boot and returning to the job at hand. The tank touched down with a hollow clang. I undid the hooks and retracted the crane. Bolting the heavy shed doors again, I looked up once more at the sky.

And then, a sound from inside.

I stopped and listened.

A thudding of some sort. Faint, as if from somewhere far away.

No rat or mouse would make such a sound.

I opened the doors again, switched on the lights and went inside.

Thud. Thud. Thud.

It was coming from the tanks.

I stepped closer.

Thud.

I put my ear to the one nearest.

Thud. Thud.

There was someone in there. Or something.

I looked around. The place was as empty as before.

They must have livestock in them, I told myself. He'd been pulling my leg when he said it was dead bodies.

Maybe someone was watching on closed circuit, having a good laugh at me.

I wasn't going to fall for it.

I went back out, closed and bolted the doors again and climbed up into the cab. My hands were shaking as I turned the ignition. I'd never been as relieved in all my life when I got back onto the main road and picked up speed to get the hell away.

VASILISA

I was a poor sleeper at the best of times, waking every other hour through the night, and tormented by it, too. But I'd never known nights like the nights this summer. It was the heat, of course. It made everything so unpleasant. The sheet clung to my skin, which was so horribly sweaty, and I suffered constant headaches. Yet the worst thing was the claustrophobia, the sense that the heat was inescapable. It made my thoughts claustrophobic too, they churned, the same paltry trivialities, things I'd said or done once, and would not be controlled but led their own small and worthless lives inside the confines of my mind.

I cycled to the village one day to see if they might have a fan in the shop there, but of course they did not. The radio spoke constantly of record temperatures. Fifty degrees had already been surpassed in Yevpatoria and Makhachkala. The water pressure in the taps was so low it took five minutes to fill a small saucepan. For the garden it was disastrous. The grass crunched underfoot. But I had managed to rescue the fruit bushes, the vegetables and most of the perennials. I bound a pole to the handlebars and cycled the two kilometres to the river with a bucket at each end. The river had shrunk into a shallow stream, islands and banks had emerged where normally its waters gushed, but there was enough for my own purposes. I filled the buckets, hung them from the pole and walked the bicycle back home again. The last part of the way was along a surfaced road, and I mounted then, cycling without wobbles or swerves as I had learned from practice.

My feelings as I poured the water onto the rows of potato plants, for instance, were ambivalent: it was so marvellous to see it run out and be swallowed by the greedy soil, the transformation from pale, dusty dirt to dark, moisture-filled earth, yet so frustrating at the same time to see how little such a bucketful could stretch.

In a few weeks, perhaps even a few days, the low front would arrive. It had to. A rumbling in the distance, a bank of black cloud slowly approaching, plummeting temperatures, rising winds — and then the cacophony of lightning, thunder and pouring rain. It had happened last year, and it would happen this.

As I awaited the release, I plodded on. My days are ordered meticulously, it is most important to me. I rise at four, having slept or not, give the cat some food and water, then sit down at my rickety table and write for a couple of hours. Writing is a cooling activity, if one does it right. It cools the mind, it cools the soul. That is how I, at least, see it. Haste gives rise to friction, friction gives rise to heat, and this is true also of one's thoughts, which so easily become frenzied and unhealthy when allowed too much leeway in a confined space. Writing slows them down, straightens them out, leads them with a gentle hand to places new, whose landscapes are open and free. Thereby comes the realisation that what exists here is by no means everything. And being here then becomes bearable, occasionally even meaningful.

At six o'clock I drink a cup of tea and eat some buttered bread before continuing my writing until ten. Then I will wash myself at the sink, get dressed and go out. If I need to buy groceries, I cycle to the shop, stopping off at the post office too, in case there are books for me to collect there, though otherwise it is to the river I go. Sometimes — every day in this period of hot weather — I walk along the bank to one of the few pools that are as yet deep enough for me to take a dip. How splendid it is, with the willow and the oak, and the meadows beyond, and the thought of how polluted the water is finds no traction, which is just as well.

Each afternoon, I sit out in the camping chair in the shade of the woodshed and read until I fall asleep. If fortune is with me, I may sleep two or even three hours. Then follows the time of day I care for the least, evening and night, before everything begins again the next morning.

It is not as I had imagined my life would be, and yet I have a hunch that it is as good as I could have expected, with the starting point I was allotted. To live is to adapt, adjust, amend; to use one's abilities and skills, and accept one's limitations. We cannot choose life, life chooses us. I could not have children, but I could write. I could not set boundaries, and so I moved to a place that did so for me.

Happiness is not to get what you want. Happiness is to get what you do not want, and learn to appreciate it.

I know people who got everything they wanted. What they have in common is that they don't know they've even got it. One of the best examples is Alya, my old student friend. She is beautiful, men look at her, admire her, want her. She had a child when she was twenty, and a midlife crisis when she was forty, which she resolved by having another child. It will keep her young for another fifteen years and give meaning to her later days. She appreciates none of these things, for the simple reason that they have always been available to her. A bit like water in the tap. Only when it isn't there do we miss it, only then does it become valuable to us — even if it has been keeping us alive the whole time.

I will not go as far as Cicero, who wrote that whoever owns a garden and a library will be happy. Now and then it feels as if a shotgun and a library would be more appropriate. But as an ideal, I believe it. A garden is life, the world, always different, always the same. A library is hope, but also comfort.

To pull up carrots when they are ready to be harvested, their tufty tops of green bringing to mind medieval knights, their slender orange bodies gleaming in their conical shape as they release the dark, fat soil, is not only an aesthetically beautiful and ethically satisfying act — I have grown them myself in my own garden — it is also profoundly meaningful. The same is true of the raspberries that sit so crimson in all the green, rumpled and matt with their many small pads of refreshing juice and tiny dry seeds; or the smooth, glassy casing of the redcurrants, startling red among their verdant foliage; or, for that matter, the potatoes that lie blind and mute under the soil and have themselves become earthlike in their dark, dry skins, staunchly concealing their secret, which is that their flesh is as creamy white as the wood beneath

the overlaying bark of a tree, or the teeth behind the lips of almost anyone a hundred years ago. To dig in the soil, to grow fruit and vegetables,
to see the cycle of the seasons, is to belong to the world, to be a part of
what the carrots, the raspberries, the redcurrants and the potatoes too
are a part of.

But how long can one be sustained by such a feeling?

Not long.

The meaning it carries comes in the blink of an eye, and is gone in
the blink of an eye.

I potter about here, tidying up and clearing away now and again,
reading and writing, thinking, perhaps thinking too much. But what is
my experience, my understanding, my insight worth if I cannot share
it with someone? I'm thinking not of friends and acquaintances, who
I can phone or go and see any time I like, but of a son or a daughter.
No one will inherit the insights I have gained. No one will embrace
them or distance themselves from them. They mean nothing to anyone but me.

Is that why meaning fails, because I am the end of the line?

Alya once spoke to me about her father, a colossal reader of literature who never put what he gleaned there to any use, never put pen to
paper, for instance, in that respect. His reading, so unique to the person
he was, came as it were to nothing, everything he gained from it was
gone when he died in the spring this year. What good did such a large-
scale acquisition of knowledge do anyone in the end?

This of course is true of all of us. What is our hard-won experience
worth, if we are only to die? What value can be attached to the things
we have seen and done? What were they for?

Some years ago I wrote a preface to a book about Fyodorov and Russian cosmism and was gripped by Fyodorov's idea of reviving all those
who have ever lived. My preface was rejected, but my editor asked me to
elaborate and expand upon it. With the exception of two month-long
hiatuses during which time I devoted myself to writing poetry, that
work has been my work in progress ever since. What do we lose when
we lose a person to death? That is its focus. I have written about the final
days of a handful of individuals. Some from my own life — my grandmother and grandfather, my mother and my younger brother — some

from history — Tolstoy, Napoleon, Woolf, Curie, Tsvetaeva, Rilke. The days leading up to their crossing the bridge into the realm of death, the days prior to life's flame being extinguished, of what they carry within, that cannot go with them, and yet cannot be left behind for the benefit of others.

Would I have been writing such a monograph if I'd had a daughter?

Would it have been necessary for me then?

I don't know.

But I have a garden and I have a library. And the longing for everything else. It would be easy to believe that longing is that which is not, that which is absent, but it is not the case, longing too is something that is, and it too is valuable. I use it in order to write.

Longing is something. Death is something

My younger brother. Mikhail was his name. Little Misha. He was nine years old when he died, and his death tore the family to pieces. I was fifteen at the time. Writing about his life, as I have done, was not the healing activity I had anticipated it would be. All it was was dreadful.

He had been playing on his own, had found a length of rope and hanged himself.

Had he simply been playing a game, without realising how dangerous it was?

Or had he, oh God, done it intentionally?

I remember Mama and Papa coming home with him, my new baby brother. I remember the first steps he took, I remember his first words, and I remember his infectious laughter.

And then: nothing more.

He has been with me in all I have written, as he is with me now, as I write these words. When the darkness opens, it opens and can never be forgotten. One may tell oneself that death is part of life, and indeed I tell myself that it is so, for there is certainly a truth in it, but it is not the case that death is an inversion of life, its shadow as it were. Rather, the opposite is true. Life is an inversion of death. It is death that rules. We are all of us death's children.

*

I forgot to mention the trains here. The ones that come in the night, one-eyed as the Cyclops, rushing through the landscape on their iron rails. I like them best in winter when the snow cloaks the locomotive in a thin, transluscent shroud of white, cast from the blades of its plough, but also in summer I like them, not so much in the day as in the night, in the darkness, for the trains belong to the dark. That evening, when the new star appeared, it was the train that woke me up. I'd been sitting in the chair with my book on my lap, my bucket hat on my head, and had slept for some hours, until a train tooted in the distance and everything seemed to tremble in anticipation of its appearance. I didn't know who or where I was, for the darkness in the garden where I sat was dense, yet the fields were illuminated in a ghostly light, as if by a full moon, and the fact that I had never seen such a light before, infused my first conscious thoughts with a fundamental uncertainty. But my chair was familiar, my little garden was familiar, and when I got to my feet and went over to the fence, already confident in myself again, the only thing I did not recognise was the new star, shining magnificently from an otherwise inky night sky.

The train approached, a metallic whoosh that rose in intensity as it emerged from out of the darkness, a beam of light projecting from its headlamps, the windows of its carriages a glow, and then it was past and all its noise subsided.

Some birds twittered and sang in the distance. The light in the sky must have perplexed them.

It perplexed me too.

The extreme heat had perhaps affected the atmosphere. Strange optical phenomena were by no means uncommon: the sandstorms of the Sahara could colour the sky red many hundreds of kilometres away, halos encircled the moon, a volcanic eruption in one place on earth could cause optical distortions in quite a different place altogether.

The heat presumably made it appear closer than it was.

Perhaps it was Venus, perhaps it was Mars. Its light bore a reddish tinge.

I didn't care for it. But it was the unsettlement of evening too, it always got to me, a small frog found dead by the wall outside could bring me to despair, a bottomless, bottomless despair that reached far beyond a dead amphibian.

I went inside, leaving the door open behind me, threw open all the windows, turned the radio on, opened a bottle of wine. I couldn't be bothered to read, and knew I could not write.

I phoned my sister, Ira. It was an inconvenient moment, she said, telling me she'd call me back, before asking if it was anything important.

'No, not at all,' I said.

I hung up and sat with the phone cradled in my hand for a few minutes as I gazed out at the strangely illuminated fields.

Then I called Alya.

ALEVTINA

Yura was standing by the window looking out as he talked on the phone. When mine then rang, he spun round, indicated with a thumbs up that I should go ahead and answer it and went into the other room still talking.

It was Vasya.

'Well, I never!' I said. 'It's been ages! Are you in town?'

'No,' she said. 'I'm at home.'

'Where's that these days? The dacha?'

'Yes.'

'Aren't you going to invite us soon?'

'Do you need an invitation to come and see me?'

'No, of course not.'

There was a pause.

'How are you, anyway?' I said.

'I'm fine. Have you seen the sky tonight?'

'No, why?'

'There's a strange light phenomenon of some sort. I've just seen it here. It looks like a huge star or a planet.'

'Are you sure it's not just local? I don't think there's anything here,' I said going over to the window just as Yura came through the door with his phone now outlined in his pocket.

'Perhaps it's just here, then,' she said.

'Unless it's on the other side,' I said. 'Let me check.'

Yura opened a drawer in the kitchen. He had a beer in his hand and held it up in the air with an enquiring look to ask if I wanted one. I shook my head and opened the door of Yegorushka's room. He was lying on his back on top of the duvet, one arm flopped over his head, the other at his side. His long hair was damp with sweat.

'Are you still there?' said Vasya.

I lifted the curtain.

'Oh my goodness, what's that?' I said.

'It's wondrous, isn't it?'

'Yes. But what *is* it?'

'I think it might be an atmospheric disturbance of some sort distorting the light we see. Something to do with the hot weather, I'd say.'

'But it's completely transluscent.'

'What do I know?' she said. 'I'm not an astronomer. But you are, almost!'

I let go of the curtain and stood for a moment, looking at Yegorushka, his little face. How strange it was that children slept so soundly. The light could be switched on, people could stand there talking, and still they slept undisturbed.

There was something healthy and good about it.

I lifted the curtain again. It was impossible not to. It was like something in a dream.

'Hello?' said Vasya.

'It looks like something in a dream,' I said. 'Something I could have dreamt.'

She laughed.

'I'm seeing it here, you're seeing it there, so it's not a dream. Unless we're both dreaming it at the same time!'

'You know what I mean, though.'

'Not really, no.'

'Everything in dreams means something, doesn't it? While you're dreaming, you know it's significant, and when you wake up you try and work out what it meant. What it relates to.'

'Yes.'

'That's the feeling I have now. That it means something. Does that sound stupid?'

She laughed again.

'You're back with your biosemiotics now, aren't you? I thought it was information from living organisms you were interested in then.'

'It's got nothing to do with that.'

'So what *has* it got to do with?'

'It's a feeling, that's all. I can't believe it doesn't have the same effect on you. It's really powerful. Look at it! It's as if it's telling us something, don't you think? That it means something.'

'I'm looking at it, and all I can say is no, not in the slightest.'

Neither of us spoke for a moment.

'Talking of biosemiotics,' she said. 'Do you remember telling me about those seminars that took place in Moscow in the seventies?'

'Yes?'

'I've been writing about death and eternal life, or at least the dream of eternal life, for quite a while now. I keep seeing a name from that time. Alexie Sharov. Does it mean anything to you?'

'I know about the seminars, of course,' I said. 'But I can't recall anything about Sharov. Who was he?'

'He took over and ran the seminars in the eighties. His name keeps cropping up, that's all. Do you know where he's been working?'

'No, tell me.'

'The National Institute on Aging, in Baltimore!'

'Good for him.'

'But don't you get it? What you were so interested in back then turns out to be related to what I'm doing now!'

'Not really,' I said. 'He worked in biosemiotics in Moscow, then started researching into ageing. The only thing that tells me is something about his career path.'

'You really can be a stick-in-the-mud, do you know that?'

'I'm aware of it, yes!'

She laughed.

'Have you got air conditioning?'

Now it was my turn to laugh. It was so typical of her.

'What's that got to do with anything all of a sudden?'

'Just wondering. Have you?'

'Yes, we've got air conditioning.'

'So the heat isn't bothering you that much?'

'Not here, no. Outside's unbearable, though.'

She paused. I heard her loneliness, breathing at the other end.

I looked up at the light in the sky one more time before closing the curtains again.

It was telling us something, I could feel it in every cell of my body.

'How's it going with *The Wolves of Loneliness*?' I said.

'You mean *The Wolves of Eternity*.'

'Yes, that's what I meant.'

'Was it a Freudian slip, do you think?'

I stepped out of the room and closed the door quietly behind me.

'I'm lonely, is that what you mean?'

'Or you think I am. Let's take you first. Are you lonely?'

Fortunately, Yura had gone back into the other room.

'I wouldn't say that, no,' I said. 'I've got Yegorushka and Yura, and my colleagues and friends. And Yura's friends too now, of course.'

'What are his friends like?'

'They're all right. And I've got two new brothers as well.'

'So you finally got in touch with them?'

'Yes. One of them's in Moscow now, as it happens. Syvert, the elder. I'm meeting him for the first time tomorrow.'

'Really? That must feel strange.'

'Yes, it does. But now you're getting away from things. Are *you* lonely?'

'I live on my own, so I'm alone. But I like it. Increasingly, in fact. So I can't say I am, no.'

I sat down on the sofa, picked up the remote, switched the TV on with the sound turned down, and started flicking through the channels.

'You didn't mention Seva,' she said. 'Is he completely out of the picture?'

'He comes here and has dinner with us once a week. We go for a coffee together now and again, if we've both got time.'

'Does he get on with Yura?'

'He does, yes. I wouldn't say they were twin souls, exactly, but they get on well enough.'

The star lit up all the news channels.

Mysterious celestial phenomenon over Moscow, the breaking news bar said on one of them.

'Anyway, to answer your question,' she said, '*The Wolves of Eternity* is almost finished.'

'That's brilliant! I'm pleased for you. When's it coming out? And when can I read it? I loved that preface you wrote, the one that started it all off.'

'No one's read it yet. For all I know, it might get rejected. But being honest, I don't think it will. It's turned out rather well, if I say so myself.'

'Well, no one else can,' I said, and laughed.

'You can read it when it's finished, of course you can. But just to be clear, I'm not interested in criticism or feedback.'

I laughed again.

'When are you coming to Moscow?'

'When the book's finished.'

'We should go out and celebrate, the two of us together!'

'Deal,' she said. 'I want oysters, lamb and Italian ice cream, chocolate flavour, with a double espresso.'

'Yum,' I said. 'Chablis with the oysters and a Barolo with the lamb?'

'We've always understood each other, haven't we?' she said, laughing now.

It was the mention of food that put her in high spirits, I thought to myself. It always had.

The first thing I thought when I saw Yura's apartment was how impersonal it was. Expensive new furniture, expensive rugs, a minimalistic kitchen all gleaming steel and shiny grey surfaces, unexciting graphic art on the walls. It was everything he wasn't, Yura, standing there with his unruly hair and unshaven cheeks, waiting for my reaction.

Flecks of dust hung suspended in rays of spring sunshine that slanted in through the big windows. It was a Sunday, we'd met up at a nearby cafe and he'd wanted to show me where he lived.

'What do you think?' he said, unable to contain himself.

'Very smart and tasteful,' I said. 'But I don't see much of *you* here.'

'I'm not smart and tasteful?' he said with a laugh.

'Yes, of course you are,' I said, and looked at him. He blushed slightly. 'But you haven't put your soul in here anywhere.'

'No, just lots of money!'

It wouldn't take much to make a fantastic place out of it, I found myself thinking as he led me through the various rooms. Colour, firstly. Cushions, curtains, carpets. Pictures. Bookshelves.

'Have you given up reading?' I asked when we returned to the living room.

'Not got the time any more, too much work,' he said. 'And by the time evening comes round I'm usually too exhausted for anything else but television. What about you?'

'Not as much as I used to.'

'You got through a lifetime's worth back then. I did, too. Do you want a cup of tea before you go? Or a coffee? Espresso, cappuccino?'

'I'd love to, only I need to be getting home. I've only got the weekends and evenings for studying.'

He nodded.

'Maybe you'd like to come round for dinner one night? It would be nice.'

'Yes,' I said.

'Yes? When would suit you best?'

'I'm not sure. Can we text?'

'Of course,' he said, and his chunky face seemed almost to light up from within.

Now he was reclining on the sofa, his feet up on the coffee table, beer in one hand, phone in the other. His T-shirt had ridden up and his stomach peeped through the gap between it and his shorts.

He turned his head and smiled at me, then patted his hand a couple of times on the sofa beside him.

'Come and sit here,' he said.

I sat down. He put his arm around my shoulder.

'Who was that on the phone?' he said.

'Vasya.'

'You mean she's still alive?'

'It's a thing she does. Disappears off the face of the earth a year or two at a time.'

'Peculiar woman.'

'Yes, she is a bit eccentric. But I'm fond of her.'

I put my hand to my mouth and stifled a yawn.

'Should we take him to the zoo tomorrow?' he said. 'Or will it be too hot?'

'I'm meeting my new brother tomorrow.'

'Oh, that's right!' he said and batted his forehead with the flat of his hand. 'How could I have forgotten?'

'But the two of you could go on your own.'

'What time are you meeting him?'

'One o'clock.'

I stood up.

'I think I'll have a shower. And then I think I'll go to bed. It's been a long day.'

'I'll be off to bed soon myself,' he said.

I gave a shudder, that funny way the air conditioning always made me shudder, as if I were hot and cold at the same time, and it felt delightful to step under the warm shower. After drying myself, I put my dressing gown on and went into the bedroom. I sat down in front of the old dressing table I'd bought when I arrived in Moscow aged nineteen, blow-dried my hair, removed my make-up, squeezed a little blob of face cream into my hand, rubbed my palms together and drew them over my face and neck. That wonderful feeling, the skin absorbing the soft moisturiser and all its healing ingredients. Even the smell had a soothing effect.

I put on a clean pair of knickers, hung the dressing gown back on the peg and went to bed. Lena had changed the bedlinen, it was cool and smooth, and smelled good and fresh. I put my glasses on and picked up my phone to look at the photo he'd sent of himself and his family a few months ago.

At first blush it was impossible to tell we were related. He was tall and well built, with masculine features that seemed to suggest a complete absence of doubt. But then, on closer scrutiny, there was something about the eyes, they had the same shape as my own and there was something in them I recognised, something they expressed. There was an imperturbable air about him, too, and he looked very much the dependable, can-do type. Yet there was something sorrowful about those eyes that wasn't immediately discernible.

The photo made me think too of the research station I'd been to once at the White Sea, it was the jetty that triggered the association, I was sure of it. They seemed to be a family who enjoyed the great outdoors, standing there in their lifejackets as if it were the most natural thing in the world, arms around each other, hair ruffled by the wind. The woman was the mother, his wife.

Would I like her?

I already liked him.

I put the phone down on the bedside table and picked up the book Lena annoyingly had closed, and flicked through to find my page again.

It was Calvino's *Invisible Cities*, one of Papa's favourites. I'd taken a good stack of his books after the funeral, and Yura had arranged storage for the rest. We didn't have room for them all at home. I wanted to find the space, but I could certainly see things from Yura's side. Sasha had wanted to sell them, of course. I told him used books were worthless, but he didn't believe me. I hadn't the strength to quarrel, so in the end I bought him out for a not-inconsiderable sum.

Yegorka would have to meet Syvert. He was the boy's uncle and he didn't have too many of them. But it would have to wait until another time.

I started reading, but found it hard to concentrate. The thought of the star seemed to prevent it. Or rather, not the thought, because I didn't think about it at all. It was just there, inside me.

Biosemiotics.

Great, sentient organisms all around us.

Why had I failed? Why hadn't I been able to write about it, investigate, conduct the research?

There was nothing in it, that was why. Or there was nothing to be done about it.

OK, the forest is a sentient being, then.

It was a bit like saying apes are just as intelligent as us, that they understand as much as we do and are only lacking a language by which to communicate the fact. It wouldn't change anything. Perhaps we'd treat them a bit better, if we knew they were more like us than we'd thought. But we still wouldn't be able to communicate with them. We could look into their eyes, yes, and see their soul there, yes. And it was the same with the forest. We can look at it. We can go inside it. But the meaning it contains is not for our concern, we can never tap into it.

Oh, how vast the difference between knowing and being!

Everyone thought I became a doctor because I wanted to be like my mother. Even Papa thought so. He never said as much, but I knew it was what he thought. There was a sliver of truth in it, but no more than that. Perhaps five per cent of it was down to Mama. Ninety-five per cent was in place of knowing.

Vasya believed it was because I wanted to break down the distance between myself and my fellow human beings and be a good person, and told me it was impossible, because it was the thought of being good that had led me there, rather than being good itself.

She was beginning to remind me of Papa, too many thoughts in too small a space.

But I was glad to have her.

When she emerged from her cave every now and then.

I turned my attention back to my book, immersing myself easily in it now, but then Yura came in after only a couple of pages.

'Do you think we'll be able to visit them in Norway at some point?' I said. 'I'm thinking of Yegorushka, it would be good for him. They're family, after all. Rather *close* family, actually.'

'Of course we can,' he said. 'When were you thinking of?'

'Not yet. Maybe next summer?'

He nodded and plonked himself down on the edge of the bed, making the mattress wobble. He took his T-shirt off, and then his shorts, climbed under the duvet and lay on his back with both hands behind his head.

'Do you mind if I read for a bit?' I said.

'No, not at all,' he said.

I read a few pages with him lying there staring up at the ceiling.

'Are you nervous about tomorrow?' he said after a while.

'No.'

'You don't think we should invite him round? For dinner?'

'I think the best thing is not to get too far ahead of ourselves.'

'Right,' he said. He turned over onto his side, his head resting in his hand as he looked at me.

I carried on reading, but it was impossible to resist the pressure of his gaze and pretend he wasn't there, so I put the book down and looked at him.

'What's on your mind?' I said.

'I was just thinking how beautiful you are.'

'That's what you always say when I ask what's on your mind,' I said with a smile. 'I refuse to believe it's the only thing you can think about.'

'Not the only thing, but the most important.'

He shifted closer, put an arm around me and kissed me.

'Wait a minute,' I said. 'Let me turn the light off.'

I reached out for the cord of the lamp, my fingers following it until I found the switch and could turn it off. He pressed his lips to mine and placed a hand on my breast. I smoothed his back. It was broad, hirsute and sticky with sweat.

'My big teddy,' I said, sensing his erection against my thigh.

'Bear,' he breathed as he removed my knickers.

'What?' I breathed back.

'Your big bear,' he said. 'Not your teddy.'

I shuddered with pleasure when he entered me, propping himself on his arms so as not to crush me, breathing heavily with eyes closed.

'I love you,' he whispered. 'You're gorgeous, absolutely gorgeous.'

And then, with a low, drawn-out moan, he came.

He flopped down on top of me without withdrawing.

We lay there for a while, entwined, neither of us speaking. Then he kissed me on the mouth.

'You really are beautiful, in case you didn't know,' he said.

I ruffled his hair, then sat up and swung my legs out of bed.

'I'll have a quick shower,' I said.

'Yes, you do that.'

When I was finished, I looked in on Yegorka. I felt such an urge to see him. His face was so pure and hopeful, as yet unmarked by any difficulty in his life.

Although I opened the door as quietly as I could, he sat up the moment I went in.

'Mama,' he said. 'Is it morning?'

I shook my head and smiled.

'It's the middle of the night,' I said. 'You should be fast asleep.'

'An old man was here,' he said.

I laughed and bent down to kiss him on the forehead.

'You've been dreaming,' I said. 'Was he a nice man?'

'I don't know,' he said. 'He didn't say anything.'

'Dreams can't harm,' I said. 'Not even bad dreams.'

He shifted his position until he sat cross-legged as he so often did.

'Lie down now,' I said. 'Papa's taking you to the zoo tomorrow.'

'What will you be doing?'

'I'll be meeting my brother, the one I told you about.'

'Syvert,' he said, and lay down again.

'Syvert, that's right. You'll get to meet him soon, too. Perhaps we'll go and visit him next summer.'

'On the train?'

I smiled.

'No, on the plane.'

'Plane,' he said.

He closed his eyes and I kissed him again. I had to stop myself from pulling the curtain aside to look at the star before leaving the room.

The sun blazed unremittingly again the next day. The temperature was already touching 30 degrees by mid-morning. Yura and Yegorushka set off undeterred for the zoo.

'We'll take a bottle of water each,' said Yura, crouching down in front of him in the kitchen. 'And a bag of crisps.'

'Why?'

'It's important to take in salt when it's hot,' he said. 'We'll take some fruit with us as well. What do you want? Peach, nectarine or orange?'

'Nectarine.'

'Right!'

He got their things together and Yegor helped him by packing their little rucksack.

'Now all we need is sunscreen and our caps, and then we can go!'

'I want Mama to come,' he said without looking at me. I was sitting on one of the tall stools at the long counter, watching them as I drank my coffee.

'Mama's coming to meet us afterwards,' said Yura, giving Yegorushka his cap to put on. 'But she's going to meet your uncle for the first time, she can't be late for that!'

He turned towards me to say goodbye.

'Give me a ring and let me know how you got on!'

I nodded.

'Bye-bye, Mama, and say hello to Syvert,' said Yegor.

After seeing them to the door and watching them disappear into the lift, I had a shower and got ready, picking out some clothes and laying them on the bed, choosing a pair of beige trousers, a white blouse and tan-coloured strappy sandals. It was too hot for trousers, but I couldn't turn up in shorts, not really. A skirt felt like I'd be showing my legs off, but I wasn't going on a date, and a dress would be overdoing it.

I took my sunglasses from the shelf under the mirror, made sure I'd got everything in my bag and took the lift down to the garage. The bus and the metro would be hellish in the hot weather, and there was a multi-storey not far from the restaurant where we were due to meet.

There was barely any traffic, so I was half an hour early when I got there. The star, so compelling the night before, was still visible, though in the daylight its aura and sway were diminished. Exactly like a dream! I thought to myself with a smile. Dreams lost their aura and sway too the next day.

I ordered a glass of cold white wine and sat looking out into the street, where hardly a person passed by, and gazing around the room, where a number of diners sat, most rather elderly, with wispy white hair and shiny bald heads. I'd thought it would be good to meet up with him somewhere respectable but at the same time not too formal, but the mood of the place I'd chosen wasn't quite right.

Too late to do anything about it now.

All of a sudden it hit home that I was about to meet my own brother. It was the first time I'd ever met anyone from my father's family. We were talking about half my genetic material.

I'd never felt any loss, never felt I'd only been half a person.

But what lay behind the door that now stood open belonged to me.

A whole new room in the house that was me. No, a whole new storey!

I sipped my wine and trailed a fingertip through the condensation on the glass.

I would have to explain to him why I hadn't been in touch before. It was important, so that he wouldn't think it hadn't mattered to me. Only when my adoptive father had died, I would say, had I been able to fully address the substance of it. Papa had stood in the way, or consideration for his feelings had stood in the way. But without me knowing! A subconscious consideraton. And it was true, because when we'd buried him and I returned to Moscow, one of the first things I'd done was to find the letter Syvert had written and try to word a reply. I didn't know why, but I'd felt it to be imperative, all of a sudden it was what I wanted.

Perhaps it all came out of the feeling I was left with when Papa died. The feeling of being all on my own.

I'd been prepared for it for some years, that a telephone would ring and someone would tell me that he was dead, I knew it could happen at any time.

What was it Vasya had written? We carry our death within us.

Papa wasn't the sort of person who would wither away in sickness. Somehow, I knew that. He would die suddenly, without warning.

And that was what happened.

Katya found him dead in his bed. He had retired as usual in the evening and never woken up again. Fortunately, he did not lie dead for days, as I might have feared; Katya had discovered him the very next morning.

Outside, a broad-shouldered man in a white T-shirt, blue denim shorts and bright white trainers lingered a moment in front of the entrance.

Something told me it would be Syvert, though I hadn't yet seen his face.

I imagined he had come early to make sure he could find the place.

He turned, and began to amble away, and now I saw his face. He was wearing sunglasses, but still I recognised him. It was Syvert, of course it was.

I jumped up, grabbed my bag so as not to leave it unattended and dashed out onto the pavement.

'Syvert!' I called out, startled by how unlike myself it was to behave in such a way.

He spun round. I waved. He waved back and came towards me with a big grin on his face.

'Alevtina?' he said, halting in front of me. He shoved his sunglasses up into his hair.

'Hello!' I said. 'So good to see you!'

He held his arms out tentatively as if to embrace me. I stepped forwards and threw mine around him.

'So good to see you, too!' he said, stepping back to look at me. 'Gosh, you're even more beautiful than I'd imagined!'

'There's a table waiting for us,' I said. 'Shall we go in?'

'Yes, let's do that!'

There was something awkward and youthful about him as he sat down at the table, perhaps it was the way he was dressed too, but looking at his face he seemed older than he did in the photo he'd sent. Lines around his eyes, a slight sag under the chin.

'Nice place!' he said.

'Yes, it is. You don't mind seafood, do you?'

'I love seafood!' he said with a laugh. 'In my part of Norway, we eat a lot of seafood. Especially in the summer. Shrimps and prawns, but they're very expensive. And then crabs in the autumn. I go catching crabs myself, by the way.'

'Do you really?'

'Yes. And I go fishing, of course. There are a lot of mackerel where we live, they come very close to the shore, almost into the little harbour below our house.'

'Wow,' I said, turning at the same moment to catch the attention of the waiter who immediately came gliding towards us. 'What do you want to drink?'

'A beer, I think, if I may!'

He laughed and I ordered him one.

Neither of us spoke for a moment, but then he looked at me again.

'So,' he said. 'Where to begin!'

'I know,' I said, beaming. 'It's so weird to finally see you!'

'Same here,' he said. 'Suddenly having a sister at my age, that's special.'

'Yes!' I said.

'A doctor, with two children, is that right?'

I nodded.

'I was a biologist to begin with, and taught for a long time. Then I went to medical school and became a doctor. I've only practised a couple of months, though.'

'Oh, I see,' he said.

'And I have two boys. Sevastyan, who's twenty-six, and Yegor, who's five.'

'Quite an age difference! My own are all pretty much the same age. I love them, of course, but they're not that communicative now that they've grown up. Too busy starting out in life.'

'You can't blame them, can you?'

'No, no, not at all. But it does make me sad sometimes.'

'Of course.'

'Do you get on all right with your older boy? Sebastian?'

His eyes didn't waver from me. It felt like I'd been caught in a search-light, as if his perceptive apparatus wasn't sensitive enough and prevented him from reading the situation in all its nuances.

I'd met many people like him and never felt comfortable in their company.

But he's your *brother*, I had to keep reminding myself.

'Sevastyan, you mean?' I said. 'Well, he leads his own life now, as your children do, I suppose. But I'd say we get on well enough.'

The waiter arrived with Syvert's beer and we chinked our glasses together.

'It's so good to see you. I still can't believe I have a sister!'

I smiled, and in the lull that ensued I opened the menu and he pulled a pair of reading glasses out of his shorts pocket, realising then that he still had his sunglasses on. He took them off, put his reading glasses on and started like me to examine the menu.

'What will you have?' he said.

'I think I'll go for the gazpacho as a starter, then maybe the caprese salad. What about you?'

'Well, I love fish soup, so I think I'll have that.'

'How about a starter?'

'I'm not really a starter kind of guy, to be honest.'

He closed the menu, removed his glasses and put them back in his pocket. I turned and nodded at the waiter, who came over and stood with his head bowed slightly and his hands behind his back as I ordered. When I turned my attention to Syvert again, he was checking his phone. I took a sip of my wine and looked through the windows into the street outside.

I had a funny feeling. It was as if something were collapsing inside me. There was no reason for it, I told myself, and smiled at him as he looked up again.

'I just need to send a message,' he said. 'I run a company at home and they don't know what to do when I'm not there.'

'It's all right,' I said. 'Take your time, by all means.'

He typed slowly with a stiffly protruding index finger before eventually tapping to send his message and slipping the phone back in his pocket.

'What kind of company is it you have?'

'Oh, just a small company. Most of my money comes from stocks and shares. I invest in various oil companies.'

'Really?'

'Yes. I was very lucky. When I was eighteen, I bought shares in some small companies with the money my father left me.'

He looked at me with a smile.

'*Our* father! For a long time nothing happened. Then, boom! One of the companies secured a major contract in Nigeria, then another in America, and my shares went through the roof.'

'That must have been exciting.'

'Yes, yes, it was, very exciting.'

Our eyes met, and we exchanged smiles again.

The street outside was drenched in sunlight, but empty too, and the combination made it look like something in a dream.

As if the pull of the star were exerting itself.

'I've been wondering,' he said. 'What was it like growing up in the Soviet Union? We heard a lot about the — what's the word in English?'

He was searching for it.

'What is it in Norwegian, I might be able to understand,' I said.

'*Undertrykking*,' he said, and pressed the palms of his hands downwards in front of him by way of illustration.

'Repression?'

'Yes, that's it! Repression. Not being able to say what you wanted, not being able to travel. Long queues outside the shops. What was it like, living with all that when you were a child? I often thought about it when I was growing up. We were afraid of nuclear war, you see.'

'It's hard to explain,' I said. 'A child takes the world for granted. What you describe was my everyday life, it was all I knew. The Soviet Union was my home. My mother was a doctor, and she did the best she could. I went to school. I had my friends, and we did what children do, just like you, I suppose. Yes, there were books we couldn't read and things we couldn't talk about. But we could travel and go on holidays. I remember the queues and there being a lot of things we couldn't buy, which of course is very different from now. But what you don't have, you don't miss. And we were afraid of nuclear war, too!'

He nodded a few times as I spoke. I only hoped he didn't feel he'd been put straight, and so I racked my brain for something easier to talk about. Fortunately, the food arrived. Which is to say, my starter did, along with a basket of bread and a small plate of butter.

'Please, have some bread.'

'Thank you,' he said, but made no move to do so. Instead, he drank up what was left of his beer, then immediately signalled the waiter for another, lifting the empty glass in the air, pointing a finger at it and giving a little nod, his eyes looking past me until he was satisfied his intention had been understood.

'What was he like, my father?' I said when I again had his attention.

'He was a kind man. A very modest man. But highly intelligent. He learned Russian, for one thing.'

'In what way was he kind? I hardly know anything about him. I'd very much like to get a picture of him.'

'I didn't bring a picture,' he said. 'But I do have copies of all the letters your mother wrote to him. Do you want them now?'

Without waiting for an answer, he bent down and took a bundle of papers from his bag and placed them on the table in front of us.

'Thank you!' I said. I hadn't the heart to tell him I didn't mean picture in the literal sense. 'I can't wait to read them, even if it is a rather daunting prospect.'

'Yes, it was hard for me, too,' he said. 'I was completely in the dark until I found the letters.'

There was a pause as I started on my soup, and he buttered himself a piece of bread, consuming it almost in one go before washing it down with a gulp of his beer as soon as it arrived.

It was like sitting next to someone on a long coach journey and feeling obliged to talk to them because you were stuck there going the same way.

It was hard to believe we had any connection at all.

'Tell me about your brother,' I said. 'Or rather, *our* brother — I keep forgetting!'

'Joar?'

'Yes.'

'It's a shame he was too tied up to be able to come. But he's much more like my father than I am. Very intelligent in the same way. Top marks at school. They even wrote a piece about him in the local newspaper, he did so well. And then he went on to study astrophysics.'

'He's an astrophysicist?'

'Yes. And I can't even pronounce it!'

He laughed.

'He's a bit strange in many ways. He says exactly what he thinks. So people often get angry with him.'

'Do you?'

'No, I'm used to him. I make light of it.'

I put my bowl to one side and wiped my mouth with my napkin. He looked at me, smiling.

'Joar got the brains, you got the looks and I got the sense of humour!'

'So it seems,' I said, returning his smile before twisting round slightly on my chair, a movement transparent enough for the attentive waiter to descend and clear my place.

'Will you excuse me for a minute?' I said to Syvert when he went away again. 'I just need to go to the ladies' room.'

I picked up my bag and went towards the stairs at the far end, which took me down into the basement. It was like a grotto there, dark and cool, with an empty bar at one end, empty tables and chairs. In the ladies' I splashed my face with cold water, dabbed myself dry with a paper towel, refreshed my lipstick and put some eyeliner on, not that I needed any, but because the familiar movements it involved gave me something to hold on to. I told myself everything was fine, that nothing had gone wrong, that he was a nice, well-meaning man and that there was nothing to get upset about, but none of it seemed to be able to alter the way I felt. Crestfallen and despondent, I stood and looked at my mouth in the mirror as my hand drew the lipstick across my lips. I realised my expectations had been far greater than I'd been ready to acknowledge. A new family. Perhaps even a new sense of belonging.

But I didn't want it. I'd never wanted it.

I sat down on the toilet seat and put my head in my hands.

It didn't matter. Nothing had changed. We'd met now, and acknowledged each other. He could go home. I could go home. We could exchange Christmas cards, the occasional photo, and leave it at that.

I had Mama's letters now. And perhaps that was what I was after, perhaps that was the whole point of our meeting.

When I returned to the table, the food had already arrived.

'I ordered you another glass of wine,' he said.

'Thank you,' I said.

'This looks very good! And it smells fantastic! I actually worked as a cook in the military, when I did my national service. I love cooking. How about you?'

I smiled and shook my head.

'Not really, no.'

'Oh, but it's such fun! You never quite know how it's going to turn out. It's almost like travelling, if you know what I mean. Each meal is like a journey. But what do you like then, if you don't like cooking?'

'I like to read. That's what I like the most, I think.'

He nodded before dipping his head towards his bowl and spooning up a mouthful of soup with plenty of shrimp and vegetables.

'Mm,' he said. 'This is delicious!'

We ate in silence for a bit. My stomach was a knot. All I wanted was to get away.

'Do you know any other Norwegians?' he said, glancing up as he leaned forward again.

'No, you're the first.'

He laughed.

'But not the last! You're an aunt to three of them now, you know. And the sister of two Norwegian brothers.'

'And you are an uncle to two Russians.'

'Yes. We should all meet up, don't you think? A big family . . . what do you call it . . . reunion? Or no, it can't be a reunion can it, not when we've never met before!'

'A family gathering?'

'Yes. A get-together.'

'Good idea.'

'I live in a big house, so there'll be plenty of room for everyone. Summer would be the best time. It's the loveliest season in Norway.'

'Sounds good,' I said. 'Let's email.'

'Yes,' he said. 'Let's do that.'

There was another awkward silence. He wiped the bottom of his bowl clean with some bread he then devoured before draining his beer.

'How about dessert?' he said.

'I don't think so,' I said. 'I have to pick up my son and his father soon. They're at the zoo, and it's so hot today. He's only five, you know, so I think I really have to go.'

He looked at me as if perplexed.

'You're leaving?'

'I'm very sorry. But we do have the rest of our lives to get to know each other. And meeting in Norway next summer really does sound fun!'

'But . . . we've only just met! We've so many things to talk about, don't you think?'

'Yes, of course. I agree. But I really must be going. Let's keep in touch, always. I'll look forward to meeting your wife and children. And you must meet Sevastyan and Yegor sometime, too.'

I turned towards the waiter, who nodded immediately.

Syvert turned his empty beer glass with one hand while staring at the table. He looked up at me and smiled.

'It's sad that you have to leave so soon,' he said. 'But I completely understand. And we do have a plan for next summer, right?'

'Right,' I said.

'It'll be fun. You'll be able to meet our brother then, too.'

'I'd like that very much!'

The waiter came with the bill on a little silver tray. I got my credit card out.

'No, no. Let me!' said Syvert.

'But you're my guest in Moscow,' I said. 'Please?'

'Well, if you insist,' he said. 'I'm not happy about it, though!'

I inserted my card into the reader the waiter held out towards me, entered my PIN, put the card and the receipt in my wallet and got to my feet, picking up the stack of letters as I rose.

'I'm looking forward to reading these,' I said.

'I remember I felt the same way,' he said, putting an arm through the strap of his small backpack, then glanced at his phone as we went outside into the street.

'It was so nice to finally meet you!' I said.

'Same here!' he said.

We hugged.

'Bye-bye,' I said, and smiled as I walked away.

'Wait!' he said.

I turned round.

'How about a selfie? So I can show my wife, too.'

'Yes, of course,' I said.

He stood beside me and held his phone out at arm's length, his other arm curled around my shoulder.

'Smile!' he said, his finger tapping the screen a few times. He checked the photos, a hand shielding the phone from the sun so he could see properly.

'Very good!' he said. 'I'll send them on to you!'

'Thanks,' I said. 'Have a nice trip back home!'

I sensed him watching me as I walked away, turned right at the first opportunity and phoned Yura.

'Hi!' he said at the other end. 'How did it go?'

'It was terrible,' I said. 'Really terrible. All I want to do is cry.'

SYVERT

Earlier in the day I'd noticed a park of some sort down by the river, not far from Red Square, so that was where I went. The grass and trees were almost eclipsed by concrete, glass and asphalt. I wandered about for a while, bought myself a can of Sprite, and people-watched. A gigantic glass dome shaped like a turtle shell covered what looked like an amphitheatre, while a strange-looking bridge without supports snaked through the area and extended out over the river. It was all spanking new and modern, a far cry from what I'd imagined Moscow would be like.

The sun blazed down and I looked for somewhere I could sit in the shade.

My phone pinged in my pocket. It was Lisa.

How did it go?

I crossed one of the grassy areas and sat down under a tree. It was just as hot there, but at least the light wasn't such a glare. I didn't feel like talking to anyone, but it was impossible to explain how it had gone in a text, so there was nothing for it but to phone her.

Maybe not just yet, though. For all she knew, I could still be having lunch.

Alevtina didn't like me.

It was the only explanation. One minute we'd been chatting away, the next she had to go. She hadn't received any text messages while we'd been at the table, so she must have known all along that she'd have to leave early. But then she'd have said so from the start. Which meant it was just an excuse.

I tried to recall exactly what I'd said, what we'd talked about. Had there been reason for her to take offence?

No, surely not.

She just didn't like me, that was all there was to it.

Did I like her?

She was a very good-looking woman. And brainy, too, if she was a biologist *and* a doctor. But there was something cold about her. She was the type who could smile while their eyes said something else.

I didn't much care for the thoughts that were coming to me now. It felt like my brain was going haywire. I didn't normally think like that. Didn't I always accept people the way they were?

If she didn't like me, it was only because she didn't know me.

No, it was too hot to be outside.

I stood up and followed the river along the embankment for a bit before heading up into the city centre, pinpointing the Bolshoi Theatre and a few minutes later returning to my air-conditoned room at the hotel.

I sat down on the bed and phoned Lisa.

'Not FaceTiming?' she said.

'Thought I'd save you having to look at my ugly mug.'

'Nonsense,' she said. 'You're a very handsome man. Understand it for once. Anyway, how did it go?'

'It didn't, really.'

'Why, what happened?'

'She got up and left. We'd only been there three-quarters of an hour or something, and I thought we were having a nice time. But then all of a sudden she had to go and pick up her son. I've come all the way from Norway to see her. We're brother and sister. We've never met each other before. And yet she gets up and leaves after less than an hour. Can you understand that?'

'Maybe it was important.'

'No, it was an excuse.'

'What was she like?'

'Good-looking. A bit arrogant, perhaps. A bit stuck-up. It was as if she didn't want to *talk* at all, do you know what I mean?'

'Not really, no. You're the only person I know who can talk to *anyone.*'

'I know, that's what I thought as well. It's weird, don't you think?'

'Yes. But she's Russian, and you're Norwegian. It's probably all to do with cultural barriers.'

'I thought Russians were supposed to be honest and direct. She wasn't though, not exactly.'

'Can't you see her again tomorrow? You're not going home until Monday.'

'When we said our goodbyes, she said she'd look forward to seeing us next summer. I take that to mean she's not interested in meeting up with me again here.'

'But that's positive!'

'What is?'

'That she wants to see you next summer.'

'It was just something she said, she didn't mean it.'

'You don't know that.'

We both went quiet.

'How's things at your end, anyway?' I said, stepping over to the window and looking into the street. A black car pulled up at the kerb and the doorman came out to open the door.

'It's still hot. But Sølvi's coming over, she's going to stay the night.'

'That's good. Have you ventured up into the loft yet?'

'No. It's all quiet up there now. So it probably was a squirrel. It just sounded like something a lot bigger, it really did.'

'The sound gets amplified up there, that's all. But nice for you that Sølvi's coming over!'

'Yes, we haven't been on our own together for ages.'

The doorman lifted two big suitcases out of the boot. He'd bowed when I left the hotel that morning. I still didn't know how much a thousand roubles was worth, but apparently it was enough to keep him happy.

'Is the star still visible there?' she said.

'Yes, but only just. The sun's so bright you can hardly see it.'

'Your brother's been on the radio about it all day.'

'Joar has?'

'Yes. He's their go-to expert now, apparently. He'll be on the television news tonight as well, I shouldn't wonder.'

I laughed.

'I'd like to see that! How's he coming across?'

'Very well! He's not at all nervous. He sounds like he's in his element.'

'That doesn't surprise me,' I said. 'Can you record it for me?'

'What, the news?'

'Yes.'

'You can see it there, can't you? And if not, you can watch it on catch-up when you get back.'

'Of course. I forgot.'

I laughed again.

'Joar famous, who'd have thought it! I was going to give him a ring and tell him how I got on with Alevtina, but I think I'll wait now. Sounds like he's got enough to keep him occupied for the time being.'

'Listen, I'll have to go,' she said. 'I can see Sølvi coming now.'

'OK, speak to you later, then.'

'Yes, take care!'

'You too,' I said, and hung up. Then I remembered the selfies I'd taken, and sent the best one to Lisa. She didn't reply, probably already wrapped up in Sølvi being there now, I thought, and phoned Jarle instead.

'How's it going?' I said. 'Did you get some help in?'

'It worked out in the end. Vidar and Sander both came in this morning.'

'Good! How's the rest of the weekend looking?'

'Reasonable.'

'Good! Keep it turning over, then, and I'll see you Tuesday!'

I plumped up a pillow and sat back, then picked the guidebook up off the bedside table and began to flick through the pages. The focus was mostly on museums and churches, which was predictable enough, urban parks, shopping streets and malls, flea markets. None of it really appealed, but I didn't feel like sitting around moping in my room either. Maybe I'd just have a wander about.

I sent the photo to the kids, the same message to all of them.

Your new aunt Alevtina and me in Moscow!

Astrid wrote back immediately.

Wow. When do I get to meet her?

The whole family are coming to Norway next summer, I typed back.

Exciting!

Leaving the hotel, I went in the opposite direction this time, ambling along a shopping street lined with jewellery shops and watchmakers. It could have been Rome or Paris, and when the next streets seemed to be more of the same I turned round and went back the other way. While the area surrounding Red Square was the only one I'd seen so far, it could hardly be more Russian. Besides, it wasn't as if I'd seen it once and for all.

There was a pleasant little street market outside the walls with a kids' merry-go-round and stalls selling food and drink. A bit further along, an escalator led down into the metro, or rather plunged down, as I discovered when I halted in front of it, mildly astonished to see how steep it was. I had no plans, so I stepped on and slid slowly into the underground.

I hadn't even found out where her mother lived when she and Dad had been together. I had no idea where he'd been to or what he'd seen.

Almost definitely Moscow, I'd have thought.

Maybe even right here?

1975 or 1976. His shirts with their long droopy collars. Tank tops and flares. Big, chunky glasses. The roll-your-own cigarettes. His calloused hands.

He'd been so much older than me then that it was hard to understand that I was twenty years older now than he'd been when he died.

Twenty years older!

He was just a kid.

A long hall opened out in front of me with little archways leading through to the platforms on either side. The station was busy, the trains were coming in and out, but what grabbed me was the space itself as I walked along. The chequered stone floor, the chandeliers that hung from the ceiling, the blocks of marble from which the archways projected, but first and foremost the statues at every opening. They were all life-size and it struck me that they represented different segments of society. I saw a seaman, a farmer, soldiers, an aviator, a footballer, workers, a bather, students.

It warmed my heart. There was something so very good about it.

Life-size, yet somehow larger than life, these people of bronze, lifted into significance.

The strange thing was that the real-life people who bustled and scurried among them lacked this completely. At least, that was my impression as I stood there surveying. Was it because the people, the passengers, were transient, coming and going, coming and going, while the statues were permanent?

I took some photos of them and went back up into the hot sun, wandered beside the sandy red wall, and stopped at the long pool that had been erected for the summer period, where a crowd of people were gathered. A young guy was wakeboarding, skimming along at breakneck speed, pulled by a wire hooked up to a system of rails overhead. Spray showered into the air around him. It looked like a lot of fun, but everyone, including the guy himself, seemed completely impassive.

I walked on to the main gate and entered the square again.

I hadn't learned *anything* about Dad's life here.

It was my fault, not hers. I hadn't asked.

But I'd thought we had so much time.

It was half the reason I'd come.

I looked around, noting the double-headed imperial eagle above the palace, the long red Kremlin wall, the fairy-tale church at the far end.

Near the middle of the square, in front of the wall, was a rather modest-looking black-and-red structure with a stepped pyramid-like design. I hadn't noticed it when I'd been here before.

Of course. It was Lenin's Mausoleum. It was here, on Red Square.

I went across. I couldn't read the lettering, but the number of characters suggested it said Lenin. H would be N, the A without the horizontal stroke would be L, the reverse N an I, and E was E.

There was no queue, just a soldier standing guard, so I went up to him.

'Excuse me,' I said. 'Is this where I can see Lenin?'

He stared at me without batting an eyelid.

'Closed,' he said.

'Ah,' I said.

I stepped away so I could get a better look at the wall beyond. The guidebook said the communist leaders were buried there, Brezhnev among them. Andropov, too, probably.

But I was too far away to be able to see properly.

Some men came hurrying by and disappeared behind the mausoleum. A moment later, some others came out, they too in double time.

Oh, it was so hot. If only I could have dived into the sea!

I crossed the square and went into one of the cafes on the other side where it was nice and cool, bought myself a cola and sat down.

I'd received three text messages without having noticed. One each from Pål and Tor, both with exclamation marks, and one from Lisa.

Nice-looking sister you've got there! she wrote. *I think you should try and meet up with her again. Not easy seeing someone for the first time with so many expectations involved. Hard to live up to. Send her a text! I think it's important, Syvert.*

But you didn't meet her, I wrote back. *I really don't think she liked me very much.*

She replied straight away.

Rubbish. She's your SISTER.

Lisa could make me feel so stupid when she told me what I should do in a situation and was so obviously right. There was a lot of *why didn't I think of that* in being married to her. It was always hard to admit, of course. Especially when we were younger I'd been loath to give in to her. She couldn't understand that. It was the case in hand that mattered to her. If a course of action was right in a given circumstance, it was right, and that was that, regardless of whose suggestion it was.

I wasn't quite as objective. *You're so stubborn!* she would always say, while Mum's line was *You're so bloody-minded!*

Astrid had inherited it. But not Tor.

It hurt a bit to see that. He did everything his wife told him and more. I didn't care for her. I'd tried to like her, and had occasionally managed to think better of her, but then I'd hear the way she spoke to him when she thought they were out of earshot. He'd decided to leave her once, had gone over to Pål's and slept on the sofa there for two days before giving in and going home again with his tail between his legs.

It's his life, Lisa always said. *It's not for us to interfere.*

I understood that. But it hurt all the same.

I went to Alevtina's messages and tapped to write a new text.

But did I *really* want to see her again?

Enough to put pressure on her? Enough to intrude and be even more annoying?

I put the phone back in my pocket and went outside into the heat again. The fish soup had been good, but not particularly filling, so I decided to have an early dinner at the hotel. Hamburger and chips, maybe. Always a good choice.

After eating on my own in the empty hotel bar, I went back up to my room and lay down on the bed, where, without intending to, I promptly fell asleep. When I woke up, it was with an indescribable feeling of despondency that seemed to have wormed its way inside me while I'd been most defenceless in sleep. My chest was heavy with sorrow. Everything was so hopeless.

I pulled the curtain aside and looked out into the empty street.

I was stranded. Nowhere to go, no one to meet.

I took a beer from the minibar and drank it while sitting on the bed.

For some reason, I thought of Mum. I ought to give her a ring. But then I'd feel obliged to tell her where I was, and that wouldn't do her any good at all. Was I going to fill her head with thoughts of Dad and his secret life here with his mistress, the fact that I was now meeting up with his love child?

Not if I could help it.

And I didn't want to lie to her. I'd never liked doing that, not even when it was for her own good.

Alevtina was *Dad's* daughter. He was her father.

If he hadn't died, she'd have grown up with him. That was what he'd planned, to come and live here. Or hadn't he meant it?

The first time I'd really talked to Lisa about Dad was after we'd been together a few weeks. And the first thing she'd asked me was if I thought he'd killed himself.

The thought had never even occurred to me, not once.

I was angry, but kept it inside. It was an anger that dissolved in the waves of ecstasy by which I was swept along in those first few weeks of infatuation. But the thought behind it remained.

Could he have felt such despair at the impossible situation he'd put himself in that he'd taken the simplest way out?

I couldn't bring myself to believe it. It would have been so gutless, so incredibly gutless, and Dad was never that.

But what did I know about it at the end of the day?

I was eleven years old when he died. Everything I'd seen then, I'd seen through the eyes of a child. I had no idea what sort of person he really was, no idea at all.

He had a daughter. She was real. She was here.

I couldn't let her go like that.

Not without a fight.

If she didn't want to see me, I'd change her mind. I'd insist until she did. And when she did, I'd insist we talked. Frankly and open-heartedly.

I got my phone out and started typing.

Dear Alevtina. Thank you for the lunch. It was great to see you. However, I feel that we didn't really talk. That's understandable, considering that we don't know each other at all. But I think we should meet again. I want to know about you. You're my sister. Do you understand? We need to be completely open with each other. Maybe we can even get drunk together or something. It helps sometimes. This comes from a very good place, so I sincerely hope you'll agree. Kind regards from Syvert

I hadn't heard back from her by the time I went to bed that night, and she still hadn't replied when I woke up the next morning. I had breakfast in the very grand dining room. They had everything, eggs prepared in all the different ways, cured meats and cheeses, bacon and sausages, fried potatoes and pancakes, yogurts, fruit and cake. It was hard to hold back, and after I'd eaten I had to go and lie down for a bit. When it got to twelve o'clock and I still hadn't heard from her, I wrote to her again. I'd got nothing to lose.

Dear Alevtina, I really must insist on our meeting again! I'm leaving tomorrow, so this is our last chance. In anticipation of your reply, your brother, Syvert

No response.

I had a cold shower and went down into the lobby to browse the leaflets there. I picked a few out and sat down on a sofa near the door. There were some river cruises that looked all right. Not a bad way to see the city, from the deck of a boat. A lot better than the top deck of a bus, at any rate.

I went up to the desk, where one of the receptionists, a young guy with a narrow, solemn-looking face, came towards me.

'Hello,' I said, putting the leaflet down on the counter between us and jabbing a finger at it. 'Is this very far from here?'

'Not at all,' he said.

'Can I walk there?'

'Yes, you can.'

'How long will it take?'

'Fifteen, twenty minutes. I can show you on the map, if you like.'

He opened a map in front of me, put a cross where the hotel was and drew the route down to the river.

'And the boats are right here,' he said, marking the spot with another cross. 'Bolshoy Ustinsky Bridge. Enjoy your trip, sir.'

I thanked him and went outside with the map in my hand, pausing on the pavement to study it closer. The departure point looked to be below the park where I'd been the day before. It would be easy enough to find. All I had to do was walk in a southerly direction.

I folded the map, stuck it in my back pocket and went left. Reaching an intersection, I followed a wide, busy boulevard. The pavements were almost deserted, and there were no shop windows to look in along the way. My hair was moist under my cap, my eyes squinting in the bright sunlight. I was still feeling full after my breakfast, so there wasn't much of a spring in my step, even though I was quite looking forward to a trip on the river.

The area felt vacant, which was odd, because of course it wasn't: there was asphalt, there were cars, kerbstones, signs and notices, tall buildings full of apartments and offices; there were doors, gateways, side streets. A whole world, and yet it felt like just the opposite, as if there was nothing there at all.

I got my phone out and called Joar as I walked along.

'Joar Løyning speaking,' he said.

'Can't you see it's me on the display?' I said.

'I didn't look. Are you in Moscow?'

'Yes.'

'Have you met her?'

'Yes. We had lunch yesterday.'

'What was she like?'

'OK. But we didn't really click.'

'Had you been expecting to?'

'Yes, of course.'

'She's not from Vågsbygd. She's Russian.'

'I know that. But still. People are people, wherever you go.'

He laughed, that dry laugh of his.

'You always smile at people, don't you?' he said.

'What are you getting at?'

'In Russia, smiling at strangers is considered fatuous, half-witted. Did you know that?'

'No, and I don't believe it either.'

'It's a fact. They probably think there's something wrong with you.'

'They can think what they like,' I said. 'Anyway, I heard you got famous while I've been away.'

'I've been in the media, yes.'

'Lisa says you seem to like it.'

'Yes.'

'So what's your theory?' I said, catching sight of the river glittering up ahead.

'There's no explanation. No one knows what it is. Which leaves only one way to make sense of it.'

'Which is?'

'It's a miracle.'

Now it was my turn to laugh.

'I thought you were a scientist!'

'I am.'

'Is it God giving us a sign? Is that what you're saying?'

'I don't know.'

'Is this what you've been saying on TV as well?'

'No. I've said what it *isn't*, and that we don't know yet what kind of phenomenon we're dealing with.'

'Glad to hear it! You won't get the sack just yet, then.'

'Does she look like Dad?'

'Not really. But she's more like you than me, I'd say. She's got two degrees. She's a biologist and a doctor.'

'What sort of biologist?'

'Haven't a clue.'

'I thought about studying biology.'

'I remember.'

'After Mum got cancer.'

'Yes. And I went the opposite way.'

'What do you mean?'

'You wanted to save her. I became an undertaker.'

'I hadn't thought of it that way before.'

'You surprise me.'

I came to a halt at the road that ran alongside the river, and waited to cross.

'I don't think she liked me,' I said.

'You're probably right about that,' he said as I stepped out.

'Out of the mouths of babes and younger brothers . . .' I said. 'But nice speaking to you, all the same. Are you coming down south again soon, or what?'

'No.'

'OK,' I said. 'Keep in touch.'

I put the phone back in my pocket, took my cap off and ran my fingers through my hair a few times, wiped the sweat from my brow with the short sleeve of my shirt, put my cap back on and carried on walking. There was the bridge, I could see, and on the other side the pier from where the boats departed.

I joined the queue for tickets and patted my back pocket to make sure my wallet was still there.

'Well, if it isn't a compatriot at long last!' a voice behind me said.

It was the couple from Stavanger, laden with shopping bags, beaming at me as if we were old friends. He was sporting a wide-brimmed straw hat, she a kind of bucket model. Their faces were red and sweaty.

'Nice to see you,' I said.

'And what a coincidence!' he said. I racked my brains for his name. Odd-Ivar? Odd-Magnus? 'A city of millions! What are the chances?'

'Not great,' I said, turning away from them as I stepped up to the ticket counter.

It would have been impolite to just walk off, so I stood to one side and waited for them after I was finished. The star shone pale, but still visible in the sunlight.

A miracle.

He meant it. He never said anything he didn't mean.

It was just a shame he had to be such a misery guts half the time. It was as if he had no idea a conversation required courtesy and consideration for others to make it work. Or maybe he just didn't care.

I'd have liked to have known what he meant by a miracle.

The two from Stavanger came up to me again.

'So, what have you been up to since we last saw you?' he said.

'Not a lot, really,' I said. 'Meandering about. Red Square. Have you been there?'

'Been there? Of course we've been there, it's a World Heritage site. I'd been looking forward to seeing Lenin, I must admit. Only the mausoleum was closed today. Did you see him?'

I shook my head.

'I was there yesterday, and it was closed then as well.'

'He's over a hundred and fifty years old now, you know. I did a bit of reading up on how they do it. The preservation is all ongoing. The technology gets better all the time, of course. Must have been an awful headache back in the twenties. I think he deteriorated rather quickly. They had a hell of a job with it, but it's all under control now. If I remember right, they replace tiny bits of the skin with plastic as and when required.'

'Sounds fascinating,' I said.

'It is,' he said. 'There's a team of experts on hand round the clock to look after him. The best in the country.'

'Maybe that's why it was closed. They were patching him up!'

I laughed. He stared at the ground for a moment, folding the fingers of his hand around the railing he was standing beside, then looked up again and gazed at the buildings across the river.

'Have you been to the museums you wanted to see?' I said.

'I'll say,' he said, glancing at his wife, who nodded and smiled. 'In this weather though, it's better to be indoors than out, so it was all right. What was the name of that painter, the one you liked so much?'

'Ilya Repin,' she said. 'But there were a lot more I liked besides him.'

'I'm sure,' he said. 'Is this our boat here, do you think?'

A large multi-deck riverboat in white and green came gliding towards the pier.

'Looks like it.'

It moored, and people filed out from inside onto the pier. I couldn't think of a way to tell the Norwegians I wanted to sit on my own without offending them, so I followed them upstairs to the upper deck and sat down in the sun alongside them.

'I think they serve dinner here,' he said.

'They put on dancing, too,' she said.

'Sounds like a nice night out,' I said. 'Would you like a drink?'

'White wine for us both,' he said. 'As dry as possible.'

I went up to the bar that was sheltered from the sun under a tarp canopy, ordered two glasses of white, and a beer for myself.

'This heat's too much of a good thing, isn't it?' he said. 'Never thought I'd hear myself say so, though. I love hot weather. We once had forty-four in Greece, but that was by the sea, which always helps. Doesn't feel as hot then, does it?'

'No, it doesn't,' I said.

The engines began to rumble again, their noise thrown back, as if trapped between the boat and the pier, a damp, muffled growl that didn't subside until the boat backed out sufficiently for it to be released.

'*Skål!*' said the Stavanger man, and we raised our glasses.

My phone shuddered in my pocket. It was Lisa.

Not heard from you for a while! Everything all right?

I replied straight away.

All OK! On a riverboat with some people from Stavanger. Call you later! All OK your end?

Yes, fine, she wrote back. *Sølvi's just gone. Who are you with from Stavanger?*

A chatty tourist couple, that's all.

Just your sort.

Ha ha, I wrote, and put the phone back in my pocket.

'I suppose the river's rather polluted,' I said. 'The water's so murky I can't see a thing.'

'It'll be no better in Paris or London,' he said.

Was he a communist? His defence of Moscow had fallen so promptly it seemed almost like a reflex.

Could he be a gymnasium teacher, a philatelist *and* a communist at the same time?

'A lot of blood will have run through this river,' I said, if only to hear his response.

'Perhaps not in this river exactly,' he said. 'But the country on the whole has seen a lot of bloodshed, certainly.'

'How many are estimated to have died as a result of communism, do you know?'

'Stalin wasn't communism.'

The same old argument.

So he *was* a communist.

'But Lenin, he was a communist, wasn't he?' I said.

'He was, yes.'

'There'll have been a few million lives lost in the Revolution, I'd have thought.'

'That was civil war. Terrible thing. But it takes two to tango, as they say.'

We sailed slowly past the Kremlin, and for the first time I listened to the voice that had been droning through the PA system ever since we left the pier. Kremlin was the Russian name for fortification, said the guide. Within the walls here were four palaces and four cathedrals, the oldest dating back to the fourteenth century. But the Kremlin, as we surely knew, was best known as the seat of political power in Russia, and its presidential residence.

'How splendid,' the Stavanger woman said.

'On that bridge we just sailed under, Boris Nemtsov was shot dead,' her husband said. 'I'll tell you why. He'd spoken out against Russian military involvement in Ukraine and corruption in Putin's government. The Kremlin can be as splendid as it likes, but it can't blot that out.'

'No, of course not,' she said, a touch offended, and turned to look the other way.

'That big church over there is certainly splendid,' I said. 'It looks like something out of a fairy tale.'

'The Cathedral of Vasily the Blessed. St Basil's, if you prefer.'

'I get the feeling you're well versed. Is that the philately showing through?'

'I've been interested in the country ever since I was a boy. But this is the first time I've been here.'

Nothing more was said for a while. The Stavanger couple sat gazing at the city, so I took the opportunity to stretch my legs and ambled to the afterdeck.

Everything had been so different from what I'd been hoping for. I'd thought meeting Alevtina would be a warm experience, full of affection, laughter and storytelling, in fact I'd taken it for granted. And I'd thought Moscow would fascinate me.

And yet here I was, out on a limb.

Nothing to hold on to.

Dad had obviously felt differently. He'd wanted to come and live here.

I couldn't understand it. If I met someone I liked in Moscow, perhaps even fell in love with her, would I be able to move over here and leave everything at home behind?

Even if I hadn't been happily married, I wouldn't have been able to do it.

Somewhere far in the distance there was a hollow rumble. I looked up in the direction from where it came.

The horizon was almost black.

A massive bank of thunderclouds.

Shallow waves raced across the surface of the water. A few seconds later, I was buffeted by gusts of wind.

I could almost feel the temperature drop.

The passengers around me were strangely enlivened.

I realised how we'd all been longing for it.

A release.

'Have you noticed the storm that's coming?' I said as I sat down with the Stavanger couple again.

They nodded.

'I hope it's not going to affect our cruise,' he said. 'I don't suppose they'll cancel it because of a bit of rain, though.'

'I'm sure they won't,' I said. 'I feel a bit cold all of a sudden. How about you?'

They shook their heads.

'It's still very hot,' he said.

'A breeze always makes me shiver, if my skin's moist,' I said.

'Really,' he said.

My phone vibrated.

It was a text from Alevtina.

There's a nice bar just by your hotel called Korobok, on Bolshaya Dmitrovka. Can we meet there at 20:00? A

Oh, thank goodness.

Of course! I wrote back. *Very much looking forward to seeing you again!*

It felt like I'd just been relieved of a heavy rucksack or something. I felt so much lighter.

Thunder rumbled again, closer this time. I looked up. The buildings stood against a backdrop of inky black.

'Lightning,' the Stavanger woman said. 'And again, over there.'

'And yet the sky's still blue above us!' I said.

'It won't be for long,' her husband said. 'Shall we go inside?'

Twenty minutes later, the storm was upon us. It didn't start gently, the way thunderstorms often do, but crashed around our ears from the outset. One minute all we heard were people in conversation, cutlery chinking against plates, the hum of the engines; the next, rain thrashing down on the roof above us, the surface of the river pelted with great, heavy raindrops that fell so hard it was easy to imagine they'd been fired by artillery. On the unprotected deck, they detonated like bursting balloons filled with water.

It was so wild, and came so suddenly, that I started to laugh.

The Stavanger couple gawped at me.

'Isn't it fantastic?' I said. 'At last!'

'We're thinking more about our cruise,' he said.

'It won't be in danger, I'm sure,' I said.

Impulsively, I stood up and stepped through the door onto the open deck for a moment, and was soaked to the skin in seconds.

It was as if the whole world had transformed. Everything had speeded up all of a sudden, the draggy listlessness of before now evaporated, and the glaring light, if not extinguished, had at least been dimmed considerably.

With rain streaming down my face I looked up to where the new star would be. The slate-grey vault of the sky was as if illuminated from within, a glow that looked as if it was in motion, turning and spinning, but it was only the scudding clouds that gave the impression.

A nerve of lightning flashed from the top of an enormous building on the riverbank and lit up the heavens, followed immediately by a crash of thunder. Oh, it was like a bomb going off. The air trembled, I laughed again, and again the sky ripped open, a new bolt angling down to strike the road beside the river.

The thunder that followed was tremendous.

But why had the lightning hit the ground? Didn't it always strike the tallest object?

Drenched and delirious, I went back inside to the couple from Stavanger.

'Looks like we'll be getting soaked anyway, so I thought I might as well get it over with,' I said, and wiped my face with a napkin before going over to buy myself another beer.

An hour later we moored at the same pier we'd departed from. The rain was still falling heavily, though nowhere near as fiercely as during those first minutes of the storm, and the occasional flashes of lightning we still saw were a lot further away now. The Stavanger couple found shelter under a pent roof where they could wait for a taxi. They weren't the only ones. The queue was long, and I decided I'd rather walk. We shook hands in parting, I wished them a pleasant cruise and set off back along the wide boulevard in the rain.

Everything that only a few hours earlier had seemed open and unfilled, appeared now as if compressed and crammed with life — cars with wipers swishing, yellow headlights, red tail lights, people with umbrellas unfolded, grass and trees verdant in the strange murk. The sounds that surrounded me too had changed, as if bound now to their sources, held down beneath the lid of cloud and rain.

I stopped at the busy intersection and waited for the green pedestrian light.

A sleek black car slowed down for red and came to a halt in front of me.

The driver turned his head and looked at me. He was wearing a monkey mask.

It was creepy. I froze.

Two passengers in the back seat were also masked, though as dogs.

I sensed it would be best not to stare, and looked away.

The light changed to green and I crossed over, my eyes fixed on the street up ahead. I didn't want to stop and look back, so I carried on walking, sensing the car then glide away through the gloom.

As I turned onto the pedestrain street a few minutes later, people came running towards me in the pouring rain. There were screams. At first, I didn't realise what was happening, but then I saw the car again. It was pulled up at an angle so as to block the street, another likewise a short distance away. A man waving an automatic pistol stood behind the first vehicle shouting. He was wearing a dog mask.

My heart raced, but I wasn't afraid; they were still some distance away and didn't seem to be targeting passers-by.

I turned and began walking slowly in the other direction.

An alarm went off. Then, shots rang out. I spun round in time to see four men emerge from a jeweller's shop and jump into the cars. A couple of security guards came tentatively after them. The vehicles pulled away along the pedestrian street without haste, turned down the first side street and were gone.

The street had emptied.

I ran towards the scene. Two figures were lying on the floor inside. The display cases had been shattered, there was glass everywhere. And blood.

I bent over the injured person who was nearest to me, a woman, shot through the cheek and throat, a pool of earthy red staining the floor beside her. I tore off my shirt. There wasn't a chance she was going to make it, her jugular was gaping and my shirt at once became heavy with blood.

Sirens in the distance.

Behind the injured woman, half hidden by a display case, the second figure moved.

I pressed my bunched-up shirt to the woman's throat. She opened her eyes and her gaze met mine. Her face was quite white, drained. But her eyes were clear and warm. I turned my head. The second person was now sitting upright. I saw that it was a man, that he'd been shot in the chest. He held his hands to the wound and stared down at himself.

The sirens approached.

Blood spurted out between the man's fingers. His heart should have stopped, his chest was blown open, and yet it pumped. He looked at me with his mouth agape. I looked down at the woman again. I couldn't help them both.

At the same moment, people came bursting in. They were shouting, I didn't know what. I stood up and put my hands in the air. A policeman grabbed me, another twisted my arms behind my back, handcuffs snapping around my wrists, and I was bundled outside as more came running, paramedics with stretchers, and this was the last I saw of what happened at the scene.

Outside, the street was a chaos of response units with flashing lights. The two policemen dragged me aside. I said nothing. They were twitchy, heavy-handed. One of them shouted something at me in Russian.

'I'm only a tourist,' I said.

They exchanged some words with each other. One of them went away, the other stayed with me and gripped his pistol. Shortly afterwards, the paramedics emerged carrying the two casualties on stretchers they then lifted into two ambulances. There were no bystanders, no passers-by stopping to see what was going on, and I realised the street must have been cordoned off. The ambulances drew away. The policeman from before returned with another man, this one in plain clothes.

'What were you doing there?'

'My hotel is just around the corner. I was on my way back there.'

'Where are you from?'

'Norway.'

'Ah, Norway. A beautiful country.'

'Yes, it is.'

'Can you prove it?'

'I have some ID in my wallet.'

He gestured to the uniformed officer at his side, a movement of the eyebrows, and he released my handcuffs. I took my wallet out of my pocket and handed the plain-clothes man my driving licence.

'Passport?'

'At the hotel.'

'Can you prove you're staying there?'

'Yes,' I said. 'Just a moment.'

I found the booking confirmation on my phone and showed it to him.

'OK,' he said, turning his back to me and tapping a number on his phone before conducting a short conversation with someone in Russian. He turned to face me again.

'Tell me what you saw.'

I gave him my account: the driver in the monkey mask, the passengers in their dog masks, the cars blocking the street, the lookout man with the gun, the four who came out, the way the cars left the scene so slowly.

He didn't take notes, but stared at me as I spoke, as if I were an animal whose behaviour he was studying.

'When are you leaving Moscow?'

'Tomorrow afternoon.'

'Tomorrow morning at nine, a man will come and speak to you again, at the hotel. Your passport will be returned once you've answered his questions. Understand?'

'Yes.'

'Then you're free to go.'

Standing under the shower in my room, I watched the blood wash from my shirt into the drain, and began to tremble. My arms shook, and my legs felt so weak all of a sudden that I had to sit down and let the water pour over me.

I hadn't been in any danger, so it wasn't that. It was the fact that without warning I'd been pulled into something terrible. As if a door had opened in the normal world and I'd been hauled through it into a different world entirely.

Now I was back, the door had closed again, and everything was the same as before.

But I would never forget the look in the eyes of the woman dying on the floor in front of me.

I stood up again and washed my hair and body with the shower gel. Lisa always said it damaged your hair if you didn't use a designated hair product, but I'd never seen any sign of that. Soap was soap, whatever they called it.

I dried myself and put on a white shirt and a pair of chinos, drank a beer as I padded about in my socks, scrolled through the movies on offer, though without finding anything I particularly wanted to watch. I realised I was hungry, and went downstairs to the bar to get myself a hamburger and chips.

I needed to call Lisa before going out. I didn't feel like talking about the robbery, it would be far too much for her to take in over the phone and she'd only worry about it all evening. On the other hand, it would come across as a bit strange if I didn't mention it before going home, as if I didn't trust her in some way and felt I had to keep things from her.

I smiled at the girl behind the bar as she came over to take my order, only then I remembered that smiling at strangers made them think you were daft.

If Joar knew what he was talking about, that is.

Usually he did, so most likely it was true.

They probably had their suspicions anyway, if they'd seen me go through the lobby earlier on, bare-chested and drenched, gripping a shirt that was soaked in blood.

At least I still had a decent body.

'Hamburger with sweet potato fries and an Amstel beer,' the girl repeated.

'That's right,' I said.

'How would you like it cooked, sir? Well done, medium or rare?'

'Medium to rare, isn't that best? Or no, I'm thinking about steaks now. A hamburger should be well done, right?'

She noted it down and went back behind the bar. While I waited, I phoned Lisa.

'Hi,' she said. 'How's Moscow?'

'Moscow's good,' I said. 'Two things to tell you. One is that I'm meeting Alevtina again. The other is that I witnessed a robbery on my way back to the hotel earlier today.'

'A robbery? You're joking?'

'No, seriously. A jeweller's shop just round the corner. I came walking along and all of a sudden there was a car blocking the street and people running away. I think I saw a guy with a gun, but I'm not sure. I just turned round straight away and ran in the opposite direction like everyone else. When I went back a bit later on, there were police everywhere.'

'That sounds awful.'

'It was, yes. I'm glad Alevtina agreed to see me again, though.'

'What did I tell you?'

'I can't remember! But you did urge me to get in touch with her again, so thanks for that. Anyway, how are you? What have you been up to?'

'Working, mostly. I bought a peach tree yesterday, by the way. I've been watering it and admiring it.'

'A peach tree? What for?'

'I've always been so fond of peaches. I just never knew they could grow here. I saw them at the garden centre and bought one on the spot.'

'Where have you put it?'

'In front of the south-facing wall. It'll get the sun all day there.'

'So you get a peach tree, I get a sailing boat. Deal?'

She laughed.

'OK, deal.'

I entered the address of the bar into Google Maps an hour before we were due to meet, just to see how far it was. It was very close, as she'd said, only a six-minute walk from the hotel. I shaved and wet my hair that had dried into a fluff, rubbing it with the towel and applying some styling wax. The unspoken rules from when I'd been growing up, that with the possible exception of a deodorant men weren't allowed to use perfume, and never under any circumstance were supposed to put any-thing in their hair, were still so ingrained in me that even picking up the tin of styling wax made me feel embarrassed, despite the fact that society now, forty years on, was completely changed, at least in such respects, and no one was going to have bad things to say or think about me on that account.

As I got myself ready, the events I'd witnessed earlier kept flashing back, each time a shock, and yet somehow they were already elusive, as if it had all occurred a long time ago and something had suddenly hap-pened to remind me of it.

And then it was time to go.

I put the key card in my wallet, put my shoes on, and a jacket, stepped into the corridor and closed the door behind me.

She'd asked me for photos of Dad. I couldn't believe I hadn't brought any with me. She wanted to know what he looked like, of course she did.

We had two albums of photos from the sixties and seventies. Joar had taken one with him when he moved, Lisa and I had the other, in the living room at home. The photos were all glued to the pages and it would have been impractical to have brought the whole album. But I should have had some copies done for her to see.

But wait a minute, all it took was a phone!

Lisa could photograph some of them and then send them on. Why hadn't I thought of it before?

I paused on the stairs and texted her. She answered immediately.

Will do.

Downstairs, I went over to the reception desk. The same earnest young man came towards me with an enquiring look.

'There was a robbery in the street here earlier on, which I witnessed,' I told him. 'Two people were shot. You wouldn't know anything about their condition, would you?'

'No, sir, I'm sorry,' he said. 'I didn't hear about that. Maybe you should call the police?'

'That's OK. Thank you,' I said, and turned towards the entrance as my phone vibrated against my thigh. Lisa, sending the photos. I stopped and looked at them. Perfect. Eight different ones of him. Quite decent quality, too.

Excellent! Alevtina would be glad.

Outside, the rain was still pouring, and the gutters were flooded. I'd completely forgotten the change in the weather. It was as if once again I'd opened a door into a different world. I had, too! I went back inside to see if there was an umbrella I could borrow. There was, a metal cyclinder containing several stood just inside the door, most of them wet and not properly closed. They reminded me of birds with curving beaks and necks that craned from great black wings.

I took one and went back out. There was no tape cordoning off the jeweller's shop, and no police presence either. The sky above me was dark, the asphalt a shimmer of reflected street lights and shop windows. As I walked, I held my phone up in front of me to make sure the little circle that was me was going in the right direction, towards the red flag that stood planted perhaps fifteen centimetres further up as I scrolled.

Five minutes later I was standing outside the bar. I was early, though not as early as last time, so I closed the umbrella, shaking it as I did so, and went inside.

The room was rather dark. With its brick walls and timberwork the place looked more like something you'd find in the country than in a big city. But of course that was the idea. The furniture looked antique, all deep chairs, and from the ceiling above the bar strange wooden cages hung with lights inside. Lamps glowed all around, and elsewhere in the room something resembling moss hung down too from the ceiling, while old-looking cabinets of dark wood contained bottles and glasses.

She didn't seem to be here yet.

I got myself a beer and sat down in a corner where I looked again at the photos Lisa had sent. I was in one of them myself, sitting astride a tricycle in a white woolly hat that was tied under my chin and a short coat the colour of mustard. Dad, clean-shaven and without glasses, but with all his dark, thick hair, held the handlebar with one hand as he turned towards the camera and smiled.

Everything about it screamed the sixties. It could have been anyone at all from that time. But it was Dad and me. Syvert and Syvert.

The door opened and I looked up.

Alevtina.

She scanned the room. In the seconds before she saw me, I saw Dad in her. The shape of her face. The way she moved her head.

A shiver ran through me.

Our eyes met and she came over with a smile. I stood up and we hugged.

'How are you doing?' she said, putting her umbrella out of harm's way before sitting down.

'Good,' I said. 'What would you like to drink? My shout this time, OK?'

'OK,' she said, and smiled again. 'A vodka, please.'

'Just vodka? Neat?'

She nodded.

It struck me again how good-looking she was, even though I'd known what to expect this time. Maybe it was why I hadn't seen the resemblance to Dad the first time round. There'd been something about the eyes, and the eyebrows then, but only very faintly, an echo, perhaps, not of him, but of the image I held of him. That would be why beauty was so often described as stunning. It stopped you from seeing anything else.

I came back to the table with two small, ice-cold glasses of vodka.

'I read the letters from my mother,' she said as I sat down again. 'They were absolutely heartbreaking.'

There was an intensity about her, a glow in her eyes, that hadn't been there before.

'Yes,' I said, and nodded. 'I was shocked when I read them.'

'They're so full of hope, the way they strain towards the future. She was obviously very much in love. I hadn't been prepared for that. I knew about my father, of course. But I hadn't ever thought about how much she must have loved him. He must have been a remarkable man.'

'To me, he was just normal.'

'Was he?'

'To me, yes.'

I looked at her and smiled.

'Thank you for meeting me again,' I said.

We chinked our glasses for our father.

I wasn't sure, but her eyes seemed to moisten as we did so.

'Tell me a bit about your mother,' I said.

'What she was like, you mean?'

I nodded.

'She was very generous and thoughtful. The kind of person who went out of her way to help others. And very non-judgemental, too.'

'In what way?'

'Oh, you know, always trying to understand people and accept them as they were.'

'She sounds like a very nice person.'

She drained her glass. I thought it best to keep up, and did likewise.

'What about your own mother?' she asked.

'My mother? She's nice, too. Though perhaps not quite as kind as yours! She's always had a bit of a temper, I think. But a heart of gold!'

'She's still alive, then?'

'Yes. She lives in a home for elderly people not far from where I live. Can I get you another?'

She nodded, and I got up.

As the bartender entered the amount in the till, I glanced back at her. She was sitting with her elbows propped against the table, her hands folded under her chin. Naturally, it was impossible to tell what she might be thinking. But it wasn't easy to say what kind of a mood she was in either.

Damn it, the photos!

I went back to the table and put the drinks down, then pulled out my phone.

'This time I brought some photos of my dad,' I said. 'Would you like to see them?'

Her face lit up.

'Really? Yes, I would, very much!'

I tapped the first photo and held the phone up for her to see.

'Oh my goodness!' she said, and looked up at me with wide eyes as if she'd been startled. 'Is that him?'

'Yes,' I said, and looked at the photo again. It was from when he and Mum got married. He was about to get into a car and was looking straight at the camera, in a dark suit and white shirt, a flower in his buttonhole.

'But I've seen him before!'

'Have you?'

She nodded.

'I've dreamt about him. Oh my goodness. How is that even possible?'

'I don't know . . .'

We stared at each other for a moment. She still looked startled.

'It must be my mind playing a trick on me,' she said. 'Some kind of déjà vu, perhaps.'

'Yes,' I said.

I showed her the other photos, and she studied them intently.

'I can send them to you.'

'Yes, please do.'

I sat down again and drank a couple of mouthfuls of the beer I'd forgotten about. She stared absently at the table in front of her. Clearly, she'd been shaken. But it wasn't so strange. It was the first time she'd seen a photograph of her own father.

'Can you see yourself in him?' I said.

'Yes. Yes, I can.'

'I don't look like him at all.'

'Perhaps you inherited something else from him, something other than his appearance.'

'I don't think so.'

'Was he a good father to you?'

'Yes. He liked doing things with me.'

'And you like doing things with your children, I'm sure.'

'We used to do things together, yes. When they were small.'

'There you go, then!' she said, and laughed.

And then she looked at me.

'How weird, me dreaming about him like that. But I can't have done. It must be some sort of auto-suggestion.'

'Do you know how I found the letters?' I said.

She shook her head.

'I dreamt about my father one night. It was so real that it was like he was still alive. I was about twenty years old at the time. I started thinking about him in a different way then. Wondering about the person he was. I'd never done that before. So I went through his things and found all these letters in Russian. I didn't even know he knew Russian! I got someone to translate them. That was when I found out that he'd had this secret relationship with a woman in Russia.'

'That must have been upsetting.'

'It was, it was very disconcerting!'

'And there I was, on the other side of it all,' she said. 'To me, it was your side of things that was secret and mysterious. My mother married another man, and it was he who became my father. Our father, yours and mine, simply wasn't a part of my world.'

'Until now.'

'Until now.'

I raised my glass towards her.

'To you, my sister, and to our having met at last.'

She chinked her glass resolutely against mine and knocked back its contents.

'I'm sorry I left so early the first time,' she said. 'I think I just wasn't prepared, if you know what I mean. There are a lot of emotions in play here.'

'Yes,' I said. 'I did wonder why you had to go all of a sudden, I have to admit. I thought maybe you were the kind of person who has a lot of feelings on the inside, but not so many on the outside.'

She laughed.

'That's a good way of putting it.'

'I think our father was probably a bit like that.'

'Do you think so?'

'When I started asking about him, his brother told me that he suffered greatly from anxiety. I hadn't known that. I think he must have hidden it from us.'

'What about you? Is that something you suffer from, too?'

'No, not at all. Never have. Unless I've been suffering all along without knowing!'

I smiled, and she did, too.

'And you?'

'Occasionally.'

'You'll have it from him, then, I imagine.'

'I don't think so,' she said, and smiled again. 'I think it's all my own, to be honest.'

I could feel myself slowly getting drunk, that wonderful rising of the soul, and all I wanted to do was sit there talking and laughing as we drank. She altered too, her features softened and she became much less guarded, though it was still me doing most of the talking.

After a while, I hit the point where I had to start concentrating in order to talk properly. Some of the fun went out of it then, and rather than going with the flow I found myself struggling against it. It was a bit like realising you were dreaming when you were still dreaming.

'Do you think we can be completely honest with each other?' she said all of a sudden.

'Of course,' I said.

'Shall we give it a try?'

'Haven't you been honest tonight?'

'Sometimes I'm not even honest with myself. Let me get another round in first.'

'Great,' I said.

I got my phone out and checked my email while she was gone. Nothing new, though it was hardly surprising for a Sunday night. I checked the football results instead. A two—one defeat to Strømsgodset, that too hardly surprising, but still a disappointment.

She came back with more drinks. I decided to slow down a bit. Few things were worse than travelling with a massive hangover.

'Were you thinking we should take turns to ask each other questions?' I said.

'Sorry?'

'The honesty thing.'

'Oh, that. No, I didn't mean like a game. But more as an obligation to ourselves. I can ask you a question if you like, though!'

She looked me in the eye.

'Do you believe in God?'

I laughed.

'No! Do you?'

'Yes,' she said. 'But I've never told anyone. Not even myself. I do, though. Yes. I do.'

Neither of us spoke for a moment.

'This might be difficult to talk about,' she said then. 'When you told me about the way your father died, my first thought, my very first thought, was that he committed suicide. But I didn't know him at all, so of course I've no way of knowing.'

'I think he did too,' I heard myself say. 'I think he realised he'd put himself in an impossible situation. Perhaps he was suffering from a depression because of it. At any rate, I think he drove his car off the bridge to escape it all.'

My eyes filled with tears as I uttered the words.

She reached out her hand and briefly placed it on mine.

'We'll never know for sure, will we?'

'I suppose not,' I said. 'It doesn't matter either, not really.'

I wiped my eyes and smiled at her. And then I laughed.

'Why are you laughing?'

'I don't know. It just felt so good to be able to say that.'

It sounded mad, but it was true. I'd known it all along, somewhere deep inside. But only by saying it out loud did it become real. And it felt good.

'How about another?' I said, and got to my feet.

'Why not?'

She looked up at me and smiled.

It was a warm smile, I thought, as I stood at the bar waiting for our drinks. And there was no indication as yet that she was thinking of leaving.

I looked across the room at her. She was staring straight ahead. Perhaps I wasn't the only one feeling a bit drunk. I knew nothing about her. I had no idea what sort of person she was.

She held things back, my new sister.

I paid and returned to the table, handing her her drink.

'So,' I said as I sat down, 'if we're going to be honest with each other, then tell me who you are.'

She looked at me rather perplexed.

'What would you say is your most defining character trait, as you see it?'

'What a strange question.'

'I want to get to know you, that's all. The way you see yourself, the person you are when there's no one else around.'

'But you're around now.'

'I don't count, I'm your brother!'

She laughed.

'Yes, you are. Hm.'

She paused and looked down at the table, turning her glass in her hands.

'I don't think I'm very good with other people,' she said. 'I get too wrapped up in myself.'

'I didn't mean a negative trait!' I said.

'Let me turn it around and ask how you see me,' she said.

'I see sorrow. Beauty. A lust for life.'

She held my gaze for a long moment.

'A lust for life . . .' she said.

'Yes,' I said.

'I've never thought of myself like that,' she said. 'But perhaps you're right.'

She smiled.

'What about you?'

'Me? My wife, Lisa, says I lack insight into myself.'

'Don't we all.'

'Good answer!'

We fell silent. I looked around the room, as if rediscovering it.

'You know,' she said, her eyes fixing on me, 'it's rather telling that you didn't answer my question. If we're still meant to be honest with each other, that is.'

'Sorry, what question?'

'I said *What about you?* Going back to you asking about me.'

'Ah.'

'You avoided the question. You said you lacked insight into yourself.'

'But it's true.'

Her gaze was unyielding.

'We all have *some* insight into ourselves. You're just avoiding it.'

'How do you know?' I said, smiling to take the edge off what sounded like a rather abrupt response.

Her expression was earnest, her eyes dark.

'Do you really want me to be honest with you?'

'Of course.'

'Don't say of course, if you don't mean it.'

'What is this?'

'I'll tell you why I left our lunch so early. I've never known my real father. You know that. In that respect, there's always been something incomplete about my life. Something has been missing. I've always felt I was longing for something, but strange as it sounds I've never really known what it was before. All my life, it's been the same.'

'Yes?'

'I'm telling you so that you know how important it was for me to see you. You may not believe it, since it took me so long to write back to you. But it meant so much to me that I feared it. You're the only link I have to my father.'

'It meant a lot to me, too.'

She carried on as if she hadn't heard me speak.

'And then suddenly we met, and I found we didn't connect. I'm not blaming you. It was a difficult situation for us both. It had nothing to do with failed expectations, I hadn't been hoping for any kind of revelation. It was just that I couldn't relate to you at all. And because I couldn't relate to you, it was as if I couldn't relate to my father either.'

'Our father.'

'Yes. Our father.'

'Where are you heading with this?'

'I think to the question you didn't answer, about the person you are.'

'I'm your brother.'

'Exactly. And so we must be able to talk.'

She smiled for the first time in a while, at the same time as her gaze passed over the table.

'Let's talk about your investments, then.'

'My stocks?'

'Our father left you some money, and that money made you wealthy.'

'Is this about money? Are you angling for a share?'

'No, not at all. But you invested in the oil industry when as everybody knows pollution from fossil fuels poses the gravest risks to humans and the environment. And there you were bragging about it.'

'I mentioned it, that's all.'

'How could you not have considered that aspect? Because you shy away from consequences, that's why. We've only met twice, and yet this is obvious to me. You are a man who shies away from consequences. And I realised that would impact on us.'

'In what way?'

'Because you were going to avoid the consequences.'

For a moment, neither of us said anything. The only thing I wanted was to get up and leave. But that would only underline her point.

'But then you cried, when you told me you thought our father had committed suicide.'

'I'm not sure I want to be psychoanalysed right now.'

'Why did you cry?'

I shrugged.

'It made me sad,' I said.

'Have you cried for your father before?'

'Of course.'

'We're being honest here, remember?'

I got to my feet and put my jacket on.

'I've had enough of this. You're accusing me of lying. I never lie.'

'I'm sorry. Please don't go,' she said, standing up to place a hand on my shoulder.

I looked her in the eye. She seemed genuinely sorry, and I sat down again.

'You see, it's a most dangerous thing.'

'What is?'

'Honesty.'

'Not for me, I'm an honest person. But I don't like accusations.'

'You're the only person who can know your own truth. And if the truth is that you've never fled from the matter of your father and his death, or from other difficulties in your life, then there's no need to be angry or insulted, is there?'

'I really don't understand why you're talking like this.'

'Because you're my brother! You grew up with my father, who I never even met! We can't just sit here and be polite and talk about nothing. We can't allow our meeting each other to be inconsequential!'

'Of course not,' I said.

'How about another drink?' she said, smiling all of a sudden.

'I don't see why not,' I said with some hesitation.

It was a lie, I realised as she went up to the bar. I could think of plenty of reasons not to have another drink with her.

I wanted to go back to the hotel and go to bed, get a few hours' sleep, before dragging myself out to the airport, falling asleep on the flight, driving home.

That was what I wanted.

Not even Lisa at her worst was as bad as this.

Joar's sarcasm was nothing by comparison, I was used to that.

Why couldn't people leave each other alone? Meet up, have a nice time, and then say goodbye?

She found me superficial, but how much had all her expensive clothes set her back? And how long did she spend on her appearance every day?

I spent exactly nothing on mine.

'Thanks,' I said as she handed me my drink.

'You're welcome.'

'How about emulating your mother a bit more?' I said, hoping I'd be hitting a tender spot.

'In what way?'

'Accepting other people for what they are.'

'But I do accept you! Of course I do! I thought this was more about you accepting yourself, really.'

'All I wanted was for us to have a nice evening together.'

'And now you're angry with me.'

'Not at all.'

Again, it was as if I only became aware of our surroundings as I paused and looked around the room. Normally, I enjoyed being drunk, the feeling of everything else receding while the faces around you become fluid and dreamlike. It went together with laughing and joking, having a good time.

Not with this.

I turned to face her.

And what I saw was Dad.

A terrible thought occurred to me. I was meeting him again in her guise. I was with him now.

It was he who was telling me I shied away from difficulty.

The moment lasted a second or two. And it had to do with me being so drunk that the walls of my conscious mind were now bearing down to such an extent that there was only room inside them for one thing at a time.

'Listen,' she said, 'I'm sorry for being so presumptuous. I'm a bit drunk, you see. Well, more than a bit, actually. I'm very drunk.'

'Some people get happy when they're drunk,' I said.

'I know. I do sometimes as well. Only not tonight, it seems.'

'That's OK. I accept you as you are,' I said.

She laughed. I laughed too.

'What time do they close here?' I asked.

'That's up to us. They stay open until the last guest leaves. Do you want to call it a night?'

'Well, travelling home with a terrible hangover tomorrow isn't the most inviting prospect.'

'Indeed.'

'Tomorrow needs doing as well, as we say in Norway,' I said, and got to my feet. She put her coat on, while I discovered I'd already got my jacket on from before.

Outside, she turned towards me.

'It was good to talk,' she said.

'Yes, I think so too,' I said.

'And we'll see you all next summer?'

'Yes.'

We hugged.

'Goodbye, big brother,' she said softly, and then walked away down the street.

The next morning I woke up to the sound of the room telephone ringing. I sat up reluctantly. My head was pounding, my mouth dry. The sudden movement made me feel sick.

I didn't know anyone here, so it could only be from reception. Maybe they were wondering why I hadn't checked out yet.

But it was only nine o'clock, so that couldn't be it.

I decided not to answer.

Then, just as it stopped, I realised it could be Alevtina.

Or no. Why would she be calling the hotel?

It started ringing again and I crossed the room to pick it up.

'Hello?'

'Mr Løyning?'

'Yes?'

'There's someone here to see you.'

'Who would that be?'

'A police officer. Are you ready to receive him?'

'Oh! Yes. Yes, send him up!'

I checked my mobile and saw that Alevtina had sent me a text.

Thank you for a very nice and very interesting evening. Love, A

I closed the messages app again and put the phone back down on the bedside table, then put some clothes on as fast as I could, the ones I'd been wearing the night before, grabbed the rest in the wardrobe, stuffed them into my case along with whatever other items of mine I could see lying about, snapped the case shut and stood it upright by the wall. That done, I quickly tidied the duvet on the bed, and by the time I heard the knock on the door I was sitting in the armchair casually studying the guidebook.

'Come in!' I called out.

The door handle went up and down a couple of times.

'It's locked,' a rather high-pitched male voice replied.

I went and opened it. A short, slightly built man wearing faded jeans and a white shirt was standing in the corridor. I motioned for him to come in and stepped aside. He informed me it was merely a formality and asked me to tell him what I'd already told his colleague the day before. I sat down on the edge of the bed, while he took the armchair. He opened the voice recorder app on his phone, which he balanced on the armrest, holding his hand poised above it for a second in case it slid off.

I repeated everything I'd said. He stopped me occasionally to ask a question, but after twenty minutes or so he was done, switched off his phone and got to his feet.

'Can I ask you something?' I said as I showed him to the door.

'Of course,' he said.

'The two people who were shot. I assume they're both dead?'

'They are both alive,' he said. 'Their condition is stable.'

I nodded. He thanked me for my help and wished me a pleasant journey home. I tried to go back to sleep, but couldn't, so I had a shower and went down to the breakfast room even though I wasn't that hungry. It turned out not to be a problem. Bacon is a treat for a hangover, and once you've got some bacon inside you, you'll invariably find yourself ravenous for all sorts of other things too.

It was still raining and I decided to clear away some administrative work before heading off. It was Monday now and the emails were already piling up. I replied to a few, and then gave Jarle a call.

'Hello, it's me,' I said. 'Everything under control? We've not gone bankrupt yet, I take it?'

'Everything under control, yes,' he said. 'But if it carries on like this, we might well end up bankrupt.'

'How do you mean?'

'We've not had a single one in all weekend. None Saturday, none Sunday, and none today yet, either.'

'None?'

'Not one.'

'Have you thought of checking the website and the phones, see if everything's working?'

'Yes, done that. Everything's fine.'

'Strange. What about our other branches, have you checked with them?'

'Done that, too. Nothing's come in anywhere.'

'There must be something wrong with the report-back systems. Maybe the server's down or something.'

'I don't think so.'

'It's the only reasonable explanation. There can't possibly not have been a single death in three days, not in four towns!'

'That's what it looks like.'

'It's never happened before, nowhere near. Listen, I've got just under an hour before I get going here. Let me make a few calls, see what's going on.'

'You'll be back home tonight, will you?'

'That's right, yes.'

'Had a nice time?'

'Yes, as a matter of fact, very nice. Anyway, I'll call you back once I know what's what.'

I ended the call and phoned our offices in the other towns, one after the other. They only confirmed what Jarle had told me. Not a single corpse had come in since Friday. And it wasn't just us either. Not a single death had been registered.

It was so weird that I phoned one of the big funeral companies in Oslo to hear what the situation was like up there. It was the same.

I sat on the bed and stared vacantly at the phone in my hand.

I'd never known anything like it.

I supposed it was possible in theory that during a three-day period not a single person died in the whole country. But theoretical possibility didn't make it any less weird.

And weird was what it was, there was no other word for it.

I slung my jacket over my arm, picked up my suitcase and bag and went down to the lobby, where my taxi was already waiting for me. Outside, the light from the new star shone in the grey sky above us, as if through a shroud.

Sources: Anya Bernstein, *The Future of Immortality: Remaking Life and Death in Contemporary Russia* (Princeton and Oxford: Princeton University Press, 2019); Brita Lotsberg Bryn, *Den russiske togmyten: En kulturfilologisk tilnærming til russiskspråklig jernbanefiksjon* (Oslo: Cappelen Damm Akademisk, 2018); Boris Groys (ed.), *Russian Cosmism* (Cambridge, MA, and London: MIT Press, 2018); Nikolai Krementsov, *Revolutionary Experiments: The Quest for Immortality in Bolshevik Science and Fiction* (Oxford: Oxford University Press, 2014); Jon D. Levenson, *Resurrection and the Restoration of Israel: The Ultimate Victory of the God of Life* (New Haven and London: Yale University Press, 2006); George M. Young, Jr, *Nikolai Fedorov: An Introduction* (Belmont: Nordland Publishing Company, 1979); George M. Young, *The Russian Cosmists: The Esoteric Futurism of Nikolai Fedorov and His Followers* (Oxford: Oxford University Press, 2012).

For other sources I've found useful and inspiring while working on this novel, see the bibliography at themorningstar.no

Thanks to Ann-Kristin Bjergene, Dag O. Hessen, Rolf-Inge Vogt Andrésen, Nils Olav Årdal and Olga Drabot for invaluable help with things I know nothing about, and to Bjørn Arild and Kari Ersland, Monica Fagerholm, Kjersti Instefjord and Yngve Knausgård for their readings as the novel came together. Thanks, too, to Charles Buchan, Andrew Wylie, and everyone at Forlaget Oktober. The editor of it all in the original Norwegian was Geir Gulliksen, and if thanks could ever be sufficient, I'd thank him here.

THE WOLVES OF ETERNITY

Martin Aitken would like to thank Professor Hans Otto Uldall Fynbo of the Department of Physics and Astronomy, Aarhus University, for his help with four short passages relating to radioactivity and radiation.

THE LEOPARD

The leopard is one of Harvill's historic colophons and an imprimatur of the highest quality literature from around the world.

When The Harvill Press was founded in 1946 by former Foreign Office colleagues Manya Harari and Marjorie Villiers (hence Har-vill), it was with the express intention of rebuilding cultural bridges after the Second World War. As their first catalogue set out: 'The editors believe that by producing translations of important books they are helping to overcome the barriers, which at present are still big, to close interchange of ideas between people who are divided by frontiers.' The press went on to publish from many different languages, with highlights including Giuseppe Tomasi di Lampedusa's *The Leopard*, Boris Pasternak's *Doctor Zhivago*, José Saramago's *Blindness*, W. G. Sebald's *The Rings of Saturn*, Henning Mankell's *Faceless Killers* and Haruki Murakami's *Norwegian Wood*.

In 2005 The Harvill Press joined with Secker & Warburg, a publisher with its own illustrious history of publishing international writers. In 2020, Harvill Secker reintroduced the leopard to launch a new translated series celebrating some of the finest and most exciting voices of the twenty-first century.

Laurent Binet: *Civilisations*
    trans. Sam Taylor
Paolo Cognetti: *The Lovers*
    trans. Stash Luczkiw
Paolo Cognetti: *Without Ever Reaching the Summit*
    trans. Stash Luczkiw

Pauline Delabroy-Allard: *All About Sarah*
    trans. Adriana Hunter
Álvaro Enrigue: *You Dreamed of Empires*
    trans. Natasha Wimmer
Urs Faes: *Twelve Nights*
    trans. Jamie Lee Searle
María Gainza: *Portrait of an Unknown Lady*
    trans. Thomas Bunstead
Stefan Hertmans: *The Ascent*
    trans. David McKay
Ismail Kadare: *A Dictator Calls*
    trans. John Hodgson
Ismail Kadare: *The Doll*
    trans. John Hodgson
Jonas Hassen Khemiri: *The Family Clause*
    trans. Alice Menzies
Karl Ove Knausgaard: *In the Land of the Cyclops: Essays*
    trans. Martin Aitken
Karl Ove Knausgaard: *The Morning Star*
    trans. Martin Aitken
Karl Ove Knausgaard: *The Wolves of Eternity*
    trans. Martin Aitken
Antoine Leiris: *Life, After*
    trans. Sam Taylor
Édouard Louis: *A Woman's Battles and Transformations*
    trans. Tash Aw
Geert Mak: *The Dream of Europe: Travels in the Twenty-First Century*
    trans. Liz Waters
Haruki Murakami: *First Person Singular: Stories*
    trans. Philip Gabriel
Haruki Murakami: *Murakami T: The T-Shirts I Love*
    trans. Philip Gabriel
Haruki Murakami: *Novelist as a Vocation*
    trans. Philip Gabriel & Ted Goossen
Ngũgĩ wa Thiong'o: *The Perfect Nine: The Epic of Gĩkũyũ and Mũmbi*
    trans. the author

Kristín Ómarsdóttir: *Swanfolk*
  trans. Vala Thorodds
Intan Paramaditha: *The Wandering*
  trans. Stephen J. Epstein
Per Petterson: *Men in My Situation*
  trans. Ingvild Burkey
Dima Wannous: *The Frightened Ones*
  trans. Elisabeth Jaquette
Emi Yagi: *Diary of a Void*
  trans. David Boyd & Lucy North

Karl Ove Knausgaard's My Struggle cycle has been heralded as a master-piece all over the world. His work, which also includes *Out of the World*, *A Time for Everything* and the Seasons Quartet, is published in thirty-five languages. Knausgaard has been awarded the Norwegian Critics Prize for Literature, the Brage Prize and the Jerusalem Prize. *The Wolves of Eternity* is the second book in his new series, which begins with the highly acclaimed *The Morning Star*.

Martin Aitken has translated numerous novels from Danish and Norwegian. His work has received many honours, including most recently the 2022 US National Translation Award in Prose for his translation of Karl Ove Knausgaard's *The Morning Star*.